Lone Wolf

More by Brooke Shaffer

The Timekeeper Chronicles

The Chivalrous Welshman
Time to Kill
Tick Tock
Windup
Stopwatch
Free Time
Leap Second
Imminence
Synchronization
Turning Point (Summer 2024)

The Hands of Time
In the Hands of the Enemy
The Hands Pulling the Strings
The Hand Holding the Knife (Winter 2023)

The Lone Wolf
Wolf Pack
Alpha Wolf
Lone Wolf

Singles
Of Saints and Sinners
Chasing the White Bear

Lone Wolf
Book Three of The Lone Wolf
The Timekeeper Chronicles

Brooke Shaffer

Black Bear Publishing

Published in Michigan by Black Bear Publishing.

ISBN:
   Hardcover: 978-1-953113-31-3
   Softcover: 978-1-953113-32-0
   eBook: 978-1-953113-33-7

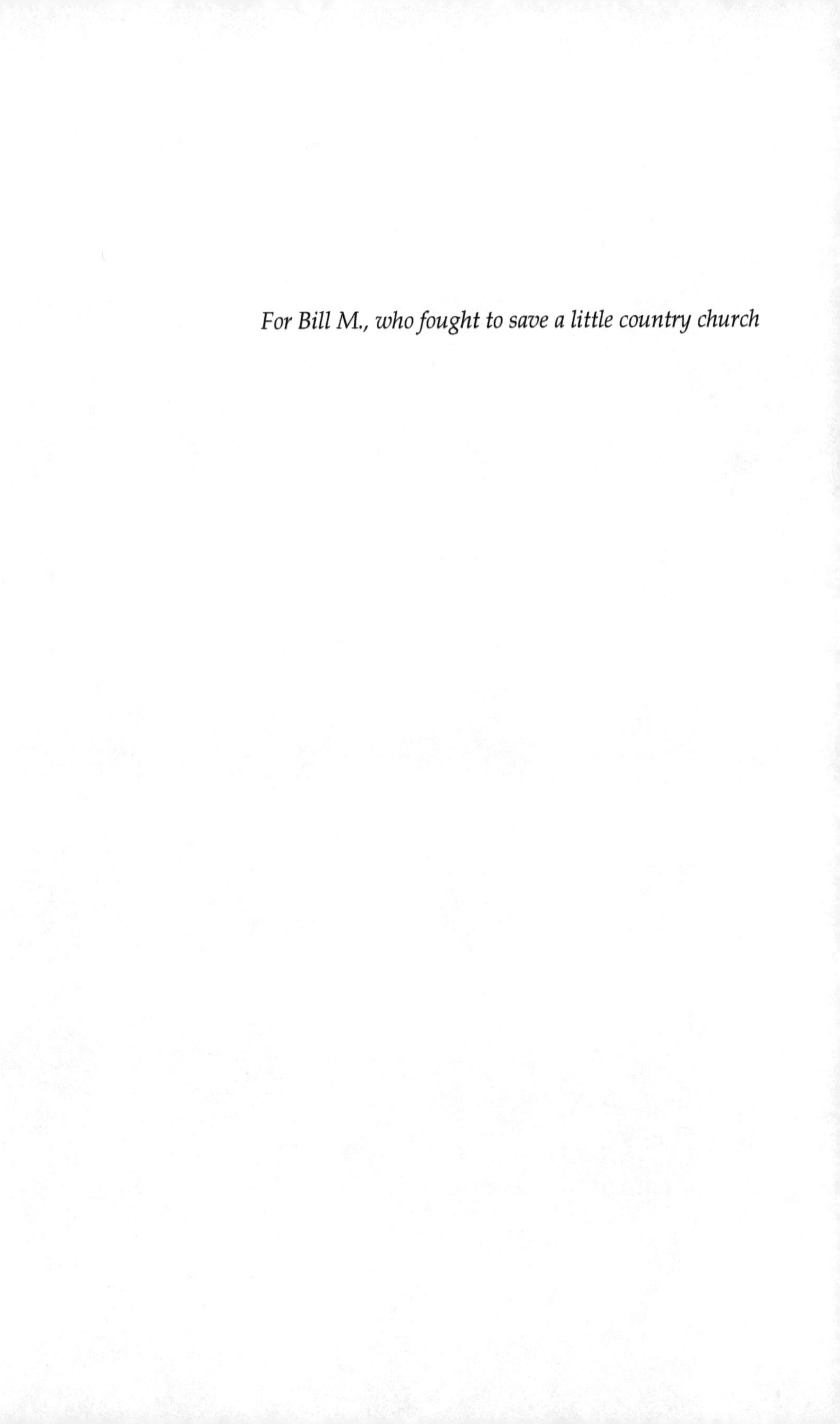

For Bill M., who fought to save a little country church

Words and Phrases

Krydik
Adelohosgi | Prophet
Agotvhdi | Sight (prophetic)
Datsitsa | (our, but not your) Dad
Dotsitsi | (our, but not your) Mom
Dutsitsa | (their) Dad
Dutsitsi | (their) Mom
Hadi | No
Hitsa | (your) Father
Hoda | (your) Brother
Humi | (your) Grandmother, Granddaughter
Ido | (my) Brother
Itsitsa | (our) Dad
Itsitsi | (our) Mom
Nattawodatnu | Seeing fruit
Tsidushi | (my) Uncle
Tsiquiyi | (my) Nephew
Tsitsa | (my) Dad, Daddy
Tsitsi | (my) Mom, Mommy
Tsituta | (my) Grandfather, Grandson
Utsa | (his/her) Dad
Utsi | (his/her) Mom
V-e | Yes
Wada | Thank you

Sorceries

Adahnesagi'a | He is conjuring/witching
Agvhalvda | Matter
Asvhnisgi | Touch, Feel
Atsvstdi | Light
Galohisdi | Doorway
Galo'ondiha ale Agi'a | Gravity
Gasadoyasgi | Force
Gayalvnga | Magnetism
Iyuwahnilvhi | Time
Nulinigv | Energy
Udilegv'i ale Uhyvtsa | Thermodynamics
Uhnvyvgi | Noise, sound

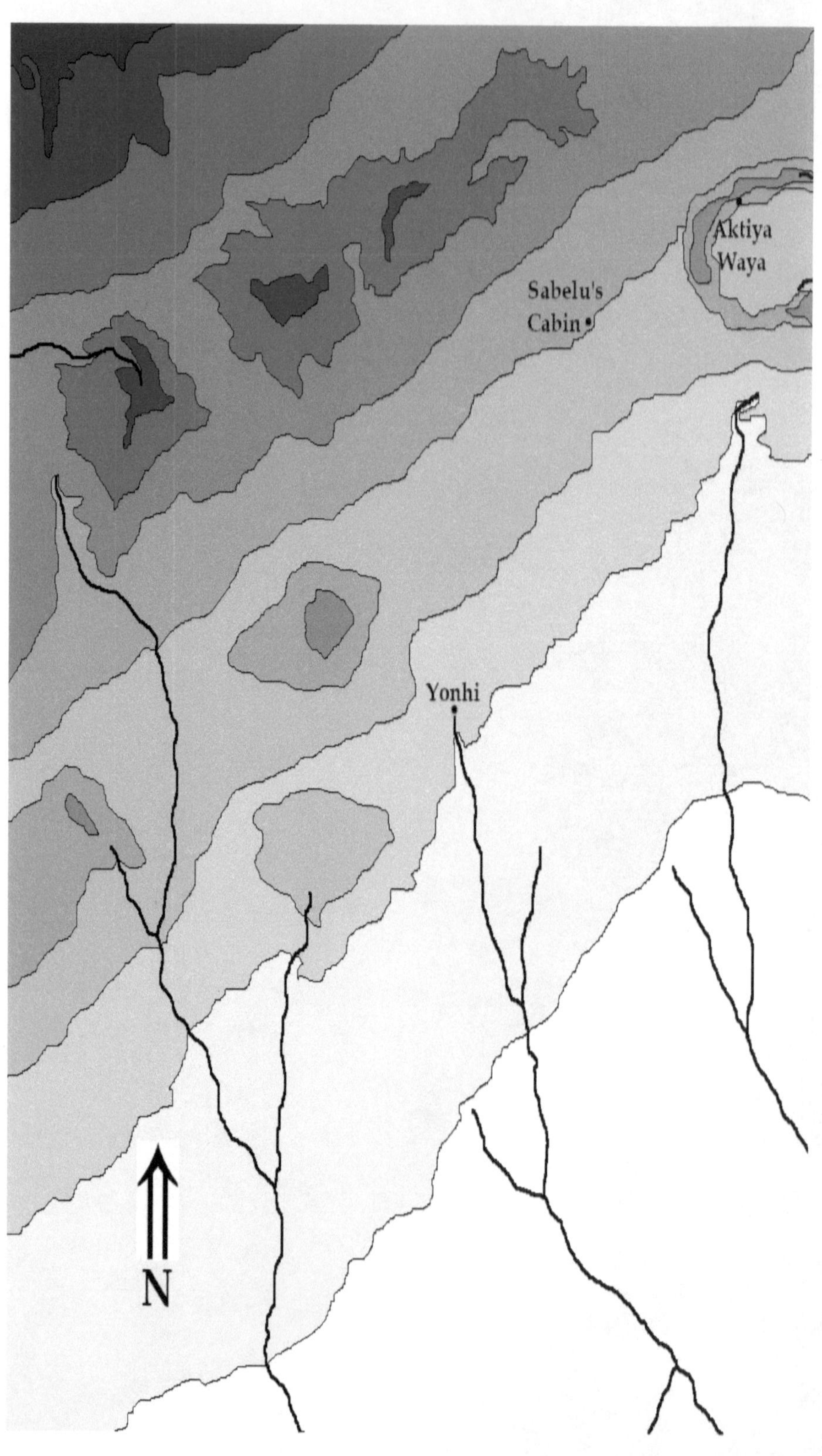

Aktiya Waya
Sabelu's Cabin
Yonhi
N

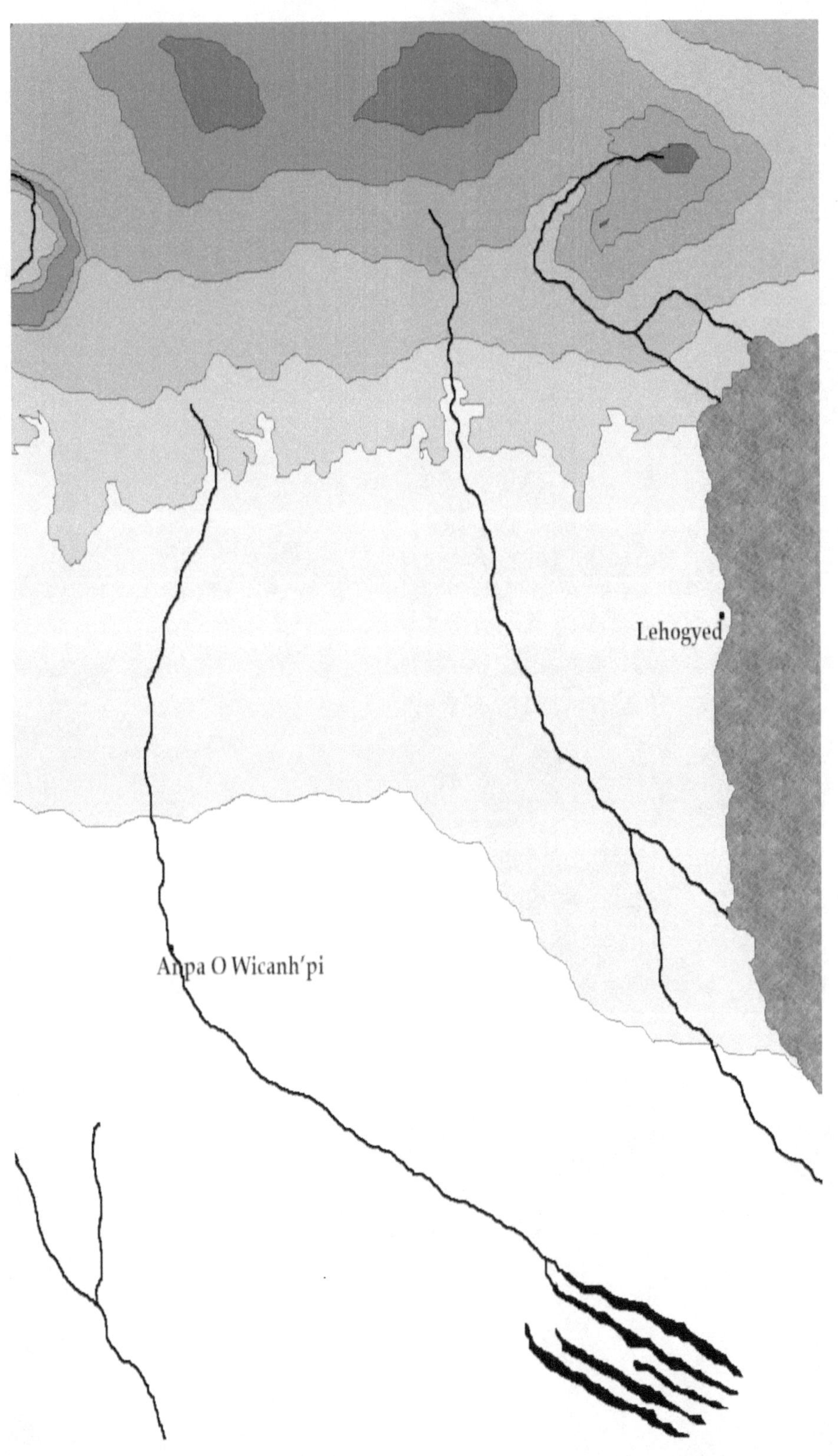

Lehogyed
Anpa O Wicanh'pi

TEΛ DVꞀT

Igvpi Adolv'i

Outcast

For her sake, he hoped she wasn't trying to be sneaky, because she was failing at it. To be fair, he wasn't trying to be sneaky either as he stomped across the hard-packed earth and rock, shoving aside small branches as they blocked his way.

"Sabelu!" she called, the word cut off by a grunt when she tripped over a gnarled root. A moment later there was a clearer, "Sabelu, wait!"

He did not stop or even slow down. He didn't know where he intended to go, and for the moment, that was just fine with him.

Unfortunately, this rare spree of fated freedom saw him straight onto an open ledge with nowhere to really run. Oh, he could jump, he supposed, and invoke Galo'ondiha ale Agi'a—or not—but his anger had waned to frustration and finally dwindled to annoyance so that he had no real desire to pull off such a trick. He sighed and turned just as Netami pushed her way through the trees and stumbled out onto the ledge beside him.

"Sabelu, stop." As if he had much of a choice. "Don't be like this. Please."

"What do you want from me, Netami?" he demanded. "What does anyone back there want from me?"

"They just want—"

"They tell me to keep the histories and hold the truth. But when they ask for the histories or the truth...at best, they ignore me, and at worst, they become angry with me."

"No one enjoys being reminded of their faults, Sabelu, even you. But that is your job."

He scoffed. "My job. It's not my job, Netami, it is my life. It is every fiber of my being. To know these things, to know them all the time, and to be hated for it!" He turned and shouted the last phrase into the valley so that it echoed. He looked back at her. "My whole life, Netami. Ever since I was born. These things that I know. I can't stop them. Sometimes, I get accused of lying, but when I look into their eyes, I know that they know I'm not. They just can't figure out how I know the thing that they've tried so hard to erase. They say they want the truth, but what they really want is the truth as they make it, not as it is."

Her expression was one of terrible pity, and she put a hand on his shoulder. "You're an adelohosgi, Sabelu. A seer. Rats run away when the light shines on them, and you are that light. It's in your name."

"But what good is it, really? To be like the sun, shining and doing good and yet to be so offensive that men cannot even look at me for fear of going blind?" He shook his head. "I can't do it. And I can't look at them either."

"You've told me before, but—"

"What good would it do to tell them, though?" he repeated. "I look at a man—or a woman—I look at anyone and I know them. I know all about them. I know who they are. I know their secrets, their lies, their dreams, their triumphs and failures. I know their people and their ancestors. And it doesn't—stop. It never—stops. The only time I get any relief is with children. So pure and innocent and full of possibilities. Then they reach maturity, and it's like a dam bursting forth to swallow me." He couldn't stop the words as they flowed, rambling, from his mouth. "But the worst is at night. The things I see, Netami, the dreams and visions of things to be."

Netami sighed and put her other hand on his other shoulder, facing him though he did not look at her. "I wish I knew how to help you, Sabelu."

"I need to go to the Old Land. I have to take the seeing fruit and commune with Anagalisgi."

"Sabelu, you know that's not a good idea. All of the teams who have gone to the Old Land have reported the hatred for our kind, especially those who try to remain faithful to the old ways. You being a priest won't go over well."

He scoffed. "The priests here accuse me of ignoring the old ways or favoring one way over another. They're so...wrapped up in the embellishments of the bow that they don't even realize that the string is broken."

"If you have trouble with the hundred or so people in Aktiya Waya, and didn't even leave the tent during the last national festival, how are you going to face thousands or even millions of people in the Old Land? You might go there, but you won't be able to get yourself back."

Sabelu closed his eyes, tried to look ahead, but everything was a terrible jumble of images.

"Maybe the Agotvhdi doesn't extend to whites," he said.

"You don't know that."

"Maybe you'll have to come with me."

Netami sighed. "Sabelu, you are my brother, and I love you because of that. You know I've always favored you. But I can't...I can't babysit you forever."

Sabelu gave her a look. "For a moment there, I thought I was speaking to Itsitsi."

She matched his look.

"What do you want me to do, Netami? I can't control it, and too many people here are too dishonest for me to trust their intentions."

"Many, but not all," she said gently. "There are honest people. You know them."

He hesitated. "Itsitsa, you, a few others."

Netami's expression turned confused. "Itsitsi is honest."

He hesitated again, then shook his head. "Her love is genuine, but her intentions are not. I'm afraid she was too influenced by the death of Yvgidahi and Tsona. She is too bound by fear."

His sister was quiet for a long moment. As he'd come to understand his abilities and interpret what he was seeing and feeling, he'd slowly drifted away from their mother. Everyone assumed it was just part of his naturally odd behavior, but only now did he admit that there was some intent of his own behind the distance.

"Blaknik?" she asked finally, diverting the conversation.

"He's a child," Sabelu said. "I can't see him, and he doesn't understand. Honestly, I think he's afraid of me."

Netami half-shrugged and nodded. "He is. Most children are. Some adults are."

Sabelu shook his head and walked away several steps, toward the edge of the cliff. "I can't keep going like this, Netami. If I don't kill someone else, it'll be myself."

She came up quickly behind him. "Don't talk like that."

He turned on her. "Then help me. Nothing here is helping. Anagalisgi is the only one I can think of who might have some answers, but he's in the Old Land. I've tried to reach him from here, but I can't. All that's left is to go there."

Still she hesitated, staring aimlessly into the valley below. Finally, "All right. It's the only thing you haven't tried, and I don't want to see you suffer like this." She sighed. "It seems like it gets worse for you every year."

"If I don't do something about it now, I will kill myself."

"Don't do that," Netami said softly, bringing him into an embrace which he reluctantly accepted. "There is an answer. You just have to find it." She released him from the hug though she kept her hands on his arms. "But we can't just go running off to the Old Land on a minor day trip. Everyone who has ever gone back and sought Anagalisgi has had to try for at least a few days. The good news is that we know roughly where to find him, but we can't expect much hospitality from the people of the Old Land while we wait."

As she spoke, mental nebulae slowly formed themselves into something resembling a plan. They would need supplies, figuring that they would have to do everything themselves. Any help they received was a bonus, not an expectation. Food was less of a concern, but they would need shelter of some kind. Weapons were also low priority because of the sorceries, but sometimes there was no good substitute for a physical blade. Unfortunately, since the war, the restrictions on the peoples were said to have gotten even worse. Given the experiences of the people before, this was saying something.

 Lone Wolf

"We have to go back to the village now," Netami was saying. "We'll pack a few things and then we'll probably have to explain what we're doing." She went on before he could protest. "It's what needs to be done. I'm going to help you, Sabelu, but I'm not going to treat you like a child and do everything for you."

He found himself grinning. "You used to be so excited to marry and have children; you begged Itsitsa and Itsitsi to have a baby you could take care of."

She grinned. "Yes, and I got you."

"Be careful what you wish for; you might get more than you bargained."

She took him by the hand and gently pulled him away from the edge of the cliff. "Come on. The sooner we get packed and ready, the sooner we can leave."

"Not necessarily, but if we never begin, then it only ends one way."

She kept hold of him until they reached the tree line. There she dropped his hand and started pushing branches out of the way.

Some people looked for smoke to tell them where an encampment or village might be. Others listened for the din of activity of people going about their day. Still others might look for evidence of foraging, hunting, or perhaps nearby abandoned sites.

For Sabelu, he had only to be near a place, sometimes as far out as a day's walk. He didn't have to see or hear anything to know when people were around. Even now, just walking through the forest, he could feel them. He felt their presence, not just in the place, but in time, and it sounded ludicrous even to himself most days. He knew that hunters would walk this path in search of game. He knew that they already had. He could feel them weaving around trees not yet grown and already gone, and yet they also walked through trees that would fall in their own time or be cut down.

At this point, he did not necessarily see anything, as phantom images, although it was not uncommon for him to glimpse something in his peripheral vision, only for there to be nothing to see. As he and Netami passed by an enormous tree that four men could not surround holding hands, he could feel a time when those four men would discuss how to fell the tree.

The closer they got to the village, the more tangible and less peripheral these feelings became. He could see the next delegation from Deer Clan, riding in on their horses, vanishing when they reached the pass into the bowl of Aktiya Waya. He saw another group of riders, this one leaving on some other errand. He saw a group from Eagle Clan to the east, and another from Bear Clan in the west.

When he'd first begun to see these images, in his peripheral and in front of him, he'd been entirely unable to distinguish them from real people standing before him, and he'd been thought quite mad, even possessed. If not for the tutelage of an elderly priest, he might have been killed, assuming he hadn't killed himself. These days, he could distinguish the real from the phantom by the fact that phantoms usually had no motivations. He did not know why the riders were coming and going, their mission or intent; he knew only their actions.

But when he looked at Netami, he knew her. He saw her memories of the last hour or so as though they were his own, felt her distress as she watched her brother storm off into the forest. He could feel it as a kind of failure on her part; she felt as though she were failing him in someway. Even now, he could feel her anxiety and confusion, the will to make things right although she did not know exactly how. He could feel the pride she had felt when he'd been born, a baby for her to take care of. He could feel the confusion of newness as his destiny was divined. He could see and feel her exasperation as the realities of that destiny manifested itself into this monster that had overtaken his mind.

If the only things he knew were the past and present, he thought that might have been fine. He might have been able to train himself to be quiet and discerning.

It was about two years ago as he really began to grow into his manhood that he began to see more. He began to see the future. At first, this was counted as a blessing as he was consulted for omens and other readings, divining the best time to plant the crops and whether a couple was suitable for marriage. It was the last time he remembered being happy. He remembered being proud of himself, that his destiny was being fulfilled and he was going to help the people. And because the council and the elders and the priests were giving him more consideration than Anagalisgi had ever been afforded, then conditions for the people might actually improve this time around.

For a while, this seemed to be the case, as far as he was concerned. Then things began to change. Over a period of about four moons, it became no longer about seeing everything separately. If the past, present, and future could be likened to pools of water, those pools began to fill up and merge together. He began to see patterns, connecting people and events, until he could not only see a future conflict but know everything about it, who the instigators were, what the outcome would be. Sometimes, when these predicted events were emotionally charged, he could feel the faintest hint of motivation.

Even now, as they passed the men guarding the pass, he knew them. He did not even have to really look at them to know them. One man was proud of himself for taking down a bear, and yet Sabelu could also see an argument that would come up between that man and another. This vision had a hint of pride mixed with jealousy and also the fear of being found out in it. The man who had killed the bear was proud of it, but it had not been strength and cunning alone that did it, as much as he bragged about such. Some other factor had played into it, a previous wound that slowed the bear down and made it easier to kill. The man he was arguing with did not know all of this and was merely jealous, but the bear man was afraid of being found out and so argued more vigorously than he probably should have.

All of this he knew in the space of half a step, as he and Netami walked past, words and images and impressions being shoved into his mind when he did not want them. The bear man himself hadn't said a word and only gave them half a glance anyway. The man he would be arguing with later was nowhere to be seen.

It was when everything started to run together that Sabelu started suspecting that he was going to need more help than the priests would be willing to provide. Things were fine when he could see everyone else, but when he started calling out the actions and motivations of some of the priests themselves, things started to get rocky. When his predictions and phantoms had begun to be tinted by motivation, this just over the course of a season, he'd begun to panic, afraid that he would soon no longer be able to tell the difference between past, present, and future. Shutting himself away had done little good, had really only made things worse when he had emerged.

Somehow, he simultaneously felt as though he were speeding up and slowing down as he walked through the village, and he began to fear that perhaps he was starting to read himself at different points in time, one point when he would be moving quickly along this path, another point when he would be moving slowly, but all of it in his head at this present moment.

He slowed to a stop and looked around. Every person he saw, and even those he didn't, were laid out before him, different points in time overlapping on their bodies and faces, a multitude of emotions and motivations washing over him like pouring rain.

Only the children remained solid. He could look at a child, and to him it was like looking at a rock. Any emotion was what was displayed on their face and in their body language. Their memories were their own, as were their intentions. He was, in a sense, blind to them, at least in his mind, and he didn't know whether he loved or hated them for it.

He didn't start getting impressions on them until they reached adolescence. When they hit maturity was when they turned into the shape-shifting phantoms.

He knew that Netami was going to grab his hand before she did, and yet he still found himself startled by it, if only because he was unsure just when it happened, or when it was supposed to happen, or that it was happening. He forced his gaze away from the people so he didn't have to look at their constantly-changing faces and bodies, but even staring at the ground as Netami led him along, he could feel them. He could feel their curiosity, their questions, their loathing, their joys. If he was grateful for anything, it was that he could not actively hear their thoughts, though he feared whether that could change and what difference it really made.

Most of the people were out and about in the sunshine, and getting away from them, hiding in the stone city, helped to ease the worst of the pressure in his mind. He was able to look up to watch where he was going, though he still deliberately avoided looking at people. Not just avoiding their gazes, but ignoring their very existence if he could.

They went a roundabout way through the city, avoiding common gathering areas and anywhere the council, priests, or elders were likely to be. It didn't help that their home was quite near to the longhouse, but that was nothing a little conjuring of Iyuwahnilvhi couldn't handle.

Sabelu loathed the conjuring of Iyuwahnilvhi, especially when there were people around. It was bad enough that he could see everything in regular Iyuwahnilvhi, but to twist and warp that aspect of reality, to take oneself out of sync with his environment and everything and everyone else, or to do the same to others, it only served to twist Sabelu's mind in ways he didn't like, even more than normal. He might have said that it literally twisted his brain, if such a thing were possible.

Earlier that spring, he'd tried to use Asvhnisgi in reverse, project his mind, what he saw and thought, to Netami, to try and make her understand. She had shrieked as no normal person should and eventually collapsed, lying comatose for four days before either she was healed or returned naturally; no one was quite sure. She proclaimed no ill will toward Sabelu for it, but that was when the real shift came, when the elders and others began to view him with some hostility. When Netami had attempted to use Asvhnisgi Sabelu, she'd claimed it was as though her brain had touched hot coals. She could feel anywhere in his body and heal any wound, but when she tried to reach his mind, she found only pain.

Rarely was he in any physical pain, but the stress he endured on a minute-by-minute basis was excruciating and often left him feeling tired by midday, assuming he stayed in the village.

He had to get out. He had to leave. He had to find Anagalisgi and get help or else he really would kill himself.

There was no one home when they arrived, and Sabelu took a

moment to simply sit down and try to breathe, staring at the floor for inspiration. He knew there were people around, could feel them pressing on his mind, their impressions, most of it mundane as people made all the little decisions that came up each day. What to eat, how to prepare it, how to fix something that was broken, how to entertain a child or surprise a spouse or annoy a sibling or get back at a sibling for being annoying. But at least without having to look at them and watch them change form through all the things they had done, were doing, wanted to do, and were going to do, the chaos in his mind was manageable. How tedious to consider that he now longed for something that had once seemed so overwhelming. He closed his eyes and tried to relax, even a little. Embrace the quiet, ignore the phantoms, count off his breaths, calm his heart that was racing so hard that if he had been a horse it might have exploded.

He could hear Netami moving around, a large, amorphous impression on his mind, filled with the same mundane worry as everyone else as she considered what to pack, but also harboring anxiety and worry. Some of it was directed at him, but some was also directed other places. She worried about their parents, their family in general, the thoughts people might have about the others because of him.

When he reached fifty breaths, he stood and started looking around for a bag to pack some of his things. He found one that his sister had laid out on his bed, grabbed it wordlessly, and began picking out a few items. He saw Netami in his peripheral vision, and only the impressions he got from her informed him that she was real.

"Is it going to take very long?" Netami asked.

He doubled over and sucked in a breath as he was suddenly struck by a tide of visions, images moving so fast in his mind he could barely process one before another took its place. He saw the places they would travel to, saw where they needed to go, saw a dozen other things he could not describe except as choices, and even he did not understand what that meant.

He put his hands out to catch him as he went forward, coming to rest on a chest at the end of his bed. Netami was by his side, though she stopped just short of touching him.

"You know I hate it when you ask questions like that," he gasped.

"I know," she whispered. "I'm sorry."

He also hated that for as much as he seemed to see, he couldn't predict things like this. If he had known about her question, he might have answered before she could speak. But then, if she hadn't asked, he wouldn't have known to answer. Then there was the frightening possibility that he had seen it at some point but it got lost in the chaos of his mind.

He let out a breath and said, "It won't be long. We're expected."

"We—" She caught herself. Instead of asking a question, she simply stated, "We are expected."

"It won't be very long at all. We won't need much."

"That's good to hear. We'll leave just as soon as you're ready."

He took in another breath as everything seemed to twist and fold, multiple impressions from around the larger cave forming into a road, like boulders filling a gap in a mountain trail or leaves on a river that pile up into a single mass. Sabelu shook his head. "No, we won't."

He could hear Netami's question as clearly as if she actually spoke the words aloud. What did he mean?

For as frustrating as it could be to know things before they happened, Sabelu came to cherish those moments, because it was like watching a puzzle fall into place as if by magic. For just a few moments, the chaotic threads of life twisted and coalesced into a single path, a single line that he could see and follow. Such epiphanies were typically followed by major events or decisions, thereby functioning as a kind of bottleneck for everything going on as it passed through some invisible trial.

Nevertheless, he seized on the moment of clarity, stuffing a few more things in his bag and shouldering it. Then he and Netami turned just in time to see Blaknik enter the house. His impression as an eleven year old was still weak compared to everyone else, only just developing as he was just developing into a young man; Sabelu had only sensed him when he was just outside the door.

Their mother, however, he'd never actually lost track of, and his sense of her grew stronger when she'd entered the city. She wasn't far behind Blaknik, her presence just one of many strong waves in the ocean of people in Aktiya Waya. All that remained was for her physical presence to crash upon the shore of his mind.

As soon as she appeared and he looked upon her, he saw everything.

"Where have you been?!"

"I was so worried!"

"Oh, my boy, you're home!"

"Wait until your father gets here!"

"The council is on their way with the priests and elders."

All of these things that she wanted to say, all the different ways she wanted to receive him, all flashing in front of his eyes, fixed on his mother's shape-shifting body and face, all of it occurring in the half breath between the time of their gazes meeting and when she opened her mouth to actually say, "Oh, you are home."

And this did not take into account that he could see everything she had done that day, tending the crop fields, fleshing hides, gathering water, being informed of her troubled son's latest mishap.

"Not for long," he said, looking away and squeezing his eyes shut so he could reorient himself to the present moment, though those moments were notoriously difficult to catch and hang onto. When he opened his eyes, he looked at Blaknik, the only safe option he had at the moment, as far as people. Blaknik gave him a sympathetic look, but even his faint impression said he still didn't understand what was wrong with his older brother.

"Yes, your bag says as much, but where are you going?"

Sabelu went to a knee as the question triggered a violent reaction in his mind. People, places, buildings, landscapes, hundreds and even thousands of images swirling in his head. He had no clue where most of them were or who the people were, and yet he knew that he would cross paths with all of them at some point in his life.

He did not blame his mother or sister or anyone else for their questions, nor his response to them. It was a new development within the last year, and it went entirely against human nature to not ask questions.

Blaknik stepped forward as if to help, but Netami held him back, saying, "Hadi. There's nothing you can do."

"What's wrong with him?" Blaknik wondered, his voice just breaking out of its boyish shell.

It was perhaps the only question that didn't provoke a response, or that didn't provoke one yet; he had a hard time believing that there was nothing wrong with him. Perhaps his mind itself didn't know what was wrong so it had nothing to show him.

He got to his feet, speaking before anyone else could. "I'm going to the Old Land. I need to seek out Anagalisgi."

"Sabelu, you know that's a bad idea," his mother said.

"It's not forbidden," Netami stated.

"It will be by the time the council gets here," Sabelu said, feeling short of breath though he had done very little. He deliberately did not look at his mother, although she still shifted in his peripheral vision as he stared over her shoulder. "Besides, there's nothing they can do to stop me, short of physical restraint." He saw and felt another ripple. It was not quite so solid as before, but he was confident as he added, "They won't be able to."

His mother took a breath and let it out slowly. "Sabelu. Please. I know this is confusing. I'm just as confused as you are—"

He barked a laugh and shook his head. "That's the thing, though. I'm not confused." He chanced to meet her gaze and immediately looked away again as a dozen variations of sorrow and hurt and fear warped ehr visage. "I'm not confused. I'm overwhelmed. Like you every year with the national festival. You're not confused. You know exactly what needs to be done. It's just a matter of getting it all done in time. I'm not confused. I just see everything all the time from almost everyone. I understand it, but there isn't enough time in existence for me to process it all and it's overwhelming. And it's only getting worse."

"Please, Sabelu, there must be something more you can do here. Anything. I know you're not overly fond of tea, but—"

"No evil spirit was ever banished because of a cup of tea." He shook his head, gripped his bag harder, and made for the door. "I have to find Anagalisgi."

As he went past her, she reached out and grabbed his arm. Immediately he was seized in pain. The memory being forced on him was excruciating enough, but given the fact that the memory itself involved unbelievably atrocious amounts of physical pain didn't help things either. At first he didn't understand it, what was going on. Maybe he was dying. Or she was dying. But that couldn't be it because his mother was still very much alive, had never brushed death like that in her life.

Except, perhaps, with childbirth. This realization hit him half a second before the pain released, and a moment later, a tiny infant was placed in his mother's arms. Him. Mostly dry though his hair still had a bit of dampness to it, blue eyes seeing the world for the first time, already seeing far beyond the physicality that surrounded them. The love and ferocity of the woman who held him was known to him, then and now.

The whole thing flashed through him in the blink of an eye. He knew the love she held for him, the fear of watching her tiny baby boy go mad amidst the divination of prophecy and guidance and being an adelohosgi.

He also knew, from the priests themselves if not the Book that recorded it, that his life had hung in the balance those first few days. Some wanted to kill him outright, proclaiming him evil. And he knew that, lately, some of those same priests were harboring a hatred and fear of him that would very likely result in attempted murder.

A tendril of thought and time began forming, and he suddenly knew with absolute certainty that one or more of the priests would try to kill him at some point in the future.

Two blinks had passed, an eternity between moments as Sabelu forced his way out of the house. He kept his eyes down, but he could still sense everyone moving around. But for as much as he sensed their presence, he was unable to overcome the intended future, and he was soon cornered by several people: three council members, four priests, and an elder.

"Where are you going?"

"What do you think you're doing?"

"Please, stop running and let us speak as respectable men."

"What have you seen?"

"Where have you been?"

"You thought you were going to run away?"

"You're brave to return here."

All of it hitting him at the same time though no one had actually spoken or even drawn breath to speak.

"Have you come to make amends for the division and slander you've wreaked here?" one of the councilmen asked.

"Truth is not slander," Sabelu said, repeating what he'd told them earlier. Perhaps if he could look them in the eye, then he could assert himself a little better, but his only concern right now was himself and just making it out of the city. "Besides, I'm not staying for long."

"Oh? And where are you going?" a priest inquired.

Again he was struck by the question, and it felt almost like a physical blow. It took everything in him to remain upright and not fall to the ground, clutching at his head as images suddenly appeared in his mind. Unlike when his mother had inquired, these were images of a vast landscape first punctured by mountains and then spread with sands and scrub brush and trees he did not recognize. Something about the visions promised pain, and he felt it even now, a kind of foreshadowing echo.

"I think the more he gets called out, the more he feigns insanity to cover it up," another priest said.

The words exploded from Sabelu's mouth before he could call them back. "You raised me for this! You divined my future for this! To know and to tell, but you don't listen! You want me to speak of power, but character is what builds trust and that is what grants a man power. Character is shaped by truth. What you seek, what you have, is a hollow vessel easily shattered. I can't help that. I can speak words all day long, but if no one listens, then what good is it? And calling out someone's lies and darkness of heart should not be a shameful act."

He didn't know whether to call his tone shrieking or sobbing, though he suspected it fell somewhere in the middle. He could see the words as he spoke them, how they knitted into roads and trains of thought; he saw them interact with each man's motives, interweaving with preformed plans and preconceived notions, his intent misaligning with their understanding or desire to understand or heed his warning.

The problem only got worse as people began to crowd around, drawn to the spectacle. More impressions, more noise, more weaving of words and emotions.

"You didn't answer the question," the first priest stated, and Sabelu braced himself for what he knew was coming. "Where are you going?"

Even knowing what was about to happen, it was like trying to hold back thunder. These images now were of a forest, although he was becoming so overwhelmed from everything else that he couldn't ponder the significance of this particular forest, other than he knew it was in the Old Land.

He was saved from having to speak by the appearance of Netami, pushing her way through the crowd and getting between him and his tormentors.

"We knew he was going somewhere, but you appear to be going with him," a councilman observed.

"That's correct," she said, her voice calm though her jaw remained set. "We're going to the Old Land."

"He can't!" another councilman barked.

"And how do you plan to stop us?"

"We cannot stop you from leaving, but we can stop you from returning here."

"Please!" the elder said, finally speaking up. He got between the two parties, using his staff to roughly tap the ankles of anyone in his way. "Are we really resorting to threats now? Are we animals to be penned and caged and led from here to there?"

"Casual visits to the Old Land have been suspended since the end of the war," a councilman reminded him. "Only specially chosen teams and delegations are permitted."

"Do you think Sabelu is going for a casual visit?" the elder shot back. "Is seeking out the seer Anagalisgi merely a casual thing to you? Look at the boy!"

Sabelu was crouched down on the ground, staring at a single, tiny pebble, trying not to scream.

The elder went on, "The only threat to you from him is his words. Now, I can't say whether or not he speaks the truth, nor can I say what he sees or knows, but I do know that he is the only one among us who acts this way. Who is able to guide him?"

"Anagalisgi never acted this way," one priest said haughtily.

"Maybe not, but he is the only one who has not yet been consulted." Sabelu could feel that the elder turned toward him somewhat. "If Sabelu does see and know these things, if he is the seer and keeper of knowledge that you divined him to be, then it appears that he has outgrown your guidance. His cauldron of knowledge is boiling over, and he does not know what to do."

"And how do we know that he isn't simply trying to make a clever escape after the chaos he has caused?" the third priest demanded.

Sabelu spoke up before anyone could respond, though he wasn't sure he was even in control of his own voice. "If you want to talk about motives, Ganhv, shall we talk about yours? Your wife is pregnant. When she bears a son, you will proclaim him an adelohosgi also, and you will plot to be rid of me. The truth is, you don't want me to leave because you want to ensure my death for yourself, and so that I cannot return later and expose your crimes. And in the meantime, you want to keep me talking, get everyone to see my insanity so that they will not only accept your son but be relieved when I'm gone." He dared to look up at the man's face, just for an instant. "Isn't that right?"

The only sound that could be heard in the entire cave was a few whistled notes from a swirling breeze. Everyone stared at either Sabelu, still crouched on the ground, or Ganhv, who appeared as a deer, frozen and trying to decide what to do.

Ganhv broke the silence first with a few sputtered protests, but it was Sabelu who spoke. "Your son will not be an adelohosgi. In fact, he will not be able to speak at all. And far from being a threat to me, he will end up being the death of you without ever having uttered a word in his life."

There was another moment of near-perfect silence, then Ganhv stormed off.

"Seeing how he was the instigator of all of this," Sabelu went on, "does anyone else really want to try and stop us from leaving?"

"Ganhv may be overzealous," a councilman said, "but he's not wrong. You are a dangerous man, Sabelu."

"The truth is dangerous only to those who are unwilling to hear it," Netami told him, kneeling beside her brother. "Sabelu is only the messenger. If you have a problem, it's not with him."

The councilman also moved forward to kneel beside Sabelu. "And what, then, do you see, now that you have exposed Ganhv's plans?"

Sabelu's heart slammed against his chest repeatedly even as his brain pulsed inside his skull. "Exactly as I have said. His son will not be an adelohosgi and will not speak. And he will cause Ganhv's death."

"How so?"

"In the river. Ganhv will drown trying to save him."

The councilman shifted position. "And does that remain true, now that you have spoken it aloud?"

Sabelu could feel the sweat on his face. "It will remain true. You will not tell him, because you want to see whether it could change. And because if it doesn't, if he dies, then you have less opposition from the priests as a whole, seeing how Ganhv is your biggest adversary in national matters."

"And what decides whether a thing shall come to pass once it is spoken aloud? What if I did decide to go and tell Ganhv now?"

Sabelu was rapidly becoming light-headed. It was not that he saw specific visions, but there seemed to be a tragic influx of knowledge into his mind that he couldn't sort all at once even as his mouth said, "I know what I know. Some things just are. Even if you did tell him, he wouldn't believe you, and he would die anyway. He couldn't leave his son to die, because he is too motivated to try and prove me wrong. But neither will he be able to swim."

The councilman made an odd sort of noise, then stood. "I do hope you find Anagalisgi and that he is able to help."

"It won't be for your benefit, Usdaglv," Sabelu said. "Truth is not a servant, it is a master. Prophecy and the messenger are servants of truth."

No one said anything to that, and the crowd began to break up. It was like removing rubble. Relief and light-headedness overcame Sabelu and he flopped over onto his back, then his side. Netami knelt on one side. A moment later, their mother was on his other side. He could feel Blaknik by his faint impression but could not see him.

"Are—" She caught herself. "You're all right."

"I will be," he said softly.

"We need to get you out of here before Ganhv comes back," Netami said, grabbing his hand and arm and helping him to sit up. "Even if he doesn't believe Usdaglv, that doesn't mean he won't still come back and try something."

Sabelu nodded, head still full of clouds. "Usdaglv is on his way to speak to him now, and he will be back."

He struggled to his feet, his sister on one side, mother on the other, younger brother in front, all trying to hold him upright. After a second or two, he got his feet under him, and some manner of coordination returned. He kept his gaze focused on Blaknik as his support was removed and he was left to stand on his own two feet.

"I hope Anagalisgi can help you," Blaknik told him. His impression was wild with fear and uncertainty.

"So do I," Sabelu told him sincerely. "So do I."

"Be safe," their mother said. "The Old Land is a dangerous place."

"We won't have any trouble."

It was true, but he knew that being unable to muster up the required confidence was unlikely to ease her fears. He met her gaze briefly and jumped as she hugged him.

"We have to go," Netami said.

Nendawagan released her son. "Go. Get help."

Nothing more was said as Netami handed him his pack, grabbed his hand, and started walking. Sabelu desperately hoped Anagalisgi could help him, if for no other reason than so he could make his way through the village without having to be led by the hand like a child. So many people, so many lives, so many impressions. He looked at children when he could, just so he could see something other than the ground beneath his feet. Outside he might try to look at the grass or the crop fields or the landscape itself, but people had a knack for getting in the way of the view and pushing more unwanted information into his brain, so he minimized these glances, especially now.

Even without his gifts—if one wanted to call them that—he could feel the stares. How quickly had word of the incident in the cave spread? Were people now taking bets on Ganhv's life? Were they even now divided, as one might be divided over the winner of a horse race?

Asking questions such as these was about equivalent to wearing heavier furs in the winter; it was just obvious. He knew the answers. Many people had heard of the incident. Few wouldn't have, by nightfall. Some of the more prone gamblers were taking bets, while the rest of the people harbored their own opinions and curiosities. He knew all of this without even having to look at them.

"Almost there," his sister said ahead of him.

He knew that. Gifts and impressions aside, he knew what the bowl looked like, what the trail looked like. He wasn't dumb. As they got farther from the village and the heavier, more intimate knowledge and impressions began to subside, he was able to look up and watch where they were going. He took his hand out of Netami's and nearly ran into her when she stopped short.

"I'm fine," he told her. "Let's go."

He again averted his gaze when they reached the pass and had to get by the guards. Again he was treated to images of an impending argument between a couple of the men, but he bit his tongue and followed Netami out of the bowl.

They traveled down the slope a short distance to a grove of trees that was designated as the place where Galohisdi were conjured. It was impolite to conjure inside the bowl, given all the activity.

Before either of them could do anything, Sabelu sat against a tree and forced himself to breathe evenly. He did not look at Netami, but he could still feel her questions. How did she ask if he was all right without actually asking a question and evoking a terrible response within him? But for as much stress as he could see she felt from it, he was not obliged to answer these unspoken questions. It would only generate more of them.

"I will conjure Galohisdi," Netami stated as Sabelu stood. "Don't worry about me, just get yourself through."

"I'll do it," he told her. "I know where we have to go."

"But you've never conjured Galohisdi before."

"Maybe, but I know how to do it."

She sighed. "Of course you do."

"Lend strength if you want, but let me direct it."

Reluctantly she agreed, then stood back a few steps and watched as he began to conjure.

DCꞨ DVꞀT

Atline Adolv'i

Anagalisgi

By all accounts from everyone who had ever traveled via Galohisdi, even just once, even if it was just from one village to another on some urgent errand, it was a horrible experience, physically and mentally. To feel compressed, as though being crumpled up into a ball, even as the air was sucked from one's lungs and all energy from his body. It was a harrowing experience, not one that was undertaken lightly. So it was that Sabelu did not feel terrible in the least about his condition once he and his sister landed on the other side.

Netami had been the Old Land only once, just to see where their grandfather and brother fell in battle. Sabelu had never been to the Old Land, at least, not physically. Yet as they stood and got their bearings, he seemed less disoriented and confused than she did. He knew this place, as if he'd dreamed of it before. Or maybe not him, but someone else. And not a dream, but memories. The memories of someone who had walked here before.

Utsa, he realized. He had walked here before, when he fought in the war. His memories were now Sabelu's memories, of a kind.

Even as he thought it, phantoms began to appear in his peripheral. Men in ragged uniforms, marching in worn boots. A small group of soldiers on horseback. Morale was low, supplies were low. If they were lucky, they would join up with another column just over the next hill, then march on to the nearby town for supplies.

"Sabelu?"

He turned at the sound of his sister's voice. She sounded distant, and yet when he saw her—quickly averting his gaze—the phantoms vanished. She stood a few paces from him, not quite leaning against a tree though she looked a bit pale and worn out from the trip.

"Well, you look better than I do," she observed.

"It's quiet here," he stated.

Even as he said it, he had the oddly stunning revelation that the pressure on his mind was—well, it wasn't gone, not entirely, but significantly reduced. He knew there was a settlement of some form in the vicinity, and several small houses dotted here and there, but they weren't close enough for him to perceive every single person, their hopes and dreams and failures and regrets and memories and ancestry and future. It was no more significant to his mind than the breeze was to his face. The only person he was truly aware of in such a sense was Netami.

She was disoriented, and he didn't need spiritual gifts to discern that. But she was also conflicted, earlier fears tentatively relieved by his admission that he was all right and his mind was quiet, yet mixing with new fears about what was going to happen next. He could feel her fatigue as surely as if he felt it himself—and he would not say he did not feel similarly—a weariness of body and mind as she waited for the next thing, wondering what it was and how she was going to react.

Sabelu looked around and noticed that most of his visions of this place were of the past, when his ancestors roamed these hills. The future was largely a mystery. This gave him pause. Even on the occasion that he went out on an extended hunt or game drive, he still knew the land, knew what it was and what it would become. Here, even the land faded away.

But in the present moment, if such a thing existed, he managed to focus on a small swath of land that was relatively flat and sheltered. It would rain over the next few days; they would need some form of protection. Without a word, he started down the slope toward that spot of land. Netami followed.

"Sabelu, where are you going?" she asked.

He stopped in his tracks as though he'd been slapped in the face. He momentarily forgot how to breathe as he watched the day play out, the things that would happen, that had to happen.

But he was also presented with something he'd not seen before: an empty space in his gift of sight. Perhaps empty wasn't the right word, for that would have implied that it was devoid of events or other intuition. No, it was more like it was blocked out, but full. Something was going to happen, and he didn't know what. It was an odd sensation, almost foreign, something he hadn't even approached since he was a child, before the impressions and waking nightmares.

He did not attempt to answer her question, just continued moving as soon as he could, still heading for the sheltered spot. Netami caught up to him, though she remained a step behind.

"It's beautiful here," she observed. "I love watching the buds unfurl into leaves."

He took her simple joy and clung to it. "You love it when the leaves change color, too. So you get both in a single day."

"I suppose so. It's funny how the seasons are so...off, between our worlds."

"It's too bad our ancestors couldn't keep their land. Grow food here in season, then grow food on Hlohi in season."

"Well, Itsitsa says that some good has come from the removals." She went on before he could speak. "I'm not saying they were a good thing; they were terrible and murderous. And you know I'm being honest. But it sounds like the peoples have made some progress."

"Good," Sabelu said curtly. "I'm glad for them."

"You see something."

He huffed a sigh. "No. I know there are people around, but I don't know the future of them all."

She didn't believe him, not entirely. "Well, I won't ask what's coming, not until you've found Anagalisgi and hopefully gotten some things sorted out. If you have trouble just with Aktiya Waya and the Krydik, I can't imagine the burden of all of the people of the Old Land."

If there was any advantage to his abilities, it what that he knew what people truly thought and felt, even if they had trouble putting it into words. Sometimes he wished others had just a shadow of his gift, enough to know when he was grateful, even when he had trouble saying so. He stopped and faced her. "Let me ask you a question. If Anagalisgi can't help me, and if this only continues to get worse, what will you do?"

She raised a brow. "You're asking me a question?"

Her question did not provoke more than a bit of amusement in Sabelu, but he replied, "I want to hear you say it."

She sighed, and he could hear and feel everything as if it were his own. First she would have to deal with his threats of suicide, which she expected to manifest shortly after this went poorly, if it did. Second, she feared having to make a decision between helping him, defending him, and maintaining the honor of the family as a whole, whether by allowing his suicide or not interfering in whatever fate the council and priests determined for him. Finally she answered, "I don't know."

"Liar."

He continued walking.

"Just because you know something about me doesn't mean I do," she protested, following. "I suspect that you're able to articulate things a lot better than I can, sort out thoughts and feelings faster than I can because I'm the one living them. So just because you know something about me that I don't understand doesn't make me a liar."

"You would rather be called ignorant?"

"I'm ignorant about a lot of things compared to you. I don't deny it. Being called ignorant is less annoying than being called a liar, coming from you."

"But still annoying," he stated, stopping at the appropriate patch of ground. It wasn't much, a relatively level spot with moderate natural protection, though the natural state of the landscape and the surrounding trees would allow for easy shelter building.

"A little, yes." She went on before he could speak, "I just hope Anagalisgi can help you so that you can articulate your own thoughts and feelings so that you can relieve me—all of us, of some of our ignorance."

He looked around at the trees. "So do I."

"You say that like you don't know."

"I don't."

He went and started gathering firewood. Netami continued to follow, not helping. "What do—? You said it's quieter here. I'm glad. But I feel like that should come with some ability on your part to take what you already know, what you've already seen, and sort through it a little better. Now that you're not bombarded by everyone else's thoughts, maybe you can have some of your own."

Sabelu paused and considered this. Then, "But considering the futures that I see for others, how do I know which one is mine? If I could see something of my future, that I definitively knew was mine, then I might be able to say, yes, Anagalisgi helps me and I don't kill myself. But I can't."

Netami sighed but said nothing more—aloud—as she went to work, helping to build a small camp. Only when the fire was burning steadily did Sabelu reach for his pack and bring out the nattawodatnu, the seeing fruit. There were none to be found in the Old Land, not this time of year, but they were just in season on Hlohi. Their cultivation and use was currently restricted to the priests only, seeing how there was only one tree that produced the fruit that gave the desired results, that of speaking to the spirits.

There was more to it than that, but Sabelu had little desire to think about it now as he peeled the skin and cut a slice.

"If anything happens to me," he said, holding the slice on the blade of his knife, "know that I've always been grateful for your help, for standing up for me."

"What?" Netami asked. "What do you mean?"

But he was already eating the fruit.

Even as soon as the juices touching his lips, the veil between worlds began to tear, and it was as though he saw the heart and mind of the earth itself. As he could look at a person and see their past and future, so he saw it around him in the hills and trees. Where back home the phantoms were isolated, fleeting, and without feeling or motivation, here now it was like walking into a city of endless people and feeling and knowing every single one of them at the same time, being all of them, even. He felt the groan and heave of the earth, scar tissue and tender flesh, memories of eons long past and epochs yet to come.

The sensation was enough to paralyze him, but the fruit—only a slice of it—was still in his mouth, its power leeching into him. But there was something more. Something else was trying to leech power out of him.

Suddenly, he felt claws on his back and teeth in his shoulder, a huge mouth nearly around his neck. He could not feel it as a person, did not know its thoughts or memories or feelings or motivations, nothing outside of chaos and kill and destroy. As the fruit's effects came more into focus, he was able to turn his head, just a little, and catch a glimpse of the beast on his back. He could not discern its shape beyond smoke and shadow, but the more he thought about it, the more he saw it, the more it realized that it was seen, the heavier it got.

Sabelu leaned forward until he was on his hands and knees. He couldn't be sure if he was there physically, or if he had somehow left the physical world. Then he was on his belly, like a snake, still under the crushing weight of the beast, its teeth and claws sinking ever deeper into his flesh.

As it did, he saw even more. He saw histories full of blood and murder. He saw futures that were more of the same. Desolation, anarchy, sheep surrounded by wolves yet denying the danger. His people, his ancestors, their neighbors, whites, blacks, everyone in between, all across a world where the amount of blood spilled was one hundred times the water that filled the oceans.

His muscles began to twitch, his body desiring to contort in pain but unable to under the crushing weight of the Shadow upon his back. He didn't know what to do, if there was anything he could do. Was it possible that the blackness, the abyss that obscured his sight was in fact a warning of his own death? Had he come looking for help in order to avoid death, only to walk right into it?

His twitching muscles began to strain, and he feared his might explode. Had he been able to, he might have startled as he heard wolves howling in the distance.

For just a moment, the Shadow on his back loosened its grip. Then it redoubled its efforts. Sabelu knew there was no way it could sink its teeth any farther into his flesh and not break bone; he was surprised it hadn't already. Surely it would soon find the artery in his neck, tearing open his meat carcass and spilling his life into the soil.

He heard vibrations in the ground, and the Shadow began to growl, deep and sickening inside a diseased chest. The vibrations grew louder and he began to feel them. White flashed in his vision. There was more growling and snarling. Soon the Shadow had to make a choice whether to keep its grip on him or face its attackers.

It chose him. With a final crunch, the Shadow punctured flesh until its upper and lower jaws met. Sabelu might have screamed, he wasn't sure. Then the weight lifted off him. It was not the Shadow leaving his body voluntarily, for the teeth were still in his flesh as the weight shifted. Sabelu was too dazed to wonder if flesh actually tore from his bones or if he only imagined it did.

The pain was initially what kept him immobile, wheezing for breath there on the ground, still on his belly, the side of his face pressed into the dirt. He could hear snapping and snarling, the sounds reminisce of fighting dogs. He was unable to move his eyes, but every so often, he saw a white paw or tail, and he figured that a pack of wolves had come to save him.

Slowly he realized the pain was reaching beyond just the bite at his neck and shoulder. Like fire or ice or perhaps an angry swarm of wasps, it moved through his body, infecting his blood, destroying his life force. His left arm went numb and his head began to feel cool and tingly, as though he lay his head on snow instead of dirt. His breathing slowed and his vision darkened. Had he truly tried to avoid one death, only to walk into another? Was this to be his great legacy, going mad and becoming scorned among his own people, only to die in a foreign land? He was only just a man and the most he had to his name was a bad reputation. Surely there had to be more to life than this. An adelohosgi was supposed to guide his people; what had he done?

He had a vague sense of his body being moved, and he put up as much resistance as a piece of cloth. The last sense he had was something soft and warm. Then he dropped into oblivion.

Sleep had not comforted Sabelu for several years now, but he found himself welcoming the chaos of his dreams over the hell that he had seen from the Shadow, the endless ages of blood and death. And yet, what he found now was not chaos. In fact, with exception of a few images imprinted into his mind, he couldn't say that he dreamed at all. And it was this confusion that began his ascent out of unconsciousness.

At first, fatigue was all he knew, such that he questioned whether he'd truly rested, not that sleep brought him much rest these days, but he usually felt better than he did now. All the same, if a little more fatigue was the price he paid for a night free of visions and madness, he would take it.

Then the fatigue began to manifest itself in his body, his limbs feeling weary as if he'd just climbed a mountain or fought a bear. He didn't know that he could lift his arm if he tried.

Eventually, he reached a point, mentally, where he decided to try. That was where he acquired another sensation, pain. Compared to the agony of the Shadow chomping down on his flesh, this pain was little more than an inconvenience, a small thorn in the finger, a minor nick of a knife, hardly the decapitating purgatory from earlier. He managed to trace the pain back to his left shoulder and side of his neck, where the Shadow had bitten him, but it did not radiate far beyond that.

The pain brought him more quickly back to the waking world. He felt a mat beneath him, but also constant coolness as if from stone. To one side, heat, as if from fire. His shirt was missing as well, perhaps to address his neck and shoulder wound. At his feet, across his lower legs, he felt more warmth, but also softness, as if from fur. Except the fur was moving. Breathing. He felt a bit of movement and a sound, as from a dog licking its muzzle.

For a long moment, he just lay there and listened. It occurred to him that he actually could not See anything, in the sense of his gift. He had to physically feel and hear the animal at his legs to know it was there, but he had no knowledge of its current state of mind. Similarly, he could not detect anyone in the immediate vicinity. Thinking about it, he couldn't sense them, but neither did he hear anything that would indicate someone nearby. Where was Netami?

His heart jumped, but his body did not, as he heard a sound. It was a squeaking sound, a heavy sound, and another sound that, if Sabelu was any judge, someone was trying to muffle. The animal at his legs moved, perhaps lifting its head, though its body remained where it was.

"No, Yawi," a male voice said softly. "Stay there."

Yawi, Sabelu thought as the animal lay its head back down. Yawi was the name of the wolf Anagalisgi had seen in his dreams when he first ventured to Hlohi.

There were some light footsteps, a bit of shuffling. Then more footsteps, and someone approached Sabelu where he lay. As soon as fingers touched his shoulder where the Shadow had bitten him, Sabelu lashed out, catching the man's wrist. He opened his eyes.

Familiarity washed over Sabelu like a tide. He couldn't remember ever meeting this man before in his life, and yet he knew that they had seen each other, even spoken.

"Anagalisgi," he stated.

"Sabelu."

They stared at each other for a long moment. Even as Sabelu tried to figure out where and how they could have met, he was also acutely aware that he could not sense the man. He did not know his thoughts, emotions, fears, triumphs, failures, none of it. It was like looking at a child, how quiet and solid he was.

"Can I have my hand, please?" Anagalisgi asked finally.

Sabelu slowly released his grip on the man's wrist. Anagalisgi began to probe the spot where he'd been wounded. "The infection seems to have cleared, but healing will be slower, I'm afraid." He sighed and sat back on his heels. "And there will be a rather nasty scar. Fortunately for you, it will only be physically seen here, else you might have some explaining to do."

"What...?"

He got to a sitting position, his attention drawn to a massive white wolf at his feet, its head and front paws across his legs. It looked up at him and opened its silver mouth in a huge yawn before staring at him with shining silver eyes. After a second or two, the wolf stood and approached, nosing his head like a dog and giving a few tentative licks. Sabelu put a hand up to block the sloppy tongue and scratched the wolf's chin.

"I don't understand," Sabelu said, looking at Anagalisgi even as Yawi lowered its head for a scratch between the ears. "Where's Netami?"

"Exactly where she was," Anagalisgi told him. "Exactly where you are. You have not physically gone anywhere in the waking world."

Sabelu blinked. "But...the Shadow. The visions." He looked at his shoulder where twisted flesh slowly mended itself back together. "This wound."

"All of it born from a world beyond the physical, though just as real. People forget that it is not only good spirits who inhabit the spirit world."

"But I don't..."

He shook his head. Everything was so quiet. He saw nothing, heard nothing, sensed nothing. Anagalisgi and Yawi, utterly opaque. Everything and everyone beyond this cave they were in, he was completely blind to. He'd longed for this for years, yet he felt naked without his agotvhdi, and his head felt empty. He'd been articulating everyone else's thoughts for so long, he'd forgotten how to think himself.

"When you were born, you were divined to be a dark seer, such as myself, but also a keeper of truth and history. Adelohosgi is the term now used, I believe," Anagalisgi said, still squatted beside him. "Although we reside on different worlds, I felt your birth and your destiny even here. I visited you when you were still an infant."

Sabelu studied the man's face, suddenly frustrated that he could not discern his motives. Finally he said, "I don't remember."

Anagalisgi's expression was gentle. "I don't expect you would." He stood and crossed the cave to a stone table and grabbed a jug of water and small cup. As he returned, he added, "I told you then to remain in the waking world as much as possible."

"It's only marginally better than the dreaming world," Sabelu said, reaching for the water as it was offered.

His uncle nodded sadly. "But even as I felt your birth and destiny, so did the Shadows."

"But if my sight is so great, how did I not notice that thing on my back?"

"Didn't you?"

Sabelu paused. He sifted through his memories, the terrible progression of his agotvhdi over the last few years. "The chaos."

"The Shadows can't stop you from seeing, but they can distort your agotvhdi," Anagalisgi told him, "force you to see so much that you have no possible way of making sense of it all. Overload the spirit to destroy the body and mind."

"Why didn't you step in sooner? Uncle, I was going to kill myself."

Anagalisgi nodded sympathetically. "I know. I imagine that the chaos of your mind was too great for you to notice, but you have been the focal point of a very intense, but invisible, war. Whites and Shadows have been fighting over you your whole life. And yet, it is still your life. The decision to get help had to be yours. The Whites would call you, the Shadows would confuse you, and on it went until you had but one decision left to make."

"Find you, or throw myself off a cliff."

"Exactly."

Sabelu shifted his stance and glanced around the cave, at Yawi who was sniffing around apparently aimlessly, back to his uncle. "So the war is over then? Now that I've found you, and you—or, I think it was Yawi and the wolves that actually did it—got that thing off my back?"

Anagalisgi chuckled humorlessly. "Oh, how I wish that were so. If only things were so easy or so simple. No, I'm afraid the war is not over. It's only just begun. All that's changed is that you have become an active participant instead of a passive victim."

"That doesn't sound like the better option."

"It is if you want to live."

Sabelu huffed a sigh. "All right, so what does that mean? Am I not going to have visions anymore? Am I going to stop seeing people's thoughts, feeling, past, present, future, all of it?"

"No. But, in getting the Shadow off your back, you should be able to learn to control it, though it won't be overnight."

"How did it get there?"

Anagalisgi made a motion to follow. At the mouth of the cave, he had built a wooden room, almost like an observation post. They left through the door and stood outside. Sabelu did not recognize the area, nor did he see Netami.

"As I said, you've been a pivotal point in a great, invisible war," Anagalisgi said, starting down a small trail. "The Whites have fought as hard as they could, but there is much darkness around the people. I imagine the beast started out small and only grew by your insanity, defended venomously by other Shadows."

"Why did coming here make a difference?" Sabelu wondered.

His uncle may have sighed; he wasn't sure. "I speak kindly when I say that there is a darkness around the people. In fact, they have become a haven for the Shadows. Not quite a stronghold, as other places, but a haven nonetheless. Every battle was our disadvantage. Here, things tend to be in our favor."

Sabelu looked around. They appeared to be in the same mountains, the trees just fluffing out into summer foliage. He saw small creatures rustling in grass and bushes for food, and a number of birds twittered in the high branches. Most of them he had never seen or heard before, yet he knew them still, from the memories of his ancestors.

He considered the sensation. It was simple familiarity, as if the memories were his own and required no nauseating flood of backstory or other extraneous information. Whether the memories came from his grandfather or someone else—maybe even Anagalisgi himself, somehow— it was just something that he now knew. Perhaps it would be different once he returned to the waking world, but for the moment, he was enjoying it.

"If there is a darkness among the people," he began, "then when I go back...it's all going to happen again, isn't it? The overflow of information, the impressions, the visions, all of it, it's going to come back."

"The Shadow did not make you a seer, Sabelu. You already were. The Shadow just distorted your perceptions, made it so you were unable to distinguish between the information you were receiving and the information you needed, making every minute detail its own grand discovery." Anagalisgi nodded. "Yes, it will all come back, and it will start just as soon as you leave this place." He continued before Sabelu could open his mouth to protest. "I can tell you that it will not be quite so overpowering, but it will be there."

Sabelu stepped over a log as they made their way up a steep incline. "I don't understand, though. There's a war over me? What for? And why would Aktiya Waya be a haven of darkness? Does it have to do with the sorceries and the Books in some way?"

"It does," Anagalisgi replied simply. "And the Author."

"I don't get it."

Anagalisgi stopped at the top of the rise and looked at him, expression unreadable. "You will."

Sabelu went and stood next to him. Where he expected to see a downslope and more mountains, he found himself facing a gentle forest dotted with white trees, and, beyond that, a lush silver-grassed meadow foaming with white flowers. Even farther beyond that, a few more white trees, these starkly visible against a thick forest of blackened and rotted husks that were once trees but somehow still standing. Dark clouds swirled above this place, a near-physical line seeming to separate the two places.

"Where are we?" Sabelu wondered.

"The world beyond the veil. The true spirit world." Anagalisgi nodded discreetly toward the area. "This is our battleground." He grinned and chuckled humorlessly once. "Well, I say 'our,' but really it's the spirits' battleground. Mortals would have a difficult time surviving, even one as experienced as myself."

"You've seen such battles, then?"

"I have. It's dangerous, but also terribly mesmerizing."

Sabelu shifted his stance. "Why did you bring me here?"

"So you could see and understand what is it you're up against. It goes beyond overwhelming visions and seeing people's thoughts and emotions. It goes beyond your own madness and whatever trouble you stir up because of it. There is more to being a seer than simply telling the people when to plant corn."

Peering at the distant, swirling clouds, Sabelu thought he could make out a huge shape, something flying up there, barely visible as black lightning flashed across the sky.

"What do I do, then?" he wondered, not looking away from the beast.

"The first step has already been taken," Anagalisgi told him. "You have been rid of the Shadow that has been riding and controlling you. While this leaves you open to help, it also leaves you open to attack. Do not make the mistake of thinking they won't try again."

Now Sabelu broke his gaze and gave his uncle a look. "How can I help the people if I'm bogged down by insanity, or trying to fend it off?"

"The next step is to know what is going on beyond the waking world." Anagalisgi again gestured to the white and black forests. "Perhaps it was my error for not telling you earlier, but we're here now."

"You can't come with me to Hlohi?"

Anagalisgi shook his head and began walking back down the hill. "I cannot, no. I am bound to this place by the will of the Author, although she may permit me to sojourn in other places for brief periods."

"Well that's convenient."

Sabelu was still at the top of the hill, staring down at his uncle. When he looked back, the white forest and meadow had gone, as had the black forest. All that remained was a downslope and mountains beyond. He rubbed his eyes once, but all appeared entirely normal, exactly as expected. He slid down after Anagalisgi.

"The Whites, however, do cross and travel wherever they wish," his uncle was saying.

"I'm guessing the Shadows do the same," Sabelu guessed.

"You guess correctly."

"Do the Whites have any havens or strongholds?"

"Small ones, few and far between. This is one such place, around my cabin, which is why you are not overwhelmed by more visions."

Sabelu considered this as they returned to said cabin. Yawi was laid out on the ground, sunbathing. A few more White wolves were also lounging on the ground or various nearby boulders. All of them looked up as the two men approached, then finally stood.

"You are safe for now," Anagalisgi said, giving scratches to some of the wolves before heading back inside, Sabelu in tow. "But I cannot imagine that the Shadow upon your back will not report this to the dragon."

"The dragon?" Sabelu questioned.

"Who rules the Shadows, who gives commands, who drives this war and all wars. Once it hears of this development, it won't be long before they attack again."

"How am I supposed to fight that if you say that Aktiya Waya is a Shadow haven and mortals would not survive?"

"When it comes to the waking world, the realm of mortal men, the Shadows very rarely attack directly. They prefer pawns and proxies. It's a game to them. As you get older and more experienced, you will understand. They will use someone or something else to get to you."

"Half the council and the priests want to kill me already."

"And one of them may very well try."

Sabelu sighed. "What do you expect me to do? If I am going to be overwhelmed again with visions and everything else, what am I supposed to do, and what chance do I have to do it?"

"I will go with you," a new voice said.

He turned, but the only other being in the room was Yawi. Then the wolf opened its mouth and spoke, the same voice, smooth but powerful. "Without the Shadow on your back, feeding on your energy and visions, it will be much easier to defend you, and it will allow us to start a real campaign against the Shadows there, turn a Shadow haven into a White refuge."

Sabelu pointed, opened his mouth, couldn't find words, looked at his uncle, and finally managed, "He talks?"

"You've read the Books, you know Ge'gwogv talks," Anagalisgi said.

"I thought...That was...But he..." Sabelu shifted his stance several times, lowering his hand. "What? I'm supposed to return to Aktiya Waya with a talking wolf?"

"Given the name, I think they should be grateful," his uncle commented.

"The humans will not see me," Yawi went on. "I will not reveal myself to them. My purpose is to defend you while your kin teaches you our ways."

Sabelu paced several times across the cave. "So, you're going to try to help me control what I see." He pointed vaguely toward his uncle as he walked, not looking at either of them. He pointed at Yawi. "You're going to defend me from any more Shadows trying to jump me from behind." He ran his hand through his hair. "And once I'm in control and have learned a few things, we're going to depose the Shadows out of Aktiya Waya?"

"They are in all the villages, encompassing all of the people," Anagalisgi told him, "but yes."

"Why couldn't I have been made aware of all of this sooner?"

"You were made aware."

Sabelu stopped pacing and sighed. "The Books."

"Yes. I saw them. Your father saw them. Now you see them."

"My father isn't an adelohosgi, though."

"Maybe not, but it was important for him to know."

Sabelu shook his head. "I don't know where to begin."

"You will return to the waking world," Anagalisgi said, sounding very matter-of-fact. "You will be confused, disoriented, and, after the peace this place has afforded your mind, a bit overwhelmed, I will not lie. Once that has subsided, and you realize that things are not so bad as they were before, you will return to Aktiya Waya. Again, you will feel overwhelmed. Brave through it. When you sleep, I will come to you again."

"How can you not follow me to Aktiya Waya, but come in my dreams?"

"One place is physical, the other is not. There is more to the universe than meets the eye."

"This is known, but...it's so...overwhelming."

"Start small," Anagalisgi said kindly. "The smallest minority is the self, and this is who must be helped first if you are to have any effect in helping the people. If a man is out of touch with himself, he is out of touch with his surroundings, and this causes a ripple effect which can harm others."

Sabelu shook his head. "I feel like my ripples are more like waves."

"And so they are. You must change your rhythm, bring yourself back in balance. You have already begun this process just by coming here, where you can see things without being accosted by the Shadows of Doubt and Fear and make a rational decision."

"Why can't I stay here, then, and learn here?"

"You cannot build strength if there is no weight to be overcome. I can speak all the words I want while we are here, but your growth would be only minimal because there is no weight."

"But when I sleep, I am crushed."

"I will be with you, as will Yawi. We will help you get through this; there is a lot of work to be done."

The thought was daunting, but, without the Shadows of Fear and Doubt hanging around, Sabelu found that he was far more agreeable to the mission, compared to how difficult it was for him just to get to the Old Land from Aktiya Waya. Had he really considered killing himself earlier that day? While he wouldn't say such musings had left him entirely, the whole notion now felt...extreme. And a bit foolish.

"Will I ever come back here again?" he wondered, looking at his uncle. "I understand that there is work to be done elsewhere, but this is the most at peace I've felt in a long time."

Anagalisgi nodded. "Yes, you will return here. But you should consider it a gift, not an expectation."

Sabelu blanched. "Did you ever experience anything like this? The constant noise in your head? The Book doesn't say anything about it, but did you?"

His uncle shook his head. "No. As a seer, I was only a messenger. You are a keeper."

"What's the difference?"

"The messenger tells the people that they are in danger of having their culture stolen from them. The keeper picks up the pieces of culture that the people have willingly thrown away."

"Was it wrong, then, for Yvgidahi to welcome so many peoples and refugees? You know I am blended from many peoples. Aniyvwiya, Chahta, Lenape, American."

"If red and white did not blend, we would never understand the beauty of pink," Anagalisgi stated. "If yellow and blue did not mix, how would we know green?"

"But some things should stay separate," Sabelu said. "Good and evil." He gestured to Yawi. "Whites and Shadows." He blinked. "You're not speaking of literal things." He went on before Anagalisgi could speak. "But if a keeper only keeps these things, why do you speak of deposing Shadows? How am I supposed to accomplish this? What am I supposed to do?"

"Again, Sabelu, you jump to the end when we are only at the beginning. You will do nothing without self-control. If you do not control yourself, someone or something else will. Remember, the Shadows rarely engage in direct combat in the waking world. Your adversaries will come as friends and family, acquaintances, clan members, none of them evil by themselves as men, but influenced by Shadows. You must prepare yourself."

Sabelu huffed a sigh of frustration.

"I understand," his uncle went on. "You wish you could make them see, to give them a glimpse into your mind, your reasoning, to show them what is so obvious to you but a mountain to them. Believe me, I understand. I wish I could do the same to you, but I can't. I can only guide."

For a long moment, neither man said anything, and Yawi simply sat down and watched them. The wolf talked. This was not uncommon in the innumerable stories of the people, Sabelu just never expected to meet such an animal himself.

"It is time for you to return," Anagalisgi stated, shifting his stance. "As I said, you will be a bit disoriented, and you will continue to see and know things. Yawi will protect you from the Shadows, and I will guide you in your dreams, but you must be able and willing to listen and learn, or else this will all be for nothing."

Sabelu nodded. "I understand, Tsidushi." He looked around. "How do I get back?"

"Get back where?"

The voice belonged to Netami, and as Sabelu turned to look for his uncle, he found himself suddenly awake, staring at his sister who looked a bit confused, but also relieved.

His senses were wholly scrambled as his body tried to reconcile having been standing with his uncle and yet now lying on the ground looking up. And, like clearing a mass of leaves from a stream, more information began pouring into his mind. Somehow, he knew more than just an afternoon had passed. Looking at Netami, he knew she hadn't slept well, hadn't eaten at all, and was afraid for both herself and her brother; the rain that had been hovering over the area wasn't helping her disposition any. She was relieved that he had woken up and spoken coherently, but there was still the lingering doubt over what had happened. She had burned incense as she watched over him and considered several times returning to Aktiya Waya for help. The only reason she hadn't was because she was uncertain whether he would actually get help or if the priests would try to murder him in his vulnerable state.

He also saw a brief vision of her speaking to their mother when they returned. Their mother was naturally worried, but Netami was trying to explain what had happened, how things were better.

It also occurred to him that he was knowing all of these things without feeling as though someone were stabbing him in the head repeatedly. More than that, he could actually look at her. Rather than a massive flock of birds diving at him, everything passed through his mind in a far more orderly fashion. He might have even said that the sharp edge of his insanity had dulled so that he no longer saw her every possible reaction overlapping on her face, or heard every word she might say. He still sensed her, still knew her general disposition and had visions, but it no longer hurt to exist in her presence.

She scooted back a bit as he sat up. Looking around, he saw that she'd cobbled together a shelter to keep off the rain, and a small fire burned steadily just out of arm's reach.

"How long has it been?" he asked.

"Four days," she replied softly, as if speaking to a stranger. She feared what had happened to him, wondered if he was still her brother. "After you ate of the nattawodatnu, you collapsed. For a moment, you were rigid, as a stone. Then you began flailing wildly as though possessed by an evil spirit. Then you went still. I didn't know whether you had died, I thought about going back for help, but I didn't know what to tell them, and I didn't want anything to happen to you, but I didn't know what to do."

"No. No, it's all right. Anagalisgi took care of me."

"Anagalisgi. You saw him?" Netami's eyes were huge.

"Yes. I spent the afternoon with him. Or rather, it felt like an afternoon. I'm not entirely sure."

"What did he—" She cleared her throat. "He told you something. Or he healed you."

Sabelu faltered for half a moment. "He...began the healing. He said he would continue to guide me." It also occurred to him that her question had not evoked a wild response.

"That's good." Netami grinned, and Sabelu couldn't be sure that the relief he felt wasn't his own. "And you look..." She made vague, awkward gestures, unsure just how to continue. "Good. You look better than you did when we first arrived. And your sleep wasn't so fitful as it normally is." She nodded slowly. "So you're saying we have to stay here a while, so Anagalisgi can guide you."

He shook his head, momentarily feeling almost disembodied. "No.

No, we should go back to Aktiya Waya. Itsitsi is worried, and the worst of the priests' anger toward me has cooled. Anything left is what has smoldered for a long time now."

Rather than feeling these things as water being poured down his throat so that he drowned, he now knew them with the calm certainty of being wet because he was standing in water. Granted, he still felt neck-deep, but it was better than drowning.

He wondered if it would last once they returned and he was again among people.

Netami nodded uncertainly. "All right. We can do that."

Sabelu looked at her as she gathered up a few of the supplies that she'd taken out of the packs. He could still feel her as a powerful presence pressing on his mind, knew everything she was feeling, knew what she was going to pick up before she did, knew the things she had done while watching over him. He got vague impressions of what she was thinking right now, blurry, dream-like images pressed upon his psyche. And yet, it remained separate from the person before him. She was no longer layered in time, but very nearly solid. For the first time in a year, he could look at his sister and not have a mental breakdown.

"Here's your bag," Netami said, handing him the bag and standing. He followed suit. "Are you conjuring Galohisdi?"

She snapped her mouth shut and huge waves of guilt and shame flooded through her. Her eyes were huge as she looked at Sabelu, silently pleading for forgiveness.

But Sabelu was largely unaffected. Rather than being overwhelmed by images of every possible outcome, he was presented with only a simple knowledge of what was to come.

"It's all right," he told her, intentionally looking at her. "I think I can handle it."

Her expression softened and she shifted her stance. "What did Anagalisgi do to help you so, that the priests have been so unable?"

"He cleared the Shadows away. And I don't think it's that the priests were unable, but unwilling."

"Why do you say that? Of course they want to help you."

"The priests might, but not the Shadows."

"Sabelu, you're not making sense."

"I don't understand it either, but Anagalisgi has promised to help me and show me what I need to do next."

Netami was still uncertain, her fear morphing into confusion as she thought about the priests and their words and actions, trying to pinpoint something that bespoke of an unwillingness to help her addled brother. He saw her, in the near future, going to the priests and asking roundabout questions, trying to get them to admit to some nefarious dealings.

"Come on," he said, readying himself for Galohisdi. "Let's go home."

ᏗᎩᏄ ᎠᎤᏏᎢ

Atsone Adolv'i

Big Brother

Sabelu had guessed correctly when he figured that returning to Aktiya Waya and being among people once more would bring him back to the brink of madness. Walking past the guards at the entrance to the bowl, he again saw the man who had killed a bear and had argued with another about it. He knew how the argument had started, he knew what was said, he knew how it ended, and he knew the discontent brewing between the men because of it. He knew that there would be a fight between them at the upcoming festival, though it wasn't going to turn into much because they would be told to take out their anger in the wrestling ring. They would, the man who killed the bear would lose, and he would be shamed in front of everyone.

And this was just one man and one event.

Looking at the man whom the bear man had argued with, Sabelu saw how harsh he was with his wife, how, even though they had four sons and three daughters, he still wasn't satisfied with their family or himself, how he was chasing some kind of elusive "more" that would bring him satisfaction, and how it would eventually lead to his death in about eight years as he would do something stupid on a game drive and eventually land under his horse's hooves to be crushed.

On their way through the grassy fields toward the village, he saw a woman. She was newly married in the last couple years, had one baby already and just found out she would have another. She was still starstruck by her husband and equally in love with their children. She carried memories of a duty-driven, mildly aloof mother and had vowed to herself to be better than that for her own offspring. And she would be, caring for them and nurturing them and their children for many years. She would be a Gigu one day, perhaps not so famous as Diwedalohi, but loved and respected nonetheless.

If Sabelu noticed any difference from Anagalisgi's interference, the Whites taking the Shadow off his back, it was that he simply knew these things, and they did not appear as a constant barrage of visions and hallucinations, overlapping the people as shape-shifting monsters. He could actually stand to look at people, adults, not just children. This was not to say that the knowledge itself was not overwhelming, for he could also still sense the presence of everyone in the village. Around one or two people, it was almost bearable, but it still appeared as though the acquisition of the knowledge was involuntary.

He moved slowly, acutely aware that the last time most people had seen him, he'd been almost curled up on the ground, going insane, still verbally beating the priests and council, before finally running away like a hunchbacked idiot being led by his sister. It actually wasn't his most embarrassing moment, just the most recent one.

No one said anything to him, though most acknowledged his presence by intentionally ignoring him, averting gazes and turning away on some suddenly important task.

The phantoms still persisted, sometimes in his peripheral and sometimes not. Unlike before, when all of the phantoms were devoid of motivation and so distinguishable from the reality around him, now they were different. Some of the phantoms had motive, and the motives were all dark. The Shadows were masquerading as his hallucinations, keeping an eye on him, confusing him, but never getting close before they vanished, disappearing before he could look at them too long but not before leaving him with a flash of a vision, like bright sunlight, that momentarily blinded him.

"We're almost home," Netami said, somewhere close to him.

"I know where we are," he replied, feeling distant from himself.

He did not relish the idea of the confrontation that was about to happen, and he instead focused on the minor revelation that he was able to see this confrontation and know where it stood in the progression of events. It was no longer jumbled in with millions of other events, but it was a fixed place in time.

They were within sight of home when they were intercepted by their older brother. He hadn't expected to find them so soon or so easily, and he stopped short.

"You're back," Galiliga stated dumbly.

"When did you arrive?" Netami wondered before Sabelu could speak.

Galiliga blinked, refocusing himself. "They sent for me after you disappeared. It was just good fortune that we were already packing to come to the festival." He gave Sabelu an accusatory look.

"If they hadn't interfered, there would have been no commotion, no reason to think anything was amiss," Sabelu told his older brother.

"Everything is amiss with you, Sabelu."

"He can't help it," Netami cut in.

"I don't need you to defend me," Sabelu told her.

"Apparently you do," Galiliga commented.

"He went to the Old Land to seek out Anagalisgi and try to get help," Netami said.

"And did he?"

"He did," Sabelu confirmed.

For a long moment, the trio just stared at each other.

"He cured you of your madness, then?" Galiliga questioned.

"Galiliga, you only come around during festival time," Netami began softly. "You haven't seen how much worse it had become—"

"I don't need you to defend me," Sabelu repeated.

"—he could barely walk through town on his own, never mind talk to anyone—"

"Shut up!" Sabelu snapped, turning on her. "Everyone knows!"

He felt her pain as surely as if it were his own, as if Galiliga had punched him in the face. Sabelu clenched his jaw shut even as Galiliga quietly asked Netami to leave, which she did without another word.

After another long moment, Galiliga opened his mouth, but Sabelu beat him to it. "That's why I went, so I don't have to be defended by women and surrounded by only children."

"I'm not saying I don't understand," Galiliga said slowly, "or that I don't want you to find help and get some relief—"

"You just want me to keep my mouth shut. It's easier for you that way." When his brother just sighed, Sabelu went on. "Everyone wants to know the truth, but they don't want to live by it. Everyone wants to know the true history, but only if it's good. Everyone wants to know the future, but only if they benefit. Just like this year, as every year around the festival, you will ask me who should be on the national council. I will tell you who would do well, and then I will tell you what's going to happen when you ignore my advice and choose someone else because you don't think the person I said would be good enough, or you don't like them for some other reason. What is the point of asking a question if you're just going to ignore the answer?"

Galiliga sighed again and rubbed his eyes. "Sabelu, I am trying to help you—"

"And I'm trying to help you! I'm trying to help the people. But the people don't want to be helped because—"

He cut himself off, wondering if he should mention the Shadows or anything Anagalisgi had told him.

"Because...?" his brother prompted.

Sabelu found himself lowering his voice. "Because of the darkness that has settled over them, over us. Over all of us."

Galiliga folded his arms. "That sounds like a matter for the priests."

"The priests are part of it. Some willingly, some entirely unwittingly. But I can't tell them because the Shadows have too strong of a hold; they will never hear me."

His brother let out a breath. "What do these Shadows want?"

"They want to destroy the people. Yes, death and destruction are good, but at the very least, they will settle for division and incompetence. Anagalisgi and Yvgidahi tried to fight them in their own time. Our father continues to fight them here, but he is a single man."

"So are you."

"Yes, but I have Anagalisgi and the Whites with me."

Sabelu could see that Galiliga wanted to believe him. Sabelu was an adelohosgi, after all, had been divined and raised for this. And though he could be crude at times, his antics a bit outlandish, he'd never actually been wrong about anything. But while the existence of spirits both good and evil were not in doubt, it seemed a strange thing that only three men were in any position to fight the evil spirits.

Galiliga sighed again. "And what are you going to do about it?"

"I don't know yet," Sabelu admitted sheepishly. "I'm still just trying to walk through town and get home without being mobbed or harassed or overwhelmed in my own mind."

"Are you even going to go to the festival this year?"

"I don't know."

He could feel his brother's confidence dwindling. "Well, at least there are some things you don't know."

"I know that Itsitsa is going to be home tomorrow," Sabelu offered. "The hunt was very successful."

Galiliga nodded, unimpressed. "Good. I expect preparations for the festival will begin as soon as they return."

"They will."

After a moment of awkward silence, Galiliga put his hands on Sabelu's shoulders. "Are you sure you're all right? You know what's going on, what..." He dropped his hands. "I don't even know what. You are my brother and I want to support you, but some days I feel like your father who needs to discipline you."

"For what?"

"I don't know. It's as frustrating for me—and Netami, and Blaknik, and Itsitsa, and Itsitsi, and everyone else—as it is for you. When you can see and know everything and everyone, everything and everyone is affected. It's not something we can understand or experience for ourselves. Just remember that."

He walked away.

There was a time when Galiliga had been proud to call Sabelu his brother. He'd been happy to show him off, to defend him when others ignored, downplayed, or ridiculed his words and prophecies and visions.

But as the visions overwhelmed him, Galiliga came to his defense less and less, and his delight in having Sabelu as a brother dwindled. Now it felt like little more than a formality, or a technicality.

If there was any comfort Sabelu could derive from this, it was that Galiliga would not turn on him. Nor, in all honesty, would he be anyone of any real significance. Oh, he was on Yonhi's council, and was one of those who chose the national council, both of which were honorable positions, but in the grand scheme of things, he was no one truly important. In Sabelu's opinion, that was a blessed thing to be. Maybe it was different for others who couldn't see as he did, but he could do without his pedestal; his visions always seemed to be trying to push him off that pedestal to his death.

Sabelu had been preparing himself to again meet with his uncle in his dreams that night, to begin learning more about his agotvhdi, the Whites and Shadows, what he should do next. What he found instead was only blackness, the first dreamless sleep he could remember. No visions, no prophecies, nothing but peace and quiet. Oddly enough, it was also the worst sleep he'd ever gotten, and that was saying something. Perhaps his mind and body didn't know what to do with a dreamless sleep. Whatever the case, while he was fatigued, he was also greatly relieved. Even if it was only temporary, his uncle had given him a greater gift than anyone could possibly imagine.

Another thought occurred to him as daily life began pushing against his mind once more—all the people still sleeping, those who were up and around extra early, even the dreams of his mother and sister—and that was the possibility of the Shadows being responsible for his dreamlessness, that they had somehow blocked his uncle from reaching him.

It was almost odd to not know something, especially something so critical as who was controlling his dreams and feeding him knowledge. Like walking around with his uncle in his cave or the forest, for as much as he despised his gift, he also felt empty without it, half the man he was supposed to be. Did anyone else feel that way, that they were missing something? Or was it simply a matter of, if no spot was carved out for it, it never looked like anything was missing?

His ability to think about the matter diminished in proportion to the number of people who started coming awake and going about their day, as well as their proximity to him. Within an hour of his waking, his mind had regressed to something a few levels above a survival mode of existence. Fleeing from Aktiya Waya the other day had been pure survival—as most days had been up to that point—but since speaking to Anagalisgi, he could maintain something almost resembling normal. He hoped to speak to his uncle again soon so that he might do even better.

"You look terrible," Netami commented as she made tea. "Bad dreams?"

"No dreams," Sabelu told her.

"Really?"

"I know, it's strange. I don't know what to make of it."

"Maybe it's a gift from Anagalisgi."

"If that's the case, then I need to tell him it's a terrible one." Sabelu glanced at the door. "Itsitsa is almost home."

Netami's eyes lit up as she grinned. "He is?"

He barely got in half a nod before the door opened and their father walked in.

"Tsitsa!" Netami exclaimed. "Welcome home!" She thrust a cup of tea in his hands before he had a chance to set his bag on the floor. "Did the hunt go well?"

Their father, Ola Achukma, gave her a look as he sipped at the tea, glancing once at Sabelu. "You mean you don't know?"

"Oh, tell us anyway."

Sabelu started to slip away, but his father was still in the doorway. Before he could leave, his father touched his arm and said, "Don't go far."

Sabelu said nothing to that, just nodded once and ducked out.

With the return of the hunters, Aktiya Waya quickly came to life. It was the unofficial signal to start preparations for the festival. The physical change was quite noticeable. Smiles, laughter, excited chatter and laughing as the anticipation was shattered, the gate was opened, and the animals were permitted to run free. Only Sabelu noticed the rest of it, mundane thoughts and routine concerns replaced by excitement, planning, hyperactivity, and a chaos that had, in an odd sort of way, become its own routine. The pressure on his mind increased tenfold as people began to plan for the setup, remembering years past, imagining themselves in this year's events, and even looking ahead to hoped for futures of engagements and children coming of age to fully participate.

Last year, Sabelu had been so inundated with everyone's thoughts about the festival, even before it began, that he'd been unable to leave the tent, had nearly been physically paralyzed as much as mentally. To be bombarded by constant visions of all the work people had put into their training or other activities throughout the year—from the horse breeding to the arrow fletching to the crop tending—plus all their thoughts about the events as they were going on—silent pep talks, strategizing, cheating or accusations of cheating—plus all of the extra concerns—wrangling children and ensuring food was kept in constant supply—plus all of the regular needs—having to relieve oneself, looking for something to eat, fantasizing about one's husband or wife—it was the first time Sabelu had honestly considered killing himself.

Standing in Aktiya Waya now, even knowing that this was only the beginning, it felt less traumatic than before. Oh, he could sense everyone just as well, and he could look at anyone and know all of those aforementioned things, but it seemed to manifest more as simple knowledge rather than moment-by-moment visions, all overlapping and vying for attention. Becoming infused with all of this knowledge was not easy, but it was easier on his mind than the visions.

He wondered if there might come a day when his mind would "catch up" with everyone. If he could look at a man and know the entire history of his performance in the festivals, then surely that history would remain a stable, known thing, and perhaps the onslaught of such information next year would be even less traumatic until it settled down into background knowledge, in the same way that he knew his mother's favorite color was purple though such information was hardly relevant in most everyday matters.

Sabelu chose a man a short distance away and focused on him, knowing he was probably only inviting trouble.

The man, Yuhpa, was not much older than Sabelu, had been participating in the games for six years, taking one year off on account of the birth of his newborn son, and then being forced to take the next year off on account of a hip injury during practice in the horse racing. The injury had been healed easily enough with the sorceries, but it was not so swift or easy to retrain muscle tone or memory. He tried again anyway, the next day at practice, but conceded his own defeat and electing to not drag the team down with his injury.

These things were more fresh in the mind, and of far more significance than his first years of participating. His first year, Sabelu knew, he'd been ousted early from the wrestling tournament. In his mind, his opponent had cheated. His hazy memories told him this was true, and he acted accordingly, yet there was a disparity between what the man believed and what was actually true. Mentally holding the memory up against what Sabelu supernaturally knew to be true about that day, that event, that match, the man's opponent had not cheated. He'd simply been bigger, stronger, faster, and Yuhpa, being a hot-headed new participant, didn't want to admit defeat. That was all. But he'd convinced himself that cheating had taken place and he had been wronged.

No, Sabelu concluded, looking away from the man, he would never "catch up" with everyone, because everyone's perceptions were constantly changing and always at odds with the real history. He would constantly have mental double vision as he compared their memories and what they believed to be true against what actually happened. And this wasn't even considering what they envisioned themselves doing in the festival versus what they would actually do.

He looked at a woman near the common pool, Atsudiya. She'd been carefully tending a gourd vine, and even now she was imagining winning first place for the best gourd. While she was not a boastful or self-centered woman by any means, she couldn't help but envision how proud her husband and daughter would be when she was announced as the winner. Even second place wouldn't be a bad run, she thought. She hadn't placed at all last year, and she'd been absolutely crushed.

But Sabelu knew that she would not win first place. Nor second. There would be a big to-do over third place, and she would ultimately be knocked to fourth, which was not considered a valid placement. All in all, she would not place this year either.

Atsudiya would be heartbroken once again. But, from this, the timing would be correct for her to conceive another child, another daughter, and she would be happy again. She would take several years off from tending gourds for the festival to raise more children. Then, when she returned to the festival in five years, she would take first place. And subsequently have yet another child.

"You look better than when I left."

Sabelu turned as his father exited the house and approached him.

"Netami told me what you did, going to see Anagalisgi."

Sabelu just nodded.

"It seems to have helped, just from what I'm seeing."

"The overlapping visions have stopped, but I still know things," Sabelu said. "I'm still inundated with the knowledge of everyone here."

"It's a start," Ola Achukma said calmly. He shifted his stance. "Galiliga also told me what you said to him, about the Shadows."

"He doesn't want to believe me. He wants to think all of the people's problems got left behind in the Old Land, whether it was the Great Migration or the War of the Old Land." Sabelu went on before his father could speak. "It's a dangerous mentality for the people to get into, and I'm afraid it's starting to become entrenched in our identity, that because of our isolation that nothing can reach us here. And if something does happen, dumping it back in the Old Land will somehow solve our problems. But it won't, not really. Evil is already here, it was here before we were, and it will follow us wherever we go."

"And somehow, you intend to stop it."

"I have to. It's not just about us. We are the focal point, but this will have far-reaching effects, to the ends of the universe in a time where neither you or I exist anymore."

Ola Achukma didn't want to believe him either, Sabelu knew, but having seen the Shadows and the Whites himself, his unbelief had far less will than Galiliga's had.

"All right, so what's the first step in this quest of yours?" his father asked finally, sounding a bit resigned.

Sabelu felt his skin burn hot, but he was thankful he was not crippled by the question. "Anagalisgi was supposed to visit me again, but he didn't. I didn't have any dreams last night."

"That's a first. I don't know that you've ever had a dreamless night."

"Not for a long time, no. Perhaps it was a type of gift."

"A calm before the storm."

"Something like that."

Sabelu knew his father cared for him, was proud of him, respected him in many ways. He knew that his father had always tried his best to be supportive, even if he didn't fully understand what life was like for an adelohosgi so in tune with the spirits. But he also knew that his father would have great chasms of doubt, his faith in his son held together only by the divination that the priests had proclaimed so many years ago. And even then, he would have dark moments in the deep hours of the night when he would wonder if things would be very much better or worse if the antagonistic priests had been correct, that Sabelu was possessed of evil things and needed to be drowned.

Looking at Ola Achukma now, the man was wary. He wanted to be happy and hopeful that his strange son had found some semblance of help and direction, but he worried over what trials this new era of prophecy would bring. The Krydik population was still very heavily skewed toward women; if there was to be a fight of some kind, their numbers were still low.

There wouldn't be much physical fighting, Sabelu knew, as he was suddenly awash with a new wave of involuntary information, but there would be a great spiritual battle which even fewer people were prepared to fight in. He felt a tingling sensation in his hand, as though feeling soft furs. When he looked, there was nothing there.

"Sabelu?" his father's voice was distant, but he latched onto it and followed it back to the present moment. "Sabelu, are you all right?"

Sabelu blinked and looked at the ground. "Fine."

His father let out a breath. "Galiliga also mentioned—"

"They're not going to ask me about the national council this year," Sabelu said. "In the minds of the council members and priests, they worry about my sanity and spiritual affiliation. Galiliga is taking a slightly more noble stand that he doesn't want to put undue stress on me, and he will cite last year as his reason. His concern is genuine, but foolish. But it's not as though they've listened to me in the past, so the people will only continue to decline."

"Perhaps if you could name a specific threat and course of action—"

"But that's the thing. I can. I have. The people don't want to listen because they—" Sabelu cut himself off and searched for words. "The Shadows have maneuvered us into a place where every known move only causes chaos. If I give them specific names, people are going to reach for their old affiliations and we'll have our own civil war on our hands. But fighting each other only kills the body, not the evil behind the chaos that killed the body."

His father shifted his stance. "That's one option, one move as you said."

"On the other hand," Sabelu went on, "if I frame it as an outside threat —a physical one, then the Shadows will be in a position to maneuver physical attacks against us and pick us off one by one. If I frame it as a spiritual outside threat, then the Shadows who infect the people now will play with us as a predator toys with its prey before having us eventually kill each other, and me, and ensure their own victory."

His father nodded. "All right. That's two, maybe three options. What else?"

Sabelu sighed. "If I do nothing, they'll kill me eventually and then there will be no one to help. The people will divide into their old affiliations and finally kill each other off."

"Sounds serious."

He gave his father a look. "You've seen the Shadows. You know they're not just here, not just on Earth. They're everywhere. The universe is their battlefield, and they have strongholds all over the place.

Hlohi is fast becoming one of those strongholds. It won't be the biggest or the strongest, but it doesn't need to be in order to destroy us."

"Well, you're up to four options, one of which is clearly not part of the discussion."

Sabelu nodded. "I know."

"So what's the fifth option?"

"The fifth option is to try and stop the Shadows myself. It's not out of the realm of possibility. Yes, I would probably die, and there would still be a civil war among the people, but the Shadows would be forced to retreat. But when the time comes for the people to spearhead the effort of truly taking the fight to the Shadows, they really wouldn't have recovered, and the fight would be harder than it needs to be."

"How about an option where the people don't murder you?" his father suggested.

Sabelu grinned humorlessly, not looking at his father. "Even in the best outcome, I'm not going to live to see the final fruit of my labor. Quite honestly, neither are you."

"Maybe so," Ola Achukma began hesitantly, "but I don't like the thought of the people who once venerated you turning on you."

"They never won't."

"Again I ask, is there an option where the people here don't kill you?"

He nodded. "There is. But it involves going to everyone individually and ridding them of the Shadows that have a hold of them."

His father shifted his stance. "If you know all of this, as you seem to know most everything, why aren't you out doing things now? Why wait for Anagalisgi? What needs to be accomplished by waiting? Why does a prophet need a plan?"

Sabelu sighed. He'd never be able to make anyone understand. "Because, on the one hand, many of the things I see...they exist all at once for me, all happening at the same time so that it can be hard to distinguish what is before and after. The non-aging of the people on account of the sorceries doesn't help things either. Not everything is like this, and some things have certain markers that I can use to say that such a thing will happen at a specific time.

"But that only works with mundane things. Looking at the Whites and the Shadows, they exist beyond us, beyond this dimension and even the in-between dimension where Anagalisgi resides. Their ability to move in their own plane muddies the water. I could no more say that one man yelling at another man is because a Shadow wishes to tear them apart than a White using one man to discipline another or effect some kind of radical change."

A rock would have understood it better, Sabelu thought. His father was trying to put all the words together to make them make sense, drawing on what he remembered about the Whites and Shadows on the battlefield in the War of the Old Land. That alone had been enough of a shock. Trying to imagine something even greater was a little beyond him. He would never understand, Sabelu knew, not really. Few would. But at least his father would remain loyal, a servant for the people. He would have his doubts, but he would not turn against Sabelu, the people, the Whites, or the Author.

"Once you start fighting the Shadows, intentionally," his father said, "they're going to start fighting back. Intentionally."

It was as insightful as the man was going to get about the larger situation, but it summed it up nicely.

"Yes," Sabelu said reluctantly.

The two of them were silent for a long moment. Finally Ola Achukma asked, "Once you start helping the people and driving back the Shadows, will it be somehow impossible for the people to help? You make it sound like you are going to do this all by yourself."

Sabelu opened his mouth, looking for words. "Imagine you are out riding in a game drive. Now imagine that everyone else, all the other riders are blind; you are the only one who can see what's going on. Now imagine that you are trying to hunt mother bears who have been separated from their cubs and are trying to kill you."

"That doesn't sound very smart," his father commented. He added hastily, "The analogy is rather vivid and, I imagine, inadequate to describe the situation you see."

"It is."

"But it sounds like you know what you need to do," his father said, trying to sound hopeful.

Sabelu nodded and shifted his stance. "Yes. I just don't know how, other than I need to speak to Anagalisgi."

"Why return home so soon, then?"

"I need to see the people for who and what they are, not what the Shadows wanted me to see. I need to know what I'm starting with."

His father nodded. "I can understand that."

He didn't, not really. He was sitting in a canoe on top of the water, claiming he understood what was at the bottom of the river when he couldn't even see the bottom beyond vague shapes and colors. But his concern and support was genuine.

"I suppose this means you'll be participating in the games this year?"

They turned to see Galiliga approaching. His tone and demeanor said he'd been listening for at least a few minutes.

"Not participating, no," Sabelu said meekly. "I have no desire to compete in the games. But I will come and watch."

His older brother nodded slowly, then clapped him on the shoulder. "Wouldn't want to give our family too great of an advantage. Netami is well-prepared for the cooking competitions."

Sabelu had learned many years ago not to spoil the results of the games. He'd also learned that no one enjoyed being accused of cheating. Even if they had done so, they always took such offense. Even if others had seen it, and it wasn't just one man's word, cheaters didn't like to be found out. Someone was going to sabotage Netami's food—and others; it wasn't a specific vendetta—and get called out for it. Arguing would ensue. But because of the sabotage, many of the entries would be disqualified.

If the Shadows felt comfortable and unopposed, they could afford to toy with their prey for a little while. Creating strife through simple division, playing on people's envy and pride, breaking down bonds which, even after a hundred years and a war, were still quite fragile.

But once they sensed opposition, true opposition, they would strike back with a fury. First they would come after him, looking for an easy victory. If he didn't give it to them, they would go after the people.

He needed to know what to do next. He needed to talk to his uncle. But he'd only just woken up and knew he wouldn't get to sleep for a while.

"...consider helping with setup," his father was saying, bringing Sabelu back to the waking world. "Marking the course for the footrace would be helpful, and it would get you away from the people for a bit."

"Tsitsa, the women and boys mark the race courses," Galiliga said. "Sabelu is no boy."

"I can help with the horses," Sabelu said. "The competitors have already chosen their mounts. There will be no accusations."

"Very good then," Ola Achukma stated. He was searching for any way to end the discussion on a happy note, though he in no way believed that this would be the end of the larger conversation. It was a way for him to push this to the back of his mind so he could focus on his own involvement in the games. Galiliga was less convinced of this false conclusion, but he, too, wanted a way out. Ola Achukma continued, "We all have our duties, then, for the games. Get sleep when you can."

He realized his mistake half a breath after he said it, but Sabelu knew that as long as he didn't react to the statement, his father could push it from his mind, and it would be forgotten by day's end.

His father and brother departed. They would walk together for a bit, until Galiliga would head to the townhouse, and Ola Achukma would make his way out to the archery fields to begin setting up the targets. Sabelu did not move from his position just outside the house.

Netami poked her head out, then approached him, offering him a cup of tea which he accepted.

"Did I hear that you will be working with the horses?" she wondered politely.

Sabelu nodded. "It's better than holing up at home. It's simple enough, and there won't be too many people around."

"Do you see animals the way you see people?"

"Not in the same way, no. They're like Blaknik, like children just reaching adolescence, or perhaps like using Asvhnisgi on an animal. I know their general disposition, I know their current state of mind, what they're thinking about, what they intend to do in the next few moments. But I don't see their future, their past, their failures and triumphs, because, honestly, animals don't have those. They know when they have failed and they know when they have done well, but they don't have the same sense of accomplishment and pride that people do."

His sister nodded. "I remember learning Asvhnisgi on animals. I remember using it on a horse, a mare with foal. She was very...simple. She had concern for her unborn foal. She had concern for any predators that might be lurking about. She was focused on eating but had some intention of going to the river to drink." She shrugged. "And that was basically it. I knew that she had memories of predator smells and other things, but they weren't so...involved as we might make them. We think about these things, but for the horse, they simply are." She shifted her stance. "What does that say about children, then?"

"It means that children are carefree, but also impressionable. Their parents tell them the way of things, and the child simply accepts them as the way things are. It's the adults who concern themselves with whether these things are correct or incorrect, if things are the way they ought to be."

"Does that mean you were never a child?"

"Physically, of course I was. The rest of me, I cannot say."

She smiled gently. "I think so. For as serious as you were, we were still able to get laughs out of you. Maybe now that Anagalisgi is helping you, we can get laughs out of you again."

"I know you will."

He decided to leave her with that and head out to start helping with the horses. Contrary to popular belief, he did want to help people, and he did want them to feel good. For the right reasons. True peace was a reason to feel good. Ignoring a threat and hoping it went away was not a good reason, and he needed to wake people up to what was going on. Problem was, he really couldn't do that, not in such dramatic fashion. He had to be smart about it. In the old days, when a warrior went to kill a man of a rival tribe, he went with the knowledge that he couldn't take on all of the warriors at once. He had to be sneaky, plan his attack, strike at the right time, and get away. He would have to do the same, but against the Shadows.

There were more people out and about outside the stone city; most were too engrossed with their own work to pay him much mind. He spotted his father in the archery field, sorting through whatever was left over from last year with a group of men. Later on, his mother and sister would join the rest of the women in the crop fields, doing some last inspections on their crops and planning the larger menu for the other villages when they arrived.

Just walking to the horse pens, Sabelu was assaulted with enough information for him to know roughly every moment of this year's events, and even the highlights from future events. He saw winners and losers, failures and triumphs, near-crippling injuries and comebacks against long odds. If he had any relief, it was that these things came to him primarily as impressions on his mind, along with a healthy scattering of hallucinations, rather than a flood of images before his eyes and shape-shifting monsters as he passed by people.

Hoshonti was the primary horse tender, though he was joined by his teenage son Hieli as they rounded up and inspected the horses. It was Hieli who first spotted Sabelu as he entered the pen. The father and son abandoned their immediate task and approached him.

"Something wrong?" Hoshonti inquired, his tone and posture guarded.

"I thought I would help you," Sabelu stated.

It didn't take three blinks for the man to nod. "V-e. It's not difficult, just tedious with so many out there. And they know the game. Any other day we could walk up to every single one of them. But they know what's coming, so good luck getting within ten feet of them."

Sabelu was given a handful of brightly-dyed leather cords to tie on the horses' halters to signify which ones were able to compete. Blue cords signified that they were able and ready, a prime candidate. These were mostly young stallions. Green signified able, but perhaps better as a second choice, such as mares and older stallions. Brown cords signified that the horse could not compete, whether because of age, injury, or a mare in foal.

Most of the competitors already had their favorites, their regular mounts for the game drives and whatnot. But, for the younger or more inexperienced equestrian competitors, or in the event of an unfortunate accident, they might not have time to pick and choose a suitable horse. Having the colored cords to denote fitness saved everyone a lot of time.

This task was perhaps one of the least impressive uses of Sabelu's talents, as he knew which horse to approach, how, and which way it was going to go to try and evade him. This didn't mean that he never had to chase one down, but his time spent chasing was significantly shorter than Hoshonti or Hieli.

"Why don't we simply conjure Time?" Hieli complained, having lost another horse as it pranced across the field.

"It's a dangerous thing to do around a horse," his father said, not the first time he'd explained it. "To us, we simply slow Time around us, slow down the horses. At best, they simply see us moving very quickly, and it alerts their instinct to run from whatever is chasing them. At worst, we are in one place, then suddenly we are beside them, touching them. The horse will panic, and it could start a stampede." He shook his head. "No. We do not conjure Time around horses."

Hieli sighed in pointed exasperation but did not argue.

Sabelu said nothing and approached another horse, this one a slightly older stallion, mostly black with gray spots on his neck and rump and some gray stripes in his mane and tail. He'd been an excellent mount in years past. Sabelu put a hand under his mane and used Asvhnisgi.

He was starting to waver. The last young male challenger in the herd had nearly beaten him, probably would next time. His standing in the herd was going to fast slip away. It wasn't that he had any major aches and pains; he was just starting to slow down. A few years ago, he could run and jump and rear and show off to everyone that he was a champion. Now, it might take him a minute to get up to full speed, jumping just wasn't a fun thing to do, and he would have to take a breath and gather strength before he reared. Even his kicks weren't as forceful as they used to be. He was by no means a poor mount, but his competition days were fading fast.

"One more year, maybe two," Sabelu murmured, tying the green cord on the stallion's halter. "What do you say?"

The stallion snorted and moved off twenty feet to continue eating.

Knowing what he did, the stallion would get chosen by a particular competitor, the same one who had ridden him since he was first broken. He wasn't ready to give up on his favorite mount. They would do well, but it would be a fall from grace for the horse. Next year, he wouldn't be chosen at all. After that, he would be retired for use by women and children.

Sabelu did not see this through the horse, but through Hoshonti. The horse tender did not actually compete in the equestrian events, citing bias, but he was a fearsome wrestler. Hieli, on the other hand, loved to compete in the equestrian events, and was constantly inventing new games to try.

"You can't just invent a game to invent a game," his father chastised. "To a child it is a game, but it must teach him something. Horse racing, showing off the best horses for the game drives. Horse pulling, showing off a horse that can bring back lots of meat and pelts and trade—"

"Yes, that's true," Hieli acknowledged, "but it doesn't have to be just about the horses. Anything done from horseback requires coordination. The game drives, as you said. I figure, if we can dye the feathers of arrows, we can do archery from horseback as well. Competitors start out standing still, then they start walking, then they start running, and then they start running and jumping."

Hoshonti waved a hand. "Far too complicated. Wrestling, one man bests another. Archery, you hit the target or you don't. Racing, you win or you don't. Pulling, you pull the most or you don't. All of this coordination...too complicated. Like the women's events. How do they judge best cooking anyway?" He scowled. "By the Sacred Wolf, you kids are becoming consumed by these games."

"It's better than being consumed by war," Sabelu said, making himself known. He looked at Hieli. "But your father isn't wrong either."

Hieli just huffed.

"You need more cords?" Hoshonti fished for some in his pack.

"No, actually, they're all done," Sabelu told him.

The horse tender looked up and scanned the field. Sure enough, dyed tassels hung from the halter of every horse. "Oh. Well then, thank you for your help."

It was mid-afternoon. Most people had abandoned their chores in favor of a cool dip in the river. Sabelu elected to take one of the horses out for a ride. It was one of the second-choice mounts, just to ease Hoshonti's fears of anything happening to the better stock. Sabelu knew nothing bad would happen, but it was surprisingly difficult for a prophet to make himself heard, even on the most mundane issues.

Phantoms fluttered around his vision as he passed through the bowl, most of them clearing by the time he was through the pass and down the slope, away from Aktiya Waya. He still saw things, future visions of the various villages come to the games, but they were ghosts only, and he continued riding.

He did not have a particular destination in mind, only far enough away for things to settle down. He still saw things. He still knew things. But here he was not confronted by people.

So it caused some slight bit of panic in him when his horse stopped short, thoroughly surprising him. His horse hadn't intended to do so, had had no inclination toward a threat or other disruption, and he'd seen nothing indicating it would happen, or the circumstances surrounding it. Suddenly he was aware that he had only a small knife on his person. Then he considered the number of things that could sneak up on him in such a way and wondered if even the greatest physical weapon would be of any use.

He held fast to his horse as a tangle of bushes rustled. A moment later, Yawi stepped into view. Sabelu breathed a sigh of relief. His horse remained a bit antsy about the situation, but something about the White's presence indicated friendship to the beast.

"I don't enjoy my visions, but I also don't enjoy being frightened," Sabelu told the wolf. He thought a moment. "But then, this time it's only you. And it's only us. It's going to be a lot worse when the Shadows get involved, isn't it?"

Yawi did not speak, just dipped its head.

Sabelu looked around at the forest. It was familiar enough, but he couldn't shake the feeling of an unfriendly presence. "They're out there. They sense something, because you're here. Because the one was taken off me." He paused. "I can't see what they're doing, or going to do." He turned his horse around, back toward Aktiya Waya, and looked at the wolf. "You coming?"

DOI DVꞀT

Anvge Adolv'i
Lesson One

"Does this mean that I'll never be able to leave the bowl?" Sabelu asked.

He sat in his uncle's cave. Yawi relaxed next to him beside the fire while Anagalisgi grabbed some bowls and utensils for stew. Unlike before, when Sabelu had gone to the Old Land and partaken of the seeing fruit, this time his uncle had come to him and brought him back to the cave by means he did not fully understand. Anagalisgi called it dream-walking.

"Of course not," his uncle said, his voice tinted with amusement. "That would not only make for a sad existence, but it would be most ineffective against the Shadows."

"How am I supposed to fight them?" Sabelu asked irritably. "I can anticipate almost every move that anyone else is going to make, but I have no such defense against the Shadows. If walking blind is how normal people function...I don't know how they do it."

His uncle chuckled, which only annoyed him more. "I know what you mean."

He returned to the fire and ladled out some stew for both of them. Sabelu took the bowl and spoon, eyeing them suspiciously. "If this is only a dream, what purpose does food serve?"

"Does the soul require less nourishment than the body?" Anagalisgi countered.

Sabelu opened his mouth, paused, then took a bite of stew. It was good, he wouldn't deny that, but his mind was too focused on other things.

"The Shadows are not unaware of where things stand," his uncle continued after a few minutes. "It was Yawi's doing that your sleep was dreamless last night. It was the only way he could protect you."

"And tonight?" Sabelu wondered.

"The Author has brought us together to begin your training. You have all the tools you need; it's just a matter of learning how to correctly use them."

"You think my agotvhdi is a tool?"

"You think they aren't?" Anagalisgi raised a brow as he took a bite.

"It might be a good tool to predict when to plant the corn, but if I am blind when it comes to the Whites and Shadows, what good is it?"

His uncle did not respond right away, and instead stared thoughtfully into the fire while he ate. Sabelu watched him for a moment, then let out a disbelieving breath and took another bite of his own stew.

When they were finished, Anagalisgi stood and motioned for Sabelu to do the same. Yawi also stood, stretched, yawned, and shook himself. Together they left the cave and headed down the trail to a stream. Yawi crossed first, but Anagalisgi knelt in the soft, wet sand. He pointed. "What is that?"

Sabelu knelt beside his uncle and looked. He shook his head. "It's Yawi's paw print."

"What made this print?"

"Yawi's paw."

"How do you know? Are you having visions here?"

Sabelu gave his uncle a look. "I watched him do it. I watched him step right there before he crossed the stream."

Anagalisgi was unfazed. He just nodded once, straightened, and kept walking along the path. Sabelu rolled his eyes and reluctantly followed. The farther they got from the cave, the more the noise in his head increased as visions ran through his mind like a flock of birds.

After another short distance, they veered off the trail into the woods several hundred yards. Again, Anagalisgi knelt and pointed. "What is this, then?"

Sabelu knelt and looked. "It's bear scat."

"How do you know?" Anagalisgi asked simply.

Sabelu blinked. "Because I know what bear scat looks like."

Anagalisgi looked around pointedly. "I see no bears here."

Again he stood and moved on, heading farther into the woods. Yawi remained close to Sabelu who also stood but waited a long moment before following. He put his hand out. As soon as he felt the wolf's fur, the overwhelming visions dissipated into simple knowledge.

This time his uncle stopped at a tree that had fallen, becoming caught in the lowest branches of another tree. He did not kneel this time as he pointed and asked a third time, "What is that?"

Sabelu sighed and looked. "Claw marks."

"From what?"

"I don't know."

"Look, and you might find out." Now there was the faintest tint of annoyance in his uncle's voice.

Sabelu, his hand still clutching Yawi's fur, looked. It appeared to be a favorite scratching post of whoever was using it. The tree looked like a recent fall, still hard when he knocked on it, yet the claw marks had stripped the bark clear to the pulp. The lines were long and narrow, coming in groups of four.

"Bobcat," he decided.

"Why do you say that?" Anagalisgi asked.

"Four toes, not five, so it's not a bear. The marks go up the tree, not down, which means the animal likes to climb. That would eliminate foxes and coyotes. They're small, so it's not a cougar. They're too narrow to be a raccoon, in addition to how frequently this animal has been scratching."

His uncle dipped his head. "Very good." He leaned against the fallen tree. "You saw Yawi make his paw print. This was obvious. But the scat and these scratches, you had to deduce by your knowledge, what you know of the animals, without the benefit of the animal being present. Knowledge is a tool, just as your agotvhdi is a tool. Sometimes it is the absence of something that speaks." He made a gesture. "The absence of a toe told you that it was not a bear. The absence of size told you it was not a cougar or a raccoon."

"The inverted direction told me it was a climbing creature," Sabelu offered. "Inversion is a type of absence."

Anagalisgi nodded. "It can be."

"And the absence of absence, too. This is a favorite scratching post."

"Excellent work."

"But...I know animals. I can observe the animals, and sometimes I see phantoms. How am I supposed to observe the Shadows? I can't go over to the dark forest."

"No, and I wouldn't suggest it," his uncle said coolly. "You understand that the Whites and the Shadows operate on a different plane than we do. Even I am not fully integrated into the Whites' existence, as I am yet a mortal man. But that is where we actually have the advantage."

Sabelu blinked. "I don't understand."

Anagalisgi held his hand out. Yawi went to him and nosed his hand.

"We see Yawi. Feel the fluffiness of his fur, the wetness of his nose, the soul in his eyes. The sharpness of his claws. And though we see and feel him, he is not bound by mere flesh."

"Neither are the Shadows," Sabelu stated.

"No, but we humans are. We have limits. There are things we cannot do, and there are certain rituals we must observe in order to maintain our mortality. The greater Shadows know this, and their hold over their assigned humans is nearly seamless. But the lesser Shadows?" Anagalisgi shook his head. "Less careful and coordinated. Sometimes it is not even a constant relationship, but one that comes and goes."

"How does this apply to the Whites, though? Yawi doesn't control me."

"The Whites are whole and complete in the Author. The Shadows are not, and they use the minds and flesh of men to complete themselves. But flesh is only temporary."

Sabelu thought about this for a long minute, studying the claw marks on the tree. Then, "So I am correct that this must be done individually.

Any large assault will be met with brute opposition." He looked at his uncle. "But won't the Shadows take notice, when their...lesser minions start disappearing?"

"Oh, absolutely," Anagalisgi told him with barely a hesitation. "But you forget that as the Shadows are removed, the Whites may fill the void."

Sabelu faltered. "In my father's Book, he saw the Whites and Shadows on the battlefield. If the actions of men are but extensions of the conflict between the Whites and Shadows, what is to keep Aktiya Waya from turning into a battlefield itself?"

"It must, if it is to recover. Otherwise, the field is dead, the soil dead, with no hope of new growth or life, and the people are but walking corpses. There is no easy path. The Shadows let nothing escape without a fight."

Sabelu sighed. "I don't know where to begin."

His uncle gave him a cheeky grin. "Perhaps you ought to start with the largest gathering of people all year."

He considered this and finally nodded. "I suppose it would make sense that the Shadows would be very active during that time, trying to turn the people against each other, either in direct accusations of cheating or long-term, burning resentment." He made a shrugging sort of gesture and nodded again. "The Shadows will be active, and I'll be able to learn their patterns." An idea occurred to him. "Is that why the Shadows were so intent on blinding me with the shapeshifting? I have to look at someone to see the Shadows that have a hold on them." He went on before Anagalisgi could speak. "No, it couldn't be. I would have seen them today when I was out and about."

"Just because a Shadow is no longer embedded within you, doesn't mean they don't still try to influence and attack you," Anagalisgi said. "Sometimes it only makes them fight harder. They may no longer control you, but that doesn't mean they will not try to blind you to their other areas of influence."

"Would nattawodatnu help?" Sabelu suggested.

His uncle nodded. "It will make it more difficult for them to hide, yes, but I would be cautious of becoming overly dependent on it."

Sabelu shifted position. "I can understand how the earliest fruit trees were not useful, due to the way they must be planted in order to be effective. But if the newest ones are viable, and the fruit works as has been demonstrated, why do the priests not see what I do? How can the Shadows still have such hold on them?"

Anagalisgi gave him a serious look. "What happened when you ate of the fruit? Did you ever actually see the thing latched onto you?"

"Not really. But surely they would see the Shadows on others."

"Would they?"

Sabelu thought about this for a long moment. His uncle spoke again. "If the Shadows were foolish, we wouldn't be in this predicament. There are ranks and hierarchy among them, yes, but why would you assume that the leaders of the people would be held by foolish, fleeting spirits? The greater the influence, the stronger the Shadow. And these Shadows are capable of terrible and glamorous things to trick the mind. Sometimes even good can be used for evil; that's what makes it difficult for people to see it as such and condemn it.

"You have to cut through all of that. You must recognize the evil, condemn it, drive out the Shadows. The Author has much work she needs to do here, with the people. But the land must be prepped before the house can be built."

Sabelu gave his uncle a look. "Then why doesn't she do it herself? Why doesn't she just write the Shadows into oblivion? Why did they have to exist in the first place?"

Anagalisgi matched his look. "Even if I didn't know that you are arguing just to argue, I would say that you are still too immature and inexperienced to handle the answer to that question. Once you have begun to fight, you will also begin to understand, but a boy does not tell a warrior how to fight."

Sabelu nodded, mildly chastened.

"Go to the festival," Anagalisgi told him. "You don't have to participate. Just watch. Observe the people, their comings and goings, their attitudes. Use the seeing fruit only as an aid, and a last resort at that.

Now that your eyes have been uncovered, see what afflicts the people."

"If I can drive away a Shadow, should I? Or do you just want me to observe?" While there was a tangible measure of genuine curiosity in the question, Sabelu would not deny that there was also a bit of spite in there as well. A lot of what his uncle was saying and showing him made a lot of sense, and Sabelu was grateful to finally have some semblance of sanity returned to him. But he wouldn't deny that there was a tiny coal of resentment that said his uncle should have been helping, should have started this work already. Maybe the people would not have had to flee. Maybe they would not have gotten caught up in the War of the Old Land and so sacrificed nearly all of their warriors.

"You may find some Shadows that you are capable of driving off," Anagalisgi answered. "And whether you start now or wait another moon will make little difference, other than you have lost a moon."

Something about the way he said it told Sabelu that he somehow knew of this coal of resentment and was countering it in some way, breaking a wave before it could crash onto the shore with full force.

"And how do I drive off a Shadow exactly?" Sabelu wondered.

His uncle's gaze turned gentle. "First, you must understand that the people have little true idea of what is going on and what is at stake. You must confront the Shadow while being kind toward the person." His uncle's expression faltered, knowing that compassion was not one of Sabelu's strong traits. "When the Shadow is confronted, it will attack, often using the person as a proxy. Do not give in to condemning the person; focus on the Shadow. This will attract the attention of Shadows and Whites alike."

"But a minor Shadow that has little solid hold on someone will likely not be defended by other Shadows," Sabelu concluded. "Making it easier for the Whites to dispatch it."

"Correct."

"Then what need is there for me?"

"Because we mortal men are naturally bound to the waking world, the physicality of three dimensions and linear time. You and I are unique in this regard, but it is only our knowledge of the greater spiritual world that is needed. No physicality on our part will cause a Shadow to depart from its host."

"Confront it in the waking world, sever its anchor, let the Whites deal with it."

"Yes." Sabelu opened his mouth to say more, but his uncle put up a hand. "I understand. You have a lot of questions and you don't want to succumb to the Shadows yourself when they attack."

"I'm not ready for this," Sabelu said, feeling a moment of weakness.

"No one ever is," Anagalisgi told him. "I wasn't. Some days, I still question whether I did enough, whether I am making any difference now, whether I shouldn't try to do more and what that more might be. Then I am reminded that everyone has a role. Sometimes those roles are not glamorous or self-aggrandizing. No one may ever understand what the role is or why it's important. But it must be done, as the Author has ordained."

"I would ask what happens when people decide to do something else, but I have a feeling that you're just going to say something along the lines of, 'Look at the mess we're in.' "

"You would be correct."

Sabelu sighed and nodded. "I suppose...for as much trouble as the Shadows have given me, to keep me confused and ineffective, I shouldn't be surprised that there would be some great task waiting for me beyond the veil. And I suppose that I shouldn't be surprised when they start to more forcefully oppose me now."

"You speak truly," his uncle said, not unkindly. "Just remember that you are not alone. Yawi is with you, as is the Author. And as you drive out the Shadows, the Whites will come to take their place, and you will have even more help. And when you sleep, I will be here. We will not meet every night, and there may be long periods where we don't speak, but I will be here on your behalf."

Sabelu nodded again. "Thank you."

"You can do it, Sabelu. I know you can."

Sabelu had to do no more than blink before he found himself back in bed. What he'd just experienced conflicted with what he was seeing now, or trying to see as he blinked the sleep from his eyes and tried to remember where he was and why. The spirit world, the Land In Between, was as real as anything in the waking world. And it was confusing. Sitting with his uncle in the cave, it was like peering into a pool of crystal water. His mind was calm, uncluttered. Simple dreams were a torrent of rapids punctuated by sharp, jagged rocks. The waking world was somewhere in between.

Sensations and unbidden knowledge entered his mind like uninvited guests as he found all his limbs, rolled over, and sat up. People were already awake and thinking about the festival and the various games and competitions. Women thought about their cooking entries as much as the food they prepared now for breakfast. Men thought about the horse racing as much as the next game drive that would take place in the next few days. Children were blessedly quiet, but simple observation said that all of their casual games had now shifted to pretending to be in the adult competitions, or perhaps practicing for next year when they would be old enough to participate. Sabelu's mother's sister had organized something resembling children's competitions, but he'd never participated.

He looked over at Blaknik, still asleep. This close, Sabelu only knew that he was having some kind of pleasant dream. And that was it. His father, in another room, was dreaming of hunting in the forest and being distracted and annoyed by numerous spider webs that tangled around his bow and arrow. His mother and sister were already awake, but he could feel their excitement over the games, very much like everyone else.

Still looking at his brother, Sabelu wondered how old someone had to be before a Shadow latched onto them. Given that he himself had been suspected of corruption upon his birth, it would make sense that the Shadows would want to attach themselves as early as possible, like a weed that has its roots intertwined with a healthy crop and grows up beside it, stealing nutrients and stifling growth. And yet, to destroy the weed would be to destroy the healthy plant.

He did not see any Shadows lingering around his younger brother, and he had no desire to eat of the seeing fruit so early in the morning. He had little desire to eat of it at all, at least before the games.

The significance of his uncle's teachings, the epiphanies that had blossomed within the clarity of a quiet mind, were fading quickly as his thoughts were besieged by everyone else's. He fully remembered the object lesson with the print, scat, and scratches. He remembered the conversation they'd had. Looking around at the room, his brother, and being empathically aware of everyone else in the village, being able to take simple knowledge and apply it to the situation seemed a laughable endeavor at best.

He got around and made his way out of the house. Still he did not see any obvious Shadows. What did he look for, then? Just because something wasn't present didn't mean it didn't leave something behind. And sometimes just the absence of something spoke of something more, in the same way that he'd never understood the Shadow on his own back until it had been removed. Perhaps such a thing could be applied in the opposite direction, the lack of Whites being indicative of Shadow activity.

It didn't take more than a few seconds for a certain sense of fear and dread to creep up on him. He'd come to loathe his gifts and yet he didn't like not having them, or having them and not knowing how to use them. He couldn't see the Shadows. He didn't know what they were planning. Did they know what he was planning? He doubted the Shadows were unaware of his meetings with Anagalisgi. Perhaps even now they were working on ways to dispatch him completely, just kill him and be done with it. But did they know what he and his uncle talked about? Did they know his thought and fears even as he stood there outside the house like an idiot?

Sabelu was happy to turn his attention to his sister who was returning from the communal pool, just about to turn the corner and see him. When she did, her face lit up and she grinned.

"Good morning," she greeted, quickening her step. "Did you sleep well? You weren't tossing and turning so much."

"I slept fine," he replied haltingly. "I'm just trying to figure it out."

Netami didn't know how to respond to that, but she tried to remain optimistic. "Are Itsitsa and Blaknik awake yet?"

"They will be shortly."

Blaknik was already slowly coming out of his slumber, but their father would be woken by Netami's cheerful presence in the house. It wasn't a bad thing to wake up to—certainly there were worse things—but he would be tired for most of the morning because of it. This fatigue was only a tiny ripple in the day and entirely inconsequential to the festival at large, or anything else. It was just a minor inconvenience for half a day.

Something nagged at the edge of Sabelu's mind as he considered this, following his sister back inside the house, but there remained a shadow between him and something significant. Whether it was simply a shadow of ignorance or a Shadow intentionally trying to keep the knowledge from him, he did not know. He did not understand just how the Shadows worked, what their limits were, if any.

He needed to observe people. More than just being aware of their presence, he had to watch them go about their business and prepare for the festival. Mentally he blanched. He had a hard enough time observing his own family at the breakfast table, and they weren't even eating breakfast this morning.

"You're helping with the horses, I hear," Netami said, glancing at Sabelu.

"Somewhat, yes," he replied absently. "It's the safest thing for me to do, both for myself and so I'm not accused of using my talents to rig the games."

She shook her head and rolled her eyes. "Honestly. You don't change the future; you only see what's going to happen."

Sabelu blinked as the veil began to lift from his mind. It didn't completely dissolve, but he was certain that just a minor touch would shatter whatever illusion the Shadows were creating to hide it from him.

Perhaps it was the realization of the illusion itself that saw him through, or perhaps Yawi had something to do with it.

The Whites and Shadows could influence people just by their presence because they were spirits. Looking ahead to some of the activities that day, if he saw an argument, it wasn't because the parties hated each other for no reason. The Shadows would be influencing them, polluting and corrupting their souls with a smoky, shadowy, evil taint.

As much as he was dreading having to observe people, he found that he kind of wanted to in that moment, if only to test out his theory. Did the Shadows know that he'd had this revelation? Were they trying to figure out how to counter it even now? Was it possible that they were using a fictitious epiphany in order to distract him from a real one, give him a false goal to reach so that he never tried to continue on to the real destination? Were they capable of doing that?

As his talents unfolded with rapidly increasing intensity, he'd slowly shut himself away. Now he was going to have to put himself back out there, embrace the chaos, and get to the root cause of the darkness enveloping the people.

All of this passed through his mind in a matter of seconds. In that time, Netami's demeanor hadn't changed; indeed, she hadn't yet noticed that he was in some distress. In the next room, Blaknik was up and around, morning fatigue swiftly giving way to general enthusiasm. Blaknik enjoyed the festival, but he was caught between the childish notion of being excited because everyone else is and he could participate in the children's games, and the adult excitement of being able to actually compete.

Sabelu wondered if there were any Shadows hanging around his brother that he couldn't see. He looked at his sister. Did she have permanent Shadows, or just ones that flitted through from time to time to cause chaos when it was not warranted? How did this all work?

Netami looked up from brewing tea when Blaknik entered the room. She grinned. "Good morning."

Blaknik rubbed his eyes. "Morning."

"Are you doing anything to help with the festival today?"

In the other room, Sabelu sensed the fading of their father's dream and the slow, unwelcome slog back to wakefulness, his mind simultaneously trying to wake up and get coordinated, as well as figure out what it was that had woken him. Once he determined that there was no immediate threat—subconsciously knowing that it was only his children but not quite aware of this fact—his mind began filling up with all the tasks he had to do that day.

For Sabelu's part, he could sense his father organizing his thoughts, prioritizing his tasks, and making his mental schedule. His first priority at the moment was going to relieve himself. Then he intended to go help with the archery, as he always did. What he did not know, that Sabelu did, was that he would be interrupted this morning, first by Galiliga, then by some of the other leaders of both the village and the festival. They would want to know about him, Sabelu, and what he was going to do. Last year he'd shut himself away, but what about this year? Did Ola Achukma have any insight so they didn't have to approach Sabelu directly and risk more humiliation and confusion?

As all of this entered Sabelu's mind, he made a conscious effort to try and identify any evidence of Shadow interference. He figured there was a good chance of Shadow activity, but what about active interference? If there was any such thing, he was unable to identify it. But just being aware of it had to count for something, right? It was a first step, better than lying curled up on the ground unable to distinguish anything, much less demonic activity.

Again, he knew all of this even before Blaknik finished replying to Netami's inquiry, at which time their father emerged. He was tired, as Sabelu had known he would be, but he was glad to see his children. There was a certain happiness in knowing that Galiliga was here as well, and a certain old sadness that Tsona was gone and had never met his two younger brothers. All of his children were here, but not all of his children were present.

This sadness manifested no larger than a pinprick on his father's heart, yet it often captured Sabelu's attention, like how an animal might watch a fly for seemingly no reason at all other than it is a thing that is moving. He had a brother he'd never met and knew only through his family's memories and feelings about him, as well as his father's Book.

"And what are you doing for the festival?" Ola Achukma asked of Netami. "Other than waking everyone else up for it, that is?"

"Sorry, Tsitsa," Netami said, embarrassed. "I'm just so excited for it."

"Everyone's excited for it," Blaknik told her, not sounding overly impressed, his masked enthusiasm tempered by the frustration of being unable to compete with the adults.

"Not everyone," Sabelu commented dryly.

"You helped with the horses yesterday," his father pointed out. "You don't intend on continuing to help?"

"Doing something and being excited about the doing of it, are two different things. The horses are fine, but I think I will have to spend some time among people today."

Just saying the words out loud were enough to sour any eager anticipation he'd had about observing people and watching for Shadows. Even if he did start to catch on to certain patterns and notice certain things, what was he supposed to do? How did he confront someone about something they couldn't see? Ask any man outright and he was almost guaranteed to believe himself a good person, if understandably flawed and imperfect. How was Sabelu supposed to explain that some of their "flaws" might be demonic influence, and that their minor influence was feeding a greater influence that was less of an influence and more of a sentient being that wanted to control and destroy them?

Sabelu had once looked at his father's childhood memories of the Old Land. They were faded and distorted, and some things had been reduced only to knowledge with no idea of the event or person who had imparted it. He'd learned a lot about the Old Land, including the Christian religion. It seemed to be highly successful around the world, telling people a similar story of demonic influence in need of cleansing and offering freedom of a kind. The details were unclear, and only the later memories from the War of the Old Land and the army chaplains offered any answers. There were rituals of blood and water involved, one man dying for everyone.

Well, the Krydik had plenty of water rituals. A lot of men had died in the war and spilled their blood. So what was it? What was the difference that kept the Shadows at bay? Or were they? His father hadn't really known about the Shadows until the end of the war, so why should Sabelu expect to find anything useful in his earlier, more ignorant memories? Even Anagalisgi's earlier encounters with the white preachers had been less than clear on the issue.

"This has to do with the Shadows, then?" Ola Achukma wondered. His curiosity was genuine, but marred by a kind of wariness. It wasn't doubt per se, but a fear of what might happen by sneaking around a hornet nest.

Sabelu nodded. "It does."

"Shadows?" Blaknik wondered.

Everyone ignored the youngest boy, instead focusing on Sabelu.

"I get the feeling that you don't want me telling the council about this," Ola Achukma stated. "Or the priests."

"That's right," Sabelu said.

"Is there anything we can do to help?" Netami inquired.

"Don't tell anyone," he repeated. "If this goes how I think it will, they'll figure it out on their own, but I don't want them to know before that."

"Why not?" Blaknik asked.

"You will do as your brother tells you," Ola Achukma scolded. "And you won't tell anyone what he's really doing, looking for Shadows."

The eleven year old still looked confused, but he agreed anyway.

"What about if someone does ask what you're doing?" Netami wondered. "Surely someone will notice that you're not being consulted for this year's leaders of the national council."

"That will be for the council to explain," Ola Achukma told her. "As for Sabelu, we don't know. He was helping with the horses and that seems to be where he is most comfortable."

No matter their former tribal affiliation, most people agreed that lying was wrong. Perhaps necessary at times, but, overall, wrong. But was it still wrong if telling the truth would be to open the door to destruction? Could the greater good be used to justify such a thing? Was it wrong if that lie was made using only the truth? His family really didn't know or understand what he was doing. He had helped with the horses, and that really was where he was most comfortable. But it was still, in principle, a lie.

Sabelu headed out of the house, but he didn't get five steps before his father called to him and he turned. Ola Achukma approached, getting close and lowering his voice.

"Sabelu, I don't know what's going on in that head of yours," he began. "I don't understand what you know or what you see. I don't. And I'm not going to pretend I do. But I do hope, for your sake, that something is going to happen. Good, bad, or otherwise, you can't just hold onto gifts like yours without something giving way, like adding rocks to a net. Eventually, it will break."

"I know that very well," Sabelu said.

"I'm sure you do. But for as much as you know, I think you also miss things that are right in front of you. You speak of Whites and Shadows, and I don't know whether it is to my benefit that I do know what you speak of. But even as the war is theirs to fight, we here in the waking world are the collateral damage. We are the ones who will be injured or killed when the spirits are disturbed. And you know that you are not immune to this either."

Sabelu nodded. "I understand that, too. I'm trying to figure out how to prevent such things." He laughed once humorlessly. "As for myself, as long as I stay away from the Old Land, I should be fine."

His father raised a brow. "You may have the benefit of knowledge, but the rest of us have yet to receive the same courtesy."

He was afraid, Sabelu knew, afraid for his son. His death had been foretold. For Ola Achukma, it was like seeing Tsona, knowing what was going to happen, and still being powerless to stop it. Maybe there was a way to stop it, maybe not, but it was out there for all to see and read.

"Well then," he said at last, "let's hope I'm right."

He walked away before his father could say anything more.

Sabelu hated the term as soon as he heard it. Collateral damage. Incidental. Expendable. Temporally-bound flesh puppets trapped on a plane of only three dimensions. He wasn't sure about that last term, but it sounded more accurate than any of the others.

The war was not theirs to fight, for they could barely conceive of it, much less participate. And yet, they were the prize to be won or lost. The Shadows sought to destroy them; the Whites sought to protect them. This was simple enough to consider, Sabelu thought. It was the manipulation of people and circumstance and time that made it unpalatable for most people.

The Whites and Shadows have their war to fight, he mused. Mortal men cannot get involved. But when the war spills over into the waking world, they are bound by our limitations, our three dimensions. He mentally shook his head. But they are still more than that. They are trying to force a fox into a snake hole. There is only so far they can go, so much they can do. And for as careful as they might be, there will still be some disturbance.

He headed to the wrestling rings. It was not the most populated venue currently while it was being built, but it was arguably the most popular sport in the games, especially now since more and more boys were coming of age to fill the participation gap that had been left in the wake of the war. Boys tried to lie about their age in order to compete. Old men staunchly held out for years past their prime. Even when they finally retired, they would often try to coach the younger men. It was the perfect spot to look for Shadow activity, a group of men trying to build the arenas where they would soon be trying to throw each other into the dirt.

Sabelu tried not to be seen. He didn't want to influence the men as they worked. Problem was, he didn't know if he would actually be able to spot Shadow activity from any great distance. Sure, maybe if there was some major catastrophe like a fistfight, but this? Would a minor argument and small coal of resentment really require legions of Shadows to pull off? Or would it be more of a whisper, a mosquito pricking the skin? He could barely see mosquitoes when they were buzzing around his face; he'd never spot them at a distance.

He dreaded the thought of actually going down and helping. He didn't mind the work, but he didn't want to be bombarded with all of their thoughts, memories, hopes and dreams for the games, fears of failure, their past victories and failures, and even their future ones. There were easily a dozen men down there, and every single one had a life story that would be pushed on Sabelu like dirt into a grave. Even from this distance, he knew who was down there, what they had done the previous day, what they had already accomplished today, what they intended to accomplish later and what would actually be accomplished.

After a few minutes of debating back and forth, he felt fur touch his hand and most of the visions quieted. Looking down, the only thing he saw was white fur where it touched his fingers. Otherwise the white wolf was invisible. His hand moved down the wolf's spine and disappeared into its fluffy tail. Just by feel he could tell the wolf was heading down the slope to the rings. Sighing, he reluctantly followed.

As it turned out, he didn't have to do much more than approach to spark something. He wouldn't say that the veil between worlds lifted as it did when he ate of the nattawodatnu, but he could certainly sense a change. It was like finding a sudden current of cold water in a warm river.

He tried to stay focused as he drew nearer, forcing himself to consciously think about the present moment and not all the moments he could glean about the men's lives just from sheer proximity. Present concerns, past games, future reality, all of it. He could sense the past, present, and future relationships between the men, those who had been friends for a long time already and those whose enduring friendships were just now being sown.

Even as he felt the cold current in a warm river, Sabelu discovered a new kind of sensation. If he had to extend the analogy, he might have said it was a sudden, out of place ripple, the current breaking around a small rock not visible at the surface. For just a moment, there was a tiny break in the constant stream of information from a couple of the men. It vanished and then reappeared in half the time it took Sabelu to even subconsciously comprehend that such a change had taken place. He couldn't even be sure that it had except that he had been intentionally looking for it amid the onslaught. If he hadn't been so intentional, if he had just sullenly approached them as he normally might have, he would have missed it. And the sudden discrepancy in the foreseen events might have just been explained away.

There were Shadows here, but small ones, fast-moving. A thought, a word, a feeling, a brief flash of an image or fantasy. Just enough to plant a seed, like lighting a fire in order to draw in something else, a larger Shadow that would settle in, make a nest, and nurse ill feelings.

Sabelu tried to look around discreetly. Where was the Shadow that had effected this change? And why had Yawi not tried to stop it? Was the Shadow too powerful, even in such a small matter? Could it be that Yawi was the reason he had noticed it at all? Did this constitute a rescue, or was there something more that had to be done?

"Well, look who it is," the leader of this particular work team, a man called Aya, said. The crew stopped working and turned to face Sabelu as he got within conversation distance. Aya grinned and folded his arms. "Come to give us some betting tips?"

A few men chuckled or nudged one another in the ribs.

"No," Sabelu said. He knew he could look people in the face again, but there was still a paralyzing fear of whether the shapeshifting monsters had truly gone, and the best he could do was stare at the man's shoulder or chin. "Actually I thought I would help."

"Help?" one of the workers questioned. "How do you propose that?"

"Just because I see things doesn't mean I'm weak. I can carry, I can assemble."

The men were silent for a long moment. They didn't know what to do with him, how to treat him. Technically, he was a priest, or an acolyte anyway. He really should have been praying for good fortune for the games and the competitors. Aside from that, he should have been afforded some measure of deference and respect, been welcomed into the group. Except the priests had largely shunned him. Or he had walked away. Personal accounts and beliefs differed.

Aya believed Sabelu to be an acolyte at odds with the priests, and the only reason he hadn't been shunned or even killed was because he was an adelohosgi and to do so would be to invite wrath from the spirits.

But simple dislike on a personal level was perfectly acceptable. Sabelu searched for any more cold currents or other indications of Shadow activity, but found nothing. That didn't mean those signs weren't there, or that the Shadow wasn't there; he just wasn't skilled in finding them yet.

Finally, personal conviction—the inherent deference afforded a priest as well as the acceptance of help on a task—won out, and Aya nodded. "Fine. Help Ahugda."

Sabelu nodded once and approached Ahugda. He was a man of perhaps forty natural years, though he only looked just thirty as the slowed aging from the sorceries began to take hold. He'd not gone to fight in the War of the Old Land, instead staying behind in Lehoyed at his wife's insistence. After the war, he regretted not fighting and moved his family to Aktiya Waya in order to learn the sorceries so he might be of use in future conflicts. His life overall would not be of particular significance, Sabelu knew—he would lead no great charges, never save the day single-handedly—but he would be a good and mighty warrior and inspire the same in his sons.

"Adolchil and Edsi will bring the boards and get them roughly in place," Ahugda explained. "We just maneuver them to set where they should." He paused awkwardly. "But you probably already knew that."

Sabelu did know that. He also knew that Edsi would injure his shoulder doing so, but his pride would demand he compete anyway, at which time he would damage it more to the point where he would never win another wrestling competition. The wound would be physically healed using Touch, but his mind would never be convinced of it, and so he would act as though it were injured or had the potential to act up. By the time he would snap out of this spell, he would be killed in a hunt.

Sabelu wondered if the Whites could change things, or if everything was fixed. Could they prevent such an injury? Could they relieve Edsi of his mental prison?

There is virtually no White presence here, he thought, or perhaps someone thought for him. The Whites need at least a foothold. Your only weapons in this fight right now are your gifts and Yawi.

Even as thought it, he knew it wasn't entirely true, or it wouldn't be true for much longer. The winds were stirring and the water was rippling. Something was being disturbed.

Adolchil and Edsi approached, bearing a large post for the fence around the arena. They used Galo'ondiha ale Agi'a to lighten the load. When they reached the designated spot, Sabelu and Ahugda carefully manipulated the post into place. The next two boards were set to tie two posts together. And on it went.

"You think Deer Clan has the better idea?" Ahugda wondered. "They built permanent arenas, let them sit out for all the years they aren't hosting the festival, but then when they do, it's a lot less work."

"There is also a lot more available land around Anpa O Wican'hpi," Sabelu said. "Space in the bowl here is too limited for such things."

"Well, I can't dispute that. And this isn't nearly as difficult as it was in Lehoyed. It wasn't even trying to dig in the hard ground, either. It was the wind. The infernal wind."

"Be glad it's only wind. In the Old Land, where your wife's ancestors came from, the wind would bring great sands that would blot out the sun."

Ahugda shuddered but said nothing more about it as they spotted Adolchil and Edsi approaching with another post.

Sabelu felt the cold current again. He was again surprised by it, but his gaze went immediately to Edsi.

"That's how this works," he murmured to himself. He looked down to where he imagined Yawi to be by his side. "Go get him."

Once more, Sabelu could not say that the veil parted as it did when taking the seeing fruit, but he did know something happened. He felt a warm current in addition to the cold one. He saw the ripple around Edsi. The man stumbled, fell, wrenched his shoulder. He cried out, but his whole disposition was less about wrath against Adolchil for leading them across poor ground, and more about concern for Adolchil that he hadn't been injured as well because of the mishap.

Sabelu went to Edsi and, once the board was pried from his fingers, examined his shoulder. It was injured, as he had seen. That had not changed. But his calmer disposition now mentally illuminated many of the actions that he would take in the future.

Sabelu had seen the future. But if he hadn't been here, hadn't told Yawi to attack the Shadow, things would probably be a lot worse. The future dictated the past. It built the past.

And this was just one small example, a voice whispered. Wait until you see what's coming next.

DᎪᏍᏁ ᎠᏫᎢ

Ahisge Adolv'i

Kah Kitowak

By the time the festival actually started, some people had come to see that Sabelu had finally gotten some kind of guidance which had begun to sort out his growing insanity. Some asked if that meant that he was no longer a priest, especially since he had not been consulted for the choosing of new leaders. Some wondered if that meant he had never been a true priest at all, that his visions had indeed been demonically inspired. Perhaps he should have been drowned as an infant, but at least he appeared, for the moment, to be almost normal.

Something in Sabelu's inner being said that this attitude was a veil in itself, a powerful Shadow sent to cast ignorance and doubt about his talents, intentions, and even his spiritual allegiances. But for the time being, it bought him a little breathing room. With everyone else, including the priests and various councils, all tied up with the festival, he was free to keep observing Shadow activity.

Once he'd begun to identify the cold currents as nearby Shadow activity, he felt as though he'd stepped into an icy river and never truly left. Blaknik had once commented that he shivered at night in spite of any blankets Netami provided. He felt the chill all the time, and he was learning to identify the ripples as well, but just knowing and observing wasn't going to be enough. With the bowl flooded with almost all the people from all the villages, was it even worth it to try and stop one little Shadow here and there? Taking a cup of water out of the river might reduce the amount of water by that one cup, but the river wouldn't notice, and the water would eventually find its way back to that river. Why bother with the effort?

At the same time, now that he knew, he couldn't just do nothing. He and Yawi had intervened on multiple occasions already. Surely those nudges had to be adding up to something more. At what point did they create a hole big enough to allow more Whites into the area, into the fight?

When he woke on the first day of competition, Sabelu found himself alone in the house. He knew his parents would be long gone to the arenas, and he might have suspected Netami to be gone or nearly so, but he was surprised that Blaknik was gone, too. He wasn't so enthusiastic about the games that he was willing to wake up earlier than necessary to go and watch. He couldn't compete yet and was no longer interested in the children's games. Yes, he supported his father and brother in their tournaments, but it was still unusual for him. Sabelu didn't know if he wished for his talents to be able to penetrate the younger generation or if he was glad that they didn't. Sometimes he was fine with being surprised, with having to figure something out. Children provided that opportunity.

An empty house provided some relief from the cold current, but the cold current provided some relief from the heat that baked the city in the height of summer, when the sun beat into the cave. He was perhaps the only person who was moderately comfortable in the cavern as he made his way to the entrance and looked out over the transformed bowl. Open pasture and crop fields had been crisscrossed with fences and littered with people.

Sabelu did not foresee or expect any major happenings during the festival. No wars would break out because one man had beaten another in a tournament. The festival, and the failures the many losing competitors would nurture, was but the air needed to stoke the flames of discontent between men. And women; they were not immune. Sometimes they could be worse about holding grudges.

Only in his periphery did he see anything that he might have considered Shadow activity. It went beyond mere hallucinations—although they still existed—to the point where he wondered if he might actually be seeing glimpses of the Shadows themselves. Beings of smoke and shadow, this was how they were described. Because he only got momentary peripheral glances, he could not say for sure what he saw, but it seemed correct. Was he beginning to hone his talents, or were the Shadows unconcerned about being seen? With so many in this place, the sheer power alone might weaken the veil that he could see more.

He made his way to the archery field where his father was competing. Blaknik was already there.

"You made it!" Blaknik exclaimed.

"Did you think I was going to sleep the day away?" Sabelu wondered.

"Itsitsi wasn't sure you'd come to the festival this year. She thought you might stay home like last year."

"I'm fine. For now at least."

His younger brother looked uncertain but did not argue, instead turning his attention to the next group of archers as they were called up. It difficult to be engaged when he knew what the outcome would be. He was not unaware that all talks of gambling and betting on the competitors ceased as soon as he entered the crowd. He just told himself that he was not here to influence the games, but to stop them from being influenced or influencing other things in a negative way.

There was surprisingly little Shadow activity concerning the games themselves, at least in the archery field. He saw only one instance where a Shadow might have directed an arrow off-target, but by the time he recognized it—he'd been prepared for influence over the archers and had not been paying attention to the arrows to catch it in time—it was too late to do anything. Rather, the activity hovered more around the disposition of the archers, toward themselves. Fear, that the older men were losing their touch. Anxiety, that the younger men were less than their fathers were at the same age. Worry, that the people as a whole were slipping further and further away from their ancestors, the same arguments that had been had for years being given new life in the next generation.

Whether the methods had been the same for years or the Shadows were having to try something new because of his newfound awareness,

Sabelu was only able to spot and intercept this activity one in maybe twenty times. His ideas of interception swung back and forth between having Yawi attack a Shadow—for which he received virtually no feedback as to its success—and approaching a competitor in the wicked throes of self-doubt and self-defeat and trying to encourage them. His lack of overall empathy in his personality made his success in this matter worse than the competitors'.

"You did good," he told one young Bear Clan man, a fourteen year old from Yonhi who had failed miserably and was an easy target for a Shadow to speak worthlessness into his ear.

The teenager gave him a look. "I did not. And if you're here, why not tell me sooner? Maybe I would have adjusted my bow, or maybe I wouldn't have competed at all. You don't have to tell me how to win, just how to not embarrass myself."

And he walked away.

If anyone had asked what Sabelu was trying to accomplish, he wasn't sure what he would tell them. He knew he would never save his own reputation and standing among the people. The most he would ever be was tolerated. If he tried to explain his crusade against the Shadows, well, that wouldn't go so well. It wasn't that the Shadows weren't aware of his meddling, but right now he was little more than a nuisance. If he announced his intentions publicly, if the flesh puppets knew, especially those belonging to the more powerful Shadows, then the physical opposition would be heavy against him. With the backing of the powerful Shadows, it would get ugly.

The only comfort he might have taken came from knowing that at least his family knew and would remain supportive, if mildly secretive. He didn't expect them to do anything physical, but for the moment, keeping his secret was more important.

Looking around at the festival, the competitions, the food, the din of conversation, the laughter and comradery, he couldn't help but feel a bit foolish. This was a good thing, a joyful occasion. Why couldn't he feel joyful and partake of the festivities?

Ola Achukma joined the next group of archers.

"You missed watching him in the footrace this morning," Blaknik commented.

"I know he advanced to the next round," Sabelu said.

"Yes, but it's still fun to watch, even if you know the outcome. Itsitsa knew you were going to be an adelohosgi and a great man, but he was still happy to see you take your first steps and speak your first words."

Sabelu blinked, unprepared for the sudden wisdom coming from his younger brother who was still largely a mystery to him. He missed the first shot from the archers and said nothing as he deliberately turned to watch the second and third shots.

Their father advanced. Sabelu had known he would, but he was still mulling over Blaknik's words. He barely noticed when Ola Achukma approached them.

"Hey now, Blaknik, you are too young to gamble and bet on the competitors," he said with mock-seriousness. "And you know you can't use your brother for an unfair advantage."

"He won't help me anyway," Blaknik complained, also with mock-seriousness.

"Good." Their father looked at Sabelu. "And I don't want you helping him. He needs to make his own way." He went on before either son could speak. "Come on, then, let's go watch your brother."

Galiliga was just entering the wrestling ring when the three of them arrived. He was a powerful man in his own right, and usually a favorite to win, but it was his opponent that actually caught most people by surprise.

His name was Kah Kitowak. Many years before the war, a group of men in Lehoyed had tried to break away from Aktiya Waya, even attack Wolf Clan out of fear of the sorceries. They'd tried to kill Ola Achukma, might have succeeded if not for Nendawagan using the sorceries to flee. After quelling the violence, Yvgidahi had given the men a choice, to return to the Old Land or die. Many had chosen death.

As for their women and children, they were sent back to the Old Land. Kah Kitowak had been a young teenager at the time, not quite a man. It wasn't until after the war that he'd returned. He had learned the sorceries, fought in the war himself though for a different regiment, and asked for forgiveness and permission to return to Hlohi.

Forgiveness was granted. Permission to return, not so much. He was given leave to visit from time to time, under a banner of peace, like a diplomat perhaps, but he was not allowed to stay or call himself Krydik. His father had tried to kill Yvgidahi, and at the time, Kah Kitowak had supported that effort. His loyalties were suspect at best.

So he returned every few years, typically for the tournaments. He was never a favorite, and his performance was usually mediocre. Whether or not it was intentional that they almost always pitted him against Yvgidahi's various male descendants was usually not commented on. The mediator cracked the whip signaling the beginning of the match.

"Why does he keep coming back?" Blaknik wondered as Galiliga charged Kah Kitowak. "No one really likes him. He's not one of us. I don't get it." He looked at Sabelu. "Do you see anything in him?" He looked back in the ring where the outsider was holding his own but destined to lose. "Why is he here?"

Kah Kitowak went down hard on the ground, the wind knocked from his lungs so that he gasped for breath, much to the delight of Galiliga and almost all onlookers. After a second, the outsider conceded the match and slowly picked himself up from the dust. No one offered him a hand, and no one was there to give him water or encouragement as he stiffly left the ring.

Only Ola Achukma was able to really get close enough to Galiliga to congratulate him. Blaknik tried, without success, but Sabelu turned his attention more to Kah Kitowak who had limped away a safe distance and was even now using Asvhnisgi to feel out any major wounds. The outsider glanced briefly at Sabelu but looked no happier for it.

"That was your brother, wasn't it?" he guessed. "Here to gloat?"

"It was literally the first round. There's nothing to gloat about," Sabelu said. "Even I could beat you."

Kah Kitowak snorted as he slowly stretched, using Asvhnisgi to work out his muscles before they knotted up. "Well, if you're expecting to goad me into a fight instead, I'm afraid I will have to disappoint you."

Sabelu studied him. "You knew Galiliga was my brother. But no one here told you that, and you don't recognize me."

"Who says?"

"I do. Because I know things. Like how your name in the war was Everett Thunder Caller."

Now the man gave him an incredulous, if disappointed look. "You're the adelohosgi, then? Last time I saw you at the festival a few years ago, you were a little boy."

"If I am as great as I am foretold to be, then either you've not heard of my greatness in which case you would not be looking for an adelohosgi, or else I've not done great things yet."

"Fair enough."

"So who told you about me?"

"You mean a prophet doesn't know?"

Sabelu gave him a look. "I know you've been run off of Hlohi, with your occasional visits the topic of heated discussion and gossip. I know you fought in the War of the Old Land, which was lost. I know you fought for your people on Earth, was even successful for a time until you were scattered to the wind. I know that you are currently living on a tiny remote island, licking your wounds and taking comfort only in a small victory that has since been mostly undone, am I right?"

Kah Kitowak's neutral, if frustrated, disposition turned to melancholy and he sighed. "Yes. Although my father's actions were his own, and the Krydik were on the same losing side in the war. But you are correct, our attempts to hold **Red River** against the Canadians failed. Our attempts to rescue the children from the residential schools, though initially successful, are likely to be entirely undone."

"I know things," Sabelu repeated. "And I won't say it has never driven me mad. Yet I find that I don't like not knowing things. So for the last time, who told you about me?"

He found the outsider's silence suspicious, but his answer even more so. "It was the Author who started me on the path, and Anagalisgi who gave me more specific directions."

"You spoke to my uncle? When? Why did he not tell me about this?"

"It was soon after we fled to the island that this began. As for why he didn't tell you, I cannot even begin to guess."

The man was uncomfortable in the situation, but he wasn't a liar. Sabelu searched the man, information pouring into his mind. He might have gone to his knees except for the blessed absence of the shapeshifting monster. He did not see or know anything of what went on between Kah Kitowak and Anagalisgi, but he saw everything else that had transpired on Earth.

"Aklaq knows of my uncle as well," he stated.

"She's mentioned him, yes," Kah Kitowak said casually. "And the white bear. She says she's been following the white bear since she was a child."

Sabelu blinked and shook his head, trying to make sense of everything. "But she herself is not a prophet."

"No."

So much to know, so much to learn. It was like inhaling continuously with no reprieve, no chance to exhale. And it wasn't just what he was learning about Kah Kitowak and his life and experiences, but about the other people and nations as well. Aklaq White Bear, Putu Canoe Maker, the Inuit, the Tlingit, the Cree, and others. He knew he was absorbing only a fraction of what there was to know, but he felt almost as bad as he had just a moon prior, and it was all he could do to sit down without collapsing and curling up like a child. Kah Kitowak gave him an odd look but made no move to help or flee.

Was this all just a coincidence, or perfect timing? What else had his uncle been up to?

Then Sabelu was forced to consider whether he was upset with his uncle. And for what? Helping others? Bringing people together to try and fight the Shadows, make the universe a better place and help the various peoples while they were at it? Was he, Sabelu, really that petty? That vain? Did he think he was going to be the sole savior of the universe? He wasn't even sure how to help his own people, never mind any others.

All the same, he was a little irritated. He was endowed with a gift to see into the lives and souls of others, and his uncle had been working with other people. Even that might not have been so bad except the best he could find was Kah Kitowak? The man had basically failed at everything, every cause he had ever put himself behind. That's not exactly someone you wanted to put in charge of a crusade.

Even just looking at him with what he knew, Sabelu could see that Kah Kitowak would not be anyone famous or especially inspiring. He would do many things, help many people, but he would never not be an outcast at the fringe of every people he would encounter and live or work beside. The best he would get was civil tolerance, which was slightly more than that he was already experiencing. Nothing Sabelu saw suggested this could be changed except by severe intervention from the Whites or the Author.

"If your conversation with Anagalisgi was only recent," he finally said aloud, "then that's not the reason you keep returning so you can be re-introduced to the ground at the games."

"No," Kah Kitowak admitted.

"It's just a more familiar pain that you can tolerate because you know what to expect, versus whatever failure you've experienced elsewhere."

The man gave him a look. "We've only been speaking for a couple minutes and I already don't like you."

"Anagalisgi might have warned you."

"He said you were troubled and difficult to work with. I thought it might be simple misunderstanding, not because you have a shit personality. I wouldn't even describe it as physical arrogance, as some of the competitors have here in the games. It's more of a...smug self-satisfaction."

Sabelu gave him a look. "I can't help that I know you better than you think. People just don't like being called out on their lies. If they stopped lying, I would have less to be aggravated about."

"At what point have I lied to you?"

"It's not me you're lying to. It's yourself."

Kah Kitowak shifted his stance. "So you want me to—You know what? Forget it. You know what I think?"

Now Sabelu intentionally turned arrogant. "You think I should talk to my uncle first before bothering you with whatever he told you."

The outsider made several unsavory sounds and gestures before walking away. At least in the festival among the other Krydik, he knew what to expect. He knew their ridicule, their stares and glares. He didn't understand Sabelu, and he didn't understand how this was all supposed to fit together. Sabelu was still blind to whatever Anagalisgi had told him, but that would be remedied soon enough, assuming he could speak to his uncle tonight.

Now distracted by this sudden turn of events, Sabelu was less interested in looking for Shadows and ripples among the general populace. He watched some of the events, watched his father and brother compete in the same horse race—both of them advancing, as he knew they would, although his brother would be eliminated in the quarter finals and his father in the semi-finals—and moseyed around the women's events, checking in on his mother and sister.

"It's good to see you out and about this year," his mother told him, stepping away from the cooking event long enough to speak to him. "I know you're not competing, but are you at least watching your father and brother?" She added quickly, "I know you know how things will turn out, but are you at least giving some semblance of moral support?"

"Yes. Blaknik and I watched both of them," Sabelu answered simply.

His mother smiled. "Good. I know that makes them happy, even if they don't show it well."

She was correct, just not entirely so. His father was glad and relieved to see his troubled third son out and about in the crowds—and Galiliga, too, though to a lesser extent—but there was also a notable current of fear and anxiety. If he was there watching, did that mean that they would win, or advance as the case may be? If they lost, was there something they could have done differently? Would he have some remarks, lecture, or commentary on their performance? Why did he show up if already knew what was going to happen? He didn't feign interest very well, so there had to be some other reason for it. Had someone, like Nendawagan, forced him to show up in some way?

And, most importantly, as most trains of thought ultimately circled around to, was there any way to change the future that he saw?

"And?" his mother prompted, breaking into his thoughts.

"And what?" he asked, knowing immediately what she was going to say.

"Aren't you going to ask how I'm doing?"

"I know how you're doing."

"Humor me," she said flatly. "Engage in conversation; you're not very good at it."

Sabelu sighed. "How are you doing? How is the competition going?"

It ate up some time anyway, and it beat aimless wandering from event to event, pretending to be interested and hanging in suspense over the outcome of the day's tournaments. And it made his mother happy, which he supposed was pretty important.

It gave him time to think about how he wanted to approach Anagalisgi and possibly confront him about Kah Kitowak. He wasn't even sure what the confrontation would be about. Betrayal? No, nothing had really been betrayed. Lying? No, Anagalisgi hadn't lied about anything. Considering that Sabelu had only been free from the Shadow on his person very recently, and Anagalisgi had been traversing the spirit world for a long time, why shouldn't his uncle have other helpers, if helper could be the right word?

As expected, they ran into Netami who was busy showing off and talking up her various entries. Nendawagan praised her and Sabelu was obligated to give her a compliment as well. His sister's cooking was good; he would never say it wasn't when it was. But sometimes he was perplexed by the basic human condition of ignorance. He knew before he took a bite what the food would taste like, through other people, and whether or not he would like it. If he wouldn't like it, he didn't subject himself to such suffering just to make someone feel better about themselves. How was it that normal people had to be surprised all the time? Didn't it get exhausting? Did they enjoy it?

Then he started wondering, not for the first time, about his influence over things. If he knew he would hate the food as it stood, but he intervened before it was served and made a suggestion that would make it better, had he truly altered the future or merely acted on some third entity that guided him to that logical end? Was he making this more difficult than it needed to be?

"Well, I'm glad you came over to see us, even if you're not really interested," his mother was saying, "but unlike you, your father and brothers can be taken by surprise. Go find them and send them over here."

He took the out, leaving the women's events in search of his father and brothers. Most of the events had wrapped up for the day and the men were busy celebrating, trying to explain to actual or prospective wives why they lost, and discussing what to do the following day. Answers ranged from various tournament strategies to placing bets on the remaining competitors.

He found his targets easily enough and sent them over to see Nendawagan and Netami, then he went home. His mother would ask where he was, his father would say he wasn't sure, and the group would move on to other things, normal conversation. They would be normal and happy, without wondering or worrying about him. They wouldn't give him a second thought until later when they got home and Blaknik found him in bed.

How can I know so much yet feel so helpless against the Shadows? he wondered, entering the house and adding a few pieces of wood to the fire. If knowledge is power, and I know more than most, how much more ignorant is everyone else?

He decided he didn't want to know. Instead he spent some time in the relative peace and quiet, etching designs into his bow and restringing it so as to be ready for the next hunt.

What was it like to not know something? To have to plan? To go out on a whim and let yourself be surprised? To eat food, not knowing what it would taste like, or explore a trail, not knowing what could be lying in wait? His annoyance over Kah Kitowak aside—because that was a larger issue than he wanted to consider right now—he'd never not known the small things.

His greatest surprise, he figured, was going to sleep, not knowing what his dreams may bring. He decided not to dwell on it, instead focusing his attention on his uncle as he headed to bed. Was there a way to let his uncle know that he wanted to talk to him, or was it just luck, whenever Anagalisgi decided to make contact? He'd called it dream-walking, well, why couldn't a path be walked both ways? Except he did not see, nor could he understand what this path was, where it led. So how did he even begin?

"You begin just by asking questions."

Sabelu didn't know whether he was rolling over in bed or turning around as if standing up, and it wasn't until he laid eyes on his uncle that he felt fully locked into the dream, if that's what it was.

"How did I get here?" Sabelu asked. He looked around the cave that was becoming ever more familiar. "Did I come to you, or you to me?"

"I saw you coming and helped you through," Anagalisgi answered, mildly amused.

Sabelu nodded once or twice, then turned serious. "Why didn't you tell me about Kah Kitowak? Or Aklaq? How many others are you seeing?"

"We're uncle and nephew, Sabelu, not lovers." Anagalisgi was grinning. "I need no one's permission to do as the Author bids."

"But..." Sabelu wasn't even sure where he was going with his anger.

His uncle relaxed his annoying mirth, turning more serious. "You think it diminishes your gifts, your ability to see."

"I thought I was special," Sabelu admitted, feeling a bit like a petulant child.

"Being special doesn't mean being alone. Your brother may have a great gift for hunting, but he cannot work a game drive alone. Your father may have a talent for language, but he needs someone to talk to. Believe it or not, but Kah Kitowak and Aklaq have their own talents.

It's a matter of using them in the correct time in the correct way."

Sabelu gave Anagalisgi a look. "But...they failed at their missions. Kah Kitowak lost Red River. They all had to flee to some remote island."

"And what specifically have you accomplished?" his uncle challenged. He was not mean, but his tone was accusing. "Are the Krydik free of Shadow influence? You have great talent, why aren't you using it? Why have you failed?" He shifted his stance. "We are in a war, Sabelu. Some battles are won, some are lost. Sometimes you have to give up a small victory in order to gain a larger advantage for a future victory. I've been watching you, you are beginning to learn, but beginning only. Aklaq and Kah Kitowak have been in the fight longer than you."

"Then why does Kah Kitowak still carry himself like a failure? If he did know about this trading of one small victory for a larger one, why doesn't he act like it? Why doesn't he act like he knows better things are coming?"

Anagalisgi's gaze softened. "Because there is much evil in the world, and human minds are small and frail. They struggle to see what lies beyond. You do see, but you still have trouble believing."

Sabelu turned suspicious. "Why do I feel like you're going to have us working together?"

"Of sorts," his uncle confirmed. "You will not be working together in the same way that Aklaq and Kah Kitowak work together. Your task remains fixed on exposing the Shadows among the Krydik, as they do for their peoples. But there will be times when you must come together for a united cause."

"Why can't you guide them?"

"Because my task is to guide you. In order to do that, I have to keep an eye on the Shadows from this side." He went on before Sabelu could speak. "We all have a task, a role to fulfill. We may all be able to do a thing, but if we all try to, it will only turn into a mess."

"Too many cooks in the kitchen," Sabelu recited.

"Exactly."

Sabelu sighed. "All right. You have a point. What do I need to do?"

Anagalisgi went to sit beside the fire and motioned for Sabelu to do the same. "What the Shadows were doing to you, trying to overwhelm and confuse you, was showing you Possible Time, the things that could be."

"The shapeshifting monsters," Sabelu stated, sitting down on one of the mats. "The things that someone might say when they walked up to me, the things they were thinking about doing but may or may not get to."

"That's right."

"Does that mean that some of my predictions weren't true, then? Was I predicting based on possibilities, not what was?"

Anagalisgi shook his head. "No. You prophesied correctly, for that is the only way an adelohosgi of the Author can prophesy. The Possible Time was simply to try to confuse you and shut you up, stop you from speaking entirely. The Possibilities have no real substance; they are hopes and wishes, thoughts and fancies. Someone may think of a stone, but that thought has no more substance than a hope that a particular girl may look our way. Only the stone itself, the girl herself, exist as substance that can be acted upon."

"Men make plans and act on them all the time, though," Sabelu said. "They are acting on something that does not have substance."

"You think too linearly, nephew. What will be has already been. Men make plans in what they perceive in the present, yet they have already acted on them in the future that is."

Sabelu shifted position on his mat. "Then what are the ripples? Can the Shadows change the future? I saw—"

"The Shadows may be as eternal as the Whites, but they are as linear as common men. They know not the plans of the Author. What they perceive as a change is merely an allowance from the Author in order to reach a certain point that has already happened."

"Then why bother with the likes of me or you or Kah Kitowak?"

Now his uncle shifted. "You've used Asvhnisgi on the minds of horses and other animals, haven't you?"

Sabelu shrugged. "Of course."

"You know how the animal thinks, what its needs and concerns are."

"Naturally."

Anagalisgi nodded. "Now imagine that animal is trying to kill you, or your family. There is no other thought in its head other than to kill."

"Then I would kill it, eliminate the threat entirely."

"Now imagine that there is an infinite supply of these animals, and the one who is causing these animals to go mad is too great for any man to defeat."

"Well, I would imagine that, as one with the infinite power to destroy this source, I would just destroy the source. Stop the supply, then whittle away at the rest."

His uncle's expression was unreadable. "Now imagine that as soon as you destroyed the source, the source, all of the mad animals, and everyone who had been touched by a mad animal and was not rescued to safety, died instantly."

Sabelu blinked. "What kind of dumb story is this?"

"A tragic one, but true," Anagalisgi said. "Men are not merely creatures of flesh, but spirit also. The spirit is sustained either by the Whites, that is the Author, or the Shadows, that is the dragon which you have not yet seen. Any soul attached to a Shadow perishes with that Shadow unless rescued to the safety of the Whites." He went on before Sabelu could speak. "Minor Shadows, the fleeting ones you have begun to observe, these are easy. The greater Shadows, those who hold those in power...the Shadows will kill a host before they give it up, because there is only one way to do so, and that is to hand it over to the Whites. There is no middle ground, Sabelu." He gestured to the fire before them. "The light is absolute. There is no struggle when the flame is lit; the shadows recede immediately. But the flame by itself is only so strong, and it must have fuel in order to stay alive. In clearing out the minor Shadows, your fire will spread to the dry tinder, and more Whites will come. There is no dead space. There is no neutral zone."

"So when I intercepted the Shadows and their ripples, I really wasn't doing much," Sabelu stated.

Anagalisgi shook his head. "Not more than wet grass that barely catches and soon snuffs out. Make no mistake, it is a start. Now it's time to do more."

"How do I confront someone, though? How do I cause a Shadow to flee?"

His uncle chuckled nervously. "What did your father do in order to force the truth from your brothers when they lied?"

Sabelu raised a brow. "All he has to do is give them a look. But there is an element of fear from our father, the authority he has over us."

"And having been given the gift of seeing Shadows, does this not also give you authority over them?"

"Well, maybe, but...not the people they're attached to. And the people have to give up the Shadows on their own; you said it yourself."

Anagalisgi nodded. "It's a delicate balance, Sabelu. An intricate dance, if you will. If it were easy, do you think we would be having a problem at all?"

Sabelu sighed. "No. But I am forced to wonder why it had to get to this point before anything was done about it."

"Many have been called. Few have been willing. Fewer still were able to follow directions and so perished in their own vanity." His uncle gave him a look. "Just something to keep in mind."

Sabelu nodded. "I understand."

"Tomorrow, seek out Kah Kitowak. Listen to what he has to say. Learn the real scope of this war, and be glad that your assignment right now is so small."

Sabelu opened his mouth to ask a question, but by the time he blinked he was back in bed and it was morning again. Was that his uncle being dramatic, or something more on his end? Whatever the case, it was a tad irritating, but there was nothing he could do about it as his mind reoriented itself to the waking world.

He wanted to understand his uncle's words. He really did. But what did it mean when he said that men were too linear? How had the future already happened? He thought of his father's Book, and the Book about his grandfather and uncle. While largely ignored by themselves, even more ignored was the fact that there were more Books listed in the front, promises of tales not yet come. What if those tales were set in the future, but because these stories here happened earlier, that's why they were there?

It made about as much sense as anything else, he thought, getting up and around. He and his mother were the only ones awake in the house, and he found her just putting some sticks on the fire to coax it to life.

"Good morning," she greeted, looking up briefly and grinning. "Did you sleep well? You hardly stirred when Blaknik checked on you."

"Slept fine," Sabelu reported wistfully.

"Are you going to watch your father and brother again today?"

"Maybe. Actually I—"

"Maybe?" Now his mother looked at him. "Sabelu, I think that's the first uncertain answer I've ever heard from you." Her expression was one of genuine concern and even alarm.

"I need to go out and find someone," he said. He was going to say more, then decided it better to just leave the house.

His mother would tell his father what had transpired, express her concern over his "uncertain answer." His father would listen, and he would also be troubled by it, but he would instruct everyone not to say anything about it, at least not right away. They didn't want to disrupt the festival by troubling the priests and leaders with something they weren't even sure was a problem. Sabelu was a bit strange and he may have had his reasons for answering the way he did. Who could know what he'd seen or heard, having spoken to Anagalisgi and encountered the Shadows? The family would agree, and about midway through the games today, the incident would be largely forgotten. By tonight, he might have some better answers.

Sabelu paused in his walk. If he didn't know the answers now, how was it that he could see anything past this evening? Was there a way to skirt the issue, come at it from a more indirect path? If he went back and intentionally studied his mother or anyone else, would he see the answers that he would give, so that he might give them later at the appropriate time, without having to track down Kah Kitowak?

If that worked, how far could he take it? Could he get the answers he needed by looking into the future and effecting them in the present at the appropriate time? He would have the knowledge because he'd already seen himself say or do a thing in the future. Was this what his uncle meant when he talked about not thinking so linearly? Would he be creating his own ripples in this way?

All that said, would his not tracking down Kah Kitowak have any real effect on things, or was it the only way to have gotten Sabelu think of things in a less than linear fashion? Where did this end? Or did it?

He continued walking but was less intent on finding Kah Kitowak. Instead he went to the top of the slope where the most diehard competitors were already out warming up and practicing. The vast majority of these were the unmarried young men trying to win a wife. The rest were the more recently married men who felt the need to prove to their new wives that they were still a good choice. Then there was also a sprinkling of boys who could not compete this year but would be able to next year and were taking in every strategy and piece of advice they could.

"So what is it like, really?"

Sabelu turned as Kah Kitowak approached, looking a bit grumpy, as if he had been forcibly roused from bed.

"What is what like?" he asked. "Looking down there and knowing how this is all going to turn out?"

"Yes." Kah Kitowak came up beside him and folded his arms as he also observed the early morning goings-on. "Do you get no thrill from it at all? Or is the end the only thing that matters to you?"

"I'm not as aloof as people think," Sabelu told him. "Or perhaps I should say, I'm not as disinterested. Sometimes I do find the details interesting. But when you know how the story ends, the journey becomes less enticing."

Kah Kitowak glanced at him. "We've all heard elder stories growing up. Maybe they're becoming more similar now, here among the Krydik, but even so, we all hear the same stories over and over again. The same heroes, the same villains, the same journeys, the same lessons. We all have our favorites. We know how it ends. You can't tell me that you have never enjoyed hearing a story over and over again, even though you know how it ends."

"You hear a story once and forget about it. You remember the basic plot, the names of the people, but it fades from you. You hear it again and your imagination is lit again like coaxing coals back into flame." Sabelu nodded to himself. "I have already heard all the stories. I know them from the past, and I have already heard them because I see others hearing them in the future. I hear them continuously. I know which stories each elder knows, I know how he will tell them, how there might be slight variations in each recitation. I know the questions his listeners will ask and I know how he will answer, what new stories it may lead to."

"But you get no enjoyment out of it at all," Kah Kitowak interrupted. "None whatsoever?"

"I do," Sabelu said, "in my own way. I don't expect others to understand."

For a long moment, they were both silent. More people were waking up and getting around. Women started cookfires, and children were laughing and playing.

"I pity your uncle," Kah Kitowak said finally. "He's got a lot of work ahead of him, taking you on."

"I don't think I have any family members who are not pitied for their relationship to me," Sabelu commented.

"Even so, I pity him. Because I think he is one of the few who does have the capacity to understand what is going on, but you're just too stubborn to want to go along with his specific direction. You want to have the last word."

Sabelu gave him a look. "And you used your own talents to deduce this."

Kah Kitowak matched his expression. "He told me so, this morning."

"So he sent you to me and that is the only reason you're here, not because you enjoy my company or know that I'm the only one who will have a prolonged conversation with you."

"Believe me, it's a conversation I could do without." Kah Kitowak shifted his stance. "But if you knew why I was here, why bother with the conversation? Or am I the only one who will have a prolonged conversation with you as well?"

Sabelu deliberately did not look at him. "I am not the Creator. I do not know everything. A lot, but hardly everything. I stand on a mountaintop and look down at a river. I see how it twists and turns. I know where it will turn, where it will split and come back together, so that when I arrive, I am not surprised by what I find for I already knew what was. But from the vantage, some parts are blocked by trees or landscape, and these are things I don't know. I know what comes before and after, what was, is, and will be, but the part in between is what is shaded from my view."

Kah Kitowak nodded. "Your uncle said you would say something like that. He also said that you would have discovered something even before I came to speak to you."

"I imagine he was speaking of my revelation about linear time."

The outsider shrugged. "I don't know. He told me not to get too worked up over your business, and I'm inclined to agree. But there is one thing he wants me to do. He wants me to take you through one of those dark places and maybe shed some light on how this all fits together."

Sabelu glanced around the bowl as it came to life, the second day of competition. He turned to Kah Kitowak. "I've no business being here. Take me wherever it is I need to see. Let us illuminate this darkness."

ᎠᏡᎾᎵᏁ ᎠᏫᎩᎢ

Asunaline Adolv'i

Behind the Cliff

Sabelu followed Kah Kitowak back to the outsider's tent, erected a respectable distance from the main conglomeration of festival visitors. There, Kah Kitowak conjured Galohisdi with some difficulty. Sabelu crossed just as soon as it appeared safe, without fully looking to see where the man was taking him. Like the crossing to Earth, it was a harrowing experience, feeling as though his whole being were being compressed into an infinitesimally tiny space. Then, just as he gave up the last of the air in his lungs, it all released, and he hit the ground.

His brain said that he was somewhere far out to sea on wild waves, or perhaps tossed about on a great wind current, even as his body said he was lying in an uncomfortable position on perfectly solid ground. It took him a few moments to figure out which to believe, but once he determined that he was indeed on solid ground, everything else quickly righted itself.

Sabelu stood on legs like a newborn fawn and looked around. He had never been here before, yet he had memories of it, owing to the man beside him who was presently on his hands and knees being sick.

The forest they were in was nothing remarkable, being very much like the forest around Lehoyed though without the terrible wind. It was the thing behind them that they had come to see, and Sabelu turned to look at it.

Like the forest, it did not appear to be anything remarkable, a slope leading below the level of the surrounding ground, like an oversize animal burrow big enough for a large child or smaller teenager, at first made of dirt, but then turning to stone. Upon closer inspection, however, one found that the stone was not merely haphazardly worn away by time and the elements, but cut and carved with manmade precision.

Kah Kitowak came beside him.

"When I was first permitted to return, I tried to go back to Lehoyed, see what remained of my friends and family," he began conversationally.

"They chased you out," Sabelu stated. "You ended up here. You did a little initial exploration, realized what you'd found, so you went to Aktiya Waya. You spoke with my father about his maps—"

"If you know all this, why did I bother to bring you?"

Sabelu did not look at the man but walked down the slope to the buried stone archway. He put a hand out to steady himself and peered inside. "Because I have no knowledge of this place. You asked about my father's maps, but they were destroyed when your father tried to kill him. Then the council confronted you and you haven't actually been back since." Now he looked back. "In short, because it's not about you."

He situated himself, grabbing some spindly bushes growing overhead, and slid feet first into the hole. This was not a smooth motion by any means as he had gotten to be a fairly large teenager by now, but once he got his chest and shoulders through, he dropped down a good four feet to solid stone. A minute later, Kah Kitowak joined him.

They invoked Atsvstdi to guide their way, drawing on the light from the entrance as well as smaller holes leading to the surface. For years the people of Lehoyed had dismissed them as simple animal burrows—which many of them had become to some extent—never realizing what lay beneath their feet.

The stone tunnel had been immaculately carved, with very little damage appearing to be caused by natural decay. It was as wide as many of the streets in Aktiya Waya, though there were places where they had to wiggle through a narrow gap, and the whole route seemed to be going downward, deeper into the earth.

They had started out heading north, but they stopped when they reached a junction, the decision to go either north or east.

"There's nothing to the north," Kah Kitowak said, "it's all caved in."

"I don't think there would be much there anyway," Sabelu mused. "Everything else is to the east. Or it was."

They turned east. There were still a few holes to the surface that allowed the use of Atsvstdi, but Sabelu soon realized that he wasn't invoking such a sorcery strongly enough to generate the light they were getting. Finally he ceased such sorcery, discovering, or perhaps re-discovering, that the tunnel was now lined with crystals. At one time they had probably stood straight and tall as great decorative monoliths; now they were broken, scattered chunks that did just enough to help refract the light and let them see, but with little beauty or enthusiasm.

The tunnel ended abruptly, opening up into a great cavern, and it appeared to be about half the size of the cave housing Aktiya Waya. More holes allowed in more light, and chunks of crystal and many pieces of metal helped to dimly illuminate the facade of what may have once been a great palace or some other building of repute.

Again Sabelu invoked Atsvstdi, augmenting the dim light, though he did so with an air of trepidation. He was not overwhelmed with visions such as he might when near the people, but he could feel something in the air, like tangible whispers, and he hoped it was just wind currents through the holes.

Immediately before them, the floor was wide and flat, clear for about forty feet on either side and maybe thirty feet in front. To the right, a sharp right angle denoted what might have been a building. To the left, a pile of rubble that blocked what looked like an old staircase, though it ascended only into stone. In front of them, the ground appeared to end, but as they got a little closer, Sabelu saw that it was only a wall, and a wide set of stairs led down to an open area, like a market, lined with stone buildings that were reminisce of Aktiya Waya but with far more flagrance and sophistication.

On the opposite side of the open market was a magnificent structure, or the facade of one, which, considering his father's memories, he might have likened to a Greek temple. Seven stone columns stretched upwards as if holding up the cavern itself; these days, maybe it was. Rubble and destruction suggested that it had been wider than that, and the boulders that tumbled down the great stone steps from the doorway reluctantly cut off the explorers from the interior. Looking at the far corners, Sabelu might have guessed that there had been a wall on either side of the temple.

Two things stood out to Sabelu, even amid this fantastical discovery. The first was the remains of the statues that had survived the collapsed rubble around the temple. They appeared as men but with the heads of bulls. One of them appeared to carry an enormous ax. Some of the buildings around the market area had smaller renditions of the same figure.

The second thing that stood out were the skeletons.

Sabelu had read his father's Book, and he knew his father's memories. He knew of the underground city east of Anpa O Wican'hpi that was guarded by the Sacred—or Cursed—Zukatopa. He knew of the fabled Tacagan people, humans but not. He knew of the fabled People Before, those who had chosen mutual destruction over slavery or extinction.

It should not have come as any surprise that the skeletons that littered the streets as densely as the crystals were human skeletons, but Sabelu could not help but shiver.

With his initial survey complete, Sabelu ceased conjuring the Atsvstdi sorcery. The light in the cavern dimmed, and his brain was spared a headache.

He knelt to examine a skeleton. Any cloth or leather was long since gone, as was most of the metal, though a small chunk remained, flecked with rust. He picked it up, saw nothing remarkable about it, and tossed it away.

"This is what my father and mother were searching for, all those years ago," he said aloud. "They just never looked in the right place. Or something happened, perhaps a rainstorm came and revealed the entrance."

He turned as if to address Kah Kitowak, but the man was still at the entrance to the cavern, rooted to the ground in awe and fear.

"Shouldn't you bless this place first?" Kah Kitowak wondered.

"Drive away the evil spirits?"

Sabelu shook his head. "There are no spirits here. Not anymore. Just as in Aktiya Waya, they're all gone." He made a motion. "Come on."

Without waiting for him, Sabelu went down the steps to the open market, carefully picking his way around the skeletons. He crossed the open area and approached the temple. The man-bull statues were ten times his size, the tips of the horns just brushing the ceiling, or so it appeared from his vantage point.

The entrance was indeed blocked, and there were no secondary entrances to be found in either direction. However, when Sabelu searched to the right, what he judged to be south, he found that the street trended downwards, and he began to notice water. The wall was discolored as from water but there was a pool at the end of the road. When he examined it, he found that it was neither stagnant, nor fresh, but salty, and he told Kah Kitowak of his findings.

"Salt water?" the Metis man questioned. "From the ocean?"

"Does it come from anywhere else?" Sabelu wondered sarcastically.

"But what is it doing here?"

Sabelu stood and waded into the pool. It was no more than six feet in any direction and never got more than ankle deep. A few small fish nibbled his toes. He got down and started feeling along the ground, finally discovering a hole a little smaller than his fist. It was covered in moss and sharp barnacles and he cut his palm. This was nothing a quick invocation of Asvhnisgi couldn't fixed, but he stood and left the pool anyway.

"This is what lies behind the cliffs," Sabelu said.

"But that doesn't make sense," Kah Kitowak insisted. "This is...this is the entrance to a city. This is the market that pops up outside a city's walls." He gestured. "This is the city wall. The minotaur is this city's protector standing guard at the gate." He shifted his stance and looked up. "If this is the entrance to the city, and we're standing on the other side of the cliffs—the same cliffs where Lehoyed overlooks the ocean—then what happened to the city?"

"Probably the same thing that happened to the underground city of the Cursed Zukatopa, or the city that is now Aktiya Waya," Sabelu suggested. "No one knows."

"But if I was directed to bring you here, then surely you must know something, or there is somethere here that you can learn?"

"Hm...maybe."

Now the outsider gave him a suspicious look. "I don't like it when prophets say 'maybe.' "

"We prophets don't particularly enjoy it either, but it's all I've got at the moment."

He returned to the temple entrance, looking up at the man-bull, the minotaur, statues.

Seeing how they were a good distance from any settlement and the only human being he had to mentally worry about was Kah Kitowak, Sabelu took the time to sift through some of his knowledge. This sifting quickly turned to simple revery, mentally bathing in the almost peace and quiet of his mind, the ability to pause the visions and the knowledge for just a little while and actually think about what he already knew.

Several cluttered visions sorted themselves out fairly quickly. He was going to bring his parents and siblings here. His parents would be thrilled and have a short period where they felt like young adults again, exploring ruins and solving mysteries, or trying to, anyway. His siblings would be less impressed, but it was all about what this meant for the people going forward.

"The Tacagans once held this world," Sabelu mused. "But I don't think they're done with it."

"What makes you say that?" Kah Kitowak wondered. "If even the spirits have departed this place, they've been gone for a long time."

"Something is going to happen. Something big."

The outsider shifted his stance and folded his arms. "I admit, I don't pay much attention to the rumors circulating about others because I know the ones that circulate about me. But if I remember correctly, you are supposed to know everything, at least about the people. If something big is going to happen that involves the people, shouldn't you know it?"

Sabelu gave him a look. "Do you understand what it's like to carry the knowledge of dozens of different peoples, and the memories of hundreds or thousands of individuals? When you return to the Old Land, visit a library and attempt to find a single sentence in a single book that you read fifteen years ago, except you don't remember the title or the author or anything about it except some minute, obscure scene or detail. And try to do this while reading a thousand other books at the same time. Granted, it is faster to search through mental knowledge than such a library, but the struggle is the same." He sighed and looked up at the man-bull once more.

"If this city is underground, though, what is Lehoyed doing aboveground?" Kah Kitowak asked instead.

Sabelu shook his head. "I don't know. And I expect that some things will never actually be known. Even men who live today cannot always be trusted with their own memories, never mind what they say is or is not the truth."

He turned and started back across the open market, heading for the cavern. After a moment, Kah Kitowak caught up to him.

"That's it, then?" the outsider wondered.

Sabelu did not look at him. "What were you expecting?"

"I don't know. A vision. A revelation. Some confirmation that there is or is not a threat to the people?" He added quickly, "Well, you said something about the Tacagans I guess, but it wasn't anything really useful."

"You say you've heard rumors about me. I know that you have heard rumors about my insanity. Understand, then, that I am having to learn how to think my own thoughts, how to formulate ideas of my own and articulate them in my own words. Have you ever tried to count something, then some idiot starts throwing out random numbers to try and mess you up?"

Kah Kitowak just grunted in agreement.

"This place, far from people, I can think. Granted, you're here and I have to be inundated with your thoughts, memories, hopes, dreams, triumphs, and failures, but one man is still quieter than a thousand. One man is quieter than ten who might go on a game drive."

"Why does it sound like you're just now discovering such a thing, getting away from people, I mean?"

Sabelu shrugged. "Children are expected to stay with the people. I am expected to stay near the priests and do their bidding, as an acolyte. My insanity actually afforded the breathing room I needed to get help from my uncle."

"But now that you're not insane, you're going to return to the priests, right?"

"I have no choice. If the people are to be saved, priests are people, too, and it's their responsibility to guide the people. If the leader is wrong, the people are led astray."

Kah Kitowak nodded. "Simple concept, yes. I'm sure they're overjoyed that you're no longer insane."

"You keep saying that, but even I am not convinced of it." He went on before Kah Kitowak could speak. "And while they may proclaim such, they will be less thrilled about it when they realize that the power that kept me insane is the same power that rules and corrupts them. Well, to be entirely accurate, the Shadows don't like to be found out. But in the mortal, linear world in which we reside, they prefer to use pawns and proxies."

The Metis man blinked and shook his head. Sabelu already knew what he was thinking. He had a number of words and concepts that he basically understood; it was just a matter of putting them all together in a way that made sense. Except even he wasn't ready to confront the truth, that the priests were corrupt and would lead the people down a terrible and dangerous path.

"So what does that have to do with this?" He gestured to the ruins behind them.

"As I said, the Tacagans may be gone, but there's still something lingering, something that they can attach to and bring themselves back," Sabelu explained. "It's a way to keep their hold on the Krydik."

"Like Galohisdi?"

"Something like that, but..." He shook his head. "I don't know. I need to speak to Anagalisgi again and ask him questions. This isn't just about the Krydik, it's...more are involved." He was searching through his brothers' eyes, their futures, but it felt so far out—decades, maybe over a century—that he couldn't put it all together, what he saw, what was happening. A sudden rush of cold air as they re-entered the cavern suggested that the Shadows may have played a part in his confusion as well.

"Does it affect the Old Land?" Kah Kitowak asked.

Sabelu barked a laugh. "Oh, it certainly does."

"Well then don't you think we might need to plan for something?"

"We?" Sabelu gave the man a look. "I don't think there is a 'we' here."

"Why not? I found this place. I brought you here. And you just said that something big is going to happen here and the Old Land is affected."

Kah Kitowak was not an ambitious man, not in such a sense. He would lead if he had to, he would charge into battle, but he was, in the end, part of the group, not its leader. Over time he would make his way into some manner of social prominence, but he would not be a leader. He would barely approach even Ola Achukma's level of influence, never mind someone like Yvgidahi.

"I need to consult with my uncle first. He knows more about the Whites and Shadows than I do. Then I will let you know, assuming you need to know."

"So that's it?" Kah Kitowak wondered. "You just speak to your uncle and get back with me? He sent me to you."

Sabelu gave him the briefest glance. "Yes."

"Doesn't sound like much of a plan coming from a prophet who can see the river of time from beginning to end."

"I try to simplify things for people who don't see things the same way I do. Most people can't handle too far beyond what they can see. A few people are capable of planning beyond what they see, and a rare few might even have the means to 'manipulate' things to that end. For you, for right now, the best course of action is simply the next step, which is wait."

"Are you calling me stupid?"

"I'm simply saying that you have a particular role. Knowing everything or most everything that is going to happen isn't it. Wait for those of us who do know to tell you what to do."

Now the outsider turned indignant. "I have served under men who didn't have your talents. I don't see that they are a prerequisite for leadership, nor do I see you as being especially capable yourself. You are, what, eighteen years old or thereabouts? Fine, so you might know things, but there is a great difference between knowing and experiencing."

Sabelu paused and turned to him. "Ah, so is that why you are still haunted by your time in the war? The fog, the noise, the shouts, the death, the sights and smells? You describe it to yourself as just like being back on the battlefield. If that is not an ongoing experience, then you are either whiny or insane." He went on before Kah Kitowak could protest. "I experience these things as well. Your memories, my father's, my brother's, any of those who survived the War of the Old Land. And I see all of the old wars from the Old Land as our ancestral peoples killed one another over land or hunting rights. I see the wars to come. Now, if you can imagine that, and somehow extrapolate your few years in the war onto a poential incoming catastrophe, by all means, you speak to my uncle and figure out what to do next. But if you can't, then be a good soldier and wait for orders."

Kah Kitowak's indignation increased proportionally to Sabelu's annoyance, though the outsider would frame it as stubborn arrogance.

Neither said a word as they navigated their way back through the tunnel to the opening back to the surface. Once they had wiggled their way back out, Kah Kitowak glowered at Sabelu for several long moments before conjuring Galohisdi back to Aktiya Waya, back to his tent set up in the outskirts of the camping area.

It was now later in the morning and the festival was in full swing. There was a nearly perpetual thrum in the ground from the equestrian events, and the din of conversation and cheering overpowered any minor sounds coming from the wrestling or archery competitors.

As soon as Sabelu regained his faculties, he left Kah Kitowak's tent. The outsider said nothing, but neither was in a mood for a fight. It wouldn't be productive; Sabelu knew it would only slow them down to let this resentment fester.

His first thought was to return home. Then he considered that it was only still morning and, now that the worst of the sickness from the Galohisdi was past, he was hardly tired. As much as he wanted to speak to his uncle right away, it would have to wait. Briefly he entertained the idea of taking some seeing fruit and going to the Old Land to speak to Anagalisgi directly, then decided against it. He was still trying to sift through everything he'd just seen and experienced. His parents had spent months, even years, searching for such a place. They even had maps from the People Before. And yet, it was one outsider who had stumbled upon it, and he had been sent to take Sabelu to that place. Sabelu was meant to go there, meant to see it. But what was so important about it, what was he supposed to learn or do?

As he made his way into the larger throng of people, searching out his father and brother, he decided that some ignorance might be a good thing. Was it really necessary for him to know every little detail about the city and its demise? Then he considered the argument with Kah Kitowak, every man believing himself to be just a little better than everyone else (which was impossible), and he rejected that decision. Information was good. Knowledge was good. Seeing how he had gifts that allowed him to know the actual truth, not just stories or half-truths that people could dig up, he really was a little bit better than everyone else. He couldn't help an objective truth.

Having to suppress everything in favor of pretending to care about the festival was more than a little annoying, but he suffered through it just so he could get to nighttime and speak to his uncle. On reflection, laying down to sleep, he could probably just conjure Iyuwahnilvhi next time, just skip through the day and get right to where he needed to be without having to deal with all the little details in between. Yes, that seemed a reasonable thing to do.

He'd barely closed his eyes to sleep before he was blinking them open in his uncle's cave, and his uncle did not look nearly as impressed with such a plan.

"He's right, you know," Anagalisgi said flatly, giving him a look. "You are supremely arrogant. And selfish."

Sabelu blinked, stunned by this change in attitude from the man who had been nothing but kind and understanding so far.

"Knowledge is power," his uncle went on, becoming more stern. "The idea behind this gift is to stop the Shadows and, as you have discovered, save not only the Krydik, but all peoples. It is not for lording over others and elevating yourself." He continued before Sabelu could speak. "Just now you were considering conjuring Iyuwahnilvhi in order to skip over the 'details' in between. In between what? There is no shortage of work to be done, Sabelu. Do you even recall your first task, about confronting the Shadows within the people? How do you expect to do that if you're just conjuring Iyuwahnilvhi, skipping from one point to the next? We speak often now because there is much to explain, much to discuss and plan, and things I must guide you in. It will not always be this way. One day you will find yourself on your own, and you must have the foundation to withstand the coming storm."

Sabelu found himself at a loss for words. Again, this stemmed more from the rebuke than the words themselves.

"The best leader knows how to follow," Anagalisgi continued. "To that end, I think I might have you help me with some errands in the near future."

"Errands?" Sabelu echoed dumbly.

"Yes. Errands. Minor tasks which you and your infinite knowledge and even more infinite ego would normally think beneath you. Such as taking messages."

"Where?"

"To the peoples of the Old Land, those who are struggling and need some guidance, some direction, for things you might consider insignificant."

"What about Kah Kitowak?"

"He is only one man, and he does not dream-walk. Nor is Galohisdi the most effective means of travel if you don't know where you're going."

Sabelu shifted his stance, feeling himself come more alive, as though warming up from being frozen and unable to move. "But then, how am I supposed to help the Krydik?"

"You can do that when you're awake," his uncle told him, entirely unconcerned. He turned as if to leave the cave, motioning for Sabelu to follow. "If you were so busy with it before, why the concern?" Once outside, he paused briefly to give him another look. "If you were so busy with it before, I might have left you alone to rest at night instead."

Sabelu glanced at Yawi, maybe four feet away, but even the wolf was giving him the look. The White turned and trotted after Anagalisgi, down one slope and up another. Sabelu sighed and reluctantly followed, catching up on the next rise and putting his hand in Yawi's fur to quell the visions that began rising like the tide.

"So where are we going?" he asked grouchily.

"This way," his uncle answered.

"Do we have a destination?"

"This way."

"Do you not know?"

This time his uncle got a cheeky look. "You mean you don't know?"

Sabelu sighed. "No. Not here I don't."

"Good."

"So you're not going to tell me."

"No. You need to learn what it's like to be like everyone else. Ignorant, seeing only what is right in front of you."

Sabelu scoffed, pushing aside a branch. "I'm not entirely ignorant, though. I still know everything I know when I'm awake."

His uncle did not look back. "And how much of that is helping you here? You still don't know where we're going or what we're doing." He glanced back briefly. "Maybe once you learn to appreciate ignorance and helplessness, then you will appreciate your talents, and you will know about this place."

They reached the top of a small hill and kept going.

"That's possible?" Sabelu wondered. "I thought I was blind to the Whites and Shadows."

"What is possible is whatever the Author wills. Many people would consider your gift impossible. But until you can demonstrate your ability to walk by faith, there is no point in walking by sight, not for this mission."

Annoyed, Sabelu said, "There's a reason I was taken to the city behind the cliffs, and I suspect it's not the only place that will have information I need to tell me what's coming. I think I need to make a trip to the underground city of the Cursed Zukatopa."

"There is a difference between information and knowledge," his uncle told him, "and fighting the physical will do nothing to destroy the spiritual. Have you truly forgotten what I've told you in just the last moon? Just a couple days ago you discovered that the ripples alone mean nothing, that you must confront the Shadows within the people, confront the people and weaken the Shadows' power. Have you forgotten? Did you misplace this knowledge? And your fears about having to help more people than just the Krydik, did you forget that, too?"

"I haven't forgotten, but it seems...slow. Tedious. Why not go directly for the heart of the Shadows? Removing a single thorn means nothing when you have to tear out the whole vine to be free."

Now Anagalisgi grinned. "Let me know how that works out for you when you have thorns wrapped around your testicles."

Even Yawi barked a laugh at that one, but Sabelu just felt the blood rush to his face.

"As for the underground city," his uncle went on, growing gravely serious, "I would warn against going there at this time. Ignorance saved your mother and father when they stumbled across it, but your knowledge and talents open you up to grave danger in that place. Danger you are not prepared to handle just yet."

"But that is where I need to go."

"Yes, but you are not ready. You have not freed a single person from the Shadows that bind them; you have no business going anywhere near that lair."

While Sabelu was partially inclined to prove him wrong, there was a seriousness in his tone and expression that gave him true pause. He'd read about the underground city in the Book, his father had talked about it a time or two, and the priests of Anpa O Wican'hpi had declared it cursed and off-limits. Nothing about the place even remotely suggested that it was a happy place to visit, even on a good day.

He continued following his uncle, up and down hills, through the forest, along streams. Yawi kept pace effortlessly, occasionally pausing to answer a call from one of the other wolves.

"Where are we going?" Sabelu asked after a while. "Are we going to the border with the dark forest?"

"That is one place we could be going," Anagalisgi replied evasively.

"But are we going there?"

His uncle did not answer.

"Are we—?"

"I heard you," Anagalisgi said.

"Where are we going?!" Sabelu demanded.

"This way."

Sabelu made a frustrated sound and briefly considered turning back. Problem was, he didn't know where he would go. He was in a dream for goodness' sake. He still didn't know how that all even worked. Did his uncle have to be the one to send him back? Did he return to the waking world automatically at some point? Was some external influence needed? He really didn't want to leave his uncle in frustration, then have to come crawling back later so he could go home.

So they continued hiking. They trekked several more miles, sometimes along gentle slopes, and other times climbing up jagged rock faces, until they reached a ledge near the peak of the mountain. The view was pristine, miles of open wilderness laid out before them like a blanket. Yawi walked along the ledge, stopping a short distance away to lift his head and howl. His voice echoed at first and then was answered by the pack somewhere in the valley. When they were done, he made another sound that was somewhere between a howl and what Sabelu might have termed a barking laugh.

"All's clear, I take it?" Sabelu guessed.

Yawi did not reply, but his look suggested that he was still internally laughing at whatever the pack had said.

Sabelu turned to his uncle. "So what's up here? What am I looking at?"

Anagalisgi glanced at him. "Creation, Sabelu. We are up here to look at Creation. We on the ground see so many trees that it can be difficult to imagine the beauty of the forest."

"It is beautiful, yes, but...I don't get it. What does this have to do with fighting Shadows?"

"You see the task of helping individual as a tedious endeavor. One at a time, that's all it is. You want to go straight to the greater Shadows, maybe even the dragon itself. But how do you cut down a forest except one tree at a time? How do you plant a forest except one tree at a time?"

"Trees, uncle. I may be able to pull up a knee-high sapling with my bare hands, but to do anything more, I will need an ax or a saw. And it takes time for a newly-planted tree to establish itself and grow."

His uncle nodded. "Not untrue. But imagine that as you pulled up these small saplings that you could twist them into the tools you need, and that others would see your efforts and come to help you? Maybe they bring greater tools, maybe they help you plant new trees or feed the planted trees." He went on before Sabelu could speak. "You are not alone in this, Tsiquiyi. But you are one of the few who is awake to the situation. You must wake up the rest."

Sabelu sighed. "Any ordinary man could do this. Why bestow gifts like this on someone, then limit them to being ordinary?"

"The ordinaries are asleep, Sabelu, chained and controlled by the Shadows. This is humanity's default state, but not its natural one. They tried to chain you as well. As I helped you, now you must help them. And, I think, in the end, you will find that your work is quite extraordinary."

"Does this mean I don't have to run errands for you?" Sabelu asked hopefully.

Anagalisgi gave him a look. "Of course not. But, because I didn't have to listen to you complain the whole way up here, I'll let you off the hook for tonight."

A sigh of relief felt like an overstatement of the actual relief Sabelu felt at that moment. He turned away from his uncle so he wouldn't see it, only to find Yawi watching him, smirking in his special wolf way.

"I bet you don't have to run errands," Sabelu grumbled.

Yawi threw his head up and bark-laughed. Finally he lowered it and gave Sabelu a look. "This is an errand, having to watch you, accompany you. This is an easy assignment. A difficult easy assignment at times, but still quite easy." He used his muzzle to point out over the valley. Somehow the landscape had changed so that the wide meadow and dark forest were now visible from their vantage. "The rest of the pack has the dangerous assignment, and even they are in better standing than those like the burrowers or the trackers or the fighters."

"I don't see much fighting down there."

"If a Shadow enters the territory of the Whites, or vice versa, the one trespassing loses both his natural advantage of being in his home territory and much strength due to the effects of the other territory. There is little actual fighting done on our own plane. A majority of the fighting is done in what one might consider neutral territory, where neither side has claim and both have the same advantages or disadvantages."

"The mortal plane," Sabelu said.

Yawi dipped his head. "That's right. Most often, humans just get in the way. Sometimes they are used as pawns or hostages."

"Gather enough hostages, and you get a Shadow stronghold," Anagalisgi added. "Free enough hostages, and you get a White sanctuary."

Sabelu considered this. Then, "What happens if a people is ruled entirely by Shadows, when they no longer heed the words of those like you or I?"

"Stronghold species. Rare cases, scattered far across the universe, but devastating in their power for either side. The Shadows raise them up as their mortal armies to spread death and devastation, though very rarely is their control overt. It is often a matter of stronghold by proxy. They do because they do not know better."

"Like the Krydik."

"That's right. The last of the light of hope is fading; you must stop it. There is no more time left to hope to raise up this man or that woman, hope to train them, hope they listen and learn. You have been given these gifts, Sabelu, you have seen it. Now that you have been freed from the Shadows, you can begin honing your gifts, using knowledge as a true weapon. You say that an ordinary man can do the things asked of you, then ask yourself why that ordinary man hasn't. I don't know what else I can say, what else I can show you."

Sabelu looked at him. "You don't have to convince me the war is real."

"Maybe not, but the others need to know, too. One man cannot fight this war alone, no matter how extraordinary. I have been here for a century myself, inundated with this war, standing beside the Whites themselves, and I cannot do it alone."

"But if the ultimate power and authority rests in the Author, why do we need to do anything?"

Anagalisgi hesitated. Then, "Because the only way this ends is in total destruction. Of the Shadows, or of the people. You, and the rest of the people, are going to have to decide whether you fear the Shadows, or whether you love the people. The Author made you. She loves you. You don't destroy something you love, but sometimes fixing a broken bone requires a little pain."

Sabelu took an even breath. He didn't understand but he felt like he should.

"We're on a sinking ship, Tsiquiyi," Anagalisgi went on. "It's not about stopping the leak, it's about saving the people. But it's the middle of the night and everyone is asleep."

"One by one," Sabelu stated.

"At first. But, like a snowball going downhill, it will gather size and speed and become unstoppable."

Looking out over the valley, the natural landscape turned into white meadow and then black forest. Blue skies faded sharply into black clouds. Lightning pulsed vaguely within them, and Sabelu could have sworn he saw an enormous shadow illuminated, however briefly. For a long breath, he forgot everything he knew, and suddenly his ideas of standing up to the Shadows and going after them single-handedly sounded incredibly foolish. Supremely arrogant as his uncle put it.

"You've seen and learned a lot today," his uncle said, snapping his trance. "I'll let you think about it for a bit, reevaluate just what you expect to do, what needs to be done. Then we'll start on those errands."

Sabelu nodded absently. When he blinked, the meadow and the dark forest were gone, leaving only natural landscape. He knew his uncle turned to leave, but when Sabelu turned to go after him, he found himself rolling over in bed, returned to the waking world.

DΘⱯI DVꞀT

Anagwoge Adolv'i

Confrontation

If the Whites had spies and other reconnaissance agents in the dark forest, then it only stood to reason that the Shadows would have the same in the white forest. It was the only way that they could have known of Sabelu's conversation with his uncle, as his peripheral vision was constantly bombarded with ripples and shadows and visions and hallucinations, all the things he knew were there but couldn't quite grasp. Sabelu had a hard time catching them in the act as it occurred mostly in his peripheral, but when he did catch the Shadows in the act, it was almost like watching small birds swoop from tree to tree, the way they, looking like little more than tendrils of smoke, slipped from person to person. They never lingered, instead being always on the move, hovering around someone just long enough to get them upset about something, cause them to be ungrateful, vindictive, argumentative, and other unsavory things. Tiptoeing around the festivities that day, the people seemed more hostile toward him as well. Either that or else the conversation and the things he'd seen had somehow evoked a similar, overwhelmingly paranoid experience as before he was released from the Shadow on his back.

It was the last day of lesser competition, the day when the quarter-finalists were decided. Up until now, a certain number had been cut each day. The second day was the largest cut, but no one wanted to be eliminated prior to the final three days. Who wanted to admit to being so bad that they couldn't last the first day? Who wanted to admit that they were so mediocre that they fell victim to the sweeping cuts of the second day? Who wanted to admit that they weren't good enough to compete with the better athletes in the higher competitions and had to be eliminated before the quarter-finals?

With the competitors all trying to work their way into the quarter-finals, tempers were short, at least among those who were worried about their chances. When there were active events, the work of the Shadows came out of the periphery and Sabelu could look at them almost straight on, like watching anything else. Sometimes it wasn't about causing active animosity between two competitors, but getting in the heads of a single competitor. Clouding a thought process as an archer tried to aim properly. Slowing judgment in the middle of a wrestling match, even to the result of injury. A misread on the disposition of a horse. Exaggerated melancholy over failing to advance.

Later on, then, another Shadow would swirl around another competitor, or even just a spectator, planting thoughts, influencing reactions. Sometimes, if two or more reactions collided just right, some form of either arguing or bullying would ensue. Sometimes it was two or more different Shadows playing with their own puppets, and sometimes it was one Shadow wafting back and forth between the two like a cloud of lingering smoke that wouldn't clear.

On the whole, the festival itself went as it always did. It never turned into a brawl, nor was there any real threat of internal war. Rather, it was a slow erosion of joy and trust, internal decay, like a log that might look fine on the outside, but, if pressed, would collapse in on itself.

Again Sabelu felt overwhelmed by the task, and he also felt a bit foolish for his, as his uncle put it, supreme arrogance over thinking he was going to take on the greater Shadows. It was everywhere, all around him, with no one left untouched in some way. He had to do something. If he couldn't banish a lesser Shadow, what chance did he stand against one of the greater ones? An image of the shadow in the clouds flashed through his memory.

He needed to find something small, something easy. A trial run as it were, just to see how this was all going to work out. He didn't even know what it looked like when a Shadow was confronted. As his uncle had said, it was a fine line between confronting a Shadow and confronting the person they influenced. Confront the Shadow, save the person. Confront the person, strengthen the Shadow.

He made his way through the festival. He couldn't start with the events or participants. In this state of competition, they were too easily influenced, too easily controlled. There were just too many variables to consider their actions or reactions, never mind how the Shadows might twist them. He needed something smaller, less consequential. A mother scolding her child. An otherwise minute fight between friends or siblings. Something the Shadows might influence but wasn't playing off such high stakes and personal pride. And, if there truly was some hierarchy to be had among the Shadows, Sabelu would expect that such tasks would be relegated to the weakest of Shadows.

Sabelu left the festival and headed up to the stone village. The front half was baking abominably, but the deeper areas remained relatively cool. Most of the people were down at the festival, but a good handful remained behind, either doing chores or errands, or avoiding the festival for one reason or another.

It wasn't five minutes before he heard the first argument, and it was indeed a woman scolding her child. He passed by them at the communal pool, then stood around the corner of a house, hidden from view. The boy was six years of age, but he had several older brothers. He wanted to go watch them and cheer them on (in spite of them either being eliminated already or ineligible for real competition, but he didn't understand this). However, in the memories of the boy's mother, Sabelu saw that he had done something against her explicit order under threat of not being allowed to go to the festival. She was simply making good on the threat.

This by itself was hardly anything evil. Discipline was a good thing. For a long moment, Sabelu considered that this was simply life as it was and to let it be. But when he peeked around the corner, he was struck by a sort of oblique attack on her, a whisper from a minor Shadow. It wasn't the child whom she would come to resent for the episode, but the father, her husband.

If only he would take them out more. If only he would teach them more. If only she had more brothers to spend time with her children because clearly their father wasn't overly interested. Sure, he'd warmed up to their oldest son now that he was of an age to compete, but what about the little ones?

Sabelu heard these whispers as surely as if a Shadow stood behind him and spoke to him. Perhaps it was the difference between the woman and himself—he was not a woman with children, so why should he be swayed by words to that effect?—that made it so he was unaffected by the whispers except to be angry about them, that a Shadow was taking advantage of what should be a normal, disciplinary, learning opportunity.

But how did he approach this? He wouldn't rebuke her for disciplining her child. And while it wasn't unknown to everyone that he had prophetic abilities and uncanny knowledge, most didn't seem to understand that it wasn't just about great events for the people as a whole or bits of information here and there, but it was everything. She wasn't going to react well to this.

Unless he rebuked the Shadow and it let her go so she might see the error of her ways and be free.

"I see you hiding back there," the woman said.

Sabelu blinked back to the present moment and realized he was staring directly at the woman. Her name was Ikoa; her son's name was Yomi. She was looking at Sabelu, Yomi was looking at his mother, still begging to go to the festival and promising all sorts of fantastical, impossible things in order to be allowed to go.

Sabelu cleared his throat and stepped out of his hiding spot. He could see many things from this woman. She'd lost one husband in the War of the Old Land. He had been the father of her first two children. Her current husband had fathered the rest. He could see that she would have three more children in her life. He knew that her second daughter was her favorite child, and her fourth son was her least favorite. This wasn't to say she hated any of her children, but any honest parent would admit to ranking their children. Few parents were that honest, however.

Trying to identify the father of her three children yet to come, however, was like trying to identify an object at the bottom of a pool whose waters are quite disturbed. If it wasn't the peripheral mess that indicated Shadow presence, an unusual chill in the air around him was another good indication.

"Why are you spying on me?" Ikoa demanded. "You've never been disciplined before yourself?"

The Shadow whispered suspicion and resentment of Sabelu's mother to the woman.

"I was simply observing the festering discontent you have with your husband," he answered awkwardly.

She blinked, momentarily caught off-guard by the change of subject and also the brief confusion over how he knew that was what was in her head. She knew well that he was an adelohosgi, but why single her out?

"Is that really the most important thing a prophet concerns himself with these days?" she asked.

He shrugged. "If a prophet doesn't concern himself with the welfare and direction of the individual person, what good does it do to direct the whole group? A herd of sick horses might be directed to safety, but they will still succumb to the sickness if not treated."

Ikoa folded her arms. "And you believe I'm sick just because I'm a little frustrated with my husband?"

"Your sickness stems from the love of that frustration," Sabelu told her. He knew he was committed to the conversation, this confrontation, but he still had no idea what he was doing. The chill had turned to ice, and he involuntarily shivered. The Shadow, now caught, was working hurriedly to muddy the waters as much as possible, whispering faster and louder to the woman, trying to distract her, confuse her. But in the midst of all of this, a small white butterfly appeared in the area, flitting around Ikoa. Any time it tried to land, the Shadow swatted at it. But the Shadow, being a minor spirit of lesser abilities, could not fight the White and whisper to the woman at the same time. Sabelu watched as Ikoa's expression twisted, however minutely, as contemptuous replies ran through her mind, mixing with genuine introspection.

The butterfly, invisible to all but Sabelu, landed on the woman's head like an adornment, working into her hair and pressing itself flat, nearly disappearing.

"Why would anyone love frustration?" she asked, her tone far less hostile now.

"Because it creates a false sense of self-righteousness, projecting blame onto someone else. It doesn't mean that something is your fault; sometimes, life is just life." Sabelu gestured to the boy. He was no longer begging, but he was too riled up to just stand still while his mother talked, and he ran in silly circles around the area. "He is a boy. Young, innocent. Many things he experiences, which we take for granted, are new to him. He still has a sense of wonder. He has to see everything, do everything, know everything."

The Shadow found the butterfly. It gave a mighty strike, but the butterfly darted away.

"Yes," Ikoa said, annoyed again. "If his father or uncles would spend more time with him, he would do all these things. See everything, do everything, learn everything."

"Would you trust a toddler with a knife?" Sabelu inquired.

Again, the odd question gave the woman pause, stalling the Shadow long enough for the butterfly to land on her shoulder.

"Of course not," she answered.

"Why not? He is a boy, he must learn these things."

"He's not ready. He has no strength to wield it, nor knowledge to do so properly."

"Surely a few lessons is all it takes."

"Years of practice are also required."

Sabelu shifted his stance, trying to keep his focus on Ikoa and not the fight between the Shadow and the butterfly. The Shadow had taken the general form of a cat and was now chasing the White, batting and pouncing, unnaturally long claws extended. "Would you expect your husband to feed your children on the breast?"

Ikoa laughed, and it was impossible to tell which spirit had prompted the reaction. "Of course not! He has none. And it would be unnatural for a man to do so."

Sabelu nodded and again gestured to Yomi. "He is learning more than you think. Everything he sees and hears, he remembers. He learns. But for now, he is still in your charge, as his mother. He is learning how to interact with others, what is appropriate social conduct. When he is ready, your husband and your brothers will guide him into manhood and teach him the finer points of discipline and provision, the skills he will need to be a successful man and husband and father and uncle himself."

As he spoke, Yawi moved from his side toward Ikoa, baring his teeth. The Shadow gave up its cat-like form, but still acted a bit like a treed animal. The White butterfly landed peaceably on Ikoa's head once more, again burrowing into her hair.

"I suppose," she said, sounded a bit chastened. "I love my sons, and even the older ones still defer to me, but I can see how they have separated from me in order to become men." She looked at Yomi who was now spinning in circles. "I should be thankful for the time that he is still with me. Even now, wanting to go after his brothers, that is the beginning of the separation."

"Your husband is already doing his duty just by interacting with your older sons, doing things and making a life that Yomi wants to imitate."

Yawi's growling grew to a level so loud it was a wonder Ikoa couldn't hear it.

"He learns respect from you," Sabelu went on. "He disobeyed your orders, and now you are preventing him from engaging with his father and brothers like he wants, like he should want. So that when he is able to go and watch them again, he has learned his lesson from you and is now ready to learn from them as well."

Yawi made a sort of snarling sound, and the Shadow flinched.

Ikoa nodded, and the Shadow fled. The turbulent water around her future settled. Her husband would be the father of her three future children.

"Maybe you're right," she admitted. She again looked toward Yomi, sitting on the ground playing with something. "As stressful as it can be, there's also something...sad, when they don't need me anymore."

"They will always need you, if you've raised them well."

He knew it was the right thing to say, but he would be lying if he said he felt any real empathetic emotion behind it.

Nevertheless, his task was complete. The Shadow was gone, the White butterfly in its place, still nestled in Ikoa's hair. The woman gathered her child and guided him away. He was still pouting and asking to go to the festival, but her demeanor and responses were far less hostile. He watched them go, Yawi sitting at his side, tongue lolling in a smile. Sabelu looked at him.

"I understand that you Whites are more powerful than your common counterparts, but will a butterfly really be able to fend off the Shadow if it comes back when you're not around?" He knew the reply before he even finished the question. "No, which is why we need to help others and make room for more Whites who can fend off the Shadows. The butterfly was just a way to get inside."

Yawi tilted his head, very much like a dog, his expression one of affirmation.

Sabelu had no illusions that the Shadow would wait long before returning. Or maybe it would. Maybe it would console itself by tormenting another villager. How would it be for someone, anyone to admit that they had been bested by a butterfly? Granted, that butterfly had a wolf to back it up, but a butterfly all the same.

He searched through the nearly endless information in his head, searching for Ikoa and her family, but for the moment, with the Shadow gone, everything remained clear, a perfect and uninterrupted stream.

"Where do I go next, then?" Sabelu asked of Yawi. "All things considered, I feel like that was as easy as it is ever going to get, and I barely knew what I was doing. I didn't know what to say. I don't know how to confront Shadows." He shifted his stance. "Maybe my uncle was right to take me on that hike, show me what it's like to not know something."

Yawi's expression turned smug, even for a wolf.

"I suppose I should keep going. One minor victory and a single butterfly won't win this war."

The wolf stood, stretched, yawned, and shook himself out, finally coming to a pose that was not quite relaxed but neither ready to attack. Sabelu looked at him. "You think you can sniff out another minor Shadow? A few butterflies ought to be worth a sparrow, right? Snowballs, like Anagalisgi said. Start small, make the opening wider and wider."

Yawi sneezed, but it almost seemed intentional. Then the wolf took off at a slow trot, weaving through the town. Sabelu took a breath and followed.

As a child, the priests and leaders had expected him to live a life similar to Anagalisgi. Priest, prophet, dreamer, engaging in daily life, communing with the spirits, and guiding the people. Unlike the ancestors in the Old Land had ignored Anagalisgi, the priests now would heed his advice and his wisdom and make life better for the people.

Now that it was obvious that they had little intention of doing so, it fell to Sabelu to do the heavy lifting, or the lifting that could be done on the mortal plane. It was one of those things that he had known for a long time but never quite understood. Visiting the cliffside city had answered those questions, but it didn't make him feel better. On the other hand, his uncle had warned and warned, but was unable to help the people in their time of need except to help them escape. Sabelu actually had the opportunity to do physical work and banish evil from their midst.

He thought about Kah Kitowak. What was he going to do in the Old Land? What were any of them going to do? What role did the Old Land play, and why did it seem like the Krydik just couldn't leave it behind? Time, distance, generations, war, and still the people were tethered to the Old Land.

Yawi rounded a corner. Sabelu followed and nearly ran straight into another young man. His name was Tayuli. He had been just twelve years old when the men left for the war. Among those men was his father, who had died just a few moons into the campaign. Afterwards, when things got back to normal, he had thrown everything he had into training for the festival and the tournaments, always keeping the focus on practical, warrior applications rather than fun and games. He married into Bear Clan and was an accomplished sorcerer as well. His demeanor at the moment was not what one would call cheerful.

"Watch out!" he snapped at Sabelu, a Shadow swirling about his head.

"What happened?" Sabelu asked, the words coming out before he was fully aware of the situation.

Tayuli stopped a few steps away, then turned to face him. "For being a prophet full of knowledge, you don't seem all that interested in helping the people."

Sabelu raised a brow. "And in what way could my boundless knowledge have helped you today?"

"You could have been there to call out Dikdali and his cheating!"

"I see." Sabelu nodded thoughtfully and approached slowly. "Wrestling match, right?"

The wronged competitor nodded stiffly. "That's right."

"And you train for war, don't you? You want to live up to your father's name and reputation, with none of the mirth and flighty gallantry of some of the others, right?"

"Of course."

Sabelu gave him a look. "In what war is an opponent going to follow the rules? What rules are there? Our ancestors lost the War of Removal because they tried to play by the same rules as their opponents and lost their advantage. Earlier in the war, when the rules were different, our ancestors had many victories."

He could see the swirling Shadow wavering, trying to come up with something. Sabelu tried to discreetly look around for any more White butterflies or other small creatures, but saw none.

"But if I had done the same, I would have been called out," Tayuli said.

"Then Dikdali is a better cheater than you are and clearly deserves his victory."

"Shall we all become cheaters then?"

Sabelu tried to choose his words carefully. The way things were set for Tayuli, he was going to die before he became an elder. All that remained to be seen was whether it was a noble, honorable death, or a disgraceful, wretched waste of life.

"I will not say that you haven't been disrespected. If Dikdali was wrestling for the fame of it, for a chance to advance and make his name known, then the shame is on him. But you participate in the games out of respect for your father and duty to your family, to train for war and horrible things. If this is the case, then you should thank Dikdali for the lesson he has taught you. There is no room in war for pride and petty ego."

He could see Tayuli wrestling with this, but his own mind was no match for the Shadow, not without a White to help him refine his thoughts into a dedicated will. And where were the Whites? A butterfly, a caterpillar, Sabelu would even accept a mosquito or a gnat.

In the end, the warrior just gave a thoughtful grunt, turned, and walked away. The Shadow remained in place around his head, and the best Sabelu could do was hope it was weakened, even a little.

Sabelu looked at Yawi. "What was that?!" He made a helpless gesture. "I had him talking, got him thinking. I never confronted or accused him directly. Is there only one White butterfly, one small White to get through such heady defenses?"

"The Shadow from the woman likely alerted the others to mischief. Any further Whites may have been delayed," the wolf offered. "But there is an opportunity here. If even three or four Shadows have left their hosts to go after the White on its way to this man—"

"—then we have an opening with three or four people to try and get more Whites in using a different route," Sabelu finished. "Can you find them?"

It was a kind of reverse tracking technique. Rather than follow the strongest scent to the creature, it was finding a scent and moving away from it. While interesting in principle, it was much harder to put into practice, like trying to find the least wet spot in the forest after a heavy rain. Even so, Yawi indicated a few possible candidates for freeing.

One was a teenage boy who was desperate to court a girl and questioning his self-worth as he hadn't found any prospects in his three years of, admittedly, poor to mediocre competition. His Shadow was whispering slippery lies of worthlessness and hopelessness.

Another was an older boy who did have a prospect, but was secretly terrified of someone else proving himself stronger or faster and taking his girl's eye. His thoughts had centered on four competitors most likely to do so. Sabelu had little doubt that his Shadow was giving him all sorts of ideas of how to neutralize these real or imagined threats.

A third was a woman who, every year, lost to the same competitor in the crafting competitions. The other woman was always a little bit better, a little bit faster, had just a little better eye for detail. Her thoughts were divided between despair over her less impressive skills, and smoldering anger that this competitor just seemed so oblivious to the pain she was causing this second place woman.

Seeing how his only success so far had come from a woman, Sabelu elected to speak to the disgruntled crafting competitor first.

He quickly discovered that while Shadows did appear to have certain people they preferred to manipulate, certain specialties or skills that they utilized, they were remarkably cooperative when it came to protecting a host from White interference, trying to take advantage of a gap in their defenses.

At the same time, trying to put a square peg in a round hole was its own self-defeat. This woman who was feeling self-conscious about herself and a little bitter over her competitor, even she found it strange that she would be worrying about an unfaithful husband when such thoughts had never really crossed her mind in her whole saga. Given more time to take root, this line of thought might have worked out. In the moment, though, it was the wrong Shadow for the wrong argument, and the confusion was enough to let in a White spider.

Competition demanded Sabelu leave before the Shadows had completely departed from the woman, but he was confident in a White victory.

The teenage boy with self-esteem issues was a fascinating case, perhaps because the two of them would be peers, yet Sabelu did not feel any sort of connection in this way. The boy was a wretched mess of hormones and raging masculine desires that were, for the moment, going unfulfilled. Sabelu should have been able to strike up a conversation easily and quickly assuage any fears or doubts the boy had. The problem was, not only did the boy not view him as a peer either, but the Shadow expanded itself, stretching itself thin so as to cloud even Sabelu's mind. If Yawi snapped at it, the Shadow just dispersed and reformed.

The kid just wanted to know whether he would one day have a wife and family. He didn't have to know who his wife would be, just the knowledge that he would have one. The ripples from the Shadow left much to be desired, and, at that time, Sabelu had no answer to give, so the boy walked away, even deeper in the Shadow's clutches.

Not two minutes later, Sabelu considered that maybe he should have spoken to the boy's mother and looked to see if she had any grandchildren from that son, a roundabout avenue of obtaining that information. But the damage was done.

By this time, whatever hubbub had drawn the Shadows away from their hosts was now finished, and the defensive gap had closed. Sabelu found a quiet spot, observed the goings-on for a minute, then looked at Yawi again.

"Did we fail?" he asked. "Was the butterfly defeated? What about the spider?"

Yawi yawned, making a sound that was almost a laugh. "Strongholds are notoriously difficult to infiltrate. That's why they are strongholds. But that is also the reason why the creepers are the first inside."

"The butterfly and the spider and, I imagine, other insects."

"That's right. They are not dislodged as easily as you may believe."

"Who comes after the creepers?"

"The burrowers. But there is a lot of work that must be done before that. After the burrowers comes the all-out war."

Sabelu swept his gaze over the field, settling briefly on each of the events and the campground. "Should we keep going, keep pushing?"

Yawi sat down. "There will always be more work to be done. Always. But sometimes, short bursts of good work are worth more than large swaths of poor work."

"The ant eating the bear," Sabelu stated. "But the bear is healing even as the ant is attempting to devour it."

Now the wolf lay down. He stuck his nose in the dirt for a moment, then looked up at Sabelu with a cheeky expression. "Only if the bear knows the ant is there."

Sabelu knelt beside the wolf and looked at the ground disturbed by the wolf's nose. A line of White ants was marching along dutifully, hastily constructing a network of tunnels.

"The first tiny stronghold of the Whites," Sabelu stated.

"Seeds," Yawi said. "Living seeds, able to go where no one else can and remain undetected by the larger Shadows."

"Why didn't they come sooner? Years ago, even?"

"They have always been here. It was just a matter of finding them. Disturbing the Shadows and creating the gap in the defense allowed them to bring in the likes of Butterfly and Spider." Yawi carefully nosed the dirt back over the ants and sat up. "The ants are perhaps the smallest of the Whites, but they are by no means insignificant in our work. They may be more important than any of us larger creatures."

Sabelu stood. "Why don't I take everyone back to the Old Land, give them the nattawodatnu, and introduce them to Anagalisgi? Why doesn't everyone have a guardian wolf like you?"

Yawi bark-laughed. "Ah, pup. How naive you are." His tongue lolled out in a smile for a moment. "It's all about choices, choosing the Whites or the Shadows. Everyone has a guardian lying in wait, but it must be a choice freely made."

"But if we were to show them the Shadows, show them what we're really up against—"

"Half would go mad, and the other half would be too wrapped in the clutches of the greater Shadows to accept what they were seeing in any good sense and would try to kill you. Only a small handful, three if you're lucky, would emerge as powerful and determined as you believe." Yawi shook his head. "Mortals are very frustrating creatures, very contradictory in their physical and spiritual matters and manners. You have all of this knowledge, and you struggle with it."

"Then why engage the likes of Kah Kitowak and the others?" Sabelu wondered.

"Because the ones hosting and planning the dance are rarely involved with the final performance," Yawi told him. "Each dancer spends a lot of time preparing their dress, their routine, their steps. There are many dancers with with many dances, many songs played by many drummers. Someone must coordinate all of this, and rarely does this person have time to partake in the very thing they are coordinating. In the beginning, perhaps, when the operation is small, but as it grows, there is less and less time for such a thing."

Sabelu considered this for a long moment and finally nodded. "I suppose I should talk to Kah Kitowak." He looked around again. "But not right now. No, he can wait, and even then, I can't tell him anything yet."

Yawi said nothing to that, just yawned hugely.

"Do Whites know the future like I do? Do you know why I'm not speaking to Kah Kitowak right away?" Sabelu wondered.

"Whites and Shadows may nudge and influence mortals in many ways, to steer them along the river as you put it. The Shadows are blind to the consequences of their nudges, and Whites only know as much as we need to know. However, we also exist on a different plane than this linear, three-dimensional one, so our sense of time is a little different than yours. I know the day and the next day as they will happen to me, because I can step out of time. My tomorrow may not be the same as your tomorrow."

"So we could already be having this conversation in the past?"

"It's a lesser version of the Author's existence outside of all of this. You see the two rivers, you see what has happened, what will happen, what you are doing now. All the same you are stuck in your canoe in your place in your river. I can get out of the rivers, run from one to another at various points in time, help steer the people in their canoes. Above it all, the Author is directing the rivers, directing us, seeing and knowing all that is in the past, present, and future, to use linear terms."

"And the Shadows?"

"Monsters in the water. They see only what is in front of them, scouring the water to steer the canoes into obstacles or break them apart entirely if possible. They do not know which river they are in, do not care. Some of the greater Shadows have a sense of time and consequences like we do, but not nearly as great."

Sabelu nodded. "So even if there are some observing us right now, some that might observe me later, they're not going to instinctively know what I'm planning, what I'm going to do, any of that."

Yawi dipped his head. "That is correct. They're not very smart, the Shadows. They never were. They have a terribly diminished sense of time, and they don't read minds."

Sabelu raised a brow. "Do you read minds?"

Yawi tilted his head. "I don't think I would call it reading a mind, but having a greater instinct about the person, informed by past and future and my own instincts."

"So Shadows don't see into people's dreams?"

"That is a complicated matter, for you know that the dream world and the spirit world are closely linked," the wolf said cautiously. "On a purely physical level, no. Their presence may influence nightmares, but they do not see or control the visions."

Sabelu nodded. "So any time we have to meet someone, dreams wouldn't be a bad place to go. The white forest would be ideal, but if there is a way to manipulate simple dreams, that could work."

"Why not stay here in your own home?" The question was not an accusation or spoken in offense, more like one asked in order to evoke a particular response of line of thought.

"Because even if my home is clear, and even with you there to protect us, there are still too many lurking in the city at large."

"Why not meet in the field after dusk, when no one is around? Or the wilderness?"

"Sound carries. The Shadows may not read minds or know the future, but they can listen and hear as well as anything."

Yawi's mouth popped open in a tongue-lolling smile, looking a bit like a father rejoicing at some mundane thing his young child has just learned to do. After a second he asked, "So, knowing all this then, after the events of today, what is your next step?"

Sabelu hesitated and avoided looking at the wolf for a long minute. Finally, "Well, I think I already uncovered that, but it's not going to be easy. In any sense." He looked at Yawi. "I need to clean my own house. Now that the Shadows know I'm involved—really involved—they're going to attack. With you here, they won't come after me directly. But my parents, my brothers and sister, they're still in the dark enough that they can be influenced and nudged. I have to wake them up first so they can be protected, even if they don't help."

Again the wolf got the fatherly expression, and Sabelu got the impression that Yawi had known that this conversation would happen, had gotten an "instinct" that this was the way it would go, and was quite pleased about it. Sabelu was still trying to get used to the idea of having a conversation partner whom he couldn't read or know what he was going to say next.

He did not confront anymore Shadows that day at the festival, although they were everywhere. A great majority of them stayed where they were with their hosts; a few sneered and snarled at him. But there were a few occasions, especially around older children, when the smallest and weakest of Shadows would flee at his approach.

Another reason he elected not to confront anymore Shadows among the general populace was so he could digest everything that was happening. He thought he saw and understood everything before, but that was merely observing the valley through a blanket of fog. Now the fog was lifting and he was seeing even more, things he never could have imagined. It was a lot to take in, and he also suffered a headache through the greater part of the afternoon that no use of Asvhnisgi could truly heal.

He arrived home that night no worse for wear, still dreading the conversation that he knew would happen. He felt very conspicuous, not only for his family around him staring at him, but also the Shadows nudging them to do so.

"I'm fine," he began outright.

"Are you?" his father wondered, at the same time his mother blurted, "You were seen speaking to no one on the hillside."

"I was speaking to a White, the wolf Yawi," Sabelu informed them.

"And what did he have to say?" his father wondered. His experience with the Whites and Shadows immediately jarred the Shadow swirling around his head. The ethereal being of smoke and shadow struggled to keep a grip, like a leaf in a strong wind. The Shadow around Nendawagan was also jerked off-kilter, if only because of her belief in the Book and the tale from her husband. As for Netami and Blaknik, their Shadows remained undisturbed. Netami's was less powerful due to her belief in Sabelu, and Blaknik was only just growing up and able to be more consciously influenced by the Shadows.

"He said that the time has come to purge the Krydik of the Shadows' influence," Sabelu replied. "He said that we will be needed, but in order for us to be of any real use, the Shadows have to go."

"I suppose he means you," Nendawagan stated. Her Shadow was not one of doubt, but of fear, as images of her dead son were pressed into her mind.

"More than me," Sabelu told her. "We must be as ants. Small, yes, but relentless, hard-working, constructive, helping one another with our tasks. I may be able to direct, but I can't do it alone."

His father was thinking about the war, the Whites and Shadows on the battlefield. It was not a matter of one side having the backing of the Whites and the other having the backing of the Shadows. Rather, both sides were driven by the Shadows to fight and destroy themselves and each other. The Whites were tasked with just containing the carnage as much as possible, bringing everything to its written conclusion.

"Why you?" his mother asked. "Why you, why now? What's coming?"

"Why me, because it is already written. Why now, because it will take time and effort to accomplish, more than just a yearly festival preparation. As for what is coming..." He hesitated, though it only served to push his mother further into the Shadow of Fear. "What is coming has already happened. It was the destruction of the People Before. But the evil that drove them to their demise still exists, and it is at work in the people as we speak. They always have been. The Shadows were hoping for an easy victory, slowly herding us to our deaths, until I came. Since I was freed from them, it is now going to turn into war."

At the mention of the People Before, his father thought of the canyon and the underground city, the mystery that had only been half-solved. His mother, on the other hand, thought of those like Kah Kitowak's father who tried to kill them because of their persistence, and she feared a similar fate for her son.

The thought of being involved at all, yet helping to eradicate the Shadows, was the last gust of wind needed to completely detach the Shadow hanging onto his father and blow it away. Simply seeing the Whites and Shadows and the scope of their influence was terrifying; the idea of being able to get involved this time and be of real help was far more encouraging.

"But Itsitsa has a Book, and that means we're special, doesn't it? Why do we have to do anything, why not let the Author take care of it for us?" Blaknik wondered.

Sabelu looked at his little brother and the Shadow resting on his shoulder. It was a minor Shadow, and Sabelu couldn't tell its specialty, but figured it didn't matter as he answered, "We sit in our canoes in the river of time and history. And it is a very tumultuous river, with many rapids and obstacles. If we do not take heed of warnings and steer ourselves, we will crash and be tossed into the waters and die. The current is always flowing, and we will always reach our destination; it's just a matter of our condition when we do."

It was difficult to tell whether Blaknik had some thought or change of heart that dislodged the Shadow, or if it was Yawi confronting it himself. Whatever the case, the minor Shadow fled the boy and left the house entirely.

"What about you?" Netami asked. Her Shadow was similar to their mother's, Fear and Loss. "I can't imagine the Shadows are just going to allow this to happen. If you're the only one who can see them, who can direct us in what we need to do, they'll come after you."

"They already have," Sabelu told her. "And they will again. That's why we need to be strong and work quickly, get ahead of the Shadows and bring the Whites in to fight alongside us."

Out of the corner of his eye, Sabelu noticed a line of White ants start marching dutifully into the house.

"There are no Whites here now?"

"Only Yawi and a handful of others. But Yawi is here to protect me, and the rest are very small, enough to make an opening for the rest, but we have to bring them in."

Nendawagan still looked uncertain. "This sounds very much like war, Sabelu. We can't afford another war, especially amongst ourselves."

"That is exactly where we're heading anyway, whether or not we do anything. If the Shadows stay, they will have us in civil war if for no other reason than their own amusement, and to ensure that we can do nothing but scrape by and meet our own needs, dividing villages and even families. If we start fighting back against the Shadows, yes, there will be conflict, but at least we as a people have a chance of surviving and helping others later."

This idea was enough to shake loose the Shadow from Netami, but the images of Tsona were too embedded in his mother's mind to get rid of her Shadow. No amount of growling and snarling from Yawi could force it to leave either. Nendawagan was holding too tightly to the fear, feeding directly into the Shadow, and it wasn't going to give it up for one meager wolf.

"All right," Ola Achukma said finally, "what do we need to do? If you are the only one who can see what's really happening, and you are going to be directing all of this, then direct us."

Now Sabelu faltered. "I don't know how right now," he admitted. "I know what I have to do, what I can do. I don't know about others yet." He looked at Blaknik who yawned. "Besides, it's late. I think we need to get some sleep."

It broke the tension in the air anyway, and the impromptu meeting dissolved, each to his own bed, though Sabelu stayed behind for a minute with Yawi. He looked at the wolf.

"I don't know what I'm doing," he said quietly.

"Regardless, now that you have pushed yourself out into this river, you must follow it. Steering or not, as you put it," the wolf stated.

Sabelu glanced at the ants that had formed a kind of perimeter around the main room. "I think we're going to need some of these ants to infiltrate my mother and start planting seeds. Her fear is strong and the Shadow heavy. I don't think I will be able to do much for her right now, but her Shadow will attract others back to the rest of the family."

Yawi dipped his head, then laid down on the floor, his nose a hair's breadth from the ants' line.

"Are you speaking to them?" Sabelu wondered, kneeling down.

Yawi looked up at him. "Well, you weren't."

"I don't know how to speak to ants."

"The same way you speak to me." He sat up. "But it's all right; they heard you. They're not offended either; they would rather not be disturbed by direct conversation. Takes time away from their work."

"They're very dedicated," Sabelu said, standing.

The wolf glanced down at the ants briefly, then back up. "They say thank you."

Sabelu nodded uncertainly. "I suppose I shall sleep soundly tonight, then, knowing we're guarded by a wolf and a colony of ants."

Ꭰᏸ Ꮄ Ꮒ ᎠᏴ Ꮧ Ꭲ

Achuchine Adolv'i

Errands

Patience was a virtue, and not one that Sabelu had in abundance. It wasn't just that his progress in confronting the Shadows and bidding them leave was excruciatingly slow, but it could also be reversed. He'd lost count of the times he'd had to return to Ikoa, who'd let her butterfly become overwhelmed by Shadows of Malcontent, chase away those Shadows, and coax the butterfly back in.

He'd recently had the idea that maybe it would take a woman to help a woman. Few men liked him as it was, and the young women weren't exactly batting their eyes at him for marriage. So after the most recent banishing of Shadows and reestablishment of the butterfly, Sabelu had asked Netami to be a friend and keep Ikoa on the right path. So far, so good.

But still, it was all very tiresome. He'd expected that once he got going, the Shadows would mount some kind of opposition. He'd expected huge confrontation, grand conflicts, and standing against them as a mountain against the wind. What he got was decidedly less exciting, instead being more of a game of cat and mouse, and he was the mouse. He could run and run and run, work and work and work, but all the cat had to do was one pounce to get in front of him or one good swat of a paw to knock him back. And if they really wanted to, it would take only the tiniest bit of effort to catch him and kill him. It was a game to them still, while for him it was life and death.

It wasn't all bad news. There were more small Whites among the people now than there had been at the end of the festival, all of them insects of one form or another. Butterflies, dragonflies, regular flies, spiders, and more. The ants were also still around, a minuscule yet powerful presence. Anyone who managed to keep their White for at least three consecutive moons eventually saw the ants move in, like a small perimeter guard. Yawi said it acted like a homing beacon, telling the next class of Whites to be ready to move in.

"Well they can move in any time now," Sabelu complained. "No war was ever won with dragonflies."

They sat at the top of the slope, northeast of the cave, beside the river that fed the crop fields. A brisk wind might have chilled him if not for his use of Udilegv'i, and Yawi's thick fur where the wolf leaned against him, blocking the worst of the breeze. It had snowed earlier in the day, but it was just warm enough now that it had since melted. Although with the sun going down and the wind picking up, more snow would fall overnight.

"Maybe not, but you've seen how their erratic movements confound the Shadows," Yawi said, a hint of amusement in his voice.

Sabelu couldn't help a small smile of his own. "Tiny distractions."

"Even the largest of creatures is bothered by the tiny mosquito," the wolf said. "Some would say they are bothered more than the small creatures."

"But don't the Shadows have something similar? Why are you not bothered by tiny Shadow ticks or fleas while we're sitting here in this Shadow stronghold?"

"Because such creatures are busy elsewhere, creating openings for Shadows in other places. You don't post green boys to guard a stronghold."

"But sending those green boys to infiltrate a stronghold is perfectly acceptable."

"Would you suspect a child of treachery?"

"Maybe not." He frowned. "In the Old Land, children would be taken to replace dead children and warriors." He looked at Yawi. "Do Whites and Shadows take prisoners?"

"We can. We have. But there has to be a purpose to it. The resources spent just guarding one Shadow are significant."

Sabelu gave him a look. "You don't have unlimited resources from the Author?"

"The policy of the Whites is strategy. You are learning well about confronting the Shadow and saving the human. We operate similarly. The Shadows' policy is destruction. They will destroy men just to spite the Author, and they will destroy us if we try to interfere."

"Can Whites and Shadows die?"

Yawi shifted position. "Not as such. It is very easy to kill a Shadow, but their essence is simply reabsorbed by the dragon and they are rebirthed anew. It buys us time in a fight, but it is not death, the true elimination of an enemy. As for us, we go through a similar process of rebirth. But it is much harder to kill a White than a Shadow."

Sabelu pondered this. Then, "In the first Book, in my grandfather's Book, Anagalisgi formed you from clay in a dream. Kind of. That was your reforming. You had been killed and remolded into a new White."

The wolf dipped his head. "That is correct."

"Were you always a wolf? Could you have been reformed into anything?"

"By the Author's word, I could have been anything. But my spirit is that of a wolf, my task is that of communication and protection, and that is how I shall be."

Sabelu looked up at Yawi who was looking down the slope. "How did you die?"

The wolf looked down at him. "As I lived, protecting the people, protecting your kin so he could make the first trek here. It was a crux in time, you see. As you have seen and are facing now. Your kin's discovery of this place was essential, and the Shadows worked hard to try and keep him blind to what he needed to see. My pack stopped the Shadow blocking his vision, and I was forced to sacrifice myself in the process."

"Does my uncle know this?"

"He learned of it eventually, yes. That's why he asked me specifically to watch over you."

Sabelu adjusted his position. "So, what is your name, then? Your real name. Anagalisgi gave you the name Yawi, but you must have been called something else before."

Yawi shifted in a way that might have been interpreted as a shrug. "I am called Yawi now, and so I am. Before I was simply called Wolf—"

"But there is more than one wolf," Sabelu interrupted. "How did you tell each other apart?"

It sounded foolish even as he was asking the question, but Yawi answered, "We have our own signatures to identify each other among ourselves. Your kin has given names to other animals to tell them apart in their groups, or to comfort his own mind. But in the big picture, wolf are pack. The pack is what matters. The pack works together as a whole, as a single thing."

"How does that go with you, alone, protecting me?"

The wolf vaguely pointed toward the town with his muzzle. "The people are the pack I protect. You are my specific charge, so we are pack as well. The rest of my pack will come in time, once there is a better White presence here."

Sabelu scoffed, his curiosity shattered by cold reality. "Right. When does that happen again? How many insects does it take to make a burrower?"

"How many flames does it take to make a fire?" Yawi countered.

Sabelu sighed, shivered, and stood. Immediately he was smacked in the face with a strong gust of wind, but Yawi was there to keep him from falling over. Grudgingly he made his way back to Aktiya Waya, the cave providing much needed relief from the wind, although the chill from Shadow activity remained ever present.

A handful of people were out and about, but they were inching their way closer to the time of year when the people would hibernate as much as the bears. Even so, only one person even attempted a greeting toward him.

He pretended it didn't bother him, at least so he could bypass any inquiring busybodies, but he couldn't lie to himself. Didn't they understand he was trying to help them? Did they even understand what his mission was, or did they just assume it had to do with the priests and that automatically made it none of their business; the full priests would interpret and disseminate information as needed? Did they even see him as a person, or more of a walking oracle or spirit, something to be respected but avoided at all costs?

Well, he knew the answers to all of those questions, but he pretended he didn't as he scurried home, past another half a dozen curious minds. What was he doing? Where was he going? What had he done today? He seemed unusually talkative these past few months, almost sounded like he was trying to help people, but he had some strange ideas of how to go about it. Well, at least he wasn't curled up on the floor like a madman, blaspheming the priests and council.

It never escaped him that no one really came to him for help; he had to seek them out. He would find them in the midst of their problems, but they would never actually walk up to him for advice on a problem they were having. No one asked him to summon or drive out a spirit. No one asked him to heal a wound. No one asked him to use the sorceries in any way. For the most part, he just existed as a ghost.

Was it possible that the Shadows were inspiring this sort of latent attack? Make him socially invisible, make him like nothing, so that if he interfered too much and the Shadows decided to go in for the kill, no one would really notice him missing. If anyone was aware of his existence, it was his family.

His father remained staunchly against the Shadows and ready to help, although he didn't know how. His mother wanted to support him, did in her own way, but her Shadow of Fear had paralyzed her to inaction. Blaknik was young and still trying to understand, but Sabelu just didn't know how to explain it all to him.

Only Netami seemed fully supportive, able and willing to help. He'd taken her to the cliffside city, shown her the wall, the statues, and the many skeletons. It hadn't taken but a few minutes for her to consider that there had once been a city where the ocean was now, and she resolved to do whatever it took to prevent something similar from happening to the Krydik.

Later she took Galiliga to the city. Their brother was a bit disturbed by the experience and hadn't said anything about it for a long time. When he did finally visit and broach the subject, he agreed to help, but he wanted to do real things to help, physical things. He wasn't like Sabelu, didn't understand how all of these spirits worked. Still, he would help the people, as he was sworn to do as a councilman of Yonhi.

Of course, when asked about what normal people could do, Sabelu couldn't come up with anything better than mere friendship and accountability. It sounded pathetic even to him, and he slunk off to bed just as soon as he could.

It had been about a month and a half since he'd seen his uncle. His absence had made Sabelu a little nervous, but then, what was he really going to tell him that was profound? Any large news, he might expect, but if he was still struggling to smuggle in butterflies, his uncle wasn't going to saddle him with rabbits.

"Welcome, Tsiquiyi."

Sabelu was barely conscious of the dream when he heard Anagalisgi speak, and he found himself standing on the slope outside the cabin portion of his uncle's dwelling.

"Tsidushi," Sabelu acknowledged. "You look enthusiastic."

"An overstatement I think, honestly, but I'm always glad to have something to do, be able to help people."

"Errands?"

"Errands."

Running errands with his uncle was hardly a difficult task. It was almost like pretending to be a White for a little while, visiting people in their dreams, influencing them in subtle ways, sometimes having a conversation if it was really necessary. While easy, it was also a bit tedious. Sabelu recalled that being dragged along was his punishment for his ego, and he might have hoped that going a month without them meant he was off the hook.

Anagalisgi made a motion and started off, Sabelu hiking a step behind to the right, Yawi trailing happily.

"Who are we visiting tonight?" Sabelu asked, more out of formality than genuine curiosity.

"Aklaq White Bear."

"The woman Kah Kitowak mentioned?"

"That's right."

"Why are we not visiting Kah Kitowak himself?"

"Because right now we are more concerned with Aklaq."

Sabelu could see Aklaq as he had seen her through Kah Kitowak's memories, though his knowledge of her personally was otherwise nonexistent. This frustrated him and he said as much to his uncle.

"Does anything not frustrate you?" Anagalisgi inquired, sounding a tad exasperated. "You enjoy your knowledge, don't like not having it. You hate your knowledge, see it as a curse and a burden. Just once you'd like to get to know someone without already having every detail of their past, present, and future being shoved into your brain. We're going to meet someone who you will have to meet and get to know, at least initially, and yet you complain about not knowing enough. You complain that confronting Shadows is difficult and slow. You resent including others because then you might not be so important anymore. Honestly, Sabelu, what do you want?" He glanced back at the question, but never slowed his pace.

"I want to know what I'm supposed to do!" Sabelu said, annoyed. "I want to know what's going to happen."

Now his uncle stopped and turned to face him. "Don't talk to me like I haven't been at this a few more decades than you. You know what I think? I think you want an easy fix that will make you look good. Something where you can save the day like the heroes of old."

"I want to be respected!" Sabelu spat. A dam broke in his chest and tears began streaming down his cheeks. "I'm destined to die alone on the side of a mountain, Tsidushi. And I know that no one will mourn my death. Even now, I am barely acknowledged as an existent being. Is it really so wrong to want a little respect and admiration before I have to lose it all and go to my death?"

Anagalisgi's expression softened and he nodded slowly. "I understand. I really do. How many times I wished the priests and council would have paid a little more attention to me and my dreams.

How many times I wished I could have explained the things I saw, the Whites and Shadows. And how many times I wished a woman would look my way and not scorn me as a bad omen." He sighed. "This is our life, Sabelu, as prophets."

"Adelohosgi," Sabelu scoffed, wiping his eyes and hating himself for his childish outburst. "Dark seers. Harbingers of destruction. Is there no good in our lives?"

"There is good where we make good."

Sabelu sighed. "The visions don't stop, Tsidushi. They never stop. The hallucinations, the phantoms in the periphery, even with Yawi beside me, it never stops. Even here, since I've been confronting the Shadows, they're starting to creep in, more and more. The battles to come. On Hlohi. On Earth." He paused. "Here." He ran a hand through his hair but said nothing more.

"I know," his uncle said quietly. "The future is frightening enough to those who have only their imagination. But it is far worse to know, I think."

"How much knowledge do I really need, though? Is it really important for me to know the names of a man's great-great-great-great-grandsons? Or the name an old woman gave a friendly fawn when she was a girl? Or a woman's favorite flower? Or the minute rituals a man performs before he sleeps? Or anyone's preferred sexual position? Do I really have to know all that?"

"I don't know," Anagalisgi admitted. "I really don't know. That would be a question for the Author."

"Well it's not as though she couldn't just use you as a mouthpiece to answer. Or maybe just make it so I automatically know." He looked up and around at the sky. "Well?! Why do I need to know all this?!"

His uncle just sighed. Beside him, Yawi whined. After a moment of godlike silence, the older prophet said, "We have work to do tonight. I know time and space work a little differently here, but our time here is limited."

"Mine is, yours isn't, and it was your idea to bring me along," Sabelu reminded him.

"Maybe when you actually meet Aklaq, you will understand her significance."

And there Sabelu found himself in a trap of his own making as his uncle resumed the hike. Did he want to meet her and know, or did he not? He cast a last angry glance at the sky before following Anagalisgi.

They crested the hill and found themselves entering the white forest. Beyond that was the white meadow and a few more white trees on the border of the dark forest. Anagalisgi said nothing, just continued straight ahead. Yawi had a look like he wanted to go trotting after Anagalisgi but knew his charge was to stay near Sabelu.

"You can go ahead," Sabelu told the wolf. "I think I'll be fine with my uncle."

The wolf's mouth popped open in a smile and he loped away, looking genuinely happy just to run and bark and frolic in the grass. When he reached the meadow, the rest of the pack appeared out of nowhere and tackled him playfully, a massive bundle of white wolves rolling around in the tall grass.

Anagalisgi laughed, and even Sabelu had to smile.

"I will leave you here with them and bring Aklaq here," the older prophet said, still grinning as he walked away.

After a minute of playful romping and rolling around, the wolves all got to their paws, shook themselves, and started out across the meadow. Their lolling smiles quickly disappeared, and Sabelu could see they were on a mission. Rather, they were on patrol. Overhead, a White hawk screamed. The leader of the pack looked up briefly and made a kind of barking noise, but that was about the only acknowledgment.

Sabelu followed them at a short distance. The pack went straight for the dark forest, turning at the last moment to walk along the border instead, but he stayed behind. There was a line of white trees at the border, and Sabelu was forced to wonder whether the foliage itself was at war, if these white trees were the only thing keeping the dark forest from spreading.

He stared into the forest, the foggy abyss, feeling very distinctly that it might also be staring back at him. The trees seemed to be the only semi-solid thing there. He couldn't even be sure that the bushes weren't just Shadows lying in wait for something, anything, to foolishly cross over. Glancing down beside him, Sabelu spotted a White grasshopper and a White field mouse, both of them staring intently into the forest as well. What were they waiting for? What did they hope to achieve? The wolves were not only stronger against threats, but they could cross the meadow in a few bounds to deliver any messages. Or just howl. Wasn't that their primary task, communication? Grasshoppers were seed planters, infiltrators, like the ants and the butterflies; what was it doing here?

"I am doing my duty," the grasshopper said, as if reading his thoughts. "As is Field Mouse. But we dare not speak of it here, lest the Shadows hear us."

Sabelu blinked and could only nod as he turned his attention back to the forest.

Something was in there. Something big. The air in the dark forest was thick and toxic; even standing just this side of the border, Sabelu could taste carrion. But he could also feel the current breaking around something. The problem was that after just the first few rows of trees, everything blurred together into darkness and smoke and shadow, as might be expected from the domain of the Shadows. He did not know what lay beyond, or what was looking at him.

"The dragon, what else?" the field mouse said at his feet. He looked down at a tiny paw on his foot. The mouse stared up at him with enormous eyes.

"The dragon," Sabelu stated. "The leader of the Shadows."

"That's right."

"Why would it be watching me?"

"You are the dark seer. You see the darkness. But you are also the one who stands in a crux of time and can do something about it. Why wouldn't it watch you?"

He looked back up at the forest. A dark seer, not because he saw bad things or evil omens, but because he saw the Shadows. He Saw them. And he was able to stand against them, one man in the gap. The dragon, in all its power, this close to him so that they were perhaps a stone's throw apart, and it could not touch him. Or would not.

A guttural noise emanated from the forest, and Sabelu felt the air current change. Squinting his eyes, peering deep into the black mist, he thought he saw something large shift position, but he couldn't be sure.

The dragon was deciding what to do with him. Maybe it would suffer any consequences in order to be rid of him now. Maybe it was organizing the Shadows in Aktiya Waya to take care of him that way. Maybe it had something else planned.

Sabelu wished he could show this to everyone. Show everyone the Shadows, bring the people here so they could see the dragon and understand what was happening, what was at stake. It wasn't just petty argument, poor decisions, bad leadership, or any of the usual excuses. There was real evil at work here, and it was trying to destroy them. In destroying them, the dragon would spite the Author, be rid of an adversary, and save itself; it had every reason to want their destruction.

The people were needed. They needed to be rid of the Shadows. If only he could make them listen, make them see!

"We're working on it," the mouse at his feet said, patting his foot, the motion barely registering as sensation on his skin. "It takes time. I know humans aren't the most patient species out there, but have a little faith. The foundation the ants provide is unmatched."

He didn't know how to respond to that, so he remained silent. He knew the mouse was right, but it was head knowledge only, hardly anything resembling faith. How was this all supposed to work together? How were they supposed to navigate these rapids? Sabelu could see everything that was coming, but the rest of the canoers he was leading were all blindfolded. How was he supposed to tell one to go right to avoid a rock, and another go left to avoid a marsh, plus give a thousand other directions, and somehow make it all make sense without people getting the orders mixed up?

"It's impossible to do on your own," the mouse went on. "You must teach the others to lead as well."

"But none of them can see as I do," Sabelu said. "That's the point."

"But you do not see as they do. You see the forest; they see the trees." The mouse made a gesture outward, as if to the grass. "You see the meadow; I see the blades of grass. You have no trouble navigating to the forest, for you can see the forest. I have no trouble navigating to the forest, even though I cannot see it. But I have other senses, other instincts, and they guide me as much as my memory of past trips." It made another gesture, this time toward the sky. "Likewise, the birds can see the whole of the landscape while you can only see the forest or the meadow. We see things from different perspectives, yet we all get exactly where we need to go."

"Even you just admitted, though, that you have instincts to guide you. How am I supposed to guide those who don't have instincts?"

The mouse squeaked a laugh. "All creatures have instincts. Even trees have instincts. A bird with a broken wing does not forget how to fly once healed, and a caged bird wishes only for freedom."

"Then birds are smarter than people, because most of the people I've helped have gone right back to their Shadows."

"Then you help them again. And it's not enough to do something for them; you must make them understand why you helped them, what you are trying to accomplish."

Sabelu threw up his hands. "What do you think I've been trying to do?!"

"If a man requires surgical intervention, all you've done so far is offer an anesthetic. It is only the first step. From there, you must act quickly. You must follow this up with action. Don't be surprised when inaction sees the anesthetic wear off and the man wakes in the same condition he was before."

Sabelu made a grunt-like sound of displeasure and turned away from the mouse. The same advice and flowery words, and he was no closer to actually helping the people. What was he supposed to do? How did he show the world to a blind man? He did he lock the cage once the bird was free so that it could not return?

He walked off several yards and stood, mostly turned toward the dark forest. He knew he was still being watched, and he might have even said that the thing, the dragon, was laughing at him. See the small human who doesn't know what he's doing. See how he struggles in vain. Sabelu was no threat. The people were no threat. The reason the dragon hadn't moved in for the kill yet was because the game still amused it.

He didn't know whether the Shadows had any greater mind-reading advantage here in this plane than they did on the mortal plane, but even if Sabelu did have some kind of plan or motivation and they could see his thoughts, he doubted the Shadows would be worried about it. Of course, with the dragon right there in the darkness as witness to his frustrated conversation with the mouse, Sabelu was willing to bet that by the time he woke up, every Shadow throughout the universe would know of his ineptitude and would redouble their efforts to undo everything he had accomplished so far, even to the point of wiping out the ants.

"Aklaq, may I introduce to you my nephew, Sabelu," Anagalisgi said behind him.

Sabelu turned to see his uncle approaching, a young woman a few steps behind. Pretty, actually, full-blooded Inupiaq from the north. He immediately knew who she was, who her people were, their history and future. He saw her as well, the children she'd left behind, the children she'd rescued, the children yet to come.

But that was all a long way in the future. For now, the best she could come up with was, "You're the prophet."

"Prophet," Sabelu grumbled. "Dark seer. Harbinger of destruction. Take your pick." He looked at his uncle. "Why are we here?"

"Because you need to work together," Anagalisgi said. His words were kind enough on their own, though his expression did not match it half so well. He was trying to be hopeful and encouraging to the woman, but how did one make war sound pleasant?

"You have shown them that escape is possible," his uncle was saying.

Sabelu shifted his stance. "They'll need it, considering the next fifty, sixty, seventy years are going to be only—"

"Silence, pup!" Anagalisgi snapped, giving his nephew a look. He turned back to Aklaq. "Escape is possible. They know this now. Like you, they are beginning to understand that where they are is not where they will always be. You have known this as both good and bad, and such is the way of things in this life. But you must show it to them for the better."

Aklaq shook her head. "I don't understand."

"Most of the time, you won't," Sabelu muttered.

"You must give the people a place to escape to," Anagalisgi said.

Aklaq blinked. "What, like Aktiya Waya?"

"Preferably not," Sabelu interjected.

Anagalisgi huffed. "Sabelu—"

"You knew what would happen. If you were really that concerned, you would have had us meet in person."

"What do you mean?" Aklaq wondered. "What happens? What's going on?"

"Dream-walking does things to him," Anagalisgi sighed. "It is the weakest, but also the strongest, barrier between dimensions. Some don't consider it a barrier at all, but a nexus of Time and Space."

She just blinked.

"I can't stop the visions on a normal day when I'm awake. It's like I'm constantly flooded with them," Sabelu stated crassly. "Coming here is like drowning."

"Then why are we here?" she inquired. "Why not have us meet in person?"

"Do you really think it would go well between Sabelu, Putu, and Everett?" Anagalisgi countered.

She considered this for a moment, then said, "Probably not."

"And anyway, the reason we're here, the reason he's here, really, and could have already been gone by now—" Anagalisgi gave Sabelu another look. "—is because there should be some coordination between Earth and Hlohi, between the Krydik and District Nine."

"How so? For what?"

"For the preservation and restoration of the people. Those schools and other policies will seek to destroy us. And, in some cases, they will be successful. You must be the force that pushes back."

"How do we even begin something like that?"

Anagalisgi grinned. "You already have. You must build on what you have already done."

Looking at her, Sabelu would admit that she had done a fair amount of work. As the children of the Old Land—or her small part of it—were kidnapped and forced into prisons of assimilation, she and her children went out to kidnap them back, delivering them back to their families or other places of safety.

She was out doing things. She was getting things done. Physical things. Tangible things. And Sabelu was, what? Trying to make friends with people? He just wasn't cut out for such a task. If anything, he should be the one rescuing children and she the one making friends. But they lived in two different worlds, quite literally. She could no more accomplish her task by trying to make friends than he could accomplish his by declaring an all-out war.

How wretched and embarrassing was that?

Even worse, she was given more tasks and greater guidance while he was treated like a child to run errands. He was the adelohosgi with the gifts. He was the one who was best prepared to coordinate the proverbial dancers. And yet, his uncle seemed to think he still needed to learn something from a woman from the Old Land.

"You said it yourself," his uncle told him later that night. "You can guide a herd of sick horses to safety, but they will still succumb to the sickness if not treated. And each horse must be treated individually."

"Yes, but—"

"You are a young stallion still learning to fight. She's a mare who has already had to defend the herd multiple times. However great you may become, you must still learn the basics. We are speaking now, but at one time you were still only a babbling baby."

Sabelu grunted as he was reminded of Blaknik's words. However great he was intended to be, his father had still rejoiced over his first steps and first words.

"Yawi said that Whites are not bound by linear time," Sabelu stated.

"That's correct," his uncle confirmed.

"Are you bound by linear time? Can you go back and forth and see where I have been, where I will be?"

Anagalisgi shook his head. "I'm afraid not. Although I know much and have experienced even more, I am yet a mortal myself, and this flesh does not respond well to attempts at time travel."

"But it is possible?"

"Doubtful." He stirred the stew over the fire. "And anyway, it was curiosity only, to see if I might go back and...save a few people."

"My brother?" Sabelu guessed. "Your brother?"

His uncle's silent expression was answer enough.

"Do you at least see the past? Maybe you cannot see the future because the Author does not allow it, but if the past is so fixed, do you ever look back?"

Anagalisgi chuckled humorlessly. "We are in the past, Sabelu. According to our future selves. And we are in the future, according to our past selves. What you are doing, you have already done. Just consider your father's Book. Consider that each page, every word he ever spoke, at one time was the present, but it was also past and future, relative to the rest of the book."

Sabelu shifted where he sat by the fire. "I remember...looking into the future in order to figure out how to do something. Because by looking ahead, I could do it now, or then, so that when I got to that point, I already knew how to do it."

His uncle nodded. "That is one way to take advantage of your gifts, yes."

"So why can't I just look ahead, figure out the killing blow as it were, and do that now?"

"If you know that the string is the last piece of the bow that you attach, why don't you start with the string and be done that much faster?"

Sabelu shifted again, evading his uncle's logic. "The problem is, I can't see myself. The only vision I have ever had of myself has been my death, and that was when I was an infant." He made a motion. "I can see all these events, looking through the eyes of others, and yet there seems to be a void. I do great things, but I apparently do them alone."

"That is possible, yes."

"But why? Do the people not care that I try to help them? If the idea is to free the people from the Shadows, why can't the people help with the load?"

Anagalisgi raised a brow but did not look at him as he began ladling stew into bowls. He set one down in front of Yawi but the wolf did not touch it just yet. "What do you want, Sabelu? Do you want to be a great hero with respect and admiration, everyone looking to you to save the day? Or do you want the people to do everything themselves?"

"I..." Sabelu closed his mouth and took a bowl as his uncle offered it.

"If ordinary men could do this, then why aren't they? The priests are the ones intended to guide the people in matters of ritual and religion, yet you know that they are perhaps the most corrupt."

"But I was under the Shadows' influence, too. They tried to make me kill myself."

His uncle nodded. "This I understand. Men will help men, women will help women, and the people will be free. But who will confront the Shadows themselves, except the one chosen to do so?"

"My void of knowledge is not limited to myself, Tsidushi. I cannot see you. I cannot see Yawi or any of the Whites or the Shadows."

"No, but you can see other people, which is how you will help them. And just as greater weight produces greater strength, so it will be when you confront stronger and stronger Shadows."

Sabelu could only guess that his uncle intended his words to be encouraging. He took a bite of stew. Then another. Yawi stood and started lapping at his bowl, perhaps trying to be polite but still a wolf in his etiquette.

"Why did you tell Kah Kitowak to take me to the cliffside city? There's nothing down there that you couldn't have simply explained here."

"You have a lot of memories, Sabelu, but very few experiences," Anagalisgi told him. "Just as you wish to think your own thoughts, so you must also live your own life, have your own experiences. You may look ahead to a future event in order to help you in the present, but in the present, you must still act in order to have the memory in the past that you will need in the future that will be needed for the past."

"But if I am to go after the Shadows, why am I blind to them? I can look ahead to prepare myself for men attacking me in the street, but I cannot look ahead to see what awaits me in the underground city? What if something were to happen here? Why am I blind to the most important aspects of this war?"

"I'm a little tired of your complaining, Sabelu," Anagalisgi sighed. "All you do is complain about how you can't see, how you don't like not knowing, and then you complain that you think you know too much because you're here and you interact with Whites and Shadows. You have been given the gifts necessary for defeating the Shadows, but it is not by your own power that you do so, and the void in your knowledge is a way to ensure that you walk by faith."

Sabelu wasn't sure quite where this was going, and the best he could come up with was, "I just want to understand the plan."

"Are trees isolated beings? Are they so separate from each other and the surrounding landscape that they do not matter? When a seed sprouts, it must draw from the soil, from the water, from the air. It one day becomes a home to many creatures. Bees build a hive on its branch and so attracts the bear. A fox digs a burrow in its roots. You cannot simply study a tree and expect it to be isolated and unimportant.

"I have told you before that mortals cannot handle the real war that goes on, how the Shadows slither and weave evil through people, how the Whites step into and out of time. Even what little you do is but a faint, shadowy echo. I am the closest anyone has come and even I am still only on the fringe of it."

Sabelu looked guiltily at his stew. "Tsidushi, I'm sorry. I'm just frustrated—"

"So am I, Tsiquiyi. And you see there, the fear? The fear of the unknown, the fear of the known, the fear of what could be, what might be, the desire to know, the desire to not know. Maybe it's time to erase all of that. Maybe it's time to give you a real taste of what you're up against."

Sabelu didn't need his gifts to know what came next, and he went to the floor of the cave, covering his head as if it might stem the tide of agony that crashed into his brain.

If he thought things were bad before when he had a Shadow on his back, clinging to his soul, it was but an annoying gnat compared to this. Images flashed through his head so quickly they were little more than a blur of color. He had no ability to slow it down or even catch a momentary glimpse of anything. Everything came more as impressions and abstract concepts: fear, war, love, peace, joy, pain, sorrow, suffering, triumph. These feelings intensified, refining like iron into steel, sharpening incessantly, until they were in their pure, natural forms. Hatred, revenge, loyalty, protection, motivation, ambition, betrayal, purity, steadfastness, doubt, faith, resolution, revolution, life, death.

Somewhere, in a distant place he knew was his conscious mind, he had a stray thought that he was diving into the very essence of the Whites and Shadows, the war that was going on here. Then he knew for certain that, yes, even the foliage was at war. Nothing was not at war in this realm. The animals, the plants, the rocks, the water, the air itself. He saw and felt how the dimensions overlapped, bled into each other, the influence of these beings on the mortal realm. He saw the marionettes of men, the lesser Shadows their strings, the greater Shadows their gimbals, the dragon the puppeteer. He saw the diligent work of the ants and other insects, cutting the strings of the people. When all the strings were cut, the people fell into a pool of Whites waiting to catch them. Or they would fall, but there just weren't enough insects to help everyone, and sometimes the Shadows repaired the strings just as fast as the Whites cut them.

The visions shifted again, adding yet another dimension. He moved through time now, following the strings through the Shadows back through time. Recycled over and through again. Suddenly Sabelu found himself simultaneously at the impossible past and the unknowable future, compressed and yet stretched thin as if traveling through

Galohisdi. He saw a past full of light, full of Whites. He saw a future as if that light had been turned inside out, like a pair of pants, yet the force of this turning was like a maelstrom in water or a tornado on the plains. It only strengthened, but it could not hold forever; eventually, something would give out. Something was going to implode. Or explode. Whatever the case, the consequences would be dire. A shield was needed, to protect those in harm's way.

Sabelu didn't know if it was even possible to pass out while dreaming, but something finally gave out in his mind; the visions ceased, the cave faded away, and all he knew was merciful blackness.

When he came to, he was back in his uncle's cave, lying on a mat, staring at the ceiling. To his right, cave wall. To his left, the fire, burning hot. His uncle sat beside the fire, shaving a piece of wood, throwing the curls into the flames.

"There is nothing more I can show you, Sabelu," Anagalisgi told him. "There is plenty to teach, but if you are unwilling to do the work with the tools you have, then you might as well walk out of my cave, not come back, and doom the people and the universe."

Sabelu groaned as he sat up. He felt terribly sluggish as he got himself situated by the fire.

"What was all that?" he asked dumbly, his head pounding, face aching, mouth and jaw feeling as though he'd been punched and lost some sensation from swelling.

"A taste," his uncle replied, still shaving curls into the fire and not looking at him. "A glimpse of the war that has been raging since long before you or I were even thought of, compressed and packaged for the benefit of a linear, three-dimensional, mortal mind."

For as much as he'd just absorbed—most of which was stuffed into his brain like eating far too much food at a meal and feeling nauseous afterwards—perhaps that statement was what hit him the hardest. They were, in fact, linear...three-dimensional...mortal creatures. The beings he was up against were none of those things. He was not going to defeat them, not truly, but he was going to defend the people from them. Sabelu knew and understood all of this, but he was still struggling to work through it. Mostly he just wanted to take a nap and get away from this dream.

"Now that you know," Anagalisgi went on, "ignorance can no longer be an excuse. You have had visions and prophecies before; you have Yawi to aid you. You have been given the greatest tool of all: knowledge. All that remains now is the choice set before you. You can step into the mortal theater, on the Hlohi battlefront, in this war. And you can use your knowledge to help the people. No more excuses, no more complaining and whining. Just diligent work. Or you can take what you have learned, ignore it, and walk away. I know things are moving quickly; I know that this has been a hard summer and it will only get harder from here. But there is too much at stake and too little time to waste on frivolity."

Sabelu nodded. "I understand. And I will help the people."

Finally his uncle looked at him. In the flickering firelight, he appeared to have aged fifty years and bore a striking resemblance to his older brother. He nodded kindly. "Good. Rest now, then. You have a lot of work to do."

Sabelu shifted position until he was again lying back on the mat. As he closed his eyes, he wondered how great a tool knowledge could possibly be. It was the knowledge of good and evil that doomed humanity in the first place.

ᎠᏃᏪᏂ ᎠᏴᎢᎢ

Asonelane Adolv'i

Burrowers

A year and a half went by.

In the beginning, Sabelu might have expected the knowledge of the universe and the history of the Whites and Shadows to really change things. As it turned out, this was hardly the case. He might have had grand revelations, but no one else had.

Ikoa still struggled with Malcontent and other unkind feelings toward her husband.

Galiliga wrestled with Jealousy and Shame, being related to Sabelu.

Nendawagan continued to feed her Fear over the possibility (and, indeed, future certainty) of losing another son.

Blaknik, getting older so that Sabelu could read him more clearly, was frequently a victim of Worry. And why not? Growing up in Sabelu's shadow, he'd been inundated with dark words and bleak prophecies; was it any wonder the boy questioned whether he would come of age and marry and have a life of his own before falling victim to the evils spoken of by his older brother?

And then there were the cares of day-to-day life, things not evil in and of themselves, but still taking up space in the mind for the average human being. Clothes that need mending, children that need tending, horses that need breaking, game that needs hunting, and the many seasonal festivals in addition to the annual national festival. And Sabelu was not immune to this mundane clutter. He was still a functioning, if weird, member of society, and he had certain obligations. He went out with his father on a hunt, did errands as his mother asked, and taught

Blaknik thirty different ways to do everything, techniques from dozens of different ancestor peoples.

Then there were his priestly duties.

The priests didn't like him very much, and the smoke that filled the private portion of the townhouse was less natural and more spiritual than Sabelu was really comfortable with. He saw shapes and shadows in the smoke, and the incense and tobacco tasted unusually sulfuric. Sometimes when he looked at the other priests and they looked at him, he did not see their eyes, but the eyes of something else looking back at him.

He blinked and looked away, trying to focus on his duties even as he wondered if such rituals weren't the cause of the madness. Just as soon as he could, he retreated to the slope above the crop fields. There was a certain spot, a large, level rock beside the river, where he and Yawi would meet to speak. He told the other priests that it was a place where he could meditate and pray alone.

The Shadows knew better, and he wouldn't doubt that the Shadows told their priest hosts what he was really doing. How they phrased it Sabelu did not know, for he did not believe the other priests to be so consciously aware of the war between Whites and Shadows. If they were, why they'd chosen the Shadows was beyond him.

"They choose it because they know nothing else," Yawi said, appearing beside him as dust on the wind forming into the shape of a wolf until he could feel the soft fur of the White. The wolf sat beside him, and they looked out over the bowl. The snow was melting fast, filling the irrigation system which would feed the crops and replenish everyone's home reservoirs. The wolf went on, "They feed it because it is familiar and because they are rewarded for it. By now, they are not feeding the Shadows so much as the Shadows are feeding on them."

"Why can't I just rebuke them outright? Surely if they saw you, saw the Whites and the nature of the war—"

"Their spirits are not so robust as you think. Spiritually, they are simply reanimated corpses under the control of another. They have no ability to stand on their own and would die before you reached them."

Sabelu frowned and said nothing to that. The one side effect he'd noticed from obtaining so much knowledge was the inability to ask meaningful questions of genuine curiosity, mostly because he already knew the answers, and asking the question wouldn't change anything.

The dragon was the head Shadow in charge of all other Shadows, but beneath it were four main generals: the cerberus, the three-headed dog; the wolf dog; the serpent; and the black phoenix. Each one had a role. The cerberus was the primary general of the army, the one spearheading the actual, physical fights against the Whites, and he was the one who had killed Yawi in the wolf's last iteration. The wolf dog's role was more internal affairs and ensuring the Shadows all did as they were told; he was the one the Shadows had to answer to when Sabelu confronted them and drove them away from their hosts. The serpent was in charge of the stronghold species, ensuring they remained stronghold species and directing his underlings in how to prepare more species for such a role, although this process could take hundreds of years. Finally the black phoenix was the one in charge of death ground. When things started going badly for the Shadows and it was time to destroy the host before it could be taken by the Whites, the black phoenix was called in to do just that.

Right now, all he was doing was creating a little more work for the wolf dog—and probably not even the wolf dog himself, but one of his subordinates. More was needed to get his attention.

"And once you have his attention, what do you plan to do?" Yawi wondered.

"I don't know," Sabelu admitted. "How do you kill a Shadow?"

"The same way you kill a White. You can't." Sabelu sighed. He knew this, but Yawi continued anyway. "Only the Author has such power to destroy. In our war between ourselves, we do not die, but are only reformed. It works the same way for the Shadows."

"Because they were once Whites," Sabelu stated. "So even if we did 'kill' the wolf dog, he would only be reborn through the dragon."

"Yes. And it will be this way until the end. But the goal here is to save the people."

"The insects are here, the needle has been threaded, we just have to do more to get the burrowers in here."

"Once the burrowers are here?" Yawi inquired politely.

"The burrowers are tasked with information, aren't they? Well, we need information. The Shadows are fully aware of what I'm trying to do. They know that I can't confront and attack the people. But if I don't see the Shadows, if they are kept hidden away in people's homes, I can't talk to the people to get the people to shake off the Shadows. Therefore, evil becomes a private affair, at least for a while. It makes confronting the Shadows more difficult, but it opens another gap in their defenses while the people are out and about."

Yawi dipped his head in a gesture for Sabelu to keep talking.

"I can't be everywhere at once. Netami is doing well to befriend people and help them, but not everyone can do everything." Sabelu shifted again. "One person to clear the field of stones, one person to till the soil, one person to plant the seed, one person to care for the crop. And just like the women pick their crops as their own personal project, so people should stand by one another, feeding and protecting their own charge. And this has to be done on Earth as well, for our kin in the Old Land."

The wolf said nothing. Sabelu searched his visions and memories, unsure which were his own life and which weren't. "One person to clear the field of stones. Kah Kitowak already has some experience in this, from Red River. And Aklaq is working with the people to warn them of danger and help them." He shook his head as if in some new revelation. "The process has already been started."

"And what of the people here?" Yawi asked.

Sabelu nodded. "I am the one to clear the field of stones. We don't have any outside enemies like the people of the Old Land; our war is purely spiritual, and I am the one best equipped to clear the field."

"And the one to prepare the soil?"

"My father. He has the rapport and the support; he is liked by most everyone. Even those who don't really like him at least respect his work and what he's done to try and help the people. He can smooth out the ruts that I make."

Yawi made a gesture. "Who plants the seed?"

"Netami. She has the care and precision to know what to say and how."

"Who cares for the crop?"

"At this point, everyone."

The wolf made a sort of nodding motion, then stood and pointed with his muzzle. "Very good. Now then, why don't you go down and help your mother?"

Sabelu's mind went blank for a moment. "What?"

"Your mother is still trapped by Fear. Why should anyone listen to you if you can't help even your own mother?"

"But...what if she still won't budge? I know we've shaken the Shadow in the past, but it always comes back. The Shadows always come back, at least to try and retake their hosts. Are you saying we shouldn't help others until we ourselves are perfect?"

The wolf gave him a look. "Our homes will always accumulate dirt; this is known. Would you rather be asked to clean your home by someone who never cleans at all under the excuse that it will come back, or someone who is diligent to clean their own home when dirt accumulates because they value cleanliness?"

Still Sabelu balked. He knew his mother would one day shake off her Fear; he'd gleaned as much from looking far ahead. He just kind of foolishly hoped that it would be someone else who talked to her about it. But then, what kind of son would he be to neglect his own mother?

Grudgingly he stood and started back down the slope. The tricky part about the confrontations was that timing was everything. He couldn't just walk up to his mother and talk to her about her Fear, especially if she were feeling joyful or determined or anything else. Well, he could, but simple human confusion over the sudden choice of topic would hinder meaningful progress and could spark an even deeper Fear, the idea that there was some sinister reason that he was bringing it up out of the blue.

The Whites were not bothered by weather on the mortal plane, so he was not surprised to see ants and grasshoppers and other insects out and about in otherwise chilly weather. The population of ants had increased tremendously in the last year or so, though they now seemed more intent on establishing a general perimeter around the bowl than singular homes, unless, of course, the occupants managed to shake off their Shadows. He also saw a few mice here and there, scurrying about the field and in the shadows around town. There was still more work to do before the burrowers themselves could establish their presence, but just the sheer number of small Whites was enough to scatter and confuse the minor Shadows, which provided some opportunities to speak to hosts left unattended.

If only it were so easy to dislodge the Shadow that had affixed itself to Nendawagan. The Shadow of Fear had been a permanent fixture on her soul ever since the War of the Old Land. The object of that fear didn't matter—fear of losing her husband and sons in the war, fear of losing her infant son because he was possessed, fear of losing her adelohosgi son because of some destiny—the Shadow of Fear was all the same, and each new target, every fear that was realized and every new fear added, only saw the Shadow sink its claws deeper into her.

It angered Sabelu in a way he could not describe. Women were the givers of life, and now a Shadow was stifling that beautiful, free-flowing energy, poisoning it with Fear.

The Shadow itself was still a lesser Shadow. More than the minor Shadows which were the small vices that could be shaken off in one or two confrontations, like the Malcontent that plagued Ikoa, but less than the greater Shadows which were the puppeteers like those controlling, either directly or indirectly, the priests. These middle Shadows, or indulgences, were typically the worst Shadows that would inhabit a common person who had little or no influence over a larger group, enough to wreak havoc in the casual domestic setting, although they would sometimes push people into such situations where a puppeteer could take over control.

Sabelu wanted to believe that his mother was not influential enough to be of concern to the puppeteers, but it was a lie. His father still carried influence, and with the slow merge of the women's council into the local village councils, there was some power to be had. If his mother allowed herself to continue to be led by Fear, soon she would not only be ruled by it, but she would be leading others in the same way. He couldn't let this happen, either to his mother or the people.

He searched the river, searched the timeline. He saw his mother being freed. He saw her future joy. But it looked so far away. He didn't want to see her suffer for so long. Where was it? When was it? Who was it that finally said or did the right thing that got the Shadow to release her? And what did they say or do?

He knew his mother would be home when he returned. He knew that she was making cornbread and thinking about everyday activities and chores, musing over this year's crops and the snow melt and everything else. She wished to see her grandchildren soon; she wished Netami would marry so that she would have more grandchildren; she wished Sabelu would marry so that he might have children and father a legacy before his death.

That was when Sabelu saw, like a turbulent pool suddenly stilling, that her final release from Fear would not come until after his death. Oh, this Shadow of Fear over her now would be shaken off, and she would have periods of Fear sobriety, but it would never completely go away until after he died. If it was any comfort to her—and him, to be honest—his death wasn't for more than a century. But how could he let her suffer for so long? The Shadows tried to nudge things here and there, couldn't the Whites do the same? Couldn't they nudge things so that she could let go of her Fear—really and truly be done with it—before he died? Couldn't he get the benefit of seeing her without Fear?

Maybe that was one small benefit to his gift; he could see her without Fear after his death.

She turned as he walked inside.

"Oh, there you are," she said, a minute allowance of relief being granted her by her Fear, perched on her shoulders like a vulture. Yawi bared his teeth at the thing; the vulture cawed and hissed at him and did not budge. Nendawagan turned back to her cornbread. "Blaknik was looking for you earlier."

"He knows I'm at the townhouse most mornings," Sabelu stated.

"Well, he went looking and you weren't there. He wants you—"

"—to go fishing with him. I know."

"So why aren't you?"

He hesitated for half a second. Then, "I wanted you to know that I'm all right."

Nendawagan paused in her work. After a moment, she looked back at him. "I know that."

"You know it, but you don't believe it," he told her.

The Shadow of Fear shifted position.

"They don't like you, you know. The other priests. Most of the council, village and national. I'm afraid they're going to try something."

"Of course they are," Sabelu said flatly. "And they're going to fail. I know their schemes. They're not going to work."

A White mouse was crawling on his mother's shoulder. With the indulgence still distracted by Yawi, the mouse went unnoticed up behind his mother's ear.

"Are you sure?" she asked.

Sabelu nodded. "Absolutely. And I have a few plans of my own, but I need you to help me, just like you helped to get the women organized for the war."

The pinch of the vulture's talons outweighed any whispered words from the mouse as Nendawagan asked, "Is there going to be a war?"

"No. Not as such. I'm just saying that you are very good at organizing people and getting things done."

"I organize people for the festival just fine. Why did you bring up the war?"

"It was a mistake, I'm sorry." He searched for words to salvage the situation. The mouse's tail brushed the vulture's foot. The vulture looked down, saw the mouse, and immediately went into a frenzy. It shifted forms from a vulture to a raptor, twisting around and snapping at the rodent with lightning speed. Yawi launched himself into the fray. Sabelu tried to block it out and not be distracted. "It's a spiritual war, one to save the culture and identity of the people."

"Yes, the Whites and Shadows, you've said it before. Your father has tried to explain it as well. But we're safe here, Sabelu."

"We're isolated. Prey isolated from the pack is the easiest to attack."

By now, the mouse had run off, and Yawi and the Shadow were going round and round Nendawagan, clawing and snapping. This was attracting the attention of nearby Shadows. Yawi would soon be outnumbered, and Sabelu would have no good way to get through to his mother as the dark thoughts began to dominate her mind.

"Will you at least consider it?" he asked finally.

"Consider what?" she wondered, a new Shadow snaking through her mind just long enough to confuse her before going after Yawi. The wolf yelped at a nip on his hind leg.

"Helping me."

Perhaps it was something about the yelp that caused the minor Shadows, the vices, to disperse suddenly, and his mother nodded. "Of course. I'm your mother, you know I'll help you. I've fought for you since you were born; I'm not going to stop now."

Yawi chased the last vice out of the house, then whirled as the Shadow of Fear returned to its perch on Nendawagan's head. Sabelu just nodded, thanked his mother, mentioned something about going to find Blaknik, and left the house.

Once out of battle, Whites healed fairly quickly. By the time they made it to the slope, Yawi was good as new. Still Sabelu inquired after him.

"I'm fine," the wolf assured him.

"Why are Whites grouped according to their task or skill, and Shadows grouped according to their strength?"

"Because Whites, like good, are absolute. We are solid. But Shadows are shifty and constantly changing, hard to pin down which makes them difficult to identify and defeat. It makes grouping them by task or skill a laughable endeavor. Force and power are all they know, all they are."

"But the wolf dog and the others, they're identified as certain forms. And the dragon is the dragon."

"Their forms are a type of shield, a protective shell that is very difficult, if not impossible, to penetrate. The cerberus killed me, and for all my might and with all the help of my pack, I don't know that I scratched it but twice. I know Griffin has also fought the cerberus, and he was terribly injured."

Sabelu grunted. "How much more powerful is the dragon then?"

Yawi did not say anything to that, just padded along quietly until they reached the river where Blaknik was sitting on the bank, watching a net and waiting. The teenager turned at Sabelu's approach, but did not get up.

"I wanted to get out here for the first run," he said. "I think I might be a little early."

"By a few days," Sabelu told him. He knelt on the bank and looked at the net. "Your net looks good, though. The knots are well-tied and secure."

"Is that why you didn't come, because you knew I wouldn't get anything today?" his little brother inquired.

Sabelu glanced at him. "Of course not." He waded out into the water until he was waist-deep, still inspecting the net. "I was busy."

"With the Whites. You weren't at the townhouse; I checked."

"That's right."

Blaknik shifted position. "Shouldn't speaking to the Whites and doing your priestly duties be basically the same thing?"

Sabelu sighed, the net in his hands. "Yes, they should."

"Yet you tiptoe around the townhouse and the other priests as if they are sleeping savage dogs." He paused. "Itsitsa's Books talk about Whites and Shadows. Are there Shadows in the townhouse?"

"Shadows are less interested in places than people," Sabelu told him, dropping the net and pushing his way back to the bank. "The land, these hills, they mean nothing to the Shadows. It is the heart and soul of the people they want."

"Why?"

"To destroy them, to destroy us. For no other reason than they can, to crush the Whites and spite the Author."

His little brother looked around. "I don't see anything. There are no fights. Nothing's falling down."

"Force is usually the last thing to happen. Just like a tree that has died and decays while still standing. It will withstand wind and rain for a few seasons, but if pressed, if examined for even a few minutes, its flaws are revealed. Then it comes crumbling down, whether through natural means or because someone pushes it over."

"That's fun to do," Blaknik quipped, grinning at him.

"It is," Sabelu agreed. "But unlike a tree, the soul of a people can be revived and come back to life, to live and thrive once more without decay."

"And that's what you're trying to do. Get rid of the Shadows because they're decaying the people."

"That's right."

Blaknik looked back at the river. "The Shadows must be very powerful then."

"Why do you say that?" Sabelu asked.

"You always look so unhappy and frustrated, even though you speak to the Whites basically every day. And I've seen you talking to people, trying to help them, but not everyone wants help."

"No, they don't."

"Of course, it doesn't help that you're really weird."

Sabelu raised a brow. "Having talents isn't the same as being weird."

Blaknik laughed. "Talent is winning the archery competition three years in a row. Talent is staying on a horse when it rears. Speaking to Whites and banishing Shadows is...weird."

"Our great-uncle Anagalisgi did the same thing."

"And he was weird."

Sabelu sighed. "We see things you don't see. We try to protect the people from threats they don't understand. And telling the people that there are Shadows hovering around the priests is...not something done lightly, or without a plan for when they get angry about being confronted."

"Then why don't the people confront them together?" Blaknik

wondered. "You obviously can't do it alone; either the work is too big or else you're just not fit for the job."

"Because I'm weird?"

"Because you're weird."

Sabelu gave his brother a look. "I've already thought of that, about recruiting others." He explained the analogy of one to clear the field, one to till the soil, and so on.

"So you are going to teach others," Blaknik stated. At Sabelu's look he went on, "Come on, Ido, you know what I'm talking about. You know everything."

"Well, no, not quite."

Blaknik gestured to the net. "You've taught me how to tie at least fourteen different types of nets. I will never want for fish in my entire life, however long I may live. You are confronting the Shadows in the people, but do they know that? What happens when the Shadows come back? Do the people know what they're fighting and how to defend against it?"

"Some do, yes. They have learned and they guard themselves and their homes well. Their diligence increases the presence of Whites."

"Are they helping others? Do they know how to help others fight off their Shadows? Yawi follows you around, you said, and helps you. Do other people have Whites?"

"Yes, but they are only small Whites. Insects and others, like mice. Next come the burrowers. And the people have been helping each other, somewhat."

His brother looked around. "Do I have any Whites with me? Are there any here?"

Sabelu also looked around and gestured accordingly. "Well, the ants maintain a perimeter, laying the foundation for all other Whites. I see a grasshopper, a couple mice here on the bank. Yawi is here as well."

"Are there Shadows here, too?"

"Not at the moment, no."

Blaknik stood sharply and nearly went in the river. "Then what are we waiting for?! We should go help people!"

Sabelu blinked. "You asked to go fishing."

"You've already said I'm early by a few days. I'm sure that's enough time to talk to at least a few people."

Beside him, Yawi had also stood and was wagging his tail, tongue lolling in a smile, expression like that of a child begging his father to do something.

"All right," Sabelu conceded, though he still did not stand. "You've obviously given this some thought; is there anyone in particular you want to speak to first?"

"Esdsi," Blaknik replied. "He never gets along with his brothers and I don't understand why. Maybe there's a Shadow clouding his judgment."

Esdsi was a couple years old than Blaknik, but they were good friends nonetheless. The older boy had taken it upon himself to mentor younger boys just coming of age, trying to help them in the festival tournaments. He felt slighted by his brothers, felt that they had never helped him. To be fair, his next closest brother was more than twenty years older than him and had children of his own older than Esdsi. It was a similar situation to Sabelu and Galiliga. All the same, the Shadows of Resentment and Pride were his constant companions and growing stronger every year.

"I'm sure you know where he is," Blaknik was saying.

Sabelu sighed and stood. "Yes, I do."

Blaknik moved past him, away from the river, and turned, still walking backwards. "You sound so reluctant. Is something wrong?"

Was something wrong? Only that a thirteen year old appeared to have more ambition than he did. Was there a reason he shouldn't let his little brother help and learn how to confront Shadows? Blaknik was right, he couldn't do this alone. But Blaknik also didn't understand the real power of the Shadows, how dangerous this could be. He really didn't want his little brother to go confront the priests and find out the hard way.

"Sometimes," Yawi said beside him, "allowing a little freedom is safer than denying it entirely. A small opening in a dam to relieve pressure can prevent a massive sweeping away later. Burning a small swath of land now can prevent greater wildfire later."

Sabelu let out a breath. Instead of answering Yawi, he looked at Blaknik. "All right. Let's go. There's a storm moving in and the water is becoming dangerous anyway." He moved toward his brother. "Esdsi is out in the horse pens."

Blaknik grinned hugely and took off running. Sabelu ran after him, and Yawi followed, barking excitedly.

Esdsi was indeed in the horse pens, looking over the more promising mounts. If there was anything Esdsi wanted to prove in himself, never mind the boys he proclaimed to mentor, it was that he was a good horseman. His brothers were always in the final round of the equestrian tournaments, were not unknown to win frequently, yet Esdsi felt terribly neglected as they had shown him very little about the sport. Others had been generous in their advice, but it was his brothers he wanted to bond with.

The Shadow of Resentment was gorging itself on his broken soul.

"Esdsi!" Blaknik called.

Esdsi and about a dozen horses looked up, but only the young man grinned and came to meet them. He might not have noticed Yawi growling at the Shadows on his shoulders, but the Shadows certainly did. One took the form of a snake and the other of a bat.

"Blaknik, how are you?" he greeted, clasping wrists with the young lad. He looked at Sabelu and nodded once. "Sabelu."

"Esdsi," Sabelu acknowledged. He looked around. "Going for a ride?"

"I was going to start showing the boys the horses," the fifteen year old said, trying to stand tall and act and talk like an adult.

Sabelu nodded. "I think Blaknik knows what a horse looks like. He's not so bad a rider either."

"But he's never ridden in competition. That can be dangerous."

"Yes, it can, which is why you've never actually done it. So why are you trying to teach these boys something you know nothing about?"

Esdsi straightened just a little more, up tight with offense, Pride sinking its claws into him though its focus remained on Yawi who was still snarling. The young man sniffed. "I've watched. I've taken notes. I've seen things, things that would help."

"A carving is refined only after the general shape has been achieved," Sabelu told him. "Anyone can critique something when they don't understand the hard work that goes into it."

If there were any "easy" vices to get rid of in boys who were just becoming men, it was Pride. Esdsi had no real accomplishments or achievements for the Shadow to latch onto and feed into his brain as a source of vanity. The problem was that shattered Pride often gave way to Depression and Self-Loathing, sometimes in the same fight. Having Resentment around wasn't going to make things easy either. In fact, chipping away at Pride seemed to feed Resentment, resentment toward Sabelu, that is.

"How is anyone supposed to learn anything if no one shows them?" Esdsi asked defensively.

"Speaking of Blaknik?" Sabelu questioned. "Or yourself?"

"Not everyone gets to have a brother who knows everything."

"I hardly know everything. But for all that I do know, how many people do you see approaching me, wanting to know what I know?" He gestured to Blaknik. "He complained when I taught him different ways to tie a fishing net. Other people complain when I tell them things they don't want to hear. And I don't recall that you've ever come to me to learn anything."

Pride was a posturing sort of Shadow, easily shattered in young boys who didn't know what to do with it, but just as easily replaced with Self-Loathing. The good news was that Yawi's presence held off the arrival of Self-Loathing, even as Pride raced away, screeching.

"I can't help it!" Esdsi protested. "You know my father and uncles are gone. My brothers don't even acknowledge my existence. Even you know that I can't hang around my sisters in the festival."

"But if you don't know something, how are you going to teach it to us?" Blaknik asked innocently. "What if you're wrong about something, and one of us gets hurt?"

"Even experienced riders get hurt sometimes."

"They do. But as you say, they have experience." Sabelu gestured to his brother. "Let's say you give instruction to Blaknik on how to ride a horse. Let's say he falls off and hurts himself. How are you going to know where the fault lies, what to correct? Was Blaknik riding incorrectly? Did something spook the horse?"

Pride was long gone, Self-Loathing was swirling around the area, kept at bay only by Yawi's snapping jaws, but Resentment was growing ever stronger.

"I know you blame your brothers," Sabelu went on. "I know you feel neglected by them. I know you harbor a bit of hatred for your father and uncles, too, deep down."

The first and second sentences did nothing to provoke the Shadow, but the third was like sticking it with a knife.

"And I know you resent your mother," he added, twisting the knife.

Esdsi dared not breathe. After a long moment he said, "I know the man she says was my father wasn't my father."

"The father of your brothers died in the war."

"That's right. She won't tell me who my father is, says it doesn't matter. But her brothers are gone, too, which means there is no one left to show me anything."

"Except your brothers who don't acknowledge you."

Esdsi just nodded.

After a long moment of silence—well, silence for the normal people, though Sabelu still had to listen to Yawi's barking and snarling as he kept Self-Loathing from landing on Esdsi—Blaknik said, "You can always ask Sabelu. He can teach you things. He can teach you more than your brothers ever could."

Esdsi made a pouting sort of motion and said, "I don't want to."

"Because that would mean letting go of your resentment toward your brothers?" Sabelu asked, naming the Shadow. "Maybe your resentment toward your mother?" He paused. "We don't get to choose where we are planted. But, like the crops in the field, we should be happy when someone chooses to care for us and help us grow. It does no good to refuse to grow because we do not like our caretaker."

The young lad gave him a look. "You're really weird, you know that?"

Sabelu glanced at Blaknik who grinned. "I've been informed of that, yes."

Resentment was steadily losing its flow of energy, but it was by no means ready to be shaken.

Esdsi looked around. "But I want to help younger boys. I can show them how to run and everything, but I want to show them the horses, too."

"Wouldn't it be better to meet them on horseback and lead by example?" Sabelu suggested. "Anything I teach you, you can teach them."

Self-Loathing, which had been fluttering around as a kind of grouse, was suddenly distracted, and the next thing Sabelu knew, Yawi's jaws had clamped down hard around the ethereal bird. The thing let out an infernal screech which he reacted to, covering his ears and going to the ground.

Esdsi and Blaknik were by his side in an instant. For a long moment, there was only ringing in his ears. Then it subsided and garbled noise came back into focus as voices.

"Are you all right?" Blaknik was saying.

"Sabelu? Sabelu!" Esdsi shouted.

Sabelu forced his hands away from his ears and waved them off. As he stood, he saw Hoshonti and Hieli approaching.

"Everything all right?" the horse tender asked.

"Fine," Sabelu said hastily. "Just fine."

Hoshonti's real concern was for the horses; he wasn't sure what to do about Sabelu.

Trying to recover some small measure of dignity, Sabelu asked, "Say, do you still have that dark stallion with the gray spots, was retired last year? And the brown mare with a black mane and white spots on its rump?"

The tender shrugged. "Sure, they're in the other pen."

"Can you bring them here? I want to show these two something."

Sabelu gestured toward Esdsi and Blaknik.

Hoshonti considered this for a moment, then nodded and motioned for his son to follow him.

Sabelu glanced at Esdsi, noting that the Shadow of Resentment appeared to have suffered a significant blow. While it did not bleed per se, something about its general demeanor said it was hurting and trying to avoid Yawi as much as possible without actually giving up Esdsi. Yawi, sitting in the middle of the three of them, was looking a bit smug, and Sabelu wondered if the wolf had gotten in a good blow to the evil spirit.

"I got a good mouth full of smoke, yes," Yawi said, not looking at him. "It doesn't taste good, but it is still immensely satisfying."

He said nothing to that, instead looking at Esdsi. "Have you ever been on a horse before?"

Esdsi gave him a look. "Of course I have."

Sabelu looked at his brother. "I know you have."

Blaknik beamed from the perceived praise. Before anyone could say anything more, Hoshonti and Hieli returned with the horses Sabelu had requested. The stallion was older and no longer competition material. The mare was younger but not suited to the high stress of competition, instead serving her days primarily as a broodmare.

Sabelu thanked the horse tenders and took the horses. He turned to Blaknik and Esdsi.

"Mount up and ride around," he said, handing them the reins. "Show me what you can do, show me how you ride."

Once both boys were on their mounts, Sabelu headed over to the fence to sit and watch. Even being two years younger, Blaknik was ten times more comfortable on horseback than Esdsi. The older boy wasn't lying when he said he'd ridden before, but it wasn't something he did with any regularity or proper instruction.

Yawi sat beside him, still looking smug.

"So is this really what it's going to take?" Sabelu asked. "Just going up to every single person here and in the entire Krydik nation and helping them work through their problems?"

"It's people caring for people, as the Author cares for all," Yawi said. "As the gap widens and more Whites come through, as the fight shifts in our favor, this will give you the opportunity to confront the Shadows as you see them. But you have to start small."

"It's been almost two years. I'm tired of small. I'm tired of baby steps. A horse may take time to get up to speed, but if he doesn't get up to speed in time, he'll trip over the jump. Confronting the Shadows is a pretty big jump, especially if the generals are going to get involved."

Now the wolf looked at him. "If ten people are canoeing in a river, and there is a rock in the middle of the river, and in various places, are you going to give the same instruction to all of the people on how to avoid those rocks?"

"Of course not. Some will avoid them, yes, but others will steer right into them."

"In the same way, not everyone here needs the same instructions. But how do you know which instructions they need unless you talk to them and know them?"

"But I do know them," Sabelu sighed. "I know them better than they realize."

"You know facts about them, in the same way anyone reading this story knows facts about you. Should they meet you, they will know well your life's story, as it is covered in this Book. But they won't know you, not truly." Yawi looked back at the boys, now trotting around on horseback, shouting to each other. "And as you have said, it is not your job to do everything. Clear the field and let the rest of the workers fulfill their roles."

"The field isn't clear, though. The Shadow of Resentment still follows him."

"The field is clear," Yawi countered. "The Shadow has been named, the problem uncovered. Next, the soil must be tilled, smoothed and prepared for seed. And from what I can see, your brother is an excellent tiller."

"As long as he doesn't till over us," a new voice said.

Sabelu and Yawi both looked down. While it did not physically change, there was a sort of overlap in the waking world and the spirit world as a small hole opened up in the ground and a White rabbit poked its head up into the sunlight.

"For the love of the Author, they sent you first?" Yawi whined.

The rabbit hopped up out of its hole and got on its hind legs, facing the wolf. "That's right. They needed a go-getter, someone who can get things done."

Sabelu shifted his position on the fence. "So, no more baby steps?"

The rabbit sighed and gave him a look. "You humans. You always overestimate yourselves and underestimate what you think you want. What you think you want, what you think you need, what you even think those things are and what they really are—" The rabbit shook its head. "—you don't get it. You think you do, but you don't."

"You don't seem to be overly endowed with specifics and details either," Sabelu observed.

"Yeah, well, I'm not known for my oration, and I wasn't sent here to bore you to death with words and talk. You do that well enough on your own. I'm here because I do things. I get things done. You want action, I'll give you action. I'll give you so much action, you'll beg me to stop."

Sabelu smirked. "I have memories of men who have said that to their wives, but I think they were referring to something entirely different. Although, you are a rabbit, so who knows?"

As he shrugged, he was unprepared for the sudden, impressive leap and flying kick from the rabbit. Considering that he was fairly certain the rabbit was invisible to everyone else at this point, he wondered how it looked to anyone watching for him to visibly react to an invisible strike. He was leaning against the fence, and the rabbit struck him square in the thigh with more force than he thought possible for the small rodent. Well, for a normal rabbit maybe, but not for a White. His whole leg went numb for a moment, then it began to burn and throb like mad, and the only reason he stayed upright was from his grip on the fence.

"And that was me being restrained," the rabbit informed him.

Sabelu used Asvhnisgi inside his leg, certain he was going to find a broken bone, even a minor hairline fracture. He didn't find anything broken, but the quickly forming bruise went all the way to the bone.

"How do you like that?" the rabbit challenged, bouncing lightly on its back legs, occasionally hopping to the left or right.

"I didn't," Sabelu hissed, shifting his weight and leaning against the fence. "Why did you do that?"

"Because you needed it, that's why. Maybe it will slow you down a little."

When he opened his eyes, he saw Blaknik and Esdsi, about twenty paces away. They were still on horseback, but now they stood side by side, facing him, watching him. He glanced at Yawi.

"This isn't helping my reputation for being weird, is it?" he asked.

"No, not really," the wolf answered.

Sabelu strangled a groan of pain and straightened as much as he could. The rabbit hopped back a pace or two.

"So why," he began, "did the Author send a go-getter who can get things done to cripple someone who wants to get going?"

"Again with the exaggerations," the rabbit sighed. "You're not crippled. Not yet anyway. This was just to slow you down so you don't go sprinting off at the next sign of trouble. And that sign of trouble should be coming upon us any minute now."

Sabelu again looked out across the pen toward his brother and Esdsi who were still staring at him. They were fine, and he saw nothing in their future to suggest distress, at least not in the next few minutes.

He used Asvhnisgi to examine the wound more thoroughly. Nothing was going to kill him or cripple him; it just hurt like mad. He wasn't so talented in the Iyuwahnilvhi sorceries, but he could do Agvhalvda and Nulinigv, and he now invoked the former to prevent the injury from getting worse—stopping bleeding and inflammation— and then slowly knitting everything back together.

He was only about half done when there was a shout. He looked across the pen, and it was like fog clearing from a valley. Ganhv was approaching.

The cranky priest had indeed fathered a son, born the previous year. Ganhv had declared him a seer and a prophet, and there had been some great to-do about it. Many were skeptical of the proclamation, but Ganhv touted his son as one of the crowning achievements of the people. Lately he'd been plotting some demise for Sabelu, nothing especially detailed yet, but he expected that his time would come when he could be rid of Sabelu in such a way that it wouldn't look like murder.

Well, his time had come. He and Sabelu would indeed be separated, never have to deal with each other again. It was just the matter of which one of them was going to be in the ground at the end of the day.

The man was harried and angry, like a father confronting his son who had forsaken some sacred tradition.

It was interesting to look at him, to read him as it were. Almost everyone else in Aktiya Waya, he saw years into their future. Ganhv just stopped. He had only hours, not even that, and it was not to be the peaceful passing of an elder. Sabelu saw the pain, the panic, the final moments of sheer terror, all the dreams he'd had, vanishing into dark water. Despite the hatred Ganhv held for him, Sabelu could not hate the man.

Seeing the disgruntled priest rapidly approaching Sabelu, Esdsi and Blaknik uncertainly nudged their horses forward, coming just within earshot.

Ganhv got uncomfortably close to Sabelu who was able to conjure Time just enough to erase any lingering clues about his leg injury from his face. Then, before the priest could speak, he said, "Today is the day one of us dies."

DᏧᎪᏢᏁ DᏙᏋᎢ

Askoline Adolv'i

Prophecy

Y ou know that for a fact, do you?" Ganhv said, not missing a beat or wavering in the slightest. "I'm guessing that in your infinite knowledge, that person is me, because it could never be you."

"My death is already foretold, it is already written, it has already happened," Sabelu told him. "But that is not the dilemma here."

Ganhv made a wild gesture, and Esdsi and Blaknik nudged their horses a little closer. "Oh? Then what is?"

"Your son is nearing death as we speak. In fact, he is already struggling." Sabelu nodded. "If I am not telling the truth, and he is not dying, and you do nothing, then I lose what little reputation I have and you gain immense credibility in your campaign against me. If he is not dying and you go to see anyway, you lose some credibility both in your opposition of me as well as the greatness with which you tout your son. If he is dying and you do nothing, then you not only lose your son through negligence but you may be accused of both murder and blasphemy. If he is dying and you do something, you save your son, but you die in the process, and much of the anger and consternation and conniptions that you have fostered against me will fall away, and your son will never be the seer and prophet you falsely claim. In fact, your wife will barely acknowledge your existence beyond your noble service as a priest."

Sabelu let that hang there for a long moment.

Ganhv said nothing, but his mind was working and he shifted uncomfortably from foot to foot. He didn't want Sabelu to be right. He didn't want to give in. But if he was right. If—he was right. If. That

                                          Lone Wolf

terrible notion of what if.

Someone was going to die today, and now it rested on Ganhv to choose.

Ganhv, in an effort to save his son.

Ganhv's son, because his father was too proud to listen to a warning from someone he hated.

Perhaps Sabelu himself, if Ganhv decided to attack.

Sabelu studied the priest's Shadow. It did not jump around like an animal, but stood beside him, almost hugging him, as if they were good friends. Quite honestly, they probably were. This was a greater Shadow, a puppeteer, approximately nine feet tall, appearing as something like a cross between a bear and a lizard with a great head fan and obscenely long claws, one of which appeared permanently set in Ganhv's spine. The size and strength of this Shadow could be felt with all the subtlety of an ice storm, and even the blowing wind and light rain felt mild in comparison. Beside Sabelu, Yawi bared his teeth but made no move to attack, and the rabbit was nowhere to be seen.

The Shadow's will intertwined with the priest's own made the next few moments murky at best, and Sabelu briefly wondered if it was possible for a Shadow to actually change something. If Ganhv attacked, no doubt aided by the Shadow, Yawi might not be enough, and butterflies weren't going to be enough to save him.

"You wanted to do something, little man?" the Shadow rumbled with some amusement. "You wanted to do something, to confront us? Well, you have our attention. Here I am. Do something. Confront me!"

Sabelu swallowed but forced himself not to react. He also tried not to give away the White ants marching across Ganhv's feet. That tiny pinprick of reason, tapping into the love of a father over the hatred for a rival.

"But if you know that something is happening," Ganhv said, "and you don't do anything, why is that different?"

"An excellent question, and it may be that I am at fault. And yet, I don't think you are entirely ignorant of the situation. Else why would you come all the way out here to kill me and make it look like an accident, except that you had an excuse?"

Behind the priest, up the hill, someone was running toward them, shouting and waving their arms. Ahead of them, Sabelu saw the rabbit crossing the field in leaps and bounds. When Ganhv and the Shadow turned, the rabbit disappeared into a hole.

"Ganhv!" the man yelled. "Ganhv, your son! We need you!"

On the ground, the rabbit again poked his head out of a small burrow, and landed a solid bite on what would be the Shadow's ankle. The Shadow jerked in pain and looked down, searching for the rabbit. At that moment, two small White birds flew through Ganhv. One went through his head, the other through his chest, and disappeared before the Shadow straightened and could see them.

The priest took off running, Sabelu forgotten, focusing only on his son.

The Shadow ignored his host for the moment and turned toward Sabelu. Now Yawi moved up defensively, truly snarling and preparing to attack. Sabelu silently wondered whether it was possible for him to be physically hurt if the two did get into a tussle, then considered the injury to his leg and decided he didn't want to meet the sharp edge of the Shadow's claws.

Sabelu blinked first as he felt a sharp, but far less traumatic, kick to the back of his other knee. He looked down to find the rabbit.

"Go!" the rabbit said, kicking him again. "Don't worry about us, worry about the kit! Worry about the people!"

Sabelu again looked at the Shadow not two paces in front of him. On the one hand, he would be happy to run away from this thing. On the other hand, he didn't want to run away from a fight, and he didn't want to run away from a Shadow fight because that was what he had been pushing for, what he had really been wanting to do. Less talking, more actual fighting and work being done.

But he also didn't want to disobey an order from a White. Gritting his teeth, he pushed himself away from the fence and started limp-running as fast as he could manage. He motioned for Blaknik and Esdsi, and the two trotted over.

"Are...you...all...right?" Blaknik asked cautiously.

"Esdsi, give me your horse," Sabelu ordered.

"I want to come with you," the older boy protested, even as he dismounted.

"Then do it on foot." Sabelu hauled himself onto the horse's back. His leg didn't feel much better in this position, but at least the weight was off it. He kicked the horse and snapped the reins.

Behind him, he heard the sickening sounds of an animal fight. One of the combatants was clearly a dog, the gruff barking and snarling and yelping hitting Sabelu harder than he thought it should have. The other combatant was not something he could readily identify, for its sounds belonged to no single animal, at once bear and at once cat and at once pure, shrieking demon. The sound almost made Sabelu nauseous, and he forced his attention straight ahead.

The tragedy had become quite a spectacle by now, with more and more people gathering and trying to figure out what to do, many shouts lost in the growing wind. Among the least helpful bystanders, there was plenty of speculation and gossip, but Sabelu knew what had happened.

Ganhv's son, Telaldhi, who was not quite two years old, had gone out with his mother while she got water, bathed, and checked the crop fields. She was not the only one; there had been a whole flock of women eager to check the fields and begin planning this year's crop. Many of the women had also brought their young children. It was quite an outing, a sort of rite of passage for the arrival of spring, and nothing unusual.

The children had gone off to play, as one would expect from a large gathering of women and children. The ages ranged from about three at the youngest to about ten years old. Telaldhi had toddled after them, eventually helped along by some of the older children. Things were going well until one of them realized they hadn't seen the toddler for a few minutes. Rather than running for help right away, for fear of being punished for such irresponsibility, the children tried to search on their own, pretending it was a game of hide and seek when the adults came to herd them back inside.

Telaldhi had gotten distracted by a small animal and followed it to the river. The child fell in the water and was carried off in the current, high and swift because of the spring melt and overhead storm. His only saving grace was Blaknik's fishing net, abandoned just an hour before, if that. The net caught the child, and the way he was tangled kept his head mostly above water, although the waves still washed over him and filled his lungs with water.

"Has anyone tried cutting the net?" Sabelu heard Ganhv demand. The priest was pacing back and forth on the bank. "Forget untying the knots, just cut it and pull it in! It's for catching fish, isn't it? My son is just a very large fish!"

"The current is very strong right now," someone replied. It was Delgwa, a man of about thirty years and good repute, who appeared to be the one in charge of the situation. "If we start cutting the net away as it is, we risk losing it and your son down the river. Winkele has gone to get more cordage to tie so we can hold the net and—"

"That will take too long! Winkele has no grasp of the Iyuwahnilvhi sorceries! What about his brother Nehnonkes?"

"Not here."

"Well where is he?!"

Ganhv looked around frantically. Every other blink he was looking at Telaldhi. By now the two year old appeared nearly dead.

For most people in the area, all that mattered was the present moment. The fear, the uncertainty, the rushing river and helpless child trapped in a fishing net. Few were thinking about how to use the sorceries to help the child. Those who did manage to bring such thoughts to mind were unable to mold them effectively. Delgwa himself was well-versed in Atsvstdi, Uhnoyvgi, and Udilegv'i ale Uhyvtsa. Winkele, whom he'd sent for rope, was skilled in Gayalvnga. This was the reason Delgwa had sent him. The idea was to not only tie off the net so it could be held, but use magnetic stones and Winkele's talents to augment the holding power. It would take fewer men to hold the net and drag it to the bank so the rest could go out and rescue the child.

As for the Iyuwahnilvhi sorceries, water was like air, finicky about being conjured. Water was less finicky than air, true, but the skill required was not only greater than what was possessed by a majority of those present, but for those who could do so on a normal day, panic had eroded the required concentration. Sabelu knew such a thing had been tried already. Part of the river was conjured, the water building up in an invisible dam upriver, but slowly seeping away downriver and giving a couple men room to try and work or cut the knots. The person doing the conjuring could not hold on long. When the sorcery failed, the current, having built up at the invisible wall, crashed into them. They were lucky to have not gotten tangled up themselves in the net underwater. For Telaldhi, the sudden watery onslaught had effectively silenced his cries, and the window of opportunity was quickly sliding from rescue to recovery.

Ganhv's gaze rested on Sabelu, watching from the back of the crowd.

A small White sparrow had landed on the priest's head, but a slithering serpent Shadow with wings was constantly darting at it, trying to chase it away. The sparrow encouraged Ganhv to ask for help. The serpent, an indulgence of Pride, was telling him to disregard all of these useless peons and go rescue his son himself.

Behind him, Sabelu could sense that either Yawi had lost the fight or the puppeteer Shadow had run away and was now flying, perhaps literally, across the field toward his host.

The next few moments suddenly came into perfect focus for Sabelu. The Shadow was making for the priest, yes, but it was going to give Sabelu a brutal blow on its way by, maybe even try to kill him. He couldn't allow that to happen, for a number of reasons. He also couldn't allow the Shadow to reach Ganhv before they got in the water.

Sabelu started running, or rather, limp-running as fast as he could toward the river, propelling himself with Gasadoyasgi, racing the Shadow toward Ganhv like a couple of horses in the tournament. He reached for Ganhv, grabbed the priest, and spun him toward the river. The Shadow missed Ganhv and Sabelu, but the sheer force of its wake was enough to make them both stumble, this dismissed by spectators as slipping on slick, wet rocks.

"Come on," Sabelu grunted, standing and dragging the priest to his feet while still moving. "You need help, and so does your son."

There was no gentle way to wade into the river. One breath they were on the bank, and in the next, sudden breath, they were waist deep in a frigid pre-spring current. Two steps in and they were swimming, the water easily up to their shoulders, forcing them hard into the net. They kept one hand on the net, though neither wanted to rely on it too much lest they get a wrist or ankle stuck. This was difficult to do as the churning current frequently inserted itself into their mouths and nostrils and clouded their vision.

"I thought you were...going to...l-let my s-son die," Ganhv gasped in between waves, teeth chattering.

"I see what is," Sabelu said, trying to use Udilegv'i to warm himself up a little, just so his limbs would move. He gulped a mouthful of water, nearly choked, spit it out, and shook his head. "I have no t-time to waste on what could be."

They reached the spot where the child was tangled. Ganhv shouted his son's name, but the boy was limp. Sabelu was working on getting his knife, not wanting to lose it in the water as a sudden wave threw them against the net. The two men crawled up the net back to the surface, mindful of their positions.

"You said-d my son will live," Ganhv said.

"That's right," Sabelu told him. He took his knife in one hand and the net in the other. He used Asvhnisgi combined with Iyuwahnilvhi to age the cordage, making it easier to saw through. Ganhv took hold of his son, but the child was slippery. As more ties were loosed and the waves came crashing into them, Ganhv frequently lost his hold on Telaldhi. The toddler was beginning to swing freely in the river.

"You als-so s-said that-t I will d-d-die," the priest mentioned, making another valiant attempt at keeping hold of his child.

"That-t's right," Sabelu said, still working in spite of numb fingers.

"From frost-t-bite?" Ganhv huffed something that was supposed to be a humorless chuckle.

Sabelu turned. His gaze went to the shore where Yawi was chasing the puppeteer, snapping at its heels. But the puppeteer was faster than the wolf, and soon the Shadow was flying—yes, literally—over the water, straight for them. Sabelu then looked at the priest. "No. Because you're about to try and kill me."

The puppeteer slammed into Ganhv with all the gentleness of an avalanche. Sabelu briefly wondered if the priest was even aware of how his thoughts changed at that moment. But the man's expression changed into something like smugness as he said, "Well, it would be better to make it look like an accident."

The priest lunged, one hand going for Sabelu's neck, the other for his wrist which held the knife. He got hold of both, hanging on with impossible strength, maneuvering the two of them so they were hanging over the cut portion of the net. Ganhv put his full weight—plus whatever weight the Shadow could provide—on top of Sabelu, forcing him under the water even as he himself reached frantically for his son, now attached to the net by only two cords.

Sabelu was stuck. The priest held him under the water, face up, the current threatening to take him downstream while the net promised an even bigger, tangled up mess if he tried to wiggle around and get creative. He tried to force his way up, move a shoulder, a hip, anything to gain an advantage. Any physical advantage he might have had was negated by the Shadow. Just the Shadow's incredible presence was making it difficult to see; he didn't know what was happening on shore, didn't know what was going on anywhere at any time except in this one moment. As his body went numb and his lungs began to burn, the importance of the present moment began to increase exponentially.

Fear slid into his mind. He tried to move his arms, wave a hand, punch Ganhv in the stomach, anything. The cold had once soothed the ache in his leg, but that time was long past, and fighting the river only diminished the effectiveness of his kicks. The priest did not respond at all, and his frantic motions said he was still working on the net in some fashion.

Sabelu searched his vast knowledge for any sorceries that might help him. He knew there was something about how water and air were related, about the air in the water, but as his body jerked once, he knew he couldn't conjure if he tried. He let out a small breath, trying to alleviate the burning, but it only bought him a few more seconds. Still the priest remained a rock over him. Did no one on shore see what was happening? Did no one notice that two men had gone into the river but only one remained? Or did they assume he was doing some kind of underwater sorcery?

Something caught Sabelu's eye in the murk. When he looked, he saw his knife sinking in the river and being swiftly pulled away by the rushing water. He threw his arm out as best he could, but it was gone. The motion had stolen some air, but it was hardly relief. His chest burned, his head ached, and spots danced in his vision.

Fatigue spread through his limbs, and he could feel himself sinking even farther. He might have said that the Shadow itself pushed him down. But he didn't care.

What did it mean if the Author was wrong? What if his death was not on a mountainside, but right here in this river? Did that mean that the Books were little more than truth wrapped in a fictional setting? Were they all wrong? Was all of his stubbornness and insistence at knowing everything all for nothing? Was all of his guidance and advice no more than good guesses?

Something pressed into his hand. After a moment of consideration, or perhaps just a reflex from his next jerk, he grasped it. Viewing it around a multitude of black spots, he saw that it was his knife. Just a few inches away was a White otter. It wasn't an otter as in the Old Land, but an otter as the Krydik knew them on Hlohi. They were more slender with longer fingers, narrower heads, and a kind of crown of whiskers or feelers around its face, floating in the water as if the current were no more inconvenient than on a calm summer day.

The otter darted forward, straight through his chest. Sabelu took an enormous breath without actually taking a breath. The fatigue washed from his body and the spots cleared from his vision. It didn't stop the Shadow from pressing down, but a Shadow couldn't possess a dead body.

Using the current to his advantage, Sabelu flung his arm up, even using Gasadoyasgi to augment the strike. He buried the knife deep in Ganhv's ribcage, piercing his heart. The priest seized and froze in position, but Sabelu was distracted more by the Shadow. It roared with such a fury that Sabelu was surprised the bystanders couldn't hear it.

Ganhv's body went limp and was promptly carried away by the current. The Shadow, now without a host, turned its attention to Sabelu. Sabelu twisted and tried to crawl over the net, heading for the surface if possible. He'd just gotten situated, clear of the threat of entanglement, when the blow came. It hit him square in the back, and for a moment, he feared the Shadow might have broken it. All the air the otter had given him was forced from his lungs in an open-mouthed gasp, and he went tumbling forward in the river. The knife again slipped from his grasp.

He broke the surface once, but whether it was the current, some debris underneath, or the Shadow still attacking, he was promptly dragged under once more. Actually, he was fairly certain that he could feel an actual hand around his ankle dragging him around, swinging him, even.

Under the water, breaking the surface, each time he could not get the air he needed. He struck unseen rocks and debris, tumbled around so much he barely knew which way was up. When his head hit a rock, he hardly cared.

Ironically, breathing clearly sent him into a panic. He sat up, gasping for air, shocked to find that there was plenty available, and even more shocked to discover that he was completely dry.

A sigh of relief, as from one who's been startled and now recognizes there is no danger, sounded to his left. He turned to see Anagalisgi.

They were in his uncle's cave in the spirit world. He was on a mat, and his uncle tended the fire, expression still startled.

"Am I dead?" Sabelu demanded, still surprised at the existence of air.

"Hardly," Anagalisgi replied, relaxing and returning his attention to the fire. "You're just sleeping." He shifted position. "You were knocked unconscious underwater, washed up on a bank near the Sacred Wolf, barely alive but able to be salvaged. You are currently being tended to in the townhouse."

Sabelu took several intentional breaths. "And Ganhv?"

"Dead. As foretold."

Sabelu blinked. "I did it, though. I killed him. I didn't understand it before because even when I looked through his eyes, he didn't understand. And I can't see myself." He shook his head as if to clear it. "Tsidushi, I killed a man. Worse, I killed a priest."

"You knew this. You always knew it was either you or him."

"He couldn't be saved, then. His Shadow was too strong. Even if it was prophesied, even if he had to die in the end, he himself could not be saved."

Anagalisgi gave him a sympathetic look. "No."

"But his death opens up a door in this war, an advantage for the Whites."

"One less puppeteer, yes, it provides an advantage for the moment. Fear not, the Whites are already exploiting it. The ants have laid the perimeter and the burrowers are working on the base and reconnaissance."

At that mention, Sabelu rolled up his pant leg.

"The wound is healed," his uncle said, not looking at him.

"Was it really necessary in the first place?" Sabelu wondered.

"You know the answer to that."

Sabelu nodded reluctantly. "What would have happened if he had won, if he had killed me, or if we had both lived?"

"He would have used his Shadow to cast a great delusion over the people, to make them believe you were a charlatan and an attempted murderer," Anagalisgi replied. "As it is, there is no such delusion. The people are aware that he tried to kill you, so you are not responsible for his death."

He nodded again, then shifted position so he was facing the fire. "You said that his death opens a door."

"That's right."

"A door, once opened, can be passed through both ways."

Anagalisgi nodded. "Vices, indulgences, they are typically pretty inconsequential. Deposing a puppeteer is a far more serious offense. You will garner more attention. The attacks will be stronger, more numerous, and come from places you least expect, and in ways that will often make no sense to you except that you can see through the veil of deceit."

"I understand, Tsidushi." Sabelu looked around. "Where is Yawi? Is he all right? I saw he was hurt."

"Yawi is being tended to by the pack. He'll be fine."

"When can the rest of the pack join us? Burrowers are great, but if we're moving past vices all the way to puppeteers, we're going to need more than butterflies, otters, and bad-tempered rabbits."

His uncle managed a small grin as he placed a pan of meat on the hot coals. "Yes, you will. And they will come, don't worry. Communications, combat, they will come in due time. But don't think that you will be fighting all puppeteers all the time. Most people are still held by vices and petty indulgences, and these must still be dealt with. Like rats, they can't be left unattended, no matter how small they seem."

"But the others priests...there are more puppeteers. They're not going to be happy."

"No, they're not. But without the delusion, with the people seeing and knowing what happened, the puppeteers are playing defense and trying to salvage what they can."

"Why can't the other puppeteers cast a delusion, make the people believe I wanted to kill Ganhv?"

Anagalisgi nodded, not looking at him. "Oh, they're trying. Make no mistake, they are trying to frame it that way. As I said, the sudden void has opened a door. You aren't the only one fighting in this war. The Whites will handle things for the time being, until you're up and around."

Sabelu let out a breath. "I know where this is going. I know what they're going to do when they fail to deceive the people, this time."

"Then I would suggest you start preparing yourself." Anagalisgi poked at the meat, poked at the coals, poked at the meat again. "Prepare your family as well. You know where the weakness lies.”

“Tsitsi,” Sabelu murmured. “Her and her Fear.” He shifted position. “How is it that I can destroy a puppeteer, but I can’t seem to touch the indulgence that grips my own mother?”

“You didn’t destroy a puppeteer,” his uncle said sharply, setting down his poker. He looked at Sabelu. “You destroyed his host. There is a difference.”

“Should I not have killed Ganhv?”

“That is not the issue here. As to your question, it is always easier to fix other people’s problems than our own. Other people, we see only the issue at hand. But we tend to be blinded by our own fears and iniquities, how our problems intertwine, how we got to be where we are. We become so consumed by the situation that we mistake it for the problem at hand.”

Sabelu blinked and shook his head. “My mother is not going to be released from her fear until after my death. How can you tell me that I have to watch her suffer for over a century?”

“What will be, will be,” his uncle told him firmly, but not unkindly. “And you know more than I do about the situation.”

“She has so much work to do,” Sabelu went on. “She is going to accomplish a lot, but I’m sure she could do a lot more if only she could really and truly get rid of her Fear.”

“Physical work maybe.” Anagalisgi retrieved a couple plates and divided out the meat from the pan. “But the spiritual work she will accomplish will be greater by far. Strength is built under repeated strain and pressure, not perpetual comfort. This applies equally to the people at large as well.”

Sabelu said nothing to that, just took a utensil as it was offered and started in on the meat. Say one thing for his uncle, the man knew how to cook.

“There is no point in asking me what you should do next,” Anagalisgi said, as if reading his thoughts. “You know what is coming.”

“I know. It’s still frustrating. I can see what’s coming. I can see where we are going, the rapids in the river. But the current now is so slow, it's almost like a slow death. Linear time is...so inconvenient."

His uncle nodded, amused. "It can be, yes."

Sabelu looked around the cave. This was a place where people came for guidance, for just enough wisdom to make it through their next big problem. It sounded small, petty, far beneath him and his talents. But it also sounded kind of nice, to have only the next big problem to worry about.

"You still need guidance, too," Anagalisgi told him. "You may know a lot about the future, but you remain your biggest blind spot."

"Is it some sort of established law that prophets cannot see things regarding themselves?" Sabelu questioned. "Anything I see about me, I must do through the lens of others."

"While this does seem to be a common theme among prophets, that's not what I meant."

Just because he was right didn't mean Sabelu had to like it, and he stabbed at the last piece of meat on his plate.

"Our time here is nearly finished," Anagalisgi stated. "You know what is coming, you know what you must do."

Sabelu just nodded and handed his plate back to his uncle. As Anagalisgi touched the plate, Sabelu felt something being pressed into his hand. His sense of direction shifted, vertigo overcoming him like a wave from the river. He went to his knees and lay down, colors blurring. He blinked once and the vertigo mostly subsided. He blinked again and the cave had changed. The light shifted, his position shifted, there were more people, and the thing being pressed into his hand was another hand. Blinking again, his vision cleared and he saw his mother kneeling beside him.

"Oh, thank the spirits!" she gasped, sitting back and relaxing.

Sabelu looked around from his position. He was, as his uncle said, in the townhouse. He was in the common area, not the partitioned section for the priests. He searched his knowledge.

"How are you feeling?" Nendawagan interrupted, touching him. She took his chin and turned his head, looked into his eyes, and she was less than subtle about using Asvhnisgi to examine him. She'd done this several times over the last day since he'd been pulled out of the river, but she still wanted to hear him say it.

"I'm fine," Sabelu told her, taking his chin out of her hand.

There was no point in asking what happened, for he already knew. Nevertheless, his mother saw fit to inform him anyway.

"We saw Ganhv try to murder you. We saw him push you under the water and hold you there. I was afraid he was going to kill you with your own knife, but he was thankfully more focused on rescuing his son still. No one wanted to go out because of the current, and we didn't know what to do anyway. How could a priest do such a thing? Telaldhi was rescued, and then Ganhv just went limp. Then someone saw you break the surface downstream. The best we could do was follow on shore and wait until you got close enough to the bank to be rescued. Ganhv was fished out as well; he was dead."

"I know," was the best Sabelu could offer.

Tears were streaming down his mother's cheeks. "Sabelu, why did you do that? You had to have known he was going to try and kill you if you went out there."

Sabelu slowly got to a sitting position, leaning against the wall. "I did know. I also knew that if I didn't do it, then he was going to hurt a lot more people."

The thought did not comfort her so much as confuse her. She shifted position, wiped her eyes, and shook her head. "But why? Sure, everyone knew of the animosity between you two, and there was some controversy about his son, but...murder? Really?" She shook her head again and glanced toward the partitioned part of the townhouse. "The priests took his body, but I don't know what they'll do with it. A dead priest deserves an honorable burial, but murderers are fed to the wolves."

Actually, the Shadows were in conference over what to do next, but Sabelu did not say this out loud. At the mention of wolves, he looked around the townhouse for Yawi. He did not spot the great white wolf, but he did see evidence of large paw prints near his bedside. Given that he did not see any other possible evidence of Whites, even the ants marching in their faithful perimeter, he guessed that even with Ganhv's death, the townhouse was still not a safe place for the Whites. More likely, it was because of Ganhv's death that the Whites stayed away. There were three angry puppeteers in the next room, and Yawi was their biggest and perhaps only warrior right now. Exactly how were the Whites exploiting this situation again?

Before he could consider anything else, the rest of his family walked in. Ola Achukma and Netami breathed a sigh of relief, Blaknik just stared with wide eyes.

Any other time, Sabelu might have been annoyed by such attention. They'd all read the Book. They all knew that he was destined to die on a mountainside, not in a river. Why such little faith? However, now that he'd actually seen and faced a puppeteer, felt that brush of death even before the actual murder attempt, questioned whether a Shadow could truly change the course of the river, he was a little more willing to entertain his family's sympathies.

"Nenda, you know you shouldn't be here," Ola Achukma scolded his wife.

"My son was almost murdered by a priest," Nendawagan replied hotly. "You thought I would stay away?"

"It's not proper."

His father was correct in many respects. Self-defense or not, Sabelu had killed someone. He needed to be isolated and purified for seven days. At the same time, the only ones qualified to tend to his wounds during that time were the other priests. If his mother wasn't there to watch over him, Sabelu was sure they would try to kill him. Only the confusion over Ganhv's actions was keeping everything in balance at the moment.

"Well, he's awake now, and I'm sure he can defend himself," Ola Achukma said.

Nendawagan still hesitated and looked at Sabelu for reassurance.

"Go ahead," he told her. "I'll absolve you of your uncleanness later."

After a moment of hesitation, she nodded, stood, and joined the rest of them. Netami and Blaknik both looked like they wanted to say something to him, but it was improper for them to even speak to him.

They left him, but he was by no means alone. The townhouse was a big place. Small groups of people sat here and there, gossiping while working on small tasks. A group of children ran around, playing a game. No one looked his way, no one spoke to him, but he knew that at least two of the conversations revolved around the fight in the river.

The strength of the Shadows in the area meant he was not privy to the quiet conversation going on in the partitioned area. He briefly wondered if it would be possible to ask one of the burrowers to tunnel into the area, listen to the conversation, and report back.

"Why would we do that when you already know the outcome?"

Sabelu recognized the rabbit's voice even before the White popped up beside him.

"We have our own tasks to attend to without having to satisfy your petty, unnecessary curiosity," the burrower went on, hopping out of his hole which magically vanished and pulling himself onto Sabelu's lap.

"So what kind of door has this opened?" he asked. "What advantages are you exploiting?"

"It's easy for you humans to get comfortable and overly trusting," the rabbit told him. "Revealing the Shadow in someone, especially someone people inherently trust, is an excellent way to make people start questioning things."

"Is that a good thing?" Sabelu wondered innocently. "What if something happened and I started questioning the Whites? An open door can be passed through both ways. What if I started questioning the Author?"

"Only a fool believes questions are evil. It's whether he is willing to listen to the answers that makes the difference. And whether he is willing to change his beliefs and preconceived notions if necessary."

"Is that all?"

"I don't like your attitude, human."

Sabelu shrugged. "It was a question. And I don't think you have much room to lecture me on being willing to do anything when you intentionally, if temporarily, disabled me."

The rabbit sniffed. "Sometimes free will needs a swift kick in the tail."

"But is it free will if I know everything that's going to happen? Was it still free will for Ganhv to kill me when I spoke of it two years ago? Was it still free will on my part to kill him?"

"Is it free will if you don't know?" the rabbit countered. "No one out there knew about it. No one knew what Ganhv was planning. Except you. And the Author of course." He went on before Sabelu could speak. "Maybe instead of looking at things so selfishly, in terms of whether it's your coveted 'free will' or not, maybe you should think of things exactly as they are. You are merely a character. The Author doesn't need you, but the story does. So you can either play your role, or you can try to fight it."

"Does that mean that Ganhv played his role as some sort of antagonist? Would that then be the Author's will, or was he still fighting because of the Shadow?"

The rabbit nodded slowly and got up on his hind feet. "You live in a terrible, fallen, messed up, chaotic, linear universe. I pity you for it. Having the gift of agotvhdi, that glimpse into how things really are..." He shook his head. "It is necessary for you, but it wreaks havoc on a linear, mortal mind."

"Are you going to answer the question?" Sabelu asked.

"I can't," the rabbit told him. "Not in any way that can be properly conveyed on this plane. Your agotvhdi would give you some advantage if I tried, but it exists solely in the realm of the spirit world and cannot be simply rendered into ink on parchment. Humans on Earth measure Iyuwahnilvhi via timepieces like clocks and watches, but these clocks are not Iyuwahnilvhi. Similarly, we can sit here and debate free will and whether Ganhv was playing a role or fighting it, but to truly understand it would take us beyond the measurement of actions using limited, inadequate words."

Sabelu wouldn't say he didn't understand what the rabbit was saying. It was a bit like trying to convey the essence of dreams. Words might describe what images a dream produced, and they might even relate how the brain rendered a dream. But there was no way to adequately convey the essence of what a dream was, what separated one dream from another, what made his dreams special and others not.

He elected to change the subject.

"Is Yawi all right? I'm guessing he's not here because of the puppeteers in there." He nodded toward the partitioned area.

"He's out patrolling with the pack," the rabbit said, waving a paw. "He was watching over you, but your mother's peacock relieved him for a while."

"My mother's peacock?" Sabelu wondered. "I have a hard time believing she shook off her Shadow of Fear. Besides, I didn't see a peacock just now when she was here."

The rabbit shrugged. "He was busy distracting the Shadow of Fear so your mother could tend to you without hysterics."

"Oh. But Yawi is all right?"

"Isn't that what I just said? Do you think he would be out patrolling if he wasn't?"

"And you said the pack was here. So there are more Whites in Aktiya Waya now. Not just butterflies and grasshoppers and sparrows, but actual fighting Whites."

The rabbit gave him a look that resembled one his mother got when his father wasn't paying attention to what she was saying. "All Whites are fighting Whites. Even I can fight when the situation calls for it. As for your implication, the wolves are here for protection and communication. Hawk has also come for high observation. Peacock and Fan Lizard are here for distraction and bait."

"Bait?" Sabelu cut in. "That seems...cruel."

"But necessary. Fan Lizard takes great pleasure in being bait, luring Shadows into traps."

Sabelu thought about this for a moment, then nodded. "All right, I can understand that."

"The point is, the work that you've been doing, moving in the insects, moving in the seeds, bringing us burrowers in, now we have the stability to introduce more Whites. Imagine the chaos if there had been no foundation before ripping away that nasty puppeteer."

"The vacuum would have only drawn in more Shadows," Sabelu said.

"Exactly. This is why the small things are important. So keep doing them."

He considered this for a long moment. Then, "Yawi alone got the puppeteer on the run, even if the puppeteer did manage to outrun him. But now the whole pack is here. Would it be possible for them to take out the remaining puppeteers?"

"The puppeteers, maybe," a familiar voice said.

Sabelu and the rabbit turned to see Yawi and two more wolves enter the townhouse. The three of them were strong and stoic, fluffed out and gleaming white. It was Yawi who had spoken. The wolves approached and sat down around Sabelu like enormous guardians.

"The eight of us could take down the puppeteers," the pack leader repeated, "assuming they had no other help, which you know is fantasy only. But we are also the best protection here right now. Even if we did take them out, such bold action would only attract greater attention. Beyond the puppeteers are the titans, and not far behind them are the generals. You are not prepared for such things. The people are not prepared for such things."

It wasn't Sabelu's agotvhdi that told him Yawi was thinking of the cerberus.

Sabelu let out a breath. "So what is our next move?" He glanced at the partitioned area. The Shadows may have made him blind to the conversation, but he could look ahead to others who heard the verdict. "The priests are going to declare Ganhv unclean and unfit for a noble burial. This will let them save face, smooth things over publicly for a while, allowing the puppeteers to quietly consolidate their remaining power and assets. They're going to publicly apologize to me, speak honeyed words that he was bewitched and deceived them and I will be accepted as a full priest and prophet as I should be. This will let them keep me close, maybe close enough that you—" He looked at Yawi. "—won't want to go near them."

Yawi smirked. "A door once opened can be crossed through both ways. They will not want to be near us."

"It's going to be several years of me not only sitting that close to the puppeteers, but years of me being put on public display. The Shadows couldn't keep me down with insanity, so instead they're going to force me to the center of attention and try to make me destroy myself, or give the perception of it." Sabelu gave the wolf a look. "They're going to try and frame me."

"Then you should make the best use of your time while you have it. Otherwise you are only going to waste several perfectly useful years."

"I'm going to be in the inner company of demons who want to kill me."

Yawi tilted his head in canine manner. "Your kin's fire is surrounded by dark and cold, yet it does not cease to be a fire as long as fuel is provided. You have plenty of fuel."

Sabelu sighed, thought a minute, then nodded. "I suppose so. And it might work in my favor to have such vocal support from them, trap them in their own professed adoration and desire to help the people. If they're going to pretend to be good, I'll force them to live up to it."

The reaction from the Whites was not the overwhelming support he'd been hoping for.

"Maybe," one of the other wolves said, "but sometimes the worst thing you can do is give someone exactly what they want. The Shadows reward their pawns, often very well, and they bribe those under the influence of vices in order to turn them into indulgences. Similarly, we do not operate by giving everyone everything they want, but what they need, and sometimes discipline, while not fun or desirable, is needed."

"The only way they can save face with Ganhv is by denouncing him," Sabelu said, "or else they all look corrupt. Since he tried to kill me, they have to admit that I am the adelohosgi I was divined to be. They can't just proclaim something like that and then ignore me. They might try to put reins on me like a horse, but I'm the one who'll take them for a ride."

"Be ever cautious," Yawi warned. "The more protection you think you have, the more reckless you become, and the worse the injuries that penetrate." He went on before Sabelu could speak. "But for now, focus only on the present moment. You will be here for seven days. Don't worry about the Shadows. Don't worry about us. The priests are in conference, which means the puppeteers are occupied. While their backs are turned, we will make great gains. You can, as you say, hit the ground running, once you are released from here. Use the time to decide which direction you will go."

With that, the wolves stood and left the townhouse. Sabelu watched them go, then looked at the rabbit, still sitting on his lap. "And you?"

"What about me?" the rabbit asked.

"Do you have some mission to accomplish, or are you willing to maybe try to burrow in there and listen to what they're saying?" Sabelu vaguely gestured toward the partitioned area.

"I don't have to," the burrower said, suddenly very serious.

Sabelu looked up just as the priests emerged from the partitioned area. The rabbit hastily jumped off his lap and vanished underground.

Standard protocol dictated that those who were undergoing purification such as he were to be served only water, fresh honey, hominy, and a sacred herb blend tea. Considering the demeanor of the priests who hovered over him now, augmented by the presence of puppeteer Shadows of varying grotesque physiques, Sabelu wondered if he wasn't going to be served an ax to the head instead. He glanced at another acolyte, a boy no older than seven, who also seemed to sense that something more was going on.

"You must be hungry," one of the priests, Asdeoha, said finally. He turned to the boy. "Amagei, fetch food and drink for Sabelu."

The boy took the out and hurried away. All the priests save for Asdeoha dispersed to attend to minor errands. Asdeoha himself, now the head priest after Ganhv, squatted down beside Sabelu.

"Looks like you were right about Ganhv's death," he said, his tone carefully neutral. "You know, it's one thing to be right about crop success or failure, the game drives, even the outcome of the festival tournaments. But now we've gotten into matters of life and death. Not only did Ganhv die as predicted, but you killed him."

"He tried to kill me," Sabelu cut in.

"No one denies this, although it might have been helpful to mention that last little detail."

Without the Shadow, Asdeoha might have been interpreted as being a little annoyed. With the puppeteer looming beside him, as friendly with Asdeoha as Ganhv had been with his Shadow, Sabelu could not entertain even the idea of giving the priest the benefit of the doubt.

"It would have only prejudiced the people against me, so that even if they knew and saw the truth, it would matter less."

"Hm." Asdeoha managed a small nod. "I can understand that. You've never been especially liked, but why make it worse? Although your friendship with the traitor Kah Kitowak is questionable." He shrugged. "No matter. The point is that you have proven yourself in the matter of prophecy and rid us of a dangerous man. A dangerous priest. No doubt people's opinions of you have changed." He stood. "But that is something to be discussed after you have completed your purification."

Amagei returned at that moment with a tray of food and drink. The boy handed the tray to Asdeoha who blessed the food but did not give it to Sabelu immediately. Instead, he made a gesture. "Stand up."

Sabelu did so. Asdeoha turned and the other priests gathered round. "Come with us. We will proceed with your purification."

Sabelu followed the priests into the partitioned area, feeling like a very small flame in a very dark cave.

DISꞀ DVꞱT

Asodune Adolv'i

Roles to Play

The last day of Sabelu's purification was also the day he was inducted as a full priest.

The ceremony weighed so heavily on Sabelu he couldn't decide if he wanted to laugh or cry. He found himself wishing that for just a moment, he wouldn't see the Shadows and could simply revel in the moment. But he couldn't. He felt an extra level of humiliation as he stripped down to nothing for his seven baths in the pool in the partitioned area of the townhouse. Afterwards, he had to stiffly suffer as the priests, accompanied faithfully by their puppeteer Shadows, first cloaked him in a white priest's robe, then handed him a staff in one hand and large beaded talisman in the other. By Asdeoha's word, he knelt to be blessed, but he couldn't shake the image of a large knife lobbing off his head.

The staff and talisman were taken and he was given a ceremonial drink to consume. He envisioned poison in the drink. It wouldn't have to kill him, just rip his bowels apart for a few days, enough to give the puppeteers a good laugh. From there, new incense was burned and the pipe was passed around. Tobacco was not the only plant inside; it was accompanied by an herb called nala. This herb, cultivated by the priests after the War of Removal, was known for its spiritual bonding. Hunters would partake of it before a hunt, to become more in tune with each other, especially important on game drives. Dancers and drummers would partake before a dance so they might be more in step with one another. Couples would partake before making love, and it was said the herb also granted a boost in fertility.

For the priests, nala was intended to not only bond the priests with one another, but also bind them more perfectly to the spirits. The reason nala was used for this and not the traditional nattawodatnu was simple availability. Nala spread like a weed and could be grown for most of the year, versus a single crop of nattawodatnu from a few small trees.

Sabelu was the last to take the pipe. After a long drag—having less to do with ceremony and more trying to take the edge off his dread—Asdeoha proclaimed another blessing and declared Sabelu a full priest.

But it wasn't over yet. From there, the priests herded Sabelu out into the larger townhouse where a feast had been prepared and everyone in Aktiya Waya invited to celebrate. Normally this would have happened right away, but Sabelu had a promise to fulfill. He spotted his mother right away and motioned her forward.

The Shadow of Fear had wreaked havoc on Nendawagan for the last seven days, but seeing her son now effectively cut off its supply of fear, allowing Yawi and the wolf pack to chase it away with some enthusiasm. Sabelu couldn't help but smile, and he was glad that the current situation allowed for it, even if the others didn't fully understand what really amused him.

"What brings you here?" he asked of his mother.

"I interfered in the purification of a man and require purification myself." While intended to be a somber affair, Nendawagan herself couldn't stop smiling.

Sabelu nodded and gestured for her to kneel. He motioned for Amagei to bring him a pitcher of water and a small tray of unlit incense. Sabelu prayed a simple prayer and gently poured the water over his mother's head. When that was done, he lit the incense and let it burn for a full two minutes before praying again. Then he bid his mother rise.

"You are now cleansed and in good standing with the spirits," he told her. "You may return to your business."

His mother had never stopped smiling. As soon as he handed the elements back to Amagei, she threw her arms around him most unceremoniously.

This seemed to be the cue to begin the feasting and celebrating.

Everyone in attendance congratulated him at least once, though their level of interest and sincerity ranged from his mother's enthralled excitement to expected formality with an undercurrent of suspicion. The Whites had done well to stir up the Shadows and loosen them from their hosts, allowing people to have a glimpse into reality, but the Shadows did not give up easily. They still fomented suspicion and mistrust, their seemingly sole mission at the moment to prevent any meaningful foundation of trust and faith in Sabelu as priest and prophet.

In terms of the feast, that was almost a good thing. It meant that the people weren't fighting with each other, and everyone could enjoy themselves.

It was Sabelu's duty to clean up after the feast and ensure everything was back in its proper order, and it was late by the time he returned home. His parents were still awake and waiting for him. His mother hugged him and he clasped wrists with his father.

"We're proud of you," Ola Achukma told him.

Sabelu's first instinct was to say, "I know," but at the last moment he opted for, "Thank you."

"You drove the Shadows from Aktiya Waya," his father went on, "and saved the people, even at the potential cost of yourself. You are a good man."

Now Sabelu faltered and awkwardly cleared his throat. "I drove out one Shadow from Aktiya Waya. A powerful one, yes, but still only one."

"What do you mean?" his mother wondered. "Ganhv bewitched the people, the other priests. Now that he's gone—"

"The other priests were not bewitched, they are trying to save face. They are conjoined to Shadows as well, of the same power and strength as the one that held Ganhv."

Ola Achukma and Nendawagan glanced at each other. It was his father who spoke.

"Ganhv's animosity toward you was quite obvious. This debacle with his son being a seer also was cause for some suspicion. After everything that's happened, his death, the explanation that's been given is a reasonable one. Without him, the bewitching has been lifted and you've become a full priest. All is well. If you start accusing the other priests of evil—"

"Then I begin to look ambitious and evil myself," Sabelu finished. "I know."

"Are you sure they have Shadows?" Nendawagan inquired. The Shadow of Fear had not yet returned, so her question was born more out of confusion over the situation than fear over what the priests might do to her son.

Sabelu nodded. "I'm sure."

Ola Achukma made a sound like a half sigh and folded his arms. "It would make sense that the Shadows would want to be rid of an adelohosgi of the Whites. But what do they really want with the people? Why are we—" He made a vague gesture. "—important?"

"First and foremost, with any individual or group, the Shadows want us just so the Whites can't have us. As for the Krydik specifically, we have been chosen by the Author through the Books, and we must be the foundation on which all else stands, so that we may act as a beacon of hope for the people of the Old Land."

Now his father scoffed and gave him a look. "Perhaps you've learned so much that you've forgotten what matters. We came here to escape our own extinction. We lost the War of the Old Land. There are others who are more powerful than us who have lost much more. As you seem to be saying now, we can barely save ourselves."

"Ants are very small," Sabelu told him. "They have no monuments, no festivals, no art. Their sole purpose, their sole desire, is simply to build a foundation, to expand, and to do this for all eternity, generation after generation. There have been fires, floods, flocks of birds and other predators, and children who deliberately disrupt their perfect lines. Yet they continue to build and thrive. Because one day that predator is going to die and his body will feed the ants and feed the earth. Faithful determination in small tasks and small bites is all it takes.

"The people have been attacked through fire and flood and numerous enemies. Yet here we are. But the Shadows persist, and they will not stop until we are useless, a wet, cracked, uneven foundation.

We have to fight back."

"If you include the children and infants, the whole of the Krydik is maybe eight hundred people across four villages."

"If you include all the people as we were originally, as we were intended to be, we number in the millions," Sabelu corrected.

"The Old Land?" Nendawagan questioned.

He nodded. "The groundwork is already being prepared, led by Kah Kitowak and a handful of others."

"Kah Kitowak has never accomplished anything in his life," Ola Achukma cut in. "He's not exactly who I would choose first to lead any kind of initiative."

Sabelu raised a brow. "Didn't you just say that we fled here from extinction and lost a war? We're not doing so hot either."

Ola Achukma grunted but could not refute the point.

"In order for us to do this building, this laying of a foundation, you say we need to throw off the Shadows," Nendawagan began, in a tone that suggested she was working through something and trying to keep everything in line. "But what are we building exactly? We're eight hundred, the Old Land is a few million, maybe, but what are we expected to do?"

Sabelu hesitated for a long moment, then said, "Wake up Netami and Blaknik. They will need to know and I only want to make this trip once."

The pair glanced at each other, but Nendawagan went to wake up her other children.

"What about Galiliga?" Ola Achukma inquired.

"I'll tell him later," Sabelu said, shrugging.

Nendawagan appeared then, followed by Netami who was a bit grumpy and Blaknik who was rubbing his eyes and trying to walk straight. Once everyone was assembled, Sabelu conjured Galohisdi to the cliffside city, directly into the open market. It was a taxing trip on a normal day, but fatigued Netami and Blaknik arguably got the worst of it. After using Asvhnisgi to ensure they weren't actually hurt, the two were moved out of the way to sit against a wall while their mother attended them. Meanwhile, Sabelu stuck close to his father who wandered off a short distance, looking around.

"This isn't the Old Land."

"No," Sabelu said. "It's a city underneath Lehoyed, behind the cliffs."

"Underneath Lehoyed?" his father echoed. "Is this what we were looking for, your mother and I, years ago?"

"That's right."

Being nighttime now, the light was very poor. Ola Achukma looked around, caught sight of the minotaur statues, reached for a knife. Sabelu put a hand on his arm. "No, don't."

"But what—?"

"It's not a beast," Sabelu said. "It's just a statue."

Sabelu invoked Atsvstdi, brightening the cavern so all could see. He understood why his father was hesitant. Even now he was considering memories of the underground city, the discomfort and unease he felt when down there.

"What place of demons is this?" Ola Achukma demanded weakly, his gaze darting back and forth between the statues and the skeletons.

"I don't know exactly, but I don't believe it to be a place of demons."

"Why have you brought us here?" Nendawagan asked, trying to be calm in spite of her genuine, understandable fear.

"First, to show you what you were searching for all those years ago," Sabelu said, trying to lighten his tone and reignite the sense of wonder. "It does exist. I don't know what happened that the entrance was not open when you were first looking, but it's open now."

"How did you find this place?" his father asked, lowly relaxing and releasing his knife.

"Kah Kitowak found it first, accidentally, after he was run out of Lehoyed. Then he showed me."

His father shook his head. "Kah Kitowak."

"Does it matter who found it?" Blaknik wondered innocently. "This is the place you were searching for."

Sabelu knew that it wasn't so much that Kah Kitowak found it— although that was certainly a secondary blow to his father's pride—it was the fact that it had been discovered so easily after Ola Achukma and Nendawagan had spent so much time searching. And if this truly was so close to Lehoyed, how had they missed it? Where was the opening and why hadn't they been the ones to find it?

"You know what this place is, then?" Nendawagan wondered, her fear slowly receding. "A city, yes, or part of one, but did you discover more about the People Before?"

"I have a few thoughts about them, but what's more important is that the evil that wiped them out is going to come back for us."

"The Tacagans?" Ola Achukma inquired.

"I don't know if it is specifically about them, but the Shadows are already here. They've been trying to slowly kill the people. I'm here to expose it."

"But why?" Nendawagan asked. "We're peaceful, we don't want any trouble. We have no neighbors to anger."

"We have Books. We have been chosen by the Author and are protected by the Whites, or we were. Even if the vast majority of the people don't understand what that means, the Shadows can't risk that knowledge getting out. We must be destroyed."

"Which is why you say the priests are corrupt," Blaknik stated. "The Shadows got to them."

Sabelu nodded. "That's right."

"But the priests with their Shadows," Netami said, still mulling it over, "they can do everything we can. They help teach a lot of people."

"The Shadows have a distorted, perverted version of the sorceries. It looks the same to outsiders, but it's not. It is harsh and demanding and only gives the Shadows more control over a man."

Ola Achukma shifted his stance, his posture thoughtful. "You say we are being targeted because we have Books. In the beginning of the Books, before the story, there are more titles listed. Did the People Before have Books? Are those other titles and series, are those people being targeted?"

"I can't imagine they're not," Sabelu said. "As for whether the People Before have Books, I don't know. I haven't found any evidence here."

"Do you think those other Books have the same list?" Blaknik wondered. "Do you think other people know about us? You think we might meet them someday?"

"I think for now, we ought to be focusing on protecting ourselves and ensuring that, if we are to meet others, that there is someone to meet and not simply more ruins."

"How are we to go about this?" Ola Achukma asked, now turning more serious. "So far, we thought that may you have just been trying to be more helpful in the community. In doing so, you exposed Ganhv's treachery. Now we learn that there is an even bigger plot afoot." He shook his head. "I have seen the Shadows. I don't doubt that you have as well, or that you may know them better than I do. We can't just move forward without a plan. I don't there there is a subtle way to do this. Once the Shadows start attacking us—"

"I thought the Shadows already were attacking us," Blaknik interrupted, a mixture of confused and unimpressed.

"They are," Sabelu told him. "They are trying to get to us now in our ignorance and weakness. Plan one, isolate us. Plan two, wipe out the men who are called to be leaders and warriors. Plan three, destroy all faith in the priesthood, prophets, even the spirits and ancestors themselves, cut us off from the Whites and the Author. Beat us down so that we are useless, if not already destroyed, by the time the physical destruction comes to sweep us away."

Sabelu's parents and siblings exchanged glances. Belief in the spirits was unquestionable, as was the Creator, but the Author specifically was not exactly a revered or even prominent deity. She existed more as a superstition than anything else, mentioned once somewhere in some Book but having little bearing on real life, not like the rest of the supernatural that could be seen, heard, or prayed to.

"I've never lied to you before," Sabelu said quietly. "Why would I lie now? After all the troubles I've gone through—really, through my entire life—why would I voluntarily take this on if it weren't true and imperative?" He gestured toward Netami. "Why wouldn't I just throw myself off a cliff?" He looked at his mother. "Or let Ganhv drown me?"

He met his father's gaze. "It would have been much easier. Believe me."

Contrary to some beliefs, doubt was not always an evil thing born of Shadows. Sometimes doubt was merely a slow-acting, divine discernment, scaled down for the benefit of mortal minds who couldn't see the future or the thoughts and motivations of their fellow man and needed time to process through thought and logic in temporally linear fashion. Even knowing this and knowing in advance that his family would doubt him, Sabelu wouldn't say he wasn't still a little hurt and disappointed. He was also a little disappointed in himself that he couldn't sway them away from such doubt, that he wasn't powerful enough to effect that kind of change, that little nudge.

It was Netami who spoke first.

"I believe you," she told him. "I know you too well, little brother, and I know you're not a liar."

"You're still weird," Blaknik quipped.

"Blaknik, show some respect," Ola Achukma scolded. "He is a priest and a prophet."

Blaknik gave their father a look. "He was my brother before he was either of those things; I can say what I want."

Before Ola Achukma could scold him again, Sabelu burst into laughter. The act startled the rest of them into stunned silence, all rebukes forgotten. Nendawagan broke first, grinning hugely and embracing Sabelu for no reason other than she was happy to see him genuinely laughing. There were tears of joy in her eyes, and they evoked such pride and joy in Sabelu that he could not explain.

"All right," Ola Achukma stated after a moment, serious once more. "So what are we supposed to do? We, us, the Krydik, at home? Like I said, we're only eight hundred in number, again, including even the babies. And I thought you said something about the people of the Old Land?"

"The Krydik are made up of many people, and we are still tied to the Old Land. The Shadows will come after us all, just to ensure that such a feat is never attempted again."

"You said Kah Kitowak was taking care of the Old Land." Ola

Achukma ground his teeth once as he swallowed a piece of his pride. "I may not like him or see anything in him, but if the Author does, I guess that will have to be good enough. There's nothing I'm going to do about it anyway. But we need to start small, clean up our own house before criticizing others."

"Isn't that why we're called the Krydik, though? Because we're so critical?" Sabelu continued before anyone could speak. "You are right. We need to prepare ourselves first."

"Talking to people and being kind and considerate is one thing," Netami said, "but Ganhv really crossed the line when he tried to murder you. The priests denounced him, opening up his family to retaliation."

"Maybe so, but such an avenue would only cement the divide between us and them, which is something the Shadows can easily exploit. If they're playing on Ganhv being a rogue priest, they can't try the same thing, but—."

Ola Achukma shrugged. "They'd just make it look like an accident."

Sabelu shook his head. "No."

"Sabelu, what are they going to do?" Nendawagan asked.

"They're going to try and frame me."

"For Ganhv's murder," Blaknik stated.

"No. That will quickly be put to rest. I don't know precisely, which I can only conclude means that there will be heavy Shadow involvement. There will be accusations of heresy and evil spirits against me."

"Accuse you of something they are guilty of," Ola Achukma said distastefully. "Make themselves look better."

Sabelu nodded. "I think, then, that the next few years should be spent building you guys up and preparing you."

"Won't they just accuse us of conspiring with you?" Blaknik wondered.

"No. I'll make sure of that. But I think..." Sabelu sighed internally. "It's not about me. I am not the hero here. I need to make sure that you guys are prepared to continue my work and expand it."

"You say that like you won't be around anymore," Nendawagan said, shifting her stance uncomfortably.

"I'll be alive, but I will be separated from the people." He went on before she could say anything. "That is for the future to worry about. We have barely made it past today."

Ola Achukma chuckled humorlessly at that and looked around. "I still don't know what to make of this. Is this real?" He touched a nearby table. "Are we dreaming? Is this the place where you meet with Anagalisgi?"

Sabelu shook his head. "No, it's not where we meet. But this is real; you're not dreaming. I brought you here so you might understand what we're truly facing. The city that used to rest behind this wall is gone. The people of the underground city and Aktiya Waya are gone. We will suffer the same fate if we do nothing."

His father turned to look at him. "Our enemy is not each other. Our enemy is the Shadows. The same as it was on the battlefield."

"Yeah," Blaknik said, looking at Ola Achukma, "but those men were still trying to kill you." He looked at Sabelu. "Ganhv tried to kill you. There are still men out there who want to see us dead, or there will be."

"Evil knows no physical bounds," Sabelu told him. "We're taking the fight to the Shadows. It will save us and free those still in bondage."

He could see his younger brother trying to understand. He wanted to understand. He was trying to put together everything he knew, everything he'd seen, and everything Sabelu had ever shown him.

"Aktiya Waya boasts the Sacred Wolf," Netami stated. "Southeast of Anpa O Wican'hpi is the Cursed Zukatopa." She gestured to the statues. "Are these man-bulls sacred or cursed?"

"They are called minotaurs, and I haven't determined that yet," Sabelu replied honestly. "Regardless, I think it would be best to keep this to ourselves."

"What about the Sacred One of the Desert?" Blaknik wondered, looking at their parents. "You were looking for that one, too, weren't you?" He looked back at Sabelu. "Have you been there? Have you seen it?"

"No, not yet. But I will."

"Well, before anyone goes on any more adventures today," Ola Achukma said, breaking into a yawn, "I think we all need sleep." He looked around. "Maybe it will turn out that this is a dream after all."

His words were hollow, but it was true that they were all tired. Netami and Blaknik mirrored the yawn, followed by Nendawagan. Sabelu led the way out of the open market, heading for the cavern. He did not conjure right away just so his parents could see more of the city, more of the place they had once searched in vain for. His parents and brother were a few steps behind, still looking around in fear and wonder, but Netami kept pace with him.

"You're going to be exiled," she stated. "Or rather, you're going to choose exile over whatever other punishment they have for you, and you will go to the desert."

"That's a possibility," Sabelu replied evasively.

"Then the Shadows will try and pick you off, once you've been separated from the pack."

"Naturally."

She nodded. "That's what you're counting on."

"It won't be a matter of my isolation making me easy prey. It will be a case where the lack of people and proxies means I no longer have to pretend to be nice and play by social rules when dealing with the Shadows. They make themselves vulnerable." He could feel her gaze and he glanced at her. "What?"

"You seem very sure about that," she commented, "for someone whose gifts are distorted and even useless when they run into Shadow interference."

He faltered for half a moment. Then, quietly, "People don't like it when an adelohosgi doesn't know something."

"Am I people?" Netami asked. "I admit, you're unique. But adelohosgi aren't gods. They're not supposed to know everything, no one is. Adelohosgi are supposed to know something so well, so intimately, that it is unquestionable in its thoroughness and undeniable in its truth."

"Then why do I know so much?"

"Because you're not simply prophesying a single event, a single warning, as Anagalisgi tried to do in his day. You are prophesying reality itself, tearing apart an enormous illusion. You said it yourself, evil knows no physical bounds. You prophesy to and of the souls of men and women who are bound in chains they cannot see. Anyone proficient in Asvhnisgi can learn how our bodies work, how our brains bring everything together and tell our bodies what to do. No one has ever touched a soul. Until now."

Sabelu contemplated this as they reached the steps and made their way up to the platform overlooking the market. He'd never thought of it that way before. He still wondered why he needed to know absolutely everything about someone, though. Why did he have to know his mother's favorite sexual position? Or his father's? Or his brother's? Netami had not yet known a man, but he knew she had fantasies about men every now and again, especially around festival time. Blaknik was growing into his manhood and couldn't stop thinking about sex half the time.

But then, didn't it all revolve around family, the desire to reproduce and make more and propagate the people? Didn't it have to do with love and security and protection and dominance? Weren't those some of the most basic elements of human behavior?

As true as it might have been, he still didn't think it entirely necessary.

"Sometimes those who speak the most have the least to say," Netami went on as they stepped off the stair onto the platform. "If you start preaching about everything as if the sky is falling, then no one will listen when it actually starts to fall."

"The Shadows are a serious matter," Sabelu insisted.

"I'm not saying they're not. But if you magnify them too greatly, you end up minimizing the ability of the people to respond. We teach our children not to lie, and we discipline them when they do, but how would it be for a mother to go into hysterics over every small lie? How would it be for her to treat a lie the same as Ganhv's attempted murder of you? That child may not lie anymore, but he will also be terrified of doing anything else. He'll be paralyzed and unable to make any sort of move."

He opened his mouth, but she kept talking. "You don't go on a game drive looking for rabbits. You don't use a horse to run down a turkey. Sometimes, it is silence, solitude, and patience that gets you what you want. Like Ikoa, who doesn't need a beating, just a gentle reminder that things are not as bad as they seem. Or Itsitsi, who will panic if you get agitated, and just needs some quiet reassurance."

"You're better at those things than I am," Sabelu stated.

"Then it's a good thing that we'll be taking over for you, in the end. Are you at least going to tell us what our roles will be?"

"Tomorrow, once we've all gotten some sleep."

Netami yawned at the mention of sleep and did not disagree. Sabelu mirrored her. Behind them, the rest of their party was noticeably lagging behind, yawning and rubbing eyes, fatigue now completely overpowering any remaining sense of wonder.

"Although we have agreed to keep this place a secret for now, could we still come back later to look around some more?" Ola Achukma asked, looking at Nendawagan who was thinking the same thing even as they were both silently reminiscing about all the adventures they used to go on.

"Of course," Sabelu told them. "Maybe later when you're not so tired."

Feeling a bit tired himself and knowing that he was going to collapse into bed just as soon as they got home, Sabelu took a breath and conjured Galohisdi. The five of them stumbled through, each to his own bed.

Sabelu felt the warmth of the fire even before he could be certain that he was fully asleep. When he opened his eyes, he was in his uncle's cave. Anagalisgi himself was just grabbing a plate and utensils. Sabelu noticed he also grabbed a pipe and several small pots of herbs. Elsewhere in the cave, eight White wolves were lounging about.

"Congratulations," Anagalisgi said when he turned and saw Sabelu awake.

"I feel like I've been inducted into a pit of venomous snakes," Sabelu admitted.

Anagalisgi measured out the herbs and lit the pipe. The two of them started passing it back and forth.

"Maybe so, but I think this recent string of events has helped to clear up any lingering confusion," Anagalisgi said. "You understand what's going on, you know what is going to happen, you know what to do. All that remains is to simply do it."

Sabelu puffed once. "It seems strange. I know I complained about nothing being done, but now it feels like it's all coming so fast. And yet, I know that we still have at least a few years before the next step. And it's still over a century before my death." He frowned. "I know what is going to happen and how, but I don't know the why. Why is it necessary for us to do this now? Won't things just regress in the next hundred years?"

"The why belongs to the Author, and it is beyond you or me," his uncle told him. He cut off Sabelu when he tried to speak. "Shut up."

"But—"

Anagalisgi took the pipe from his lips. "What did I just say?"

Sabelu shifted position uncomfortably and turned his gaze toward the fire. After a moment, his uncle sighed.

"I know you struggle with your own future, Sabelu. I know what you see."

Sabelu shifted again, still not looking at his uncle. "So many people...they say that if it would help their children, help the people, help someone, that they would endure all these terrible things. Almost all of them are liars once the pain starts, because they always wonder if they truly made a difference, if their misfortune truly prevented tragedy for the other person. Even those who believe it often wish there had been another way, so that no one had to get hurt."

"But you know the absolutes," Anagalisgi stated.

"The Shadows don't like absolutes; it's why they don't have a solid form. Evil itself comes in so many forms that it is formless." Now Sabelu looked up. "You told me a couple years ago not to go to the underground city because I couldn't handle what I would find. Yet my death was foretold at the end of my father's Book. Could the Shadows—the truly powerful Shadows like the cerberus or the dragon—really make such a change? Altering a moment, a day, a month, those seem rather inconsequential, assuming it truly happens. But changing a century of the future? Or more? Could the premonition at the end of the Book not be a premonition at all, but a catalyst of some kind? If I believe myself protected until then, would it cause me to do something that I might not have otherwise? Would all my visions of the future, the oblique ways I observe myself, be erased? What about the rest of my visions? What about the Krydik?"

Sabelu took the pipe and put it between his lips while his uncle looked on sympathetically.

"You see things," Anagalisgi said gently. "And you understand them. For the most part. You are able to put things in perspective. But you are so focused on the horizon that you don't see the land right in front of you. You will get there, Sabelu. Just because the forest is thick with trees does not mean they have brought down the mountain."

Sabelu thought about this, then finally nodded and passed the pipe. "Thank you, Tsidushi." He hesitated. Then, "Do we have any errands tonight?"

"Of course not. We're celebrating your induction into the priesthood. You can take the night off."

"How are Kah Kitowak and Aklaq and the others doing?"

"Slow, stumbling progress, as expected. But they're moving in the right direction."

Sabelu hesitated. Then, "The people don't really see a difference between me and the other priests. They expect that we all believe the same thing, serve the same spirits, the same Creator, and perform the same rituals to such effect. But we don't."

"No," Anagalisgi agreed quietly.

Sabelu sighed. "There's no real point in complaining about what's going to happen. It is what it is. It's the future. I might as well complain about the course of a river; all the complaining in the world won't change its path. I'm just trying to help people navigate around the obstacles, maybe remove a few if I can."

"It's not always about the best outcome, just the least bad."

Sabelu shifted position and looked at his uncle. "I know you don't see things as I do, but what do you see of the future?"

Anagalisgi puffed thoughtfully on the pipe. "I see many independent threads weaving together, in and out of each other's lives and stories, like a dreamcatcher, all bound together by the circle of eternity, crafted by the Author's hand. If any one thread is cut loose, it all falls apart, and the spirits, both good and evil, which bombard this dreamcatcher, have no impact, no stakes, nothing to fight over."

Sabelu gave Anagalisgi a look. "I thought dreamcatchers were supposed to let the bad dreams pass through and catch the good dreams?"

His uncle shrugged and handed off the pipe. "Your brother's net will catch a fish of any kind if it is large enough, and it will let any small fish pass through regardless of its species."

"Makes sense, I suppose." Sabelu shifted position again. "The people have lived with the Shadows for a long time. Our net of discernment had enormous holes in it that the puppeteers have been able to pass through unimpeded. Now the net is being repaired, and the fish that are being caught are starting to fight their entrapment."

He puffed one last time on the pipe, then handed it back to Anagalisgi and stood. "We could sit here all night spouting analogies and pithy advice and words of wisdom, but it won't actually get anything done. I know what's going to happen, I know what I need to do."

Anagalisgi did not stand up as he puffed, looked up at him, and asked, "The question is, are you willing to do it?"

"The circle of eternity, Tsidushi, crafted by the Author. I can only run as far as the fences she's erected. It doesn't matter much what I want because it's going to happen one way or another."

"Maybe so, but a willing horse enjoys a ride far more than an unwilling one, regardless of destination or provocation."

Sabelu said nothing to that. He was tired of the conversation, tired of the analogies and words. His uncle may have had the time and energy—

or lack thereof—to spend hours or days contemplating time and the future and the meaning of life and the universe, but he, Sabelu, was the one in the fight. Anagalisgi couldn't do much more than watch and wait and observe the skirmishes of the Whites and Shadows, but Sabelu was the one on the ground on the battlefield in the middle of the proxy war on the mortal plane. He had the advantage of being able to see the whole battlefield, all of the combatants. He could see the weak spots and the advantages, knew what had to be done. It was just a question of how to get reinforcements where they needed to go without leaving anything exposed.

He mentally shook his head. Again with the analogies.

"I expect this will be the last time for a while that we will speak to each other," Sabelu stated.

Anagalisgi nodded. "It is. Training is over, Sabelu. Once you leave here, you are stepping onto the battlefield, where you will be the one responsible for—"

"I know what I will be responsible for," Sabelu cut in. "I know."

"You don't," his uncle said, not unkindly. "But it is something learned only through experience." He stood, and the two clasped wrists. "Be well, Tsiquiyi. Yawi and the wolves will continue to watch over you, and so will I."

They released wrists and Anagalisgi clapped him on the shoulder. "Good luck, Sabelu. Live up to your name."

Sabelu nodded and turned to leave, only to find himself rolling over in bed. He was familiar with the sudden wave of vertigo, but that didn't mean he was especially accustomed to it or liked it.

Blaknik was still asleep. Netami and Nendawagan were out of the house. Ola Achukma sat at the table with a hot cup of tea. Upon Sabelu exiting his room, still recovering from vertigo, Ola Achukma motioned for him to sit. Sabelu did so, but it was a long moment before his father spoke.

"Why did you take us to the cliffside city yesterday?"

"It was necessary," Sabelu answered simply.

His father leaned back in his seat. "Many times I've told myself to take things on faith. I've seen only a glimpse of the world you walk in, and I have to accept that you have been called to something greater than I can fully understand. And I cannot deny that it makes sense for our destiny to be tied to the People Before in some way. Of all the worlds that exist, it cannot be a coincidence that we were brought here. I knew that when your mother and I first discovered the cliffside city. And I suppose it makes sense that the Sacred One of the Desert would also factor in."

Sabelu nodded. "When Anagalisgi first discovered this place, he declared that all the spirits had departed this place. I have a suspicion that it was not time that saw their departure. I think their souls were destroyed."

"I will not pretend to know what a priest knows, but what I do know is that there are very few forces in this world that have the power to destroy a soul."

"That is correct, which should tell you what we're up against," Sabelu said seriously. He hesitated for half a second. "You know that I am blind to myself, with exception of my death. I am also blind to the Whites and Shadows. I can see them in the present moment, but I could no more tell you their plans or thoughts or intentions any more than I could tell you the same of a child or a rock. They exist outside of our plane, our entire reality. They have no need for us except that the Shadows wish to destroy us because the Author has written us. And the Whites are here to defend us, if we let them."

Ola Achukma was silent for a moment, searching Sabelu's gaze. Sabelu would not characterize his father as being doubtful or lacking faith necessarily; rather, it was mostly sheer frustration and confusion. He had a thousand tiny pieces of a complex machine laid out before him, and he was struggling to put everything together. Meanwhile, Sabelu's machine was fully operational, but he was unable to explain just how it got that way.

He internally shook his head again. Always the analogies. He was turning into his uncle.

"Evil exists everywhere," Ola Achuka stated. "This is known. You have said it yourself that the Shadows are less interested in places and more interested in people. The cities would not mean anything except that there is some physical danger to us that the Shadows are going to try to use to try to destroy us. Something to do with the Tacagan people, the same way the People Before were destroyed."

"I would believe so, yes," Sabelu agreed. "And once we're gone—or even before—the Shadows would try to do the same to the Old Land, to ensure that our kind can never return."

His father stood, walked a few steps as if going toward his room, stopped, walked a few more steps in another direction, stopped, and finally faced Sabelu.

"Helping people overcome their own problems is one thing. It's good and noble and expected of everyone. Exposing one corrupt priest is another thing. Painful and shocking, but necessary if we are to maintain harmony with the spirits." He switched from one line of thought to another. "We have no armies here. We have no competing kingdoms or nations. And it's not unreasonable to think that just because we exist on a smaller scale that these Shadows wouldn't still seek to conquer us through different means. But what you're talking about..." He let out a breath and gestured with his arms helplessly. "Sabelu, you're asking a horse to pull a mountain. You are suggesting that at the next festival, we hook up our strongest pulling horse to the Sacred Wolf itself and expect it to move."

Sabelu nodded. "I know. And how surprised will people be when it does." He put up a hand. "Speaking figuratively. The horse would never be able to do it."

Ola Achukma just sighed.

"Tsitsa, not everyone needs to know or understand this," Sabelu said. "Even if they knew, even if I took everyone there today, within six moons, ninety-five percent of them would have shrugged it off and returned to their own cares. Why? Because they are common soldiers. Their only concern is what is right in front of them, their current enemy. You know how this works. And that's fine. For most of them, all they need to know is that there is a fight to be had and it needs to be won. They need to understand the evil spirits, the Shadows, and they need to know to fight them. Let the rest of us worry about the larger maneuvers."

"Us?" Ola Achukma raised a brow.

Sabelu nodded. "In a few years, the priests are going to frame me for heresy and witchcraft, and I will be exiled. Rather, I am going to choose exile as my punishment."

"What?"

"This will give me the freedom to do what I need to do."

"Which is what?"

Sabelu ignored him. "On the part of the family, Netami is going to step in with great apologies, saying I bewitched you."

"Nonsense!"

"You won't be exiled, but you will be shunned. This will give you some leeway to begin the next step in your own missions."

Ola Achukma folded his arms. "And what is that going to be?"

"More work in the Old Land, I'm afraid. But it will be good work. You're going to work with Kah Kitowak—" Ola Achukma scoffed. "—in helping rescue and restore the peoples whose children fell prey to the residential schools."

"Sabelu, we've been through all of this before. We can't just scoop up every stray dog—"

"No one is going to come here. This is helping people in their own land, their own people, not whisking them away to some fabled city. Kah Kitowak is doing what he can, teaching the people about the sorceries. You are going to teach the people about themselves, help them hold fast to their cultures that are fast eroding and being taken away."

"How does that help the people here?"

"Because mercy and joy and helping people is just as contagious as fear and suspicion, and the Shadows hate it. It might not do anything to directly free someone, but it will shake the Shadows' hold." Sabelu went on before his father could speak. "But it will take time. You cannot change what is in a man's heart overnight. It is an ongoing process, in the same way that guarding against the Shadows must be continuous because they can and will return if given half a chance."

His father thought about this for a long moment. Finally, "I'm guessing you don't want the other priests to know about this."

"That's right."

"I can't imagine it's going to be easy for you, going to the townhouse to perform your duties, knowing you're surrounded by such evil forces."

Sabelu met his father's gaze. "It's easier than it is for you, to think that the people you're supposed to be able to trust the most with your soul are more interested in destroying it. I've always been in the waking world—the real waking world. You've seen it a few times, but only now are you really waking up."

Ola Achukma nodded, sighed, and made a motion that said Sabelu was dismissed.

Sabelu left the house and made his way to the townhouse. The other priests and acolytes were already there. He saw their smiles and heard their congratulations, but he also saw the strings that moved them and the voices that spoke through them. And he considered that his uncle was right; the priests were long dead, their souls withered away to nothing, and all that inhabited them now was smoke and shadow. Maybe there was a way to save them in the end, maybe not. In the moment, with three puppeteers on one side and Yawi on the other, all Sabelu could think was that maybe exile wouldn't be so bad.

DℒS∩ DVᎢT

Atladune Adolv'i

Inquiry

For the next few months, once the initial shock of Ganhv's treachery had ebbed, everything ran smoothly among the priests, in the same way that a mother dragging an obstinate child across the ground was smooth. There were no arguments and no scandals, but there was still some tension in the townhouse. Like the exhausted mother, only those involved could appreciate just how much tension there truly was.

But it was, for all intents and purposes, smooth. It had to be. For the sake of the people, all of the priests had to live up to the image of being rid of evil influence and getting back to normal. They went house to house, performing rituals and incantations to drive out any evil spirits that might be lurking about because of Ganhv's influence. Where Sabelu went, the Shadows were shaken, all vices and many indulgences driven out entirely. Where the other priests went, indulgences were strengthened and new vices introduced, even if the residents did not yet realize it. By the time they were done, the spiritual landscape of Aktiya Waya was less of an incoherent swirl of black and white beads thrown haphazardly into a pot, and more like a black canvas with distinctive white patches. Lines were being drawn, territory established, but few had noticed it yet.

Where once the Shadows moved freely, by themselves or in groups, now they roamed in packs, like territorial dogs, very reminisce of the Whites who did the same. When two people passed by on the street, the sides clashed. The Whites wanted the people to look at a familiar person and be reminded of the good things, the positive traits and memories of that person. The Shadows wanted the opposite and worked to dig up past hurts and old grudges, no matter how old or how small. For the humans caught in the middle, the exchange was little more than a glance and a fleeting thought over just a few seconds.

For the festival that year, Sabelu was again consulted for his opinion concerning the new national leaders, and his decisions were publicly praised. Sabelu desperately wanted to enjoy it. He wanted to revel in the appreciation, but he knew it was hollow and fake. There was much ado made about Ganhv's treachery, his attempt on Sabelu's life. More ado was made about the spiritual restoration that the priests had to carry out in all the villages. They had become too lax, thinking that they were safe from spiritual problems in this land. They had to be more vigilant, more aware. Sabelu watched it all unfold, and the only thing he could think of was a theater play his father had once seen as a child. Actors, all of them, telling a story with scripted lines in order to evoke a particular response, but none of it real.

"After so many years of being scorned, this sudden praise and adoration must be overwhelming," Asdeoha observed, a few days after the festival had ended and everyone returned home.

"I was praised as a child," Sabelu stated, keeping his tone neutral as he went about his duties in the townhouse. In the corner, a vice Shadow was chasing a White mouse.

"Yes, that is true. Then it seems Ganhv became jealous and bewitched even you, sent you into madness."

It wasn't entirely a lie, but it also wasn't quite true either. Sabelu elected to say nothing.

"Oh, come now, Sabelu," Asdeoha said, slapping him on the back. "Nothing to say? Seer of all things, keeper of all history and wisdom, slayer of evil, and you have nothing to say about any of it?" He laughed. "Or are your thoughts more fixed on Yukpa?"

Sabelu felt his face burn hot before he could stop it. He deliberately looked away from the head priest, but the man had caught it all the same.

"Well, well, has our all-knowing little prophet finally been blindsided by love?" The man roared with laughter.

"I wasn't blindsided," Sabelu mumbled. "I knew who she was. I've seen her before."

The White mouse darted across the townhouse, running over the feet of another priest, Dikdi. The puppeteer took note but made no move to go after it.

"Oh, come on, Sabelu," Dikdi chuckled. "We all grew up with someone who, one day, suddenly meant something to us. You are not so special that you are immune to love."

The best Sabelu could rebut was, "I'm not going to marry her."

"That makes it all the more interesting, then," Asdeoha commented slyly. "He knows it will never be, yet he fawns after her all the same."

Now Sabelu turned to face Asdeoha, hackles raised. "Just because I'm not going to marry her doesn't mean that—"

Asdeoha put his hands up in mock surrender. "Am I making threats? I may look young, but I am still older than you, and I have been married a long time. I find it amusing when young men discover love for the first time, especially when they're so old."

"I'm not that old."

"Your younger brother has already discovered the existence of girls," Dikdi said. "You should be showing him how things are with women, not the other way around."

Sabelu just scowled, much to the amusement of the other priests and anyone within earshot.

Yukpa lived in Yonhi, formerly Deer Clan though now associated with Bear Clan. A few years older than him, her father and uncles had died in the War of the Old Land, leaving her mother and grandmother to care for her and her seven siblings and numerous cousins in a new and strange town. Despite seeing her only at the festival each year, it wasn't any of her competitive talents that had caught his eye. Truth be told, she wasn't especially talented in any of the competitions and rarely competed; she came mostly to support her brothers and sisters in their events and keep their camp tidy. She was, however, quite skilled in the sorceries, especially the war sorceries, as befitted Bear Clan.

There was no rhyme or reason that Sabelu could point to as to why he looked at her versus any of the other Bear Clan women, or any of other other female war sorceresses. Trying to puzzle it out was like trying to discern the ripples around an active Shadow. What made it worse was that he knew he wasn't going to marry her. She was going to marry a man from Eagle Clan; they were going to live in Yonhi and have many children together.

At the same time, she was pretty. She was powerful and skilled in the sorceries. Any time he saw her at the festival, she always appeared attentive to her family's needs while they were competing, and she watched her nieces and nephews while their parents were busy. He knew her many secrets and annoying habits, but they seemed somehow less important.

Of course, how did he even approach a woman when he already knew everything about her? He watched other young men and women meet and talk at the festivals. What's your name, where are you from, who is your family, what is your ancestry, what are your hobbies, can you cook, can you hunt? He already knew all that about Yukpa. True, she didn't necessarily know so much about him, but conversation tended to require another person. He wasn't good at small talk, or empathy, or anything that might make him even remotely attractive. He really didn't have any friends, so his prospects in any other social endeavors were somewhat limited.

"Oh, don't feel bad," Asdeoha said, his tone somewhere between dismissive and condescending. "With our longer lives, it's no hurry to marry, not like it used to be. After all, look at your mother. And with your duties, your prestige as adelohosgi, I'm sure there are more important things to worry about right now."

Their gazes met, and Sabelu couldn't help but glance a time or two at the puppeteer standing just behind Asdeoha's left shoulder. The first time, the priest did not react to Sabelu's shifting gaze. The second time, he looked a tad suspicious. The third time, he turned to look as well. To no surprise, he did not see the Shadow.

"Something wrong?" Asdeoha inquired.

By the time the priest turned back round to look at Sabelu, Sabelu had gathered up a few things and made some excuse to leave, an errand they would normally send the acolytes to run. He wouldn't say that he was afraid necessarily, but he got the distinct feeling of the walls closing in and a kind of dark energy—darker than normal anyway—radiating from the Shadow. Was it a laugh? A threat? Something else? He didn't want to stick around to find out. He'd had to pretend to get along with everyone for too long. The Shadows taunted him for it. He needed to get rid of them, but helping people deal with their minor vices didn't seem to be making much progress on that front.

"Running doesn't make the best impression either."

Sabelu had run the easy errand, then headed to his favorite spot on the slope, overlooking the bowl. Yawi sat beside him, and the wolf had spoken.

"I'm not concerned with impressions," Sabelu said. "I'm concerned for my own sanity. You've seen what I've had to go through. You've gotten in a few scuffles on the street; you don't have to pretend."

"Quite frankly, neither do you."

"No, but sometimes it's necessary."

Yawi made a grunting noise and lay down. "So then, what's next?"

"Now, we sit and wait until Asdeoha comes up to talk to me."

"Oh? What is he going to talk to you about?"

Sabelu glanced at Yawi, and the wolf glanced back. Yawi tilted his head. "What?"

"If I told you the conversation we're going to have, and then Asdeoha came up here and we had that conversation, which one do you think the Author would record in the Book?"

The sound that came from the wolf was a bit like the sound he made right before a yawn, but elongated and trilled in a way that suggested puzzlement. Finally he said, "I don't know. I'm only a White. I have my task and I do my task. You are the ones with choice and destiny."

"I think it would be the second one," Sabelu finally decided. "Assuming any of this is recorded at all, it would be more significant than just a conversation between me and you."

Yawi crossed one paw over the other. "Well then, what's he going to say when he comes up here?"

Sabelu only got about halfway through the conversation before spying Asdeoha. He made to stand, but the priest put up a hand and instead joined him sitting on the ground. For a long moment, the two of them just looked out over the bowl. The puppeteer loomed behind them, and for Sabelu, it was like standing under a cold rain. Yawi got in a defensive position, fur standing on end, but made no aggressive move beyond baring his teeth.

"It's a nice view," the priest commented. "I can see why you like it, why you come here."

Sabelu did not look at him as he repressed a shiver. "It's peaceful. And quiet."

"Yes, it can get a bit stuffy in the townhouse during the summer."

"But you didn't come out here to make small talk."

Asdeoha sighed in somewhat serious resignation. "No." He shifted position. "I'm going to be honest, Sabelu—"

"I hope you've been nothing less so far," Sabelu cut in, giving the priest a look.

The priest gave him a look of his own, then went back to staring across the bowl. "There is some concern about you."

"And water is wet. Get to the point."

"Your lack of social graces is somewhat concerning. If we are to guide the people, we must understand them. Now then, you might say that you understand them very well, understand them better than they understand themselves. This is fine, but you lack the inherent empathy to make them understand. If it makes it easier on you, you can tell us your visions and we can relay them in a way that is more empathetic, more palatable to the people."

Sabelu gave him another look. "The words you speak are different from your intentions. Doing that, you could shut me away and make up whatever you wanted, just as you've already done with the others. Pretend it came from me and the people will accept it."

A twinge of frustration passed through Asdeoha, but his external reaction was minimal. He covered it up with a shrug and said, "It would save your image, anyway. Look at you up here, putting yourself above everyone else, sitting here and speaking to no one. Just now, it appeared as though you held half a conversation. We all want peace and solitude at times, and maybe you need it more than most, with everything you claim to see. Or maybe it would help if you had someone to talk to who could understand. Although a woman and not as prominent as you, I understand your sister has some shadow of prophetic ability as well. She cannot be a priest, but if it would help, we could arrange for—"

"You will leave her out of this," Sabelu cut in sharply. "This fight is between us." He let out a breath. "But it doesn't have to be."

A strange thing happened then. The puppeteer Shadow behind them began speaking—hissing, really—and Asdeoha echoed the words just half a breath after. "Of course it does. You don't see things the way we do. You don't worship the way we do. Oh, you may perform the same rituals, but your mind, your heart, your soul is elsewhere, on other gods, other spirits. The Whites, I believe they're called in your fabled Books?"

"You don't believe things happened the way the Books say?" Sabelu asked rhetorically. Out of the corner of his eye, he saw the rest of the wolf pack making their way up the slope.

"Your great-uncle Anagalisgi followed the Whites and our ancestors lost the War of Removal, and they had to flee here. His brother, Yvgidahi, touted the Whites in his bid for unity which nearly ended in an assassination and another war. Your father claimed to see Whites in the War of the Old Land, and we lost the war, nearly all of our fighting men."

"Then you openly admit to following the Shadows."

"Sabelu, you may possess a great trove of knowledge beyond what someone your age should know and understand, but you lack real, practical experience. You barely even grasp the concept of love. You are too young and naive to truly appreciate what the world is like. We've been here for over one hundred years now, and what do we have to show for it?" Now Asdeoha stood. "Whenever one of Anagalisgi's line rears his—or her—head with some prophetic mantra and starts speaking of the Whites, bad things happen. War happens. I would be willing to bet you spoke of Whites and Shadows to Ganhv before he died; what does that tell you?" He went on before Sabelu could speak. "Yvgidahi said the past is the past. Now, the present moment, is what matters. We're not Cherokee or Choctaw or Lenape or American anymore. We are Krydik. We have no need for the Whites or the wars they bring. And we have no need for their prophets. And if you continue to preach the Whites, it will only bring war again."

Now Sabelu stood, eye to eye with Asdeoha. "Is that a threat?"

Yawi and the pack surrounded the puppeteer, barking and snarling.

Even if Asdeoha did not see the Whites and Shadow, the nervousness of the puppeteer caused him to be nervous as well, though he tried to keep a strong face. The Shadow no longer spoke through him, and he was momentarily at a loss for words. The best he could come up with on his own was, "Consider it a warning."

"You say that as if I don't know how this all turns out," Sabelu said. "I know what you're going to do to me."

One of the wolves lunged at the Shadow, snapping at its heels. As it swung with its huge claws, another wolf took a turn.

"You may know a lot, but you are no god," Asdeoha replied, now more nervous, though the part of him that was still human was having trouble figuring out why he was so anxious. "Things can change."

"Yes," Sabelu told him. "Things are going to change."

The puppeteer fled, Asdeoha with him. Three of the wolves gave chase while Yawi and the rest howled their approval over the minor victory. Once they were safely gone, Sabelu sat back down in the grass. Two of the remaining wolves trotted off while Yawi and the others lay down around him, smiling as they panted.

"I think you're right," Yawi said. "That was much more exciting than our conversation."

Sabelu sighed. "You and your pack could have torn that puppeteer to shreds. But it would have shattered Asdeoha. I saw the hold the puppeteer has on him, the connection that allowed the Shadow to put words in his mouth." He shook his head in disbelief. "Is there any way to safely break that?"

"Anyone still alive has the chance," one of the other wolves said. "In the same way that an animal in a trap still has a chance to escape as long as it is still alive. It is just a matter of wanting it badly enough, being willing to do what is necessary, even if it means chewing off a limb."

Sabelu sighed again. "But animals know when they're in a trap."

"Humans long before you made their choice," the third wolf said. "They traded the ability to see for the ability to know."

Sabelu nodded. "A blind man may know a lot, but he will never have the full picture. And a man born blind is at a special disadvantage. Which is why a man born with sight, among a population of the blind, is a reviled oddity."

The wolves grunted and nodded their approval. Sabelu looked at Yawi. "Are analogies just part of being an adelohosgi? I've sworn to not be like my uncle, yet here I am."

Yawi made a motion that might have been interpreted as a shrug. "How does a man with sight explain what he sees to a man without sight, except that he must relate it through words and other means that the blind man does understand?"

Sabelu just sighed.

There was a lot that needed to get done. Minor chores, small errands, preparation for a wedding. But for the moment, Sabelu just sat and looked out over the bowl, the life going on in Aktiya Waya. The festival was fun and all, but the end of it sparked a sudden urgency among the people. Summer was just about gone and now was the time for the full harvest and preparation for winter. Any crops that had been left through the festival were now being harvested, with only a few select plants or varieties permitted to remain until the first frosts. Meanwhile, more hunts were being organized, with a large group of men in the horse pens choosing their mounts.

"With the sorceries, your people have no need for such frequent sustenance," Yawi observed. "Feeding the pups aside, why do they do it?"

"It's tradition," Sabelu answered. "It is the way of our people."

"But why do something if it is not necessary?" Yawi glanced at the other wolves. "We hunt and eat, fight and protect. We find shelter and sleep."

"You also run around and romp and play," Sabelu cut in, giving the wolf a knowing look. "Pups might play because it begins their training to fight. Why do you do it?"

If a wolf could look embarrassed, Yawi was certainly embarrassed as he admitted, "Because it is fun. It is part of being pack. It part of the hierarchy."

"That's why we do the things we do." He gestured to the men in the horse pen, most of them mounted now and preparing to head out. "It is part of being pack. It is part of being Krydik. To provide food, to strengthen the pack bonds and establish the hierarchy, to help others who are struggling."

"Wolves have no need for bows and arrows," the second wolf said. "We have no need for horses."

"Of course you do. Horses are messengers and transportation. I would be willing to bet that you have worked with a White horse before, to relay a message quickly when you yourselves are out of range. Perhaps a wounded animal has ridden on its back to safety. As for the bow, you work alongside other fighters. Maybe you've fought beside a White bear or some other fighting White because they possessed a skill you did not."

The second and third wolf glanced at each other.

"You have the benefit of cooperation," Sabelu went on. "Other than the horses, we don't have that benefit."

Yawi sat up and stretched. "Then why do you not keep livestock anymore?"

Sabelu blinked and stood, suddenly annoyed. "Because it's not our way."

"Why?"

He couldn't decide if Yawi was trying to bait him into an argument, guide him to some realization, or if he was genuinely curious, but the question still irritated him as he started walking away, back down the slope. "Because we have to keep our skills sharp."

The wolves trotted after him. "Why?"

"Because it is our way."

"That is circular reasoning," Yawi said. "You hunt so you can eat. Is the goal to hunt or to eat? If the goal is to eat, then plants and livestock would be far easier. If the goal is to hunt, then why do you only do so when food is low?"

"It's disrespectful to take more than necessary." Sabelu went on before Yawi could speak. "Why do wolves hunt in packs? Why do bears hibernate? Why does anyone do anything except that it is who they are, their way of doing things?"

"It was once tradition for your people to kill each other. Why stop doing that? It was your way."

"It was a bad tradition."

"Was it bad for your kin to go to war in the Old Land?"

"We were trying to save our people in the Old Land, trying to help them."

"It was observed that there were Whites and Shadows on both sides. Was it a bad tradition to kill some men but not others?"

Sabelu sighed dramatically. "Only my father and grandfather had the benefit of seeing the Whites and Shadows. The rest had to make do."

"Does ignorance excuse a crime?"

Now Sabelu stopped and turned to face the wolf. "What are you asking, Yawi? What are you trying to get me to say or realize?"

Yawi just looked at him. Then it dawned on him.

"I know I have to help people," Sabelu said defensively. "I know I have to drive out the Shadows but spare the people. I know. I understand. The puppeteer with Asdeoha..." He let out a breath and rearranged his words. "The people don't understand that their rituals and worship are incorrect; they're going to the wrong place, feeding the wrong spirits. We have to educate them, strengthen the pack in the right way. It's not enough to drive the Shadows out; we have to bond the people to the Whites, as you and I are bonded." He paused. "As Anagalisgi is bonded to Ge'gwogv." He nodded. "Because it is our way."

Now the wolf looked pleased, almost smug, though it could have just been how the expression presented itself on the canine face.

Sabelu nodded. "And I know just where to begin."

The three wolves barked in delight, each one giving a small romp and wagging their tail.

"Keep Asdeoha busy," Sabelu said. "I need to find Pakanli and Nonya."

The three wolves ran off, still barking in delight and romping for another twenty feet before settling into formation, Yawi at the head.

Pakanli and Nonya had grown up together, both fatherless from the War of the Old Land, and it had been clear from the beginning, even without consulting the spirits and family members, that they were meant to be together. They had denied it with much embarrassment over the years, but finally gave in to fate and declared their marriage intentions.

Sabelu found Pakanli's mother, Abonta, outside her home, preparing the harvest. Some went to be preserved for the winter, while some was set aside for the wedding.

"Ah, greetings, Sabelu," Abonta said, barely looking up from her work as he approached. "To what do I owe the pleasure?"

Her words were kind enough, but her real fear was that he was going to tell her that the union between her daughter and future son-in-law was ill-advised and should be stopped. While Asdeoha was the head priest and had declared the marriage sound, and Sabelu only just inducted as a full priest, Abonta was accompanied by a small White songbird on either shoulder which gave her subconscious partiality to Sabelu's opinions.

"I was wondering if you had found anyone to conduct your daughter's wedding," he told her.

Abonta made a kind of scoffing sound as she picked up an ear of corn to inspect it. "Pah." She gave him a look. "It was supposed to be Ganhv. But we see how that worked out. At least he was able to complete the blood taking ceremony, though I admit I'm a bit dubious about that." Sabelu did not know how to respond to that, so he remained silent. Abonta picked up another ear of corn and continued, "Are you offering yourself?" She grinned. "So eager to step into your role as priest, eh? I understand."

"Ganhv died moons ago," Sabelu observed. "Why wait so long to find a replacement?"

Abonta laughed. "In the Old Land, my mother said, the villages were so far apart, it would take a moon to travel from one to another, trying to bring bride and groom's families together, trying to get everything coordinated so the food was hot and fresh for the celebration." She gestured around and picked up a gourd. "These days, we have everything we need right here. The families, the food, the priests." She set the gourd down and looked up at him. "But I will admit, I never expected you to volunteer yourself. You've never been especially...social. Oh, you perform the rituals, but you always seem very...detached, very distant from what is going on. You always look happiest when you're by yourself on the hillside there. Or, I think you're by yourself. Sometimes it looks like you're talking to someone, but I never see anyone there." She waved a hand. "But that's no matter. I suppose you talk to the spirits, and I should not interfere or inquire into that."

"Um, yes," Sabelu said awkwardly. "Anyway, I thought you might want something, a revived tradition."

"Oh?" Abonta grabbed an ear of corn, but while her fingers worked, her eyes remained fixed on Sabelu. "Sabelu, surely you know that our family is traditionally Choctaw and Nonya is traditionally Cherokee. Where does this tradition originate?"

"That's why I call it a revived tradition, for the Krydik."

"I'm listening."

He explained the idea. It was a modification of the Cherokee wedding, where the groom would present a knife as a symbol of his protection for the bride, and the bride would present an ear of corn as a symbol of her provision for the household and family. But it also incorporated elements similar to the Choctaw tradition of draping the bride in ribbons.

He already knew Abonta would agree to it, but there was something exciting about seeing her eyes light up at the mention of the revived tradition. He did not miss how the White songbirds on her shoulders sang their delight as well, and perhaps it was this which influenced her to say yes.

"It will take a lot of hard work to pull it off in the short time we have left until the wedding," Abonta mused, pausing in her sorting of food, "but I have a few young nieces who aren't doing much for this wedding." She stood. "I'll grab them and have them sort all this out while I..." Her attention left Sabelu and she wandered off to find people and assign duties.

Sabelu left the area and went on his way. A few minutes later, as he was walking around town, Yawi caught up to him. The wolf trotted happily, mouth open in a huge smile while his tongue lolled contentedly.

"I don't suppose you managed to chase off the puppeteer and destroy it?" Sabelu asked.

"No," Yawi replied, though that fact did not do much to dull the wolf's joy. "We did manage to chase a flock of vices out of the townhouse, and a couple indulgences. It was great fun. It kept the puppeteer busy while you tended to your duties."

"Well, I'm glad you enjoyed yourself. Chasing out some of the vices and indulgences should make things smoother for the wedding. For the guests, anyway."

"What wedding?"

Sabelu looked up, seeing that he'd returned home and it was his mother who had spoken. She watched him from where she sat and worked on repairing a pair of pants for his father, where a stick had torn a hole in the shin.

"Um...I'm performing the ceremony for Pakanli and Nonya," he answered. "It was supposed to be Ganhv, but obviously he can't do it."

The Shadow of Fear was perched on Nendawagan's shoulder, the vulture form a huge contrast to the little White songbirds that accompanied Abonta. Elsewhere in the house, the ants maintained their perimeter, the mice scurried from here to there, the spiders worked to catch the tiniest of Shadows that sought to avoid the ants, and there was evidence that the rabbit had been by recently.

Yawi bared his teeth at the vulture who hissed and shifted position on his host's shoulder to face the wolf.

"This is your first wedding, isn't it?" Nendawagan asked. The Shadow of Fear told her that something was going to go horribly wrong—he would forget something, drop something, or otherwise mess something up—and he would make a fool of himself, after working so hard to shake off the negative reputation he'd garnered, and from that, he would disgrace the wedding, which wouldn't reflect well on anyone. But with the Shadow distracted by Yawi, however briefly, this fear was more like inarticulate background noise rather than an active thought.

He nodded in response to her question. "Yes, it is."

Yawi took a swipe at the Shadow, his paw passing through Nendawagan's shoulder just below the vulture's talons. The vulture spread its wings wide for balance as it hopped on one foot, nearly falling backwards.

Nendawagan grinned. "Oh, lovely." The vulture regained balance, both feet on her shoulder. She frowned. "Was there a reason they asked you?" Fear told her that it was because they were hoping to humiliate him in some way.

"I offered it. There is a tradition that needs reviving, and in doing so, I hope to drive out more of the Shadows from this place and establish more Whites."

The statement got the attention of the Shadow who turned and hissed at him. But from that distraction, Yawi was able to grab the ugly bird in his teeth and rip him off Nendawagan's shoulder. The vulture let out a screech, and the Shadow began shifting forms, now fully intent on the attacking White. Using the distraction, a white Mouse scurried up Nendawagan's leg and hid in a pocket in her dress.

Nendawagan's grin widened. "That's a good thing, right?"

"Of course it is."

"When is the wedding?"

"Three days."

She nodded. "Good. And maybe afterwards you can tell us—myself and your father and siblings—what we can do to help you? You take us to this cliffside city, tell us all these things, but we've done nothing productive since."

"It's coming, I promise," Sabelu told her.

His mother looked uncertain but finally nodded. "Well, it took you this long to look at a woman, so what's a little longer to wait?"

Sabelu sighed and looked away, much to his mother's amusement.

"Oh, come now, Sabelu," she teased. "Who says you can't look at a woman? There is no rule against marrying and having children. If not for your grandfather, the prophetic line would have died out."

"Then it's a good thing Galiliga, Netami, and Blaknik are here," Sabelu stated.

"Well, Yukpa might be in Yonhi, but she is looking at you, not your brother. If I understand correctly, she is some relative of Pakanli, so you might see her at the wedding."

"A distant relative."

"That doesn't mean much. Families used to have to travel for days, all over the place, to coordinate a wedding. Young men would go on long expeditions just to impress a girl. A few days to and from Yonhi is nothing. She may come under the assumption that it's for Pakanli, but I suspect she would be looking at you. That's what weddings are for, after all, for the single men and women."

He sighed. "Tsitsi..."

His mother shrugged. "Give it a chance is all I'm saying. You can't go through life alone, not with your destiny."

He did not respond, and he tried not to react too greatly to the fight still raging in the middle of the room. Yawi had the Shadow pretty well defeated, and the Shadow was making some ghastly noises. The wolf delivered a final, devastating bite, and the larger Shadow of indulgence erupted into half a dozen smaller vices. The vices screamed in fury as they slithered away, out of the house, disappearing through the rock.

Sabelu left the house, Yawi again trotting beside him, stopping occasionally to paw at his mouth and noise or give a few quick licks to minor wounds.

"I need water," the wolf complained. "Shadows taste terrible, leave all sorts of rot taste in your mouth."

"I wouldn't know," Sabelu said.

"Sure, rub it in, why don't you? I'll be back."

The wolf broke into a run, heading for the slope and then vanishing. Sabelu watched him go, then turned and headed for the horse pens.

"They left this morning," Hoshonti said as he approached. "But if you want to catch up, I've still got a few good mounts."

"I'm not going to join the drives," Sabelu told him, "but a sturdy mount would be most welcome."

The horse tender huffed a sigh and addressed his mutter to no one in particular as he flagged down Hieli. "I keep telling you, you have to decide what kind of horses you want. Do you want fast? Do you want strong? Do you want sturdy? The characteristics for these are not always compatible if you want specialty horses. Hanepi understands this."

The mutterings were intended to be rhetorical, but Sabelu couldn't resist adding in, "That's because Anpa O Wican'hpi only has use for fast horses, like Hanepi breeds. Aktiya Waya has more use for sturdy breeds, but our competitive nature tells us that we can't let them win the horse races every year."

Hoshonti waved a hand. "Bah. Kids are too focused on the tournaments. Breed for what we need, what we have use for. A horse may be fast, but we don't have the plains like Deer Clan. We need the sturdier mounts, the ones that can handle the rocks and the sharper turns, avoid trees and obstacles while on a drive." He sighed. "But that won't win the horse race, as you said." He shook his head. "Damn tournaments. It's gone from a unifying force to an obsession, almost a new religion among the young people."

Sabelu did not say anything to that, and Hieli returned in short order, leading a brown and white mare. Sabelu mounted up and was on his way in short order.

A few of the wolves had taken up sentry positions at the entrance to the bowl. Their expressions said they were less than enthusiastic about listening to the conversation between the human sentries. One wolf, presumably the senior one of the group, was more than happy to break off and follow him out of the bowl into the wilderness.

In the old days, Sabelu knew, sentries were expected to stay quiet while guarding a place. On Hlohi, there weren't any threats that wouldn't smell them before hearing them, but it still felt lazy and disrespectful.

"Changes need to be made," Sabelu said aloud, glancing at the wolf beside him. "Everyone should have a White who accompanies them, not a Shadow. And we should learn from them, reconnect to tradition in a new way. The right way."

The wolf glanced at him but said nothing.

Sabelu had no real destination in mind, but he found himself on a rocky ledge overlooking the forest to the south. He looked at the landscape, how the mountains descended into gentle foothills and, eventually, into plains. To the west, about four days' walk, was Yonhi in the forest. To the east, about seven days, was Lehoyed on the ocean.

Here was the Sacred Wolf, still slumbering peacefully. Near Anpa O Wican'hpi was the Cursed Zukatopa, lying in wait. The ruins near Lehoyed were fascinating, but the entrance to the city only, the rest of it obliterated. Only the Minotaur remained, its holiness yet to be determined. What other Great Ones were out there? There were rumors of one far to the south, in a desert, but no one had ever actually sought it out. What else was there to find out there, and how did it tie in with the Whites and Shadows?

He thought about his father's Book, the story of his parents' courtship and their adventure into the underground city. Although he intended to consider the story itself, both what was recorded in the Book and what his parents had told them over the years, he found his thoughts going in a new direction. What if he and Yukpa sought out the Sacred One of the Desert? She was capable, and it would be—

No, he mentally chided himself. No, he couldn't do that. He wouldn't do that. A childish fantasy only. He knew for certain that they would not be going on such an adventure. He knew that just like he knew everything else.

On the other hand, sometimes better discoveries were made when in pursuit of something else. That was how the Lehoyed ruins and the Cursed Zukatopa had been discovered.

He had his task. He knew what he needed to do, and he only had a limited time to do it. He didn't have time for this.

"Everyone has time for love, Sabelu."

Sabelu jumped and whirled to see Anagalisgi standing beside him.

"Tsidushi?" He questioned. "I thought you couldn't come to Hlohi?"

"I can go anywhere by directive of the Author," his uncle told him. "But in this instance, you fell asleep against a rock and didn't realize it."

Sabelu blinked. "Oh." He shifted his stance. "Then why are you here? Why not take me to your cave? What words do you have for me?"

Anagalisgi grinned and looked out over the forest. "This is just a social call on my way from here to there. Thought I would check in since we haven't spoken for a little while. Thought you might need some encouragement with this girl you like."

Sabelu groaned. "Why now, Tsidushi? It's so...inconvenient. Surely this wouldn't be the Shadows' doing? Shadows don't love."

His uncle nodded. "You are correct that they don't, but that doesn't mean they've never taken advantage of such things. You're a man, Sabelu. And whether you are an adelohosgi or a fletcher, you still have the desires that all men have. A little late, maybe, but still there."

"I'm not going to marry her, Tsidushi. Why bother?"

Anagalisgi laughed. "Did you expect to kill anything with the blunt arrows your father gave you when you were five? Maybe you would pretend you could, but no one really expected a five year old to hunt. It was simply practice. You observed others who did it well, imitated it to the best of your abilities, and built up your own skills. Love is no different. You have watched your parents, and others through the people and throughout time, and now the same desire has welled up within you at the sight of Yukpa. Maybe you won't marry, but the experience will be invaluable."

"But why now?" Sabelu whined. "Not only is it distracting to me, but Asdeoha is going to try to exploit it. I don't need that kind of stress when I'm already trying so hard to figure out this problem with the Shadows." He added quickly before his uncle could get in a sound, "What's out there?" He gestured to the south. "What do the Great Ones have to do with the Whites and Shadows?"

For a long moment, his uncle just looked at him, studied him. Then he looked at Yawi who had appeared by means Sabelu did not know. Yawi did not say anything, but something in the wolf's expression must have spoken to Anagalisgi.

"This place. This planet that you call Hlohi. It was once a haven of mortal Shadows."

"Mortal Shadows?" Sabelu questioned.

His uncle nodded. "When a White or Shadow 'dies' so to speak, they are reborn. The Whites are rebirthed by the Author, and the Shadows are recycled by the dragon. In the original fallout between Whites and Shadows, the dragon did not have the strength or ability to both fight the Whites and recycle the fallen Shadows. Some of those Shadows sought refuge in mortal creatures, thinking that if they could suspend themselves long enough in a fleshy being, they could be recycled later.

"It isn't known whether they couldn't be recycled, or if the dragon simply refused. I don't think it matters except to be glad that so many Shadows were culled from the ranks. What does matter is that the union of Shadow and fleshy creature produced a mortal being capable of taking the form of any creature it came into contact with."

"A shape-shifter," Sabelu stated.

Anagalisgi nodded. "That's right. They couldn't travel across dimensions and had no communion with either Shadow or White. Because they had been rendered mortal, their desires shifted into mortal survival."

"They created a civilization."

"Yes."

Sabelu shifted his stance and nodded thoughtfully. "When the Tacagans arrived, the dragon used it as an opportunity to get rid of such abominations. Or the dragon used the Tacagans and brought them here for that specific purpose."

"I thought the same thing," Anagalisgi agreed. "Get rid of the half-bred creatures as the dragon desired, and pave the way for the Krydik to take up residence, clean the Shadows from this place, and do the Author's work. A kind of poetic justice."

For a long moment, the two stood there in silence. No one believed that he was the first to walk upon any ground on Hlohi, but there was a chilling effect to consider that the previous people had not been just some unknown people, but a civilization built from half-bred Shadows.

"Was there no redemption for them?" Sabelu asked at last. "After a hundred or a thousand generations, when the shape-shifters had long forgotten their terrible origins, was there no hope of redemption for the part of them that was mortal, or were they doomed from the start because of their immortal ancestry?"

Anagalisgi hesitated. Then, "I don't know. That would be a question for the Author herself. Though I am curious about your interest in it. It's been a thousand years since they were wiped out. All that remains are their broken cities."

Sabelu did not answer for a long moment. Finally he said, "I think they could. I think the dragon refused to recycle them, because it thought them weak and frail, or else I would expect there to have been more fighting over this place. But you said they had no communion with either Shadow or White, and if the dragon abandoned them, why not send in the Whites to finish them off, cull the ranks entirely as you put it?" Sabelu nodded. "I think they could be saved. I also think maybe they were starting to come around. I think the Shadows held some kind of veil over them, to stop them from reaching the Whites. But the ants prevailed, faithfully building that foundation. When the half-Shadows finally got a glimpse of things beyond the Shadows' veil, maybe they tried to ally themselves with the Whites, and that's when the dragon sent the Tacagans to finally destroy them.

His uncle looked thoughtful. "It's an interesting theory." He glanced at Yawi but the wolf betrayed nothing. "But I don't see how it makes a difference in the here and now, the work you have before you."

"About their redemption? No, it doesn't make a difference. Understanding the history of the Great Ones and the underground city..." Sabelu nodded. "Well, it does put things in perspective."

"You're still not ready for that," Anagalisgi warned.

"Maybe not, but it's the first live target I've had to aim at with my blunt arrows."

DKSᏁ DVᏆT

Atsodune Adolv'i
Veiled Threats

Sabelu had memories not his own of old Choctaw weddings. The bride's family would line the streets from the location of the wedding as far out onto the road as possible to welcome the groom and his family. Food and gifts were brought for attendees, and it could take hours to get everything sorted. He knew all of the weddings ever held from his father's mother's family, including her own, first when she'd married John Aberdeen, and then later when she married Chilita.

He also had memories of old Cherokee weddings, most of them informed from his mother's father's family. He knew well his grandfather's first wedding to Advtowa. He had presented her with a haunch of venison, and she had presented him with an ear of corn. Midway through the celebration, they had stolen away to consummate their union, then returned to the party. He also knew of his grandfather's second wedding to Mesim, an unusual combination of Cherokee, Lenape, and American.

There was no standard Krydik wedding, nothing plain or ordinary about any of the unions that took place. Most of it had to do with the prevailing historic people in each clan. For Deer Clan, their weddings leaned toward traditional Sioux. For Eagle Clan, Navajo. For Wolf Clan and Bear Clan, Cherokee and Choctaw.

The wedding as it was currently laid out was a fascinating mix. With exception of the single revived tradition that he had proposed, Sabelu had no part in the extraneous wedding plans, anything that didn't have to do with the actual union of man and wife before the spirits.

The women of Pakanli's family lined one side of the road. Their dress was rather plain with minimal jewelry or adornment, but each one held some manner of harvest or homemaking: a basket of corn, a large gourd, a decorated pair of moccasins, and so on. On the other side of the road, the men of Nonya's family were dressed as if for war, or maybe just a small skirmish. Each one wore tough leather armor and carried at least a pair of knives, and some of the younger men also sported a bow.

Pakanli arrived first, escorted by Nonya's mother and sisters. The escort was also plain, for Pakanli was the real beauty. She wore the softest doeskin dress, bleached almost white and decorated with much silk, bead work, and quill work. Around her shoulders was a beautiful woven shawl, dyed many bright colors and decorated with beads. She had feathers and flowers in her braided hair which fell over her shoulders and went nearly to her knees. In one hand, she carried a basket of many vegetables.

Sabelu, watching and waiting at the door to the townhouse, noted that while everyone paid proper attention to Pakanli as she walked by, several of the young men from Nonya's family were still looking at some of the girls from Pakanli's family. He found himself looking too, wondering if Yukpa was nearby. He chastised himself for his distraction, blinking back to the present just as Pakanli approached and paused at the door.

"Welcome, Pakanli," Sabelu greeted formally, taking a bowl of red paint and marking a wolf's paw on her hand before she went inside.

Nonya arrived second. He was escorted by Pakanli's brothers. As before, the escort was comparatively plain, looking prepared for nothing more menacing than a fight after a bad night of gambling. Nonya himself was dressed for war. He had armor made of leather and bone, large cages of antlers protecting his shoulders and making him look that much bigger. He had half a dozen knives on him, two bows, and even the old pistol his father had used in the War of the Old Land. He carried one end of a spit on which rested a large carcass ready for roasting. The other end was supported by one of his escorts.

"Welcome, Nonya," Sabelu greeted. Nonya did not set down the spit, merely shifted the weight so Sabelu could paint a blue bear print on his hand before going inside.

He let Nonya go first, then followed the couple and their escort groups inside. Behind him, a small group of people consisting of other close relatives who were not part of the escorts also filed in. The rest of the people, he knew, were busy portioning out the gifts for the attendees and would then line the streets from the townhouse to the house Pakanli and Nonya would share.

In the townhouse, a fire had been built, and Sabelu went to stand between it and the couple, with a low table between him and them. Pakanli had not let go of her vegetable basket, and Nonya and his helper continued to shoulder the weight of the carcass on the spit. On the table were two bowls. One held white paint, and the other held fresh tobacco and other herbs.

Sabelu lit the tobacco and said a prayer, asking for a blessing on the couple. Then he addressed the gathering at large.

"We are here to witness and celebrate the union between these two." He gestured to Pakanli who set down her basket of vegetables on the table. "Pakanli of Wolf Clan, with this basket of vegetables, you promise to be a good wife and mother for your children, that they will live and thrive and bring honor to your family, your clan, and your people."

He turned to Nonya who made a small motion to his helper. Together they slipped past Sabelu and maneuvered the spit over the fire. Once it was positioned, the helper retreated to the rest of the group and Nonya returned to his bride's side. An acolyte added a couple more logs to the fire, sending sparks leaping into the air.

"Nonya of Bear Clan, with this roast, you promise to provide for your wife and future children, that they may live and thrive and bring honor to your family, your clan, and your people."

Next Sabelu turned to the women who had escorted Pakanli. Each one had produced a brightly colored ribbon. Some were authentic silk from the Old Land, others were of a kind of silk that was made on Hlohi, and a couple were simply fine leather. The ribbons were decorated with either beads or embroidery, each with a specific animal.

"Pakanli, you make this promise before the spirits. As they watch us and guide us, as they teach us the way of the world and how to live in harmony with each other, so we must be open to their teachings. We must be as enthusiastic to learn as they are to teach."

He gave a nonverbal cue to Abonta who led the procession of women, each one laying a ribbon over Pakanli's head and speaking.

"The bear, fierce and protective of her cubs," Abonta said, draping the bear ribbon.

"The wolf, the teacher and former of the pack," another woman said.

"The deer, patient and gentle."

And on it went until approximately a dozen ribbons graced Pakanli's head.

The townhouse had been largely devoid of Shadows during this whole endeavor. The only one that remained, that was any kind of threat, was the one hanging around Asdeoha as he observed silently from the corner. If asked, he was merely watching Sabelu, seeing how it was his first wedding.

Yawi and the wolves kept the rest of the Shadows at bay, and as the ribbons were heaped on Pakanli's head, more Whites were escorted into the building. It was a small rodent-like creature, like Hlohi's version of a rabbit, that finally took a seat at Pakanli's feet.

Now he turned to the men who had escorted Nonya. Instead of beautiful ribbons, however, the men took their knives and gave Nonya a small cut on his hand, only a couple inches long, while reciting similar platitudes.

"The wolf, loyal and brave."

"The bear, strong and unyielding."

Sabelu had suggested using animal claw or tooth pendants and draping them around Nonya's neck. Pakanli's brother had insisted that was too weak. Their fathers and uncles had fought and died for the people; Nonya could at least know pain. By the time it was over, a dozen cuts later, Nonya, having weathered the ritual rather well, was bleeding all over his hand and arm, and drizzling on the ground. A larger creature of Hlohi that was somewhere between a wolf and a deer was posted by his side. The White Hlohi rabbit and the White Hlohi wolf-deer exchanged a glance, like two warriors promising to have each other's backs.

The couple was then brought under the single sacred blanket and made to drink from the two-spouted cup. Sabelu said another prayer and declared the couple fit for marriage.

From there, Nonya and Pakanli turned and ran out of the townhouse, through the streets lined with people, to the home that they would share. Once inside, all of the guests filled the townhouse to start eating and celebrating and giving out the prepared gifts. Nonya and Pakanli would consummate their marriage, then return to the party.

Sabelu's role was basically finished. The only other thing he might do was announce the couple's return and say another blessing over them. Otherwise, he was free to eat and leave if he so chose.

The carcass that Nonya had brought was actually for the couple themselves, the food that would sustain them for the first few days of their marriage (in order to make time for more, ahem, important things) and would be brought to them once it was done. For the guests, more food had been provided, on top of the take home baskets.

Sabelu watched the people mingle for a bit, let the elders of the families procure food for themselves before getting in line. A few cuts of meat and a variety of fresh, roasted vegetables graced his palette.

He didn't realize it until the music started that Asdeoha had vanished from the corner where he had been silently observing. No sooner did Sabelu turn his head to look for the priest than he appeared at his side.

"Interesting blend of traditions," the head priest commented levelly, his voice just loud enough to be heard by Sabelu and no one else.

"Familiar enough to both sides," Sabelu agreed, trying to come off as at least neutral. No need to upset the guests with feuding priests.

"What do you see for the newlyweds? Many children?"

"Nine, in fact."

Asdeoha nodded. "I hope they are all happy and strong."

They paused long enough to greet a few guests, nod along with some thanks and well wishes, and make some comment about the good food. The whole time, Sabelu could feel Asdeoha's Shadow looming over his shoulder.

"One thing I don't understand," Asdeoha murmured once they were again left alone. He turned slightly toward Sabelu and inclined his head. "Why invoke the Whites only? I thought this was a crusade for the Author and the Books; surely you wouldn't leave out the great creator from your prayers."

"If the people read the Books and understand them, they will know it is not the Author they should be praying to, nor the Whites," Sabelu said firmly.

The Shadow hissed, and Asdeoha shifted his stance uncomfortably.

"Then you are as much a heretic as I," the priest said.

"We work with what we have. We exist in this limited form and are bound by it, but only in the body. Our souls stretch far beyond that. I think you know this, but you're afraid to admit it. You're afraid of what's out there. Like looking at the ocean, you are content to get your feet wet, but you are afraid to swim because your real fear is drowning. Or being pulled apart by dangerous water creatures."

For the first time, Sabelu saw what he might have characterized as a tiny gap between man and Shadow. But this Shadow was not fooled by petty trickery, nor dazzled and distracted by the many Whites in the townhouse, some of whom were keeping one eye on the current exchange. This Shadow was not only powerful, but capable of multitasking. It kept the Whites at bay while hurrying to cover up the gap before Asdeoha could act on it.

"Does your Shadow have a name?" Sabelu pressed, hoping to widen the gap just a bit, just big enough for an ant. "We know of Yawi the White wolf, Ge'gwogv the White woodpecker, and there are others who have been given names. What about you, your Shadow?"

But the Shadow had closed the gap and now threw everything into reinforcing the wall it had built around itself and Asdeoha.

"Names are dangerous things, Sabelu, you know that," the priest said. "In Lehoyed, the old southwestern people won't even tell you their true names unless you are a very close relative. That's why you have to call them by their profession or skill or talent or anything else, out of fear of their name being invoked in a curse. They even dropped the 'g' from the town name because they didn't want people invoking it and cursing the town and its occupants."

"And your Shadow is afraid of the same," Sabelu stated. He tilted his head. "Do Shadows know fear? Is your Shadow afraid of the Whites in this room?"

Another small gap. Again the Shadow worked to cover it up.

"The Shadows do know fear," Asdeoha answered, at the Shadow's bidding. "And if the Whites are smart, they will mirror that fear and leave before things get worse."

"Worse how?" As if he needed to ask.

"You're causing problems. You know too much and you've seen too much. You've worked out how important the Krydik are, how important all the people in the Old Land are. Keep doing what you're doing, and you're going to attract some very unwanted attention."

"I already have," Sabelu said stubbornly.

"This?" Asdeoha made the smallest of gestures which only confirmed that he, too, could see the Whites and Shadows and was as aware of his Shadow as Sabelu was of Yawi. "This is the first day of competition. Ganhv was the practice round. Do you know what waits for you in the final round?"

"The dragon itself."

"Do you know what you have to go through to get there?"

"The cerberus, the black phoenix, the wolf-dog, and the serpent."

"And do you know how many have made it even that far?"

Sabelu gave him a look. "It only takes one well-placed arrow to kill."

Asdeoha nodded. "Maybe." He gestured to the wedding guests. "But here are all your arrows that missed. All these people, unaware of the true magnitude of things, the real stakes of this competition. All the people of the Old Land, eliminated in the first day or two of competition, the sweeping culls, the removals, the oppression."

"And now the Shadows attack the remnant that was saved, the

spearhead that will pierce them."

"You seem very certain of that."

"I've seen it," Sabelu told him, hoping his confidence masked his bluff. "It's already happened. I know what you're going to do to me, the plan that the Shadow is planting in your mind because it doesn't know what's coming. It wonders. It's afraid. It wants to head it off, but it is doing exactly what I know it will."

"Then why not buy yourself some time and save yourself some trouble?" Asdeoha wondered. "Why engage in this conversation? Why not use silence to cover your actions?"

Now it was Sabelu's turn to gesture discreetly. "Because it is as you've said: I'm causing trouble. I'm attracting attention. But a warrior is not afraid to look that trouble in the eye and challenge it."

Asdeoha grinned, but it was not a pleasant smile. "That must be your American blood, your white blood. Our people have always been cowards, Sabelu. Strike fast, then run away. Do not be seen, do not be taken alive if you can help it. It worked for us in the past. It was when we tried to adapt to white ways that we began to lose the war. Bravado got us nowhere."

"Then it's a good thing I am well-versed in all the old ways."

The head priest continued to smile, and it continued to make Sabelu's skin crawl. "You have much knowledge and great talent, Sabelu. No one denies this. Even the Shadows acknowledge that you are favored. But even your father has said that you can see everything except what is right in front of you." He made a tiny nod toward the guests. "Take Yukpa for example."

Sabelu's stomach did an uneasy flip. "I told you to leave her out of this. There is no future for us in any respect."

"Are you sure?" Asdeoha asked. "Do you know why? Does something happen to her? Are you incapable of saving her? Surely even if you are not meant to be, you would try to save her. If she is destined to live, then what does it matter what happens?"

"Leave her out of this," Sabelu repeated in a fierce hiss.

"Arrows, Sabelu," Asdeoha said, shrugging. "One arrow to kill, yes, but so many more that miss. Where is it that you will lose her? The second round, when things get a little harder? The later competitions, when the Shadow kings decide to put a decisive end to things? Could it be the dragon itself that does her in?"

The priest never raised his voice, yet Sabelu felt an explosive anger in his heart. Sweat broke out on his head and chest. Even Yawi by his side had his teeth bared, much to the amusement of Asdeoha's puppeteer who did little more than laugh.

"Think about your actions, Sabelu," Asdeoha said, his tone suggesting the conversation was ended. "Consider the consequences." His smile now was a little more genuine as he made a sweeping motion around the wedding party. "This is a very good thing we have here today." He lowered his voice as he turned back to Sabelu. "I would hate to see what such a thing would look like if the black phoenix decided to purge all of these Whites."

With that, the head priest departed. Sabelu was left standing there, skin burning hot, sweating atrociously. Then a clamor outside announced the return of Pakanli and Nonya, now consummated husband and wife, and Sabelu had to throw himself back into happy festivities.

He prayed for a blessing on the newlyweds which served as a cue for another, more lively round of singing and dancing. Sabelu stayed and watched, if only to be in the presence of the Whites who looked as enthusiastic as the guests. Some of them even looked like they might have been dancing or otherwise moved by the music, but Sabelu was not fooled into thinking they were being lax in their duties.

His eyes wandered to Yukpa who was across the room, speaking to a gaggle of women, relatives she might normally only see at the annual festival. Her gaze darted over to him a time or two, but she did not approach and he likewise refrained.

"Why do you resist the idea of a mate?" Yawi wondered, sitting beside him and following his gaze toward Yukpa. "True, the use of the sorceries makes it a less pressing matter, but you appear to resist even the thought of a mate."

"I don't want Asdeoha to hurt her, for one," Sabelu said, leaning forward so he could stare at the ground and speak quietly, hopefully so he wouldn't look or sound like a lunatic. "Besides, I already know we won't marry. Anagalisgi says it would be good experience anyway, except I know that I will never get married."

Yawi looked at him and tilted his head, expression genuinely confused. "Why not?"

"I don't know. I know the facts, not necessarily the reasons for them."

"Are you resistant to the idea of love?"

Sabelu looked up briefly. "Of course not. It is for the love of my people that I am doing all of this."

The wolf made a guttural sound. "Oh, human, you know there are different kinds of love. There is the love of the pack, the love of a parent, the love of a child. And there is the love of a mate. All different."

"Then it is for love that I don't want to risk Yukpa."

"Would it not be for love, then, that you would cease your endeavors, given the Shadow's threat? One kill strike, but many missed arrows."

"That would only be what is easy, not what is done for love. If I do nothing, millions will die. If I do something, slightly less than millions will die. There is no good answer."

"Then why not enjoy the happiness of a mate while it would last, even if it did not last forever? The pack has lost many members. Your kin have lost mates and pups. But they continue to do these things because of the joy it brings them, even not knowing what will happen."

Sabelu sighed, feeling slightly annoyed. "Except I do know what will happen. Right now, I have only a few years until my exile. I need to do as much as I can to prepare my family, prepare the people, and bring in the Whites." He paused and let his gaze linger on Yukpa as she, still in conversation, stood, twirled around twice, then bent over to grab something. "Chasing after a girl only takes me away from that task."

Yawi gave him a look. "What if chasing after the girl is the task?"

Sabelu shook his head, just slightly. "No. It's not. I appreciate the concern and the encouragement, but it's not going to happen."

The wolf still looked uncertain but said nothing more about it. After a moment of just sitting there, Yawi stood, stretched, yawned, and started nosing his way around the townhouse. He occasionally spoke to the other Whites, made a few interior patrol laps, then headed out of the townhouse to do the same outside.

Finally Sabelu himself stood, stretched, and left the townhouse. Yawi trotted up to him, but Sabelu put a hand up, saying, "No. Stay here. This pack is more important right now. Protect the Whites and the people in there."

Yawi dipped his head and returned to the party.

It was getting late but not yet fully night, though the growing darkness provided little relief from the heat, and most of the people who weren't at the wedding party were somewhere along the river for a refreshing swim.

Sabelu saw the Shadow before he saw the man. Or rather, men.

"If he knows what is going to happen, why doesn't he avoid it?" one man said, stepping behind him on the street.

"Maybe this is an important event," a second man said off to his left, blocking a side street.

"Good," a third said, stepping in front of him. "Means we're not completely wasting our time."

"Dilegwa," Sabelu acknowledged the third man. To the second, "Doltsi." And the first, "Debetsqua." He turned so he could keep all three of them reasonably within sight. "Hired by Asdeoha to push me around a little, try to scare me, send a message."

The three men closed in on him, their Shadows forming a smoky wall so as to fool outsiders into thinking nothing was amiss, at least at a first glance.

Debetsqua pushed Sabelu's shoulder so that he had to step back once to balance himself. "Seems like you already got the message then. Know what we're going to say before we even say it."

Dilegwa pushed him from the other side. "You know what we're going to do next?" Another push. "What about what we're going to do now?" Another push. "How about now?"

Sabelu gave him a look. "Do you know what I'm going to do?"

He barely uttered the last syllable before he dropped his shoulder and drove it into Dilegwa's gut, right at the bottom of his ribcage, feeling the slight flex of the bottom of the man's sternum in his shoulder. Dilegwa stumbled back several steps and fell to his seat. Sabelu ducked and twisted out of the way as Doltsi and Debestqua lunged for him. Still Debetsqua managed to grab hold of his left arm, but Sabelu came up swinging, delivering a perfect right hook to the man's jaw.

Debetsqua released Sabelu's left arm, but Doltsi was just as quickly locked onto his right, yanking it back and trying to pin it behind him. Sabelu dropped and slid around behind Doltsi. The assailant still had hold of his arm, but as Sabelu grabbed the knife on Doltsi's waist and got around behind him as if to cut his throat, Doltsi released his arm and danced away.

There was now a good four feet between Sabelu and his attackers. Dilegwa was back on his feet, standing beside Doltsi. Debetsqua was off to one side, whimpering and holding his jaw, trying to invoke Asvhnisgi to heal it, though he was sorely lacking in that particular skill. Meanwhile, Sabelu just stared them down with a small knife.

"Dilegwa and Doltsi," Sabelu said, not relaxing his ready stance. "You're cousins from the same clan. Your family is one of the oldest in Aktiya Waya. My grandfather's brother personally spoke to your great-great-grandmother, reassured her that the crossing from the Old Land would be safe for the baby she carried inside her." He glanced at Debetsqua who was meekly rejoining the scene, the pain in his jaw lessened even if it was not completely healed. "Debetsqua, your uncle spoke against the treachery of the rebels in Lehoyed, defended my grandfather."

"And yet you keep the company of that bastard traitor Kah Kitowak," Debetsqua said. It was unclear whether he spit in distaste of Kah Kitowak or because of his slurred speech.

That statement was used as a cue by the Shadows to prompt the men to attack again. This time, Dilegwa drew his knife and made a full lunge for Sabelu, pitching his shoulder just as Sabelu had done. Sabelu dropped to the ground and rolled to avoid the blow, but it cost him every other advantage he had as a passing kick from Dilegwa's foot dislodged the knife from his hand. At the same time, Doltsi was flying through the air at him, landing on Sabelu as he untwisted from the roll and pinning him to the ground. Debetsqua, a little wary and distracted now because of the pain in his jaw, jogged over to act as more of an intimidating threat than a combatant.

Sabelu wasted no time invoking Galo'ondiha ale Agi'a, a short burst of force that got Doltsi off him so he could breathe and scramble to his feet. Dilegwa had scooped up the knife he'd dropped and gave it back to his cousin.

A wolf howl split the air, though of the four of them, only Sabelu could hear it. He flinched at the sound, but his attackers took pleasure in their apparent victory over him.

"What's the end game here?" Sabelu asked, his gaze darting to the wolf which was a short distance down the street. "What are you hoping to accomplish?"

"You're the prophet," Dilegwa sneered. "You tell us."

The lone wolf trotted down the street, head down, teeth bared. Two more wolves showed up.

"If I told you, you wouldn't believe me," Sabelu said, his gaze darting toward the wolves again. Two more had shown up to bring the total to five. He glanced back at the men. "At least, not yet."

"Try us," Dilegwa challenged. "Asdeoha thinks you might be a dark prophet, maybe an evil witch. Looked all over to find a few warriors brave enough to challenge you and find out."

Now Yawi joined the pack, sprinting down the street to take the lead and lead the charge against the Shadows hovering around the three men. Only when the Whites and Shadows were fully engaged did Sabelu speak.

"Asdeoha didn't look all over," he said, heart hammering as he tried to stay focused on the three men. "He hasn't told anyone yet. He wants all of this to go away quietly, after what happened with Ganhv. But in his fear, he cast a spell of his own, to find men with Shadows, evil spirits, strong enough to challenge me."

"You're saying we have evil spirits hanging around us?" Dilegwa questioned, his hostility still present, but now with a twinge of doubt, not something he would recognize until later.

"Sounds like something an evil witch would say," Doltsi said. "Deflect the blame." His words were spoken partially out of true belief and partially as a man who wanted to save face with his friends and act tough in order to impress an older cousin.

One of the wolves landed where Debetsqua was standing. Even in the middle of a fight with teeth and claws flashing, the wolf still had a positive impact on the man with an injured jaw. "Evil witches lie," he told the cousins. "Sabelu doesn't lie."

With the flurry of fighting Whites and Shadows, Sabelu wouldn't hold it against them that their thoughts were muddled and racing too fast to catch.

"Whatever," Dilegwa said finally, sheathing his blade. "We did our job; we made our point." He turned as if to leave, but gave a last look at Sabelu and said, "I suggest you don't walk the streets alone."

Sabelu met his gaze and replied, "I don't."

The three men retreated, walking hurriedly away from the scene. The Shadows that had been hovering around them tried to go with them, but Yawi and the wolves and several other Whites who had been attracted to the area ran them down and kept them from reattaching to their hosts. They would eventually rejoin them, Sabelu knew, but the ants had been deployed, the seeds planted.

Sabelu himself returned home. A few minutes later, Yawi joined him. The wolf was panting heavily but looked excited and ready for more action. After a thorough inspection of the house, he stretched and lay on his side at Sabelu's feet at the table, resting his head on the floor.

"I'm here to protect you from things like this, you know," Yawi said, not moving.

"You are here to do the Author's work, not mine," Sabelu told him. "You didn't have to stay at the party."

"You left and sent me away, knowing that they would attack you."

"You left me, knowing that I was going out alone, away from the safety of the pack. What did you think might happen?"

Yawi looked up long enough to bare his teeth. "Do not presume to lecture me about the pack, nor of making choices and sacrifices."

Sabelu felt his ears burn hot and he nodded. "You're right. I'm sorry. That wasn't fair."

The wolf relaxed his lips and lay his head back down.

"Will you tell me the story of your fight with the cerberus? You said you were defending Anagalisgi."

For a long moment, the wolf did not speak, did not even look at him, just lay on the floor and panted. Sabelu was just debating whether to repeat the question, or perhaps rephrase it in a nicer way, when Yawi shifted, sat up, stretched, yawned, and got comfortable.

"The Whites and Shadows had long fought over your kin, since he was just a newborn pup, when the Author touched him," Yawi began.

"It is said that he was struck by some kind of lightning at his birth, hence his name," Sabelu said.

"And so it was." Yawi vaguely gestured out of the house. "Most pups come under the protection of their kin and the pack. The Shadows surrounding their kin attach more easily to them, making them easier hosts when they mature. The Whites and Shadows will still fight for each person, but everyone is born with certain advantages or disadvantages to each side. When your kin was touched, it launched a fresh wave of war just as you see now. Over a pup.

"It was the one Anagalisgi calls Ge'gwogv who secured him, aligned his spiritual lens with the Whites so he could see the Shadows and have an understanding of things."

"The Shadows never give up so easily," Sabelu commented.

Yawi barked a laugh. "No, they don't. They rarely give up at all, and they would never give up someone like your kin, not without a fight. They learned of Nathan and Andrew's plan to bring them here and staged an ambush. Nathan and Andrew are bound to the Author through the sorceries, yes, but they still lack the sensitivity to our greater war, the reality of it."

"And with the lingering Shadow stronghold here, from the old civilization of half-Shadows, it gave the cerberus an advantage."

"Yes," the wolf confirmed. "It was a hard battle. The cerberus is a powerful foe by itself, but there were legions of Shadows involved. I was not the only one rebirthed that day."

Sabelu nodded and shifted in his seat. "But what actually happened? How did you come to be fighting the cerberus at all? Don't the Whites have equals among the Shadows?"

"Griffin was busy with the black phoenix. Chimera was battling the serpent. Minotaur was occupied with the wolf dog."

"That's only three, though. Who is the fourth?"

Yawi looked uncertain. Then, "You know it."

Sabelu blinked. "The dragon?"

"Indeed. After the dragon's betrayal, the Author raised up the pack, the wolves, to replace it. We are not original Great Whites, but we have been endowed with the same power in order to fight against the Shadow generals. Our unique dynamic has proven advantageous in many battles."

"Hornets around a bear rather than two bears."

"Yes."

"So the Shadow generals aren't really generals, not in the same way of the Great Whites. The dragon is the general, and the cerberus and the others are comparatively lesser."

"Yes, but still very powerful. Hate is a tragic motivator and a worse prison."

Sabelu nodded, mulling over the information. "Your reluctance about the puppeteers, then, really does have more to do with the sanity of the host than the toughness of the Shadow."

"Yes."

He nodded again. Then, "How did you die?"

The wolf gave him a look as if he would rather not answer. Finally he did. "We stopped the cerberus from rampaging through a part of the battlefield where we held the advantage. It would have crushed dozens or hundreds of Whites under its paws. We maneuvered it away from the battlefield, trying to isolate it from the Whites but also from your kin. We had eight wolves against three heads, four paws, and a tail, and the cerberus knows how to use them all.

"The cerberus is capable of regenerating a head if the head is defeated; the only way to truly defeat it and force the dragon to recycle it is to go for the heart. Of course, regenerating a head is not an instant thing, and we had gotten it to a point where one head was dead, another terribly wounded, and we were mainly fighting the last head.

"Something to note is that each head of the cerberus controls a different part of its body. The center head is responsible for the front paws, the right head is responsible for right rear paw and tail, and the left head is responsible for the left rear paw."

"So when you say you had it weakened," Sabelu cut in, "you had it really weakened."

"We did, but the cerberus is still a fearsome creature, even in such a state. The dead head was slowly restoring itself, and the weakened head was also regaining strength. The middle head was making it difficult for us to get to its heart. It made a snap at one of the other wolves. It would have killed him, but in that moment, I saw the opportunity. I confronted the cerberus. It was in a vulnerable position for just a moment, but without the other heads to help consider such things and correct this mistake—"

"You sacrificed yourself so that the other wolves could take advantage of the vulnerability and destroy the cerberus," Sabelu guessed.

Yawi nodded. "Yes."

"And the only thing my uncle knew about it was your rebirth."

"Until such time as he joined us and learned more about the war, but in the moment, yes."

Sabelu nodded slowly. Then, "How big is the cerberus? Asdeoha's puppeteer is intimidating enough, and your pack would bury me in a second."

The wolf's expression was grave. "I told you of the heads and how they control different parts of the cerberus. The left head does not only control the left rear paw.”

“What else does it control?”

“When the Shadows came to eliminate the half-Shadows, the cerberus was there. After the war, when the Shadows were victorious, the cerberus came and mated with the Sacred Wolf in order to humiliate her.”

“How do you know this? I thought the Whites weren’t part of that war? Was the Sacred Wolf once a White? I don’t understand.”

“The ants told us. And the Sacred Wolf is not a White necessarily. She is something of an homage, an altar, a shrine if you will, built in the early generations after the fallout when the half-Shadows still remembered their origins.”

“Some begged to be taken back by the Author,” Sabelu said. “Others, like those who built the Cursed Zukatopa and the underground city, begged the dragon to rescue them. All of them were turned away and ultimately destroyed.”

Yawi’s silence was confirmation enough.

Sabelu shifted in his seat. “Is that why we were brought here? I know you said Nathan and Andrew are not so sensitive to the Whites and Shadows, but what are the odds that of all the planets and creatures in the universe, we would end up here?”

Now the wolf turned cheeky. “Seems impossible, doesn’t it?”

Sabelu leaned back, turning it over and over in his mind. On the one hand, he was puzzled. On the other hand, he found himself excited by the fact of the puzzle itself, something important that he didn’t know and had to think about and figure out. Granted, it was a little frustrating that something so important was hidden from him by the fact that it involved Whites and Shadows solely so that he couldn’t see it, but that only added to the intrigue.

“The Krydik are being targeted because the Author favors us,” Sabelu stated, staring at the wall. “But we are not the only ones with Books. If the location weren’t important, I don’t think we would be having this conversation.” He looked at Yawi. “There is something about the planet, the land itself that we have to redeem, to rid this place of the stench of the Shadows." He sat up. "Anagalisgi said that it was ignorance that protected my parents in the underground city. But the war was over a thousand years ago, and this city when Anagalisgi explored it was said to be so old that not even spirits remained. My parents explored the ruins not fifty years ago. What's down there in that city?"

"You will find out soon enough, and you don't have the luxury of ignorance," Yawi told him.

"I don't have the advantage of knowledge either," Sabelu retorted. "I know what is said in the Book, and I have their memories of it, but that doesn't show me anything about any Shadow activity down there."

"Perhaps your focus should then be on how you might manage the consequences of what you do find down there and how you will protect the pack."

Sabelu glanced toward the doorway. "There may be many members of a pack, each in his place in the hierarchy, but wolves are not helpless." He did not miss Yawi's mouth popping open in a smile. "I need to speak to Kah Kitowak, I need to get my family ready." He glanced at Yawi. "And we're going to need more Whites to keep the puppeteers more interested in the goings-on here than what we're doing."

The wolf simply answered with a tongue loll and a couple swishes of his tail on the floor.

"I need to get a message to Kah Kitowak, tell him I want to meet," Sabelu said. "Can you do that? Or can Anagalisgi?"

Yawi sneezed in such a way that it somehow conveyed the message of, "Duh."

"Good. Now I just need the rest of my family."

"What for?" a new voice asked.

Sabelu looked up as Netami entered the house, her hair still wet from where she'd been swimming in the river. She gave him a look and continued, "Sabelu, it is unbelievably hot out and you're sitting in here all alone."

"Yawi is here with me," he offered lamely.

Her expression turned apologetic and she made as if to leave. "I see. Do you want me to leave?"

"No, not at all. I was just going to come find you."

"And Itsitsi and Itsitsa and Blaknik, too?"

"Yes."

Netami shifted her stance, faced him, and folded her arms. "A new revelation from the Whites, then?"

Sabelu shook his head and couldn't stop a small grin. "No, just me getting my act together, knowing what I need to do."

Now her expression was puzzled. "Sabelu, we keep doing things, helping people, all at your behest, and yet none of it ever seems like it's what you really want us to do. You say we make progress, and I won't say that I haven't noticed a change in people in general—for the better, I will say—but it never seems to be enough for you. You say that you need to figure something out or there must be something more or there is something more or we need to work here or there or whatever it is. It's like a skin that continues to fill with water, and I keep expecting it to burst but it somehow never does. Sabelu, I don't understand. What more is there? What are you not telling us?"

He sighed. "It's like the festival of tournaments, Netami. People train for it all year. Some people treat the practice rounds like the final rounds. And people will watch the practice rounds and the early rounds and they will cheer and gamble until you would think they expected to die that night. For practice rounds. And we both know what the final rounds can turn into.

"We're only in the early stages of this, Netami. Ganhv was only round one, maybe even just practice. There is a long ways to go, a lot more to do. And we're not going to win if we run this race at an easy jog, or hold back our strength in the wrestling."

Netami took in a measured breath and slowly let it out. "Sabelu. What—do—you—want—from—us? There are times when you treat us like children, trying to distract us from some terrible fate with stories and lies and false reassurances, never wanting to get us directly involved, the same way you pretend not to look at Yukpa."

Sabelu groaned when she brought up Yukpa. He sighed and shook his head. "That...she is not part of this."

"Liar," Netami said. "More than lying to me, you're lying to yourself. Now then, why don't you stop treating us like children and get us really involved? Fine, so we don't see everything the way you do; that is where your calling as a priest and teacher comes in, to educate us in the ways and wants of the spirits."

"I'm trying," Sabelu told her through gritted teeth. "I'm really trying. I've been trying for a couple years now, trying to establish a force of Whites without pushing our hand so far that it brings down catastrophe on us."

Netami made a vague gesture. "Hoshonti has a few foals out in the field right now, and he does an excellent job of breaking them. Any one of those horses will take a rope around the neck and let itself be led about by men and women, elders and children. Any one of those horses is easily ten times stronger than the strongest warrior and can kill with a single strike." Her gaze was gentle, but there was an underlying mask of accusation. "You were born into this world small and helpless but still with great power. The Shadows tried to break you, tried to tame you, tried to get you to kill yourself if possible. But you got away. Now you are growing stronger, and you have decide what you are going to do with your size and strength when they come for you, if you are going to take a rope around your neck, or if you are going to fight back." She made a gesture toward him. "You are the leader here. You are the only one who can truly see what we're up against, and you have to make the decisions. The longer you wait, the easier it will be for the Shadows to pick off the rest of us, regardless of whatever menial task you have for us."

Sabelu closed his eyes and took a breath. "You're right. And it just so happens that I have a plan."

DOSᏘ DVᏗT

Anvdune Adolv'i

Reconnaissance

"Two lost wars wasn't enough for you; now you want to go for a third?" Kah Kitowak asked disbelievingly, leaning back in his seat. "I suppose that's why you wanted to talk to me, just to rub my face in my own failures and cowardice, is that it? Or are you just going to give orders to a good little soldier, seeing how you are the superior leader with infinite knowledge here?"

Sabelu sighed. "I won't say I don't deserve your scorn, but can we please focus?"

It had taken a few days for Kah Kitowak to respond to Sabelu's message, though it was not for lack of time on either end. Kah Kitowak just didn't like Sabelu and had hoped to put it off. Curiosity and boredom had finally gotten the best of him. It was now six days since Sabelu had initially sent the message.

Sabelu had not specified where he wanted to meet. While waiting for Kah Kitowak's response, he had finally informed his family of the roles they were expected to play. Though not anyone's idea of exciting, several points were made: it would help the people, and if something went sideways, they had a way to escape.

It had been a hard sell, because the plan once again involved the Old Land. It wasn't that they didn't want to help the people of the Old Land, it was that every time they tried, things tended to get worse.

Netami suggested meeting in the cliffside city. Ola Achukma and Nendawagan were less enthusiastic about the idea, and it was Galiliga who suggested going to Kah Kitowak's home. The excuse he gave was that it would be Blaknik's first time seeing the Old Land, and if they were supposed to do work in the Old Land, then they might as well start there. What he actually wanted to do was gather up ammunition to use against Kah Kitowak, to deride him for being a traitor and a coward and everything else. Sabelu had confronted him about this, but the Shadow of Pride was an indulgence his brother was not willing to give up just yet.

Instead, it was Kah Kitowak's home that started chipping away at Galiliga's Pride. He lived with the Tlingit people on a small island off the west coast of North America. His home was little more than a small hut with a mat for sleeping and an assortment of necessities. He had a few small personal possessions, but otherwise, his entire worldly wealth was kept in a ten by ten hut.

This ten by ten hut got considerably smaller with Sabelu, his parents, and his three siblings all crammed inside, plus the addition of an Inuit man called Putu. Putu did not use the sorceries, instead preferring a simpler, watered-down, safe but heretical version simply called Time. Comparatively speaking, he had only the barest of skills in Time, none whatsoever in Matter or Energy, but he was not ignorant of the greater sorceries. Given that he was one of the ones currently in charge of such training for this particular village, he was included in the conversation.

Kah Kitowak sighed in response to Sabelu's words, leaning back where he sat. His expression was not disinterest, but stress and fatigue. "We're already doing what we can. Aklaq is out east, speaking to the eastern peoples. We've not heard anything from her or the ones who went with her."

"She's fine," Sabelu said, waving a hand. "A little over-ambitious, but fine."

"It's just as well that she's out east," Putu, a gruff bear of a man, said flatly. "We've got our own troubles with the oilmen who've started coming around."

"You will always have trouble with them. They may come and go for the time being, but eventually they will be here permanently."

Putu just grunted.

"That's all well and good," Kah Kitowak said, "but that's not why you brought your family here."

"We came to help," Nendawagan stated.

Putu barked a laugh. "Help? Child, I'm inclined to agree with Everett; have you Krydik learned nothing from the last two wars?"

Sabelu spoke up. "You knew that rescuing the children from the schools was most likely a doomed endeavor. No matter how many you rescued, the soldiers only had to go back and kidnap them again. And that is what they're doing, even as we speak. Of course, you only wanted to save your grandchildren, and here they are, safe and sound. The rest were just extras, bonuses. Right?" He met Putu's frustrated gaze. "The people are needed, Putu. All of the people. You deride us for the wars we lost. But we have gained so much. We have the knowledge and traditions of the old ways. And we have a way to help those freed from the schools, those who have lost their way."

"No one wants to go to Aktiya Waya," Kah Kitowak interrupted. "I don't know if you know this, but as far as most Old Land people are concerned, you are the ones who have lost your way. Once a proud forest of many different trees, you have burned yourselves to ash. Now all the same, yes, but worthless."

Sabelu gave him a look. "I did know that, thank you."

"Kah Kitowak, you know me," Ola Achukma cut in, his tone slightly rebuking. "You know that I was not born in Aktiya Waya, but I was raised there. You know I have American blood. You also know that I am more Indian than most of those coming out of the schools."

"What do you know of the schools?" Kah Kitowak asked lamely.

"Nothing first-hand, but I believe my son and the things he sees. Aktiya Waya once opened its doors to take in many various peoples, in order to preserve them. Yes, it nearly destroyed us. But now we have the opportunity to take those things that we have saved and bring them back to those who are suffering here."

Kah Kitowak and Putu glanced at each other. It was Putu who spoke.

"The children are stolen at gunpoint. The soldiers don't even bother with pretense or stealth anymore. They're taken hundreds of miles from home, forbidden from speaking their mother tongues, beaten if they sing their songs or tell their stories. They are forced to wear white clothes, wear their hair in white style. They speak white languages, play white games, and worship a white god. And you think you can help them?"

"Some will never recover, it's true," Sabelu admitted slowly. "But their children will. There will one day be a fire, a hunger for the ways of their ancestors. But the less we do now only makes it harder to help those future generations. You know it is already difficult to show the people the sorceries. It will not get any easier."

"Why do they need more than the traditions? Why do they need to learn the sorceries?" Kah Kitowak asked. "That is something we are constantly asked, but we have never been able to come up with a sufficient answer. Simply another tool or another weapon doesn't work for everyone. Some view it as white religion or white witchcraft; others say that it should be reserved for the special few, the chosen shamans, as it was in the old ways. Why does everyone need to be a shaman?"

Sabelu looked him in the eye. "Because each man is responsible for his own demons. A great concentration of Whites may deter certain Shadows, but a man's soul is his own responsibility. If the Shadows remain attached to him, if he continues to feed them, not only does he doom himself, but he continues to be the poison in the well." He continued before anyone could object. "The return to tradition will give them the strength of spirit to start the healing process. Learning the sorceries will help them to fulfill it. From there, a man has only the choice whether to help or hurt the people with his great power."

"Kah Kitowak told me of the Authored Books," Putu said. "He even showed me once, tried to explain everything, convince me of it all." He looked at Ola Achukma and Nendawagan. "I know all about your lives, your courtship, the ruins and the underground city you discovered. And I know about the Whites and Shadows on the battlefield."

"How is that?" Nendawagan demanded. "How did you read our Books?"

Kah Kitowak shifted uncomfortably, thinking about his words.

"There is another copy of each Book. Nathan and Andrew have them, collect them, so that all of those who have Books can one day reference each other's works."

It was a blatant lie. Sabelu knew the things Kah Kitowak had seen, the places he had been. But the man didn't know how to explain such things to them, figured that Sabelu would have the better words for such a task.

"And?" Ola Achukma prompted, looking at Putu. "What did you think of our adventures?"

"I haven't decided. I believe in the spirits, and I don't believe you to be a liar. I don't believe Aklaq to be a liar when she says she has met with Anagalisgi and been given instruction by him. My fault lies with the girl, this Author you espouse. White, blond, what does she know about any of this? If she does have such power, why direct our paths so destructively?"

"Strength is not gained without resistance," Sabelu told him. "All of the people have faced much resistance, been beaten individually and scattered. But now is the time we unite. As District Nine. As the Krydik. The Shadows come for the Krydik because we have Books, and they come for the people here in order to ensure that nothing like us can ever happen again."

"Sounds more complicated than just ensuring our children know nursery rhymes."

"What is the body but a capsule for the soul? We must revive their spirits, show them the way things are. We could sit here for years, discussing, debating, telling stories, but it means nothing without action, without experience. I hold many memories of the past, the present, the future, of hundreds of different peoples. I have memories of the ocean. You can sit here and describe what it is like to go out in a qayaq, on a calm day, on a stormy day. But until I go and see it and experience it for myself, all the words and all the imprinted images mean nothing."

That, at last, cornered Putu. He wasn't convinced, but he was quiet.

Sabelu looked at Kah Kitowak who sighed. "What's your plan, then?" He reluctantly added, "It would be nice to have more than a handful of us working toward this goal.”

“The children are one priority, yes, but we’re going to start with a second priority: the people and families left behind to rot on the reserves. The children may be returned, but it must be a place they want to go, a place of life and spirit and culture.”

“If the people are caught singing songs and holding festivals and doing things the old way, they could be arrested,” Putu threw in.

“Then we will go to them in the jails,” Ola Achukma told him. “You can tell them that this is one of the advantages of the sorceries, that we are not bound by mere physicality. True, our usage was more passive in the past, but after the War of the Old Land, we’ve taken it more seriously. We can conjure Galohisdi to go from one place to another. We can invoke any number of sorceries to get us in or bring them out.”

“Start small,” Sabelu continued. “Stories. All of our peoples love to tell stories, and the white men can’t monitor everyone at all times.” He gestured. “My father will teach the languages. My mother will teach the stories.”

“And your brothers and sister?” Kah Kitowak eyed Galiliga warily.

It was Galiliga who answered. “Netami and I will continue your work of rescuing the children from the schools.”

“And Blaknik? You’re, what, fourteen now, fifteen?”

“He will help where needed, but most likely that will be with us.”

Kah Kitowak glanced at Sabelu. “I didn’t hear what your role will be, master of knowledge.”

“I have business to keep in Aktiya Waya,” Sabelu answered, meeting his gaze. “This isn’t going to go over well with the council or the priests.”

“No, I would think not,” Kah Kitowak said at the same time Putu said, “You didn’t clear this with your elders?”

“You say you believe in the Shadows.” Sabelu looked at the proud Inuit man. “Even if you don’t believe in the Shadows, the Shadow of Depression that follows you around believes in you. The Shadows wish to destroy us, for no other reason than we exist. That the Author has favored us, and that we have been called to be the fire keepers of the people, only fuels an already intense hatred. Do you think that a council and a priesthood that has been infiltrated and run by those controlled by Shadow puppeteers is going to be just fine with what we're doing? They tried to use the war to wipe out all of our warriors. They used it to try and divide us. Now they use the loss of two wars to try and isolate us from the rest of the people, from the Old Land."

"You're saying it was a mistake to go to Hlohi?" Kah Kitowak interrupted.

"Nothing is a mistake; it's all about the ensuing exploitation of circumstances. There is only necessity. Whether by the Whites or the Shadows, there is only necessity."

Putu grunted. "I've never been one for complicated strategy. Few of us are so naturally inclined."

"Few of us have to be."

"Just follow orders, soldier," Kah Kitowak grumbled.

"The Whites are the ones doing the real fighting, where and how it really matters," Sabelu told them. "That which happens in the waking world is merely an echo of what happens in the spirit world. Restore the people, bring in the Whites, and let the battles fight themselves."

After a moment of silence, Kah Kitowak asked, "Where do you intend to start? Aklaq has the greater influence here in the north. I might still have some pull in the east, but I don't know that I want my name to surface there again quite yet."

Sabelu shook his head. "You don't, not yet."

"We'll be starting in the south," Ola Achukma answered. He hesitated for half a second. "We're going to the end of the Trail, where thousands were taken to die. Where I would have died, if not for my wife." He looked affectionately at Nendawagan who blushed and looked away.

"Logical enough," Kah Kitowak conceded. "And you've got more than thirty peoples to choose from, though I imagine you'll start with the Chahta."

"That's right."

"So if you were going to start there, why bother telling us?" Putu wondered, mildly annoyed.

"Courtesy," Galiliga said, his tone unimpressed with Putu's attitude and apparent stonewalling. "We're all supposed to be working together, saving the people together, so let's actually try to come together and learn what we're all doing, make this a group effort."

Putu sidestepped that issue by bringing up another one. "There is also the matter of the Timekeepers."

"Timekeepers?" Nendawagan questioned, biting off her word so as not to appear rude.

The man did not look at her, only Sabelu. "If you know as much as you claim to, if you know Aklaq at all, you know the troubles we've had with them."

"And the troubles you will have in the future," Sabelu said. "There is a trap brewing, I know."

"We have enough problems with the regular soldiers. We don't need to cause extra problems with the Timekeepers."

"Who are the Timekeepers?" Ola Achukma inquired.

"They fancy themselves as, well, the keepers of Time," Putu answered distastefully. "They fashion rules governing the use of sorcery and enforce those rules on anyone with even a shred of talent. You haven't had any problems with them because of your isolation. We've been hounded relentlessly for years. They haven't yet found us on this island, but it's only a matter of time, if this operation spreads beyond our own kind of isolation—and it will, if those oilmen stick around, or if the gold prospectors come back."

"There are rules to the sorceries?" Netami questioned.

"Arbitrary ones only, much like the rules of land and hunting that the white men imposed on our peoples, rules that never existed before, that have never needed to exist."

"The Akari is superior to these Timekeepers as a matter of principle," Kah Kitowak added, "but a well-trained Timekeeper can outmatch a poorly-trained Akari-bearer. And poorly-training Akari-bearers make up the bulk of our force."

"Many of them work double duty," Putu cut in. "Now that they know that we have sorceries, the Timekeepers have inserted themselves into the soldiering and policing forces, if they weren't already. They'll be able to enforce their rules in more ways than one."

"Start small," Sabelu repeated emphatically, looking back and forth between Putu and Kah Kitowak. "The trap will be sprung, but it will catch nothing if you start small. You will learn what I mean, but for now, simply heed my words."

"Do we have a choice?" Kah Kitowak asked.

It was intended to be rhetorical; nevertheless, Sabelu answered, "There are no mistakes, only exploitation of circumstance."

"And necessity?"

"And necessity."

"When do you expect to begin your work?" Putu wondered, looking at Ola Achukma.

Ola Achukma shifted position. "In the next few days. We will be making multiple trips back and forth, trying to figure out what we're up against before starting in on our plan."

"Your all-knowing son hasn't told you?" Kah Kitowak asked sarcastically.

"We want to see for ourselves," Galiliga informed him.

The Metis man just chuckled and said, "O ye of little faith."

Galiliga did not take kindly to the jest. He was unable to stand well in the hut, but he got up on his knees, facing Kah Kitowak and somehow making himself appear larger. "How would you like to help me practice for next year's wrestling tournament?"

"I would not," Kah Kitowak said coolly, "although I'm sure there will be plenty of potential opponents waiting for you in the south." He stole a glance at Ola Achukma, then Sabelu. "Not everyone is excited to receive help, even from their own people." He relented just a little and nodded. "But saving their children, that would be an act that could not be matched in any physical way."

"We're not asking for thanks," Ola Achukma said.

"Good," Putu said, "because you're not going to get much. No one likes a proud critic."

"Are we done here?" Galiliga complained, looking at Sabelu.

"Before you go," Kah Kitowak cut in, "a word of advice. And your father can attest to this as well. If you ever have to deal with the whites, the Europeans, pick a white name to use for yourselves. It will cause a lot less trouble."

"Wouldn't that defeat the purpose of why we've come?"

"You'll find that a lot of people have two names," Putu told him. "Some do it just for ease of relations. Others do it to protect their true names from ending up on the tongues of devils."

That gave Galiliga pause, and he slowly got himself seated and situated once more.

"With Aklaq working here in the north, our focus is going to be the south," Ola Achukma reiterated, "but don't hesitate to get a hold of us if you need something."

"Thank you," Kah Kitowak said, dipping his head once and making a small gesture that prevented Putu from speaking. After a moment of consideration, the Inuit man let go of whatever he was going to say and mirrored the nod.

Sabelu glanced at his family. His parents were well focused on their mission, ready to begin, like a new adventure being written just for them, just like their Book. Galiliga was currently struggling with Pride as he considered the conversation and his general dislike of Kah Kitowak. His Shadow was busy trying to fend off a White fox and was unable to maintain a decent hold on him. Netami was filled with wonder and curiosity about the Old Land and all the people, and she held an almost motherly desire to scoop up the kidnapped children and bring them to a place where they could learn the songs and stories of their people, as safe and loved as she had been growing up. Blaknik was more curious about the land itself, the mountains, the trees, the animals, and everything he was experiencing for the first time, having heard about it only in such stories.

The Krydik took their leave of their hosts and departed. It was Ola Achukma who conjured Galohisdi, taking them south to the miserable land where he had once marched and almost died.

Sabelu helped to guide the Galohisdi so they didn't end up in the middle of a town or a lake or other unfortunate feature. Blaknik fared the worst, if only because he was still inexperienced, though it was not a pleasant journey by any means.

They were on a hill overlooking a small town. While the overall landscape was tinted a permanent shade of beige, there was some green life to be found in small garden patches that surrounded shabby houses and tents.

"Where are we?" Netami wondered, putting a hand to her eyes and squinting against the sun.

"A small nameless town on a Chahta reserve," Sabelu answered. "The people from the Trail were dumped here, given a couple sacks of grain, half a dozen chickens, and left to their own devices."

"It looks terrible," Galiliga commented.

"They've fared better than most."

The six of them started down the slope.

"Do you think we should do it?" Blaknik wondered, skidding down behind Galiliga. "Do you think we should take white names, even though we're supposed to be helping the people?"

"White men are people, too," Ola Achukma said off-handedly.

Sabelu did not need to turn to know Blaknik gave their father a look. "You know what I mean."

Their father met his look. "It's not a bad idea. If we're supposed to be helping all peoples throughout the universe, then we should attempt to maintain good relations."

"Why can't they just call us by our names, though? Blaknik, Galiliga, Sabelu, it's not difficult."

"You grew up with all these languages and sounds. These men haven't, and that goes for the people as well as the whites. We speak differently than they do, even here, and I'm sure we'll mispronounce others' names as well."

"But we'll still call them by their names."

Ola Achukma sighed. "For the time being, we don't appear to need them. If we do, your brother and I already have names to use, and we can do the talking."

The town wasn't much better looking up close. There were thirty homes in all, some of them wooden construction and others a mix of modern construction and old style; a stable with a few horses in the adjacent scrub field; a trading post or general store; a small church that had certainly seen better days; and a number of outbuildings that had gone to rot as the owners gave up trying to fight the storms. If there was any hope to be found, it was in the crop fields. While not as beautiful and perfectly maintained as the ones in Aktiya Waya, these fields were nevertheless robust and productive, tended with great care and pride.

It was the women in these fields who spotted the visitors, and by the time Ola Achukma led them into the town proper, half a dozen men were there to meet them.

Only two of the six wore shirts, and only one wore leather boots such as the white men wore. The rest were shirtless and wore either moccasins or nothing at all on their feet. Five of them sported tattoos, and one was heavily pierced. There were no guns to be seen, but the improvised clubs in their hands could still do some damage, though when they recognized fellow indigenous, their beating arms relaxed. One man tossed his club off to the side where it skittered across the ground and came to a stop near the sagging porch of one of the houses.

Despite knowing more about the situation and what was expected of them socially, Sabelu elected to let his father lead the ceremonies, greeting the men and exchanging appropriate gifts and other pleasantries.

"You bear our name, yet your family does not, and they speak with accents and odd twistings of words," the lead man, Ihika, observed. "I can only conclude that you are Krydik."

"We are," Ola Achukma acknowledged simply.

"Have things gotten so bad in the fabled land of plenty that you seek refuge here in the Old Land now?" a second man, Fiopa, laughed. He was the second youngest of the men and the newest member of this particular welcoming party.

One of the older men hissed a rebuke, but Ihika carried the line of thought. "Indeed, it would be an ironic twist of fate. Though with the way you handle your wars...it wouldn't be surprising either."

"We are not seeking refuge, and we have physically recovered from the war."

"But not spiritually," a third man, Fichik Shobota, mused. He was the oldest man in the town, approximately seventy years old, with long, blazing white hair like the comet he was named for. He wore a plain shirt that was part cotton and part leather, with leather pants, expertly beaded moccasins, and a large beaded medallion around his neck. He nodded and looked at Sabelu. "And you seek to rekindle the fire."

"I do, Tsituta," Sabelu answered humbly.

The five younger men gave absolute deference to Fichik Shobota's words. Whatever comments or misgivings they might have had about the visitors would now have to wait.

The old man made a motion. "Come. We will discuss this matter further."

Without another word, the group turned and started walking. Ola Achukma led the rest of the Krydik after them. Sabelu looked up at a familiar scream and saw a White eagle hovering in the sky.

Fichik Shobota lived in a house that was part modern and part traditional. The modern part, about sixteen by twenty feet, was clearly for daily living, with modest accommodations for a bed and assorted furniture, a small kitchen, all of it much like what would be found in some poorer white homes. The traditional side, about twelve feet in diameter, while built with bent branches and covered with bark and animal skins, was more modern than what the Chahta would have used three centuries ago. It had a rough wood floor with a ring of large stones around the outside, a metal bowl to line the center fire pit, short modern tables on which lay a number of shamanic paraphernalia, and comfortable cushions to sit on. Herbs and various animal parts were hung from the ceiling, and Blaknik let out a huge sneeze as Fichik Shobota guided them in. His cushion was made of animal skins and stuffed with feathers, but the ones he kept for his guests were modern textiles stuffed with cotton, feathers, or straw.

As the six Krydik and six Chahta got situated, they found themselves short one cushion. Blaknik, being the youngest, was made to give up his seat, which he did without complaining. Fiopa offered to grab a cushion from one of the chairs in the house, but Fichik Shobota refused the idea with an emphatic no.

The Krydik had taken many plants from the Old Land to cultivate on Hlohi. It would only stand to reason that, even with careful cultivation, the new environment would alter the plants some. The smudge that Fichik Shobota burned now as he said a prayer was different from what they grew on Hlohi; it looked and smelled different. The tobacco that he added was also different from the stuff on Hlohi.

"You were expecting us," Ola Achukma stated when it was finally safe to speak.

Fichik Shobota nodded somberly and was wordless for a long moment. He added a log to the fire before speaking. "I was. Some years ago, after the war, I had a dream. There was much about it that I did not understand, but now I do. There was a war, of light and shadow, good and evil spirits. They walked the same lands, but they fought a different war. What we saw here was but one image, almost a reflection, like when you look through an icicle and see many facets of the same focus. Always just around the corner, always sitting in one's periphery, always just out of sight until the focus is revealed.

"In one facet, the good spirits had won, for life had been preserved. In another facet, the evil spirits had won, for they had decimated life and settled over the land like a heavy blanket. But when the focus was revealed, so, too, was the mystery. As the flow of life turns, it is the death of one which brings about the life of another. As ash brings forth life from the soil, as the wood gives of itself to bring light, so the good spirits had to step away. For the greatest strength is born of the greatest opposition. The good spirits tricked the evil spirits into thinking they had won, for it is only in such an environment that this kind of power and unity and resistance is born."

The smoke from the fire drifted up through the chimney, and Sabelu wasn't convinced that he was the only one who could see the

White eagle perched on the bent branches.

Fichik Shobota looked at Sabelu. "You are the strength born of this opposition, but you are only the tip of the arrow."

Sabelu nodded, not breaking the old man's gaze. "We're here to bring the rest of them in."

"I know. Ossi told me."

"Ossi is your eagle."

Fichik Shobota dipped his head once even as the White eagle overhead chirped. Sabelu wondered if Yawi was nearby. He probably was and just wasn't showing himself.

"You know what we intend to do, then," Ola Achukma ventured.

"I do. And we are going to help."

The elder looked at the five Chahta men as he said it, his words and tone, if not his age and status, spelling out clearly that there was no room for argument.

"What's the plan, Itsituta?" Ihika inquired politely.

Fichik Shobota looked at Ola Achukma and made a motion for him to speak.

"Galiliga and Netami—" He gestured to each in turn. "—are going to steal the children back from the schools."

"That was tried in the north," Fiopa interrupted. "The soldiers just came back and took them again."

"Then we will return and steal them again," Galiliga informed him.

"That was one woman breaking into one school at a time," Ola Achukma added. "But we're not going to stop there. Myself and Nendawagan—" He motioned to his wife. "—will be helping the people here to restore the old ways. Although—" He looked around emphatically. "—it seems you have managed better than some."

"That much is true," Ihika muttered.

"The point is, we don't want this to be just us. We want this to spread. We want to teach the people to become teachers, to teach you how to help other settlements."

"And when the soldiers come?"

"That is where the sorceries come in," Fichik Shobota said.

If it had come from anyone else, any of the Krydik, the idea would have been hotly debated, if not rejected outright. As it was, the only resistance came from Ihika who said, "With respect, Tsituta, the sorceries have done little to help the Krydik. How are they going to help us?"

"The Krydik were not only unskilled with a powerful weapon, but they were not fighting the same war as the spirits; therefore, the sorceries were of little help. But now, the focus has been revealed. We are now fighting the same war, with weapons intended for this war." The old man got excited. "It is a war of the spirits, a war for the souls of men. This will make it no easier than what we went through in the northern war, but it will be more effective." He faltered in his enthusiasm. "It will also be more consequential."

"If we don't win, everyone loses," Sabelu said.

The Chahta men glanced at each other.

"It will be as you say," Ihika declared, looking at Fichik Shobota rather than Sabelu or any of the Krydik.

"How shall we begin?" one of the Chahta men who had been silent thus far, Uti, inquired. "Are the Krydik to stay here with us?"

"Not at first, no," Ola Achukma said, assuaging some subtle fears. "We have our own issues in Aktiya Waya which we must tend to first. We also wish to start small, this way we will not overwhelm you and so we won't draw so much attention here too soon. As for how we shall begin, I would propose, with your permission, Fichik Shobota, that we convene everyone in a central location this evening. We should learn as much as possible—about the children, about this town, about the state of the history and traditions—before we try to teach anything new or begin any endeavors."

The answer satisfied the men, but they still looked to the elder for guidance. Fichik Shobota merely agreed. He said a simple blessing over their departure before dismissing them to wander about the town.

"Sabelu," he said as they all stood. "Remain with me, please."

No one questioned the old man or Sabelu, and the rest of them filed out of the room, out of the house entirely. Soon it was only Sabelu and Fichik Shobota in the room. Sabelu looked up as the eagle chirped once.

When he turned his attention back to Fichik Shobota, Yawi had also materialized.

"Something you need, Tsituta?" Sabelu inquired.

"Only a question to ask and a warning to impart," the elder answered, "to you specifically."

"I'm listening."

"I see the spirits as you do, the White animals and the shadowy shape-shifters." He gestured to Yawi. "The wolf." He gestured upwards. "The eagle." He lowered his hand. "And others, occasionally, roaming here and there in town, most of them small creatures, rabbits and the like." He shifted position on his cushion. "All animals have spirit, yet the true nature of these Whites elude me. I know they are good, but there is something more, something deeper that all of my prayers cannot seem to penetrate. But I know you understand the truth."

Sabelu nodded and shifted position himself. He spent the next couple hours explaining the Whites and the Shadows, the spirit world in which his uncle walked. He described the Books and the Author to the best of his abilities, and the mysteries contained therein. He told the old man about the People Before and the Great Ones and their cities. He also did his best to explain his gifts, the knowledge he had been endowed with so that he might be able to confront the Shadows and drive them away.

"And this is why these Shadows seek to destroy us," Fichik Shobota mused. "They seek revenge in the past for great deeds we will do in the future. Killing a babe before he becomes a dangerous man." He looked pointedly at Sabelu. "Or attempting to kill a babe before he has a chance to oppose evil."

"That's right."

"I don't envy you, Sabelu," the old shaman said sincerely. "I do not. These things make sense to me, and I accept them. The work your family does here will ease much suffering and it will strengthen the people. But the trials you will face in your own town, your own land..." He shook his head.

"You said you had a question and a warning," Sabelu said. "You have spoken your question. What is the warning?"

Fichik Shobota nodded. "Tell me, are you familiar with the four horsemen?"

"In the Christian Bible?"

"Mhm."

"Are you asking if I believe in them?"

"What you believe about them is irrelevant, for they are already among us, although they appear differently to us than horsemen."

Sabelu blinked. "The four Shadow generals. Or kings, I think they were called once."

"Two have come to pass," the elder said. "Two are yet to come."

"War, famine, pestilence, and death. Which of these have any of our peoples not experienced?"

His mildly flippant attitude garnered a look from Fichik Shobota. Sabelu felt his skin burn hot with embarrassment as he quietly searched through his vast knowledge and the memories of generations now long dead.

"The War of Removal," Sabelu stated. "Famine. The British burned thousands of acres of land, burned the crops, halted trade, tried to starve the people into submission." He thought a minute more. "The serpent, using the Shadows to speak sour words into the minds of kings and their armies, to expand terrible influence."

The elder merely nodded and gestured for him to continue.

"The War of the Old Land," he said next. "War. An attempt to destroy the men of the people, the main fighting force. Seeing how the people of the Old Land were reluctant to accept any of our help, it was also a lesson in failure and even an attempt to pit the people against each other as the different tribes took different sides. That would be the cerberus, head of all confrontations."

Sabelu leaned back. "What remains, then, is pestilence and death. Do you know which one is coming first?"

"No," Fichik Shobota said slowly. "But I think you do."

Looking ahead at the things to come, Sabelu applied what he'd just worked out, that individual incidents mattered less than the big picture.

The forest, not the trees.

"Pestilence," he said finally. "And we're sitting in the middle of it. The slow decay of the people that we are even now trying to fight. The wolf dog, trying to maintain control of the stronghold the Shadows have forged on Hlohi and Earth, keeping the Shadows in line so they aren't thrown off, trying to block the Whites and stop us."

"And what does that leave?"

"Death. The black phoenix. One final, tremendous attack with the only intent to destroy."

"And after that?"

"The dragon itself. Come to oppose the people, the Whites, the Author herself."

Fichik Shobota nodded. "Seven generations, Sabelu. Learn from the wisdom of the seven generations before you. Act with wisdom for the seven generations after you. Look at the big picture. Do not look at a drop of water, but see the whole river. Prepare the people in this way. This is why the Krydik will succeed here where they have not succeeded elsewhere. Before, it was a concern over this person, that place, this fight, that victory or defeat. Now that you have seen the real war, the Whites and Shadows, now you understand."

Sabelu considered this for a long moment and finally nodded. "Thank you, Tsituta."

"Thank you, Tsituta. I am happy to guide you."

Sabelu stood, then paused. "Do you know my uncle, my great-uncle? Have you ever spoken to Anagalisgi? You sound a lot like him."

"I cannot say that I have," the old man said. "But if we are both servants of the Whites and the Author, does it really matter?"

"I suppose not."

He thanked the old shaman again and left the house.

He found his family touring the town, meeting everyone who would talk to them. Sabelu took his father aside for a moment.

"I am going to return to Aktiya Waya," he said.

"Is something wrong?" Ola Achukma wondered.

"No, but my work is there."

"You know we're going to need your help. I know a lot, but you're the one with all the truly traditional knowledge."

"I know, and I will help you. But my place is back home, wrestling with the other priests."

His father sighed but nodded. "All right."

"It'll be all right, Tsitsa," Sabelu told him. "We're going to do a lot of good work."

His words were more confident and inspiring than his tone, and his father was only mildly reassured.

Sabelu returned to Aktiya Waya, stumbling through Galohisdi and collapsing into his bed. He lay there for a long moment, arm thrown over his eyes, until he felt a wet nose nudging his forehead. He reached up and gave Yawi and small scratch under the chin, then slowly got himself to a sitting position.

When he sat up, he found himself in his uncle's cave, the fire crackling spectacularly with fresh wood. Anagalisgi himself was just getting himself seated on the other side of the fire, brushing the bark and dirt particles off his hands.

"Welcome, Tsiquiyi," he greeted.

"Tsidushi," Sabelu said, sitting lazily. "Do you know Fichik Shobota?"

Anagalisgi's thoughtful yet blank look was enough of an answer, but he replied, "Can't say that I do."

Sabelu opened his mouth, but it was Yawi who spoke beside him. "He is as you would be, had you remained in the mortal plane."

"Ah, I see." His uncle nodded. "Judging by the name, I would guess he is Chahta, like your father."

"That's right," Sabelu said. "Ossi, a White eagle, is his companion, and it's been slowly teaching him about the Whites and Shadows, even if he didn't fully understand it. I had to explain it to him."

"This is excellent news."

Sabelu shifted position until he was sitting properly, facing his uncle. "I didn't know there were others like you."

Anagalisgi blinked, but his expression was mildly mischievous. "Well, I am currently the only full-time human resident of this dimension, but I don't think that's what you mean."

"I didn't expect to find another teacher of the Whites."

"Why not? Is that not what you aspire to become? Why shouldn't there be others who are also raised up in their own lands, their own peoples? Everyone has a role to play." Anagalisgi went on before Sabelu could speak. "They have the social standing that you do not. They have the influence and respect of their peoples that the Krydik do not. They are who will hold their peoples together."

Sabelu blinked. "They are the workers in their own fields, those who will tend their own crops." He paused. "Does this mean that my family shouldn't be working with them, that Fichik Shobota should be leading this?"

"What the Shadows intended for evil, trying to isolate the people on Hlohi, the Author has turned for good, to ensure that all of the old ways have survived to some degree. You may know much, but you are one man, and not very well-liked at that. Your family is simply giving back what has been stored up."

"Knowledge being stored up like grain, now feeding the people in famine."

Anagalisgi dipped his head. "And so you see, nothing is wasted. All things that we do, we do for a two-fold reason. On the one hand, we till the land and plant the crops so that we may eat and survive the winter, as it has always been, and this is known. But we also prepare ourselves and each other, to grow and flourish as we are planted."

Sabelu nodded. "I understand, Tsidushi. Having teachers like Fichik Shobota will also help those like my father and mother in their work, and others when they join. And it will allow me to focus on my work in Aktiya Waya." He met his uncle's gaze. "I've always known the what, and most of the time I've known the how. Now I'm starting to understand the why."

His uncle said nothing, just smiled.

"We really are going to finish the work that you started," Sabelu continued, "emerge from this valley of the shadow of death."

"The work that the Author started," Anagalisgi corrected, "but yes.

The people will emerge from the valley." His expression and tone tempered. "Do not forget, however, that although we know dawn is coming, it is darkest just before the break of the sun."

"I know, Tsidushi."

Sabelu said it not unkindly, and he relayed the discussion he'd had with Fichik Shobota, about the four not-quite-horsemen, including his conclusion that they were in the middle of the third horseman.

"An astute observation," Anagalisgi mused. "I am glad to see discernment and wisdom growing within you."

"Thank you. And now that my mother and father and siblings are beginning their work in the Old Land, I need to start working at home, distracting the puppeteers as much as trying to confront them and make them leave the people entirely."

His uncle's gaze was kind. "I wish you well, Tsiquiyi. I know you will prevail."

Sabelu did not more than blink before he was home again. He yawned and sat up, for real this time.

The house was empty. When he wandered out into the street, he saw that it was evening now, the sky turning from red to indigo. A few people were still out and about, some making last minute runs for water for the night, others heading home after visiting with friends or family.

His own family would not be back until morning, because of the disparity between Hlohi and the Old Land. Sabelu took the opportunity to go to the townhouse. It was largely empty, the fires burned low. A couple of the acolytes remained, charged with tending the fire and seeing to the needs of whichever priest was also there that night. The acolytes stayed in the main room, but Sabelu made his way to the private area.

Asdeoha was the overnight priest this night, and he was just adding a couple logs to the fire. He looked up as Sabelu entered. His Shadow loomed large behind him, but Sabelu thought, just for a moment, that it shrank back half a step at his appearance.

"Sabelu," Asdeoha said, mildly surprised. "Is something the matter?"

"Not at all," Sabelu told him. "I just thought I would come to pray. If you want, you can leave and go home. Your wife misses you."

The head priest was uncertain inasmuch as his Shadow was uncertain. The appearance of the rest of the White wolf pack was enough to make the puppeteer nervous, and this prompted Asdeoha to accept Sabelu's offer. He said some vague words of farewell and left the townhouse.

Once he was gone, Sabelu went to work adding more wood to the fire and preparing an herb bundle. As he burned the bundle and inhaled the sweet-smelling smoke, he happened to look down at his hands and saw that they were glowing.

DᏤSႶ DVᏔT

Ahidune Adolv'i

Organization

Sabelu did not visit the Old Land often, instead preferring to spend his days trying to covertly undermine the other priests and their puppeteers. This was accomplished primarily through helping the people. This was more than just striking up random conversation and trying to help someone with a problem. With a solid group of people who were more firm in their faith, Sabelu was free to take over major events, steering things toward the Whites. This included things like weddings, gatherings, and minor festivals.

The problem was that the random acts of kindness were beginning to evolve and expand. People started to notice Sabelu's interest and intent in everyday life and the way he seemed to cut off the other priests. People started to noticed that his family wasn't always around when they normally would be. People started to sense that more was going on. Sabelu did his best to explain things to those who were well protected by the Whites, those who were of a level head and could appreciate his words, but his words always made it to the ears of lesser, more easily manipulable men.

His trips to the Old Land, to the little nameless town, were something of a vacation, a chance to get away and relax and enjoy the company of those who were slightly more receptive to the ideas being taught.

Walking through town with the heat cooking his skin, Sabelu noted a presence of Whites that was comparable to that of Aktiya Waya. Snakes slithered through the grass or sunned themselves on rocks. Hares and mice scurried from here to there. The ants kept a faithful perimeter while Ossi the eagle hovered overhead, content on the mild wind current. A couple White coyotes had their noses to the ground as they criss-crossed the town, following some scent.

This was not to say that there were no Shadows present, but on a cursory glance, he did not see any lingering. Darting through like an arrow, running in for a swift attack on one man as he spoke to another, then running away before the Whites could catch it. Shadowy termites sought to destroy everything the ants were building, and a tiny war was going on far beneath the noses of man and animal.

Sabelu stopped short as a group of children darted into the street, chasing each other and laughing. There were two girls and three boys; the boys' hair was just starting to brush their shoulders again after being cut for the schools. From the porch of a home, an older woman barked something about watching where they were going. When the children did not pay her any mind, she just shook her head and went back to sweeping, her scowl holding almost no real malice.

On the other side of the street, a couple of men were busy cleaning the siding on another house, preparing it for a new coat of varnish. A few houses down, a more traditional home was partly dismantled, old, decaying branches being replaced by fresh ones prepared in the way Sabelu had instructed so they would last longer than a couple years.

A woman stood on the steps of the church that doubled as a school and called for the children. Like mice they appeared from all manner of nooks and crannies in the town, clamoring into the building, eager for "a real education in a real school" as one man put it once. Reading, writing, math, yes, but in the care, safety, and language of their own people, alongside the traditional arts and stories.

He headed to the stable where one man was busy trying to repair a hitching post that had been nearly snapped in half when a horse bucked and kicked it.

"Do you need help, tsidushi?" Sabelu offered.

The man, called Itukawiloha, looked up, straightened, and stepped back from his work. He'd tried nailing pieces of wood over the break, but dry rot had destroyed the post. The horse couldn't have gotten more than a glancing blow if it didn't snap completely in half. The horse tender sighed, wiped sweat from his brow, and looked around.

"I suppose I should just go out and find a branch to serve as a new post," he mused, half to himself. "Town fixes up well enough, this'll stick out like a sore thumb and make me look like a lazy louse."

Sabelu squatted down and inspected the break and the work.

"Don't suppose your sorceries can fix that rot," Itukawiloha said, making a vague gesture with the hammer in his hand.

"It would involve reforming the Agvhalvda that remains, and forcing foreign Agvhalvda to change and assimilate into it," Sabelu said.

"I take it that means no."

Sabelu stood. "In the interest of time and ease of conjuring, it would be better to find a new branch and mold it."

The man sighed, nodded, then made a motion for Sabelu to follow. "All right, might as well do it now. Should have done it from the start, but I thought..." He shook his head. "I don't know what I thought. But with you here, maybe we'll get it done before the riders gets back." He glanced at Sabelu. "You're a prophet I hear. Will they have good news for us?"

Three riders had gone out to the nearest Indian town, trying to spread the idea, spread the hope, spread the work that had begun here. Sabelu nodded. "Yes."

"Like spreading the gospel, the Good News of the Lord."

He was sarcastic, but not malicious. Still, Sabelu seized on it. "You don't know what to make of these things."

Itukawiloha sighed. "I was happy to believe in God and go to church up until they started taking the children. How could God authorize these kidnappings? And I've seen your father conjure sorceries that, by any standards that I've ever heard, would be classified as witchcraft, evil sorceries and heresies. But yet, listening to Fichik Shobota, hearing about the sorceries and the Books, and knowing what I do...I don't know how I feel about it...making sense."

"You don't want to believe the wrong thing, yet you are disappointed in yourself for having so little faith in anything."

The horse tender thought a moment, then nodded. "That's a fair way to put it. Even if my ancestors were wrong or misguided, they never doubted. They always knew what they believed."

They reached a small grove of trees a fair distance from the town and set to work searching for a tree or branch of good size for the new hitching post.

"Doubt is part of life, even for the ancestors," Sabelu told him, inspecting a particular tree. "And asking questions is how we get answers. If we don't know why we believe something, then believing it at all is almost meaningless."

"Why do you believe, then?" Itukawiloha asked. "I know you have prophetic gifts, but what else compels you? What is it that you act on, that you are confident in?"

"Because I've seen the war, and I've experienced it, albeit on a very small scale. I have had Shadows try to kill me. I've read the Books."

The man sighed. "I also feel guilty about asking a prophet to justify himself. In the old days, the word of the priest was law."

"In the old days," Sabelu said pointedly, "our ancestors thought written words had magic powers and could never lie." He vaguely gestured back toward the town. "Yes, we want to bring the people back to the right road, but only inasmuch as it is their heritage, their culture, their land and ancestry. But it would be a sin to ask them to go back to such ignorance as believing written words are magical and always truthful."

Itukawiloha nodded. "I will agree with you there, but where does it end? Shall we all go back to the old huts made of branches and furs? Or should we all live in white housing?"

"That will be up to you. We are preparing the people, but it must be done in the words of the Author with the protection and direction of the Whites. The sorceries hold no favor for this people or that one, what kind of home they live in."

"Evil is evil, no matter how it looks. Like you've said a time or two, the style of the bow matters less than the arrow or the target."

"Yes."

The man made a sort of huffing sound that summed up an attitude of awed disbelief.

Sabelu turned and indicated a certain tree. "This looks like a good, sturdy tree. What do you think?"

Itukawiloha inspected the tree, knocked on it a few times, then looked to Sabelu. "What does the priest say?"

Sabelu ran his hands along the gravelly bark. He did not know the tree as he knew people, but he could still feel the life in it. He nodded and looked at the horse tender. "This one will do nicely."

The trunk of the tree would be used for the post, and the branches were cut and divided into firewood and kindling for various community members.

Sabelu and Itukawiloha took the rough post to the stable where Sabelu demonstrated the sorceries by gently stripping the bark from the pulp, then using the tree's own sap to coat the post and make it more weatherproof than the previous post. The horse tender was fascinated by the display and asked questions, but he was not yet ready to commit to anything.

They had just finished tamping the dirt around the freshly set post when hoof beats alerted them to incoming riders. There were three of them, and the smiles on their faces as they trotted into town spoke of good news. One of the riders was halfway off his mount before it was even fully stopped.

"Slow down there, and keep your head on your shoulders," Itukawiloha scolded him. "That way it doesn't end up under his hooves."

"Sorry." He was hardly worried. "But we bring good news."

"Well, let's keep the news good. I don't want to have to explain to your mother that your mission was a great success but it was you who did you in."

That sobered him up the tiniest bit, but by now the other riders had dismounted and were more polite about handing off their reins. Sabelu took one horse, Itukawiloha grabbed the other two. The three riders wished them the faintest of thanks and farewell before running off into town, gone to gather the council.

"Shouldn't you be with them?" Iyukawiloha inquired as the two of them started dressing down the horses and got them water. "You're the prophet and all."

"It's going to be a few minutes before they get everyone together and settled down," Sabelu said. "First they have to find everyone, then get them all in one place. Seeing how they use the church for large gatherings, and the children are currently using it as a school, well…" He shrugged. "It's going to be a few minutes, longer than what it's going to take to settle these horses back in." He looked at the horse tender. "Besides, I wasn't sure our conversation was finished yet."

"You've given me plenty to think about," the man assured him. "I'm sure I will recall this day for a long time, whenever the people take the horses out to whatever town needs saving next."

"That's good and all, but don't let your mind become stuck on this day or this conversation. Whenever the people take the horses out to whatever town needs saving next, think about what they're doing and why."

When the horses were unsaddled, watered, and brushed out, Sabelu and Itukawiloha turned them out to the scruffy pasture. Two trotted out contentedly to the herd to start grazing while the third, a young male still hyped up from the run back to town, decided to continue his run and started galloping along the fence line, intent on making laps and impressing anyone who was watching.

Meanwhile in town, activity had more than doubled as people started milling around the church, talking excitedly. The horse tender looked at Sabelu. "You weren't wrong about it taking time to get everyone together."

"That wasn't anything especially prophetic, in case you were wondering," Sabelu told him. "That's just understanding people."

Itukawiloha chuckled. "Well, I guess so. Are you joining us, or was this just a prophetic trip to aid a spiritually ailing stable master?"

"I guess I could stay for a few minutes."

"Is the meeting going to go well? The three of them looked so hopeful."

Sabelu looked again at the mass of people that was slowly filtering into the church. Among them was an equally excited throng of Whites. "Hope is just as contagious as fear. Their eyes are opening, their spirits are coming alive again, and they want others to know the same joy."

"That's good, isn't it? Your tone makes it sound not good."

"Dead leaves always burn faster, and sickness is only a problem for the living."

The horse tender said nothing to that, and the two of them left the stable to head to the church. They were among the last to enter, taking a seat in the very back.

The three riders were practically tripping over each other in their bid to explain all the good that had happened, not just in the next nameless town itself, but also on the ride out and back. A certain fortuitous cloud formation, the good omen of a certain bird call, and how one of the riders spotted a white deer roaming in the forest just outside the town. Sabelu glanced at Yawi, lying in the aisle between the pews. The wolf looked up at him but said nothing.

"The people are as thirsty as we were for hope and knowledge and fire," one rider, the one who had dismounted prematurely, said, never losing an ounce of enthusiasm. "They saw the fire of our spirits as we rode into town, and they are ready and willing to learn."

There would be several different responses to the riders as the mission spread, Sabelu knew. There would be those who wanted nothing to do with it, even acted hostile toward it. There would be those who were initially excited, but when the traditional ways and the new sorceries failed to turn back time four hundred years and they found themselves still in the same nameless town in the same foreign land, they would drop back into the Shadows' clutches, tormented by Depression and Resentment. Then there would be those who were excited and talented, but still weak in spirit, who would succumb to the pressure of others to give it up, for a variety of excuses: heresy, witchcraft, not being part of the traditional ways, or just flat-out fear.

It was good that the first mission was very much like this town, enthusiastic, destined to become a White haven. Sometimes, a boost of confidence really was all that was needed. Sabelu also knew that when they hit their first hostile opposition, there would be a period of chaotic unproductivity as the people tried to reconcile the idea that not everyone was so excited as they were, regardless of how desperate the situation.

"Ola Achukma and Nendawagan will be here tonight," one of the council members was saying. "We can ask them."

"And what of Galiliga and Netami?" someone asked. "Beyond us, we will need more help to rescue the children from the schools."

Murmurs of agreement.

"That will be a question to ask when they get here."

"Sabelu is here," someone called out, pointing to him in the back, shifting all eyes his way. "He's a prophet; we can ask him."

"We do not abuse our prophets," Fichik Shobota said sternly, "nor anyone else's. He is here on other errands."

Still the old man looked at Sabelu with a question in his eyes, permission for Sabelu to counter him and give the caller the answer to his unvoiced question. Sabelu did not do this. Fichik Shobota was right; he was here on other errands. He wasn't here to lead these people; that was the job of his father and mother and siblings and, now, those who would be called on to do the same in other settlements. His primary work was still back in Aktiya Waya.

His refusal to espouse prophetic wisdom disappointed some of the people, but they would be revived once his father arrived and gave them a plan of action.

Once conversation swung back toward the riders and their journey, Sabelu slipped out of the church. A few people were out and about, these ones being the most skeptical of the sorceries and what Sabelu was asking them to do and learn. They watched him suspiciously, trying to discern his motives, his reason for being there, his reason for leaving the meeting early, wondering what he was going to do next.

He paid them no mind as he headed to the outer edge of town to conjure Galohisdi. That was one of the first rules established, Galohisdi must be conjured away from other people, unless it was a true emergency. Aside from not wanting to surprise people, get them caught in the middle of Galohisdi, it was just a courtesy thing. People were trained to accept others entering and exiting by certain means, and suddenly appearing through a door in the air was not one of those accepted means of entry or exit. It would be a couple more centuries before that happened on a large scale.

This did not mean that he did not conjure directly into his home, right into his bed that he might rest just as soon as he ceased conjuring. In the next room, he heard his mother and Netami speaking. His father was out, Blaknik was at the river, and Galiliga was home in Yonhi. For the moment, everything was exactly as it should be. Sabelu closed his eyes and breathed a sigh of relief before getting up, knowing that he intended to disrupt all of that.

"And where have you been?" Nendawagan asked as he ventured out into the main room.

"The Old Land," he answered tiredly. He yawned, then recounted his visit to the town, finishing with, "They're waiting for you."

His mother sighed. "It's bad enough trying to explain where we go and why we go there, but the difference between our days and theirs is wreaking havoc on my body. All of ours. I just woke up not long ago and half the day is gone."

"Galiliga is having troubles of his own in Yonhi," Netami mentioned. "His wife doesn't like him going to the Old Land."

"No matter what we do, it's going to cause division," Sabelu said, still a bit grumpy.

"But why are people upset that we're trying to help?"

"You weren't old enough to really understand the War of the Old Land," Nendawagan answered, cutting off Sabelu. "We were trying to help there, too. But sometimes intentions aren't enough to overcome the consequences of an action. Among friends, small actions may be easily forgiven. Something like war, when we weren't much wanted in the first place, it's a little harder."

"Last time, it was the people here who wanted to help and the people there who didn't want our help. Now it's the other way around."

Their mother grinned. "And such is life, full of contradictions."

Netami looked at Sabelu as if for support or insight, but he just shrugged and said, "She's not wrong."

Still his sister looked frustrated. "In all of the stories I've heard, the evil spirits are all the same, they work in generally the same way. They want to lure people into the darkness, they eat children, they cast evil spells, they turn people into animals, they turn themselves into animals, they do all sorts of bad things. This kind of petty stuff..." She shook her head. "I don't doubt you, little brother, I just...don't understand."

"If a man doesn't tell the truth, then he is part of the lie, willingly or unwillingly. The means may be different, but the goal is always the same."

"The same Shadows across the universe, just adapting to whatever situation causes the most destruction."

"Exactly."

Now her expression changed. "You expect something to happen. You're using the willingness of the people of the Old Land to learn in order to get the people out of Aktiya Waya long enough for you to expose the Shadows here and confront them."

He nodded. "That's a good way to summarize it. The people of the Old Land are thirsty for revival. We have what they need, physically. It's a matter of reviving the spirit as well."

"Revive the people here, bring in the Whites to sustain them, send them to the Old Land to help. Get them out of here, anger the Shadows here, expose the Shadows and banish them, and keep as many people out of harm's way as possible."

"That's right."

"And salvage our own people," Nendawagan added. "Sabelu may have great knowledge, but even those of us who fully support him can only take him at his word. The people still look to the priests for guidance. Ganhv's treachery was a strong wind against a mighty oak. But if that trust in our priests shatters, we'll be left adrift."

Now Netami looked at Sabelu with wide eyes. "That's why you're going to go into exile." She turned puzzled. "But why would you want to save a corrupt image?"

"Maybe I'm not saving any corrupt thing," Sabelu told her. "Maybe I'm buying myself time and distance to do the real work that needs to get done."

"But exile will take you away from the people."

"Away from the people and into the Shadows."

With the work being done in the Old Land, Nendawagan had managed to starve her Fear indulgence down to more of a vice, or perhaps something between the two, so it was less of a great vulture and more of a large owl. With Yawi keeping the Shadow busy, a White ferret was able to run around between the two women, snaking around their legs, up their backs, over their shoulders, and back down. There was still fear in his mother's mind about what was going to happen to her son, but there was also a great allowance of hope and motherly pride in what he was doing. This in turn fueled a desire to get to the Old Land and continue the work there.

Sabelu headed out of the house and made his way through the town. Whites stood sentry on top of the buildings, a hawk looking around with its keen eyes, an owl peering through the dim light, a leopard poised to pounce, motionless but for its eyes tracking something on the ground. Up above, clinging to the cold stone, Shadows in the form of bats, rats, and other nebulous creatures timed and coordinated their attacks.

Around the townhouse, however, for at least a couple streets, the Shadows held fast. To Sabelu's eyes, there was a perpetual smoky haze around the area, to the extent that it was nearly impossible to distinguish one Shadow from another as they roamed around in regular patrols. Passing through the haze was akin to jumping in an icy river, and he got a certain feeling of walking to his death. He wondered if this was how Anagalisgi felt when he was to be taken to hang, and he wondered if it would be possible to escape his fate as well.

Bird-like creatures with long, sharp beaks and shredded, leathery webbing where there should have been feathers watched him from their perches around the townhouse. A large predator paced back and forth over the entryway. Sabelu flinched as something slithered around his feet, but he was not blind to the fact that nothing actually touched him. Some came close, swooping low or sprinting just behind him, but nothing actually touched his skin. Still his flesh bunched in unease and he found himself wishing for Yawi, or any White, to be near him. Even a White mouse in his pocket would have helped to ease some of the anxiety.

It wasn't as though he were planning anything especially sinister. He wasn't going to the townhouse with the intent of openly challenging the priests and causing a huge fight. At this point, he was simply going about his business, as were others going in and out of the townhouse or just passing by on their way from here to there.

Sabelu smiled to himself as he observed a couple of women walking down the street. Within the haze, within the Shadows' influence, all evil and negativity was amplified. Pain, sorrow, fear. The Shadows were fortifying this section of the town. The problem was, the people would react to such things. If they feared a place, they wouldn't want to visit it. There would be some explaining to do.

His smile faded as he entered the townhouse, forcing himself not to react to the slobbering beast that rested near the door and snapped at his ankles. He knew the excuse they would give. He just had to make it through the next few years and all would be well.

Sure. If it wasn't one obstacle, it was another. But at least he only had to save his people once.

"Where have you been all day?" Dikdi wondered. He was busy tying herb bundles.

"Out helping people," Sabelu answered simply. He went to a basket of small animal bones and began sorting them.

"Which people? No one has seen you." He paused emphatically, and Sabelu saw his puppeteer whispering in his ear. "Have you been going to the Old Land?"

"The council has not approved such missions," Sabelu said evasively. It wasn't a lie, really. Trips to the Old Land were supposed to be limited to formal delegations, though few had been sent out recently.

Dikdi's tone remained mostly neutral with only an undertone of accusation. "Your father and mother have also been acting strangely lately, coming and going at odd hours, sleeping in the middle of the day."

Sabelu picked up a small skull and examined it. "I didn't realize we were dictating when people should be awake and when they should sleep."

"Maybe not, but it's only a recent change." Another emphatic pause and more whispering from the Shadow. "And there have been murmurings about the Old Land recently."

"More bad news?"

Dikdi gave Sabelu a look which he returned.

"More talk about helping the people of the Old Land," the priest stated.

Sabelu pulled out another bone, a vertebra from a small animal like a squirrel. "You don't think we should help people?"

"I have no problem with helping people if they want to be helped, if they want our help." With each use of "want," the priest jerked a little harder on the string holding the bundle. "But every time we try to help, we just make things worse. And if they don't want our help, then why should we force them?"

"What if they did want our help?" Sabelu asked casually, tossing a couple tiny skulls into a specific basket. "Perhaps their fathers were ungrateful for our help, but maybe now it is the children who have seen the light and are ready for the revival we thought would happen in the War of the Old Land. Shall we punish them for their forebears' obstinance?"

Dikdi gave him another look but did not answer right away. "Why should we turn our attention outside when we have enough problems here as it is?"

"What problems? I thought Ganhv was a rogue priest? And we can't pretend that we will ever be rid of common daily frustrations."

The priest sighed. Sabelu could see that his puppeteer was trying to decide where to take the conversation. Did it continue with this passive aggressive nonsense like two wolves circling each other, or did it strike and begin the real fight?

It chose a third option, call in reinforcements. Whether it was intentional or not based on the conversation, Asdeoha walked in at that moment, and he spoke as if he knew exactly what had gone on. He deposited a basket of fresh herbs between them and looked at Sabelu.

"Let us stop beating around the bush, Sabelu, what are you really doing? What are you really up to with all of this Whites and Shadows nonsense?"

"Let's not pretend that any of you are oblivious to the greater war here," Sabelu countered. "You have already admitted loyalty to the Shadows; I can't imagine that anyone greater than a priestly candidate would be caught entirely off-guard to learn that these things are going on. The difference is, I know what you're up to."

Then the head priest said something Sabelu didn't expect. "We are only trying to continue your father's and grandfather's work. You've read the Books; you know your mother's argument." He put his hands out. "In one culture, the rabbit is a sign of life and fertility, something to be admired. In another, he is a dreadful trickster, something to be scorned. Which is it?" He brought his hands together. "We are finally achieving cohesion."

"A well-made bow can be used to strike down one's foes and one's friends, whichever he has a mind to kill. You are trying to make this about the bow. I am trying to keep you away from your intended target."

Asdeoha grinned. "You remember what I said about the arrows that miss?"

Sabelu gave him a look. "I don't forget things easily." He continued before Asdeoha could speak. "Have you thought about what will happen to you, in the end? You think you're going to get out of this unscathed, but you will not. The Shadow of Power—" He did not miss how the puppeteer flinched. "—is not protecting you; it is using you. It is using you to get to me." Sabelu deliberately turned his gaze to the Shadow at the head priest's shoulder, knowing the head priest (probably) couldn't see it. "Because it knows that I am the only one currently standing between it and the ultimate goal of the Shadows, which is the destruction of our people."

Being in the heart of Shadow fortifications, it was no surprise that the priest's Shadow had an easy answer and ready supply of Confusion and Self-Justification to feed into Asdeoha's mind.

"You're, what, twenty winters, twenty-two?" the head priest questioned. "Granted, the Shadows may have failed in their first attempt to be rid of you as an infant, but why stop there? Why wait so long to be rid of you?" He shook his head, his expression suddenly turning grandfatherly. "You may see many things, Sabelu, but you might be thinking too highly of yourself. Anyone who is that great a threat would have been dealt with by now. If we have learned anything from our forebears' mistakes, it's waiting too long to respond to a threat."

"And yet I have the backing of the Author."

Rather than get upset, Asdeoha chuckled. Even Dikdi smiled as he sorted herbs. Asdeoha's expression was one of false bemusement. "The Author. The Whites and Shadows, good and evil spirits, yes, this is known. Even the Creator is known. But the Author? A white man's religion." He gestured to the many herbs, bones, feathers, sticks, and other assorted spiritual paraphernalia. "The ways of our fathers and grandfathers. Blended, yes, some compromises made, but it is the legacy we must uphold. The legacy you are teaching the people of the Old Land to uphold. So which is it?"

"Once again, you would have me believe that the big concern is the bow. If it works, what it's made of is of little concern, and the decoration and embellishment even less. My real concern is the target." Sabelu quickly added, "And as for why they should wait to be rid of me, well, after they realized that they couldn't influence me away from the Whites and use my gifts for their own purposes, I expect it has something to do with wanting everyone to know about the Whites and the Author before making a full attempt at discredit and destruction, so that anyone who may come along in the future speaking of such things will be immediately hated and run off."

Naming a Shadow was a serious blow to its influence, but correctly guessing their plans and motives could be just as devastating.

Asdeoha's puppeteer had no readily-available rebuttal, so it settled for a generous amount of general disdain and dismissal.

"What do you plan to do, then?" the head priest asked finally.

Sabelu grinned. "Why would I tell you that? I will say that I am going to stop the Shadows and save the people, but why should I disclose any specifics? I'm sure your Shadow of Power—" He felt immense satisfaction at watching the puppeteer flinch a second time. "—is already getting regular reports from the other Shadows that are out and about. And I'm sure it's already feeding you that information and suggestions for plans on how to stop me. I see no reason to clear any debris from that river."

He didn't like the look the priest got on his face, and he felt a chill creep up his spine as he knew that the first seeds of the Shadows' final plan for him were beginning to sprout in Asdeoha's mind. More than just an annoyance, a buzzing gnat telling him that Sabelu needed to be dealt with, now the first fuzzy images of treachery were beginning to take shape.

"I see," the head priest said finally, his tone indicating that the conversation was over. "Well then, I suppose I will leave you to your work." He gestured toward the bones and herbs. "Meli is nearly ready to give birth and I promised I would deliver some charms for her to use for a quick delivery."

"Her mother is more than proficient in Touch to be able to help her," Sabelu said.

The priest chuckled as he turned, but it still wasn't a light-hearted as Sabelu might have hoped. "One thing you should learn is to never argue with a pregnant woman." He glanced back. "But then, you did say that there was no future for yourself and Yukpa, and never have you mentioned anyone else. Could it be that you die with no legacy?"

Sabelu met his gaze. "The people will be my children, their survival my legacy."

The puppeteer made a sickly growling sound and Sabelu turned his eyes to look at it. After a long moment, Asdeoha departed without another word. It was another moment still before Sabelu returned to his work sorting bones.

"He's not wrong," Dikdi commented. "You do think very highly of yourself. Some might say too highly."

"Just because one is confronted with the truth does not mean that the one speaking it is arrogant," Sabelu said. "It may be that the one listening is too arrogant to accept correction. I have spoken truth to common people and they have received it with joy. Some rebuke, some resentment, but once they finally let go of their vices, their indulgences, they realize that they were in the wrong, but now things are better."

The priest glanced up from his work. "Do you think us malicious, Sabelu? Do you think that I concoct plans to go out an attack men and brutalize women? Do you think I pray for crop failures just out of spite?"

Sabelu shook his head. "Not out of spite. Nor are you so specific. If you pray for a crop failure, then you are an obviously evil man who wishes harm upon the people. But if you pray for yourself and your own elevation, your own pride and vainglory, then in your mind you free yourself from any consequences. Whatever the Shadows might do to create a situation where you are elevated in some way, you can justify it in your mind as not something you really wanted, but you took the opportunity to help yourself by helping someone else."

Dikdi's puppeteer, Vainglory, having been named, was not ready with an immediate reply.

"Or you might create a ritual you say will protect the people. The blood-taking of women when they become engaged, for example. You invented that one, didn't you, after the War of the Old Land, when women outnumbered men three to one? Protect them from rape or affirm their purity by ensuring that their blood is pure for their husbands. A brother if she has one, a priest if she doesn't." Sabelu spat. "Sickening. An affront to the life-givers."

"You can't say that you have never looked at the women when they become engaged and hope that they ask for you. Considering how well it has been received, you're going to have a hard time convincing the people to give it up. The women's council itself was one of its biggest defenders, and even the women who have served on the village councils have not seen fit to rescind the practice." Dikdi shrugged. "I was merely the voice of an idea."

Sabelu shook his head. "You were not always malicious and spiteful. Even now, the weight of the Shadow is heavy on you, because for all its promises, it has done nothing for you." He continued hastily, as if the Shadow itself might suddenly protest. "It started out as a vice of Pride. You, out of all your brothers, were chosen to be a priest. Then it morphed into a indulgence of False Humility, when they died in the war, but your status as a priest protected you. But secretly, you were quite happy to have not gone, for you were slowly succumbing to this puppeteer of Vainglory, seeking to elevate yourself, to be noticed, and to very slowly start working against the people and even the other priests. Again, you don't pray for them to fall ill or succumb to other misfortune; you just ask for some opportunity to be above them in some way and let it all work itself out."

Now defensive, the Shadow was quick with a reply, and Dikdi asked, "If there is a puppeteer on every priest—except, conveniently, for you—then why would they work against each other?"

Sabelu gave him a look. "They're not. They don't work against each other, they work against you, against us, against the people. It doesn't matter if you have a Shadow or a White, the Shadows only come to destroy. The Shadows are at war against us—" He couldn't help but shift his gaze around to the many Shadows crawling over the walls and ceilings, gnashing teeth and ready to pounce. "—but they play a very long game, generations in the making."

In his uncertain glances, his eyes caught movement in the reflection on a polished silver pot. A short line of a dozen or so White ants was marching into the townhouse, using everything possible for cover as they made their way to Dikdi, creeping over his feet and disappearing safely into his moccasins.

"It's like watching a child play with dolls," Sabelu went on. "If a child takes two dolls and makes them fight, he is not fighting against himself; he is making the dolls fight each other."

He knew Dikdi would not suddenly be freed from his Shadow and fall to the ground weeping, but Sabelu could tell the ants were having an effect against the puppeteer. Just tiny pinpricks of light and knowledge. Like poking a small needle into a waterskin, the leak would be evident, but it would be impossible to see where it came from initially. He wondered if the Shadow was aware of the ants yet, how much water would have to leak out of the skin so to speak before it noticed.

He could only conclude that the Shadow was aware, for it made a hasty motion. Dikdi, just as hastily, swept up a large basket of herbs and made to leave, saying only something about having to make some deliveries to some people.

Sabelu saw none of the other priests after that, and it was an otherwise peaceful day. The acolytes were terrified of him, and he did his best to encourage them and send them on meaningful tasks in an effort to stave off the Shadows that were slowly sinking tendrils into the boys.

"I hear you talking about them," one of the boys said as Sabelu prepared to leave for the evening. "About the Whites and the Shadows." His expression said that he hoped he wouldn't be punished for admitting to eavesdropping, although Sabelu wasn't exactly subtle himself. "Asdeoha and the others don't like it when you talk about them."

Sabelu opened his mouth to reply, but the boy added, "Do you think they're evil, the other priests?"

For a long moment, he was only aware of all the Shadows still staring at him. Finally, "They are only men. As we are only men, all of us. And women. But our spirits need outside guidance, for we cannot hope to guide ourselves. Asdeoha and the others are guided by the Shadows, and these Shadows influence them to do many terrible things."

"Did they influence Ganhv to try to kill you?"

Sabelu nodded. "Yes, they did."

The boy shifted his stance. "Does that mean that we are entirely at the whim of the spirits? I heard you talking about a child playing with dolls. Is there a Shadow on me right now, telling me what to say? Or maybe a White?"

"That was a different illustration for a different argument. To your question, I might say that we are like horses—you know, the horses that Hoshonti takes care of? Our rider will tell us where to go, what to do. But, like the horses, it is only a suggestion. A horse that doesn't want to do something when it should—or does want to do something when it shouldn't—can and will put up a fight. A bad rider, an evil rider, will abuse the horse terribly. A good rider will work with the horse, praising it, being gentle with it, but still correcting it when necessary. A bad rider thinks of himself and his needs. A good rider is concerned for the welfare of the horse."

"And the Shadows are abusing the people while the Whites want good for the people," the acolyte concluded.

"That's right."

After a moment of the boy shifting from foot to foot, thinking about everything, he said, "You say that the Whites serve the Author. Authors write words. My brother likes to write down stories."

"I know he does, he's very talented and creative," Sabelu cut in.

"He tells all of the people and animals in his stories what to do. Does that mean we're only doing things at the whim of the Author?"

It was a question that had been asked a thousand times over as everyone tried to reconcile predestination and fate and luck and free will all at the same time. Even Sabelu would admit to having his own doubts from time to time.

"Time and life is a river," he told the acolyte. "The vast majority of the people only see what is right in front of them. There are obstacles, rapids, fast parts, slow parts, and all sorts of stuff. The Author has determined the course of the river. We are all going to the same end. How we get there is similar, but no two trips down the river are ever the same, even if you've canoed the river a hundred times. Some people may have to go one way around an obstacle, and some people may have to go a different way. What determines our fate is our condition when we arrive at the end. Have we paid attention to the obstacles and any warnings we have been given? Have we listened to instructions on how to navigate this river? Failing to heed instruction leads to natural consequences. Maybe your canoe is damaged, your paddle breaks, you yourself are injured. But still we go down the river. The Author may give an instruction, but if we fail to yield to it and crash into a rock, it was not the Author's intent that we are harmed, but that is what happened because we didn't listen."

"But the Author could just direct us away from an obstacle, right?" The boy added, "My mom doesn't like the Author or the Books. She was glad I was chosen to be a priest. She said it might help offset any taint you brought to the priesthood because of your father or grandfather, and maybe I could be a better traditional priest than you."

Sabelu smiled. "I know. And yet, here we are. At the whim of the Author."

The acolyte paused for a long moment, then absently muttered some kind of farewell and took off. It would be a few days before he actually relayed the conversation to his mother, at which point she would be absolutely livid. But the boy's curiosity had been ignited, and the cricket on his shoulder was intent that it stay kindled.

Sabelu himself left the townhouse and headed home, spotting Dikdi down one of the roads on his way back to the townhouse for evening duties and overnight care of the fire. The priest did not notice him, but the puppeteer did. Sabelu smirked at it but kept walking.

The house was devoid of people when he arrived, but this did not surprise. Having no people did not mean that it was empty, necessarily, as the house had become something of a small haven in itself for the Whites. Several burrowers, a number of birds, and two wolves currently made themselves at home, resting in between shifts as it were.

"At ease," Sabelu said as everything lifted its head when he walked in.

Heads went back down.

"Is Yawi around?" he asked of one of the wolves; it lay at the entrance to the room he shared with Netami and Blaknik.

"On patrol," the wolf answered. It sat up. "I can call him in."

Sabelu put up a hand. "No, that's all right; I was just wondering."

The wolf looked uncertain but lay back down. Sabelu stepped through the ethereal wolf, enjoying the warmth emanating from its thick fur, a welcome relief from the chill of the cave and the Shadows. Then he was through, into the room, and the best he could get under his own blanket was lukewarm.

DᏪᎾᏚᏂ DVᏗT

Asunadune Adolv'i
Group Effort

Aktiya Waya and Yonhi remained close-knit towns, mostly for the fact that both still practiced the sorceries regularly, but being the closest in proximity factored in as well. Anpa O Wican'hpi held strong ties with Aktiya Waya on account of their great participation in the national council and national affairs, though some grumbled that their participation was more like bullying.

Lehoyed was more isolated, always had been, always would be. There had been no further violent uprisings since Yvgidahi put down the one Kah Kitowak's father was involved in, but they were always the most resistant to anything the national council decreed, if for no other reason than the national council decreed it. Overall, though, Eagle Clan remained fairly low-key, happy to live apart from everyone else and continue their national task of preserving the people, discovering the stories of Hlohi, and forging the less tangible aspects of Krydik identity. There were only a handful of real books to speak of on Hlohi, but for what few books there were, the vast majority of them came from Lehoyed.

Lehoyed did not outright ban the use of sorceries, but it was greatly frowned upon. From this, the people lived fairly normal lives, requiring more frequent hunting and gathering and all the tasks associated with such activities that took up much of one's time. Crafting the paper, ink, and binding for books was not high on the priority list, and this task was outsourced to the sorcerers in Aktiya Waya or Yonhi, who, according to Lehoyed, "had nothing better to do with their sad, empty lives devoid of all traditional, physical meaning of the people."

Desiring to take a break from the stress of Aktiya Waya and the Old Land, Sabelu volunteered to take a small shipment of bookmaking supplies to Lehoyed. He made the excuse to Asdeoha about collecting new books in Lehoyed, any new volumes of stories or other tomes—one of the Lehoyed elders had once written an extensive guide to the helpful and harmful plants of the eastern cliff region—and generally seeing what they were up to on the spiritual side of things.

It was an obvious excuse, and either of them were too in touch with the Whites or Shadows to not know what was spiritually going on in Lehoyed, but from a more physical standpoint, it made sense. Actually, Asdeoha, the priests—the Shadows really—were curious to see if he would even survive once he got out of the safety of Aktiya Waya. The Whites were protecting the people; what would happen if he wandered away from the people for a while? Lehoyed was still very much a Shadow haven; how would he fare there?

It would be a change from the mundane anyway, Sabelu figured as he secured the packs to his mount. All evil might be the same Shadow of a different color, but there was something appealing about dealing with new problems he hadn't encountered before. True, he wasn't the only person running offense for the Whites right now and there were plenty of White-endowed people doing battle though they weren't entirely aware of it, but he was a little exasperated from hearing that such-and-such had given in—again—to their old Shadow, or that so-and-so had exchanged one vice for another, or that someone was being hard-headed and locked in the throes of a particularly powerful indulgence.

He needed this, he decided, mounting up and taking the reins. He needed to get away and find some new problems to worry about. He internally rolled his eyes. Because that would help with his headaches.

With a last glance at Aktiya Waya, he turned his horse in the proper direction and nudged it forward. The chestnut stallion snorted and pawed once, then leaped into a fast trot.

About half a mile outside the bowl, Sabelu noticed Yawi keeping pace a few yards off to one side. The wolf did not give any indication of wanting to stop and speak; in fact, he looked quite content to trot alongside them. Nevertheless, Sabelu slowed the horse to a walk. He thought Yawi looked a little disappointed as he, too, slowed.

"You're coming with me?" Sabelu questioned dumbly.

"I've been assigned to protect you," Yawi reminded him. "Of course I'm coming."

He should have expected that, honestly. "What can you tell me about the situation in Lehoyed? Is it going to be like Aktiya Waya was when we first started our work?"

"Very much so," the wolf answered, "although they are not entirely unworkable. Their participation in the annual festivals and encounters with the Whites in such events has put the seeds in that ground."

"So the ants are already there, maybe some other White insects."

Yawi just nodded.

They traveled in silence about a quarter mile. Then Sabelu asked, "Were my father and grandfather right to charge Eagle Clan with inventing new histories and stories for the people? We're never going to be truly free from the Old Land; why pretend otherwise?"

The wolf gave him a bemused look. "You know the tongues of the many peoples, all the different stories throughout the ages. How many of them, when describing themselves, call themselves original people, first people, or something of the sort? And yet, there are hundreds of different peoples, some allies, some enemies. All with different stories, different versions of the same events. Should they have isolated themselves because their stories tell them so?"

Sabelu sighed but shook his head. "No. Either they would have died out naturally or they would have died horrible deaths because they could not come to terms with sudden change."

"And so it is."

After a few more minutes of walking, Sabelu kicked his horse to a gallop. Behind him, Yawi yipped with delight and started to sprint. Sabelu glanced back once to see the wolf in a full stretch and stride, easily catching up. He turned his gaze back to the road, keeping his head just high enough to see through the horse's ears.

The landscape around Aktiya Waya was rugged yet majestic, the gentler slopes covered in pine and birch with plenty of scruffy undergrowth. Long-standing exposed rock was bleached white while newly-exposed rock or caves varied in color from red-brown and pink to black and gray.

As he made the seven-day trek to Lehoyed, the landscape started to change. The birch and other deciduous trees thinned to nothing, and the pine changed from full, thick conifers to tall, scraggly jackpine with little undergrowth. The rock all started to turn black and the ground was covered in needles and bark. While still rugged terrain, the mountains were less distinct, now more like rocky rises and jagged almost-cliffs.

It wasn't what Sabelu would call beautiful, or maybe that was just the wind talking. Once the undergrowth cleared, the wind blasted him like a slap to the face. If it was one thing Eagle Clan was proud of, it was their ability to produce deadly archers. With the wind they were constantly fighting near the cliffs, it was nothing for them to sweep the field at the festivals. When it was time for Lehoyed to host the festival, many non-Eagle archers advanced by technicality only. Even the wind in Anpa O Wican'hpi wasn't so bad. A few years ago, a group of young archers from Bear Clan asked Eagle Clan to maybe put up walls, windbreaks for the archery field, to make it more fair. Eagle Clan laughed in their faces, and the more experienced Bear Clan archers took special pride in sabotaging the bows and arrows of those young archers to teach them a lesson in both archery and clan honor. Sabelu knew what they did, as did a number of other people, but no one ever said a word. The young archers never raised a voice in protest.

The only windbreaks Eagle Clan saw fit to build were for their crops and their horses. It had taken a lot of effort to make the soil as nice as it was, but there was still some concern for the corn, and the horses needed a break from the wind as much as the people in their dug-out town.

Sabelu turned his mount over to the horse tender and grabbed his packs. He used Galo'ondiha ale Agi'a to adjust the burden some on his back and shoulders, but he didn't miss the disapproving look from the horse tender. Sabelu understood. It didn't mean he wasn't going to help himself some, but he understood.

The crop fields and horse pens were still inside the tree line, many of the windbreaks built between the trees. The town itself was situated in the fifty yards between the edge of the trees and the edge of the cliffs, and the walk to the stairwell that would take him into the dug-out town was more of a grudging trudge against the wind. By the time he finally got down below ground level, he felt as though he'd just walked through a freezing ice pellet storm and the skin had been torn off his face.

"Welcome, visitor," someone said.

It was a man, not much older than him by appearance, holding out a piece of leather. Sabelu took it and, finding it pleasantly warm, pressed it to his stinging face. After a minute, when he felt much refreshed, he handed the leather back to the man who was more smirking than smiling. Before either could speak, another voice spoke up.

"Sabelu of Wolf Clan," the man stated, walking up. "What are you doing here?"

"Bookbinding materials," Sabelu answered, indicating his packs. "And other trade goods. I've only just arrived."

"We could tell," the first man, the one with the leather, laughed. "Everyone here knows to keep a wind cloth about their neck and face when going out."

Looking around, Sabelu noticed that a good number of people did indeed have pieces of leather tied around their necks, ready to be pulled up to shield the face from wind.

"To the townhouse, then," the second man said, taking Sabelu's arm. "This way."

It was not Sabelu's first trip to Lehoyed, nor his first visit to the townhouse. Granted, he only took these eastern excursions when Lehoyed hosted the annual festival, but he wasn't an idiot. Although, given that he hadn't thought to bring a wind cover, nor had he even attempted to invoke any sorceries, he wasn't exactly proving his vast intelligence either.

The dug-out town of Lehoyed had been a more than natural fit for the southwestern refugees, and the flavor of the town was much different than that of Aktiya Waya and Yonhi, even Anpa O Wican'hpi. The people here thrived in a scarce, unforgiving environment, and were perhaps more closely aligned with the old ways than any other town.

But for all of that, it was, as Yawi had said, just as rife with Shadows as Aktiya Waya had been in the beginning. Vices, indulgences, even puppeteers hanging around the council, priests, and elders. Same Shadows, different town. Some deferred to him on account of Yawi, others became agitated and hostile. On the part of the people, this manifested as fear and suspicion, that the dark seer had come to their town. Why him, why now, and what did he want? What bad omens did he bring that couldn't wait until the next festival?

The Lehoyed townhouse was very much like the one back home except the partitioned area for the priests had two floors. When Sabelu entered the stone structure, he spotted several groups of people: one group of older women almost working on beading or sewing but getting more caught up in the latest gossip; another group of younger women who simply wanted to do some of their crafting and chores in a more communal setting; and a group of children playing some game in the dirt using pebbles, pine cones, and a small skull as from a mouse.

There was a man in the townhouse as well, perhaps thirty years of age or so, sitting quietly against the wall, thinking, a book in his hands. Sabelu approached him and offloaded a pack beside the man, saying, "You may find this useful."

The man, called Tlistso, looked up at him, then at the bag. He waited a moment before peeking cautiously inside. Then he grinned and started eagerly pawing through the supplies. He again looked at Sabelu, eyes shining.

"I've been waiting for this, yes. Oko has been dictating stories to me—his fingers are too arthritic to write—but I'd run out of supplies. Oh, I love to hear his stories, and I love to share them."

"Pah," one of the old women from the nearby group scoffed. Sabelu turned to look at her where she threaded a line of beads. "Books and writing. Our stories have always been spoken aloud, passed down on the wind." She did not look at Sabelu, but she addressed him all the same. "Your father. Learned man. White man. Bringing white man's ways, even here."

"Don't worry about her," Tlistso said apologetically. "Not everyone appreciates what your father and grandfather have done for the people. I guess that's what happens when you live in safety for so long." He looked around Sabelu toward the older women and raised his voice on the last few words. The women did not react beyond snide facial expressions, though their eyes remained fixed on their various crafts.

Tlistso looked back at Sabelu. "I guess you're looking for Oko, too."

"He's one of the people I've come to find, yes," Sabelu said.

"Follow me." He started moving, glancing back only once as they left the townhouse. "He'll be able to help with your other goods, too; he'll know who to talk to."

Only once they were well clear of the townhouse did Sabelu see a White weasel-like animal pop out of the ground and start jumping over and around Tlistso's feet as he walked.

"You're not afraid of or hostile to me," Sabelu observed calmly.

"No," Tlistso affirmed. "I have no reason to be. Anyone from a lineage with Anagalisgi and Yvgidahi and Ola Achukma must be great. True, I only see you during the annual festival when you're supposedly consulted about the next leaders of the national council, but..." His expression turned distasteful and he shook his head. "I don't know, there's something not right about it. It looks more like show than truth. They ask your advice out of formality, not because they're going to heed it."

Sabelu casually glanced around at life in the dug-out town. Other than decoration, life here appeared similar to that of home with children playing, women cooking, and men either gambling or refining their weapons. "Do others make similar observations?"

Tlistso shrugged. "Mild curiosity at best. Most tend not to question the priests."

"And those who do?"

"Don't do it aloud."

"Do they question me?"

The man gave him a look as if uncertain where this line of questioning was going. Then, "Well, most would agree that you're weird. Like I said, you're known to us only by reputation and anything we see of you during the festival once a year."

"What do they say of me?"

"That you're weird."

Sabelu rolled his eyes. "I know. Besides that."

Tlistso gave him another sideways glance. "Few would argue that you're an adelohosgi and that you have visions; even those who don't like you would never call you a liar about what you see and dream. Some might even say that you are Anagalisgi's restless ghost that reincarnated after the death of Yvgidahi. Others have argued that, because you carry the knowledge of all our ancestral peoples, that you are the manifestation of our history, ancient souls, spirits, and gods walking among us."

Sabelu had a sudden flash of a vision, some time far into the future, near the events of his death. All he got from it was his sister making the statement that his death would be like putting all past hurts and wrongs to death once and for all. He shuddered involuntarily, just for the consideration that such words would not be spoken until after he was gone, yet, somehow, such words had already been spoken. He was yet to die, but he already had.

"What about you?" Sabelu asked, trying to bring himself back to the present moment. "I've come here as a simple trader, brought you supplies you needed, and we've been having a normal conversation. Now that we're away from the festival and all the chaos associated with that, what do you think of me?"

"You're real enough, flesh and blood," Tlistso stated, "but anyone would be a fool to think there isn't more to you." He continued, "My father and uncles stood against those who tried to kill your father, rebel against Yvgidahi, and separate Lehoyed. They believed in the Books and the Author, that we had all been brought here for a purpose. They were not so enthused with the sorceries, but the rest of it they would defend." Another glance. "I don't think you're Anagalisgi himself reincarnated, but one of his line, powerful in the spirits, walking with the Whites and Shadows." He nodded. "You didn't come here on accident; you're looking for something. Or someone."

Sabelu grinned. "I've kicked a few spiritual hornets' nests in the last couple years. I've come here to kick a few more."

"Good. If you need help, I'll be glad to assist any way I can. Oko might have a few things to say about it as well."

Even as he spoke, they approached a house and entered, Tlistso calling out in a familiar tone, as though he visited the elder every day, which he did, or near enough. There was a response from an adjacent room and the two younger men filed into a small bedroom.

Oko had been too old to fight in the War of the Old Land, and a lack of sorcery use meant he had aged considerably since that time so that he was near one hundred years old. Still he got around with the aid of a staff and the help of his thirteen daughters and even more granddaughters.

"Oh, Tlistso," the elder said in a frail voice. "I didn't expect you to come today. You were almost out of supplies, weren't you?"

"Sabelu brought more," Tlistso said proudly, grinning.

The old man turned his attention to Sabelu, peering at him through fading eyes under bushy eyebrows. "Sabelu, hm?" He looked back at Tlistso. "Boy, when I told you to fetch me a priest, I didn't mean the priest of death. I'm not that sickly."

"He's not a priest of death," the younger man said gently, somewhat amused. "He's here on a mission from the spirits."

"You say that like there's a difference. One of Anagalisgi's line, is it any wonder?"

Sabelu shifted his stance, also amused by the old man's rather lively attitude. "The way Tlistso was speaking of you, I was under the impression that you were going to help me."

"Help you?" Oko waved a hand. "Adelohosgi or not, you're still just a whelp. I've been around a lot longer than you. You should be helping me."

"That is what I've come to do," Sabelu informed him, trying not to smile too much. "Believe it or not, but I do want to help the people."

Where the elder was crotchety and difficult before, with a certain air that said it was mostly for show just to give Sabelu a hard time, now he turned deathly serious, his gaze as crystal clear as Anagalisgi's. "The people welcome your help, Sabelu. But the priests and the forces behind them will eat you alive."

Sabelu nodded, his grin vanishing. "I know, Tsituta. That's what I'm counting on."

Oko studied him for a long moment, then gestured to a basket sitting on a low table. "Grab that and follow me." He looked at Tlistso. "You, too, young'un. Help me now and you can sit down and listen to more stories later." He shook his head and gave Sabelu a look. "I don't understand the youth fascination with words and books. Magical words were what bound our peoples in the Old Land. Who or what are the youth trying to bind?"

"Printed words are useless on their own," Sabelu told him. "It is the spirit of the men behind the words that give them power and meaning."

"What does that say about the Author, then, I wonder?"

Before anyone could come up with an answer, Oko was already moving. He did not move quickly, but he was determined to get wherever it was he wanted to go. Sabelu and Tlistso followed him out of the town to the north where the forest quickly thickened so the wind wasn't so brutal. There he directed them to gather certain leaves, plants, and other forest goods.

"Lehoyed may be more isolated from the rest of the towns," Oko began, "but we're not so aloof as you may believe. Granted, I don't travel to any of the festivals anymore, but I listen to the gossip that comes back, and I listen to the goings-on when the festival comes here. I had my doubts about some of the priests, and I recruited Tlistso here to keep an eye and ear out for me. You may have noticed that I don't move as fast as I used to. Then we heard about what Ganhv tried to do, tried to kill you."

"And you confronted the priests here," Sabelu stated, picking a particular leaf.

Oko nodded emphatically. "That's right. It's disrespectful if one of you whelps does such a thing—maybe not you, Sabelu, since you're one of them, but it is for Tlistso—but if an elder does so, well, the priests better listen."

"Except they didn't listen."

"Right again. Oh, they humored me the first time, proper deference and all that, but I knew there was something more."

Tlistso interrupted the old man, saying, "The priests were never directly involved with the rebellion and trying to kill your father, but they never condemned it either."

Oko markedly cleared his throat. "That spirit still lives in them, not necessarily one of rebellion against the nation or the people, but against you and your family."

Sabelu shook his head. "That's only the physicality of it, what the normal people of the waking world perceive. The spiritual roots run far deeper; their Shadows don't appreciate the Whites or the Author. But because they are bound by the rules of this world while they are here, they have to come up with something. The rebellion is just an excuse."

The old man scoffed. "I could have told you that, young'un. I'm old, not stupid. You don't need to be a priest to notice things." He waved a hand. "Anyway, after that I started talking to Tlistso here and finally agreed to participate in these magical words. Figured if the Author can conjure magical words that get the Shadows all riled up with a rock in their shoe, maybe we can do something similar."

Sabelu grinned. "The printed words mean little by themselves, but your spirit of defiance to the Shadows gives them power. And seeing how the Shadows seek to destroy the people, the fact that you are inscribing our stories and culture to make them more permanent and less prone to the whims of the wind only enrages the Shadows further."

"Well then I'm happy to do so."

"But it's such a small offering," Tlistso said, his expression concerned. "I've written plenty of pages, several volumes' worth, but it wouldn't be difficult to destroy them."

Sabelu hesitated for half a second. Then, "I know you don't use the sorceries here in Lehoyed, but you should know from the dressing of animals that even the largest animals have some very tiny bones, like the ones in the ear. But those tiny bones play a crucial role in survival. How would it be for those bones not to exist; how would a deaf animal survive even one day if it couldn't hear predators or prey?"

The man looked mildly relieved. "There must still be more we can do. Should we confront the priests again, demand to expose the Shadows?"

"No. That will happen in its own time."

"But why wait? Should there be another attempted rebellion or murder before we confront evil?"

"Evil is a master of games and glamor," Sabelu told him. "Ganhv was chosen to be the sacrifice so that the Shadows hanging around the other priests could continue their work. Nothing has really changed, although the people might have believed it so for a time. The same thing would happen here. Remember, the Shadows want to destroy all of us; we are only the pawns. The Shadows would choose a sacrifice, someone on which to pin all the blame and take the fall so that the people would be satisfied in their bloodlust without actually changing anything."

"What do you expect us to do? You didn't come here just to leave things the way they are."

Sabelu knelt beside a decaying log and indicated for Tlistso to do the same. He gestured in turn. "These two mushrooms look very similar. This one is a cure for diarrhea. This one, which looks deceptively similar, will cause the worst diarrhea you've had in your life. This one here is unrelated but, to a novice, could be mistaken for either. It is edible and good for flavoring meat, but is overall useless to us." He again gestured to the medicinal mushroom. "This is the real thing. You know it by its stem, its cap, its gills, where and how it grows, and many other things. It doesn't matter what this mushroom—" He indicated the poisonous one. "—looks like, or that one—" He indicated the edible one. "—because they are not this one." Another gesture to the good one. "There are infinite ways to make a counterfeit; it does you no good to learn all the ways because there will always be a new deception. If Oko were to ask you to come out here and find this mushroom to cure diarrhea, all that matters is that you can identify this one, identify what is real."

Tlistso had begun to relax more and more as Sabelu gave his explanation, and Sabelu noticed that the White weasel had apparently found a playmate in a White butterfly. The weasel gave chase, but in a friendly way that said it wasn't actually trying to harm the butterfly if caught.

"You must bring reality back to the people," he went on. "You must show them what is real."

"Not everyone likes those Books of yours," Oko said severely.

"The Books don't matter," Sabelu repeated. "They hold our stories, yes, but the Books are objects. A map holds the same information, but it means nothing if a man is not prepared to go on a journey. The books you are making with Tlistso are very good, but they are not a substitute for right living. It is not enough to talk about something; you have to act on it. Reading words never saved anyone; understanding the words and using the knowledge contained in them does."

Tlistso and Oko glanced at each other. With the weasel and the butterfly still playing between them, a look of understanding passed between them.

"We'll help," Oko stated. His expression turned cheeky. "But I think you already knew that."

"Know that once you start helping, they'll come after you, too," Sabelu warned. "The rebellion and all that is only an excuse; it's me they're really after—the Whites and the Author, truly—and they're going to hate you for helping me."

"Not unexpected," Tlistso said, trying to sound optimistic.

"Good. Then I don't want to hear any complaints when the Shadows do start opposing you."

They finished up their minor foraging expedition and returned to

Oko's home. To no one's surprise, one of the priests was waiting for them.

"Help you with something, Atsos?" Oko inquired politely enough.

"I was beginning to worry," the priest, Atsos, said. "First I hear that Wolf Clan's adelohosgi of death is here, and then someone said they saw you leaving town."

"And you thought I went out to lie down quietly in my grave? Pah! What nonsense." Oko pushed past the priest to get inside his home, Tlistso and Sabelu following. "Merely making use of young hands. And backs."

"There are plenty of young hands in town," Atsos commented, trailing them and standing just inside the doorway. He glanced once at Sabelu but still addressed Oko. "What is the adelohosgi of death doing here?"

Oko made a flippant gesture. "He's standing right there. We've been conversing so I know his ears work. Ask him yourself."

Atsos' puppeteer was not so strong as Asdeoha's, and it was far more wary of Yawi, making the priest more leery of Sabelu as he faced him. "Well?"

"I came to deliver some trade goods," Sabelu answered simply. "Tlistso was out of bookbinding materials, and there is plenty of other stuff in the bags." He gestured to the bags still on the floor. "Oko was offering to distribute the goods as needed, but we got distracted by herbs and forage."

"Oko has plenty of granddaughters to do his foraging," the priest stated, his Shadow finding a piece of its spine. "Anyone could deliver goods, and we have regular visitors who do so, most often your town's young men hoping to catch a glimpse of an Eagle girl they met at the annual festival. Considering the trouble you've been causing for your own priests, it is no accident that you are here today."

"You sought me out, which means you came looking for trouble." Sabelu smirked. "Because the White in your shoe wants to be rid of the puppeteer so it doesn't have to hide in your shoe but can instead come out and guide you and help you like it should."

He noted the way the Shadow bristled at the mention of a White hiding in Atsos' shoe. It was a lie; the White snake was actually hiding in the priest's pocket. But he saw the conflict of the puppeteer. It wasn't much stronger than a decent indulgence, having grown weak and lazy in the safety and isolation Lehoyed provided. Unlike the puppeteers in Aktiya Waya, this one wouldn't be able to split itself effectively to both hunt for the White and maintain control of its host. It appeared to decide that the present conversation was more important, and it would hunt for the White later.

"I'm only trying to keep Eagle Clan safe," was the best Atsos could offer in the absence of his puppeteer's full attention.

"Safe from what? What danger is there?" Sabelu asked. "The Krydik have no enemies here, no physical ones, anyway. This gives us a chance to hold fast to our history and culture, but it also provides a terrible avenue for dark spirit predators to pick us off. One by one, through internal decay."

"Is that why you've been working in the Old Land again? Have you consigned us to death, as the adelohosgi of death?"

"My intent is to help everyone. The Shadows want all of us, everyone, Hlohi and Earth, from all peoples. We were chosen by the Author to lead the fight against them. I intend to see it through."

"You speak of preserving history and culture, then you come here and speak of the Author. Which is it?"

"The Shadows have blinded you to the war we fight, the war we were truly made for. You despise any mention of it because it threatens you, because you know that you have been listening to evil spirits."

Atsos searched Sabelu's expression for a long moment. Then, "Wolf Clan and Bear Clan both use the sorceries quite extensively. If the sorceries were of the Author, why would she allow your evil priests to use them?"

"For every good mushroom, there is a counterfeit," Tlistso piped up, stealing a glance at Sabelu.

"As I told Asdeoha," Sabelu added, "you focus on the bow, what wood it is made of or what embellishments are carved into it. These are trivial matters intended to avoid the real issue. I am focusing on the target, the one who will be dead when the spiritual arrow is released. Right now, the arrow is still aimed at the people. We don't matter to the Shadows. We're playthings, prey in the paws of a cat. You think the Shadows are going to spare you in the end?" He shook his head. "They won't. Whether you are eaten first or last, you will be eaten."

"And so it is," Atsos said. "We all die in the end. You fancy yourselves heroes in Aktiya Waya because you have longer lives? Is that where this is coming from?"

"The body dies, but the spirit lives on. Isn't that part of the old traditions?" Sabelu gave him a look. "Those who die with Shadows still attached will be devoured by those Shadows. That includes you."

The best the puppeteer could do was simply erect a wall of spiritual deafness with a fog of indignation clouding the priest's thoughts. How dare this young prophet speak to him this way! This prophet of death speaks of life?! What madness! What insolence! He was keeping the traditions of the people, the traditions that had seen them through countless generations and just as many catastrophes and triumphs. And this pup had the audacity to chastise him!

But because that was the best the Shadow could do, the most Atsos did was give an annoyed huff and leave the house. Tlistso was less than subtle with his sigh of relief. Sabelu just looked at him with brow raised. "That was easy. That was only the beginning of opposition. Do you think Ganhv went from a minor dispute like that straight to attempted murder?"

"Well, no," Tlistso offered lamely.

"He's not backing out," Oko promised, looking at Tlistso more than Sabelu. "It's just something he will have to be ready for."

"Of course I'm not backing out," Tlistso said defensively. Then he faltered. "It's just...it's improper to question the priests. But what do you do when there is such division among the priests?"

"That's another way the Shadows will try to confuse and attack the people," Sabelu admitted. "For every rule that exists, they will either try to defy it or exploit it. On our part, that means that we will either have to decide whether the rule is worth keeping or else figure out how to work with it."

"So which is it? Even Oko is toeing a line, but his age affords him some leeway. No doubt Atsos is going to spread some rumor that you're fomenting rebellion, questioning the priests, causing me to question the priests. We're in Lehoyed. Word gets back to Aktiya Waya, that evil word 'rebellion,' and you can bet that Asdeoha and the others are going to try and take advantage of it."

Sabelu nodded. "I know."

Now Oko spoke. "What do your prophetic eyes see?"

Sabelu looked at Tlistso. "They will try such a thing. But they're not going to take it out on the people, yet. First they're going to come after me, in the same way Yvgidahi only went after the physical perpetrators of the old rebellion."

"And?" Tlistso wondered, eyes wide.

"They're going to exile me, leave me to be picked off in the wild."

Oko waved a hand. "Bah. Something tells me an adelohosgi like you already has a plan in place for what he's going to do when no one is looking."

Sabelu grinned. "You would be right."

"What about the rest of us?" Tlistso asked. "Obviously they're going to expect that we're just going to settle down quietly, like the old rebellion. If they're exiling you, I'm guessing it means that no one is going to go with you. Doesn't that say something?"

"Yes. It says they can't exile everyone, nor could they execute everyone. Believe it or not, but it will be very freeing for both me and you to do our respective work."

He could see Tlistso mulling it over, trying to make it fit together in his mind. Meanwhile, Oko was smirking as though he, too, had already seen the events of the day and was happy to see them play out.

"Do you have a place to stay while you're here?" the old man asked. "I don't think the priests would be enthusiastic about receiving you in the townhouse just now." He waved a hand as Sabelu opened his mouth. "Bah. Stay here with me. I insist. I'm sure this one—" He indicated

Tlistso. "—is tired of hearing my stories; he can listen to your stories for tonight. Your stories and whatever stories the spirits have imparted into that big head of yours."

So it was that in addition to helping Oko as requested, Tlistso filled page after page of Sabelu's stories. Many of them were stories of the old ways of the old peoples, and Tlistso took great joy in relating them to more recent traditions, and how seemingly different peoples had very similar traditions that blended easily within the Krydik people. Sabelu also told stories of the War of the Old Land, memories he held of those who had died. He related their bravery, their hopes and dreams, triumphs and failures.

"I think you'll have to make another trip to Aktiya Waya for paper," Tlistso commented, picking up another page. "You've only just delivered these today, but this is more than I've written in the last moon."

Sabelu glanced at the papers lying neatly on the table, the ink drying slowly. To Tlistso it seemed like a lot, and compared to the normal volume of written material that was produced, it was. But it still only scratched the surface of everything Sabelu knew and could share, to say nothing of the things he knew but wouldn't be able to speak of sensibly.

He stood, stretched, and went to actually look at the pages. It was not an alphabet, such as the Americans used—or the peoples of the Old Land as they lazily transcribed their languages—but neither was it the syllabary that the Cherokee used. The system his father had developed bore more similarity to the latter, but he'd swapped out several symbols that, in his opinion, were far too similar in appearance and could easily create confusion if misformed while writing in haste.

Sabelu appreciated the gesture—truly, he did—but that didn't make it much easier for him to read it as several of the shapes still insisted on changing places. Or he thought they did. He could blink five times and, somehow, the letters could be in different positions each time. When his impediment was first discovered, the first idea was to examine his eyes. Touch revealed that his eyes were fine. His brain, then, they said. Many more moons of examination and rituals and herbs and testing, to no avail. Even for their superior anatomical knowledge, the problem was two-fold: a lack of understanding of exactly how the brain worked and no desire to potentially cripple an otherwise powerful prophet; and an entrenched taboo of potentially harming one's soul in the pursuit of repairing the flesh. The limbs, the skin, and most organs were fine, for they were flesh only. The heart and brain remained the carriers of the soul, though which one, or both, was often limited to personal belief. And to experiment on an adelohosgi was akin to blasphemy.

No doubt one of the many pursuits that Asdeoha and the others now regretted abandoning.

Eventually, Tlistso returned home, and Oko announced his intent to go to bed. A granddaughter who was tasked with such a thing this evening saw to whatever he needed while Sabelu quietly made himself ready in the area the old man had designated. He fell asleep back-to-back with Yawi, the wolf's soft fur tickling his skin.

The air around him changed, and when he opened his eyes, he was not surprised to find himself in his uncle's cave. Sabelu sat up. Beside him, Yawi stretched and shifted so as to take up both spots.

"Thanks a lot," Sabelu told the wolf.

"Your fault," the wolf said. "You moved." And he huffed a breath that said he wasn't going to give it up.

Sabelu shook his head and stood. A moment later, the door of the cabin opened and his uncle walked in with an armload of wood and a dead rabbit, a regular rabbit.

"Welcome, Tsiquiyi," Anagalisgi greeted.

"Tsidushi," Sabelu acknowledged. "What news?"

Anagalisgi dropped the wood in its place, then took the rabbit to his prepping table. He glanced over his shoulder at his nephew. "What do you mean, what news?"

Sabelu walked over to the table and stood across from his uncle. "I assumed you brought me here to tell me of some development here in the spirit world, something I should be watching for."

With a deft hand, his uncle ripped the rabbit fur off the carcass in a clean sweep, creating a perfect tube. Then he took up a knife and started dividing the meat, carefully needling the knife point until the larger joints gave way. "Sabelu, you know what's coming. You know what awaits you when you return to Aktiya Waya. You understand the predicament you will be in, the trap they have laid. You understand the consequences, the road you must follow."

"Yes," Sabelu agreed, "but you are more aware of the movements of the Shadows that will necessitate these things." He put his hands on the edge of the table and leaned forward slightly. "Tsidushi, this involves more than just the puppeteers of the priests. Yes, they can conspire and plan, and they have, but what they intend requires far more coordination."

"Who are the dragon's four generals?" his uncle asked, still slicing the meat.

"The cerberus, the black phoenix, the wolf dog, and the serpent."

"Which one is in charge of maintaining the order of the Shadows, keeps them in line, ensures that they're not succumbing to the Whites?"

"The wolf dog."

"Do dogs hunt alone?"

Sabelu blinked. "No, they typically hunt in packs. Are you saying there is more than one wolf dog?"

Anagalisgi gave him a look. "Which general is in charge of the actual fighting?"

"The cerberus." Even as he said it, Sabelu understood. "The wolf dog is herding me toward the cerberus."

There was a huff and a low growl from Yawi though the wolf did not move or open his eyes.

"The wolf dog is herding us toward the cerberus," Sabelu corrected.

His uncle's silence and Yawi's continued growl was confirmation enough.

No more vices that fled like mice. No more indulgences that had to be corrected like misbehaving children. And the puppeteers were fed up with his constant meddling. Rather than risk another one of their hosts, they were calling in reinforcements. Given the level and intent of his meddling, the Shadows weren't going to waste time and effort on just going up the ranks further one by one; they were taking him (almost) all the way to the top right now.

After a minute of silence, Sabelu asked, "How long does it take for a general to be recycled?"

"I don't know," his uncle admitted. He looked at Yawi. "How long did it take the cerberus to be recycled?"

"Between the time of your discovery of this place and what you call the War of the Old Land," the wolf answered, stretching and standing. "In your linear time, it was about one hundred years, I think." The wolf seemed genuinely puzzled by the concept of linear time.

"One hundred years," Sabelu echoed.

"It is a bit of a coincidence," Anagalisgi said cheekily, sticking the strips of rabbit meat on a kebob with half a dozen vegetables. His grin faded. "How do you intend to do it?" He glanced at Yawi now beside him. "An entire army of Whites and Yawi's whole pack had a tragic time of it, and Yawi had to sacrifice himself in the process."

"That's what a leader does. He sacrifices himself for the pack."

"Yes, but you're not a White. You won't be reborn."

"And yet, I have the advantage of knowledge."

Sabelu moved around the table, motioning for Yawi to follow him. Behind him, he could feel his uncle's curious and worried gaze, his conflict over whether he should follow his nephew or simply let him go. In the end, he decided not to follow.

Sabelu and Yawi headed out of the cabin to the open slope where two of the wolves lounged in the sunlight, resting from a long day. They looked up lazily at their exit, then sprang to their feet at an apparent cue from Yawi.

"I know that linear time is frustrating for you," Sabelu began, finding a sandy spot and smoothing out a drawing plane, "but know that it's even more frustrating for those of us who have to live with it, and worse still for those who know what's coming and can only watch it happen. This is what's going to happen, and this is what we're going up against..."

DƟⱯSᏌ DVꞀT

Anagwodune Adolv'i

Opposition

Sabelu stayed with Oko in Lehoyed for a total of four days. In that time, he managed to tell enough stories to use up all of the pages he'd brought for Tlistso, but he also assuaged many of the more irrational fears that the locals had about his presence. He wasn't there to predict doom and gloom and condemn the town to death; he was there to tell stories, both of the entertaining and educational variety. It was not lost on anyone that some of his stories challenged or outright contradicted some of what the local priests said, and it certainly wasn't lost on the priests that some of the people were starting to prefer Sabelu.

Sabelu made them feel proud of their history and their present, the people said, not obligated or shackled to it like the priests. He made them feel alive again, that there were good spirits to be found, not merely bad ones to be avoided or vanquished. He gave them hope, not rules. The Books were not more important than holding faith in one's heart. The sorceries were not more powerful than simple acts of kindness.

"You are going to alienate your own people, Sabelu," Atsos warned, stopping him as he tried to leave the dug-out town. "Aren't your precious Books the center of your religion?"

"A map on paper is less important than the land under your feet and before your eyes," Sabelu told him. "It is a good guide, yes, but it won't take you anywhere if you do not physically move. It is the destination that matters."

"Regular missionary, aren't you? Just like your bastard American grandfather."

"My grandfather was a diplomat, but even so, he was respected by all peoples because he showed them respect."

"Then maybe you should take a lesson and show some respect to me," Atsos said lowly. "You undermine me here. I don't care if you are a full priest in Aktiya Waya; these are not your people, not your charges, you don't know them."

"I do know them, very well in fact," Sabelu said. "Even if I didn't, all Krydik priests are in charge of all Krydik people. Even if we weren't, I'm not undermining you. I'm undermining the Shadow within you. The Shadow that whispers power and control and safety for self and family."

The last four days had been harrowing for Atsos' puppeteer, its own laziness making it unable to keep up with the Whites that had swarmed into the village. The Whites had had a field day with the puppeteer, toying with it, tormenting it, teasing it. For Atsos' sake, they didn't completely annihilate it, but his brief glimpse at freedom, allowing more Whites to work on him, had certainly opened up a possibility of true freedom from his puppeteer.

The wolf dog was not going to like that.

"You are not excluded, Atsos," Sabelu continued. "As long as you still breathe, you can get back on the right road. I am not asking for your title, your status, your possessions, your family, or your life. I am asking for your heart, your soul, your commitment. We are the gatekeepers of the people in this war. We should be guarding the people from the Shadows, not letting the Shadows in. You've heard the stories of what is happening in Aktiya Waya and the Old Land. You've seen what has happened here in just a few days. I know that the Shadows whisper that their victory is inevitable, and they make tempting offers to protect you from some terrible fate if they were to succeed. They won't win in the end; as for this waking world and our narrow, linear moment in time, they won't win if we don't let them."

The puppeteer was hanging on by a thread, a stray thought, a feeble doubt.

"The other priests will never believe me," Atsos said weakly. "They know I've opposed you. The people know I've opposed you."

"And men will continue to have conflicts with each other. This is how the Shadows work. But I choose not to give in to petty spite. It's not me you're opposing, and it's not really you opposing me. It's the Shadows and their war on the Whites, the dragon against the Author. We are the prize to be won, but we can choose who wins us. What is this fleeting life compared to the next?"

And just like that, the Shadow floated away, like an autumn leaf breaking free of its twig. With the connection severed, Yawi and the rest of the Whites tore into it with remarkable savagery. It took everything in Sabelu not to flinch or react at all to the unearthly sounds it shrieked out as it died, disappearing like black vapor into the air and finally vanishing entirely, pulled back to the spirit world.

"Keep the work going," Sabelu told him. "Help the people as I have done. Oko will show you if you need it."

Humble shame enveloped Atsos, and the most he could do was nod once and walk away quickly. Watching him go, Sabelu knew the man would have several relapses, where doubt and fear would cause him to question his apparent conversion. But there was little to convert, and this realization would ensure that he was never taken hold of by another puppeteer.

With no further delays, Sabelu pulled a hood and mask over his head and face and headed out of the town, being blasted by the wind almost as soon as he was clear. He headed to the stable and retrieved his horse. The steed needed no convincing to turn its back to the open cliffs and head in the direction of home.

Even with the hood and other protection, once they were far enough inland that the wind no longer bothered them, Sabelu couldn't help but feel a bit like beaten dough, and he found himself slouching a bit. He straightened when he noticed Yawi trotting up alongside.

"Sorry I'm late," the wolf said enthusiastically and not apologetic in the least. "Had to go hunt something to get the taste of Shadow out of my mouth."

"But it was worth it, right?" Sabelu asked, raising a brow.

"Absolutely. I'm insulted you thought it wouldn't be. I'm just sorry you can't know the same pleasure."

Sabelu shifted on his horse, trying not to off-balance himself too much as he faced the wolf. "Do you ever feel guilty about it, though? I mean, the Shadows were Whites once."

"Once," the wolf agreed, "but no more. No amount of sympathy will make them turn their path."

"What about the half-Shadows who built the civilizations before us?"

"In the hands of the Author now. And the way you describe them says it all: half."

"Are there, or were there, half-Whites?"

Yawi made a noise. Then, "No. We are reborn too quickly to worry about needing to find refuge in a fleshy host, and our duty is all that matters. This does not mean we do not get enjoyment in our lives—you've witnessed it—but our first priority is stopping the Shadows." He added, "And there is no such thing as a half-White. It is either White or not White."

Sabelu considered this but didn't get a chance to say anything before Yawi spoke up again, saying, "Your front is this part of the mortal plane. Leave the rest of it to us and the Author."

"But it's hard," he said, mildly whining. "It's like carrying around an enormous bag of tools, watching others struggle with their own projects, and not being able to help everyone at the same time."

"Is everyone else struggling?" the wolf questioned. "Or are they learning from each other as you help them, as intended?" He went on, "You've said it yourself; you are only the tip of the arrow, forging the way through the Shadows for the rest to follow." Even at a brisk trot along the trail, Yawi managed to give him a look. "You know what's waiting for you back in Aktiya Waya. You know what's coming. Focus on the battles in front of you now, and let the rest lie in the Author's hands."

Sabelu let out a breath and could only nod. He did know what was waiting for him back home, and it wasn't Yukpa. Well, not only Yukpa.

He sighed and shook his head. Was it still coveting another man's wife if she wasn't married yet? He knew who her husband would be, and it wasn't him. She was starting to catch on that Sabelu was unlikely to be her husband, but that didn't mean that he didn't feel guilty about how it was slowly hurting her. Nor could he rightfully say that he didn't still look at her and wonder. As his uncle had said, he was still a man and had the normal desires of a man. Was it really the Shadows playing tricks on him, or should he pursue it while he had the chance? It was sorely tempting to give in to Dikdi's blood-taking game, especially because he knew how this was going to turn out.

His thoughts were not the most pleasant company, and Yawi was not always visibly around to talk to. Besides, he had an idea of what the wolf would say. Love is good. The pack is good. Having pups is good. But his mission right now was the war against the Shadows. Better the pack was small and united than large and corrupt.

When his father was younger and unmarried, he did a lot of work among the people. His mother had helped him in some of his work because she also had no other pursuits. But when they got married, especially when they started having children, the focus changed. They still worked a lot, but it was more for the family than the people.

It would have to wait a few years, Sabelu told himself. The men who fought in the wars thought about their families often, but in the middle of a battle was not the time to think about women. The first priority was always survival. Right now, he just needed to survive.

It was less like night and day and more like the twilight in between trying to keep his thoughts on track, but the closer he got to home, the easier it became to consider what was waiting for him and push Yukpa to the side.

The Sacred Wolf loomed large as he broke through the trees and followed the trail to the pass between the wolf's nose and tail. The sentries barely acknowledged him as he passed by. Once he was out of earshot, he looked down at Yawi, padding along silently beside him.

"Just tell me one thing," he said. "Considering all the progress we've made over the last few years, how could this have happened here in just the short time I was gone?"

Yawi glanced up at him. "That's what war is. You fight; you go back and forth. Some you win, some you lose. Sometimes, when you think an area is secure and you turn your back, the enemy takes advantage of the distraction."

"But I am only a man; it's the Whites who are doing the fighting."

"As I said, it is the nature of war. The Shadows need this place, these people, more than they need a little place like Lehoyed. You saw how fat and lazy the Shadow had become there. But this is the epicenter of souls and struggle. The mountain peak matters not if the foundation collapses."

Sabelu nodded. "And they're striking at the foundation."

He returned the horse to Hoshonti, then turned to face the mouth of the cave. He could feel the darkness as surely as he could feel the icy wind sweeping over the hills. A scream turned his attention to the sky where a flying White and a Shadow were locked in furious battle. There were similar fights going on elsewhere around the bowl, but it did not appear to be a full on battle just yet.

"They're coming," Yawi said, lowering his head and baring his teeth.

Sabelu did not react to that, just started up the slope, heart hammering in his chest. He instinctively ducked as two more flying creatures swooped low over his head, this time a Shadow chasing a White. He did not notice Yawi had dropped back until he heard the howl. By the time he turned, Yawi had already stopped and stood with his ears pricked forward, head tilted, listening for the replies. Sabelu counted at least four distinct howls, but had no idea what they said.

"Go, human," Yawi told him after a moment. "Leave the defense to us and do what you must."

They parted ways.

He knew what he was going to find, but to see it unfolding around him, the hazy darkness billowing out of the townhouse like heavy smoke and filling the cavern, was still terrifying to behold. A White fox was backed into a corner, snapping at a couple Shadows. A swift chase was playing out over the rooftops, though it was impossible to say who was chasing whom.

The atmosphere of the people as they walked around on their daily errands was one of apprehension, uncertainty. Sabelu delayed just a few minutes by going home to return his bags. There he met Blaknik whose overall demeanor suggested he was hiding.

"The others are in the Old Land," Sabelu stated.

Blaknik nodded. "A few days after you left, Asdeoha unveiled it in the townhouse. Said it was the pup of the Sacred Wolf, a new spirit for a new generation of people living in Aktiya Waya, said it would bring unity to the people and a decisive end to this war that you had seeded."

Sabelu slipped the bags off his shoulders. "It would, but he neglected to mention that the people would be unified only in death." He studied his younger brother. "You can feel it."

"It's been getting worse over the last few days. At this point, I think I can almost see it, around the townhouse. Netami's been affected the worst; she hasn't been home in four days. Itsitsi and Itsitsa haven't been home too much either. Anyone who supports you...they haven't been hurt in any way, but...just..." Blaknik shrugged helplessly. "You can feel it." He went on, "I don't know that anyone can't sense it, and few are pleased with it. And yet, there are plenty of people who are more interested in this supposed unity that Asdeoha preaches than any sort of discomfort."

"They're afraid. But they want things to go back to the way they were before."

"But why? I mean, it's not like you're really changing anything. Yeah, we're helping the Old Land and stuff, but it's not like we're moving there, we're not bringing people here."

"I'm not changing anything physically, but I am meddling in spiritual affairs. We are meddling in spiritual affairs, and the spirits don't like it. What we see here is only an echo of what happens in the spirit world."

"What's going on in the spirit world?" Blaknik asked. "I know you can see it."

Sabelu hesitated. Then, "The cerberus is coming. And the wolf dog."

"How do you intend to stop them?"

"I'm going to kill a puppy."

He knew his brother had a thousand questions, but there was no time to answer them all. Assuming Sabelu survived the next few hours, he could explain everything later.

He left the house and made for the townhouse. For the average person, it was an average day, but with a crackle in the air like the static before a thunderstorm. For Sabelu, it was like wading through tar and smoke. He tried not to react to the Whites and Shadows around him, but refraining from flinches and other instincts only made his muscles tighter and his lungs and heart heavier. By the time he reached the townhouse, he was having flashbacks of being held underwater, his lungs screaming for air, his muscles doing everything they could to try and propel him in any direction to safety, even as his vision blurred and the darkness closed in.

No otter was going to come and rescue him now. Right now, the pack was all that mattered. Yawi and the wolves were prepared to take on the cerberus and the wolf dog for the good of the people; Sabelu as an individual didn't matter much. No doubt the priests' puppeteers would understand this, and they would also understand that he would be very, very alone in a fight.

He entered the townhouse.

It looked very much like any ordinary day. Though it remained open to the public, there was a conspicuous lack of public. No groups of women sat around with their beading or sewing, no children played hide and seek. There did not appear to be any patrons looking for absolution for one sin or another, which was also quite strange.

The biggest change was the addition of a new figure, though Sabelu knew there was a second identical one in the priests' partitioned area. The public one was about two feet tall or so made from stone molded through the use of Asvhnisgi and other sorceries. It was in the shape of a four-headed dog. It wasn't quite sitting, not quite standing, the posture somewhere between ready to play and ready to pounce and kill, each of the heads in a different pose and expression. One was snarling, another barking, another howling, and the fourth almost looked like it was smiling. Each head had different colored eyes which had been painted, and each of the heads had over it a skull from the ones that Sabelu had sorted before he'd left. The tail was also covered in small bones, almost like armor, as were the lower part of the front legs.

Staring at the figure, not quite the center of the swirling darkness, Sabelu could have sworn he saw the thing move, the four heads turning to look at him, each one baring its teeth. When he blinked, it was back in its regular pose.

Then there was the second figure, in the partitioned section. It was easily twice as big as the public one, exquisitely carved from obsidian with jeweled eyes for each head. The covering bones were necessarily larger, and no less terrifying. This was the source of this new darkness, Sabelu knew, even without seeing it. It was like a homing beacon for the cerberus and the wolf dog. The chanting prayers of the priests, which he could hear, only added fuel to that fire.

Fortunately for Sabelu, tradition wasn't limited to artwork and language. There were plenty of weapons on display in the townhouse, showcasing many generations of weapon evolution, a variety of styles from the various peoples, and certain mementos from the wars, such as a couple rifles and pistols hung up on the wall. These were nonfunctioning anymore, but not his target anyway. His gaze instead wandered to a particular club. It was his grandfather's club, although not the one he'd used to avenge Sabelu's dead brother Tsona, for that had been buried with Yvgidahi.

Sabelu grabbed it off its wall rack, feeling the old wood in his hands, the grooves his grandfather had worn. On its own, it would never do what he was about to, but that was where the sorceries came in. True, he could have just gone up to the statues and done something quiet and innocuous, but just as the priests were chanting loudly, hoping to draw in the Shadows, Sabelu was going to make a point that they really weren't wanted.

With a whoop that he hoped would please his grandfather, Sabelu swung the club around his head once and brought it down on the smaller statue. He conjured Iyuwahnilvhi, looking for the exact moment that wood met stone. He found it, saw the energy connect, saw the ripples in the air, the wood, felt the vibrations begin to creep up his arm. Taking a breath, he whooped again, grabbed the energies, and forced it back the other direction, into the stone.

He watched the ripples move out of the wood and pass back into the stone. The rock, being far less flexible, cracked, shifted, and, in slow motion, so that Sabelu could count the shards of stone and bone, exploded. The four heads were severed from the spine between the front legs which broke off individually. Reaching for Nulinigv again, as each piece hit the ground, he took the energy from the impact and reversed it, sending the ripples up from the ground back into each piece so that they exploded. Four full heads were reduced to at least eight halves and numerous smaller chunks, the front legs reduced to dust.

He raised the club again and brought it down on the part of the body that was still standing. He repeated his efforts with the Nulinigv conjuration, the body shattering into innumerable tiny pebbles, the tail virtually disintegrating into dust and bone powder.

Then it was as if the darkness did the same thing to him as a spiritual earthquake rocked the townhouse. Although nothing physically moved— or he didn't think it did—Sabelu momentarily lost his balance and nearly fell over.

The chanting in the partitioned section abruptly ceased.

Sabelu regained his composure as fast as he could, knowing he would only get one chance. He charged toward the partitioned area, bursting through the door like a charging horse, club raised, chest full of air ready to be released into a fine war whoop.

He conjured Iyuwahnilvhi, beating Asdeoha to the punch, and brought his club down on the larger obsidian statue. He couldn't even see it because of how shrouded in darkness it appeared to him. But as wood touched stone and he reached for the energy to force it back, it was as though the darkness were also a solid thing that suddenly ruptured. The flash of light was real enough, and it blinded everyone in the room momentarily, including Sabelu.

When he brought his hand down from his eyes, he saw that the statue had been sheared, separating one head from the rest, the split going from the left shoulder to the right hip. The black stone gave up the Shadows it had been collecting, the dark brilliance fading to a natural obsidian gleam.

Sabelu suddenly became aware of the other priests in the room, and two acolytes. They all stood, hemming him in and blocking the door. It was Asdeoha who spoke, addressing the others.

"Deal with the remains of the other," he ordered calmly. "I will deal with this."

The men left, but Sabelu noted that their Shadows—from petty vices to master puppeteers—remained. In fact, they seemed to link themselves with Asdeoha's puppeteer, as if fusing into a single titan. Less than a general like the cerberus, but far more than just a puppeteer.

For a long three seconds after the room was emptied, the two men just stared at each other.

Then Asdeoha lunged. He wasted no time with words or lectures or stories, simply pounced. Sabelu brought the club up in front of him for protection. Asdeoha latched onto it and barreled into him. Whether the brute force came from Shadows or sorceries, Sabelu did not know. He just knew that they were far greater than what a single man of Asdeoha's size and stature should have been able to exercise normally. When his back finally hit the wall, it was like his navel kissed his spine and his tongue tasted the stone behind him.

He tried to suck in air but all he could do was gasp as Asdeoha, with both of them still grasping the club, swung him around—again, with far more force than he should have been capable of. Sabelu was determined to not let go of the club. He reached for Nulinigv sorceries once more, locking on to the forces keeping them in a circular motion. He managed to get Asdeoha around so that he was the one who would hit the other wall, but he himself was unprepared for just how much force he invoked. Both of them tumbled to the ground, the club falling between them.

With the titan's aid, Asdeoha recovered first, snatching the weapon from Sabelu's outstretched hand and giving it a good uppercut swing as he got to his feet. Sabelu dodged, but the titan tripped him up, and he wasn't even fully up before he was down again. He rolled away as Asdeoha brought the club down, chipping the stone where his head had been just a breath before.

He managed to get to his feet in a squatting posture, giving him good enough leverage to jump out of the way when Asdeoha whipped around with a follow-up swing.

Now they were both on their feet, but it didn't make the room any bigger, nor give Sabelu a weapon. In the middle of everything, he found that his one fury was that Asdeoha had his grandfather's club, and the corrupt priest had no right to even look at it, let alone wield it against the owner's own grandson.

Somewhere outside, a wolf howled and more answered. The atmosphere seemed to shift, the haze of darkness beginning to lift like morning fog.

Either Sabelu was the only one who noticed, or else he was the only one who reacted as the priest came for him again. This time, instead of leaping away, Sabelu leapt toward the priest. Suddenly the priest's calculations were thrown off, giving Sabelu a big enough window to conjure Time and duck the blow, then turn into Asdeoha, grabbing the priest's arm as he did so. He forced Asdeoha's arm down with one hand and grabbed the club with the other. The sudden change in physics and force saw them both stumble into the wall which broke Sabelu's conjuration. Asdeoha released one hand from the club and Sabelu grabbed it in both his hands, forcing them into a lopsided tug-of-war.

When Asdeoha turned to reached for the club with his free hand, Sabelu danced to the man's outside, just brushing the energy so that the man would think he was in danger of having his wrist broken when he really wasn't. The ruse worked and the priest let go. While the man was off-balance, Sabelu gripped the club and jabbed it in the man's ribs, then again in his chest. Then he spun it around and used the ball to strike the priest's throat. He was gentle enough that it wouldn't cause any lasting damage, but it stopped him in his tracks anyway.

Sabelu wouldn't say he didn't want to see Asdeoha gone at that moment, but his real goal was to invoke simple survival instinct. If he could make the man believe that this wasn't a fight worth having, then the titan behind him would have to literally force him into suicide to get him to continue attacking.

The wolves howled again. Sabelu watched as the titan paused and seemed to weigh its options. On Asdeoha's part, he was busy trying to breathe and regain his composure, still trying to decide what to do exactly.

The atmosphere shifted again. The titan made its choice. The beastly Shadow dissolved back into its myriad of puppeteers, indulgences, and vices. Asdeoha's puppeteer returned to its host while the rest dispersed to find their hosts. Asdeoha conceded the fight, but, as one might expect, looked no happier for it.

"The people," Sabelu said quietly, "were chosen by the Author. We were separated, united, and restored by the Author. We work with the Whites. No statue of Shadows will touch this place while I'm here."

Asdeoha, still rubbing his neck, said nothing.

Sabelu left the partitioned area. The remnants of the smaller statue had been cleaned up and it was as though it had never been there in the first place. There was no one in the townhouse.

He headed home. About halfway there, he realized he was still gripping his grandfather's club. He paused, looked at the thing in his hand, and physically peeled his fingers off the wood. The thing clattered to the ground, but when he picked it back up, his grip was much more relaxed.

"Sabelu."

He turned to see Yukpa approaching. Of all people, it would be her.

"Are you all right?" she asked timidly. "We heard a commotion in the townhouse, then all the priests left, though we didn't see you or Asdeoha. And then you left and..." Her gaze drifted to the club, then back to him. "Is everything all right?"

Sabelu looked down at the club once more. "V-e, everything is fine."

Her expression softened. "It's not good for priests to lie."

"Just doing a little housecleaning," he said evasively.

"The statue?" she guessed. When he nodded, she mirrored him.

"Good. We knew they were bad news when the priests first unveiled them. But what can we do, blaspheme the priests and the townhouse?"

"The priests are only men, and the townhouse is only a building," Sabelu told her. "The spirits are everywhere; they are the ones to watch out for."

"Maybe so, but shall every man or woman be his own priest and act according to his own law? We need guidance; that's why we have priests. That's why we have you."

He could not rightly refute her, and he was too tired to try even if he wanted to. In the end, he just nodded.

"Are you all right?" she repeatedly honestly. "I don't think anyone even knew you were back yet which means you walked into this off the road without even a chance to rest from your journey."

"I knew what I was coming back to," he told her. "And the road is not so treacherous."

"Even so. Your mother and father and siblings work hard, put in a lot of time and effort helping the people here and in the Old Land, but they still find time for rest and fun. You never seem to have a spare moment; it's a good thing sorcerers require less food or else you would waste away."

She poked his ribs once, hoping to elicit a more mirthful response than the half-smile he managed to dredge up. He could feel her disappointment even without his abilities. She wanted to help, and he wasn't responding. He became aware that he was trembling, the adrenaline slowly leaving him. Yukpa took his hand, the one that wasn't clutching the club, and put it under her chin. He could feel her pulse in her neck and he let out a slow breath.

"Your sister has told me that they're going to exile you," she said. "She said you yourself said that."

He nodded. "That's right."

"She said that you were looking forward to it."

"I'm looking forward to finishing the work I've started here. In an odd sense, exile will help with that. But I'm not looking forward to it."

It was only half-true. She was right. He was tired. He was exhausted.

He was sick of looking at people and Whites and Shadows. He was annoyed by the petty cares of daily living, not only for himself, but everyone around him. True, he was no longer suicidal over it, but it was still a burden he figured he could do without. Maybe it would be lifted once this was all over. He knew it wouldn't be, but he could hold out a small hope, right?

Yukpa pressed her lips to the back of his hand, though it was by no means a kiss. Then she moved his hand to her cheek. "Where will you go?"

He hesitated, wondering how much he should tell her. Finally, "There is a ridge, about a day's hike west. Good hunting, protection from the elements. I will build a small cabin there."

"You've given this some thought, then."

"It's one of the easier things to think about, really. Better than murderous priests."

"Better than me?"

Sabelu's throat closed up as his mind suddenly went blank. There was no good answer here. Years of observing other young men and carrying the memories of previous generations all screamed the same thing; he should deny it, say something nice about her, give her some reassurance, and steer the conversation in any other direction.

But as she said, it wasn't right for a priest to lie.

"Your silence betrays you," Yukpa said, her tone half-accusing. Then there came a shadow of a smile. "But so does the heat from your skin."

He only blushed harder at the remark.

"We both know I'm going to be exiled. Even pretending that your mother and grandmother approved of me in such a way normally, it would be no life that I would want for you."

Yukpa sighed and let his hand drop down, though she still held it between them and stared at it, her eyes occasionally flicking to the club in his other hand. "I know." She looked up at him. "If you weren't going to be exiled, would it be different?"

"I'm afraid I have too much knowledge and responsibility to entertain hypotheticals."

She gave him a look. "Humor me."

Sabelu sighed. "I don't know."

"That's not an answer. If you weren't going to be exiled, would you pursue me? I'm not stupid, Sabelu, I know you look at me across the room when I'm here. Considering the work that your father and mother have done and continue to do, I can only assume that it's the exile which has put a hold on any thought of you marrying and having a family."

Sabelu did not believe in simply telling people what they wanted to hear. The problem was, he didn't have any other real answer, and he couldn't be sure that the one he gave wasn't the truth.

"Things probably would be different, yes," he said. "I might not be so reserved about it if I didn't feel the time of exile looming over me like a storm cloud."

Yukpa nodded. "I understand. Now answer me this: if you were to be brought out of your exile—in this fight against evil spirits, it is only logical to assume that it is the work of the Shadows that you should be banished, and once they are defeated, why shouldn't you be hailed a hero and brought back to Aktiya Waya? Or any of the other villages? Or even a new village, if that is a good possibility? When this is all over, if you were to be brought out of exile, then would you consider it?"

Maybe. "I believe so, yes."

She nodded again and averted her gaze for a moment. "All right." She played with his fingers. "Well, if what you told Netami was true and she relayed it accurately, you don't have much time left here. But that's all right. You aren't the only one fighting the Shadows. I think I can busy myself for a while when I return to Yonhi."

Now he smiled.

She turned away, then looked back and noticeably cleared her throat even as she lowered her voice. "Might I suggest you hurry home and do something about your bow? It appears ready to fire, and we've just established that there is still some time before I can take your arrows."

His grin turned stupid as a fresh wave of heat languished his body. He turned around and, at her suggestion, hurried away, using the club to distract any eyes from his, ahem, taut bow.

Blaknik was still the only one home when he arrived, and his expression went through several phases before he finally just raised a brow and asked, "What sort of mischief have you been into exactly? And who was the woman?"

Sabelu scowled even as his brother grinned. "This wasn't..." He fought for words. "I destroyed the statues in the townhouse. I just...didn't put the club back before I left; I was too angry."

"Obviously not."

Sabelu briefly looked down at himself. "That was afterwards. I ran into Yukpa."

Blaknik was still smirking, the bastard. "Oh, you 'ran into' her? How many times?"

Sabelu had a notion to smack his brother upside the head with the club, and his annoyance effectively killed his arousal. Instead, he pushed past his brother into the bedroom, laying the club beside his bed.

"All right, all right," Blaknik said behind him with mock exasperation. "So you destroyed the statues?"

Sabelu straightened. "Yes. The smaller one was easy enough."

"I don't imagine the priests took kindly to it. And I'm guessing they were still in there chanting around the larger one."

"That's right. Asdeoha sent the other priests to clean up the first mess I made, then he attacked me."

"Did you kill him?"

Sabelu shook his head and turned. "No."

"Why not? Ganhv tried to kill you and you killed him, and I don't think Asdeoha was going to let you off with a stern warning."

"Maybe not, but in this way, it wouldn't be able to be used against me. I was there for the statues, not the priests."

"So does this mean you won't be exiled?" Blaknik asked.

"No," Sabelu said, "it means I will be only exiled and not targeted for clan vengeance had I killed him."

That, at least, gave his little brother pause before he asked, "But the people were frightened by the statues. They may not be overtly celebrating, but it is a good thing."

"They celebrate now, but they misunderstand what I've done, what I'm going to do."

His brother didn't understand, and a part of him didn't want to, Sabelu knew. Scheming was for white men and dealing with spirits was for priests. Blaknik was happy to help people, but he didn't fully grasp the connection between the spirit world and the waking world, and he certainly didn't see the river as Sabelu saw it.

"Is it safe for the rest to return?" Blaknik inquired instead.

Sabelu nodded and saw his brother off to the Old Land. He did not wait for their return, just lay down on his bed.

He woke in his uncle's cave before he realized he was even asleep. His first thought was that it was unusual for there to be so many Whites in the cave. A second look showed that many or all of them were injured in some way. Anagalisgi himself went from White to White with salves and bandages. Sabelu stood and went to his uncle's side.

"I thought Whites healed faster than this," he commented, kneeling with his uncle beside a cat-like creature with a long gash in its side and several bite marks.

"In the waking world, they do," Anagalisgi said, gently applying a resin-like substance over the gash. "And they do heal faster than normal here. But an injury is an injury, and I help where I can."

His uncle gave him a look and he nodded. Sabelu stood and made his way through the maze of Whites to his uncle's shelves where dozens of pots and jars contained various healing elements. Between the two of them, they were able to treat all of the Whites, and most were able to leave with rapidly-healing wounds. Only a few required any kind of extended attention, and they moved to lie beside the fire. Sabelu followed Anagalisgi outside on an expedition to replenish the supplies.

"That was a lot closer than I really would have preferred," Sabelu stated. "The cerberus and the wolf dog were nearly there."

"They were, yes," Anagalisgi agreed, kneeling in the dirt to gently dig up a root. "But you knew it was coming."

"I knew it had to happen; I just don't understand why, or why it had to cut so close. Why shouldn't I have opened Galohisdi from Lehoyed, gotten home that much earlier, destroyed the statues sooner?"

"Weren't you the one telling Yukpa that you knew too much to entertain hypotheticals?"

Sabelu blushed as his uncle stood and moved on to a new area, directing him to gather this or that item. Sabelu knelt to gently pick a couple leafy plants, then moved on to gather some blooming flowers.

There were any number of things he wanted to ask his uncle, but knew there was no point. They were approaching the rapids before the waterfall; if he didn't know what to do by now, he never would. Maybe the cerberus hadn't broken into Aktiya Waya, but they were very close by.

"Did you see the battle?" he inquired instead.

"I heard it," Anagalisgi answered, not looking at him as he cut a strip of bark from a tree. "Even here, I heard it. I had no illusions that I would be able to fight, so I simply prepared the herbs and bandages, and I waited."

"Are they still fighting?" Sabelu asked, carefully lifting a bed of moss from a log. "I didn't hear anything."

"Regrouping. On both sides."

"Is it only the cerberus and the wolf dog, or are the others involved, too?"

"From the reports I've heard, it was only the cerberus and the wolf dog, though there were a few rumors that the serpent was lurking around."

Sabelu grunted. "The cerberus is in charge of the attacks, the wolf dog in charge of the Shadows. The serpent deals with stronghold species; why would it be lurking around this battlefield?"

Anagalisgi glanced at him. "I don't know. Does it really matter?"

"Well, if we're dealing with vices, one hundred is only slightly more challenging than one. They are as numerous as leaves on trees and fall just as easily. I'm a little more concerned about the generals. If they are as big as mountains, there is a significant difference between destroying two mountains or three."

"Or four."

Sabelu huffed a sigh. "Or four." He hesitated. "Is the dragon involved yet?"

His uncle's expression said he was uncertain, but it was contorted in such a way that made Sabelu afraid.

"The Author alone knows how everything is to be, how everything will turn out," he prefaced. "But I would be lying if I said I didn't suspect that the dragon has gifts echoing yours, an uncanny ability to know and learn and understand. I think it's not involved now because it knows a more advantageous opportunity awaits it. The difference is, you know how it turns out."

"Maybe the dragon does, too," Sabelu said. "Maybe it's getting involved at such a time in order to try and change it."

Anagalisgi nodded. "Could be." He shifted position and stood from where he'd cut a few more roots. "All I know is that the supplies I used today are only a fraction of what I'm going to need when you go to confront the cerberus."

"In the underground city."

His uncle's look was response enough.

They made their way to a new area and continued foraging.

"You were right about something, though," Sabelu said, raising his voice since their backs were to each other.

"I usually am," his uncle replied. "What have you learned from your elder, pup?"

"Maybe I should have taken time out for Yukpa. She thinks it will be just a few years and then we might be together, but it's not going to happen. She's going to spend enough time doubting and worrying about my exile that she'll fall in love with her husband. When I am finally permitted to return from exile..." He let out a breath. "There really won't be anything for us."

"There are other women, you know," Anagalisgi said, moving to a new spot. "And you've said it yourself that you have difficulty seeing your own life and have to view it through the eyes of others. Maybe your wife hasn't been born yet, so you can't see yourself as being married. The Book only says you die on a mountainside; it doesn't say who you leave behind."

"Maybe." Sabelu shrugged though his uncle couldn't see. He glanced over his shoulder. "Did you ever wish you were married, when you were in the waking world?"

"You know I did on occasion. You know that I still hold some regrets that such things never came to be."

"If you did have children, what do you think they would be like? Would they have your prophetic and spiritual gifts? Would mine be needed? Would I be who I am today?"

His uncle's tone was guarded and carefully neutral. "I can't say for certain."

"Your mother and grandmother had some sharp spiritual senses; did you know that? And your great uncle was quite the prophet and priest."

"I'm guessing that no one listened to my great uncle either." Now he sounded mildly amused.

"No," Sabelu said. "Like watching people canoe straight over a waterfall."

"Well, you're about to do the same thing."

"Yes, but I'm doing it in order to stop catastrophe, according to the Author's will."

Anagalisgi looked at him. "Who says that any other time wasn't the will of the Author?"

Sabelu opened his mouth but found no words.

"It's time for you to go," his uncle said abruptly, standing. Sabelu followed suit, straightening just as his uncle approached, sounding suddenly hurried. "The time is coming, Tsiquiyi, and where you go, I do not know that I can follow."

Sabelu nodded. "I know." He clasped his uncle's wrist. "But we will see each other again."

"Yes," Anagalisgi said, though there remained a flicker of doubt in his eyes. "We will see each other again."

DⱵ ʳS∩ DVꞀT

Achuchidune Adolv'i

Challenge

The festival that year was hosted in Anpa O Wican'hpi. Out on the plains, the tournament grounds sprawled out in all directions, seemingly with no end in sight.

Deer Clan was the most flamboyant of the clans and loved a good party. They prided themselves on their festivals at all times of year, not just the festival of tournaments. Visitors to Anpa O Wican'hpi often made the comment that it was more rare for there to not be a festival or celebration on any given day than just an ordinary day.

So it was that where any other host would see their guests file in quietly and then begin the festivities later on, giving everyone time to make camp and settle in, Deer Clan welcomed their guests with dancers all the way out in the tall grasses along the trail that led to the campsite. The dancers followed the guests, getting everyone excited and riled up and ready to compete. Many of the men abandoned the incoming procession to head to the dancing grounds where the opening ceremonies would take place, leaving the women to claim a campsite, pitch a tent, and so on. Many of the women simply picked a campsite, deposited their stuff, turned the horses over to Hanepi, then joined the men at the dancing grounds. The vast majority of the visitors would sleep under the stars that first night.

Sabelu watched everything with a cautious eye. The Shadows were strong in Anpa O Wican'hpi, puppeteers clinging tightly to many of the priests and the local council members. Because Sabelu had been consulted and heeded for his choice of national council members the previous year, the national council was fairly tame on the part of Shadows. Oh, they all had their vices and a few indulgences, but there were no puppeteers among them.

The puppeteers were looking to change things. The priests of Aktiya Waya and their titan may have failed to summon the cerberus, but that didn't mean that any of the Shadows or the cerberus itself had just quietly gone home to wait for the next incantation. They were still lurking out there. And Sabelu knew right where they would be.

Although a priest, he was still a guest in Anpa O Wican'hpi, so his role was minimal. Of course, his role as spiritual support was somewhat detrimental to the rest of the priests as he prayed to the Creator and the Whites, inviting in more Whites, rather than the Shadows. Still, he had to sit with the other priests and the various councils, listening to the speeches and reports, and all the regular dull monotony of opening up a festival. The boredom was largely relieved when the dancing competition actually began, though that didn't mean he could leave his seat.

Asdeoha leaned over to him, speaking as low as he could while still able to be heard over the drummers and singers. "I wonder what would happen if each group was given a particular song or chant, and it was these chants that brought in the cerberus and the wolf dog and drove out the Whites. Would you really smash the drums? Would you destroy these grounds? Would you attack the drummers, the singers, the dancers, as you did me?"

"You attacked me," Sabelu reminded him.

"But would you? It's one thing to root out a rogue priest, or to have disagreements over minor points. Would you really condemn all those dancers down there for heresy or witchcraft?"

"I think it would be more prudent to look for the priest who gave them the song or chant. And condemning men does little to stop the evil behind it." He gave Asdeoha a look. "And I have to admit, it would be interesting to see your expression when you do try such a thing, but the cerberus doesn't show up. I'm just sorry I won't be around to witness it."

"If you think we've packed more idols and brought them here—"

"I'm not talking about painted stone, bones, and gem. I'm talking about the Shadows themselves."

Asdeoha chuckled, but Sabelu did not miss the twitch of nervousness he and his puppeteer shared. "Well, you have grown arrogant, haven't you? Gone from overseeing weddings and solving minor relationship problems to crushing the military general of the Shadows, all in just a few short years. I never knew the Whites could actually be so ambitious. Or maybe there is a Shadow of Ambition in you somewhere."

"My only ambition is to help the people, and that means destroying the Shadows. Helping them deal with minor vices and indulgences is good. Breaking the power of puppeteers is better. But crushing titans and generals is what will make the real difference in the long term."

Asdeoha made a kind of grunting sound as the puppeteer whispered in his ear. "Anyone can crush an ant. But even the white men could not make the mountains move."

"Then it's a good thing I'm not a white man."

The priest grinned. The puppeteer continued to whisper. "If you do what I think you're going to do, then you understand that you will not be coming back."

"I know what must be done. You can't scare me away from it."

Asdeoha hummed a kind of disappointment. "Another of the line which bore Anagalisgi, shamefully destroyed."

"Anagalisgi is not dead."

"No, but he is far from here where things matter. He may reside with the spirits, but we mortals are the ones who pay the price for the wars the spirit wage." He gave Sabelu a look. "I think you know who the People Before were."

"I do," Sabelu said stiffly.

"If you do what I think you're going to do, maybe you should first think about all of the others, many of whom are here—" He looked pointedly at the crowd. Sabelu followed his gaze and saw Yukpa, cheering on her sister who was dancing. "—who may also become just a Person Before."

Sabelu took a deliberate breath and grinned. "It must be frustrating for you, not knowing how this ends. Your puppeteer can whisper and scheme and pull you here and there and make many threats. Because it's afraid. And you're afraid. Because you don't know. But I do. And I am going to do what you think I am. And you can't stop me."

The puppeteer was indeed afraid, but that also made it far more dangerous. Sabelu didn't know if he wanted to make an excuse to leave for a few minutes or stick it out, stare down the Shadow as it were. His bladder made the decision easy enough.

By the time he returned, Asdeoha was wrapped up in something else, speaking to a priest of Yonhi. Sabelu reclaimed his seat and tried to pay attention to the dancers. He'd lost track of Yukpa in the crowd, but he knew that she was congratulating her sister and helping her out of her regalia. Afterwards, they would return to their campsite and tidy it up for the rest of the family who was still quite enthralled with the competition, even if it was only practice.

Sabelu did not have to stay all night, nor as long as the local priests, but he did so simply for the fact that this was the last festival he was going to see for quite a while. He waited until he knew his family would be asleep, if only because he didn't want to listen to their excited chatter or answer any of the more mundane questions that had become so unimportant to the situation that they annoyed him worse than a gnat.

At the same time, the festival was important. It was not only an enormous part of their identity, but the spiritual disposition of the participants could stir up some incredible energy in the spirit world. While the mortals competed on the tournament fields, the spirits fought on the battlefield. Asdeoha was more accurate than Sabelu would have liked to admit when he spoke of using the singers and drummers to channel energy to summon the Shadows. Summoning spirits was the whole point of such songs and dances; it was just a matter of which spirits were summoned.

The tents were pitched, but that was all that had really gotten done around the campsite. Netami got her own tent while Ola Achukma and Nendawagan shared one, and Sabelu was forced to share with Blaknik. His younger brother stirred some and rolled over as Sabelu lay down and made himself comfortable, but that was all.

Sabelu did not fall asleep immediately. Instead he lay awake for some time, wondering if he shouldn't say goodbye to people before he left. He knew he would see everyone again, but it just seemed like the right thing to do. Just because he knew what was going to happen didn't mean anyone else did, and the situation he would return to, while he had been telling people about it for some time now, would only make them anxious which would open the door for more Shadows. He knew instinctively that Fear would rip into his mother just as soon as it could.

He slept and did not dream. When he woke, the sky was cloudless and just light enough to see by. Sabelu remained where he was for a long moment. He looked down at a wet nose nudging his foot. It was Yawi. The wolf nudged his foot again and stared at him.

Sabelu quietly slipped out of the tent and crept through the campsite. He spied only half a dozen people who were up and around, and four of them were sentries. He made his way to the horse pens. Hanepi was sleeping soundly, and Sabelu saw no reason to disturb him.

Sabelu's mount was a retired black stallion. The beast had evidently found his preferred company and favorite grass, for he initially resisted Sabelu's attempts at haltering and leading. After the fourth try, the stallion had had enough fun and stood patiently. Sabelu mounted up and turned toward the gate.

Hanepi still did not react as Sabelu rode past him, opening and closing the gate on horseback. He wouldn't even notice the horse gone. If it wasn't a competition horse, he didn't notice unless someone came to him and informed him that their horse was missing.

Trying to be as quiet as possible for the sake of everyone still sleeping, Sabelu kept his horse at a walk while he circled the camp and the main village, nodding to the sentries as he passed. Even once he was basically clear of the village and heading southeast, he kept up a walk for another half mile or so, thinking through everything that was about to happen. He brought nothing with him but a couple small knives and a length of rope. These were more useful as tools or minor self-defense against any predators lurking in the grass; it would do virtually nothing for him in a spiritual confrontation. He knew all of this very well, but he couldn't help but think that just the physical feel of a larger weapon might bolster his courage some.

The grass rustled, and Yawi and the wolves made themselves known.

"You know where we're going," Sabelu said, unsure if he intended it as a question or a statement.

"Just follow the stench," one of the wolves replied distastefully.

The pack erupted into a sprint, and Sabelu kicked his mount to follow.

Sabelu had galloped before, and he had been on a number of game drives. This experience now, simply galloping across open plains, the village fading into nothing behind him, the horizon stretching out for eternity before him, it was peaceful and surreal. He used Asvhnisgi his horse, felt his smooth muscles gliding across the ground, the pounding of his heart and lungs, the exhilaration of the free run. But there was also a certain sense of dread within Sabelu. It wasn't the inherent fear of a game drive, the possibility of being thrown and trampled. It wasn't even the fear of the unknown, but the fear of the known. He was willingly throwing himself into danger here.

The sun broke the horizon, and Sabelu had to invoke Atsvstdi to shield his eyes and keep track of the wolves. Once the sun was high enough that being blinded was no longer an issue, Sabelu elected to conjure Iyuwahnilvhi.

All of the horse tenders would have a fit if they saw him conjuring Time around a horse, but the way he figured it, there was so little out in the plains here that there wasn't enough movement, or sudden lack thereof, to spook a horse. There was the argument that he might accidentally expose a horse to too much sorcery and so condemn it to death, but at least it would provide some meat for his first few days in exile, one less thing to worry about.

By now they knew of his departure. Most weren't overly worried for the simple fact that the festival was chaotic and maybe he had some business to attend to. Or maybe he was just wandering around, or maybe he had wandered off to find some peace and quiet, find something like the hillside back home where he could sit and talk to the spirits.

Asdeoha would know, though. His puppeteer would inform him of Sabelu's whereabouts; he already knew his intentions. The head priest would know. He would go to the other priests and they would begin cooking up the next part of their scheme. Well, they'd had it mostly planned for a while now; they just had to put it into practice.

Sabelu rested his horse for a bit, then continued galloping, off and on as needed. He ceased his conjuring when the wolves slowed. The ground turned rocky. At the top of a small rise, Serpent Canyon spread out before him, seemingly as far as the eye could see. Five parallel canyons, the middle one just half the size of the other four, leading to the underground city.

Sabelu dismounted and patted his horse on the shoulder. "Good boy. Go find yourself some nice grass."

He again used Asvhnisgi the stallion and impressed upon him images and desires to that effect. The horse snorted and meandered away to find something to nibble on, sampling some small scrub bushes along the way. Sabelu turned his attention back to the canyons. The wolves had spread themselves far and wide across the rims of the various canyons, barking, yipping, howling, and carrying on in conversation. Only Yawi remained by his side.

"Few humans have ever even attempted what you're about to do," Yawi told him. "Fewer still have survived."

"But it needs to be done," Sabelu said.

No more was said.

Galo'ondiha ale Agi'a saw Sabelu safely across the southern canyons to the middle canyon, then down to the ground. The sun was high overhead and provided light, but his proximity to the evil that lurked below meant that he could neither feel the heat nor enjoy it even if he could. He stood facing the yawning mouth of the Cursed Zukatopa, two fangs on either side and one in the middle.

He was suddenly assaulted by an image of a snake as long as the horizon being knocked to the ground, its teeth digging into the earth on impact. As the serpent righted itself and lifted its teeth from the dirt, it gouged out five enormous canyons.

"Is that what happened here?" he wondered aloud once the vision had fled.

Nothing answered, and he counted it a relief.

Sabelu forced himself not to stare at the serpent longer than he absolutely needed to. Memories of the dog statues coming to life still made his skin crawl, and those had been small dogs. He didn't want to chance it with a serpent that was big enough to swallow him whole. It didn't help that he voluntarily walked into the serpent's throat.

From his parents' Book as well as their verbal recitations and memories, he knew that Atsvstdi would only last so long as he descended into the tunnel. He held onto it for all he was worth, pausing when he faced its end.

He heard things in the darkness. Whispers and laughter, hisses and growls, scratching on the rock, some of it subtle, and some of it feeling as though something moved just behind him. His heart pounded in his chest. He looked back, wondering if he might still see the exit, knowing it was a foolish hope. He jumped as he felt fur brush his hand. Even though it was probably just the wolves, he couldn't suppress a shudder.

Then he saw something. In the darkness. Light. A tiny pinprick, like a star. Then there were more. They got bigger, until it appeared they were heading straight for him. They floated through the air, illuminating the rock in a bluish-white light, each one no more than a candle, but a great blue-white flame when combined. And yet, they did not burn his eyes to look upon them.

When they got close enough, Sabelu saw that they were not fireflies, as he had expected. Rather, they were like tiny fish with appendages that were not quite fins and not quite wings. They moved like fish but flew through the air like birds. They were definitely Whites, but he'd never seen their kind before.

No explanation of their kind or appearance was offered, but their purpose was fairly obvious. The group of them—a school? or a flock?— split into three, one swirling around his head, another around his feet, and another stretching out to light the way forward. Sabelu could hear the hisses from the Shadows, and he noted that the temperature in the cave dropped considerably so that he could see his breath puffing in the air.

Forcing himself to take a deep breath, Sabelu pressed forward, following the line of bird fish. When he attempted to invoke Atsvstdi to augment their light, he was startled by a sudden, scratching blow to his upper arm. Stunned, he ceased conjuring Atsvstdi and held his arm, as if unable to process that an ethereal Shadow had just wounded him, drawn blood in fact. He healed it with no trouble and did not attempt Atsvstdi again.

He felt the change in wind and acoustic dynamics even before the bird fish illuminated the end of the tunnel and the opening of the immense cavern that housed the underground city. Only a few dozen bird fish accompanied him, and it would have taken thousands more to show the full grandeur of the place. As it was, the farthest he could see was to the edge of the ledge, the stone balcony overlooking the city. He glanced to one side where he knew the trough was. There was no resin material in it anymore, so even if he had a means of making fire, it would have done no good.

The wolves appeared on either side of him, ears flat, teeth bared. The bird fish regrouped, forming a narrow circle at the edge of the ledge and moving slowly around, always clockwise.

Something moved in the darkness, something big. A crack, an echo, another crack, a huge, reverberating crash, the sound of stone scraping on stone, another crash, more echoes, a rush of wind.

Then there was the sound of a flint striking stone. The trough erupted into flame, but it was not a familiar, comforting orange flame. This was black fire, and it seemed to act as a terrible magnet for the light emitted by the bird fish, though in irony, the spreading of such light only helped to illuminate more of the area, like a luminescent fog.

The black fire raced through the trough, utilizing the system the People Before had used to light the cave. Then Sabelu noticed something about the trough. It was moving, the stone slowly turning into smoky scales. Shifting and coiling, only a split-second warning from the wolves saved Sabelu from being snapped up by the serpent as it lunged from the darkness, one fang easily twice his height. The great Shadow general slithered across the stony ledge, blocking the exit tunnel, resting at the edge of the ledge along the wall, turning and rising to look at him. The beast still appeared to be strung through the cavern, covered in black fire, or maybe he was imagining things. A glamor, as his uncle called it.

His gaze settled on a particular section of serpent or trough, whichever it was. The fire was molding into a shape. Halfway through, he knew it was the black phoenix, and it was the phoenix who had lit the trough and awakened the serpent. Near it, on the ground, a figure Sabelu recognized easily only because of the pack standing beside him. The wolf dog watched him but did not approach.

Before he could think about it too much, his view was blocked by three massive heads rising from beneath the ledge, huge noses and mouths huffing out cold, putrid breath.

"Well, well," the cerberus rumbled. "Look who it is."

"Asdeoha might have warned you," Sabelu said.

"A small man," the right head mused.

Sabelu looked at it. "A puppeteer controls Asdeoha and has bled him spiritually dry. Most people are trapped by indulgences. The weakest cannot break through even a small vice. Yet I have fought a titan and gained an audience with all four of you. I can't be that small."

"You are nothing," the left head said, lowering itself so that its breath could have knocked Sabelu over. "You are but a mortal sack of flesh. You step into a war you know nothing about."

He grinned. "I'll bet you I do know something about it, though. I know that just as I am bound by the rules of a three-dimensional, linear, mortal world, so are you. The difference is, I'm used to it." He gestured to the wolves. "We are used to it." He continued, "And every moment that you're here trying to destroy a small, know-nothing human, the Whites in the spirit world are decimating your forces."

Truthfully, Sabelu had hoped to catch the generals off-guard with such a comment. Instead, the center head said, "Then we'll just have to make your death swift."

Several things happened at once. The right cerberus head made a snap for Sabelu. When it got to within a foot of his body, one of the wolves barreled into it. In the dim light, Sabelu couldn't be entirely sure, but it almost looked like the wolves had doubled or tripled in size. With his life in immediate danger, he didn't really care.

The left cerberus head tried the same thing and received a similar result, a second wolf slamming into the side of its head. The combined force, what one might normally liken to a mouse attacking a dog, pushed the cerberus back. The cavern was filled with the sound of crumbling, crushing rock as the cerberus fought for balance and tried to snap at the wolves at the same time.

Meanwhile, the serpent struck again. This time, Sabelu was forced to conjure Iyuwahnilvhi, trying to dodge the fangs which he did not doubt were venomous. Another pair of wolves ran, jumped, and latched onto the serpent, careful to avoid the fire along its spine. Sabelu ducked as the serpent reared up and swung itself around, trying to dislodge the ferocious canines. The beast slammed into a large stalactite, causing it to crack and ultimately fall. Sabelu ran to avoid being crushed.

Only at the last minute did he consider Galo'ondiha ale Agi'a. Whipping around, he reached for the sorcery, grabbing hold of the massive, heavy object and, most ungracefully, altering its path so that it struck the serpent along its body.

The next thing Sabelu knew, something sharp was digging into his back and chest, holding both shoulders in an iron grip. He had only to look down to see the talons of the black phoenix. The giant bird with fire on its wings and tail made a sharp bank before it could hit the cave wall, though Sabelu was not given such consideration. He felt both legs break as he hit the rock like a child's toy. He cried out, suddenly oblivious to the way the phoenix carried him up and up, into the heights of the cavern.

The phoenix's fire continued to absorb all light from the bird fish in a brilliant dalliance as the creatures writhed about the cave, though the most he was able to see through tear-blurred eyes was streaks of blue-white light. His broken legs hung limply from his knees, and every twitch that the phoenix made, whether it was swooping about the cavern or just gliding, sent arrows of pain stabbing into him.

The vice-like hold on his torso released, but then he was only falling. With his brain still dealing with torrents of pain, it was all he could do to reach for the sorceries. Before he could get everything in order, something struck him, and he thought it might have actually been an arrow piercing his lower back. It was the phoenix again, snatching him out of midair. Sabelu tasted blood, but with the phoenix's talons in him, he could not cough to clear it from his lungs or stomach. Even spitting was painful, and he felt the blood dribble over his chin.

The phoenix dropped low, twisting this way and that. The wind helped to clear the tears from Sabelu's eyes, but his mind still couldn't make sense of what was going on. He saw only snapping teeth and flashes of white, all flowing together in a chaotic river as the phoenix twisted and banked. At one point, a huge paw came just inches from eviscerating him. Somehow, Sabelu managed to put together that the phoenix was twisting through the fights between the wolves and the other generals.

Even in his dazed state, he became aware of heat. Terrible heat, in the coolness of the cave. The light taken from the bird fish narrowed and twisted like a fine cord, and somehow he was able to make out that the phoenix was burning itself. Burning him. Or, perhaps as it sucked the light from the bird fish, it was sucking the soul right out of his body.

Then he was in free-fall again, but not for long as he soon slammed into the ground and started rolling. He went limp as his head hit rock. Was it his head that erupted into a great burst of light, or was that the bird fish? He heard a loud rumbling, a crash, and then he was being showered with dust and small rocks. The air thickened to the point where he almost couldn't breathe.

He didn't know what hurt the most. In the moment, everything hurt and nothing hurt. His head made it so he barely knew which way was up, or if he was even on the ground. He knew there was a hole in his back, blood going where it wasn't supposed to. There was something wrong with his legs, too, but he didn't think that was important right this second.

He couldn't see, couldn't breathe, but in that moment, he had an odd thought. It was something from his father's Book, and also one of the first things someone learned about sorcery and animals, specifically the horses. The horses didn't have complex thoughts like people did. They didn't understand logic and argument. Their minds were simple, their needs basic. You didn't try to orchestrate a full sentence to tell a horse where to go, you just impressed upon it basic directions or, if it was a familiar place, an image of that place.

Something about that line of thought brought Sabelu enough clarity that he found himself invoking Agvhalvda. Not much, just enough to stitch his skin back together to keep his blood from pouring out onto the stone. The broken skin on his scalp was healed easily enough, and even his chest wasn't too difficult, though he got an impression of a waterskin. His skin wasn't the only thing that was bleeding, and he was going to bloat with blood and die if he didn't do something more.

But in order to do that, he had to be able to think. The brain was one of the few things that people, even the healers, didn't like to touch unless to not do so was to guarantee death. Well, now seemed like such an appropriate situation.

Prolonged use of the sorceries caused headaches, and using the sorceries to investigate a concussion was little different. He used Asvhnisgi just enough to tell him where the problem areas were. Inflammation, minor bleeding, having to process an overload of sensation, nothing that was going to kill him in the next minute. That alone relieved a marginal bit of pain, at least from that part of his body.

Uhyvtsa had a more immediate and more radical effect, drawing the coolness of the stone into his body, relieving the worst of the pressure in his head and taking the edge off the pain in his body. With his head somewhat clearer, he was made aware of the blood bloat in his torso.

Feeling inside himself, Sabelu was momentarily shocked again by the damage. He needed to do something quickly, but when everything was a priority, where did he begin?

The blood. He had to stop the blood. With the skin repaired, it had nowhere to go, and it was pressing on his heart and lungs. He needed to repair the blood vessels, get everything flowing the way it should.

Normally the body itself had enough Agvhalvda reserves, often in the form of fats, that could be converted into the appropriate tissue. Sometimes, if the wound was great enough, any food in the stomach or intestines was carefully repurposed, although this technique required a great deal of both skill and time. Sabelu wasn't sure he had that much skill, and he certainly didn't have that much time. He also had no choice.

Then he had the idea to use the blood itself. As far as the vessels, they were similar enough that it was less effort than trying to draw in fat and restructure it from the inside out, to say nothing of the cleanup that had to be done afterwards. He threw himself into the work, praying for the spirits to guide him because he certainly didn't know what he was doing in his half-concussed state.

The larger vessel repair was easy enough, but the sudden correction in blood flow overwhelmed him with a tide of nausea, augmented by a sudden, rumbling earthquake, and he twisted to vomit up blood and stomach bile.

When he tried to sit up, he smacked his head again on rock and immediately lay back down. Putting his arms up, he discovered that he was trapped in what felt like a small cave or pile of rubble. Or a tomb, a small voice in the back of his mind whispered.

He was feeling better, but he wasn't clear yet. He still had terrible internal damage, plus his legs were yet broken. Ignoring the new throbbing in his head, Sabelu again invoked the sorceries.

When manipulating Agvhalvda in such a way as to completely restructure it, there were always leftovers, little bits and pieces that were not easily recycled or even not needed. In the smallest conjurations, these leftovers could be safely left to be naturally filtered out by the body through the kidneys or intestines. With everything that Sabelu was doing, leaving that much waste behind would only poison his body. He might last a day or two, but no more. Reluctantly, he pushed the leftover material into his stomach where he promptly heaved that up as well.

His torso taken care of, his broken legs made themselves known once more. The bones were sticking out every which way. This would not be such an easy fix.

Taking a breath, Sabelu carefully reached inside himself, finding the nerves in his leg, and used Nulinigv to effectively cut off all communication between his brain and his leg. The sudden sensation, or lack thereof, spooked him enough that he lost his hold on the sorcery. His leg erupted in a thousand thorns tearing into him, and he scrambled to reinstate the block while still leaving enough sensation that he could feel what he was doing.

His skin prickled uneasily, fear shivering through him that maybe he wouldn't regain the use of his legs when he was done. But for the moment, it was the only thing he had as he had to blindly finagle the bones and tissue into place. Because he couldn't sit up to actually reach his legs, the best he could do was feather the use of Galo'ondiha ale Agi'a and other minor sorceries, doing everything remotely with only a sliver of sensation. The block he instated on his nerves opened or even failed entirely several times, causing him wrenching pain. But the more he worked, the less it hurt, until he was able to drop the nerve block entirely and just grit his teeth.

It took him far longer than he thought it should have, but he really didn't want to get it wrong and have to rebreak his legs and try again later. As it was, he could only go by what he hoped was right as he pushed his legs together and attempt to splint off of each other back and forth while he made minor adjustments and stitched everything back together.

When he was as confident as he was going to be, Sabelu took in as large a breath as he could manage and bent his legs. His knees still worked, anyway, as did his ankles. As for that part in the middle, it still throbbed, and he was exhausted in almost every way a man could be exhausted, but he no longer felt like he might die of his physical injuries. He let his breath out slowly and allowed himself to relax flat on the rock floor, allowing the natural coolness of the stone to work on him as he released all use of the sorceries.

Were the Shadows still out there? He hadn't heard or felt anything in a while, and nothing had come searching for him. Maybe they believed the rock fall had crushed him. What of Yawi and the wolves? If they were alone here, how were eight wolves—even if they were one of the White generals, for lack of better term—going to handle four Shadow generals?

Well, he couldn't stay here forever. His head still didn't feel great, but he felt as though he'd spent a lot longer than necessary trapped under the rock.

Sabelu felt around, trying to determine just how big his tomb was, and if there was an opening somewhere. It was just long enough that if he stretched out his arms and legs, he could just brush the stone there. To his right, he had a little less than an arm's length. To his left, he felt no wall.

Making some grunting noise of displeasure, he began wiggling. Upper body, lower body, use his arms and legs as much as he could to slide along the ground. The ceiling lowered at one point so that he was scraping skin off his nose and back, but then it opened up and he couldn't feel anything above him anymore. He tried to sit up, but the ceiling was still low enough that he couldn't quite make it all the way. He was, however, able to situate himself so that he could crawl out head first instead of sliding sideways.

Every time his head bumped something, it caused a new ache to add to his headache. He tried to comfort himself with the fact that he believed the air to be getting clearer the farther he went. At the same time, he was a little worried that he couldn't see anything, either the bird fish or the swirling light from the black phoenix sucking their light into its fire. How much farther did he have to go? Where was he, even? Was he in the cavern still? Had the phoenix dropped him in a hole, or perhaps one of the side tunnels?

The rubble opened up enough that he was able to crawl on his hands and knees, though this lasted only until he reached an enormous boulder blocking the way forward. It stretched from wall to wall, and there was only a hand's width of space underneath. He put his head to the ground, tried to peer underneath, and was relieved to see a faint blue-white hue.

"Yawi!" he called. "Yawi, I'm here!"

An excited bark answered him.

Sabelu began feeling around the immediate vicinity more frantically, looking for anything. The blue-white hue grew brighter, and he invoked Atsvstdi to illuminate the tomb. As he feared, there was no other way he could see, other than the direction from where he'd just crawled.

There was the sound of scraping rock, some grunts and groans, and then a myriad of indeterminate noises just on the other side of the boulder.

"What's it look like out there?" Sabelu asked. "Can I just use Galo'ondiha ale Agi'a?"

"You can't see what it looks like out here," a familiar voice said. "I'll handle it and get you out of there."

Sabelu shifted his stance though no one could see. "Tsidushi? What are you doing here? Are you really here? How?"

"The Author sent me for you, Tsiquiyi. We'll get you out, don't worry. Just stand back."

Sabelu stepped back as far as he could, which was only a few feet anyway. His heart jumped into his throat as the rock suddenly shifted. Smaller rocks bounced down to the ground and dust filled the air, obscuring the light of the bird fish. There were more sounds outside, some moving, some crashing, some shifting. A shadow appeared under the blocking boulder and Sabelu heard sniffing, like a dog.

The shadow vanished and there was most heavy shifting. The large boulder moved, half an inch out, another half inch out. There were grunts of strain and effort, a heavy sigh of partial relief, as when one man helps to shoulder another man's load. The boulder shifted another inch out, then two inches up. More light streamed into the tomb even as more small rocks and dust clouded his view.

A gust of wind suddenly swept into the tomb-turned-cave, swirling the dust so that Sabelu was wiping his eyes as he stumbled out. Even before his vision cleared, he was pulled into an embrace with his uncle.

"I thought you couldn't come here?" Sabelu said, stepping back to look at Anagalisgi.

"I'm not dead, Sabelu," his uncle laughed.

"But your place is in the spirit world."

"I'm not dead," he repeated. "I'm alive, as flesh and blood as you, and the spirit world is as real as the waking world. I do as the Author bids, go where I am needed. Right now, I was needed here. For you."

"What about the Whites?" Sabelu looked around. "What of the cerberus and the phoenix and—?"

"The battle is won," a new voice cut in.

A great beast with the head, wings, and front legs of an eagle, and the body of a lion, descended from the air. On the ground, it was easily two or three times the size of a horse. Another creature with the head and body of a lion, but another head of a goat, and a tail that was actually a snake, also made its way into the light. It, too, was of tremendous size. Finally there appeared a man-like beast, although it was arguably nine or ten feet tall and had the head of a bull with great, twisted horns, and its hands more resembled hooves. It was the winged creature—Griffin, Sabelu knew instinctively—who had spoken. The other two were Chimera and Minotaur.

"Won?" Sabelu echoed. "All four generals—"

"Not dead," Minotaur interrupted in a harsh, baritone voice, "for they do not die so easily. But they are wounded."

"Why are you here, then? Why not pursue them and kill them?"

"A retreat, even when necessary, can still be used as bait."

Sabelu took a slow breath and nodded. "Understandable. What's our next move, then?"

"You know," Anagalisgi said beside him.

Did he have to admit to it? Still, he nodded again. "I understand."

"The wolves will escort you from here," Griffin stated, taking to the air. Even with the blustery beats of his massive wings, he kicked up no dust to irritate those on the ground. "We will be waiting for you."

Griffin vanished into the air, while Chimera and Minotaur were swallowed up by the darkness on the ground. Sabelu turned to face his uncle.

"I suppose this means you'll be returning to your cave."

"I like my cave better than this one, yes," Anagalisgi observed mildly.

The two of them looked around. Where once there had been a thriving city filled with people, it had been reduced to ruins. Now, it was little more than a cavern filled with boulders and rubble, only small pieces of the city spared the upheaval caused by the cerberus and the wolf dog.

"What of this place?" Sabelu wondered. "Are the dead laid to rest finally?"

"Few of the dead are truly at peace," Anagalisgi mused, his tone bordering on a lament. "But the Shadows have been driven from this place."

"Of course they have. There are no bones left to inhabit." Sabelu kicked at a small bone splinter. "Nothing left of these People Before." He gave his uncle a look. "Is that what happened to the people at Lehoyed, the cliffside city?"

His uncle's expression was gentle even as it was also serious. "You will learn in time, Sabelu. Focus on the moment and what comes next."

Sabelu let out a breath. "Exile. Then bait."

Anagalisgi nodded. "I will be waiting for you in the spirit world."

"You can't come with me? Even just out of this cave?"

His uncle hesitated a moment, then finally nodded. "I can do that. But know that I am always with you, in this cave, in exile, awake or sleep."

Yawi and the wolves formed a protective circle around the two men, and the bird fish again split into three schools to light their way through the darkness.

The going was much slower than it had been on the way in. With everything destroyed, they had to be mindful of where they stepped or climbed. Sabelu invoked Galo'ondiha ale Agi'a a few times when he believed it safe. Soon enough, they were standing on the ledge facing the tunnel that would lead them out to the canyon.

"What happened?" Sabelu asked. "Eight wolves, four generals, and the next thing I know, the black phoenix snatches me into the air and..." He shook his head. "I don't really know. I hit rock, I fall, I'm snatched up again, I fall, there's crashing, and then I'm trapped under the rock."

"Once the battlefield in the spirit world was well cleared for victory, Griffin, Chimera, and Minotaur came here to reinforce the wolves," Anagalisgi explained.

"The black phoenix had hold of you when Griffin challenged it," one of the wolves continued. "Becoming trapped actually saved you. The generals either believed you dead or decided we were more important."

"Divide and conquer, then," Sabelu stated. "On the battlefield, they would have had assistance from a legion of Shadows. Bring them here, and it's a more even fight. And it stopped them from attacking the festival."

"Something like that, yes," Anagalisgi confirmed.

"But why not finish them off? Why give them a chance to lick their wounds and heal? Is this really the least bad option?"

"Not the least bad. The most good."

Sabelu sighed. "I see what will be. You see what could be."

"And look how well we work together." His uncle looked around, what little could be seen in the tunnel, even with the glowing bird fish leading the way. "I will admit, it's a nice change of scenery, even if there isn't much to see."

"Why doesn't the Author let you out more often? Couldn't you be of more use helping others as you helped me, rather than remaining trapped in the spirit world on the fringes of a war you cannot fight?"

"I'm not a warrior, Sabelu, you know that."

"Yes, you're a dreamer, prophet, dark seer, whatever you want to call it. So am I. But I am still a warrior of Wolf Clan."

"Then you have gifts I could never possess. And that's all right. We all have a role to play."

Sabelu wasn't convinced, and he knew his uncle could see it. But

Anagalisgi said nothing more about it, and they continued walking through the tunnel toward the entrance.

Eventually a pinprick of light appeared, natural light from outside. It wasn't especially bright light; the only reason it was noticeable was because it wasn't the pitch black of the cave or the blue-white hue from the bird fish. Late afternoon or evening, then, when the sun was no longer overhead in the canyon. There was something different about the light, however, and it wasn't until they got closer that Sabelu could pinpoint what it was.

The giant serpent head that served as the foreboding entrance had collapsed, mostly blocking the tunnel. All five teeth had fallen which brought the head down with it in several large chunks and a multitude of smaller ones.

When they got close, the bird fish left them and went to circle the rubble, weaving in and out of the many small holes leading to the outside, almost like a line of dancers.

Sabelu inspected the rocky pile, looking for an opening he could squeeze through. He tried a couple, but it always came down to his shoulders being too large. He stepped back and glanced at his uncle. "Looks like we'll need Galo'ondiha ale Agi'a again."

"That is what it looks like, yes," Anagalisgi agreed.

With the two of them working together, it was nothing to shift the rocks enough that Sabelu was able to shimmy out. His uncle climbed out behind him, dusted himself off, and looked up at the sky which was beginning to darken.

"I know you said you aren't a warrior and that you simply follow the Author's direction," Sabelu said, "but do you never wish you could walk with the people again like this, in the flesh?"

His uncle sighed and looked at him. "I would be lying if I said I didn't wish for it sometimes. I wished I could have helped your brother on the battlefield, but I couldn't."

"You're speaking of Tsona."

Anagalisgi nodded and his expression took on a certain unique sorrow. "I wished I could have helped my brother."

Sabelu tried to reassure his uncle. "They died honorably."

"I know they did. And I know that they did more for the people through their deaths than they would have in another fifty years of life. But they are dead all the same." He went on before Sabelu could speak. "I think that's why I was taken to the spirit world and charged with my duties there. The sorceries are good and have done many good things, but men were not made to have such long lives that only end in loss. There is only so much a man can handle. I will watch over the people, and I will guide them as best I can, but I don't believe that I could walk among them as I once did."

"I told the people who travel to the Old Land to seek you out with the seeing fruit and by smudging and other means. Should I not have done so? Have you told them to stop?"

Anagalisgi shook his head. "No, no. It is well you did so, for it is another blow to the Shadows and those who work for them. And many of the people will have good, long lives."

Sabelu frowned. "Uncle, would you like to know how your story ends?"

His uncle's expression was gentle yet sad. "You told me once that it is a happy ending, and that is enough for me. I will get there in my own time."

"Would you want to hear it if it wasn't a happy ending?"

"No, I don't think so." He added hastily, "It will happen when it will happen. For now, there is only the present moment and the present work."

Sabelu looked up at the tall canyon walls and stifled a sigh. "Rarely a moment of rest."

"Rest will come, Tsiquiyi. Just take it one step at a time."

Sabelu looked back to reply to his uncle, but Anagalisgi had vanished.

Feeling a bit dejected, he wordlessly used Galo'ondiha ale Agi'a one last time to lift himself up to the high ground. His horse had taken up with a nearby herd of tsuyoniyvgi, though he still trotted over at a whistle while the rest of the herd fled.

"Sometimes I envy my uncle," Sabelu said aloud as he brushed off his horse's coat and prepared to mount.

"What for?" Yawi wondered, sitting down.

"I only see what is. He sees what could be. Sometimes I wish I had that sense of wonder, the ability to entertain possibilities. Should I have said or done something differently? I've always known that this would happen, and I know that I am walking into exile even now. Was there anything I might have missed out on? Should I have entertained the idea of marrying Yukpa? Should I have pursued that? There will always be work to be done, as you have said, but there won't always be time for love and family."

"There will still be pack," Yawi told him. "And there is much time to be had after this Shadow business is taken care of. You have seen that much."

Sabelu huffed a sigh and mounted up. "You're right. And I suppose it does me no good to distract myself now with such things. The pack needs to be kept safe, and sometimes that means sacrifice, even self-sacrifice."

The wolf's expression was one of total understanding.

"You stay with me," Sabelu ordered. "Send one or two of the pack to Aktiya Waya, and send the rest ahead. I think they know where to go."

Yawi nodded once, then lifted his head and howled. He howled several times, every one sounding slightly different, and Sabelu assumed that each one conveyed different information. When he was done, the wolf sat very still with his ears pricked forward and attentive, listening to the various replies as they came in.

"They will do so," Yawi reported at last.

Sabelu turned his horse around in the direction of Anpa O Wican'hpi. He looked down at Yawi who was now standing and ready to run.

"Is your pack suited to the desert?" he asked. "You've always seemed a bit...thick in the fur for even this climate."

"You forget that your mortal weather doesn't bother us," Yawi reminded him. "We can go anywhere."

"Even Hell?"

"Especially Hell."

Sabelu fixed his eyes on the horizon. "Well then, what are we waiting for?"

He nudged his horse forward, slowly at first, so it could warm up its muscles, but soon enough, they were gliding through the tall grass, riding straight into exile.

DIᏟSᏟ DVᏋT

Asonedune Adolv'i

Consequences

Sabelu elected to travel at a normal pace without conjuring Time on his return trip. From this, he bypassed Anpa O Wican'hpi where he knew the festival would be at its end, and instead made his way directly back to Aktiya Waya.

While this mode of travel would see him return to Aktiya Waya a couple days after everyone else, it also forced him to think about his return, perhaps a little too much. As much as he told himself he needed to remain focused, that he was still on the war path and should not entertain frivolous ideas, he could only hold his attention so long before he became distracted by one thing or another. Sometimes it was movement in the grass, sometimes Yawi, sometimes just the beauty of the landscape, the deep red sunsets of the plains or shining white rocks of the mountains.

"In the cavern, when you attacked the generals," he said to Yawi as they neared the pass that would take them into the bowl of Aktiya Waya, "your pack looked a lot bigger than you do here beside me. How do such small rocks take down a mountain?"

"How does a formless thing like wind take down a tree?" the wolf countered. "How does a bee defend its hive? How does your body defend itself from sickness?"

Sabelu did not reply, but this did not mean that he was at ease. As they ascended the trail to the pass, clearing the trees to view the Sacred Wolf, it was as though storm clouds, complete with lightning, came down from the sky and formed themselves into four distinct shapes. The serpent draped itself over various cliffs and crags, like soft sinew, its head resting near the end of the wolf's tail, as if ready to open its mouth and swallow all visitors to the bowl. The wolf dog occupied most of the bowl itself, like an animal bedding down for the night. The black phoenix was perched on the Sacred Wolf's head, talons digging into her ears, feathers ablaze with black fire.

Finally, the cerberus stood like another looming mountain over the Sacred Wolf, massive paws outstretched like a predator rejoicing over its kill. Had it been a solid form, it would have blotted out the sun. Even as an ethereal form, with the power it exuded, it acted like heavy afternoon clouds, its breath like a chill breeze. Normally this might be a welcome relief from the summer heat, but Sabelu felt only sickening dread.

The serpent hissed at him as he entered the bowl, trying not to look abjectly terrified as he passed by the sentries. Suddenly, the serpent struck, striking his horse so that it stumbled on a small rock. Sabelu, not paying attention, lost balance and went to the ground, landing hard on the stone. The sentries rushed over to him as if to help him, but held up at the last moment.

"You all right?" one asked uncertainly. The second sentry hit his shoulder to scold him.

"Fine," Sabelu said, hurriedly dusting himself off and scrambling to his feet, trying to hide his embarrassment. He put up a hand as he went to grab his horse's reins. "I know. I have summons waiting for me."

His acknowledgment of the situation seemed to calm the sentries' nerves and they returned to their posts. Sabelu simply turned, reins in hand, and led his horse the rest of the way through the pass.

All his thinking and planning and wondering, and now it was all unfolding before his eyes. Looking up at the three heads of the cerberus, all of them very much alive and well, Sabelu decided once and for all that he liked his gifts. He liked knowing things. He didn't like the wall he ran into when faced with the Shadows, the shifting, the uncertainty, the could be, the maybe, the should have, all the things the shapeless Shadows used to confuse, confound, discourage, enrage, and finally overtake people.

At the same time, he also knew for a fact what was about to happen, and he wasn't too thrilled about that, either.

"Is this the true size and form of the generals?" Sabelu asked Yawi quietly, as though the Shadows couldn't hear him.

"No," the wolf replied, also keeping his voice down. "They can get much, much bigger. Remember, we are in the mortal plane now, bound by mortal rules. In the spirit world, things are a little different."

"And this was the decision that leads to the most good?" He looked at the wolf dog to his right, then the black phoenix still perched on the Sacred Wolf's ears. "What was the one that was only the least bad?"

"Like you, Whites only deal in certainty. Your kin is the one who is gifted with the knowledge of possibility."

When Sabelu reached the horse pen, Hoshonti and Hieli just watched him from afar. Neither one called out to him or made any move to help him as he undressed his horse and turned it back out to pasture. Likewise, he did not call out to them, though he couldn't help but glance their way a few times.

"Where are Chimera, Griffin, and Minotaur?" Sabelu wondered as he left the horse pen, still keeping his voice low.

"Gone ahead to where the work is finished," Yawi explained. "This is merely the lull."

Although he knew it was untrue, while on the road back, Sabelu had gotten an image in his mind similar to that of the first wedding he'd done, where men and women had lined the road to the townhouse, waiting for the bride and groom, only in his mind, it was perhaps more like the walk his uncle had taken when he'd gone to be hanged. None of this materialized. Life went on as normal in Aktiya Waya, as evidenced by the sentries at their posts and horse tenders in the field. Even now, approaching the town, Sabelu saw men and women going about their business, children playing games of various flamboyancy.

His summons was known, however, and the people cut him a wide berth if they couldn't avoid him in some other way. A few offered him the smallest bit of encouragement—a smile, a nod, mouthing "Good luck" or some other platitude—but most awkwardly ignored him.

Traditionally, most crimes were dealt with between the wronged parties or the clans at large. The Krydik had modified this somewhat so that, aside from the wronged parties, it was the party of historical peoples who might deal with a larger issue. From minor theft to assault, most things could be dealt with internally, and the priests got involved only to cleanse all parties and affirm whatever decision had been made. Many times the priests were consulted as to the best course of action according to the spirits, but there was little concept of judge and jury among the people.

There were two notable exceptions to this rule: murder and witchcraft. Either charge could result in a trial that lasted for days, even up to a month, as arguments were made, evidence was presented, and spirits were consulted. The big difference between the two was that a guilty murderer was subject to clan vengeance, and the punishment was left up to the family of the victim, with virtually no limit to what they could do to the murderer. Meanwhile, a guilty witch was subject to spiritual vengeance at the hands of the priests, the priests being the mortal liaisons for the spirits who had been wronged. They, too, would have nearly unlimited options to punish an offender.

Sabelu had already been subject to such a trial once in his life, when he was just an infant. Brand new to the world and he had been put on trial for witchcraft. One priest, controlled by Shadows, had sought to drown him, but the head priest, a friend of the Whites, overruled his interpretation of the omens and saved Sabelu. The good priest had died some years later. The evil priest was finally getting his second trial, and Asdeoha was not keen on letting Sabelu slip away again.

Whatever Shadows remained in Aktiya Waya, they abandoned their individual hosts for the time being and reforged themselves together as titans and puppeteers, covering the townhouse and the surrounding block in a thick, nearly impenetrable, black haze, claws and fangs bared, like pikes surrounding a military camp. No White was permitted entry though they surrounded the Shadows, their own claws and fangs on display. The two sides appeared locked in a stalemate, though Yawi's appearance encouraged some to test the line of Shadows.

Had it been only the titans, Sabelu might have thought there was a fighting chance, even a slim one. With all four generals present, there was nothing to be done. The serpent slithered around the bowl, positioning itself at the mouth of the cave, and struck like lightning. This was followed by a quick burst of fire from the black phoenix.

Butterflies and other insects were incinerated instantly, as were the mice and other small creatures. A few burrowers took to their holes. Some of the larger animals ended up on the ground, writhing in pain as they tried to use the stone to douse the flames. Beside Sabelu, Yawi ended up a grotesque, furless wretch, though still alive.

The injured Whites were quick to swap out with fresh reinforcements, many of them limping away or vanishing entirely, perhaps to go to Anagalisgi's cave for some quick care.

Sabelu did not move until Yawi had returned, fluffed out and shining white once more. The other two wolves he had sent ahead from the canyon joined them.

"Go ahead to the next place," Sabelu told the wolves. "There is nothing for you to do here."

The pair was reluctant but, at a look from Yawi, agreed. As they trotted off, a fair portion of the Whites followed them, and the Shadows expanded their reach to cover more than half of the town.

"I am here for you," Yawi said before Sabelu could speak. "You are the pack I am protecting now."

"I just watched you get almost incinerated," Sabelu stated. "We know what is to happen here; you will be more helpful later."

"You are blind to Whites and Shadows and yourself. You know what will happen, but you do not understand the why." The wolf nodded flippantly toward the Shadows. "They will not touch me. They are not here for me."

Sabelu hesitated but finally nodded.

He entered the townhouse. Asdeoha and the others had been expecting him. At his appearance, the acolytes were sent out to announce the commencement of the trial.

In all the years the Krydik had been a functional people—which, honestly, wasn't actually that long—there had been fewer public trials than Sabelu could count on his fingers. The most recent one had been about ten years previous, and it was the thing that had really established him as an adelohosgi as he was called upon to testify to things he could not have known about the murder. Other than that, the only one of real note was the attempted uprising against his grandfather, and that resolution might have been more appropriately classified as clan vengeance.

So it was for curiosity that many of the people showed up. Even those who were so intoxicated by the Shadows that they would demand blood were, at this moment, drawn simply to the spectacle itself.

The fire in the middle of the room had been stocked well with wood. Asdeoha and the priests stood behind three tables in front of the fire so that they appeared as more ghostly silhouettes than men. Their puppeteers had again reforged into a titan, and it looked no better for the ambient lighting. On the middle table, where Asdeoha stood, was a small tray of various paints, multiple cups full of herbs and various smudging blends, several large feathers, a handful of teeth, a small knife, and a smooth stone ball. On the side tables, where the other priests waited like inferior members of the pack, were laid out more smudges and incense as well as some personally preferred icons. A majority of the items had nothing to do with the trial, as far as presenting evidence or making arguments, and instead served to try and ward off any trickery that Sabelu might try. It was a show, really, simply the priests reaffirming their devotion to the Shadows and feeding their dark power.

Sabelu made eye contact with Asdeoha, but neither man said a word as people began filing into the room.

If Sabelu had ever hoped that there was some way to separate man and Shadow, he could now only come to the conclusion that such a feat would be a bona fide miracle. Whatever wedge he had once glimpsed was now firmly sealed shut, like a broken bone twice as strong. Man and Shadow were fused in all but flesh, and Sabelu had a deeper understanding of the People Before who lived in the underground city than he had when he had been in the underground city.

Once the townhouse was as full as it could get and then some, the acolytes fetched some chairs for the interested parties. Asdeoha made a grand show of his opening prayer, invoking this and that spirit for protection, guidance, and justice. Sabelu kept the head priest locked in his gaze, not daring to blink even as he watched the Shadows move in his peripheral. When the prayer was over, Asdeoha bid everyone sit. The priests sat comfortably enough, the crowd pushed and shoved and elbowed for room on the floor, but it was Sabelu who sat last, slowly, still maintaining eye contact with Asdeoha.

For a long minute, no one said or did anything, and the only sound to be heard was the crackling of the fire.

"Sabelu." Asdeoha blinked first. "I never imagined that the day would come when you sat before us like this."

He'd done nothing but imagine it since he failed to have Sabelu drowned. Sabelu said nothing.

The head priest shifted in his seat and made a motion. "Blindfold him. I don't like how he's staring at me."

Even before Asdeoha finished speaking, one of the other priests practically leapt from his seat. Already having a blindfold on hand, he crossed the room in a few strides and jerked the cloth around Sabelu's eyes, tying it tight and not missing the opportunity to wrench a few hairs into the knot as well.

"Lift your hands and I'll have them bound also," Asdeoha warned. "We need no trickery or curses here."

"If I speak, are you going to gag me?" Sabelu asked snidely. "How shall I defend myself then?"

In spite of the blindfold, Sabelu knew well what was going on in the room. He knew where his parents were, his brother and sister. He knew Galiliga had arrived via Galohisdi just before the trial so he might know the fate of his little brother. He also knew Asdeoha shrugged in response to the question as he said, "As long as you speak no curses, I think you have a chance at defending yourself. Speak curses and you only prove yourself guilty."

They'd made up their minds long ago that he was guilty; all they were doing right now was going through the formalities of getting rid of him, a little cleaner approach than Ganhv's outright attempted murder.

When Sabelu would not speak, Asdeoha continued, "Sabelu, you are charged with witchcraft, of consorting with demons, of bewitching the people, of undermining the priests, of sacrilege and desecration of holy artifacts, and assorted similar charges too numerous and evil to speak aloud."

Only because they were speaking of spiritual crimes was Sabelu unable to challenge such vague charges, for it would only risk the wrath of the spirits to speak such blasphemies, even in rote formality. Otherwise he could have demanded that every charge be named so he wasn't defending himself from ghosts and general ill feelings.

"What say you before we begin?" the head priest inquired.

Sabelu could not look the man in the eye physically, but he made sure his posture was as stern as possible. The Shadows and Whites were not deterred by something as trivial as a blindfold, and though the generals were here, there was a sort of anxiety among the Shadows as they tried to discern what the prophet already knew.

Asdeoha wanted him to challenge the trial, challenge the priests, challenge the Shadows themselves. They wanted this place to be the battlefield, the decisive move of this years-long game as the souls of the people were won or lost. The bow, the arrows, and the targets. Asdeoha wanted a spiritual bloodbath because the cerberus wanted a spiritual bloodbath.

Three things were needed to keep a fire going: heat, fuel, and air. The atmosphere of the townhouse provided heat enough in the form of curiosity, anticipation, and hatred. The charges and any so-called evidence would be their fuel. But a fire needed all three elements, and Sabelu was going to rob it of the third.

"I say nothing," he answered at last.

Push Asdeoha and the priests back into the spotlight and let them destroy themselves. Or this was Sabelu's reasoning anyway. He tried to focus on the one thing that was bringing him pleasure at the moment, and that was the nervousness of the Shadows. Why didn't he speak, even to defend himself? Why didn't he fight, try to bring everyone into the light in one last spectacular crusade? What ploy was this? Of the many things he could do, why choose silence? The cerberus needed no excuse to attack, but it certainly made things easier. What was the Author doing that this great weapon of hers, who had done so much damage in just a few short years, had suddenly gone mute?

"Very well," Asdeoha said, his tone tinged with discomfort. "We will begin the trial, then."

Any mild, disinterested, or light-hearted curiosity evaporated instantly from the room. The common man might have assumed this was from the general shift in atmosphere to a more serious affair, but Sabelu knew that the sudden, crushing weight was from the Shadow generals as they moved in as close as they possibly could to smother the townhouse. Even Yawi, who tried to keep a strong stance, seemed to shrink beside Sabelu as he sat down slowly. Sabelu told himself it was a predator trying not to spook its prey, though it was more likely prey trying not to draw the attention of a predator.

"I don't think there is anyone here who can deny your abilities," the head priest began formally. "Your uncanny insight into the present moment, your prophetic musings of the future, and, perhaps most unusual, your seemingly perfect knowledge of things past. The intimate details that you carry of these things has been frightening at times, maybe even to yourself.

"We recognized this within you as an infant. We likened you to Anagalisgi for this new post-war generation. Unlike Anagalisgi in his day, however, we were committed to ensuring that you were not ignored and scorned. We wanted everyone to know of your gifts, and to respect them, to anticipate the changes that might have to be made by a prophet's word."

Asdeoha paused, and Sabelu knew he was going for some expression of lament, even if it was only to cover for his desire to laugh and boast of his apparent victory.

"It is not unknown that the priests were divided over you. I was the most vocal opponent of your divination, believing you to be an evil witch, an agent of evil spirits. At the insistence of the head priest at the time, Ganhv's predecessor, Amgadosgv, we held off on drowning you until we received a clear sign from the spirits and could be of one accord in our actions. This is a reasonable course of action, for no one wants to murder an innocent."

Another pause.

"Perhaps you were conjuring even then, fresh from your mother's womb. You were often described as a very serious child, like an elder in a body too immature to physically communicate, yet the spirit remains strong. We were convinced, through prayer, that you were indeed a good child. A dark seer, like your great-uncle, but good in nature. You were to hold the truth of our past, the stories of all our peoples. And yet, if there were no evil spirits, we would have little use for priests and prophets.

"The great majority of the evil spirits we encounter are interested in one of two things: mischief and destruction. A man may cast a minor spell to trip up a rival or perhaps play a prank on his friend, invoking a spirit of mischief. This alone is a concerning affair. Evil men invoke evil spirits of destruction to maim or kill other men, women, and children, and was often used in times of war in the Old Land. But there is another class of evil spirit, one that binds to a single man or woman and yet undermines the very fabric of society by relentlessly promoting the individual, the thought of self above all others, and the desire for power, even the belief that one single man knows what is best for all."

Now they would be getting into the real arguments.

"It seems that the escalation of incidents began with your madness, of which you were sorely afflicted when you became a man. You claimed to see creatures which, it will be noted, originated in the Books of your father and grandfather and are referred to as Whites and Shadows. The Whites are solid beings, appearing as any common animal though white in color. The Shadows are more formless beings made of smoke, shadow, and, sometimes, lightning. You also claimed that men and women themselves—average people, whom you knew in town—

appeared as shape-shifting monsters. This went on for several years until you managed to escape Hlohi with your sister and go to the Old Land where you claim to have spoken with Anagalisgi himself and were magically cured.

"Before you left, however, you threatened Ganhv, predicted his death —"

"I did not realize that prophesying was not part of the duties of an adelohosgi," Sabelu cut in, "nor that all prophecies were supposed to be good."

"Yes, but the timing was rather convenient, wasn't it? Just as he was trying to stop you from leaving Hlohi—which was forbidden at the time, for casual visits—you threaten him with a terrible prophecy. Threatening a priest and breaking established rules."

Asdeoha let that hang in the air for a moment before adding, "Your prophecy specified that Ganhv would die before his son was able to speak. The child was nearing the point of speech when he became trapped in the river. In a net your brother set out before the fish run season." The head priest shifted position. "So even if your prophecy were true when you spoke the words, you neglected to mention that it would be your hand which slew him."

Asdeoha paused once more, clearly expecting Sabelu to jump in with some kind of defense, maybe reiterate the point that Ganhv had tried to murder him and it was all self-defense. Sabelu didn't need his prophetic gifts to know how that conversation would go.

"It will also be noted that it was you who began this latest campaign to help the people of the Old Land, this done without the approval or even consultation of the priests or the councils—village and national. There it is reported that while you may help the people retrieve their children from the boarding schools, or teach the people the old ways of crafting or hunting, that you also instruct them in the ways of the Whites, the Books, and of some bastardized version of Christianity which still prevails in the Old Land, with little regard for the ways we observe, or even that they have traditionally observed. Now why would a prophet with the knowledge of all histories of all the peoples, who is giving such traditions and life back to the peoples, suddenly hold back on matters of the greatest spiritual importance? Why would he seek to change them?

"But then we consider your trip to Lehoyed, your apparent attempts at turning the people against the priests there with your talk of Books and Whites. Are these the seeds of rebellion? Is Lehoyed too great of an opportunity to pass up to cause division? Have you forgotten what they tried to do to your father and grandfather?

"Then there is the matter of your destruction of the artifacts which we—I—placed in the townhouse, to channel the spirits and guide them back to us. This was not an argument that got out of hand. You walked into the townhouse, grabbed a club—your grandfather's club—off the wall, and smashed the statues to pieces!" It was the first time Asdeoha had shown any sort of raging emotion, but he was smart enough to keep it mild. "You then attacked me, while I sent the other priests for help!"

Another pause and a sigh.

"Speaking of priests, it must also be noted that you speak blasphemies to our own acolytes, trying to confuse them about the ways of the spirits before they are spiritually mature enough to make wise discernment. This corruption of youth is tragic in its own right but worse when we know that you are one of those charged with guiding the priestly acolytes appropriately.

"Finally, we have this last incident, which has finally prompted this trial. You disappeared from the festival at Anpa O Wican'hpi. You were tracked to the canyon where you entered the Cursed Zukatopa. The Cursed Zukatopa has been off-limits since the end of the war. It was also noted that after you entered, the Zukatopa itself crumbled and crashed to the ground. The scout feared you had been swallowed, eaten alive.

"Were this the case, then we might have been content to simply call your death and leave you to rest in peace. Yet here you are, having illegally entered a cursed place and now emerging without a scratch. Yes, the sorceries may have healed any physical wounds, but with your spiritual affluence, I would contend that something far more nefarious took place down there. I think the Cursed Zukatopa did not eat you; it welcomed you as a spiritual brother."

There was some shuffling and shifting, both from the priests and the crowd at large. Some of the people gathered had become quite staunch in their faith in the Whites and were not so easily fooled by the Shadows, but if a man's thoughts could not be turned to evil things, then simple confusion would do. Those with little faith would be thinking about how to punish him in many terrible ways; those with great faith would, at best, simply be unable to capture a coherent thought and think deeply about the situation, the false accusations. They would know that something was wrong, both with the interpretation of past events and the trial going on now, but they wouldn't be able to articulate such things until later, when it would no longer matter. Only those with the greatest faith and most intimate knowledge of things would be able to see through what was going on. Unfortunately, there were very few in the crowd would could say such a thing. Fear was embedded within Nendawagan, Worry in Blaknik, Shame in Galiliga. They wouldn't turn on him necessarily, but their thoughts were more focused on their own problems and how they related to this trial and the man being tried. Of his family, only his father and sister would have the fortitude needed, and what good would it do them?

"Now we consider," Asdeoha went on, "that it was your sister who helped you to escape Hlohi, defying rules and threatening a priest. It was your brother's net which snared Ganhv's son and ultimately led to the demise of the respected head priest. It is your father who leads many efforts in the Old Land, his Books that your knowledge and reference of Shadows and Whites come from. And if you were indeed conjuring as an infant so as to fool even us priests and allow you to live instead of being drowned, then one must also call into question your mother. She has always been a bold woman, but there was that incident when she touched you while you were impure after killing Ganhv. It seems, then, that the only one of your family members who has not been an accomplice to your schemes is your brother Galiliga. Is it possible that he had some subtle, unconscious knowledge of your destiny and this was why he chose to go to Bear Clan?"

The fact that most men went to live in their wife's village upon marriage—or that Galiliga had already been engaged at the time of Sabelu's birth—was but dust on the wind, or maybe that was the work of the Shadows to obscure that inconvenient fact for the time being.

Asdeoha did not give Sabelu a chance to speak, even if he had wanted to at the moment. "And there is another incident to be considered, such as your attack on Doltsi, Dilegwa, and Debetsqua, right in the street, using some sorcery to avert the eyes of any passersby. And afterwards, it seems as though you had another accomplice to help brush off any wrongdoing: Yukpa of Yonhi. It seems as though any time it would be inappropriate for your family to intervene on your behalf, she was more than willing to lend a hand.

"Of course, we cannot fault Yukpa entirely, for young women are malleable to the whims of the young men they adore, though one is forced to wonder what it is she sees in you, given your madness and everything else you've displayed. Perhaps that is also some sorcery on your part?

"And then there are your accomplices in Lehoyed, again, encouraging rebellion. The elder Oko and the man Tlistso, once defenders of your father and grandfather, as well as the Books and your Author.

"Speaking of Lehoyed, we must also address your acquaintance Kah Kitowak. A suspected traitor at best, he has been the one coordinating efforts in the Old Land, encouraging work which no one here has authorized. Is this, then, showing the true nature of your followers? Rebellion and disregard for our ways which we have fought painstakingly to maintain, even through war?"

The head priest went silent, giving time for the crowd to react according to the whims of the Shadows that meandered through the place. Much of it was confusion, but there was a growing hatred for him and suspicion for his family. It was improper for anyone other than the priests, the accused, and any witnesses to speak, though it was not improper to grunt and grumble and mutter things under one's breath. Sabelu heard it all.

"Naturally, these are very serious allegations," Asdeoha said at last, and Sabelu wondered if it was just him that heard the undercurrent of mocking pleasure in the priest's voice. "Therefore, you may take as much time as you need to attempt to prove these allegations false."

If Sabelu defended himself, he would have to invoke the Whites, the Author, the Books, everything that the priests were pointing to as heresy and witchcraft.

If he attacked the priests and accused them of heresy and witchcraft in worshipping the Shadows, it would be nothing for anyone to accuse him of making a power play, attempting to depose the entirety of the priesthood and seize control for himself.

There were only two ways out of this. The first was by some miracle of the Author, sending in all of the Whites from every corner of the universe to take on the Shadows, lift the veil of confusion, and expose everything and everyone. Unfortunately, this would be the equivalent of grabbing an embedded porcupine quill and yanking it out, rather than performing a more careful removal. Or, in the case of some, removing a knife from the heart without the ability to invoke Touch and heal the wound before all the blood spilled out.

Then there was the second way out.

In the underground city, Sabelu had taunted the Shadow generals, that every moment they spent trying to be rid of him in that cave, their little forces in the spirit world were being decimated. A similar philosophy had been playing out over the last few years as he kept the attention on himself in Aktiya Waya and off his family and the work they were doing in the Old Land. This did not mean they had no opposition from the Shadows, but the generals had to pick and choose their battles, figure out what the bigger prize was.

The third horseman, Pestilence, the wolf dog, in charge of strongholds. Maintaining the stronghold on Hlohi was the priority; they would worry about the Old Land later. Right now, Sabelu was the blight in their plans.

If he fought back here, he would only be fighting against flesh. Right now, the Shadows had every advantage, and everything he had worked for would be crushed. He had to draw them out, just like the underground city. But there was one big difference between the underground city and what lay ahead.

"Have you ever been to the south?" Sabelu asked.

The question caught the priests off-guard, if only because the puppeteers had been expecting something more physical to happen.

"We've been to Anpa O Wican'hpi many times," Asdeoha stated, his passionate tirade interrupted.

"Not Deer Clan territory, farther south. To the desert. Have you been there?"

Sabelu could envision the priests blinking and trying to figure out where this was going, though Asdeoha, through the titan, had an idea. Finally he replied, "Ganhv went once, when he was a young man. Even then, he only went to the border, where it comes close to Deer Clan territory. They prefer to keep the southern hills between them and the sands. What does that have to do with this?"

"I think that's where I'm going to go."

Some shuffling, a little murmuring.

"Are you not even going to attempt to defend yourself?" one of the other priests wondered. "Witchcraft is a very serious charge, and your accomplices—"

"If I am the evil one here, and I can influence many people, then it should only stand to reason that removing me will break whatever spell I have on them. After all, my brother in Yonhi does not appear to be affected."

"A trick," another priest hissed. "He has some trickery he is attempting on us. He is trying to escape so he might conjure evil sorceries from afar. We should gag him and drown him. Then do the same to his family and the woman, just to be sure."

Asdeoha made several noises of dissatisfaction. Then, "You deny nothing, then? You are not going to fight any of these charges?"

"Just because I do not fight them does not make me guilty," Sabelu said. "It simply means that I am choosing my battles. You, Asdeoha, are not my enemy though you conduct this trial. The people here are not my enemies though they may oppose me."

"The only battle you will fight in the desert is one of survival."

"We should kill him," the one priest repeated. "We should not give him a chance to—"

"Enough," Asdeoha cut in. "We are still in the defense stage. Or that was my understanding. I realize that we have very few trials of this nature, but you do understand what is at stake here? This is the part of the trial where you explain to us why it was not heresy or witchcraft to do the things that you have done."

Sabelu nodded slowly. "I do understand." He paused and looked around though he couldn't see. "Evil takes many forms. It takes so many forms, in fact, that it is very nearly formless. That's why it is so easy for you to claim that this or that thing that I have done is heresy or witchcraft. But, for instance, in the matter of the statues that I destroyed here in the townhouse, for me to prove that I was in the right would also mean that you were in the wrong, for carving them and praying to them and invoking the spirits associated with them."

There was an instant reaction from the Shadow generals. The black phoenix gave a scream as it took to the air. The heads of the cerberus snarled and snapped at each other as if in common agreement on a heated subject. The wolf dog also shuffled and snapped, furious. The serpent slithered around, coiling tighter around the bowl. Even the titan inside the townhouse, the conglomeration of the priests' puppeteers shifted and shuffled, like a competitor in the wrestling tournament who couldn't wait to be told to begin the match.

"And if you believe yourself in the right, how is not defending yourself going to help your cause? Wouldn't that be your goal, to prove yourself in the right and to depose these evil spirits you believe surround us even now?" Asdeoha sounded nervous. "Wouldn't you want to rid the townhouse—this spiritual center of our village, of our people—of these evil spirits?"

"That will happen," Sabelu promised. "When I leave to go to the desert."

"Trickery..." the same priest growled.

"Let him go!" a new voice piped up.

Hissed whispers and quiet murmurs grew louder at the sudden interruption as everyone turned to find who had spoken.

"Atsos?" Asdeoha questioned. "What is a priest of Lehoyed doing here at all? And what brings you into this trial?"

"The wolf called to me, and I answered," Atsos said.

"The wolf called you here to defend him?" another priest wondered. "He won't even defend himself."

"He is a dark seer, one committed to the spirits. We as priests should understand that. He has no time for petty mortal squabbles. Let him go to the desert. If he is evil, the evil spirits will follow him there, and the people will be spared any more of his villainy. If he is not evil, then we are still obligated to let him continue his good work. If he believes his work will take him to the desert, then to the desert he must go."

"Or he could retreat to the wilderness to work evil from afar."

"If he cannot vex even his own brother in Yonhi, which is four days from here, how shall he vex anyone from the desert?"

"And what of his family?" Asdeoha inquired.

"What of them?" Atsos wondered. "If they are vexed, then his removal will surely cure them. If they are not, then their blood would be on our hands for the murder of innocents."

The only sounds to be heard were the crackling of the fire and the contemplative sighs of the priests.

"We can't murder innocents, especially an entire family," one priest said slowly. "If they are under some spell, then removing Sabelu would relieve them of that spell. And they are good, hard workers. Whatever this business with the Shadows and Whites, they are doing good work in the Old Land without the need for war."

"And you can't murder an adelohosgi," Atsos added. "Anagalisgi was merely ignored in his time. Shall we murder Sabelu in ours, without even considering the good he has done? Everyone knows the stories, how evil witches come to steal, kill, and destroy. What evidence is there of that in him?"

"You are welcome here as a priest and a spectator, Atsos, but now you speak out of turn," Asdeoha interrupted coldly.

His sudden sharpness silenced everything in the room except the fire. No one dared to breathe.

"Apologies, Asdeoha," Atsos said finally, taking a few steps back and falling silent.

The head priest made a sound of disapproval. "You've got us in quite a conundrum, Sabelu. We could kill you outright, yes, as would be fitting for such heinous charges. Witchcraft is a terrible offense. And yet, we run the risk of offending the spirits ourselves if you are in the right, turning punishment into murder. As Atsos just pointed out, Anagalisgi was only ignored. If we murder you, then what shall we do to the next adelohosgi who comes along? He may never make it past infancy. He may never be born. And what would become of your family and the woman you love?"

While it might have been tempting to believe that Atsos had completely reformed himself and chosen to follow the Whites after Sabelu left Lehoyed, that was not entirely accurate. The priest still had a Shadow with him, but it was the same lazy one he'd had when Sabelu first visited, and it still hadn't gotten rid of the White snake that was presently hiding coiled around the priest's left leg beneath his pants.

The Shadows all wanted Sabelu dead. They couldn't risk any more of his words, his teachings, his actions, nothing. They wanted him dead. The White snake, however, was the one throwing a wrench into things, feeding an idea of revenge, of going after Sabelu for a second round, a chance to make up for the humiliating defeat in the underground city. It toyed with Atsos' Shadow, and it was the Shadow who was feeding the idea to the others. Any other small Whites hiding in people's pockets or their hair joined in on the quiet whispers. To the average person, nothing was happening. For Sabelu and the priests, it was like a small rush of wind blowing through the room.

If the Shadows enjoyed any of their own sins, it was Pride. Boasting and gloating, they loved to flaunt their victories. A simple murder wasn't good enough. They wanted to rub it in. They wanted to humiliate Sabelu and leave his body to be eaten by the desert scavengers.

It was the cerberus who answered first, its voice rumbling like thunder and quieting all of the Shadows and the Whites.

"If the small man thinks he can win, he is welcome to try. In the desert, there are no caves to protect him, nowhere he can hide."

Of course, Asdeoha couldn't just announce exile and walk away. With such a serious charge as witchcraft, they at least had to make a show of consulting the spirits. This was not only a man's life, but an adelohosgi as well. They had to be careful.

"Have him bound and gagged," the head priest ordered. "I want no witchcraft or trickery while we deliberate. Put him on a mat over there and choose two men to watch over him. Make sure no one but the priests and council enter while we deliberate."

Two huge arms suddenly came under Sabelu's arms and hauled him up out of the chair. He did not resist as they bound and gagged him; in fact, he found the whole thing rather tiresome. He knew what was going to happen, so why did he have to bother with all of this in between monotony?

Wait. He didn't. One of the more overlooked uses of conjuring Iyuwahnilvhi was Adahnesagi'a Asganola Iyuwahnilvhi, or, as it was said colloquially in English, Slow Banding. He would be moving on a slower plane of time than everything around him. The priests would deliberate for nearly a day, but he would only experience a few minutes, or less if he so chose. That is, assuming he was permitted to do any conjuring.

Well, he thought as he was pushed down onto a mat on the floor, if he kept the Band tight enough around himself, maybe even feathered it just beneath his skin, they wouldn't notice. But no way did he want to have to endure this kind of boredom longer than he had to. As long as they didn't expect him to do anything, he should be fine.

He conjured. Everything went quiet. Several breaths into the Band, the same huge arms grabbed him again, breaking his concentration and the conjuring. Sound roared to life around him. Before he could process it, he was plopped down in the chair. All ties except the ones on his wrists were unbound, the gag removed, but the blindfold remained.

"A decision has been made," Asdeoha announced loudly, bringing the anxious whispering of the crowd to a close. "It was not an easy one, but it is decisive and final."

He let the pause go on too long for real dramatic effect, Sabelu thought, but maybe it was just him, or perhaps a lingering effect of the conjuring of Time.

"Sabelu, you are to be exiled beyond Krydik lands. Whether this means the desert, across the ocean, over the mountains, the Old Land itself, or anywhere else, we care not. But you are not to return to this place, nor any other Krydik village, nor the surrounding grounds or hunting lands. You are not to show your face here. Similarly—" The head priest raised his voice. "—no one is to seek him out. If you do, you will be considered complicit in heresy and witchcraft and will quickly join him in exile." He lowered his voice again and addressed Sabelu. "You have until sundown to leave Aktiya Waya, and three days to leave all Krydik lands. If you are found after that time, you will be treated as a hostile enemy and dealt with accordingly."

"Does this mean you've found me guilty of witchcraft," Sabelu challenged, "or is this simply you compromising with your own conscience so that you have to admit nothing of yourselves to the people?"

An icy stillness came between him and Asdeoha as the priest replied, "You have until sundown."

The blindfold was removed. Sabelu rubbed his eyes and face as he readjusted to the light from the fire before him. All around him, the crowd was slow to break up, but his family soon swarmed him.

"Sabelu, what's going on?" his mother demanded, tears streaming down her cheeks. "I don't understand. Why didn't you defend yourself?"

He groaned as he stood, stretching cramped muscles. "I didn't defend myself because I need to defend the people first."

"It's already well past midday," his father told him. "Sundown will be here soon."

"Then I guess it's a good thing my bags are already packed."

He led the way out of the townhouse.

DᏞᏧAᏁ DVᏐT

Atlasgone Adolv'i
Preparations

The cabin wasn't very big, only two rooms, just big enough for him to live semi-comfortably while in hiding. Of course, he wasn't really living there, not yet. He was just getting everything ready so that when he finished his work in the desert, he would be able to come back and fall straight into bed with no problems.

One of the many advantages of having such extensive knowledge of people and goings-on was knowing when any scouting parties would be coming through the area who might see the place. So far, no parties had come through, and they wouldn't for a few more days. He planned to be gone by then.

After the verdict, Sabelu had gone home, grabbed his bags which really hadn't even been unpacked from the festival, said hasty goodbyes to his parents and siblings, and left the bowl, escorted by half a dozen warriors. He'd not even been given a horse and had to make his way on foot. He had gone south, at least until he knew he wasn't being watched. Then he doubled back and followed the ridge northwest all night. In the morning, he found the place where his little cabin now stood. It had been easy enough to build, utilizing the sorceries to place the stone and timber. It wasn't much, just a place he would return to when it was all over.

Yawi was pacing by the front door while Sabelu finished up some work on the roof.

"You are not given to easy distraction like some," the wolf said, sounding both irritable and confused. "Nor have you ever been especially concerned about having certain luxuries or amenities." He stopped and looked up. "So what purpose does it serve to build this den before going south?"

"The Cursed One of the Desert has stood for thousands of years; it can have a few more days to say goodbye," Sabelu replied, not looking at him. "Make the Shadows wonder, make them nervous."

"The vices. Maybe the indulgences. Not the puppeteers or the titans, and especially not the generals."

"You think? Then why don't they come for me here? Why wait for me to come to them?"

"They want every advantage. I don't think you understand what the Cursed One of the Desert represents."

"It represents the rise and fall of the civilization of the People Before," Sabelu said. "Short of the spirit world and the dark forest itself, it was one of the greatest strongholds the Shadows had, before they killed everything and everyone."

"And let's not forget that you were nearly killed in the underground city," Yawi commented dryly.

"Yes, but it's not about me."

"No, it's not. If it were, I would be trying to stop you from going at all."

Sabelu looked down at the wolf. "Then what are we arguing about?"

"Your natural propensity to rush into danger because you think death is the only consequence that matters. True, you are not reborn as Whites are reborn, but a spiritual death while alive is a much worse thing."

Something about the wolf's tone told Sabelu that he knew exactly why the cabin was being built, and it wasn't just some temporary halfway house to use while running off on adventures.

"Do you understand the concept of choice, Yawi?" Sabelu asked, not unkindly. "Do you ever wake up in the morning and wonder what you're going to have for breakfast, whether it might be one thing or another?"

The wolf sat and tilted his head. "We take what the Author provides."

"That wasn't the question. Do you wonder what you're going to eat, or do you already know?" He did not wait for Yawi to answer as he slid down to the ground. "Do you know the night before? The day before? A week, a month, a year before?" He gestured to the cabin. "I knew that I was going to build this cabin in this way for this purpose. I knew it years ago. Not because I can see myself, but because I can see others and how they see me and the conversations we will have. Now, you might expect that with this knowledge, maybe I could change something. Maybe I would choose one stone differently, one stick. Something small. Maybe I will choose one word differently in an upcoming conversation. And yet, everything happens exactly as it should, exactly as I have seen it, like canoeing down a river. There are no other options; I am compelled to do something."

Sabelu sat down and leaned against the wall of the cabin, one knee drawn up. "I think that's why the Author gave me the gift of knowledge and insight. She knew that the burden would be so great that I would seek out the things I did not know, could not know. The confrontations with the Shadows. The underground city. The Cursed One of the Desert. Such a void of knowledge would draw me in to accomplish a work that the other priests have shied away from and even turned against." He slapped the wall with his palm. "This solitude afterwards. Because I don't know. I don't see. Yes, everything will happen in its time as the Author decrees, but for me, just as little scribbles of ink on paper, it gives me the illusion of choice. I decide what I eat for breakfast. I decide when I fetch water and from where. I decide." He sighed and closed his eyes. "I think I am beginning to understand why my uncle prefers to stay with you in the spirit world."

Yawi let out a soft whine as he lay down and rested his chin on Sabelu's leg. Sabelu gave him a scratch between the ears.

"Your kin worries about you," the wolf stated. "He does not have the knowledge that you do, of physical things, but he has a knowledge of spiritual things."

"He sees possibilities."

"Yes, in a limited sense. But his service to us lies more in interpretation. We fight the war with the Shadows. Everything that happens in the mortal plane is an echo of our wars, and yet, it is also almost like a prediction as well. It is difficult to explain in a linear sense —"

"You influence people," Sabelu said, shrugging. "You get your horses ready at the starting line. You know who's faster, who's slower, who's more on edge, who's calmer. You know the training that you have instilled in the horse. Then the race starts. You fight and jockey for the win, but for all that training, all that work, sometimes things just don't go as expected. In the mortal plane, you influence people, line them up, train them, get them to work well in certain situations. But when the Shadows come along with their mortals, whom they have also trained, sometimes things just don't go the way you expect, especially when the competition is a fairly even match."

"Your kin helps us to understand how mortals think, how they work. He helps us understand you so we can help you better, which in turn helps us." The wolf gave him a look. "You have seen many Whites bond with humans. Birds, rabbits, deer, otters, you have seen us work. And most people do just fine with them. Have you never wondered why the pack was sent to protect you?"

Sabelu shrugged again. "I assumed it was because I was going up against the generals."

"You have seen the generals. You have seen their true size and nature, and you have faced them in combat. The Author alone preserved your life, but why would you be needed in the first place? Why were you singled out? Your kin was merely a vessel, a warning, a prophet for the people that was ignored. Why are your actions so important?"

He sighed and shook his head, eyes still closed. "I don't know. Why?"

"Because it takes a mortal to save a mortal. Or break one. You are pack. But almost none of them see beyond the pack. They have no understanding of invisible matters, spiritual matters. Yes, I could gather my pack, bring in Griffin, Chimera, Minotaur, all Whites from across the universe, and we could tear apart the Cursed One of the Desert. But it would mean very little, because it is only a place. The universe will fall away; it is mortals who are the prize to be won. You yourself said that a man is responsible for his own demons. It must be a mortal who tears that place asunder and scatters it to the sands. Only then is the stronghold truly broken."

"And the puppeteers will be gone from Asdeoha and the other priests?" Sabelu asked.

"No," Yawi admitted. "Every man is responsible for his own demons. But the darkness that ties them to this world, that feeds them throughout time, beyond this linear plane, will be broken, and they will be more easily confronted and deposed." The wolf sat up and stretched. "You are well attuned to affairs beyond this plane. The possibilities that your kin foresaw were...not all pleasant."

"If I had chosen to embrace the Shadows as Asdeoha had, I could lock this place into becoming a stronghold until the end of time," Sabelu stated bluntly.

The wolf just looked uncertain.

Sabelu sighed and stood. "Well, you don't have to worry about that." He gave Yawi another scratch between the ears. "We are pack, and the strength of the pack comes before the lust of the individual. Only a fool would seek to destroy the pack."

Yawi's mouth popped open in a smile, tongue lolling, as he stood, tail wagging a few times.

Sabelu turned as if to go back inside the cabin, but movement in his peripheral vision caused him to stop, and he instead turned to face Netami who came hiking up the narrow trail.

"There you are!" she hissed, quickening her pace.

The first thing she did on approach was grab him and pull him into a crushing embrace.

"How did you know where I was?" he asked when she finally released him and he could breathe again.

"A White rabbit told me," she replied. She took a step back. "I thought you were heading south? What are you doing here? You're a day's walk from Aktiya Waya; Asdeoha's men will find you eventually." She gestured to the cabin. "What is this?"

Sabelu glanced at the cabin. "A project for later. Actually, I was just getting ready to leave. But what are you doing here? Itsitsi is covering for you as long as she can, but you know the family is under scrutiny. And surveillance."

"It's just that you left so fast..." Netami wiped her eyes. "When the rabbit told me where you were, I had to come make sure you were all right. Maybe get in a proper goodbye before you do head south." She continued without being prompted. "Itsitsi spent the first night weeping, and I think Itsitsa was contemplating murder himself, of Asdeoha and the other priests. Galiliga tried to argue with Asdeoha, and even Atsos got involved, but they ended up being dragged out of the townhouse and told to leave to their respective villages. Blaknik...he went to the Old Land, I think to talk to Fichik Shobota and some of his friends there."

He gave her a look. "And you?"

She shook her head and looked away. "You told us this would happen, that you would be exiled, but..." She wiped her eyes again. "I did exactly as you said I would. I denied you. I had to convince the priests that you had vexed us, that you had some lingering curse over us. It prevented any violence, but I feel horrible."

He hugged her tight. "It's all right. You did what you had to for the family. You have to watch out for each other now without me."

Netami sniffed and looked up. "Why are you building this cabin? You make it sound like you're not coming back to Aktiya Waya ever."

He shrugged. "Well, it might be beneficial for me to stay away for a little while. Even once I've done what I need to do in the south, it will still take some time to convince the others that I'm not evil."

She studied him. Then, "You're lying. You don't plan on coming back, not to town, anyway." Her expression turned offended. "What is it that you don't trust us—trust me enough to tell the truth?"

"You're upset enough as it is. I'm trying not to add to it."

"Well, now instead of having to bear the truth, I'm having to bear the truth as well as the fact that my brother keeps lying to me."

That hit him harder than he thought it should have. She took his hands in hers. "I love you, little brother. I have cared for you since the day you were born, since even before then. I have stood by you through everything, your insanity, your work, your trial, and now your exile. I don't know what else I can do for you to earn your trust."

If he told her she already had it, she would demand to know why he lied. Even he understood that much.

"Is this the real reason you don't pursue Yukpa?" Netami asked. "Because you know too much about people and their Shadows to trust them?"

"I know people and their Shadows and I still love them," Sabelu countered. "As for Yukpa, she—"

"Not Yukpa. You. I understand that sometimes it doesn't work out for one reason or another. Galiliga's wife was not the first woman he laid eyes on. My concern is for you who doesn't seem to want to look at a woman."

"I just want to get through the next couple moons first. And I told Yukpa that once this is resolved, then maybe we could talk."

Netami gave him a look. "I'm not an adelohosgi like you, but there are some things I know. And I know that you weren't serious." She added, "If not Yukpa, then who?"

Sabelu tried to sidestep the issue. "Why are you bringing this up now?"

"Anagalisgi died with no children, and he never got to be an uncle to his nephews. Galiliga lives in Yonhi, and Blaknik doesn't have children yet, nor do I. Who will you be father or uncle to before you die?"

"We have a hundred years before that happens."

"You didn't answer the question."

He sighed. "I would really like to focus on the task at hand. I'm going to finish this, and then I'm going to head south."

Netami, her tears dry on her cheeks, sighed and nodded. "All right." She wiped her face and tried to make herself a bit more presentable. "Is there any way I can help, while I'm here?"

Sabelu nodded. "Water, as much as possible. There will be no water in the desert and little the sorceries can do about it."

She asked questions while he retrieved several skins. "Is the south desert very much like the Old Land, the towns where we've been working? How can there be no water?"

"No," he answered, handing her four skins. "Not like the one in the Old Land, the towns. And that isn't entirely a desert. No, the one in the south is just sand, an ocean of it. You've been to Lehoyed. Imagine sand instead of water as far as the eye can see. No trees, no grass, nothing green of any kind."

"But the People Before lived there somehow, didn't they?"

"They did, before it was a desert. Then, when it turned into a desert, they died out."

"Oh. How—"

"Water, please. I don't have a lot of time."

He could feel her embarrassment, as well as her curiosity, as she turned and hurried down the trail and vanished into the trees. The stream wasn't far away. It wouldn't take her very long to fill the skins, but her own thoughts would keep her there a few minutes more.

He'd thought about sneaking back to Aktiya Waya and stealing a horse, make his trip a little faster, even if he couldn't ride in the desert. Then he considered that Galohisdi would do just as well, at least to get him in Deer Clan territory close to the south border. He might have considered pushing his luck, seeing if he couldn't conjure into the desert where he needed to go. Then he decided it was too much of a risk, that the Shadows would take advantage of his weakened state when he finally passed through. He didn't know if the exhaustion from the trek through the desert would give him any more of an advantage, but it probably wouldn't be any worse.

He tried to pack as lightly as possible: a second pair of moccasins, a couple knives, a bit of dried meat and nuts, a length of rope, and the skins of water when Netami returned with them.

"You're going to want shelter," Yawi told him. "The Shadows are not limited to living things in their influence. They will try to bury you in the sand. You will suffocate."

Sabelu didn't doubt the wolf; he just didn't like the idea of packing more. At the same time, he didn't need to die of thriftiness. A battle against evil spirits, fine, but he didn't need to be the cause of his own demise.

Reluctantly, he headed back inside the cabin where he had several large skins freshly tanned. He'd planned for them to be blankets and floor and wall coverings when he returned, to keep the chill of the stone at bay, but now he was forced to quickly fashion them into a haphazard tent. Of course Netami would have something to say about his sewing job, but he figured he would be more surprised if the thing survived the coming encounter.

"Sabelu?" Her voice sounded outside. A moment later, she poked her head in the door. "Oh, there you are. What are you doing?"

He hesitated a moment before explaining. As expected, she crossed the room in short order, shoving the bulging water skins into his hands so as to part him from the makeshift tent. This she yanked from his lap, then sat to examine it.

"Honestly, Sabelu," she scolded. "I understand that men need only the most basic of sewing knowledge, but did you really learn nothing from our mother? Do you have no sewing knowledge in that big head of yours?"

She made a motion and he handed over what tools he had. She snatched them from him and set to work, saying, "If you're worried about time, then you may as well conjure it so I will finish faster."

Faster to his eyes, anyway. Truthfully it took her a little more than half the day, but with the conjuration of Iyuwahnilvhi, it seemed to him no more than half an hour. When she was finished, he had a well-made, perfectly functional tent. Not only that, but it was even neatly folded so it could fit well in his bag.

"Not that I expect it to fit this well again after you've taken it out—" Her look was equal parts accusing and amused. "—but it will offer better protection than whatever you were going to get."

"Mine would have worked fine," he protested.

She gave him a look. "You're going up against the Shadow generals, Sabelu. 'Fine' isn't going to work."

Well, he really couldn't deny that.

"Anything else?" she asked. "I see you packed a second pair of moccasins, and they look good. How about the ones you've got on?"

"They're fine."

She made a motion. "Let me see."

Sabelu sighed but removed his moccasins and handed them to her. "You want my pants, too?"

"Well, since you offered."

He rolled his eyes but stood as if to go to the other room.

"Honestly, Sabelu," Netami said, not looking up from where she rummaged for some more sinew to repair a seam in his moccasins. "I've mended your pants before, and we've seen each other on hot days at the river."

"That was in a public place," Sabelu pointed out, though he stopped and did not go into the other room to undress. "With just the two of us here, I don't need any more wild charges against me. And you don't need any more suspicion or hostility against you."

He tossed the pants down beside her and she looked up. "Was I followed here? Is anyone watching?"

He sat back down. "No."

"Are you going to try anything with me?"

"Of course not."

She made a motion and gave him a look. "Then what are you worried about?" She turned her attention back to the sewing.

"It's the appearance of it."

"Considering that I think you would know if anything actually came of this—charges, hostility, or otherwise—and yet here you are anyway, I think it's just your own discomfort that you don't like." She pulled the needle through the leather. "Go in the other room if you really want, but it's all you." She chuckled. "On the other hand, if anyone did happen to notice, you could claim that you were performing the blood taking, as both brother and priest. Reverse psychology, maybe the priests would claim it a barbaric witchcraft practice and end it."

Yawi, who was watching from the doorway between the two

rooms, just smirked. That smirk, as well as his own stubborn pride, made Sabelu stay where he was, watching his sister mend his clothes. They weren't in horrible shape, but she was determined to ensure that he had as few problems as possible while out traveling. That, and it helped to ease her own mind about his trial and exile, reassure herself that he was fine. And a man who wasn't fine probably wouldn't be sitting stark naked in front of his sister complaining about minor sewing repairs. Or maybe he would.

Even so, he didn't waste time redressing once Netami was through with her inspection and repairs. She just grinned, shook her head, and said, "You just aren't comfortable around women, are you?"

"Some men wish they knew what their wives wanted," he told her. "Most days, I wish I didn't know."

"Only most days?"

He fumbled for his words even as his skin burned hot. Finally he elected to not say anything and instead focus on not getting excited in front of her. Netami, not a little embarrassed herself, stood slowly.

"I think I understand what you mean," she said awkwardly, putting her hands on his shoulders. "Maybe while you're gone, I will talk to Yukpa for you."

That was the last thing he wanted, but he still couldn't find the words to say so.

"I'll see you when you get back, little brother. Go finish what you've started."

She left the cabin, heading for home. Sabelu just stood there like an idiot, bow taut, thinking about Yukpa.

"Your excuses for not having pups are quickly running out," Yawi observed coyly.

"This is not helping things," Sabelu complained. "I should be heading south."

"You should."

"I need to focus on destroying the Shadows."

"You do."

"Instead I'm standing here thinking about Yukpa."

"You are."

He gave the wolf a look. "You're not helping things."

Yawi tilted his head. "Aren't I?"

Sabelu sighed and managed to let go of his thoughts, the ones paralyzing him at least. His awkwardness about leaving the cabin with a taut bow helped to clear up the rest of his thoughts. He knew several men who had no qualms about such things and would go to their wives in the field if it suited them. His older brother was one of them. He couldn't imagine it, but maybe it was just one more way in which his weirdness was put on display.

"Is everyone ready?" he asked, looking at Yawi.

"I think the only one who isn't is you," the wolf said candidly.

Sabelu looked at the wolf. "I'm afraid, Yawi. At this point, I've lost basically everything but my life."

"And what is your life worth?"

He hesitated for half a second. "Not much if the people are still in the dark. I know Asdeoha isn't making things easy for them."

"That's putting it mildly."

He still didn't rush off on some heroic adventure. He remembered very well the confrontation in the underground city, the antics that should have gotten him killed. He looked around, searching for Shadows.

"They're all waiting for you in the desert," Yawi told him.

"Then why am I still afraid?" Sabelu wondered.

Yawi sat down. "Fear is not an inherently evil thing."

"Yes, yes, it keeps up from jumping off cliffs, warns us of danger, so on and so forth."

"It lets us know when a challenge might be too much for us to handle alone," the wolf said gently. "To a child, simply walking through tall grass may be frightening. It isn't really dangerous, but he is afraid all the same. But when his mother arrives, he knows he can take those steps and face the danger. Going to the underground city, you were afraid, but you knew that the pack and the Whites were with you, and so you confronted the cerberus."

"I know that you're going to be there again this time, so why is it so much harder?"

"Because like the ants planting the seeds of faith, fear plants the seeds of courage."

"My mother is going to be a tremendous hero one day, then."

"She will be, and you know it."

Sabelu opened his mouth to say something to that, paused, then quietly closed his mouth and settled for a nod. After a moment, "She will. But there is only one way she's going to get there."

"And the only way to get to that point is by going south to the desert," Yawi said, not unkindly. The wolf nudged his hand. "Do it for your mother."

Sabelu nodded again. "She brought life to me. Now I must bring life to the people, and to her."

The fear did not magically dissipate from his chest. Indeed, he couldn't say he felt all that much better about what he was going to do. Instead, as he went back inside to gather up his things, he tried to reframe it as simply helping out his mother.

His father had some vague memories of his American father telling him stories of ancient peoples of faraway lands, how whole kingdoms would go to war over the love of a woman, how leaders would wage war at the behest of their wives or mothers. In the Old Land, in Yvgidahi's time, the women's council was responsible for dealing with the aftermath of the war, the slaves, the prisoners, the spoils, but while they might have given advice about actually going to war, they never gave orders to go or not go.

These days, there were only two women on any of the Krydik councils, though the regular and women's councils had been formally merged some years ago. Little had changed, it seemed. Any womanly input was typically given by the councilmen's wives, daughters, and mothers after they got home from the meetings, as Nendawagan and Mesim had done to Yvgidahi.

Sabelu was doing this for his mother, to free her from her Shadow of Fear; with the support of his sister, who was always so confused and hurt by his lack of trust; and the hope from Yukpa, that when he got back, maybe they could be together. That was his reason for going, he decided. And it was this line of thought that managed to break through his own fear and turn his forced, mechanical motions into purposeful acts as he gathered his things and left the house, Yawi rising to meet him.

He conjured Galohisdi, focusing his energy to the south, to the hills at the south end of Deer Clan territory, and stepped through.

The southern hills were not so different from the forest between Aktiya Waya and Yonhi. Less hilly than true mountain foothills with a little more grass, and the trees themselves were a little more sparse and of a different variety, but still a hilly forest with undergrowth and all manner of wildlife.

Sabelu sat against a tree to wait out the nausea and orient himself to the landscape. From his vantage, the landscape to his right remained somewhat hilly but never developed into anything more than that, that he saw. To his left, the hills remained but with an overall tapering effect that suggested the proper plains were within a day's walk. Directly ahead of him was a mix of the two, and he guessed that the plains were maybe two days away. He did not have any memories of this particular place, suggesting that no one had ever actually been this way, at least no Krydik.

The problem was, the plains were to the north, and he needed to go south. Sighing, he stood, stretched, and turned around. The only landscape he saw was more hills and more trees. Yawi was about twenty feet ahead of him, nosing around in the undergrowth.

"Is that the direction to go?" Sabelu asked.

Yawi looked up at him. "This is south, yes."

"I expect you know where we're going. Lead the way."

The wolf did not actually move until Sabelu caught up to him.

"Have you ever actually seen the Cursed One of the Desert?" Sabelu wondered. "Have you actually been to this place?"

"I have not, no," Yawi answered, "but Minotaur and Chimera have. They came soon after the destruction of the People Before, to see what, if anything, was left."

"The cliffside city at Lehoyed, that was where the People Before made their last stand, wasn't it?"

The wolf's expression was answer enough, but he still spoke. "As you know, that shoreline wasn't always there; there was an entire city where the ocean is now.

"The People Before were indeed, in the early days, split between those who wished for mercy from the Author, and those who wished for another chance from the dragon. Of course, the details faded to little more than superstition and religion by the end, but many stories contained kernels of truth."

"Four cities," Sabelu stated. "One for each of the Shadow generals, or the Great Whites. Or split between them. The Sacred Wolf in the mountains, the Cursed Zukatopa in the canyon, the Sacred Minotaur at the cliffs. What was the Cursed One of the Desert?"

"It was dedicated to the black phoenix, though not rendered in its image."

"Pretty even split," Sabelu observed. "Two for each side, one aboveground, the other underground."

"Indeed," Yawi acknowledged. "The four city-states always had their feuds and disagreements, but it was the arrival of the Tacagans that really forced their hands. The two southern cities first tried to ally with the Tacagans. They made the city of the black phoenix their base, their central government if you will. They wiped out the people of Aktiya Waya. Then something happened where they turned their sights, not on the city of the Minotaur, but the city of the serpent."

"Let me guess," Sabelu cut in, "Any and all survivors after that, of the People Before, fled to the city of the Minotaur to regroup. Then they tried to attack the city in the desert, failed, retreated to their city again, but the Tacagans wiped them out."

The wolf nodded. "Yes, but there is one minor detail. The desert was not always a desert. It was not a desert at that time, but a rather lush landscape, thick and green, like a jungle. Whatever they did to destroy the city of the Minotaur and rend a massive hole in the ground where the cliffs now stand, it not only obliterated the old city, it burned up a sizable portion of the planet."

"Including the city of the black phoenix. They destroyed themselves."

"Unintentionally of course, but yes."

"That's why there were no bodies in the aboveground cities, but there were in the underground cities," Sabelu mused. "And I'm sure it took time for the vegetation to grow back, but why has the desert been left? Maybe I wouldn't expect a jungle—or maybe I would, I don't know—but is it just the last part of the world to recover or is it something else?" He answered his own question before he even finished speaking the words. "City of the black phoenix, death ground, the destruction of everything. If the city still stands, it would stand to reason that the area around it would remain dead and barren." He gave Yawi a look. "You expect me to destroy an entire city while dodging attacks from creatures the size of mountains?"

"Most of the city is gone," the wolf told him. "There is just one piece remaining that must be destroyed."

"And what's that?"

"A piece of technology that continues to link this place back to the Tacagans, even if they ignore it or are unaware of its existence."

"After a thousand years, you think it still works?" Sabelu wondered. He went on before Yawi could speak, "I know, if it didn't, I probably wouldn't be here. Was there one in the underground city, too? I'm guessing it was destroyed in that confrontation?"

"It was."

"But what does destroying the underground city and the city of the black phoenix have to do with defeating the wolf dog, this third horseman so-to-speak?"

Yawi huffed a sigh, like a parent who is tired of having to explain something to a child yet again. "What is the wolf dog in charge of?"

"The Shadows themselves, internal affairs, making sure they do their jobs." Sabelu paused. "Is there Galohisdi in the city, a way for Shadows to
—"

"Whites and Shadows have no need for such things," Yawi cut in.

Sabelu hummed. "A link to the Tacagans. A way for them to keep track of us?" He stared at a spot between the wolf's shoulders as they walked. "The Tacagans are a stronghold species. That link between us and them is what is making it easier for the Shadows to come here and infiltrate Hlohi. Destroy those links and the Whites can come in and protect everyone properly.

"Of course, if we're really that special to the Author, the Shadows aren't going to just sit idly by. And the more we destroy their stuff, the angrier they're going to be."

"That does tend to happen, yes."

"Must be frustrating, for Whites and Shadows alike. You're immortal, so you can afford to play the long game over hundreds of years and multiple generations. But all the other side has to do is influence one of us fleeting mortals into frenzied action and we can bring it all down in just a few years."

Yawi gave him a look. "You know better than that. Yes, you have done a lot of work over the last few linear years, but you are also playing the long game, looking ahead at the next hundred years of work and influence. Seven generations before and after. And don't forget that in order to get this far, you needed help from a lot of people, the same ones who were tangentially on trial with you just a few days ago. All this work you've been doing over the last few years, just one battle in a war that spans all of Time. Everything that you might consider a battle, just individual maneuvers."

Sabelu considered this for a long moment.

"When we get to the city, or whatever remains of it, do you know where this technology is that I have to destroy?"

"I do not, but Minotaur does, although it may be a bit too busy to guide you there."

"Can he come and tell me tonight when I make camp? Even some vague directions would be beneficial. Had I known that there was one in the underground city—"

"The one in the underground city was destroyed easily enough in the fight."

"Then why couldn't you do it yourselves? If you could cause a massive cave-in like that—"

Yawi looked back at him briefly. "The Tacagans do not believe in anything beyond the physical. They loathe anything to do with superstition or religion. The Shadows have taken advantage of this. The technology can only be destroyed if a mortal is involved. If the generals were not involved to enforce the point, it wouldn't be an issue at all."

"So the Shadows are taking advantage of the Tacagans' atheism and lending their own dark power to reinforce this atheism, making it a sort of shadow religion?"

"Exactly. And what a perfect stronghold species, wouldn't you agree? As I said before, it takes a mortal to save a mortal. It also takes a mortal to destroy a mortal. Whites and Shadows only influence."

"Where does the dragon come in?"

Now Yawi stopped and gave him a long look, one that was mostly serious, a little annoyed, and terribly aggrieved. "For now, just focus on the task at hand."

"But you know the answer," Sabelu said as the wolf started walking away. "Can we talk about it later, after the city?"

"After the city," Yawi said, not looking back or slowing down, his tone impossible to determine whether he was truly agreeing to a future conversation.

The journey after that was mostly silent save for Sabelu occasionally making benign observations of new creatures he hadn't seen before. The hills did not seem to really change in either their overall height, frequency, or vegetative cover.

"In one of the Books, it was said that the Tacagans formed this world, intending to colonize it," Sabelu said. "Why would they destroy it?"

"They changed the world, yes, through technological means," Yawi replied, not slowing in his trot. "The soil, the vegetation, they made it more like their world, which resembles their original world, Earth, the Old Land. The Shadows intended to use the Tacagans to wipe out the People Before, the half-Shadows. When things didn't go as smoothly as planned, they sent in the black phoenix and abandoned the effort."

"Why keep it as a stronghold, though?"

"So no one else could. If they can't have it, no one can. Certainly not us."

Sabelu made a grunting sound of distaste and said nothing to that.

He conjured several times throughout the day, shaving off a few hours of overall travel. By the time it got dark and he sat to make camp, he hadn't so much as glimpsed the desert, although the trees were starting to thin, the undergrowth was all but gone, and the heat had become far more intense. Sabelu wondered how much worse it was going to be once there was no cover left.

"It will be better to travel at night while in the desert," a familiar voice said as if reading his thoughts.

The Minotaur appeared from behind a nearby tree. Even when he finally sat down at Sabelu's fire, he was a terribly imposing figure. The way Sabelu figured it, if there were equals between the Shadow generals and Great Whites, the Minotaur was the equal of the cerberus. He guessed Griffin rivaled the black phoenix. He wasn't sure about the others.

"The heat does seem to dissipate fairly quickly once the sun goes down," Sabelu observed.

"Sleep by day in your tent, travel by night when it is cool," the Minotaur affirmed.

"How far to the city? First, how far to the desert?"

"Half a day to the desert. Travel there, then rest, and travel again by night. It will be three nights before you are within striking distance of the city. The Whites will show you where to camp and guard you so you are not besieged during the day. You will tire too quickly, and the desert plays many tricks in the sunlight."

Sabelu leaned over to sweep clean a patch of ground, then reached for a pointed stick from his meager firewood pile, the tiny fire being for light only anyway. "What is the layout of the city? Where is this piece of technology? More importantly, how do I destroy it once I've found it?"

The Minotaur grunted. "The city is not what it once was, and the sands change its landscape every day."

"There must be something I can look for, some reference. A particularly tall building, some odd feature, something that appears only once in the city, anything out of place?" Sabelu shrugged. "Who knows? It might be that I get close to the city and the answer is magically revealed to me, but until then, I need you to explain it to me."

The man-bull snorted and glanced at Yawi who just looked at him, tilting his head like a dog. After some inaudible conversation, Minotaur unsheathed his dagger and put the point in the dirt to draw.

"The original city was laid out as a circle with a spiral sun," he said, drawing a circle with a dozen rays spiraling out around it. "Inside, there were a number of different districts, laid out like so."

Sabelu watched him draw, and it looked to him that the districts resembled feathers, and the whole depiction looked like a dreamcatcher turned inside out.

"In each of these districts was a center, a large building for district affairs." He poked several holes in the drawing at approximately equal distances, twelve in total around the circle. "There were four more state buildings here in an inner circle, or perhaps diamond—" One for each of the Shadow generals no doubt, which meant the last one... "—and then the final tower in the center, for conducting affairs pertinent to their home world."

"If the device was intended to link this world and that one, I'm going to guess that it's in that center building," Sabelu sighed.

"It would be a good place to start looking."

"You don't know for sure?"

"The desert sands change things every day, and they have been changing things for over a thousand years. It might be in the same place, it might not."

"How far could it have gone?" Sabelu added quickly before the Minotaur could speak, "This isn't going to be a leisurely search for a lost hairbrush; I'm going to be running for my life while looking for this thing. I can't stop to investigate every rock and piece of pottery. How big is this thing anyway?"

Minotaur again used his dagger to draw a line, connecting the four diamond buildings. "It will not be outside this area; of that I am certain. As for its size, it is smaller than me but bigger than Wolf." He gestured to Yawi.

Sabelu nodded slowly. "That's...a good start. At least I won't have to look under every rock; it should be fairly obvious."

"Unless it is buried."

"Unless it is buried, yes." Sabelu rubbed his eyes. "Is there no way to make this easier, some idea of where it might be, how to find it, what I'm even looking for?" He swept away the map. "Can you draw a picture of what it looks like? Shape, features, something?"

The Minotaur grunted again, considered the dirt, then used his dagger once more to draw...something. It almost resembled a dagger itself with a hilt and guard, but then it looked as though someone replaced the blade with something egg-shaped.

"And this thing is supposed to be bigger than Yawi and smaller than you?"

"Yes."

"Well, it's better than nothing."

The man-bull shifted in his seat. "Know, too, that the closer you get, the more vehemently the Shadows will defend it. The greater your opposition, the closer you are."

Sabelu sighed, closed his eyes, and pinched the bridge of his nose. "Minotaur, fire and ice is a game that children play when they hide things from each other. The closer you get to the item, the closer you are to the metaphorical fire, and vice versa, the farther you are from the item, the closer you are to the ice. I don't know how I feel about it being a viable descriptor for this mission."

"The games that children play ought to prepare them for life, train them in the skills they will need to survive," Minotaur asserted.

"Yes, yes, Hoshonti has said something similar many times, lamenting the festival of tournaments." Sabelu let out a breath, staring at the picture of the device. "But there is only so much you can tell me without actually being there. I guess I will either have to take this to heart or else hope that the Author endows me with supernatural knowledge to take me straight to it."

Minotaur stood. "Do both." He sheathed his dagger with a satisfying metallic slide. "I will be there with you, defending you from the Shadows while you search. You need not worry."

Sabelu strained to look up at him and nodded. "Thank you."

With that, the man-bull departed the camp in two huge strides, heading toward the desert and vanishing once more behind a tree. Sabelu and Yawi were left alone in the tiny camp. Yawi lay down beside the fire and yawned.

"Half a day to the desert, then three nights to the city," Sabelu stated. He looked at Yawi. "Do you suppose that there would be any drawbacks to conjuring Iyuwahnilvhi and continuing? If I travel by night now, I am wasting less time over the next few days."

Without waiting for a reply, Sabelu stood, packed up his tent—Netami was right that it only folded perfectly once—and kicked dirt over his fire. He did not even glance at Yawi as he started off south, in the direction Minotaur had gone.

DᏞᏧᎯᏌ TEᎴ DᎶᎢT

Atlasgone Igʋpi Adolv'i
Desert Secrets

The closest that Sabelu had ever come to a desert was some memories of the old southwestern peoples of Lehoyed, the Navajo, Apache, and so on. Their idea of a desert was a landscape that was, overall, fairly flat; dry in such a way that what wasn't literal rock was hard as a rock beneath maybe half an inch of soft dirt; almost completely devoid of grass but still covered in small bushes and crunchy lichen. Then, when it did rain, the dry ground was so hard that it was incapable of absorbing the moisture well, resulting in dreadful floods and mudslides.

Far be it from Sabelu to tell the southwestern peoples that their idea of a desert was pretty tame. At least they still had vegetation and got rain. Even the rocks would be a luxury compared to the landscape before him now.

When he was told that it was an ocean of sand, he'd had a hard time imagining such a thing and thought it perhaps an exaggeration. It was not. Mountains of sand stretched as far as the eye could see, but the way the wind tickled the sand on top and pushed it around made it look like ripples in water. Here there did not seem to be any ground. Oh, at the border, he could still dig and reach common dirt. Just a few strides into the desert and he couldn't seem to reach any sort of bottom. Admittedly he didn't dig farther than his elbow for an irrational fear that he might not get it back again, but it was still disconcerting that he seemed to be standing on top of a bottomless ocean of sand. It didn't help that with the sunrise blazing to his left in the east, the sand had a red tint to it, as though mixed with dried blood.

This had once been lush and green and thick with vegetation? He couldn't picture it, and he wasn't getting any supernatural revelations about the area either. Minotaur had said that the sands changed every day, which made imagining anything even more difficult. Sabelu looked down. Where had the ground gone? Was it really down there somewhere? What did the natural landscape really look like? Was it more hills such as he'd traversed over the last day or so? Was it flat? If half the planet had once been wiped out and reduced to this kind of sandy wasteland, where did the sand go when the vegetation reclaimed it? Or was that the point, that all the sand had been pushed here and that was why it was so deep? Had some of this sand once covered Aktiya Waya, filled in the bowl?

Sabelu knelt again and pushed his arm into the sand. It was just starting to warm, and there was something almost comforting about it. He decided to go deeper this time, lying down and pushing all the way to his shoulder. He found a surprising amount of resistance, but still nothing to suggest that there was solid ground, or a bottom of any kind.

He pulled his arm out but remained squatting on the soft ground.

"Are you quite ready?" Yawi asked, sounding a bit impatient.

"I've never encountered a place like this," Sabelu told him. "I have no memories or knowledge of this kind of place; I know nothing about it. Before I start running for my life, I need to understand my surroundings, what I have to work with. Just this short distance we've trekked so far, it's difficult to walk. How am I going to run from Shadows? How can I invoke the sorceries to help myself?"

The wolf did not argue, just lay down, resting his chin on his paws.

Sabelu remained where he was, watching the sun come up, feeling the sand turn hot, watching as the air itself began to crinkle and wave with heat. He felt the sweat break out on his body, the prickle and burn of his skin, made worse with the odd breeze that tossed the sand into the air and caused it to scrape his skin. Finally he pitched his tent.

The tent was helpful to keep the direct sunlight off him, but it did little to keep him cool. Yawi remained where he was outside, keeping watch, occasionally speaking to small White insects that flitted past, once howling and then listening for a reply.

"What does the pack say?" Sabelu wondered as the wolf trotted toward the tent.

"The Shadows are amassing over the ruins like a great storm," Yawi reported. "All of the generals are there already."

"Any sign of the dragon, or suspicion that it's coming?"

"No sign. As for whether it could show up, there is that possibility."

Sabelu shifted position. "What are the odds that we're going to have time to chitchat before they actually attack?"

Yawi sat down at the entrance of the tent and tilted his head. "Shadows are victims of their own Pride. It may be that they want to gloat before killing you, or they might be too excited about it to bother with a preamble."

"You could have just said you don't know." Sabelu sighed. "I'm guessing that it really doesn't matter who kills me as long as it gets done."

"In this instance, the dragon showing up might be the better bet," Yawi explained. "Because if something gets the dragon's attention, then it wants the honor and joy of killing whatever it was that somehow made it all the way to its ears. If it doesn't show up, then no, I don't think it really matters. The generals might say they want to do it, but in the frenzy, I don't think it's going to matter, no."

Sabelu turned his attention from the wolf to the sand beyond. He was still wretchedly hot inside his tent, and he only managed to get in short naps. He didn't want to waste his water, but he couldn't say that he didn't want to slurp down everything he did have.

"On the other hand," he reasoned aloud, "having traveled this far, and now understanding this area better, I suppose I could just conjure Galohisdi to a river, refill my water, then come back and sleep some more, because of the exhaustion from using Galohisdi." He looked at Yawi. "Any reason not to?"

"Only your own fatigue," the wolf replied neutrally.

"I'm tired from the heat, but I can't sleep because of the heat. I'm parched, and how many days do I have to endure this?" He gathered his skins. "I'm going."

The wolf made no move to stop him as he brought to mind the river near his cabin. With water and cool shade the only thing on his mind, he conjured Galohisdi and stepped through.

Between his existing fatigue and the stress of Galohisdi, Sabelu landed directly in the river. He didn't mind, though the shock made it so he almost wasn't able to turn over. Memories of Ganhv trying to kill him swarmed through his mind and he found himself thrashing about in the shallow water, struggling to free himself of an enemy that no longer existed.

Finally Sabelu got himself upright, drawing in huge gasps of air as he dragged himself up the bank. He found a warm rock to sit on. He faced the river, initially confused as to why he wasn't in the bowl and where Ganhv had gone.

He rubbed his face and the delusion receded. It was easier these days. It had taken him all summer to be able to go anywhere near that part of the river again.

Yawning, Sabelu forced himself off the rock and waded back into the river, the deepest part barely over his waist. The chill helped keep him awake as he dumped out the hot water in his skins and refilled them. More prepared this time, he immersed himself, seven times in each direction, praying for blessing, wisdom, mercy, and a little more specific guidance than what Minotaur had given him. Not that it wasn't helpful— at least he had an area to look for and search in—but the faster he could find and destroy this device, whatever it was, the faster he could break the Shadows' power, and the sooner he could leave the desert. Sabelu had been to a lot of different places, a lot of different landscapes, but this desert was the first one he could honestly say he truly loathed and wanted to be rid of. Even the scrub desert around the towns in the Old Land didn't seem so bad now.

He lingered in the river a bit longer, enough to get him chilled. When he finally conjured Galohisdi again and returned to the desert, the warmth was welcome, and the trip was stressful enough that he was actually able to get to sleep.

Sabelu had hoped to visit his uncle before confronting the Shadows, but maybe that would come the night before the fight. It wasn't unreasonable to think that even with all the generals currently here in the desert that there weren't other things happening in the spirit world which demanded his uncle's attention.

He woke at sundown, the burning red ball on the horizon painting the sand bloody in a way Sabelu didn't like. It wasn't that he feared for his life or what was happening in the desert; rather it seemed to be that something was happening at home. Not his cabin, but with the people.

"I'm guessing the puppeteers around Asdeoha and the others aren't coming to this party," Sabelu stated uneasily as he packed up his tent.

"No," Yawi said simply, a bit uncomfortable himself. "They await the return of the generals from their perceived victory. Until then, they have to get things back in their order, since you are no longer there to disrupt it."

Sabelu nodded thoughtfully. "The wolf dog, keeping the Shadows in line, making sure everything runs smoothly in their own ranks." He straightened and arranged his packs and skins. "Well, we're one day closer to shattering those expectations, and as long as we're keeping the titans and generals here, the Whites in Aktiya Waya and the Old Land can do their work to stop the puppeteers and lesser Shadows."

Unlike the forest or the plains, Sabelu did not move any faster than a walk. There was too little reward for the effort. Even walking felt like a terrible chore in the heavy sand. Yawi, however, kept up a trotting pace, frequently darting out in one direction or another, looking for any threats that might challenge them before they even made it to the ruins, then returning for a short time.

"I can understand why the Shadows would want to isolate me for their attack," he puffed, cresting yet another dune, "but why let me go all the way to the ruins? Why not attack me here? The device they're protecting isn't here. Am I going to run all the way to the ruins? Where am I going to go?"

Yawi gave him a look. "As I have said before, Pride."

"Take me all the way to the end, then crush me just before I crush them?"

"Yes."

Sabelu shook his head. "The Krydik like to gamble, it's true. The festival of tournaments is proof of that. But why would they even want to risk me getting that close to their device?"

Yawi gave Sabelu a mischievous look. "Never interrupt your enemy when he is making a mistake."

Sabelu considered this for a moment, then nodded. "Good advice."

If Sabelu didn't feel it for himself, he never would have guessed that anyplace could have been so blazingly hot during the day, only to get so frigidly cold at night. Even the desert in the memories of the Old Land peoples had not been this extreme. Even the land around the Old Land towns that they were helping did not get this way. He understood why, thanks to his knowledge and use of Udilegv'i ale Uhyvtsa sorceries, but as he had said often enough, there was the difference between simple knowledge or possessing other people's memories, and experiencing it for himself.

"Half the planet used to be this way?" he asked when Yawi returned from another scouting trip. "Hot during the day, cold at night, covered in sand?"

"Not at first," the wolf said. "Immediately after the destruction, there was only barren rock. All the trees and the grass and the vegetation was gone. With nothing to hold the rock together, it began to crumble. The untouched vegetation has reclaimed most of the land, but not quite all."

"Do you think this device might be part of the reason? Once it's destroyed, do you think this land will...more swiftly return to normal?"

"It would not surprise that the device would be involved in some way, though it would be the darkness of the Shadows that is the true root cause. They have a way of destroying things."

"Maybe that's why they want to draw me all the way out here. It's the last stronghold they have on Hlohi, and they want every advantage."

"Of course."

"And seeing how they have what we want, or want to destroy, we have to play by their rules."

"They think so, yes. But one of the best things an attacking force can do is, once an area or certain advantage has been secured, is to change the rules to favor them."

"I thought you wolves were in the business of communication? Yes, yes, all Whites are fighting Whites, but I thought communication was your specialty, like war is Minotaur's specialty?"

"That doesn't mean that we have not learned from others, nor that we have nothing of our own to contribute. Minotaur hunts alone. Griffin hunts alone. Chimera hunts alone. Wolves are pack."

Sabelu thought on this. "So it's not about communication, but coordination, making sure everyone gets where they need to be, creating the advantage."

"Exactly."

"And Minotaur is like the cerberus, leading the fight on the ground. I imagine Griffin takes care of your aerial coordination with any flying Whites, and is probably the only Great White to match the black phoenix in flight. What about Chimera?"

"Chaos," Yawi said. "The Shadows know that Whites are absolute, and they can prepare for many things. Chimera, being so many creatures at once, causes them much confusion."

Sabelu made a face, though the wolf was turned away from him and couldn't see. "They can't understand an animal having many different parts? I may be a mortal man, but even I am less confused or frightened by him, now that I have seen him and understood."

"But did you see him fight?"

"Well, no. But I would think that, after how many centuries, they would see him as being his own creature."

"No. They cannot. They cannot comprehend such a concept from a solid being. It is like constantly looking at themselves in shapeless form and yet still being assaulted in many different ways."

It was frustrating enough for Sabelu to try and make sense of other people's confusion over normal things, things that he knew he supernaturally understood that they did not, things he considered reasonable (if annoying) doubt for the average human being who did not know the things he knew. But for the supernatural beings themselves to not understand such basic concepts as—

"Is it because form is a three-dimensional construct?" he wondered aloud. "Your talk of being solid or shapeless, these forms you take, the shape-shifting of the Shadows, you are not referring only to these three-dimensional shapes in the physical plane, are you? There is something deeper, within your essence, that is solid or shapeless. It's not that Chimera has different parts—even Griffin is part eagle and part lion, and Minotaur is part bull and part man—it's that his essence is more than a singularity. In your case, it's not about one Wolf, it's Pack."

"Now you are beginning to understand," Yawi said.

"But why only him? Are the Shadows also confused by Griffin and Minotaur?"

"To a far lesser extent. Even us wolves give them some pause. But Chimera was made solely for the purpose of chaos and confusion among the Shadows."

"And I'm guessing that the cerberus is the dragon's attempt at something similar?"

"Yes, but we are not fooled."

Sabelu let out a breath. "Maybe not, but that doesn't mean it isn't still a challenge."

"True enough."

"But I do have a question. In the underground city, or even outside, like here...is this your full size? I know we have spoken about the work of the ants, but I have this vague recollection of you attacking the cerberus, except you were much bigger. And even the cerberus seemed a bit...small, and not just because it's a big dog in a small space."

Yawi glanced back at him. "You will understand when we reach the ruins. Then you will wish you didn't understand."

Sabelu didn't like the sound of that, honestly. Of course, sometimes the worst thing a man could get was exactly what he asked for. He wanted to know and understand. Well, it sounded like he was about to get his wish.

In the forest, there was often a delay between when the sun rose or set and when the heat accumulated or dispersed. This had to do with vegetation cover, keeping the heat close to the ground at night and delaying its escape, or preventing it from reaching the ground when the sun appeared once more. With no such vegetation in the desert, there was no such delay. In fact, the sky was only just turning colors—the sun hadn't even appeared—and already Sabelu could feel the temperature rising. He paused on top of a dune and glanced toward the horizon where the sun was just about to pop up.

What if he did as he had earlier? Go back to the river, lie down, refresh himself, refill his skins with cold water, and come back later. That would be the smart thing to do.

He decided against it for one simple reason: tradition. His ancestors had never had such luxuries, and the trials they faced were far tamer. He was going to face this with the absolute determination of the proud, honorable, warrior line he was descended from. True, he might duck out one or two more times for water, but, he reasoned, his ancestors had never had to face this kind of unforgiving landscape. He needed to be smart, not just proud.

He pitched his tent and ducked inside as the sun rose, lying down and hoping to fall asleep before the heat kept him awake.

The heat he felt next was familiar and comforting, a cookfire. Sabelu sat up in his uncle's cave just in time to watch Anagalisgi place a spit over the fire, raw meat twisted around several vegetables on the stick.

"Did you think I had forgotten about you, Tsiquiyi?" Anagalisgi teased, studying his spit.

"I thought maybe you were busy preparing for the coming battle," Sabelu said when his uncle glanced at him.

"This is me preparing." He gestured to his cabinetry which appeared to be overflowing with supplies. Then he turned back to his food. "Now is the time for patience, reflection, and preparation of the spirit for what is about to happen."

Sabelu stood. "I don't know how much more prepared I can be, Tsidushi, except that I am given very specific directions to this wicked device."

Anagalisgi gave the spit a quarter turn. "You can prepare yourself by learning to calm down and focus."

Sabelu blinked and shifted his stance. "I am focused. There is nothing else on my mind except this mission."

"And everything that could go wrong with it." His uncle gave him a look. "Every worry about being caught by the Shadows, of not finding the device, of not being able to actually destroy it, all these phantoms, these Shadows sent to confuse you."

He hesitated. "I suspect as much, but it's hard. I can see many things, but I can't see myself. Except for my death."

"Considering that the Shadows who await you are very intent on killing you, does that give you no measure of hope or peace?"

"I'm sure they would have loved to have killed me in the underground city, but obviously they didn't."

"Yet because you knew your ordination, you were far less fearful about confronting them." His uncle folded his arms. "So what's changed?"

Sabelu thought a minute and sighed as he relented. "Because this time, it's not just about me. The people have always been the target, true, but now..." He searched for words. "If I don't succeed here, it will be the end of the people, the end of the Krydik, in very short order. And considering what I know about the peoples of the Old Land...the destitution, the death, the poverty, the hunger, the alcoholism, the despair...how can I not wonder about my success here, even a little?"

His uncle sighed in a way that suggested that he was trying to make a point or get Sabelu to think of something, but the message wasn't getting across. "You say you cannot see yourself, that the only thing you can see is your death."

"Right."

"You have mentioned before that in order to see yourself, you must do so through the eyes of others."

"Right...?"

Anagalisgi sighed again and gave him a look. "So why not make it a point of telling someone where the device is?"

It hit Sabelu like a rock in the face. "Use the future to help the past. I make the decision now to tell someone where the device is, so that I can look into the future and figure out where I said it was so that I will be able to find it so that I can tell them later so I can—" He nodded. "I got it now."

"Precisely." His uncle looked relieved. "Now, who are you going to tell? One of your relatives?"

Sabelu shook his head. "No. They are going to be under scrutiny for a while; I don't need to confuse or distract them. Actually, I don't think I want any of the Krydik to know. Few are so adventurous, but I don't want to risk any of them coming this way, be it their own curiosity or some prompting from the Shadows."

"Who are you thinking, then?"

"Kah Kitowak. He's doing some work, but he's still not very well-liked, by Krydik or Metis or Cree or anyone else. No one will care what he has to say, what he knows about any of this."

Anagalisgi nodded slowly. "Interesting reasoning."

"Am I wrong to think or do so?"

His uncle's expression twisted into something resembling a serious smirk. "You tell me. Where is the device?"

Sabelu closed his eyes and tried to focus on looking ahead. He couldn't see himself, but if he could find his next conversation with Kah Kitowak...

"It's in the southwest area of the inner ring," he recited, even as the conversation played out in his mind. "There is a ruined building, one wall tipped into another, across from three ruined pillars. It's in the farthest room, partially buried. It resembles a very large egg, the size of a man, but the shell is covered in cracks. This is how it's supposed to look, though it is understandably very old, and many of the cracks have become real."

"And how do you destroy it?" Anagalisgi's voice sounded distant.

"Use the knife to peel back the pieces of shell. Take a rock and start beating it. Don't stop until the whole thing is in tiny pieces. Then gather the pieces and set them on fire. When the fire is burned out, soak everything in water and beat it some more until everything is a fine powder. Use the sorceries to break everything down into fine dust and scatter it to the wind."

Sabelu blinked back to the present moment, shaking his head slowly. He looked around, his gaze settling on his uncle. Anagalisgi gave him a knowing look.

"Now then," his uncle stated. "Are you still worried?"

"No," Sabelu said.

"You think you can focus a little better now?"

"Now that I know what I'm doing, yes."

Anagalisgi turned the spit. "And do you now have a better understanding of how Iyuwahnilvhi works?"

"I understand why Yawi and the Whites get so frustrated and confused by linear time. I'm also starting to think that maybe they do on a regular basis what I did just now."

"Not as much as you think, but they do."

Anagalisgi turned and went to gather some plates and utensils, then returned to divide out the meat and vegetables on the spit. The two of them sat to eat.

"After this meal, we will both be heading to the battlefield," Anagalisgi observed.

Sabelu looked around. "Was it like this for my father and grandfather, when they fought in the war? Just sitting and waiting for something to happen, and then when something did, just praying for it to be over?"

Anagalisgi nodded. "There was a lot of that, yes. But you knew that."

Sabelu shrugged. "I guess I might have hoped to be wrong."

"The difference between knowing something and experiencing something?"

He could only nod.

Even after they were done eating, the two of them just sat there by the fire, neither really wanting to leave. More to the point, neither was too excited for the impending battle.

"The southwest area of the inner ring," Sabelu repeated to himself. "Across from the three pillars. Pry it open, smash it with a rock, fire, water, turn it to dust, scatter it to the wind." He looked at his uncle. "Should I return to the underground city, then, and search for the device there to do the same thing? Yawi said it was already crushed from falling rocks in the fight, but should I make sure of it?"

"The many falling boulders already took care of that," Anagalisgi said.

Sabelu set his plate and utensils beside him, then stood. His uncle followed more slowly, gathering up the dinnerware and taking them to a wash basin. He did not wash them right away, but returned to speak to Sabelu.

"Be safe, Tsidushi," Sabelu said as they clasped wrists. "I know that whatever I am dealing with in the waking world, it will be much harder in the spirit world."

"In this instance," Anagalisgi said gravely, "I think they shall be very similar in nature."

As if on cue, Ge'gwogv, the White pileated woodpecker who had been Anagalisgi's companion, appeared, swooping through the cave and landing on a root snaking down one wall.

"What is it?" Anagalisgi's words formed a question, though his tone said he already knew the answer.

"They're on their way," Ge'gwogv stated simply.

Anagalisgi looked at his nephew. "We will speak again."

Sabelu dipped his head. "I know we will. All the same, good luck, Tsidushi."

"And you, Tsiquiyi."

The sensation that Sabelu felt next, however, was not the restful darkness he would normally experience before waking. Anything resembling this expected restfulness was quickly replaced by an unexpected, crushing weight. It conformed to his body like clothing yet felt as heavy as a mountain.

Sabelu opened his eyes to darkness. When he opened his mouth, his lips brushed leather and fur. His first instinct was to gulp down a huge breath of air, but a second instinct warned against such a thing. He tried to move his arms, but they felt pinned. Anything he could move, the weight quickly filled in so he could not move back into a previous position, this monster hugging him tighter and tighter.

Sand, he realized. He was buried in sand. His tent had stopped it from getting in his nose and mouth, but it was also preventing him from digging his way out. He would never be able to open up the tent, and the air wasn't going to last forever.

Galo'ondiha ale Agi'a, he decided, just lift himself and all the sand up out of the dune.

Before he could begin, he heard rustling above him. Rustling, shifting, and then the total darkness began to lift to a dull gray. Then he heard the snuffling.

"Yawi?" he asked, unable and unwilling to go any louder than his normal voice.

An excited bark greeted his ears and the rustling intensified. Sabelu concluded that the wolf was trying to dig him out. Taking a risk, he forced his arms to move and push upwards. There was only a small area of give over his shoulder area, but he took it. A second later, sharp claws met the outside of the tent. They raked the leather a few times but did not puncture it. The digging stopped for a moment, then resumed near his waist.

"Yawi, I'm going to invoke the sorceries," Sabelu said, starting to feel the lack of air as his chest grew heavy and his mind began muddying with fatigue. "I'm going to use Galo'ondiha ale Agi'a."

The digging stopped.

Sabelu did not know how deep he really was, but at least he had a little bit of light to work with.

Sand, at least this much of it, proved to be somewhat elusive as he invoked the sorcery. The tiny grains seemed to multiply endlessly, and he was unable to capture them all. After several unsuccessful attempts, with the fatigue quickly overcoming him, Sabelu decided to simply force the issue. He stopped trying to manipulate the sand, instead rigging a line on himself and his tent and forcing everything upwards.

The easiest way he might have described it was like sticking one's hand in sucking mud, perhaps at the bottom of a river or maybe on the bank, and then lifting one's hand up and letting the mud slide through one's fingers. The weight quickly released and a breeze rushed into the tent from the bottom. Sabelu gulped down a breath of air as he released the sorcery.

Unfortunately, he did not realize just how high he had forced himself, and all the air he had sucked in was promptly knocked out of him when he fell and hit the ground. For being so soft while trekking, the sand was remarkably firm when it wanted to be.

Sabelu fought his way out of the tent and was immediately assaulted by both the light from the setting sun and a massive ball of white fur as Yawi tackled him.

"All right, all right," he said, shielding his face from the wolf's tongue. "I'm glad to see you, too." Yawi got off him and he sat up. "What happened? Sandstorm?"

"An attack by minor Shadows, to distract me while the black phoenix caused the sandstorm in an attempt to bury you alive," Yawi explained.

"Hm." Sabelu frowned. "Seems kind of weak. I don't think this was much more than a message, or a warning." The wolf did not look entirely convinced, but he did not argue. Sabelu nodded to himself. "Anyway, we have to keep moving."

He knelt in the sand and dug around for his things, most of them still wrapped up in the tent which was less of a tent now and more of a giant lump of furs.

"Will we reach the city by morning?" he asked, looking at Yawi.

"It is possible," the wolf said.

"I'll just leave this here, then." Sabelu stood, his waterskins now the greatest encumbrance on his person. "Once we're done here, I'm just going to conjure Galohisdi to return home. No sense in walking back." He put his hand up to shield his eyes against the sun which was rapidly descending. "And I am sick of this desert anyway."

Yawi shook himself. "I don't blame you."

Sabelu turned southerly and began walking. He looked at Yawi. "What are you complaining about? You're not affected by mortal weather, the heat or the sand."

"Maybe not, but the scenery is terrible. No trees, no grass, no water, no prey. Just...lifeless. It's awful."

"I hope it recovers faster once the device is destroyed," Sabelu agreed.

"We will do our best to shield you while you search."

"I know where the device is."

Yawi looked at him. "You do?"

Sabelu explained what he had done, making a decision to tell Kah Kitowak something in the future so that he could search for it in the past. When he was done, the wolf made an amused sound that was somewhere between a whine and a laugh. "Now you are beginning to understand Iyuwahnilvhi. Though you will never understand it as we do."

"I don't know that I could handle it. Simple knowledge has driven me mad on more than one occasion."

"That's all right," Yawi told him. "Not everyone needs to understand it. Most just need to trust those who do."

Kah Kitowak immediately came to mind. Sabelu gave Yawi a look, but the wolf just smirked.

Sabelu figured they had to be getting close to the city. The sky looked just a little too dark, and they were starting to run into other Whites. They first met a party consisting of deer, large cats, and a large raptor hovering overhead. The bird, too high up to be reliably identified, let out a screech, perhaps announcing their arrival.

"What news?" Sabelu asked of the patrol. "Any sign of the dragon?"

"None," Deer reported. "But there was a skirmish earlier."

"Yes, the black phoenix tried to bury me alive out there."

"The other generals are here, though?" Yawi inquired.

"They are," the large cat, Cheetah, confirmed. "Just waiting for him."

Sabelu was flattered and horrified at the same time. He looked at Yawi. "I still have a hard time figuring out why they would let me get so close to the device. Why not bring the fight farther out into the desert?"

"Remember what I told you," Yawi said.

"Don't interrupt your enemy when he is making a mistake. This just feels like an enormous mistake." He searched through all of his visions and premonitions, everything he knew about what was coming next. "It feels like a trap somehow, like there is a way that—"

"Enough," Yawi snapped. "One thing at a time."

"Yes, I know, but is it really going to be that simple?" Sabelu continued before Yawi could speak. "I am going to destroy the device; I am not disputing this point. But I fear that the Shadows already have a plan in place for when that happens. They're already moving on to another plan, hoping that this will lull us into a false sense of security."

"And now that you are aware of it, you can prepare. At that time. For now, face this foe and destroy the device."

Sabelu stared at Yawi, wanting to say or do or know something more, but unable to come up with exactly what.

It was Deer who broke the silence. "Griffin, Minotaur, Chimera, and the rest of the pack are here and ready. Just waiting on you."

Something. Anything. Anything to bring this to a more decisive finish. But even if they did somehow slay all four generals, it would only buy them time, a century, maybe a little more. And they were only on the third horseman. Like it or not, there would be a fourth, and then there was the dragon. Just one battle in a very long war. Just one maneuver in a very fierce battle.

"All right," Sabelu relented, letting out a breath. "Let's get this over with."

Yawi led the way up the dune, the rest of the patrol taking up a formation around Sabelu.

The sky was already darkening with the disappearance of the sun, and only now did Sabelu really see that what he originally thought were stormclouds were actually massive conglomerations of Shadows, circling in the sky as if ready to form a tornado.

When they reached the top of the dune, Yawi paused to howl. The rest of the pack answered him in turn, though Sabelu could not readily locate them. He was too distracted by the Shadows falling from the sky like black flame boulders.

There were no vices here. There were no indulgences. Sabelu was hard-pressed to say that there were any puppeteers in the mix. If there were any of these things, they had all melded together into an army of titans, their nebulous shapes an abominable conglomeration of pieces and parts belonging to no single animal. They were not even mildly recognizable, as a bear or a lion or some other being. Rather they were grotesque creatures with clusters of eyes, far too many arms and legs, various appendages of unknown use, and an appearance of rotting flesh. There was no need to pretend to be friendly, to attempt to seduce or coerce. With the facade unnecessary, only the truth remained, and it was ugly.

It was difficult to make out the shape of the city, as it was covered in this dense Shadow fog. Only the most prominent features, such as evenly-spaced, towering buildings, really stood out, though even from the top of the dune, Sabelu could not see the whole thing.

Part of this may have had to do with the four mountains that loomed in the center of the city. Without the constraints of a cave or any other physical factors, the Shadow generals were free to flaunt their true size and power.

The cerberus and the wolf dog, each a mountain in itself, with claws like jagged boulders on paws the size of knolls. They stood so tall, Sabelu strained his neck trying to look up. Perhaps the most eerie thing, however, was that although they should have caused small earthquakes with every shift of weight, there was nothing. It was like they weren't even there, though they clearly were.

To the left of the wolf dog, perched on one of the spires poking up from the sand, the black phoenix sat, watching him with eyes like burning coal. Its form and posture put Sabelu in mind of a peacock, but he knew well the grip of its massive talons, the heat from its black fire. Now no longer constrained by the cave, he could easily imagine its enormous wings producing a terrible wind, enough to cause a massive sandstorm to try and bury him alive.

But that was only three generals. Where was—?

Sabelu jumped at movement in his peripheral. To his left, the serpent slithered silently up from the dunes, a seemingly never-ending creature with five fangs bigger than old growth trees and sharper than broken glass. The beast seemed to slither away, out of sight. Then, a moment later, it was coming back from the other direction, sliding behind Sabelu, using itself as a barrier around the city so that he could not run away, at least not physically. Looking at the spot where it had come out of the ground, there appeared to be still more of the serpent buried beneath the dune.

But the Shadows were not the only supernatural beings showing off their true selves. A great wind signaled the arrival of Griffin, the Great White beast circling the area like a flying mountain in its own right. Small earthquakes in the pattern of footsteps alerted everyone to the approach of Minotaur, no longer a meager ten feet tall but instead greater than the serpent, so that all it had to do was step over it like an inconvenient log. More erratic tremors heralded the arrival of Chimera, the strange beast clearing the serpent in a single bound and skidding to a stop on the inside of the circle, prompting a snarl from the wolf dog. Chimera responded with a snarl of its own.

Then there were the wolves. They were not so big as the wolf dog, as Sabelu might have hoped, but they were indeed greater than any wolf he had seen in his life. They stood at intervals around the outside of the circle, front paws on the serpent as if holding it down or claiming a prize. Only Yawi beside him remained small.

"You see now," the wolf stated, looking at him.

Sabelu nodded. "I see now."

It felt as though the very pressure of the air changed as the cerberus took a step forward and lowered its heads toward Sabelu, a mountain crumbling to the ground. Even when its chins rested on the ground, Sabelu could not have measured himself against even the smallest of its teeth, and he still had to look up to see the eyes of the any of the heads.

"You have made a grave mistake," the middle head rumbled. The smell of sulfur floated in the air. "We should have taken care of you long ago, you and your kind."

There were any number of things that Sabelu could have said to that, and he entertained at least a few of them. But whether it was some divine influence or else just his better judgment taking over, he elected to say nothing. He needed to get to the device, but he didn't need to really provoke the Shadows any sooner than he had to. There was going to be a fight; he just didn't want to be the one to start it.

"We let you walk away last time," the left head said. "Not this time."

"The Whites stopped you last time," Sabelu blurted. "The Author stopped you last time. They stopped you when you tried to go after Anagalisgi over a century ago, they stopped you when you tried to destroy us in the war, and they'll stop you this time, too."

The cerberus lifted its heads, each head making a noise that might have resembled a threatening laugh, though it was still very close to a growl. The three heads swung around, looking at each of the greater Whites, noting their positions. Elsewhere, the lesser Whites, those of seemingly normal size—although they, too, were still abnormally large for what they were—got in offensive or defensive positions, each one picking out a titan to target.

"Pup," Yawi said. Sabelu did not want to look away from the cerberus, but he did. "Do not stop for anything. Do not try to fight the Shadows. You run, and you keep running, until you find that device and destroy it. And when that's done, leave the city. Run, use the sorceries, whatever you must do. Do not linger here longer than you must."

"I understand," Sabelu said simply.

"Good. We will meet again afterwards, in your den."

"You seem very certain of that," the cerberus said, its tone mockingly amused. "But perhaps you were not properly introduced to the reality of our war. Allow me to enlighten you."

Two things happened at once. First, the cerberus made a lunge for Sabelu, its three heads vying for the privilege of being the one to snap him up as a tiny morsel. Second, a massive ax buried itself in the sand just in front of Sabelu. The side heads stopped themselves before they hit, but the middle head fully struck the side of the ax, creating a sound like metallic thunder. Looking up, Minotaur was the one wielding the ax. Now, even as the middle cerberus head yelped in surprise and pain, Minotaur let out an earthshaking bellow.

Fighting broke out immediately, Whites streaming down the dunes into the city, the titans rising to meet them. Minotaur propelled himself effortlessly down the slope in a single bound, taking his ax and going straight for the cerberus. Griffin and the black phoenix took to the skies, each making high-pitched whistling sounds. Chimera slammed a massive paw into the head of the serpent, then jumped away easily as the serpent struck back, breaking the circle it had held around the city.

The wolf pack divided its attention between helping Minotaur with the cerberus and taking on the wolf dog. Yawi remained at Sabelu's side.

"Shouldn't you be helping them?" Sabelu asked, momentarily frozen as he tried to process this clash of the gods.

"My duty is to protect you. I am sworn to you. You are pack," Yawi stated. "Now move!"

The wolf butted into the back of his legs, breaking his trance as he went to all fours. Run, he'd been told. Run and don't stop for anything. Don't walk, don't stop, don't try to fight. Look for the device and destroy it, then escape. As he scrambled back to his feet, he shrugged off his water skins and anything else he had on him, short of his knife. He would need that to pry open the egg and destroy the device.

Before he could get more than three steps into the run, he already had to pull up short. A White tiger had hold of a Shadow and had thrown it down into the sand just in front of him. The Shadow twisted free, took a swipe at the tiger which jumped back at least thirty yards. The Shadow made another lunge at the tiger, clearing the way for Sabelu to slide down the dune into the city.

DᏓᎫᏗᎯᏅ ᎠᏓᏅ ᎠᏴᏗᎢ

Atlasgone Atline Adolv'i
What Will Be

From the top of the dune, Sabelu had not been able to look over the entire city. He had initially attributed it to the presence of Shadows the size of mountains blocking his view. Now he wasn't so sure.

Running down the dune as fast as he could, constantly risking that he would suddenly pitch forward and go rolling down out of control and possibly break his neck—never mind the risk that he might not be able to stop if something came at him or he had to dodge any sudden obstacles— he never seemed to actually get any closer to the city. It just kept growing and growing and growing and growing, until even the ruined peaks of buildings were small mountains unto themselves.

Unfortunately, the scenery and ability to sight-see were a bit marred by the presence of warring giants. Sabelu had just reached an area that was leveling off when he had to slide to a stop and change course, swerving to the left. Something had struck one of the buildings and a hail of boulders rained down. Whether it was his own instincts, Yawi's guidance, or something else, he managed to get clear of it and have only a coat of dust on his skin to show for it.

One of the cerberus' enormous paws landed about a hundred yards ahead of Sabelu, but it was the subsequent sweep of its tail that caused Sabelu to dive face-first to the ground. This close to the city, however, even with the years of burial and uncovering, the ground was much harder, more like sandstone than straight sand. He gritted his teeth as he felt skin peel from his arms. None of the wounds were very deep, but sometimes the wide surface ones hurt the worst. Mixing them with the gritty sand wasn't helping any either.

Getting to his feet once more, there was a blur of White as Yawi launched himself at a titan barreling down on Sabelu. Flying through the air, the wolf grew larger until it took down the Shadow like a spider clinging to a fly. The Shadow deformed and slithered away to find another fight. Yawi returned to Sabelu, and his smaller size.

"Why not stay full-size like the rest?" Sabelu puffed as he continued running.

"Because you are my charge," Yawi answered easily. "This is how I may best protect you."

Sabelu wasn't sure, but now was not the time to argue about it. Later he would think about how they twisted and turned through the rocky mess that was the very outskirts of the city and come to the conclusion that it really was better for both of them to be small and agile like mice. Like the underground city, the small cracks and crevices would save him.

On a normal day, there weren't too many cracks and crevices to be found. Most of the indeterminate piles of rubble caused either by the initial destruction or ensuing decay were buried in the sand. Now, however, there were plenty of new piles being made. As much as Sabelu wanted to keep his eyes focused straight ahead, he found himself staring up more often than not.

The wolf dog, still engaged with Yawi's pack some distance ahead, lunged for one of the wolves, swiping a massive paw at it and taking out at least five buildings in the process, sending rubble tumbling to the ground.

Was this how ants felt when a child went around stomping on their hills, or when anything wasn't watching where it stepped? For any large creature, it was simply displacing a few grains of dirt or sand, maybe a pebble. For the ants, their entire world might be collapsing.

And yet the ants kept working, Sabelu reminded himself, pressing himself flat against a wall to avoid being taken out by a Shadow on the run. The ants never gave up, never stopped, barely rested. They labored all the more, their task never-ending but of infinite importance. Laying the foundation. That was all they did, just lay a foundation. They did not concern themselves with walls or roofs or fortifications, because it all meant nothing if the foundation was anything other than solid.

All Sabelu was doing here was laying a foundation. As much as he might have wanted to believe that everything ended here, with this battle, this victory, that just wasn't the case. For one, this was only the third horseman. His grandfather had endured the first, his father the second. If he wanted his people to have a chance to getting to the fourth, never mind surviving it, he had to lay his part of the foundation and slay this horseman.

His grand self talk was cut short as the cerberus' tail swept low over the ground, razing the buildings in its path like cutting grass. Sabelu had no chance to run; he immediately reached for Galo'ondiha ale Agi'a, propelling himself upwards with more force than he was prepared to control. He did not see what happened to Yawi as he reached the end of his track but still flew upwards for a short distance before going into freefall. He invoked Galo'ondiha ale Agi'a again, bringing himself to rest in midair. Then, without thinking beyond being fearful for his life, he conjured Iyuwahnilvhi, slowing down everything around him. Whether it was his own fear or something in the nature of the Whites and Shadows he did not know, but he found he was unable to bring them to a complete halt, that is, he was unable to make himself move fast enough that it brought everything outside his plane to a standstill.

Minotaur was just completing a swing of his magnificent ax, the blade apparently having come within inches—and considering they were the size of mountains, this was still quite impressive—of the right cerberus head. Meanwhile, the center head was ducked so the left head could try to get in a bite, its maw still wide in hateful snarls, going for Minotaur's arm or shoulder. Failing that, the front left paw was poised for a heavy strike.

The wolf dog had managed to get one of the wolves on its back and had drawn blood, but was currently being ripped off by two more wolves, one getting very near its throat.

Chimera was still facing off against the serpent. The great snake had ceased trying to maintain a ring around the ruins and now zigzagged here and there as it went after the chaotic creature. From their current positions, Sabelu surmised that Chimera was trying to set up the serpent as a trip line for either the cerberus or the wolf dog.

In the air, high above where Sabelu hovered, both Griffin and the black phoenix had talons locked into each other, each one trying to snap at the other's neck while protecting his own. Griffin had the advantage of having rear legs in addition to his front talons; in lieu of the black phoenix's neck, he would settle for trying to rip open its stomach. But the black phoenix still had its fire, and it looked very near to combustion, not that Sabelu was an expert in such matters.

He turned his attention back to the city. If the sand wasn't enough, the chaos of mixing Whites and Shadows made it even more difficult to locate the tall buildings. It also stood to reason that a few of them might have been knocked over just from the cerberus' tail swinging around. So how was he supposed to locate the device?

Northeast. The northeast section of the inner ring. That was where he needed to start. The problem was, the wolf dog and three of the wolves were dancing around in the northeast area. The wolf that was still on its back was likely crushing hundreds or thousands of ancient buildings into dust.

He had to get a closer look.

Galo'ondiha ale Agi'a needed to be utilized along a track of some form. In practice, this was little more than a slight visual distortion, very much like conjuring Iyuwahnilvhi. Trying to judge the movement of the Whites and Shadows still in slow-motion, Sabelu snaked his track in a general northeast direction, toward the wolves and the wolf dog, aiming for a tall-ish building that hadn't been completely destroyed yet.

He looked around for Yawi, found him flattened to the ground, the cerberus' tail sweeping just over his ears. Was there any way to let the wolf know what he was doing? Would Yawi find him missing, then go searching for him in vain? Would the Author give the wolf supernatural knowledge of his plans and whereabouts? For as much as Sabelu hoped he was saving himself a lot of time, he was also losing his dedicated protection.

He had no time to consider the decision. With slow-motion the best he could do, he had to go now. He finished his track, attaching it to the tall-ish building, and let go. Unlike his panicked grab for Galo'ondiha ale Agi'a, he was more prepared for the jolt and sudden change of direction as he went flying through the air along his track.

It wasn't impossible to modify a track in mid-air, but it was certainly more than he was prepared to handle at the moment. With his mode of transportation currently taken care of, Sabelu's attention was more focused on the activity around him and ensuring that he wasn't suddenly taken out by a slow-moving White or Shadow. He had to twist a couple of times as a stray paw or other appendage brushed the track, and he wondered how that brush affected the intended attack, though he did not dwell on it.

His problem came when he noticed a Shadow—who apparently had the time and attention span to notice him flying through the air, and possibly saw and judged his track—leaping up from the ground, gaping jowls ready to snap him up for a snack as he went by.

Sabelu had no choice. He snapped the track like an old string. Natural forces took over, and as he fell, he lost control of Iyuwahnilvhi as well, and he found himself heading straight into the middle of what might have been an eight-way fight between titans and Whites.

He managed to throw out a small Galo'ondiha ale Agi'a track, enough so he didn't land square on the back of a White bear. By the time he actually landed, he found himself rolling through a black mist with the consistency of dirty honey and as cold as standing on top of the mountain in Aktiya Waya in the middle of a winter ice storm. The shock of going from mildly chilly to impossibly cold was enough to cause him to freeze and lose any and all sorceries he had at the ready. He hit the sand beneath with all the grace of a corpse, flopping away from the Shadow which snapped at him. That distraction proved advantageous for the White that leaped onto the Shadow to deliver a severe or even fatal blow.

Just as soon as he could figure out his limbs, Sabelu was moving. The Shadow that had tried to leap into the air and eat him had spotted him again and was making its way swiftly through the sand toward him, like a fish through water.

Sabelu used every trick he could think of to make himself move faster. Iyuwahnilvhi, to slow down the Shadow; Gasadoyasgi to propel himself faster; Galo'ondiha ale Agi'a, to push or pull him in a certain direction over shorter distances. He tried zigzagging through the ruins, hoping to confuse the thing. It bought him some time and distance, but the titan was fixed on him worse than a hunting dog. Maybe he could conjure Galohisdi, jump somewhere else entirely.

He dared to look behind him and found the titan much closer than he was comfortable with. With no good options, Sabelu conjured Galohisdi. Somewhere, anywhere, he didn't care where. Author help him because he was about to dive through.

He was still in the ruins somewhere, perched in some kind of window or door opening about twelve feet off the ground. Judging from what he knew about where he was, he surmised that he was somewhere in the northeast section, though not especially close to the center. Once again, the wolf dog and the wolves were between him and his goal.

He conjured Iyuwahnilvhi, trying to buy himself a few seconds to pick out a destination. His head was starting to hurt, his adrenaline was roaring through his ears, his heart was pumping wildly, and the sand made it difficult to see, and that wasn't even including the Shadows' haze.

He set his sights on a tall-ish building, maybe even the same one as before, and committed its general location to memory before leaping from his perch to a relatively clear location below, using Galo'ondiha ale Agi'a to slow his descent.

Because his initial entrance had been from the southwest, the northeast part of the city was less crowded, and he was able to make some decent progress, ducking down old, abandoned alleys, hiding for a moment in a rubbled corner alcove while one Shadow flew overhead and another ran down the street past him.

This was not the way his people fought. This was not the way any of the peoples fought. The people fought with either stealth or a surprise and run away. This kind of open warfare was foreign to him. Well, three-quarters of him. It was not foreign to the part of him that was American, and they were the people who had won wars with open combat.

Before he could search his knowledge and memories for anything useful, a cold draft alerted him to Shadow presence. If not the draft, then the ugly, wet snuffling and snorting noises it made as it moved. Judging by these sounds, it was getting closer.

Sabelu's cover really wasn't much, and it would be too easy to trap him in his little alcove. Not bothering to wait and see where it was, Sabelu conjured Iyuwahnilvhi and slipped out of his hiding spot. He took off at a sprint, continuing toward the tall-ish building. He did not invoke any other sorceries right away. He didn't want to risk a migraine, and there wasn't enough action to make him think it absolutely necessary.

Even as he thought this, there was a crash of rock on rock. The wolf dog had thrown down one of the wolves. The wolf struck a building and sent large boulders of rubble flying, their general trajectory heading right for Sabelu. Because of the size of the Whites and Shadows as well as the city, it was entirely possible to watch the boulders as they soared through the air.

This made it easier to dodge the large boulders themselves, but did little to help with the ensuing spray of sand and rock when the boulders landed and cracked open. Sabelu reached for Galo'ondiha ale Agi'a, not to try and throw each one out of his way, but to mix it with Gayalvnga. It was a dangerous conglomeration of sorceries, but if he used it correctly, he might be able to invert the energies around himself, using his knife as the magnetic center. It was like trying to force two magnets together; they just wouldn't do it and would even repel each other. Galo'ondiha ale Agi'a was primarily for added power, so that the rocks really would get out of his way rather than just fall by the wayside.

Sabelu never slowed as the boulders continued to fall. His use of sorceries worked well enough, at least to keep the smaller rocks away and the dust from his eyes. The larger rocks, however, proved to be a little more forceful than his counterforce. One rock brushed the back of his head, a shard catching his braid and yanking him to the ground. He was too stunned to even cry out in pain, but the move actually saved him as another boulder landed right where he would have been a moment before. He ripped his hair free of the shard and was soon up and running once more.

The wolf dog still had the wolf pinned, but this was short-lived as three more wolves slammed into it from the side. The wolf dog rolled over, creating a small tsunami of sand, flinging rocks and even whole buildings into the air.

At the same time, a horrifying bellow split the air. Minotaur had taken a bite directly to the thigh, but it was likely a known sacrifice as the right cerberus head had been severed from the body. Smoke billowed from the wound, clouding the atmosphere even more so the sky was like a night of no moon.

Sabelu turned his attention back to the tsunami, now a shadow against black canvas. It wasn't coming directly at him, but the indirect strike wasn't going to be much fun either. The buildings that had not been struck directly by the falling general were now broken or dislodged by the ripples in the ground. Where once there had been more or less distinct roads and buildings, now all was laid to waste in a rocky blanket.

The next wave of boulders began falling from the sky, their position and appearance blurred by a wall of sand. Sabelu's little trick with Galo'ondiha ale Agi'a and Gayalvnga wasn't going to repel this. He slowed to a stop, unable to see, sand stinging his nose.

The wall of sand hit him, knocking him back a good ten feet. He twisted and landed on all fours, back to the brunt of the force, using all his strength to not go to his belly and be instantly buried. The ground heaved beneath him and he gritted his teeth against the small rocks that struck him. He knew he couldn't stay there; boulders rained over him, some landing uncomfortably close.

He managed to crawl over to one of the boulders, hoping to use it as a shield. It provided a small reprieve so he could clear his eyes and relax his muscles a little. He could probably wait it out here.

As luck would have it, this was not the case. In all the chaos of the sand tsunami and flying boulders, Sabelu did not hear or see the serpent as it burst through the wall of sand, trying to use said chaos to hide itself from Chimera still attacking it. The serpent was pouring smoke-like blood and had multiple gaping wounds.

The serpent passed within feet of Sabelu's position, pushing up sand on either side of it as it slithered by. What was only a minor consequence of its normal actions was another devastating, potentially fatal, disturbance for Sabelu as the ground rose a good thirty feet, and he and the boulder he'd been hiding behind went tumbling down the slope, all the while trying not to be crushed under the paws of the Chimera that pursued the serpent.

When Sabelu finally came to a complete stop, about halfway down the slope the serpent had pushed up, he decided to just lie there for a minute or two, staring up at the hazy sky and watching the terrible dalliance of Griffin and the black phoenix. He could feel the tremors in the earth as the Whites and Shadows fought, hear the screams of creatures he had no names for. But he was exhausted. His head hurt, his body hurt. Even the thought of rolling over onto all fours felt like a chore.

A wet nose bumped his ear. Absently, he reached up and scratched Yawi under the chin.

"Are you hurt?" the wolf asked seriously.

"I don't know," Sabelu admitted, taking a breath into heavy lungs.

Yawi circled him once. "You are fatigued, but not hurt." The wolf nudged him in the ribs. "Get up."

The wolf's tone left no room for argument or complaining, but Sabelu was still slow to stand.

Everything in the outer ring of the city had been leveled. A fair portion of the middle ring had been destroyed as well, if not leveled and buried entirely. The tall-ish building was gone, obliterated, and left to be consumed by the desert. Minotaur and the cerberus remained in the northwestern to western part of the city. The serpent had retreated south with Chimera chasing. The wolf dog and wolves were now more politely out of Sabelu's way, though still staunchly in the northeastern section. As for the titans and greater Whites, the majority of them were still in the western half of the city, though the cerberus and Minotaur were driving many of them to the center or eastern parts.

"The northeastern section," Sabelu repeated to himself, "the inner ring, in a building across from three pillars." He looked at Yawi. "Do you know where that might be?"

"I might," the wolf said, "but you need to stick with me this time."

"I was just trying to get there faster, save myself some time and trouble."

"This time, do it the right way."

The wolf's words held no real malice, or so Sabelu told himself, and the two of them started off at a brisk trot. Yawi remained full of energy while Sabelu kind of wanted to sit down and rest a while.

The dangers of the unknown alleys and unstable buildings quickly morphed into the dangers of sharp stones and unstable boulders, as well as the danger of being so exposed. More than once, a titan came after them, if for no other reason than it was able to see them, with no buildings in the way. At Yawi's instruction, Sabelu just kept running. He did not try and fight, did not even stop to really defend himself beyond dodging blows. He let the wolf take care of everything, instead keeping his gaze fixed on another tall building, one of the four marking the inner ring he saw, barely visible in the smoky sky.

Sabelu cried out as the ground beneath him suddenly heaved and massive jaws penetrated the space around him. A titan, maybe even the same one as before, came up under him like a massive fish, intending to swallow him whole. Sabelu's only saving grace came from all the boulders also in the beast's mouth. He ran across the unstable, rocky surface. He aimed for the gap in the teeth which was quickly narrowing as the creature forced itself to crunch through the stone.

By the time he got to the teeth, the gap was too narrow for him. Thinking fast, he grabbed onto the teeth and started climbing. Each one was like grabbing a massive icicle, and he knew he lost skin every time he peeled his hand off one to grab another. He shimmied up the toothy ladder just as fast as his body could carry him, acutely aware that the titan had nearly crushed the boulders to dust and the gap at the top was narrowing considerably.

The beast's mouth suddenly opened wide and pitched to the side, throwing Sabelu clear and back out onto the rocky ground. When he chanced a look, he saw that Yawi had struck the beast broadside and ripped it open in short order. The wolf left the titan to disintegrate and ran to Sabelu. Yawi was not full size like his monstrous kin, but still of good size in Sabelu's opinion, perhaps ten feet tall at the shoulder. Yawi skidded to a stop and lay down, ordering, "Climb on."

Sabelu did so without a second thought, pulling himself onto the softest blanket he'd ever felt in his life, with a faint hint of spice, in spite of any fighting the wolf had done. The only thing he had to hold onto was the fur itself.

Yawi hardly waited for him to be ready before leaping into action, powerful legs thrusting them forward with incredible force such that Sabelu nearly lost his grip. Thinking fast, he ducked low into Yawi's fur, hoping to hide and not draw attention to himself as the human who was trying to destroy the Shadows' device.

There was little to see, hiding as he was, but he could hear just fine. The predominant sound was the fight between Minotaur and the cerberus. With one head out of commission, as well as whatever part of the body that head controlled, Minotaur now had a real weakness to exploit, assuming his own injury wasn't slowing him down too much.

But there were plenty of other sounds as well, a majority of them being the sounds of war. Every so often Sabelu heard what he thought was a crash of a building or two or more boulders striking one another with great force.

The ride overall was remarkably smooth, not unlike some of the horses bred in Anpa O Wican'hpi that had very smooth, same-sided gaits. This smoothness was interrupted when Yawi had to traverse a particularly rough patch of ground or climb or jump over a boulder, but on the whole, it wasn't a bad ride. Certainly Sabelu had had worse rides on a couple horses just following the road out of Aktiya Waya.

He was jolted as Yawi suddenly jumped sideways. A huge, shadowy paw came down beside the wolf, and Yawi ducked and slid to the side to avoid a massive maw of stinking, putrid, icy breath and snarled teeth. Sabelu looked up to see the wolf dog hovering over them.

Yawi and the wolf dog began circling each other, the other wolves forming a circle, waiting for some silent cue from their leader. Sabelu, still tucked in the fur between Yawi's shoulders, swallowed hard and tried to stay hidden even as he felt every ripple of muscle beneath him, and he couldn't be sure Yawi hadn't grown to full size. The wolf's skin vibrated with every growl.

The wolf dog yelped and looked back, perhaps at a cheap shot by one of the wolves. At its distraction, the other wolves attacked as one, driving the wolf dog to the ground. In that moment, Yawi turned and bolted, away from the fight, shrinking again and continuing toward the inner circle.

A moment later, there was a tremor in the ground, and Sabelu looked back just in time to see a massive black paw coming down over Yawi's back, and a slavering jaw ready for a secondary snap.

As soon as the paw made contact with fur, Sabelu jumped. He threw out every sorcery that came to mind to try and slow his fall, or make the landing easier. If anything worked, it was only to keep him physically alive as he landed on frustratingly hard sand and kept going, rolling over sharp rocks and finally slamming into the side of a building.

Getting himself upright, he saw that the wolf dog had gotten Yawi down, but Yawi had shaken off any remaining constraints and was again his full size, the same as the rest of the pack. Their full attention was now on the wolf dog, their only intent to kill.

Sabelu did not need to be told to keep running. He scrambled toward the safety of an alley, keeping low so as not to be spotted. Once he figured he was a good distance away from the fight, he stood up straight and looked around. The tall building of the inner ring was much closer now.

Sabelu knew that his adrenaline could only keep up for so long;

sooner or later, he was going to crash. He had to keep going, had to press on, had to survive. He had to destroy the device; he'd come too far and gone through too much today alone to do anything else.

There were more small battles here, more titans and large Whites. Many times, the titans, upon spotting him, would try to break away from their opponents and chase after him. This chase did not last long, as the Whites were quick to pursue and attack once again, buying time for Sabelu to disappear.

At one point, Sabelu found himself hiding in a ruined husk of a building, invoking Atsvstdi to bend light around him and make himself nearly invisible. He was worried it wouldn't work, if the Shadows could track him by some kind of scent, but in the moment it worked, and they ran right past him, not to return. He breathed a sigh of relief but still did not move for a long moment.

It was not uncommon for those who could use Atsvstdi in this way to experiment with making it more useful. As it was, Sabelu could only make it work if he was sitting still and concentrating, or else moving very slowly and concentrating even more. It was unclear whether it could be invoked in such high-action situations, but the three times that Sabelu attempted it now, just trying to get out of the building while remaining more or less invisible, all were failures.

Well, it would have to wait. He'd made it this far well enough, he could finish it out the same way. Sabelu barely looked around as he exited the building and kept running down the street. Every part of him just wanted to collapse and sleep for a moon. Adrenaline alone was starting to fail. If he was surprised one more time by a Shadow, he feared his heart might just stop completely. He didn't know how much more of this he could take. With any luck, Yawi would catch up to him and give him another ride, straight to the device.

He looked up, wondering if he might be close enough to use Galo'ondiha ale Agi'a again. He wasn't trying to traverse over an entire city, just this small part of it. He might be able to see the three pillars better from up high.

Behind him, there was an earth-shattering screech as the wolf dog fell to its knees, then to the ground, smoky blood billowing from a fatal wound. The White wolves all lifted their heads in a victorious howl, but this was cut off by an equally awful shriek from the black phoenix, high in the sky.

Sabelu skidded to a stop and watched as the black phoenix ignited, an enormous ball of black fire. The ignition caused the Griffin to move back, giving the black phoenix the room it needed to turn and head straight for the wolves. Or Sabelu assumed it was heading toward the wolves. Instead, he saw it change course and go directly for the smoke where the wolf dog was disintegrating.

As soon as the black phoenix's fire touched the corpse, the smoke ignited into an impossible mountain and column of black fire that torched the sky. Any smaller titans who were also dead and disintegrating that were touched by the fire also ignited. The wolves jumped clear of the fire but made no move to touch the black phoenix as it went past. The only light in the desert at that moment was a faint glow from the Whites, this sucked into the fire like a dazzling, glowing river, and ironically providing even greater light to the area.

The black phoenix circled around, igniting all of the Shadow corpses, and finally returning to its more solid, bird-like form to re-engage Griffin, the closest thing to a sun or moon in the sky at that moment.

Sabelu, plunged into darkness and hardly able to see where he was between two buildings, stumbled along the road as he remembered it. The Whites were fairly obvious now, but the Shadows had virtually disappeared. As Sabelu passed into what he believed to be the northeastern section of the inner ring proper, he found himself slowing to a fast walk, both for exhaustion and suspicion. What was a common shadow cast by the light of the Whites, and what was an actual Shadow, taking advantage of the darkness to try and surprise him?

Three pillars, three pillars, three pillars... Where were they? In the dark, everything looked the same. No wonder he could only describe it as such to Kah Kitowak. Otherwise he might have given himself directions that were a little more specific. But there was nothing specific about this. Darkness and Shadows, every form and yet formless.

Were there any clues to be found, or would this truly be a blind search, absolute luck? Sure, the Author would guide him where he needed to go, but did it really have to be this vague? Didn't the Author want him to succeed? Didn't she want the people to thrive? Couldn't she just—?

Sabelu's body reacted before his mind did, jumping and twisting out of the way of a Shadow that leaped at him from the darkness. This almost put him in the claws of another titan that rose to meet him. A third also formed from the darkness. As they faced him, they took on the shadowy likenesses of the three men who had attacked him in the street.

"Does he know what we're going to do next?" one hissed mockingly.

"You would think he would have known better than to come this way if he knew we were here," the second agreed.

"No Whites here to save you," the third rumbled.

"Are you sure about that?" Sabelu asked, hoping he sounded more confident than he felt.

Time was like a river. All people set upon this river in canoes. The destination was always the same, though the journeys could vary somewhat, and it was your condition on arrival that determined what happened afterwards. The Whites could move here and there, get in and out of the river, and they saw things from a very broad, relatively non-linear perspective. The Shadows were beasts that lurked in the river, drawn to the things floating on the surface. They did not move so freely, nor did they have the advantage of foresight.

Such as now when Yawi swooped in, snapping up two of the titans in his mouth and crunching them in half while crushing the third under his paws. The whole encounter was over in less than fifteen seconds. Then the wolf shrank back down to a more manageable size and again lay down.

"Get on," he ordered.

Sabelu wasted no time pulling himself back up between the wolf's shoulders. "Do you know where the device is?"

"No, but someone else does."

Sabelu looked around the wolf's head to see the White rabbit popping up from a hole in the ground.

"Device located," the burrower reported. "Mole is working on digging it out."

"Take us there," Yawi said.

With the goal finally feeling within reach, Sabelu gripped the wolf's fur tight as they sprang into a run. In the darkness, another shriek echoed eerily.

"The cerberus has lost another head," Yawi reported. "It won't be long now."

"The wolf dog, the cerberus," Sabelu said. "What about the serpent? Or the black phoenix? Do you think it's possible to take all four of them out?"

"The serpent will more likely flee before it allows itself to be killed. And the black phoenix will simply burn to ash and resurrect itself later. The serpent has been killed before, but I don't know that the black phoenix ever has."

Sabelu frowned. If that were the case, if the black phoenix had never been killed, then how had any of these battles ever been won? What were they supposed to do if it decided to ignite once more and come after them as a raging ball of fire?

And how were they supposed to take on the dragon afterwards?

The ride this time was less smooth than before, if only because they were not running across open ground. There were still buildings and alleys here, although it was apparent where the cerberus had swept its tail a time or two. There were also sudden diversions to avoid areas of heavy fighting.

A thunderous roar rumbled through the air, followed by a bird-like twittering.

"What's that?" Sabelu dared to ask.

"The black phoenix has given up on Griffin and goes to aid the cerberus against Minotaur."

"If the serpent is just going to flee, shouldn't the rest of the pack help Minotaur?"

"The pack knows its role," was all the wolf said to that.

Because who was to say that the serpent wouldn't just circle back around and catch one of them off-guard? Sabelu peeked through Yawi's fur at some of the smaller battles as they flashed by, blurs of light in the darkness. He had little doubt that there were enough Whites and Shadows in the universe to keep both sides busy for quite a while, but was there no way for the smaller Whites to get involved and help Minotaur and the others? It sounded like Rabbit and his burrowers had been busy searching for the device; perhaps if he, Sabelu, hadn't tried to run off on his own so quickly, they would have been there already and this could have already been over. But were there no other clever and clandestine operations going on? Or were there such operations, and it was because of those operations that Minotaur was as successful as he was so far?

Sabelu was nearly flung from Yawi's back as the wolf suddenly leaped to one side, narrowly avoiding both a titan that was battling a large bear-like White, as well as a falling building, struck down by a mostly-lame cerberus as it flopped away from Minotaur's ax, surprisingly nimble for having only one functioning leg.

Sabelu saw Rabbit only briefly as they scattered to avoid being crushed, but in the moment, he was more focused on just staying on the wolf. A jump in the opposite direction helped him to right himself. Yawi never really slowed and did not allow himself to get distracted by everything going on around him. Sabelu noticed several instances where a struggling White might have benefited from the wolf's intervention, but no intervention was given.

He looked around, squinting into the darkness. Three pillars, three pillars, three pillars... Obviously, if he conveyed this information to himself from the future into the past, then those pillars should still be standing. Were there no other markers or directions he could use? Could he still influence himself using events that, for him, hadn't happened yet? Was there a reason he hadn't? He now understood that the darkness could make it difficult to point out greater geographical features to watch out for, but what about the things he glimpsed from Yawi's back? Was there nothing so distinct to mark how close they were getting?

Sabelu closed his eyes and tried to focus on his future conversation with Kah Kitowak. Maybe instead of trying to jump to the very end of the conversation, he should consider the whole thing in context. Kah Kitowak believed in the Author, Whites and Shadows and all, but there was bound to be a certain air of disbelief that would prevent him from fully grasping the magnitude of the situation, and his end of the conversation would be punctuated with questions, doubts, and a few sarcastic comments.

The concentration required for such a detailed search was just beyond what he could manage while riding through battle on the back of a giant wolf, and every little jump, jolt, or twist that Yawi made only broke this already fragile concentration. All that time in the desert, and he had still arrived unprepared.

He wanted to ask Rabbit how much farther. The tower at the very center of the city had been long destroyed in the fight, although its location was still quite obvious. Even so, they were coming upon it rather quickly. If the device was in the northeastern section of the inner ring, well, there was only so much of that section remaining.

Sabelu remembered having a thought that this city was impossibly big, and yet he was willing to bet that more than half of it was still buried, outer reaches where there were no towers and the buildings had been long consumed by the sands. Aktiya Waya, for as large as it was, would still fit in this place more than a thousand times.

It was unclear whether Yawi's next jump was in reaction to Minotaur's sudden bellow of pain, or if it was all just a coincidence. The black phoenix screamed a victory chortle, and Sabelu could only just make out its vague shape against Minotaur's glow. The black phoenix had gotten in a blow to Minotaur's face, and the cerberus, still hanging on, had followed it up with a strike to his leg. If the cerberus had the ability to properly stand, shift weight, and put some power behind the blow, Sabelu could have seen the large man-bull going to the ground. As it was, it only gave Minotaur another distraction while the black phoenix came in for a secondary attack, striking the other side of Minotaur's face, tearing at an eye.

Yawi slowed for a moment, looking up, but never actually stopped.

"This way!" Rabbit said from his vantage on a low wall about ten strides ahead. "Not far now!"

Yawi picked up the pace and Sabelu tightened his grip as much as he could. His legs and lungs were grateful for a reprieve from the constant running, but the rest of him was still ready to collapse and fall off the wolf.

They drew ever nearer to what was once the central tower and closer to Minotaur and his foes than Sabelu was really comfortable with. Watching Minotaur move, just lifting one leg, he noted how slow they seemed to be moving. Of course, for Minotaur, he was simply moving a leg, but to Sabelu, it was like picking up a mountain. Sabelu found himself wondering if time moved differently depending on one's size. Flies were fast-moving nuisances to humans and animals, and yet they intentionally made every move; did time go faster for them because they were smaller? Was this principle why Sabelu had such a hard time Banding the Whites and Shadows?

A thought for a different day, he decided. Right now, he had to focus on what it was going to take to destroy the device. He felt the knife on his person. Use the knife to pry the shell off the egg, beat everything with a rock, set it on fire, beat it again, soak it with water, beat it some more until the whole thing was a powder finer than the sand in the desert. It sounded silly, true, but it also sounded quite thorough, and he had little desire to do anything like this a second time.

They turned a corner. Sabelu only had time to register six massive pillar-like structures before they were suddenly split crossways by Minotaur's ax. Three of the pillars were completely destroyed, as if they had never existed. The other three remained more or less in tact, at least recognizable as pillars.

The building which contained the device was not difficult to discern, as multiple burrower heads popped up from the ground on the approach of the White rabbit. Yawi slowed to a trot, not fully stopping until Sabelu was directly in front of the door. He slid off the wolf's back and somehow managed to land on his feet.

"We've dug it out the best we could," Mole reported as Rabbit hopped by, leading Sabelu through a crumbling doorway into what might have once been a room about the size of three houses in Aktiya Waya. Half the building was gone, so there was very little protection from the elements. The burrowers had moved the sand they dug up to the open side of the room, blocking any wind or prying eyes.

What could be seen of the device was fairly true to description. It was about four feet tall above ground, though there was more that was still hidden, and more burrowers continued to shovel sand to the best of their abilities, scooping out two handfuls and enduring the one that rolled back in. The device did indeed resemble an egg, although it was anyone's guess what kind of bird it could have come from for it appeared to be made of solid metal. It was dark gray or black, at least in present light, but there were veins of blue running through it. These veins appeared to glow, but it may have also been a reflection of the glow of the Whites; Sabelu could not readily tell. From what he could see of the burrowers' progress, it was set into some kind of base or pedestal.

He gingerly reached out to touch the egg, as if afraid it might suddenly come to life. It did no such thing, and the most that happened was that he could feel a faint pulse of energy, or maybe that was his racing heart. He couldn't tell that either until he invoked the sorceries. It was the energy of the sky and storms and lightning, though incredibly faint, hardly more than the little tick of static one might get from rubbing furs together and then touching one's sibling. Not that any of them had ever done that of course.

Whatever this was and however it worked, it was nowhere near as powerful as it had been a thousand years ago. This was not surprising; actually, it was more surprising that it had lasted this long. It would probably last another century or so and die naturally if he left it.

The wolf dog was gone, and the cerberus was nearly dead as well. It would be a century or so before they were recycled. This device here was almost dead, but it would take a century or so for it to fully die. If he did nothing, Sabelu was willing to bet that the Shadow generals would come back just before the device died, and would use it for one last terrible act against the Krydik. Whoever the Tacagans were, a thousand years ago they had wiped out all of the half-Shadows and taken half the planet with them. Who knew what the Shadows would do the second time? Sabelu was also willing to bet that it wouldn't be just the generals next time either. After the black phoenix came the dragon, and this fight here was hard enough.

The device was not standing upright as it might have been when it was brand new, but instead was sunk into the sand at an awkward angle so that Sabelu could not easily see all the way around it. He ducked and turned and twisted, but from what he could see, the egg was the same all the way around.

Something large hit the ground just outside the building, causing Sabelu to jump.

"Hurry!" Yawi urged.

Sabelu didn't need to be told twice. Brandishing his knife, he stabbed it into the blue veins that ran between the metal panels.

Dying or not, it was still a powerful device. Energy flashed through Sabelu, throwing his hand back and causing his arm to rattle and twitch wildly just long enough for him to register the movement. He gasped for air and went to his seat, heart pounding.

After a moment of just trying to figure out what happened and recover his faculties, he looked up and saw his knife still stuck in the egg. If he tried to just grab it, well, fool me twice. He had to corral that energy.

His whole body was trembling as he again got to his feet and faced the egg. Nothing about it had really changed except for his knife sticking out of one of the blue veins and an occasional spark popping up from the edge of the hole.

The people had many stories about the sky and the storms that raged. Thunderbirds, lightning snakes, sea monsters, the tales were endless. The one theme that remained constant throughout all of them was that the spirits were in charge, not mortal men. Well, the Tacagans certainly appeared to have captured a piece of that energy in this device, and now he had to try to harness it himself long enough to get his knife back and destroy the egg.

Letting out a breath, Sabelu touched the device, just the metal panels. He was not again shocked by the energy, which relieved a significant portion of his immediate anxiety. He could still feel the faint pulse of energy, although it felt more erratic than before, which, he supposed, was to be expected. But this erratic pulse actually helped him to focus on the energy and differentiate it from anything he was feeling naturally.

If he could just interrupt the energy between pulses, and somehow keep it away from himself, he might have a chance. He had no real clue how to do this, and he didn't suspect that there was any real halfway between what he felt on the panels and what he'd experienced just a second earlier. There was no wading into this.

His first attempt ended very much the same way as before, though it took a few more seconds for him to stagger back to his feet. He looked at Yawi.

"D-do you know how t-t-to do this?" he stammered involuntarily.

"If I did, would you be here?" the wolf countered, paying more attention to what was going on outside than what he was doing.

"But this is sky energy. I thought the spirits were the masters of wind, waves, and weather?"

"As with many things, we may influence them, as the black phoenix did with the sandstorm, but we do not control them."

"So...there is no thunderbird?"

Few had dared to venture into any sorceries involving the sky, but those who had reported that they could not find thunderbird or the lightning snakes or whatever it was that dictated the weather, only copious amounts of energy they did not understand. A couple disregarded it, decided that they were just unworthy of seeing such things and to back off before the spirits became angry about it. One disavowed the spirits entirely, though he kept it to himself. And a couple more still ventured out from time to time to try again.

Sabelu had only attempted such a feat once. Although he had not found a literal thunderbird clapping his wings to produce the rumbling in the sky, he still maintained a general belief. His hope for a real thunderbird had been renewed with his introduction to the Whites.

"Not as you understand it," Yawi told him, giving him a sympathetic look. "Griffin was once a creature you would call Thunderbird, but that did not mean that he could summon or drive away storms as a potter might mold clay. The universe is governed by rules and the rules are determined by the Author."

A sensation that Sabelu could only describe as despair flooded him. There was no thunderbird, not really. Even with Yawi's admission that Griffin had once been Thunderbird, the whole revelation was still greatly disappointing. Maybe it had nothing to do with the thunderbird itself and more to do with the idea that it was, really, powerless. Truly everything traced back to the Author. There was no pantheon, no one else to talk to about complaints, no one to appeal to when things didn't go as planned. Even Yawi was only here at the Author's bidding. He was loyal to her and served her and would not deviate from that charge. Sabelu was only an assignment.

Another large crash outside snapped Sabelu from his trance, and he turned his attention back to the egg. He had to do this now or never and stop worrying about everything else.

He put his hands on the egg once more, intentionally focusing on it. He needed to feel and understand the energy. It was self-contained, but now there was an outlet for it to travel through. What if he gave it a new outlet, a bigger one? But what did he have?

He looked around and spied a thin sliver of rock, about arm's length, a short distance away. He snatched it up and weighed it. It felt solid enough, he supposed, not prone to crumbling on impact.

Sabelu stuck the rock in the ground a few feet from the egg. The burrowers had mostly freed the rest of the pedestal by now, allowing Sabelu to get under it and pivot the base, first straightening the device—it was heavier than it looked, or maybe he was just that exhausted—then tipping it over. He invoked Galo'ondiha ale Agia to ensure it fell squarely on the rock. A cascade of sparks shot into the ground as the rock was buried almost completely into the device.

Sabelu approached and immediately grabbed his knife. Was there a clause for fool me three times? He didn't know and he couldn't think of any as energy once more shot up his arm. But his idea had worked to a limited extent. It still hurt tremendously, but he was able to keep control long enough to wrench his knife out of the device. He stumbled back several feet and collapsed, going all the way to his back to stare up into the darkness.

"We've got company!" Rabbit yelled suddenly.

The burrowers scattered and Sabelu jumped to his feet. He had moved beyond trembling to completely shaking, and he was grateful the device was almost on the ground now. In fact, it looked as though the egg had come detached from the pedestal. More energy sparked from the bottom of the egg.

Before he could do anything, the rock dagger crumbled at the base and the device dropped the last few inches into the sand.

Peel the panels off, like an eggshell, Sabelu told himself. Don't stab into the muscle, just peel away the skin, like dressing any animal.

He picked a vein that hadn't been ruptured, sliding his knife edgewise into the glowing blue vein and twisting it just under the lip of the panel. At the same time he twisted the knife and felt the satisfying give of the panel, a titan roared into the building, smashing a wall, only to be met by Yawi. Sabelu conjured Iyuwahnilvhi to buy himself a little breathing room, but a little was all it was.

The egg had eight panels, each one coming off cleanly once he knew how to do it. Each one revealed a small compartment filled with twisted metal and small, glowing glass beads. The glow was so dim, however, that he again wasn't sure whether it wasn't actually a reflection of the Whites' glow.

"Set it on fire," he whispered to himself.

He'd worried about not being able to really get a fire going, especially as the Shadows focused all their attention on this building, smashing through walls, crawling through the sand, and scratching through the ceiling. The good news was, now that the compartments were open, the contents were highly flammable. A strike from his flint combined with the sparks from the damage already done yielded a flash of white flame and a series of pops like multiple guns being fired at once.

The device went up like dry tinder. Sabelu could only watch in fascination, shielding his eyes once from a pop of sparks.

The Shadows continued to pour in.

"Go, Sabelu!" Yawi ordered, tearing a titan off another White. "The device is done. Come back later to finish it!"

With a sudden wall of black fire descending from the sky just outside the building, Sabelu didn't need to be told twice.

DᏞᏢᎪᏁ ᎠᏦᏁ ᎠᏙᏗᎢ

Atlasgone Atsone Adolv'i

Return

Sabelu returned to his cabin, and he slept.

He did not dream, which did not bother him, but neither did he see his uncle. Of course, Anagalisgi might have still been busy with the aftermath of the battle, but still, Sabelu had hoped.

He lay abed for a long time after he woke, replaying the battle over and over and over again. He knew well the feeling of entrapment from the men who had survived the War of the Old Land, but this was not that same feeling. Somehow, he was having a hard time just making sense of what had happened. In the War of the Old Land, it had been man against man, the same except for the color of their uniforms. They both wielded basically the same weapons, or at least understood the weapons the other had. The tactics and strategies had to be adapted, but were familiar in their usage as they were made for humans.

What he had witnessed had not been man against man, or even man against god. This had been god versus god, mountains rising against each other and paying no mind to the insects below. All the peoples whose histories he held, all the stories he knew across all of time, and none of them could compare to what he'd just seen. They couldn't even scratch the surface. All this time, the people had envisioned their gods and spirits as being, if not animals themselves, then usually no bigger than a bear, with very few exceptions. But no, the spirits were the size of mountains, and Sabelu couldn't help but wonder if they were somehow still being modest about it, being confined still by this mortal plane and the height of the sky.

And on top of it all, death was not a real problem for the combatants, more of a minor inconvenience. Sure, the Whites would be reborn faster than the Shadows would be recycled, but it was still more of a blundering misstep to die rather than a true consequence of a fatal mistake. And there he was, the only mortal, running around in the middle of it all. His uncle was right; mortals would never survive such battles, at least, not without an escort.

The Shadows had been determined to kill him, but would it have been possible for one of the Whites to accidentally kill him? What if one of the wolves had stepped on him? Would he have been crushed, or were there certain protections in place for favorites of the Author? It seemed like a very silly thing, to send someone into such a battle only to have him be accidentally killed by the side that had so painstakingly protected him for the last several years. Either that or else Sabelu had gotten ridiculously lucky, either in his own right or because of Yawi's protection.

Sighing, Sabelu dragged himself out of bed. His whole body ached, and no amount of Asvhnisgi to relax his muscles, right his spine, or ease any pain senses seemed to last more than a few minutes. This was just straight fatigue, a perfectly natural and expected response to the hell he'd just put his body through. He hated it. He'd accomplished his mission, yes, but if any of the Shadows got the idea to track him down and finish the job, he didn't know how much of a fight he could give.

He arrived at the small river without incident and waded in to bathe and purify, immersing himself seven times in each of the four directions and saying a prayer before and after each immersion. Because of the nature of the battle he'd just fought, far beyond a simple raid or skirmish or even the War of the Old Land, he repeated this ritual six more times just to be sure.

Afterwards, he elected to just sit in the water, slowly freezing but grateful for it. He knew Yawi said he would have to return to finish the job, and he would, but he had decided that after that, he would never again go to a desert. Even the desert towns of the Old Land weren't high on his list of places he wanted to visit again in his lifetime right now. It was a miserable place unfit for human habitability. Actually, judging by what he saw, it was unfit for habitability of any kind, human, animal, or spirit. With any luck, once he'd ground the device to powder and left it to the wind and time, the surrounding forest and landscape would hastily reclaim the area and no one would have to worry about a desert ever again. He wondered what the land would look like once it was covered in grass and trees instead of sand.

Shivering broke his daydreaming trance, and he got out of the river on shaky limbs. He found a warm rock to lie on, letting the sun filtering through the trees bring life back to his limbs. He was still quite slow and tired, but the worst of the exhaustion had gone. This lasted only until he was faced with the daunting task of climbing back up the slope to his cabin. On a normal day, just a normal task. Now, it was running through the desert city all over again. At least he didn't have any Shadows chasing him this time and he could take his time and go slow if he wanted.

He might have hoped to find Yawi waiting for him when he returned. Or maybe he'd actually fallen asleep on the warm rock and was now dreaming, so Anagalisgi would visit him again. Neither proved to be the case; he found his cabin as empty as he'd left it.

If he wanted to, Sabelu could bring to mind all the things he knew about the people in Aktiya Waya. He knew what they would be doing. He knew basically what was going on, his understanding of the situation greater than theirs on account of his involvement with the spirits. And yet, out here, he was not inundated with the knowledge like an endless tide. Here, things were quiet. Well, quieter. Looking around, he could see phantoms of future visitors, few though there were. Netami, mostly, sometimes his mother or father, maybe his brothers. And Yukpa. She would come to visit him as well.

But these were phantoms only, not something he could interact with or understand intentions or motivations. Quiet. It was almost enough to make him believe in the illusion of choice.

What would happen if he chose not to go back? The device was destroyed well enough, so why was it so important that it be ground to dust and scattered to the wind? What if he just decided not to do it?

What if he decided not to talk to Kah Kitowak and tell him about the device, its location and instructions for destroying? Would he somehow undo everything that he had done? Would he somehow literally turn back time, un-destroy the device, un-kill the cerberus? Could he break time? Was that possible? Was he a bad person for just wanting to see if it could be done? If he broke time in that way, by undoing something, could he un-undo it again and put time back together?

He shook his head as if to clear it. Maybe it was better for him to be around people listening to their thoughts, because having his own was proving to be dangerous if he was considering all the ways he could try to break time.

His stomach chose that moment to grumble a complaint. Well, he had been trekking through the desert and dodging evil spirits the size of mountains. However great his proficiency in the sorceries, such endeavors could take a toll on a man. Maybe a quick hunt would take his mind off everything.

The shadows were long as he roasted his two rabbits over a spit. His fatigue was slowly ebbing, though he would admit he may have used sorceries to aid him in his hunt. But now that things were quiet and seasoned flesh was making his mouth water, he also found himself growing a bit worried. Sure, he knew that it might have taken a little time for the battle to wrap up, but all night and another day? The device was destroyed, and he was gone. There was nothing left for the Shadows. Unless the black phoenix had gone scorched earth and just burned everything to cinders. Maybe the Whites had all been destroyed and were in the process of being reborn. Maybe that was why Yawi did not visit him.

But again, why would the Shadows not come for him next? Why go through all the trouble to lure him out to the desert to kill him, only to not follow through, especially after he had completely thwarted their plans and destroyed the device?

He didn't like not knowing, and he wondered if the silence in his mind was really all he had hoped.

He did not see any Whites, Shadows, or anything else that evening, and he went to bed feeling a tad worried. He again did not visit his uncle in his dreams.

He might have woken up worried, except it was a wet nose to his temple that actually woke him.

"Where have you been?" Sabelu demanded. "I've been worried about you."

Yawi tilted his head in a wolfish way. "I thought the battle might have proven that even if I were in danger, there is nothing you would be able to do to help."

Sabelu sat up, stretched, stood, and stretched again. "That doesn't mean I didn't worry. I mean, what if something happened to you and the rest of the Whites, and the Shadows came to assassinate me?"

The wolf's mouth popped open in a smile, letting Sabelu know his next words were intended as jest. "You humans, always thinking of yourselves first."

"Yes, yes." Sabelu waved a hand. "How selfish of me to prioritize the survival of my people and the universe over the destruction and chaotic reign of the Shadows."

Yawi barked a laugh.

Heading outside, Sabelu found the rest of the pack lounging around the area, all of them, well, not normal size necessarily, but even their slightly bigger than normal was still far, far smaller than their mountainous size they had unleashed in the desert.

"So what happened after I left?" Sabelu asked, giving the wolf nearest the door a few scratches between the ears.

"Chaos, pandemonium, and things on fire," the wolf answered, leg beginning to twitch with the scratches.

Sabelu glanced at Yawi who gave him a wolf shrug. "That is the short of it."

"Did the black phoenix—?"

"Yes."

Sabelu nodded and started down the slope, heading for the river. "Now that I've had time to think, Chimera disappeared at some point."

Yawi dipped his head. "Chimera fell, yes. Rebirth has already commenced. But it will be a long time before we hear from the wolf dog or the cerberus."

"A century or so, at least. And the serpent?"

"Fled, as expected, but not without severe injuries."

"How long will they take to heal?"

"Not a century, unfortunately. In your time, a few days."

Sabelu grunted. They reached the river where he knelt to drink and get his water for the day. He looked up at Yawi. "What's next, then?"

"The device must still be taken care of," the wolf reminded him.

"Yes, turned into powder and scattered to the wind. But why? If it's already been destroyed, why go through the extra hassle?"

"It must be eradicated. It may no longer function technologically, but a message must be sent to the Shadows as well."

"Turning the desert black with their metaphorical blood wasn't enough?"

Now Yawi flattened his ears in annoyance. "All traces. After the effort it took to be rid of the cerberus, would you suffer even a vice in your town? Remember, it was the ants who laid a foundation for the Whites."

"But it was just a chunk of metal. Technology."

"Just because the Tacagans have forsaken the spirits does not mean the spirits have forsaken them."

Sabelu sighed and rubbed his face. Before he could speak, Yawi added, "You have seen more of the spirit world than almost any mortal aside from your kin. But there is still so much more you do not comprehend about our relationship to the mortal plane." The wolf lowered his head and got nose-to-nose with Sabelu. "Destroy the device. Pulverize it and scatter its dust to the ether."

Sabelu would have liked to have said that, having seen Yawi and the wolves in their full size battle glory, that he was not intimidated by the wolf's minor show of irritation, but that would have been only half-true. In fact, it was probably because he had witnessed what the wolves were capable of that he was as frightened as he was.

His biggest hesitation, surprisingly, had more to do with the idea of going back to the blistering heat of the desert. He was happy to be home in the forest and mountains. Yes, it was warm, but there was shade and water and vegetation.

One of the wolves approached and dropped a water skin beside him. Sabelu sighed, but picked it up, filled it, and stood. He gave Yawi a look. "I'm guessing the desert didn't disappear overnight."

"It did not," Yawi confirmed, sounding slightly less annoyed, his ears only half-flattened against his head.

Sabelu hesitated only a moment longer before reaching for Galohisdi. He remembered well the room in which the device was kept, the building the room was in. He recalled the area around the building, the row of pillars, how all but three had been obliterated. At least he wouldn't have to actually go trekking across the desert again. He could just pop in and pop out. But why did it have to be now? Why couldn't it have been sometime in the night when it was cooler?

Galohisdi opened, revealing the three pillars. One of them looked to have been cut in half since he left, but the area was still recognizable. He stepped through, enduring the compression of the body and sapping of strength, landing on the other side in a heap. This was partly by choice as he instinctively went to the ground, made himself small, and started looking around even before he could see straight.

It was, to his dismay, still blastedly hot. He could already feel his skin begin to burn. A light wind kicked some sand around. Otherwise, everything was eerily quiet. Other than damage to the buildings, there was no evidence whatsoever of the battle. No pawprints, no bodies. As he got to his feet, his head slowly sorting itself out, he wondered how far the sounds of battle had carried. Had anyone noticed the mountains at war? Or was this something only he was mortal witness to? People were going to think he was insane. Maybe he shouldn't speak of it at all and wait for his Book to reveal everything. He couldn't imagine there wouldn't be a Book about such a significant event.

He turned around and entered the building. The device was

basically where he'd left it, now a charred husk. The wolves kept watch around the building, but Yawi sat beside the device.

"Why can't you do this?" Sabelu asked, kneeling beside the device and grabbing a nearby rock to start smashing it. "Fine, so the Shadows had some kind of hold on it before, but it doesn't work anymore, right? Whatever rules said that only a mortal could disable it, does that mean dismantle it, too?"

"Mortals were given the power of choice," Yawi stated. "It is a choice that must be made."

"And the spirits weren't? Then either the Author created evil when she created the dragon, or else the dragon once made a choice, too. So which is it?"

"This device connected mortals and spirits in a way that the Tacagans did not know or understand, and they would not have believed it even if someone told them. Such mortal devices must be destroyed by mortals."

"There are more of these?"

Yawi gave him a look. "This is not the first such thing you have destroyed."

Sabelu thought a moment. Then, "The dog statues in the townhouse."

"Altars, temples, shrines, artifacts, talismans, they are not so powerless as many believe."

"The Sacred Wolf," Sabelu stated, continuing to beat the device. "The Sacred Minotaur. The Cursed Zukatopa." He paused and looked around. "What, then, was the Cursed One of the Desert? I've seen no statues or monuments. Was it buried, or destroyed before we arrived?"

"The Cursed One of the Desert was the tower at the very center of the city. It was mostly destroyed when the Tacagans here were destroyed. Many of the pieces have been buried, yes, and that which remained has been worn by sand and time so it is no more distinguishable than the rest of the rubble."

"What was it, do you know?"

"Minotaur said it was a statue of a man, a Tacagan man."

"The idol of self," Sabelu mused.

Yawi dipped his head. "Yes."

Sabelu leaned back on his heels. "My guess is that this device was in that tower, right? It was the heart or head of the idol. Unlike the other Great Ones where their destruction was simple, this is the thing that really drew in the Shadows." He gestured to the device, now in pieces. "Not because it was mechanical, but because it was focused and called to the rest of the Tacagan civilization. The serpent, overseeing the creation and expansion of stronghold species. As long as this thing exists in any recognizable form, it is still a testament of power and idolatry, something the Shadows can use at a later date, to draw in unwary explorers." He sighed. "Like my parents."

The wolf's expression was confirmation enough.

He gathered up the pieces of the device, pushed them all into a pile, and continued pounding. "I understand this. But is it really necessary to destroy the whole of the city? Or is that an inevitable outcome? Would it be possible to one day return to the underground city? Will it always remain an evil place? Surely with the Zukatopa gone, this device destroyed, we could learn more." He added, "Evil will continue to exist in one form or another. Being rid of this thing may sever the free connection to the Shadows, but could we learn something from the People Before? Surely you would not condemn the living paint in the canyon?"

Using a curved rock as an improvised bowl, Sabelu dumped the pieces inside, then added the water from his skin. It didn't look like much, and it became much more work to grind the pieces down into something like a paste.

"You are correct that the Shadows are less interested in things and places and more focused on mortals themselves," Yawi said, "and no, the living paint in the canyons is not evil in itself, no more than regular paint. Few objects are inherently evil." The wolf looked around. "Is this place evil? It is a ruined city in a desolate desert. Is the underground city evil? It is a city built deep underground. No. Was evil done in these places? Yes. The spirit that resides within you knows that. It goes beyond physical fear as from a predator and instead warns you of something more, something deeper."

"You didn't answer my question," Sabelu said, still mashing the pieces. "Could we return to the underground city? Could we come and explore this city, later, once the trees have reclaimed this sand?"

Yawi barked a laugh. "It will be a more than a century before that happens, before this desert is reclaimed."

"And the underground city?"

"One day, maybe," the wolf said. "But it will happen in its own time."

Any pieces that had been well and thoroughly charred mashed into a nice paste easily enough. Anything that still had some stability to its original Matter form had to be broken down via Touch. It was mostly just a matter of going down to its more basic structures and either forcing them apart or forcing water between them to break them apart. One piece became two, two became four, then eight, sixteen, and so on until a single piece of metal became a pile of sharp, glittering sand in the palm of Sabelu's hand. These tiny grains did not mix so well into the paste, but, he figured, by the end of the day, baking in this heat, all the water would be sucked out of it anyway, leaving everything to the wind.

"Is there anything more that needs to be done?" Sabelu asked once he was finished. He wiped the sweat from his face, likely smearing some of the gray-colored goop on his face and neck.

"No ceremony is necessary," Yawi told him. "Just toss it outside to be devoured by time and nature."

Groaning, Sabelu stood, stretched, then grabbed the rock bowl he'd been working with. Even with the partial shade of the building, it was still hot. Stepping outside into the sunlight was horrendous. He tossed the goop as best he could, tossed the rock bowl and used Force to ensure that it shattered when it hit the ground, then retreated back into the building, suddenly grateful for the meager shade.

"Is there anything more that needs to be done here?" he wondered. "I'm not coming back to this desert. Ever, if I can help it."

The wolf's expression was amused as he answered, "You don't have to be here anymore."

Sabelu wasted no time in conjuring Galohisdi back to his river. As before, he simply submerged himself in the frigid water, closed his eyes, and enjoyed it. He jumped when he heard someone else sigh contentedly. His eyes flew open, but it was only Anagalisgi, also sitting up to his neck in the cold water about five feet away.

"You know, there are many cultures on Earth that prioritize hot baths of one form or another, including our own, make no mistake," Anagalisgi said, his eyes still closed, "but there are surprisingly few who understand the benefits of an occasional cold bath."

"Did I fall asleep?" Sabelu wondered dumbly.

"You did."

"Am I going to freeze to death?"

His uncle grinned and gave him a look. "Hardly."

Sabelu shifted position. "Did you see it? Did you see the battle? Was it very different from this side of things?"

Anagalisgi nodded. "I saw it, yes."

"What did you think?"

"I think it was a little more dangerous and a little more consequential than anything I ever did in my lifetime. And I'm proud of you for stepping into your role."

"Tsidushi, I thought I was going to die. I was truly afraid that the Shadows could change things."

Now his uncle frowned. "Tsiquiyi, your death is already foretold. It is foretold and it has already happened. For as powerful as the Shadows are, they are not going to change something that has been fixed within a Book."

"But they can change things that aren't explicit in the Books?"

"Do they change them, or does it only seem like it and it is all to the Author's purpose anyway?"

Sabelu opened his mouth, but nothing came out. Instead he asked, "What now? The battle has been won, the device thrown to the desert, both Cursed Ones of the Shadows destroyed." He made a shrugging sort of motion. "And yet, won't Asdeoha and the other priests and their puppeteers still keep power in Aktiya Waya?"

"I don't know," Anagalisgi replied coyly. "Will they? Maybe you should return to Aktiya Waya and see." He gave Sabelu a look. "Come now, Sabelu, you know what is to come."

"Well, yes," Sabelu admitted. "I just want to hear you say it. I want to know that I'm not the only one who sees or knows these things."

"But it's not your power. Of course you aren't the only one."

Sabelu thought about this for a moment, then nodded. "But do I really have to go now? Are you going to send Yawi after me if I delay a little?"

His uncle shifted position. "I don't know why you would want to delay, what appointments could be holding you up, but no, I am not going to send the wolves after you to chase you back to Aktiya Waya this very moment."

"Oh, good." Pause. "What will you do now?"

Anagalisgi raised a brow. "What do you mean?"

"Now that the battle is over. What will you do?"

"The battle may be over, Tsiquiyi, but our work is hardly finished. True, your work will be far less glamorous going forward, but it is by no means unimportant. The black phoenix and the serpent are still out there, still running the show. And you can bet that the dragon will not simply let it slide that the cerberus and the wolf dog were taken out of commission for over a century. Hlohi has been returned to the Whites, and it will fast become a sanctuary. But revenge is a terrible thing."

"The Old Land," Sabelu cut in. "More wars, and an unrivaled destitution coming to all the peoples."

"Yes."

Just three seconds ago, Sabelu had wondered at what next, worried that everything was finished and he was somehow out of a job for the next century. Now his uncle reminded him of the things to come, and he found he didn't want to deal with that either. Was it really impossible for people to get along for just a few minutes?

"It's all right, Sabelu," his uncle said, cutting into his thoughts. "Take a break, enjoy the victory for a day, and then prepare yourself for the next phase of the mission."

Sabelu nodded slowly. "Will I see you again, Tsidushi? Surely if the mission continues, then we may also continue to meet?"

His uncle grinned. "Of course."

When Sabelu next blinked, he found himself coming awake, for real this time. His uncle was gone, and he remained in the cold water. When he stood and moved to get out of the river, he saw something near the spot where his uncle had been sitting in the dream. It was a leather thong with a wolf tooth pendant, and Sabelu knew that it wasn't his.

Sabelu straightened and strung it around his neck, then headed back to his cabin. No one was waiting for him, no man, woman, animal, or White. He was alone, his only task right now to savor the victory in the desert, a battle no one would ever really understand, and few would believe even if he told the story with himself as its only witness.

But then, he was kind of curious about what was going on in Aktiya Waya. Well, he knew what was going on, but he kind of wanted to be there.

Maybe he should go to the Old Land, find Kah Kitowak, and have the conversation that he would reach for in order to locate the device. He considered the temporal implications of this, but only for a few moments before deciding that maybe it wasn't best to dwell on such things.

Kah Kitowak still lived on the small island with the Tlingit people, though he was yearning for his homeland back east and would soon make his way there. He was about as enthused to see Sabelu as he was to still be on the island.

"What do you want?" He cast his fishing line back into the water. They were about thigh-deep in ocean water, the sky still early morning gray, just bright enough for Kah Kitowak to make out the face of the man he wanted to see the least. He turned his back to Sabelu and jiggled his line a bit. "More orders for the troops?" He added, "To be fair, I hear they're having better success down south than we did up here."

"Numbers and time," Sabelu said wistfully. "You worked for a summer. Galiliga and Netami and the rest have been doing so for a couple years now, and they've recruited others to the cause."

"Come to gloat, then. See, the Krydik are good for something after all. What we fail at, you fail at slightly less fantastically."

"Actually I came for a couple reasons. First, to distract myself from a more present dilemma. And to help myself in the past."

Kah Kitowak glanced back at him briefly. "That makes no sense." He scoffed to himself and turned back around. "Of course, it's not something we commoners are intended to understand."

"I destroyed the Cursed One of the Desert," Sabelu cut in.

The Metis man gave him half a regard. "From your father's Book?"

"It was mentioned briefly, but yes, the same."

"How? The Sacred Wolf is literally a mountain. The Sacred Zukatopa is a cave."

"Was a cave," Sabelu corrected.

"What was the Sacred One of the Desert, and how did you destroy it?"

"It was a man. A Tacagan man. And at its heart was a technological device that tied the Tacagans and their Shadows to Hlohi. I destroyed it. First I had to dismantle it, then set it on fire, then soak it in water, then turn it to dust and scatter it to the sand and wind."

Now Kah Kitowak turned, as if giving in to his curiosity and regretting it. "Was there a city, then? Like the other places?"

"Yes, a very big one. When the greater statue was destroyed, the device landed in the northeast section of the city, in a building across from three pillars."

"And how does telling me this after the fact help you?"

"Because in the past, I had to use my knowledge of the future to get this information. I saw this conversation, through you, and acted on it. I needed to make sure that we had this conversation so that I could use it."

Kah Kitowak blinked. "What would happen if you hadn't told me? Would things somehow...be different? Is it possible to break time in such a way?"

"I've told you now, so does it matter? And would you really want to find out something like that?" Sabelu gave him a look. "I can't imagine that breaking time is a pleasant experience."

"No, I suppose not."

Before either could say more, there was a tug on Kah Kitowak's line. A minute later, he pulled up a plump fish. Sabelu congratulated him, then headed to shore.

He thought about going straight to Aktiya Waya, then decided against it. Instead he returned to his cabin and started down the slope toward the trail that would take him to Aktiya Waya.

His conversation with Kah Kitowak bothered him, but he could not immediately figure out why. Initially he thought it was because the whole thing had essentially already happened, and it almost felt scripted, as predictable as a child's defensive lie when he was caught in some mischief. But then, this was not the first time that he had participated in such conversations.

Perhaps it was simply the lack of reaction from Kah Kitowak. The man wasn't overly fond of him, Sabelu, but there was no true loathing or hatred there. The best reaction he got was simple curiosity. Sabelu had confirmed the existence of another city, revealed another Great One, claimed to have destroyed it, and gotten only mild interest for it. The fishing was more attention-consuming. Kah Kitowak was not the most ambitious man to ever live, true, but there was something disheartening and even suspicious about his distinct lack of interest. He had barely even acknowledged what it had taken to destroy the device, never inquired for details about the statue and the city and everything else.

Well, his task was complete anyway. He'd chosen Kah Kitowak for such a conversation because he was fairly inconsequential, because it would allow him to keep the secret for that short time period. And it was that disinterest which had prompted the lack of specifics. Otherwise, Sabelu might have told all about the battle, what to expect, what to look for, what to do, what not to do. And it might have actually changed things a little.

But still. Would a tiny bit of interest have really killed him? Should

Sabelu have chosen someone else to impart the information? His father would be more interested by far.

Yet there was still that chance of changing things. Would it still change things, even now?

It was a dilemma to occupy Sabelu's mind the whole walk to Aktiya Waya.

He'd never really appreciated the peace and quiet in his mind until he returned to Aktiya Waya, or any town, really. Whether he was just returning from a minor hunt, a short trip, or exile, he was never more surprised by the quiet than when it was no longer there. Perhaps it was because when he left a town, other people's lives were quickly replaced by his own, and he simply glided from one line of thought to another. On the other hand, when he returned to a place, his mind was so full of his own thoughts that suddenly things felt very crowded, until most of himself was pushed to the side in favor of whomever was around him.

This feeling was only amplified when he considered his time in the desert. Before battle, during, even afterwards, he had felt nothing in the desert. He had seen nothing, felt nothing, knew nothing. No phantoms, no mystic knowledge of the People Before, absolutely nothing. Even around his cabin, he could see phantoms of future visitors, past hunters, anyone who had or would come to be in that area. The desert after the battle was the first time he had truly felt nothing. No phantoms of bygone epochs, no thoughts of anyone around, no prickling of the skin warning him of looming Shadows, not even the dread of an impending battle. Nothing. Absolutely nothing. It had been like staring into a crystal clear pool and seeing the bottom for the very first time.

Returning to his cabin after that had been returning to a comfortable routine. Returning now to Aktiya Waya, even just approaching the pass where he knew the sentries had already spotted him, was like jumping into a stormy ocean and wondering how he had ever learned to swim in such waves.

The two sentries predictably blocked his path when he entered the pass.

"We're not supposed to let you in," one told him.

"And yet you're going to," Sabelu replied.

"We're supposed to run you off, or kill you if you don't go," the second added.

"And yet you're not."

Sabelu stared them down for a long minute.

"Nothing will happen to you," he told them.

The sentries shifted their stances and glanced at each other. After a long moment, and a little persuasion from a couple of White birds, they lowered their spears and stood aside, neither one quite sure they were doing the right thing. Sabelu said nothing as he brushed past them into the bowl.

As far as appearances went, absolutely nothing had changed in the time he'd been gone. The wind still blew, the water still flowed, and the people still went about their daily business. The sun was setting, so many were returning from the fields, often gathering up rowdy children in the process. Some went home, others went to a different part of the river to swim and bathe. Sabelu briefly wondered how they would all feel if he took them to the desert, let them experience that kind of heat. Then they might feel a little differently about going to swim after working the fields a bit.

Sabelu turned just in time to catch Netami as she threw her arms around him. A second later, their mother joined in.

"We had to do this before the priests get a hold of you," Netami said when she stepped back.

"Asdeoha is going to kill you," Nendawagan agreed.

The Fear attached to his mother was rubbing off on his sister, and probably everyone in the family, though its hold was certainly shaken just at his appearance.

Sabelu shook his head. "No, he won't."

"You should speak to your father first, before the priests," his mother went on. "He wants to see you."

"Galiliga is home in Yonhi, and Blaknik is in the Old Land," Netami added. "We should—"

"There is nothing stopping them from visiting me, you know,"

Sabelu cut in. "Besides, important matters should be seen to first."

"What is more important than family?" his mother asked incredulously.

"I do this for the family," Sabelu told her. "Just trust me."

Fear told Nendawagan to worry incessantly, but Yawi appearing at Sabelu's side—visible only to him and the Shadow—forced the Shadow to back down. Nendawagan nodded, and Netami reluctantly agreed.

Sabelu turned and made for the townhouse. By now, someone would have reported his presence to Asdeoha.

By law, it was not impossible for someone to challenge an exile. The burden of proof for overturning such a ruling, however, was tremendous, even greater than it would be during the trial itself. Seeing how Sabelu had offered up virtually no defense during his trial, and given that the priests themselves were staunchly against him, he had no hope, beyond divine intervention, of being accepted back.

As before, the priests were not the only ones waiting for him in the townhouse. A fair crowd had been drawn in, looking and hoping for a spectacle. Many were mildly curious, some rooting for one side or the other. Sabelu knew that most of his supporters had been intimidated into silence, and many, like Blaknik, had, in an ironic twist of fate, taken refuge in the Old Land. Asdeoha and the priests had initially made a promise that his supporters would not be persecuted upon his exile, provided that they did not seek him out in his exile. Sabelu also knew that such a promise would have been broken had the Shadows won the battle in the desert.

Seeing how the Whites had won, and the Great Whites were even now surrounding the area, the puppeteers around the priests were panicking. The cerberus and the wolf dog were gone. The serpent was still injured. The black phoenix was nowhere to be found, perhaps enduring some horrible punishment from the dragon for its failure. The puppeteers here were alone, easy prey for any of the Whites. They had no smooth answers to feed to the priests about what to do with Sabelu, and the best the priests could do was stand there in the middle of the townhouse and try to look intimidating and mildly annoyed by this disruption to their day.

"Do you think the rules don't apply to you?" Asdeoha asked. "Do you think you can just come and go as you please, as if exile was merely a suggestion and not a punishment for your crimes?"

"My so-called 'crimes' are nothing," Sabelu said calmly. "I am but one man." He shifted position as if addressing everyone in the room, though he still kept the priests in his peripheral vision. "This was never about the reputation or glory of one man. As Yvgidahi once said, Gvnagadoga is dead. And Yvgidahi himself is dead. Our ancestors are dead. Though we use sorceries that grant us long life, we, too, will die. I will one day die on the side of a mountain.

"Some of you feared that I was trying to replace the old ways, bring in white man ways, white man religion. You feared the bow, but it is not the bow that matters. A bow may be fashioned any number of ways, but what matters is the arrow. Does it matter what food we eat, the language we speak, the names of our grandfathers? Does it matter what stories we tell our children, whether the rabbit is to be trusted or feared? Perhaps, as these things help to bring people together socially. But is it not more important that we are aligned with the same spirits?"

Sabelu turned slowly, trusting Yawi to keep an eye on the priests as he turned his back to them. "Many of you are suspicious, even hostile toward the Books of my father and grandfather. More of the white man's ways. But these are only a recording of our history. A recording of the truth. And these stories are known beyond us.

"This war goes beyond us. What we see here is only an echo of what goes on in the spirit world. This is not new or unknown. All I have tried to do is restore the people to the right road. I have not asked you to stop telling stories to your children. I have not asked you to change this or that in your diet. I have not asked you to change your bow. I have asked you to change your arrow, to align with the good spirits, to align with the Whites and the Author. We have been called to a greater purpose."

He again faced the priests. "I have destroyed the Cursed One of the Desert, the Cursed Man, the idol of self. The cerberus and the wolf dog are gone, the serpent gravely injured and the black phoenix fled. The Whites are here, and they are here to stay. Hlohi is a haven, a sanctuary, and the Whites are going to start doing a little housecleaning. Do you want to be clean, or do you want to be cast out?"

Before any of the priests could answer, someone piped up, "They tried to kill you, sent you into exile! Tradition dictates you may have right of clan retaliation. Or are you asking us to change that, too? Is that bow or arrow?"

Sabelu turned a bit, keeping the priests on his right and the people on his left. "Discipline is not evil, however much a child may believe so at first, because he does not understand." He gestured to the priests. "They did not know what they were doing, for the Shadows worked evil. But the Author knew what had to happen. It was the only way to get to this point.

"As for clan retaliation, what do you seek to do? Do you want to discipline the priests, for they stepped out of line and followed the wrong road? Or do you want to punish them and so fulfill your own angry lusts?"

"Once a witch, always a witch. And it seems that these are the witches we have been looking for all these years," someone else added.

"How would you define a witch, then? One who invokes sorceries, manipulates the world around him? That's most of us here. Both Whites and Shadows have great power. One who consorts with Shadows? Not all Shadows are alike. They may come as grand as mountains or as small as vices. It does not take a full demon to elicit impure thoughts. Would that not make everyone a witch?

"If you try to bind the spiritual into something physical, the evil spirit has already won. But whether Asdeoha is alive or dead, it will not stop evil. Evil existed before he did, and it will continue to exist after his death. Evil existed before all of us, and it will exist after us. But we here in the moment, have a choice.

"My father once pondered the mystery of peace. What is it? Is it an object, a state of being, the horizon, elusive prey? If you ask him, or if you know his Book, you will understand that peace is a tool. As war is a tool. As clan retaliation is a tool. As mercy is a tool." Sabelu looked again at the priests. "And choice is the greatest tool of all."

For a long moment, there was dead silence in the townhouse save for the crackling of the fire.

It was the acolyte who stepped forward first, out of the shadows of the priests. "I choose the right road."

Dikdi hesitated but nodded. In the invisible realm, three of the wolves tore into his puppeteer. Before Dikdi could speak, Asdeoha spit at Sabelu's feet and said, "I spit on your white Author." He spit again. "I spit on your white sorceries. The spirits have taught us everything we need to know, as they did for our ancestors for time immemorial."

Sabelu made a motion, and Dikdi and the acolyte stepped away from the others. Asdeoha and the rest of the priests never stopped glaring at Sabelu.

"I will not turn away, I will not step down, and I will not revoke your exile," the head priest stated.

Sabelu dipped his head once and held out his hands. He could hear the shuffling in the crowd. "So be it. But your puppeteers have no power anymore, not over anything but you. The Whites are here, and this is their home now. Once they have cleaned the rats from their home, they will go to work building up the people and preparing them for when the Shadows do return. And they will, because they do not take such losses lightly."

He did not give the priests a chance to rebut, for he simply turned and left the townhouse. The crowd parted for him, most of them silent. Many had burning questions, but no more than four were voiced aloud. Some people were focused on him, others focused on the priests. All were trying to process what had just happened and what to do next.

The sentries gave him no trouble on his way out, though he knew they were confused. He had been in exile, presumably returned in order to challenge his exile. There was no way a retrial could have gone that fast, however dismal the case, and even if he had been overruled, he would have been escorted out again. Just what had happened up there?

Yawi caught up to him about a mile outside the bowl, his faint glow illuminating the path.

"So when they ask why you didn't stay, what will you tell them?" the wolf wondered, his tone suggesting he already knew.

"If I do, they will only rally behind me, a physical person. Useful sometimes, but not now. If they want to follow the right road and again align themselves with the Author and the Whites, they need to do so by themselves, without latching onto something physical that can and one day will be destroyed. I've given them all I can. They have my father's and grandfather's Books, they know what I have said and done, and there will be more Books coming. My presence will only make things harder right now."

"You know some of those Books will be controversial."

"Only because of the Shadow of Pride. Yes, the people have been chosen for a great purpose, but we are not the only people to exist. There will be other great characters, but they won't all be us, and that's fine. We can share the glory and the honor because it's not about us."

"The Shadow of Ego says otherwise," Yawi mentioned.

"If it's not Ego or Pride, it will be something else. There will always be something, and the Shadows will keep trying to break the people. But they will survive. They'll be all right, even if they don't believe it." At Yawi's look, he sighed and added, "I worry about them, Yawi. Even when Aktiya Waya was a Shadow stronghold, the White ants were still here, keeping an eye on things, laying a foundation. I have no reason to think the Shadows will not try something similar."

"Such is the nature of war," the wolf said. "But at least for a little while, things will be just fine."

Atlasgone Anvge Adolv'i
Solitude

It was not uncommon for the clans to take on shadows of the traits that their clan namesake was known for. In Eagle and Bear Clans, there was more of an attitude of independence, every man making his own way. This was not the same as selfishness, where one never helped another in need, but a subtle emphasis on being the best one could be with as little help as possible. Bear Clan tended to emphasize strength and intimidation, as in wrestling, while Eagle Clan preferred swiftness, silence, and precision, as in archery.

Meanwhile, Deer Clan and Wolf Clan tended to emphasize the herd or the pack, and greater cooperation so as to elevate the people as a whole. This did not mean that individual accomplishments were not applauded, but it was always for the good of the group, be it a single family or the whole village. Deer Clan sought group harmony through maintaining the crop fields, to ensure everyone had enough space to grow what their family needed to eat, but Wolf Clan focused more on great hunts and protection from danger.

By this logic, then, Sabelu probably belonged in Eagle Clan more than Wolf Clan. He had never really fit into the group, and he had all the knowledge the people would ever need about their ancestors and the traditional ways.

He put that knowledge to good use around his cabin, making a new bow for himself, fashioning a fishing net and a few poles, rigging traps, and decorating inside, all to prepare for his first winter alone.

Several people had been out to tell him that regardless of what Asdeoha said, he was welcome back in Aktiya Waya. As far as the people were concerned, he was no longer exiled. Sabelu had thanked them, said he would give it a little more time, and returned to whatever he was doing. Truthfully, he had no real intention of going back, not permanently. If he had to give the most honest reason, it was because he had grown accustomed to the quiet in his mind. He liked having his own thoughts and having them be, by and large, the only thoughts in his head. True, he still dealt with visions and hallucinations, and he had a vague idea of what was going on in Aktiya Waya, but he didn't have hundreds of other people all heaped on top of that.

He'd also had a couple visitors call him selfish for not coming back. Why would such a great teacher abandon the people he purported to care about? Somehow, the idea of the message being more important than the messenger didn't quite seem to satisfy. Some people didn't know what to do and wanted guidance. Others didn't want to do anything, whether they knew or not, and wanted someone else to do it for them. But they wanted someone else to do it in their way and their timing. Sabelu reminding those people that he was not a prophet for hire went over equally well.

The frost vanished with the appearance of the sun, and Sabelu reflected that he hadn't had any visitors for about a moon now. This was going to change very soon, but, if he wanted to be honest, he kind of liked it. He enjoyed being left alone. All his life, doted on, observed, recorded, pandered to, then reviled, hated, and driven off. Now it was just him. He didn't have to talk to anyone, answer any questions, nothing.

He checked his nets, bringing in five good-sized fish and releasing the rest. His bigger concern for the winter was actually gathering enough firewood. With Fichik Shobota's help, he'd acquired a cast iron stove from the Old Land. He liked it better than the open fires in Aktiya Waya homes, if not for the wood burning efficiency, then for greater control over his cooking. He didn't eat much, didn't cook much, but when he did, he wanted it to be good. It was difficult to control fire with the sorceries, but with the cast iron stove, he had better control over the heat itself.

He cleaned his fish by the river, then took them back to the cabin to start smoking. Then he started out on yet another wood gathering expedition.

Sabelu could not say that he had ever not appreciated his mother and sister. Aside from being his biggest supporters through his many difficult years of trying to live with his overwhelming visions, they always kept the household running smoothly. Food was always prepared when needed, tea was constantly available, blemishes in clothing never lasted longer than a passing thought, and almost all comforts were seen to, usually without complaint. They tended the fields, worked on any projects they intended to take to the annual festival of tournaments, and, in all of this, still found time to go out and gather firewood. Many men helped with this chore, too, but it was always under the direction of the women. Different woods were needed for different meats, different flavors. Even if a man were out gathering wood, he was under strict orders from his wife or mother about what to grab.

If Sabelu didn't possess the knowledge from his mother ancestors, he wouldn't know where to begin to look for certain woods for certain uses. He would just grab any stick he saw and throw it on a pile. Well, he was going to do that anyway, but there was some organization to his woodpile. He had the hotter woods on one side for general heat and the sweeter woods on the other side for cooking. Oh, he knew which woods would flavor which meats the best, he just didn't feel like going to the same lengths his mother and sister did.

Maybe that was his loss, but he would have plenty of time to think about it, and he could make changes if he really had to. Maybe next year, once he'd gone through his wood, start fresh with a new pile.

He'd already picked through everything on the ground within a reasonable distance of his cabin, and he'd invoked the sorceries to knock down a few dead trees or dead branches. It was a good start, but he knew that he was going to go through a lot more wood than the average house in Aktiya Waya; he was far more exposed than those in the cave.

He'd thought about relocating to one of the other caves he knew existed in the area, maybe building a small cabin-like structure on the outside like his uncle had done with his cave. He decided against it more for the fact that he already had his cabin, and he didn't feel like building a new one so soon. There was also a certain irony in being criticized by the people for living in a foreign house, even as they themselves lived in houses that someone else had built. He'd pointed this out, too, and it went over equally well.

He found one last decent, dead tree and conjured Iyuwahnilvhi to more completely rot its base. The tree fell the ground, dead branches snapping off on the other trees as it passed by, raining down in a flurry of pulp and leaves. When it hit, the trunk burst apart into two sections. Sabelu gathered the smaller stuff, took it back to his cabin, then returned with a hatchet and an ax to process the rest.

Yes, he could have used the sorceries to cut and split the wood. He knew how to find the weak points, the split lines, and he knew how to weasel everything apart. But he could also appreciate the need for and the joy of physical labor. He processed the wood where it was, then began the first of many trips to carry it back to the cabin.

When he was finished, he headed down to the river to wash the sweat from his body. He did not sit in the water or wade out past his ankles; it was getting far too cold for that. Just a few splashes of water was enough to cool him down from all the work.

He did not return to his cabin right away. He knew what was waiting for him, but he wanted to emphasize that it was his time and his schedule out here. He had been exiled, so he no longer had to adhere so strictly to other people's rules. It sounded a bit childish, even to him, and he couldn't help but chide himself for being so petty, even after several moons of living on his own. He'd done it; he knew this would happen. Very little came as a surprise to him. Still there remained a part of him that really wanted to rub it in and show off, to make sure people knew what he had done. The problem was, among normal people, if they couldn't see or know what he did, he was just being selfish and stuck up. To those who did see and know, he was being selfish and stuck up.

But he knew his guest well, knew that he would not be denied a conversation. Sighing, Sabelu stood and left the river, starting yet another trek up the slope toward his cabin.

Since the destruction of the cerberus and the wolf dog and the takeover by the Whites, all puppeteers had been torn apart, and the greatest Shadow anyone could take with him was an indulgence. Asdeoha's indulgence was a particularly strong indulgence, true, well fortified against most average White attacks, but no more than that.

Sabelu hadn't actually seen or spoken with Asdeoha since that day in Aktiya Waya, but the man hadn't changed much. Dressed the same, walked the same, carried himself in the same manner that said he knew he held social and religious authority.

"Quite the place you've got here," the head priest observed, standing about five feet from the front door, looking around.

His Shadow was about seven feet tall, currently a nebulous cloud. Yawi's sudden appearance caused it to shift from Asdeoha's left side to his right, but that was about it.

"I'm surprised you didn't utilize one of the caves in the area," the priest went on.

"I have everything I need here," Sabelu said, still approaching, keeping one eye on the Shadow at all times. "It's close to the river." He made a vague gesture in that general direction.

"I'm also a bit surprised you haven't come back. I know several people have been out here to tell you that you are welcome, regardless of what I say." He added quickly, "But then, you've never been the most comfortable in crowds, doing enough to fulfill some task and then retreating. Is that what this is, then? You've destroyed two Sacred Ones and two Shadow kings, so you've come here to comfortably retire?"

"There is no retiring from this war, except in death," Sabelu informed him.

Asdeoha chuckled and shifted his stance. "You've left the people in quite a bind, you know. Half of them don't like me—any of the priests— and yet there is still the demand for respect, either for our position as priests or because of what you did, or didn't do. So, what are they supposed to do with us? How do they know to trust us and our rituals? Which is ironic because many of your supporters go to Dikdi now. We perform the same rituals, say the same prayers, but they trust his arrows more, or so the saying goes."

"It's all in the delivery," Sabelu said smartly. "Some people are better suited to public speaking than others."

The priest's expression said he was not amused. "So why don't you come back? It's in no one's best interest to try and kill you now; it would only make you a martyr. At this point, you would be treated as the closest thing to a god among men."

"And that's the problem. It's not about me. I may have helped the people to see and understand, but it is not about me. I know some have made it out to be so, which is why I haven't come back."

"You did what you did because you see and understand things most people only hear about and know as a vague concept. Spirits, wars, gods, stories for children, beliefs around which we structure society. But you understand. And you would leave behind the people who don't understand and hope they'll just get it?"

"As it was once told to me, only a mortal can help mortals. I opened the door. I can't walk through it for them. For those who do, they will understand, and they will help others."

Asdeoha raised a brow. "I've yet to hear of anyone claiming to see Shadows and Whites, or anything else bizarre."

"Maybe. But that doesn't mean they don't understand."

The priest studied him for a long moment, then made a motion. "Walk with me?"

Sabelu looked around. "Is anyone going to eavesdrop on us here?"

"Please?"

Well, it wasn't as though Sabelu had any real pressing matters to attend to. He'd gathered his wood and the fish would still need some time to smoke and cure. Finally he dipped his head and gestured for Asdeoha to talk the lead. The Shadow remained just off Asdeoha's left shoulder while Yawi padded along lightly between the estranged priests. Sabelu could tell that the Shadow's attention was mildly distracted by Yawi, and he might have hoped this would allow for more White intervention within Asdeoha.

"When your parents brought your older brother to us to divine his destiny, do you know what we saw?" Asdeoha began.

"Which brother?" Sabelu asked pointedly.

The head priest grinned, pleased with himself that he'd provoked such a prickly reaction. "My apologies. Your brother who still lives."

"Galiliga. What about him?"

"We saw that he would be a great warrior and a leader. Indeed, he has turned out to be just that. He survived the War of the Old Land and has become quite the figurehead in Bear Clan, or so I hear. He's been on and off the village council over the years, still not quite getting up the courage to really put his name out for the national council, though I expect that will be within the next few years, now that this dramatic saga is over. Or it appears to be."

Asdeoha gave Sabelu a look, silently probing for some reaction or answer. When Sabelu did not reply, he went on, "And do you know what we saw in your other brother, the one buried on the slope with the rest?"

Sabelu did know, but still he said, "Enlighten me."

"He would also be a warrior, but not like Galiliga. Galiliga would be very forthright, very bold. Tsona would be greater in stealth, picking off enemies from afar. This also made him an exceptional hunter. Unfortunately, he found himself in a situation where his skills meant very little. There is no real opportunity for stealth in the middle of a battlefield, and he was struck down."

"Yvgidahi was divined to be a warrior and leader, and he was also killed in that battle," Sabelu cut in, "avenging my brother."

Despite just having the legs cut out from under his argument, Asdeoha continued, "If a man strays from his destiny, he will die."

"Everyone dies in the end."

"Do you know what we saw when we divined for you?"

Sabelu internally rolled his eyes as he entertained the conversation. "A dark seer, dark prophet, storyteller, truth keeper, priest, all those things. Interestingly enough, anyone who has read my father's Book, or who knows about me at all, knows this."

"But isn't it also interesting that your father's Book never mentions your golden eyes?"

"Maybe they're not important."

"Why wouldn't they be?"

Sabelu sighed and stopped to face the priest. "Are you trying to make a point or just waste my time?"

Asdeoha donned an expression that was mock-offended. "I'm sorry, I didn't realize you had so many pressing matters to attend to. I know people come from all the villages to hear your wisdom and your visions of their futures. Or perhaps you are referring to all the household work you have to do since you have no woman to look after you."

"As much as I do not wish to mislead the people in some false worship of me, I also have no desire to strike up nonsensical banter with you or any of the Shadow priests," Sabelu informed him. He went on before Asdeoha could speak. "Your puppeteer is gone, Asdeoha. All the puppeteers are. Even if you do not unshackle yourself from your indulgence of Petty Ego and Resentment—" The Shadow, even in nebulous form, flinched upon being named. "—it will still be torn apart upon your death. The same for the other indulgences, among priest and person alike. Hlohi, the Krydik, will never be perfect in this life. But this place is a haven for Whites, and that is how it shall remain. The land has been redeemed, the people freed."

The Shadow fed evil thoughts into Asdeoha as priest gave him a look. "Do you believe in fate, Sabelu? Are all things fixed, or can men and events change?"

"There is some flexibility on both sides, but what has been written will be. It must be."

"And yet the Books skim over days, months, even whole years. Considering how much is not covered by the Books, it seems, then, that fate is a bit porous."

"Interesting way to put it."

"And in those dark passages, those giant leaps of empty time and space, do you ever wonder what really happened, how much changed?" He went on, "If you say, perhaps nothing important, then does that make us entirely unimportant except when we become convenient for the Author to tell some grand story? And if you say, perhaps something important, then why wouldn't it be covered?"

"Life happens all around us," Sabelu said. "Every moment of my life, every breath, every thought, every action, now multiplied by everyone in the universe. Not just Hlohi, not just Earth, but every living thing. Every man, woman, child, animal, and blade of grass, everything to ever exist all at once. And considering that we exist in this moment and only this moment and every moment, how would it be for us to tie ourselves to everything that ever happened in previous moments, making the present the constant past?"

Asdeoha opened his mouth, but Sabelu beat him to it. "You speak nonsense, Asdeoha, but I know why. You want to understand. You want to learn. The Shadows are every form and no form; they cannot comprehend the absolute, so you can't either. But you want to."

"And yet here you sit, alone in your cabin in the woods, speaking to no one, helping no one."

"I'm speaking to you. It's up to you to let me help." Sabelu shifted his stance. "As for anyone else, I'll help anyone who asks, but it's not up to me because it's not about me. If I go back now, it will only cause trouble."

The priest sighed and shook his head. "Aren't you just the perfect martyr?"

"Few will weep over my death."

"And what about mine? You were so eager to tell Ganhv of his tragic demise." Asdeoha grinned. "Tell me of my death. Put it in your own Book. Write it in stone. Then we'll see if it can't be changed."

Sabelu smirked. "What I tell you of your death will not be recorded in this Book. And the agony of not knowing how fixed it is will eat at you for years."

So it was. Sabelu told the high priest about his death. Though the discussion was short, Sabelu could see that Asdeoha was already distracted by the implications of it not actually being recorded. What if it really wasn't recorded? Was it still fixed? What if it was recorded and this was some kind of sadistic psychological revenge? If the Books were false anyway, did it matter whether or not it was recorded? What did this all mean?

When Sabelu was finished relating the tale, Asdeoha's disposition was about as agreeable as a cat who has been thrown in a river. His indulgence was feeding him all manner of lies, half-truths, and twisted thoughts, all wrapped up in the murk of confusion and self-righteousness, trying to block out the buzzing of the White honeybee circling his head.

"Well then," the head priest said at last, regaining his composure, "as I said, we will see if things can't be changed. After all, if you speak the truth, it should be the truth whether it is recorded or not."

He turned and walked away before Sabelu could say anything, and Sabelu did not go after him. Yawi barked once, a lilting sort of noise that made it sound like some sort of mockery or insult to the Shadow as it fled.

Asdeoha had only just disappeared when Netami approached from the same direction.

"Eavesdropping?" Sabelu asked smartly.

She gave him a look. "Asdeoha rarely leaves the bowl as it is, and I could think of only one reason why he would conjure Iyuwahnilvhi when he did."

"And you have no prophetic abilities telling you to be up in the middle of the night."

"I have a messed up sleep cycle thanks to all my venturing back and forth to the Old Land."

"And prophetic abilities owing to our lineage, though apparently not enough to let you know that everything would be fine. Besides, my death isn't for another hundred years or so."

Netami folded her arms. "That's supposed to make me feel better? And death isn't the worst thing someone could do to you."

Sabelu shrugged. "Honestly, I think you just missed me."

She sighed dramatically, then relaxed, nodded, and moved to embrace him. She was a head shorter than him, the same height as Blaknik. After a moment, she stepped back and studied him, saying, "I have missed you, yes."

"I don't recall that you were ever so affectionate toward Galiliga," Sabelu teased, "except perhaps once when he finally returned from the war. But you've never pleaded with him to bring his family back to Aktiya Waya."

"Because he married and stayed with his wife's clan and village, as he was expected to do. He helped found Yonhi. He did what was normal and expected of him."

Sabelu shifted his stance. "Well, I can't say that what I've done is normal, but could anyone really expect normal things from me? I did as an adelohosgi was expected to do."

Netami pinched the bridge of her nose. "Prophets divine the destinies of infants and auspicious days for ceremonies and tell us when to plant and harvest the corn. If you think I'm going to let you put yourself on that level, far beneath what you've actually done for us, you have another thing coming."

"Netami—"

"You're right. My prophetic gifts are nowhere near as sophisticated as yours. Sometimes I don't know that it isn't more than just a really good guess or hypersensitive intuition. I mean, if the spirits have you, why would they need to impress on me, too? But I knew when you had done something great out there. It was like...rays of sunlight breaking through the worst of storms, blinding and beautiful. It was like a veil tearing in two, and I could see beyond. I saw the Whites and the Shadows. I could understand as you understand, at least for a few precious moments. I knew you had done something wonderful, something beyond what even Anagalisgi himself had done. He had communed with the spirits, but you confronted them. Everyone could sense the change, but I think I was the only one who experienced what I did."

"You are, yes."

"And you're just going to walk away like nothing happened?"

Sabelu sighed and tried not to get short with her. "Nothing didn't happen, Netami. You know that, I know that, everyone knows that. If nothing happened, then I don't think I would be in this exile in the first place. I would be divining the futures of infants and everything else. What I've done is all to help the people, but that's all."

He again tried to explain how it wasn't all about him, and the strife he would cause if he returned. Netami was not convinced.

"That's fine for the first few days, when it would be easy to seize power from the priests. But you spared Asdeoha, haven't done anything about him. Some think that means—"

"I know what they think it means," Sabelu cut in.

"People will act more on what they think is true than what is true," Netami said forcefully. "You may have spared him to give him time to change and provide an example for others so we don't devolve into paranoid chaos, but you know how it will be interpreted. You know what has already become of it."

Some days, Sabelu hated his gifts. Like right now, he hated that his motivations for leaving Aktiya Waya, although clearly spelled out from his own mouth and perfectly reasonable, would always be analyzed, debated, and derided for the rest of his life and a few decades afterwards. He couldn't even bring himself to argue with his sister anymore. Sensing this, Netami relaxed her posture.

"Tell me this, Sabelu: is Asdeoha going to change? Do we have that to look forward to, at least?"

He took an even breath and chose his words carefully. "I don't see the Whites and Shadows like I do people. I don't know Yawi's comings and goings like I know yours, and I couldn't tell you how a Shadow will react to one thing or another. I ran into the desert entirely blind. But I can see the effects of the spirits, how the people in the mortal plane react to their suggestions.

"Looking ahead at Asdeoha..." He made a helpless sort of shrug. "—his actions and words do not suggest that he is going to change. From what I can see, he is going to follow his Shadow to the grave."

"Then why let him continue to lead the priests and guide the people? If you are so worried about the implications of you taking over, then name Dikdi as head priest."

"You say that as if I have that power. I do not."

His sister gave him a look. "The way things are is because of the way things were. If the way things were produced such evil and chaos, then maybe those ways need to change."

He met her look. "Not all people observe our ways, yet all people suffer evil. Physical changes will yield little if not spiritual changes are made."

"But you made the change!" Netami protested. "You defeated the cerberus and the wolf dog! I don't even fully understand what that means now, but I know that at one time I did."

"Yet even you know that you were the only one who experienced what you did, who got a glimpse of the bigger picture, who saw the forest and not just the trees. The rest of the people need time to understand."

Netami folded her arms. "And you're just going to leave them out there to hopefully maybe get it? If we could solve our own problems, we wouldn't have needed such...dramatic intervention, don't you think? You may have helped the people spiritually, but we are still mortals with day-to-day lives and problems."

"And you have been doing a fantastic job of helping them through all that." Sabelu barked a laugh. "The battle is over, Netami. The people belong to the Whites. Yes, we should always be vigilant, and there will always be those who are more strongly aligned with the Shadows, who seek evil things, but the people are secure for now." He went on before she could speak. "I know you want me to come back. That's really all this is. Everything else, you're arguing just to argue, trying to convince me with some greater reason."

Tears formed in her eyes and she made a vague gesture around where they stood on the narrow trail leading to his cabin. "Do you really have to be alone? This isn't our way, Sabelu; a lone wolf is a dead wolf. Why would the Author choose you, choose us, and then have you ignore some of our most basic principles?" She hastily added, "Surely one of the other villages would take you. Lehoyed, Eagle Clan, perhaps. Or what about going to live with Fichik Shobota?"

"I'm not going to be a lone wolf forever, Netami. I will be spending plenty of time in the Old Land, too, with our father and brothers, working on the next part of the mission."

"And what's that?"

"Well, I won't tell you what we're going to be doing yet, but..." He hesitated. "The Krydik belong to the Whites, but the war continues in the Old Land. The work continues there. My role, however, is considerably less than it was here."

She shook her head. "But why? How?"

"How, because there are far more opportunities for exploitation in the Old Land. People, policies, laws, hates and hurts. The serpent will have a much easier time moving against the people of the Old Land than it would here. As for why my role is diminished, it's because I already fulfilled my primary purpose. The Krydik are secured in the Whites, and we have time and ability to prepare for whatever comes next. I'm not here to be some great hero and leader. I'm not here to be the next Aganstata or Yvgidahi. I am here to help Anagalisgi and the Whites and fulfill a spiritual mission."

He knew her thoughts, knew that she was tossing around words like "quitter" and even "coward." Instead she opted for, "So why won't you help us prepare?"

"Why didn't Anagalisgi come to Hlohi except that he had another purpose to fulfill, and someone else would come to carry on his work and make it twice as effective?"

This, at least, gave Netami some pause. "Itsitsa carried on Yvgidahi's work to unify the people. You carried on Anagalisgi's work to confront the Shadows and secure the people in the Whites. Who is going to keep that going?"

"I can't tell you that."

"What? Why not? Is it because you don't know or—?"

"It's because you do. Or you will."

His evasiveness did not enthuse her. "Then why not tell me now? Do you not want me to influence him? Or her?"

"Oh, you'll do that just fine on your own. I don't want to influence you."

Netami blinked. Then, "Will it be a child of mine?"

"I'm not going to say one way or another. He will come in his own time."

Before she could say more, he turned and started back toward his cabin. Netami jogged up beside him. "So that's it? You're just going to sit here in your cabin, alone, for another hundred years until you die?"

"Oh, I'll be out and about doing work; don't worry about that."

"But you're never going to return to Aktiya Waya. Ever?"

"I'll go there, sure, but I'm not going to live there again."

"But—"

"I am to Hlohi what Anagalisgi is to the Old Land. Part of it, but apart from it. I'm just a little easier to reach and talk to."

Netami scoffed a laugh. "Easier to get to, maybe. Easier to talk to? Up for debate."

He looked at her and raised a brow. "Why, because I don't tell people what they want to hear? Because I don't dispense answers like pouring water from a pot?"

"It's more like syrup in the middle of winter," his sister grumbled. "Or honey when it's crystallized."

"We've had this discussion before, many times. People think they're ready to hear something, they're not. I showed them how to help themselves and each other, and I even made it easier for them to overcome those like Asdeoha, or his indulgence anyway." He went on before she could speak. "And so on and so forth, nothing I haven't already said multiple times, and it's a conversation I'm tired of having."

They reached his cabin where the smell of smoking fish lingered in the air.

"Well, at least you can cook for yourself when you need to," Netami observed mildly. She went to the door and looked inside. "Looks reasonably clean."

"It's only me living here, not five of us."

"Doesn't mean your house won't get dirty and need to be cleaned."

"Which I can do."

She turned, her expression very reminisce of their mother. "Oh really?"

"Who else is going to do it? You?"

"I'm sure Yukpa—"

"—is already entertaining the idea of someone other than me, the man who will become her husband."

Netami shrugged nonchalantly. "Not Yukpa, then. Another woman. You've saved the people, Sabelu. You have a great legacy to pass down to your children. Galiliga may be a bit abrasive about it, but he speaks well of you to his sons. They admire you." He opened his mouth, but she quickly added, "And you can't say 'not yet.' You just said you accomplished what you set out to do, so you don't have any more excuses."

He had said that, hadn't he? And he did appear to be making a big point of wanting to just settle down and live peacefully. Sure, this might not be a village, but it wasn't too far out of the way for a woman if she desired to visit friends or relatives in Aktiya Waya or Yonhi.

But, just as his abilities were causing problems in his normal relationships with his sister or other family members or people he generally knew, it wasn't going to get any better with a life mate. In fact, it would only get worse, and he didn't need his prophetic abilities to know that. Add in children, and things would go downhill even faster.

Sabelu would not marry. He would not raise children. He knew this and he had no real desire to change it.

"Come on, Sabelu," Netami goaded. "Just because you're an adelohosgi doesn't mean you're not a man. I'm sure that Galiliga or Blaknik or myself could ask around and—"

"Now that would be entirely improper," Sabelu cut in. "It's not right for a man to send anyone looking for a wife on his behalf, but especially his sister."

"Please, sisters do that all the time. We know women."

"That's fun and fine at festivals when time is short and introductions are necessarily fast in coming, but it's improper here. If I want a wife, I know where to look, and there's a good chance that I will know how to win her affections."

Netami gave him another look straight from their mother as she shook her head. "I don't understand you, Sabelu. Sometimes I tell myself that it's your gifts and that you can see things we don't. Other times I think you're just a stubborn idiot."

"I've been called worse."

Yet another look. But instead of pursuing the matter further, she just sighed, looked up at the sky, and said, "Well, just because you don't want anything to do with the people anymore doesn't mean the people don't want anything to do with you."

"I didn't say—"

She continued as though he hadn't spoken. "And if I'm going to do anything to help, I guess I should be getting home."

"Itsitsi could use some help, yes," Sabelu offered.

It was considered extremely dishonest, almost a punishable offense, for anyone to alter their appearance via the sorceries, as in a Disguise. And yet, the resemblance between Netami and their mother right now was perhaps even more unnerving. Sabelu hoped his unease didn't show on his face.

"We'll see what we can do for you," was all Netami said as she took her leave and headed back down the trail.

Sabelu could only watch her go. Just because he knew her past, future, and even some of her present thoughts and motivations did not mean he understood women. What was the reason for the difference? What was it that separated women from men and made them so much more difficult to understand, even for him? Maybe that was another reason he didn't want to really marry. Yes, he would know her feelings and desires, but it was like having all the pieces to build something but no instructions for how to put it together. Or worse, those instructions would keep changing and even negate themselves at times. For normal men, it might be an exciting adventure (and he knew that even those feelings only lasted a few years), but for him...

He checked on his fish. The smaller fillets were done, but the larger ones still needed a little more time.

And that was the way it was with solitary living. Do the things that needed to be done, do the things he wanted to do, and don't worry about other people.

Frost turned to snow and began to accumulate. Sabelu started a fire in his wood stove, first only at night, then continuously. He thought it was actually really nice, but he knew he would never get enough people to accept such a thing. It wasn't "traditional." They weren't miners. They might go after some easy or convenient stones or metals, maybe explore some caves, but they didn't break deep into the earth searching for stuff. Besides, the only people who had any real complex smithing knowledge were Eagle Clan, and they tended to stick to jewelry, nothing big like a stove. And what was wrong with a regular fire anyway?

Well, Yawi enjoyed it anyway, and Sabelu decided that was all that mattered. He had never known the joy of simply sitting in front of a warm stove, large wolf at his feet, and some part of him came alive with both hope and fear.

"Are you just going to stay with me my whole life?" Sabelu wondered one evening. The fire was hot, the cabin sealed off from the storm that raged outside.

Yawi stretched but did not look at Sabelu as he answered, "That is my task. Protect the pack, and you are the pack now."

"Yes, but the cerberus and wolf dog are defeated. The people are secured. My job here is basically done. Is it really necessary for you to be here? Aren't there other things that need your attention?"

"You forget that linear time means little to us Whites."

"So you...what? Jump into battle at some point in the past or present, then come back here for some rest and relaxation?"

One silver eye popped open. "Jealous?"

Sabelu shifted in his seat. "You mean to say that you've probably already fought in every battle the people are going to face in the future, and then you come back here just to lie at my feet and protect me from battles that are already won?"

"Mortal, I protect you so you can face those battles when they come. And when they do, I'm already there fighting for you."

A wind gust rattled some tree branches outside. A minute later, there was a crash as an older, partially dead tree went tumbling to the ground. Once the storm cleared, he would probably go out and collect the wood from it, the dead pieces at least. He was not hurting for wood; he would have more than enough for the winter and well into the next summer, but the dead stuff was just as good as kindling for starting a fire or coaxing coals back to life in the morning.

"The people have always been very pack-oriented," Sabelu said, looking at Yawi again. "Even Bear Clan is still centered around the people as a whole. But they don't seem to understand that the forest is not a tree."

"The pack still follows a leader," Yawi told him, sensing his inquisitive intent. "The leaders they thought they had turned out to be no leaders worth following. They think you are."

"That's great, I'm flattered, but it's not about me." Sabelu shifted in his seat. "I feel like a servant who's gone out to open the door to welcome people fleeing a storm, only for people to thank me and not the person who gave the order to have the door opened in the first place. It would be like someone from the Old Land—" He stopped and shifted again. "It would be like my father following around one of my mother's brothers after being rescued from the Trail, worshipping him, treating him like a great leader, when it's Yvgidahi who sent out the rescue parties in the first place. I'll take a thank you, sure, because I did what I was told, but it wasn't up to me. Why don't others see that?"

"You have read your father's Book." Yawi did not lift his head. "His first encounter was only with your kin. He had no knowledge of the pack or its leader, only its representatives. That was all he saw, that was all he knew. Their actions, their kindness, were what led him to make a choice and to trust that the pack leader he had not yet seen was good enough to want to rescue him. You are correct that the Books are the

520

past written in the future. They exist, but not yet. Right now, all anyone has is the words and actions of the pack."

"Do they? That won't be true forever."

"Maybe not, but in this time, in this present, the people have all the opportunity to exploit what you have done."

"Yet we both know there is no such thing as free will."

"Are you certain of that?"

Sabelu opened his mouth, paused, then let out a frustrated sigh. Yawi yawned, though it sounded more like a cover for a laugh.

"I've had a lot longer than you to come up with stuff like that," the wolf said, amused.

"I have the memories of all past Native peoples and knowledge of the future," Sabelu protested.

"Yes, but you have only used such knowledge for practicality, rarely for fun."

"Fun?"

"Yes, fun. I know you know what that is."

"I do, but a lot of 'fun' comes from the surprise and spontaneity of not knowing an outcome. I don't get that."

Yawi sat up, stretched, and repositioned as he lay back down. "Far be it from me to tell you not to use the gifts you have been given, but it is possible to ignore them for a while, I do believe. A man may be very strong, but he will restrain himself for the sake of playing with his pups."

Sabelu took a measured breath. "It's a little late for that, I think. People know me too well; they know what I can do and they'll never let me do anything less."

"Are you sure?"

"Women become frustrated with their husbands, saying they don't know what they like, what they want. Except I do know what they like and what they want."

Yawi tilted his head. "Why is this a problem?"

"Because they don't know what they like and what they want, and what they think they like and want is not always what they actually like and want. Do you have no female wolves in your pack?"

The wolf tilted his head the other way. "Whites have no inherent sex. We are rebirthed through the Author, not procreated. We exist to serve the Author and carry out a mission. Our immortal existence is slightly different than your mortal one."

"I'm guessing the Shadows are the same way, except, didn't you say...about the cerberus and the Sacred Wolf...?"

"Every form and no form, whatever it takes to corrupt, deceive, and dominate."

"How can you help people, then, if you don't understand the differences between men and women?"

"Because there are very few, if any, real problems that are so exclusive. Some may be more frequently experienced by one or the other, but there is almost nothing a man will experience that a woman will not, and vice versa. Pain, loneliness, betrayal, fear, lust, pride, weakness, but also joy, relief, courage, love, loyalty, strength. They are simply expressed in different ways at different times."

Sabelu thought about this for a long moment, genuinely puzzled. "So are you saying there are no differences between men and women? At all?"

"Of course there are. But you are thinking of the physical only. The trunk of a tree may hold it strong against the wind, but it is the leaves which gather the sunlight, the roots that harvest the nutrients of the soil. All part of the tree, all important to its survival, but not the same. If some terrible damage is inflicted, the whole tree suffers, some parts more than others."

"So then what am I? Where do I fit in? Where do you fit in?"

"We may be likened to the sap of the tree, ensuring that the tree has what it needs for roots and leaves to meet. But the Shadows will try to cut off parts of the tree, kill them and become a drain. You, and your kin in the spirit world, may be seen as the tree bark. You are what is seen. You protect the inner workings of the tree from wind, rain, even disease to some extent, and you take damage so that the interior is protected."

He thought a moment, then nodded. "I suppose so."

Yawi did another big stretch and yawned. "Sometimes there are benefits to linear time, human. This storm has passed. Now is the time to enjoy the sunshine as intended."

DℒꝹAՈ DꙄꝹI DVꞀT

Atlasgone Ahisge Adolv'i
What Should Be

Sabelu did not intend to attend the national festival that year, although he did end up playing host to a small group of those traveling from Yonhi to Lehoyed. The majority of the group ended up being his brother or someone from his brother's family, while the rest of the travelers continued on to stay in Aktiya Waya.

"Solitary living appears to suit you, little brother," Galiliga observed, clasping wrists. "You look good."

"Well, when I don't have to listen to everyone else's thoughts, I'm free to have my own," Sabelu told him. "I've discovered that I am not simply a vessel, but a human being myself."

His brother's expression said he wasn't sure how to respond to that, so he changed the subject. "Your demeanor says you don't intend to come to the festival, but I don't understand why. Surely they would listen to your recommendations on the national council."

Sabelu waved a hand dismissively. "They'll be fine without me this year."

"Then you do intend on returning to normal life?"

"I may visit from time to time, but this is my normal life now. Here."

Another tired argument, another tired conversation, and Sabelu was grateful when it passed them by.

"So this is the first year Agwelsa is participating in the festival, in the cooking competition. She wanted to wrestle, and Akdodi had to explain to her why that was a bad idea."

"Well, keep her away from Netami," Sabelu said, half-laughing.

Galiliga made a sound of reluctant agreement. "She wants to come with me the next time I go to the Old Land, too."

"More feasible, but still a Wolf Clan responsibility, and she's Bear Clan."

"And Bear Clan is responsible for war sorceries. But if there are no wars here..." Galiliga gave his brother a look. "There aren't going to be any wars, are there?"

Sabelu hesitated. Then, "The Krydik are secured for the Whites. Our isolation now proves useful. The people of the Old Land have no such assurances."

Galiliga grunted. "I can already hear the arguments back and forth. Help them or don't help them? If we're the special ones, why do we need them, considering how they treat us? Ugh." He shook his head. "How many wars between now and whenever it is we're really needed?"

Now Sabelu gave his brother a knowing look. "Don't ask how many wars. Ask how many years the war is going to continue."

"Do I want to ask that? Do I want to know the answer?"

"There is only one war, Galiliga, going on for a long time across innumerable fronts."

His brother sighed and pinched the bridge of his nose. "Now I remember why I don't visit you."

"Don't worry about it. Your place is here, leading the people, raising your sons, and keeping your daughters out of trouble."

"They're all going to be trouble, not just Agwelsa?"

"I'm afraid so. It's just that she's the oldest."

Galiliga sighed again and shook his head. "And my wife was so happy to finally have daughters after four sons. Dotes on the girls, shows them all about being a woman. Their aunts and grandmother also. Still they seem more akin to Netami."

"Even Netami will make a good wife. She's a good sister and daughter to our parents."

"Oh, my girls are happy to take care of their new baby brother, but they really would much rather run around with the boys their age."

Sabelu grinned. "Just tell them that if they go off with the boys to hunt, they better bring back prospects for a husband."

Galiliga barked a laugh. "Maybe I will."

Sabelu was respected among the people, but he wasn't necessarily liked. It wasn't that Galiliga's wife hated him, not like Asdeoha or his more vocal followers, but she had a Shadow of Fear hanging around, coupled with a Shadow of Loathing. She did not regard him as a god necessarily, but certainly more than an ordinary man, and she didn't like it.

Fortunately for him, she was the only one of his brother's family who felt this way about him, and his brother's sons—and oldest daughter— were more than happy to sit and listen to his tales of Whites and Shadows and the battle in the desert.

"Are there other Great Ones, Tsidushi?" Akdodi asked. "Is the world full of them?"

"Only four," Sabelu told him. "The Wolf, the Minotaur, the Zukatopa, and the Man. And of the four, only the Sacred Wolf remains in its proper form."

"Like Wolf Clan," Agwelsa piped up.

"That's right."

"Should we carve a bear for ourselves, then?" one of the younger boys wondered. He stood suddenly, throwing his arms high. "A great bear for Bear Clan, as tall as the trees and as mighty as a mountain!"

Sabelu shifted position even as the other children laughed. "Why would you do that? The Cursed Zukatopa never moved, and the Man was half-destroyed already. Even the Sacred Wolf did not rise from her slumber to help me against the Shadows. Such things may be beacons and dwelling places, but they are nothing by themselves. What matters are the spirits behind them. It was Yawi who protected me, Rabbit who guided me to the device, and a whole team of burrowers who found it in the first place."

"But if the spirits are as big as the mountains, why couldn't they destroy the evil device?" Agwelsa asked.

"Because it takes a mortal to help a mortal. The Whites and Shadows know and understand things beyond what we can comprehend. Their war permeates our lives and we barely recognize it for what it is. We build things and go places, not always understanding why, but we are being guided by one side or the other. The People Before had built a terrible device and linked it to the Cursed Man, an ironically demonic way of renouncing all spiritual influence. Only a man could have destroyed it."

His audience was far less curious than himself and accepted his explanation with a simple yet enraptured faith. Galiliga's wife said nothing because it afforded her some time to ensure everything was ready for their trip to the festival. Galiliga himself was presently down at the river.

With the visit from his brother's family, Sabelu found that he still generally preferred the company of children, if only because he was still deaf to their thoughts and motivations. With only the children before him and no adults, he genuinely did not know how they would react to the stories he told beyond vague impressions from the older two. He probably could know the younger children, if he wanted to search through the future and see if any of them brought it up ever again, but he refrained.

The family departed early the next morning. Galiliga said something about possibly visiting again on the way back, but Sabelu knew they wouldn't. Other things would come up, and Sabelu would be forgotten. That was fine with him.

Galiliga had made the comment that he remembered why he never visited, and Sabelu made the quiet observation that he really preferred to live alone with no visitors. He liked this normal life.

"You know, rest and relaxation is fine for a time, but this isn't why the Author made you," Yawi said, materializing beside him and sitting down.

They stood just outside Sabelu's cabin, looking out over the landscape as the sun made its arc across the sky.

"My primary purpose has been fulfilled," Sabelu defended himself.

"Yes, everyone dreams of grand adventures such as yours, but even you have said that sometimes the greater impact comes from acts of kindness and goodness in daily life, the people helping to lift one another rather than pursuing their own selfish heroism."

"But I like the peace and quiet."

"And I like lying by the fire, but that's not what I am intended to do with my existence."

"Yes, but you can jump in and out of Time at will."

"Yes, and you can't." Yawi gave him a look. "You have a limited time to do things. Every mortal does. I don't understand why that seems to make you so lazy about accomplishing great works and all the things you are capable of."

Sabelu laughed. "And you may have noticed that the longer lives we have and the more powerful sorceries, the lazier we get."

The wolf just snorted.

"You say you've jumped ahead to future battles; you know what's going to happen. You know my legacy."

Yawi gave him another look and made a disapproving sound that bordered on a growl.

"How am I supposed to accomplish that if I go back to Aktiya Waya, or even Yonhi?" Sabelu asked.

"I think you know," Yawi said. "It is not a feat that can be accomplished only here."

"Maybe not, but why take a chance? I am but a mortal character; why should I seek to change the mind of the Author?"

The wolf let out a low, grumbling growl, but said and did nothing more.

Each day, Sabelu mentally tracked the festival. He knew when everyone arrived, knew all about the opening ceremonies, the songs, the dances, the light sprinkle of rain that passed through to cool everyone off before turning the entire grounds into a humid hellscape. He tracked the progression of his siblings through their various tournaments, watched his father and older brother face off in the wrestling tournament, victory ultimately going to Galiliga, though not without a serious fight. He would lose in the quarterfinals. His mother and sister did not get very far in the cooking competition, unusual for them, but not the end of the world. Blaknik was edged out of the quarterfinals in archery. All in all, not the best year their family had ever had.

Then there were the closing ceremonies, the presentation of the new national council, the accouncement that Lehoyed would host the next national festival, and everyone dismissed to their respective villages. This was rarely an instant thing as people had conversations to finish, gifts to give, promises to make, eyes to catch, children to corral, and so on, and this didn't even consider the time it took to pack up camp.

It was the middle of the day, a few days after the end of the festival, when there were footsteps on the trail. Sabelu looked up from where he was working on his arrow fletching to see Yukpa approaching. He stood to meet her, unsure what to say or do.

"I didn't see you at the festival," she began.

"No," he said, too quickly. "Um...it was better that way. This year."

Her expression alone was enough to convey her confusion. "So, now that everything is over, whatever it is, and it's been almost a year since your adventure into the desert, will you return to Aktiya Waya?" Her gaze darted to his winter wood pile which he'd been steadily rebuilding.

He let out an even breath. "No."

"Will you ever return?" she asked quietly.

He shook his head. "No. Not more than a visit."

Yukpa was silent for a long moment, then took his hands in hers. She did not look at him right away as she said, "I met someone."

Now Sabelu nodded. "I know."

"He's a good man. Good hunter. He was knocked out of the semifinals in archery, but it really is difficult to best an Eagle Clan archer."

"You're not wrong there."

She looked up. "And...he's there. He's around when I need him, when I want him."

He hoped his expression conveyed a sense of understanding. "He's also someone you can get to know, and who will get to know you. He doesn't know everything about you even before you've met."

"Well, there is that, too."

"I know he suspects that you still care for me, and you do. This is practicality, not love. Not yet. But he's a little jealous, which is why he's not with you. You didn't tell him you were coming to see me."

Yukpa shrugged, tried to make it look casual, hastily wiped away a tear. "You said that after your work was done, then maybe we could talk. Is there something more coming, did you not know this was coming, or did you lie to me?"

"I didn't want to upset you."

"You didn't want to upset me because it would only distract you while you were out saving the people." Her tone was somewhere between frustrated disbelief and quiet understanding. "Because you do care."

She shook her head, withdrew her hands, turned around, and walked three steps. "My mother says I'm being foolish and fanciful. I need someone stable who is part of the community, someone who will help build the people up, not tear them down with divisive rhetoric and then run away."

"Well, your mother wasn't exactly one of my biggest supporters."

Yukpa continued as though he hadn't spoken. "And he is good. I like him. I do."

Sabelu went up behind her and put his arms around her. "You need the people. You need the community and a family. And the community needs you."

She put one hand over his and patted it gently. "Well, this isn't exactly making the decision any easier." She spit a small laugh. "And pardon me for saying, but it feels like you might need something, too."

Sabelu felt his skin burn hot, which only made things worse. Then she turned around, which didn't help things either.

"After all these years of hardship, everything you've been put through since you were an infant, I can understand why you might want to escape," Yukpa said softly. "But you are still a priest. And the council has not officially gotten rid of the blood taking, even if Dikdi himself has denounced it. Many have changed it to simple proof of a woman's flower, kept by the oldest brother to be presented at the time of the engagement. Others think the original way was best."

For a long moment, Sabelu's mind was entirely blank, and he could barely process her words, never mind try to conjure up any of his own to reply. Finally he came up with, "I know you have brothers. I know you were resistant to the idea of the original way. You came out here for another reason."

She shrugged as best she could. "I wanted to know if you still cared, if you were going to come back, tell you about Washachi."

"So he does have a name."

"You say that as if you didn't know."

He did not reply to that. When she sighed, he said, "You came here, and you told me. You knew you didn't have to, but you did anyway. I appreciate that." He loosened his grip but did not completely drop his arms. "But this is my home. You have to be the one to leave. When you're ready."

Yukpa took an even breath but let out a nervous chuckle. "I'm not sure, but I think I'm ready now."

Truth teller. Dark seer. Adelohosgi. Savior of the people. Whatever title people slapped on him, Sabelu was still a man. It was also the first time he'd really considered the implications of having all the knowledge and memories of his ancestors but no actual experience of his own. This consideration lasted all of fifteen seconds at which time his mind was overcome with a singular thought, or perhaps a singular grouping of thoughts as he tried to process every sensation at the same time. The one advantage he had over his ancestors, however, was that he knew what she was feeling, too, and, to a limited extent, felt it himself.

There was no ceremony to their lovemaking, and barely any privacy as they were out in front of his cabin in broad daylight. That was fine, though, he thought. They were the only ones around. And when they were done, no one was around to see them lie naked in the grass either.

"Will Washachi and I be happy together?" Yukpa asked.

Sabelu sighed dramatically. "We just made love, and you're asking me about another man?" When her expression turned embarrassed, he laughed and said, "Yes, you will, in time. Right now, it may be to please your mother, but you will love the man you are going to marry. You will have good days and bad days as all couples do, but you will love each other."

"Will we have children?"

"Yes."

Yukpa nodded silently. Then, "Well, I guess I should be going, then. If you're going to stay here and I have another life waiting for me. My blood has been taken and purified by a priest."

Sabelu rolled onto his side and laid his hand on her hip, gently rubbed her a bit. "Maybe so, but at least you know where I'll be."

He didn't know exactly what he intended to say, but the way it came out, that wasn't it. Still, it got her to smile as she stood, dressed and otherwise made herself presentable, and left quietly.

Sabelu remained on the ground, still naked, watching the spot where she disappeared. He looked up at a rustling beside him to see Yawi standing there. The wolf gave him a look.

"What?"

"You know what."

"You're the one telling me it's good to make pups."

"Anyone can make pups. But pups alone do not produce strength. The pack produces strength. The pack must raise the pups and teach them."

Sabelu got to his feet. "Then it's a good thing no pups were made today."

Or the next time, when Yukpa visited a little less than a month later. Her claim was that she wanted to be ready to receive her husband when they were married on the half moon only five days away. Her mother had given her all sorts of strange advice, and she didn't want to seem the fool when she lay with her husband. Sabelu didn't care, and he knew Washachi wouldn't either, but he also wasn't going to argue as he spread her legs and pushed inside.

It was just as well he'd pushed off thoughts of finding a wife until after he defeated the Shadows, because it was like discovering a whole new side of himself, very much like when he discovered he could have his own thoughts and develop his own personality when away from the suffocating intrusion of other people.

Yukpa visited him infrequently as summer turned into fall, then stopped when the cold set in and the snow began to accumulate. When she stopped visiting was when Anagalisgi started again.

"I admit, I wish I could read ahead and figure out just what is going on in your head, what it is that you are actually accomplishing here," his uncle said flatly, expression unamused as he worked on some leather pieces.

Sabelu raised a brow as he sat up and got himself situated by the fire. "You lament that you never had a wife and kids, now you're coming after me for—"

"Taking advantage of a woman and facing no consequences for it?" Anagalisgi gave him a look. "Please tell me her husband punches you in the face at least once."

"Well, he isn't overly enthusiastic about it."

Anagalisgi rolled his eyes. "And you couldn't find any other woman at all? Come on, Sabelu, the Krydik are still majority female—not as much as after the war, but still. You should find someone properly."

"What should be and what must be are two different things, Tsidushi. You know that as well as I do." Sabelu gestured around. "So, what's going on here? Or did you bring me here just to lecture me about sex?"

It didn't take prophetic gifts to see Anagalisgi wanted to punch Sabelu in the face.

"Just because the grand adventure and excitement is over doesn't mean you get to slack off and indulge in your own fantasies," his uncle warned. "How do you think Shadows gain power? It's not always by force. You know that wars have been started over the love of a woman, and it's just what the Shadows would need to sneak back into the people."

"The people are secure, Tsidushi—"

"The Krydik are secure for the moment," Anagalisgi cut in. "The people of the Old Land are not only vulnerable, they are under attack."

"They've never not been under attack. They will always be under attack of some form. And we're helping them. My parents, my brothers and sister—Blaknik especially—they're all doing good work there, and they're helping it to spread, training others so this whole...operation is not dependent on singular figures like you and me."

"That doesn't mean that us singular figures stop working. Men may teach boys to hunt, but the men don't stop hunting just because the boys have learned."

"Men also don't spend their entire lives tied to the bow or club or net," Sabelu countered. "They have fun, too. They race horses, gamble, look at pretty girls or fuck their wives."

"Their wives. Not other men's wives."

Sabelu had no real good answer for his uncle, other than, "It's what I have seen. It's what will happen."

Anagalisgi snorted indignantly. "As I said, I wish I could look ahead as you do to understand why it must be this way. I don't suppose you would be willing to enlighten me."

"Not since you dragged me here only to berate me immediately. If you'd asked first, I might have told you."

His uncle still did not look amused, though he did not push the issue.

"So, how are things here?" Sabelu asked instead, his tone deliberate.

"Better than they have been in a long time," his uncle replied evenly. "The black phoenix and the serpent are still causing much trouble, as you know, but it's nice to have a rest from the cerberus and the wolf dog for a while."

Sabelu raised a brow. "Do you know anything about the wars that are coming?"

"I do," Anagalisgi said. "I also know that they will be wars of chaos. The black phoenix is the master of wanton destruction, scorched earth. It doesn't know how to direct things like the cerberus does. There may be more wars, and they will be devastating, but they will still be less tragic than anything calculated the cerberus could come up with."

"The cerberus maybe. What about the dragon?"

His uncle chuckled. "In a bit of a bind, I'm afraid. The dragon is powerful, but still finite in itself. It can't recycle the cerberus and the wolf dog and conduct such large-scale operations at the same time."

"And Chimera?"

"Back out on patrol, causing chaos for the Shadows wherever and whenever possible."

"The Whites have the advantage then, universally."

Now his uncle's expression turned amused. "The Whites have always had the advantage; they just have a more significant advantage now than they did a year or so ago."

"So if the black phoenix is focusing its attention on Earth, that means it's only the serpent looking at the rest of the universe. So why is the next century going to be so terrible?"

"The Shadow generals are stretched thin, but they are not so helpless and vulnerable as you think," Yawi said, walking in the cave and shaking himself. "Remember, this is not the first time the cerberus has been defeated."

"But—"

"What you see as war, we see as a battle. What you see as a battle, we see as single maneuvers or instances within a battle. And the war is ongoing."

"You ducked out because you thought your part was finished," Anagalisgi added.

"I only have two parts left to play!" Sabelu protested. "And there is a good amount of time between those two events."

Anagalisgi shook his head. "Selfish pup! Even in your solitude you manage to make it all about yourself. Just because a man's part is small does not mean it is not important, or that it has no lasting effect. You just don't want to do it because you think it's beneath you. Just like you didn't want to run errands with me because you thought them too small."

"A man who has proven his skill in battle is not tasked with carrying water."

"And yet your father was both warrior and messenger in the War of the Old Land." When Sabelu did not respond, Anagalisgi continued, "The minor roles are not glamorous, but they are important. How do soldiers know where to go, except that they receive orders? And how will those orders get there? What happens if there is no one to feed them?"

"You speak of white men's wars," Sabelu cut in. "Moving thousands of men here and there, drilling, marching. Even in the days of Taliwa, raiding parties were small. The greatest warriors fought alongside the greenest boys. Messages were sent through bird calls. Warriors fed themselves and each other. Boys may have been tasked as scouts, but they were all part of the same body, the same pack."

His uncle got a look he didn't like. It reminded him of his mother when she'd cornered someone in an argument. "Who mends your clothing for you?"

"I do..." Sabelu answered suspiciously.

"And who cooks your meals, gathers your firewood?"

"I do."

"Aren't these chores for women?"

Sabelu blinked. "I live alone, Tsidushi. I have to do them."

"Of course. Not like your mother and father."

"Tsidushi, you speak in riddles. Say what you want to say."

"If your mother were overwhelmed with tasks—mending clothes, cleaning house, preparing a meal, looking out for children, and other things, and your father did not lift a finger to help, instead citing his work to bring down a whole herd of tsuyoniyvgi last fall, what would you think?"

"I would think him—" Sabelu stopped himself and gave his uncle a look.

Anagalisgi returned the look. "That is life, Sabelu. It is not all about heroics and universe-shattering feats. Sometimes it is the mundane that means the most."

"Wolves and Minotaur and Griffin and Chimera may have brought down the cerberus and the wolf dog," Yawi added, "but it was the ants who kept vigil while we were kept out."

Sabelu huffed a sigh. "So what do you expect from me? What do you want me to do?" He gestured toward his uncle. "Do you expect me to come on errands with you again?" He looked at Yawi. "Are we going to go after Asdeoha and his indulgence, tear it out of him, expel it from the mortal plane, and sacrifice the mortal man in the process?"

"You can start by respecting another man's wife," Anagalisgi said hotly. "I know you're better than that." Sabelu scoffed, but his uncle did not relent. "What is one thing you may have noticed about people and their Shadows? Anything strike you about it?"

"Should it?"

"They're always just out of sight. Overhead, just off the shoulder. On the back."

Sabelu blinked, then twisted as if to look behind him.

"Don't think that because you are the Author's chosen that you are somehow immune to temptation," Anagalisgi warned. "In fact, it just makes you a bigger target."

"And you think returning to Aktiya Waya would make it better?" Sabelu asked.

"At least then you would be back in the fight. The Shadows don't need you to be dead, just useless. I'd be willing to bet that they're going to try this subtle temptation for the next century, just enough to keep you alive but apathetic so the cerberus can finish you off when it returns." His uncle nodded thoughtfully. "Go back to Aktiya Waya, Sabelu, or even the Old Land. Get back in the fight."

Sabelu sighed. "Well, it's winter anyway, so—"

"That's not an answer," Anagalisgi interrupted.

"Fine. I'll get back in the fight. Somehow. Once winter is over. No one does much in the winter anyway."

His uncle wasn't pleased with his response, but he let it slide, if only because consciousness and the waking world was beginning to overtake Sabelu. The next thing he knew, he was awake.

Sabelu wasn't lying when he said no one did much in the winter, and he found himself spending whole days brooding over their conversation. The more time men had, the less they did with it. That was a sad thought to consider. One hundred years and he was only going to accomplish two more things in his life? How sad.

That didn't mean that when Yukpa showed up the next spring that he didn't willingly take her. He was more than happy to lift her dress and bend her over, though he couldn't deny that he still wondered why she came to visit, and he asked her as much afterwards as they reclined on his bed.

"I might have thought that a winter with your husband would have chased away any lingering fancies involving me."

Yukpa squirmed a little. "Well, truthfully, I didn't really intend to do it when I came up here. Actually, I—" She gave him a look. "Wait, you know all this, don't you?"

Sabelu sighed. "Your husband wasn't happy. You talked about it over the winter, even conceived a child which is now in your belly. Originally, you intended to come here and tell me that you wouldn't be coming back." He raised a brow. "And yet, here we are."

She chuckled nervously. "Here we are." She got off his bed, stretched meekly, then turned to face him. "I really didn't mean it. This time, I mean. I mean, it wasn't right in the first place, but..." She shook her head. "Things don't always go the way we want them to, and what should be isn't always what is."

"Yes, it is," Sabelu said, standing himself. "And right now, you should be with your husband. That is what should be."

"You're not angry?"

"No."

The departure was more awkward for her than him, if only because he had the benefit of knowing that she would be back. Off and on again for years, they would never actually stop being lovers until his death.

Just their brief exchange told him he probably wouldn't find a regular wife. She knew that he knew. She would wonder why he didn't already act on that knowledge. She would wonder why he didn't pretend not to know so that she could pretend to have an authentic conversation. This coming from a woman who had sought him out; a woman whom he pursued would have an even harder time of it. Just a courtship would be a nightmare.

No. He knew what would be, what had to be. He had no real desire to change it. He was happy where he was. Really.

He probably should do something with himself, though. Gathering firewood was the biggest consumer of time, but it was hardly continuous. He didn't need to hunt and fish constantly, and he kept only a small garden. There was only so much busy work he could make for himself. If such ease of living had ravaged the people, it wasn't going to be any kinder to an individual.

Maybe he should go out and explore to the north. The south had been well-traversed and he had no desire to set foot in that desert ever again, but maybe there would be something of interest in the opposite direction. Minor scouting parties had only ever reported mountains, but they also hadn't traveled for more than a few days, and traveling one day through the mountains was far less productive than one day across the plains. The mountains couldn't go on forever, could they?

Or he could go west, past Yonhi and their hunting grounds, see what was out there. Maybe they could expand and have their own land that stretched from sea to shining sea. Maybe they could get their population above two thousand and keep it there for more than five years. Maybe they could have seven clans again.

Or maybe he should, as his uncle said, get back in the fight. If one project was done, go work on another.

He still wasn't keen on the idea of going back to Aktiya Waya, or any of the villages. They knew him, he knew them. He wouldn't say he was afraid necessarily, but it felt very tiresome, like going home to a spouse who not only wanted to argue, but brought up an issue that had been decided years ago and no longer mattered, nor could it be changed.

He scoffed at himself and shook his head. He knew too much to entertain hypotheticals. All he had to do was look ahead, pick out certain figures to piece together a timeline of things he would be doing. There were very few mysteries in his life, except for now when he was all alone here at his cabin. Days and even whole months where he could not see himself, where his every move was a surprise. The problem was, there were only so many things he could do in a day. Go here or there, hunt, fish, minor chores. Even the "surprises" had become mundane.

Maybe he should get back in the fight, do small things to help people and occupy his time. Maybe not in Aktiya Waya; he didn't feel like confronting Asdeoha. On the other hand, he didn't want to go to Yonhi either and have to look at Yukpa. Lehoyed, then. They were traditional and appreciated his knowledge. Maybe he could help with writing more books and keeping record of the past. That sounded reasonable, a less flamboyant way of helping people, but one that would carry through multiple generations.

It would also fulfill some of the conversations he knew he would have with some of the people in Lehoyed. If he stayed long enough, he might fulfill his predicted duty of presiding over Oko's funeral.

Sabelu looked at his cabin, sitting quietly in the sunlight. He wasn't going to leave forever, just a little while. But this wasn't a stone cave like those in Aktiya Waya, neither was it easily packable like the tipis of Deer Clan. He had to keep it secured somehow so he didn't come back and find it had been converted into a den of foxes.

Was this going to become a regular endeavor? He knew the answer even before he finished the question. Of course it would, and he would need to secure his cabin during those ventures as well. Now how did he do it?

Just as he had done to find the device in the ruins, Sabelu looked ahead to— Wait. He couldn't find anything. He didn't see himself, and apparently no one in the next hundred years was going to— Yes, they would. Because he looked ahead now, couldn't find anything, so he resolved now to bring someone here in the future so they could watch him secure his cabin for an extended leave so that he could see it now in the past and use that information. Had he just made a change, or was it always going to be this way?

It gave him something to think about as he again used that information from the future to expedite his activities in the past. Or present. He shook his head and tried to focus just on what he was doing.

On the other hand, what if he just used Galohisdi to get where he needed to go? Go to Lehoyed every morning—or a respectful distance away so no one saw him use Galohisdi—and then return to his cabin at night. That was feasible, wasn't it? And he wouldn't need to secure it for extended periods of time.

Time on his own seemed to have produced an unusual side effect for him, and he couldn't decide whether it was indecision or a tragic desire to change what he saw. Used to be that he did because he saw and there were no alternatives. He was like an arrow that traveled exactly as expected, or maybe a horse that continued to follow a certain trail in spite of whatever the rider was doing. This, now, was somewhere between being hesitant to do something and absolutely convinced he wanted to do something else, and neither option was getting him anywhere.

Well, he was already packed up and his cabin was already mostly sealed off. Once he got to Lehoyed, if he decided that Galohisdi would be better, he would simply come back and unseal his cabin. Having long periods of solitary living was not helping him figure out exactly when he made certain decisions. Looking ahead, it appeared as though he would have both extended stays and jumps back and forth. He couldn't decide if this lack of precision was a help or a hindrance.

He used Galohisdi to get close enough to Lehoyed to walk, but not so close that he would be rebuked for using sorcery.

One might think that, being a smaller town with more traditional observances and a White-led priest, Lehoyed would be a great haven for the Whites, more so than Aktiya Waya. The problem came when considering that the Shadows were well-versed in the traditional observances and had centuries of experience deceiving the people through those avenues. It was still a haven for Whites, yes, but there were more Shadowy serpents slithering around Lehoyed than Aktiya Waya.

Many of the serpents scattered when Sabelu walked into town—less bedraggled than before, as he had remembered a face shield this time—

but some remained defiant. He ignored these and instead set about looking for Oko or Tlistso. Well, he didn't really need to look; he knew they were in the townhouse. To no one's surprise, Oko was getting older, and Tlistso was ever more desperate to record everything he had to say. As for the old man, while he was grateful for the attentiveness of the younger generation, he was also perpetually annoyed by the self-styled historian and scribe, and his posture and tone reflected this.

"And so Fox said to Turkey—" Oko was saying. His gaze shifted to Sabelu and he broke into a near-toothless smile. "Sabelu!"

Tlistso, with his back to Sabelu, stopped writing. He shifted position. "Sabelu? That's—" He noted Oko's gaze and turned around. He grinned and stood hastily. "Sabelu!"

"That is my name, thank you for reminding me," Sabelu greeted.

"What are you doing here? More trouble?" Tlistso asked, expression turning worried.

"No, no trouble." Sabelu took a seat between the two, Tlistso slowly following suit. "Just thought I would pay a visit and see if I couldn't rescue Oko from his tale." He handed a string of beads to the elder who took them with a nod. "There are others who have stories, you know."

"Yes, but most of them don't like me writing them down," the young man lamented. He altered his voice. "You can't write down traditional stories; they won't be traditional anymore." He shook his head.

Sabelu just gave Tlistso a look.

Tlistso raised a brow. "What?"

"I think he's talking about himself," Oko chuckled.

"Wha—? Oh." Now Tlistso did a slow nod. "Ooh, I get it now." His expression turned confused. "Is that why you're here, then? Is that all?"

"The major fight has already been won, but the people still need help. We may be secure in the Whites, but a wall must be maintained for it to remain strong."

"And you still think these stories will help in some way?" Tlistso went on before Sabelu could speak. "We heard you went far to the south, to the Cursed One of the Desert and destroyed it." He sighed.

"And here I am, writing down stories."

"We're all stories in the end," Oko told him. "Kept alive by our voices on the wind, the telling of stories, and now the reading of them. If we were to perish, our stories would as well. But if they were written, and someone found these written stories, we would be alive again. This is how we knew of the People Before, how they were kept alive, and how we knew the Cursed Ones needed to be destroyed.

"As we are captured in stories, our history remains with us, our ancestors speak to us. How will we know what to fight for if we don't know who we are? How will we know who are if we don't know who we were? Why do we do the things we do, except that it is in the stories?"

Tlistso nodded. "I understand."

Sabelu stood and helped the old man as he struggled to his feet. "Good. Then I will leave you two alone and see about getting some help from my granddaughters."

Oko took his staff as it was offered and shuffled out of the townhouse. Sabelu and Tlistso watched him go.

"How much longer does he have?" Tlistso wondered.

"A couple years," Sabelu answered.

"Will it be peaceful?"

"Yes."

Tlistso nodded. "Good. You know, he talks a lot about his wife, too, how much he misses her." Sabelu could feel the young man's eyes on him. "Is there an afterlife for characters in books? Do we become Whites, or maybe Shadows? Will Oko see his wife again?"

"Unfortunately, I don't know the answer to any of that," Sabelu admitted. "My knowledge stops at the end of this life."

"Oh. Well, what do you think happens?"

"I try not to think about it."

"But you're the chosen one of the Author, aren't you?"

"Chosen to help the people, yes. And I've done that."

Tlistso shrugged. "Well, I just thought that...people like to know that doing good things and keeping the old ways alive and whatnot, that it will all be rewarded, you know? I thought maybe you had some insight on that, some way to encourage people when they do good things but it seems like they are only attacked for it."

"Speaking of yourself," Sabelu stated.

"Well...yes." Tlistso sighed as he sat back down. "I'm not saying that no one reads my books because they do. And there are other writers in the community and the people at large. But...I'm attacked by the very people I'm trying to help. I want to preserve the stories of the elders, but a lot of them call me names and refuse to talk to me. Oko usually has a few words for them about it, but he won't be around forever."

"Neither will the naysayers." Sabelu also sat. "And upcoming generations will be more appreciative of your efforts."

"Yes, but what about the other writers? I try to preserve what we have. There are others who write their own imagined tales. One of them has real storytelling talent, but they're fictional adventure stories about a rabbit who discovers and explores the caves and tunnels in the area. One of the elders, if he had been younger or used sorcery, he would have taken that book and burned it, I just know it." He shook his head. "I don't understand why they're so against it. Is it the Shadows?"

"Part of it is the Shadows, yes, but not all for the same reasons. Some of it is simply blatant hostility, trying to drive a wedge between the older and younger generations and separate you from the very thing you're trying to save. But some of it is also the Shadows working on the fear of the elders, those who remember the Old Land."

Tlistso rolled his eyes. "There are no white men here. There are no other people here. It's just us. And they're just books."

Sabelu shifted position. "Do you know, my father doesn't like to travel if it's not on horseback. In the war, he was on a horse—well, for part of it. But anywhere he goes outside of Aktiya Waya, he wants to be on horseback. Whether it's on a hunt, going to another village, or just visiting me, all on horseback. When he was on the Trail, he was not on horseback. He had to walk until his feet bled. Cold, snow, rain, sickness, death, all on foot. He knows he's safe here. He's fed, he's secure, he's not being forced to go here or there. But it's that fear that he learned early on that drives him to ride."

"But they're just books."

"Just books. Just guns. Just a little land. Just this, just that. Life on Hlohi is probably the most secure they've ever been, and they don't want that to change. You don't see anything sinister because it has never harmed you. A child is fearless because he is ignorant. The elders are not ignorant. Misguided, maybe, but not ignorant."

Tlistso looked at the pages in his hands. "I offered to read the books to them. I offered to teach them to read so they would know my words were true. They refused."

Sabelu nodded. "I know. Unfortunately, not everyone wants to be helped. But the one you are trying to help, is not always the only one who is watching, nor is it always the one who is being helped." He made a mild gesture to a few boys not quite men sitting a short distance away, writing something on papers of their own. "Honor your elders and teach your juniors. In that order."

Tlistso considered this for a long moment, then managed a nod. "I should be able to handle that. Although I'm not sure what I'm going to do once Oko dies. He's always had the greatest collection of stories." His expression was an unasked question.

"You'll find something," Sabelu told him cheekily. "Now then, are we just going to sit here gossiping like a couple of women, or are you ready to put more words to paper?"

The young man took quick stock of his supplies, shifted position, then readied his quill. "I'm ready."

"Good. This is the story of the Hare and the Grasshopper..."

ᎠᏝᏍᎪᏁ ᎠᏑᎾᎵᏁ ᎠᏙᎸᎢ

Atlasgone Asunaline Adolv'i

Haven

You know, sometimes I look ahead at things, and I wonder exactly what it is that propels me to certain places or situations. Then I come here and you clear up all mystery."

"Solitary living hasn't been kind to you."

Sabelu stood in his uncle's cave, feeling very much like a child who has been brought to his mother for some punishment, or perhaps his father or uncle for a stern lecture.

Years had passed. Decades, since Sabelu had destroyed the Cursed One of the Desert and defeated the cerberus and wolf dog. After those brief years of excitement, Sabelu's life had dwindled to, basically, running errands.

Oh, there had been plenty of excitement in the Old Land as the whole world was consumed by war. Sabelu had gone there a few times, thinking he might be able to help in some way, maybe even take out the black phoenix that was no doubt stirring up all of the conflict. No such luck; it only resulted in a second world war.

"I'm exhausted, Tsidushi," Sabelu sighed. "Why did you bring me here?"

"I need you to do something for me." Anagalisgi was busy packing a small bag. "Go to the woman Aklaq and tell her something."

"Something...specific, I assume?"

His uncle scowled at him. "I think you know what. She will be presented with a decision to either save the world or end it."

Sabelu nodded joylessly. "Ah, yes, her fateful marriage."

"Just do it, please. I have my own tasks to attend to."

"Why do I have to do it now? She won't even be leaving for the south for a couple weeks."

"Sabelu!"

Sabelu scowled himself and left his uncle's cave most unceremoniously.

He'd been grumpy for no real good reason when he went to bed, and that seemed to have carried over into his dreaming self. Remaining cranky even in the dream stuck with him as he returned to consciousness, resulting in a mild headache, which did not improve his disposition whatsoever.

He lay in his bed for a while, staring at the ceiling. Down to the river to wash, gnaw on a bit of jerky just to have some taste in his mouth. Then what? Firewood, maybe. Yawi didn't visit much these days unless Sabelu was actively doing something, going among the people either on Hlohi or in the Old Land. Netami visited the most out of anyone in his family, gave him updates on the state of Aktiya Waya although he already knew. She seemed to think he was lonely.

Was he lonely? Not necessarily. Yukpa still came to him. They would see each other about every four days for a season, then she would stay in Yonhi for the winter. Guilt or pregnancy might keep her away for a few years, but then she would be back, as wet and willing as ever. She had just been by a few days ago, might show up today, might not. Did he want to put off his uncle's request until after Yukpa visited next, or do it now, get it over with, and come back to hopefully find her waiting for him?

Of course, he knew when she would be by; he was just procrastinating in his own way.

Grudgingly, he pulled himself out of bed. Whatever he was doing, he still had to get up and around. Down to the river, nibble on some jerky, move a little bit of firewood just to say he did. Then, reluctantly, to the Old Land where Aklaq was about as enthusiastic about her day as he was about his.

She'd left the Tlingit some years ago, moved back to the land of her people, the Inupiaq. Her little cabin very much resembled his, although it stood on stilts so as to sit above the snow, and it looked out over the ocean. Very picturesque, really. The woman herself was sitting on the bank, brooding.

"Frustrating, isn't it?"

She looked up from where she sat on the bank.

"Am I dreaming?" she wondered. "Or are you really here?"

He sat down a couple feet from her and looked out at the horizon. "Does it matter?"

She shrugged. "I don't know. You're the one who has trouble controlling what he sees, and I thought that dreams only made it worse."

"Please, you think I don't try to make things easier on myself, or that I haven't had some margin of success in the last few decades?"

"Maybe, but that doesn't explain why you're here. You've never come across as the social type."

"Believe me, I'm not, but my uncle sent me."

"Trying to get you to develop your social skills?"

"He gave up on that a long time ago."

"Then why send you?"

"Because he's busy."

"What about the white bear?"

Sabelu grinned but did not look at her. "I'm starting to think you don't want to talk to me." He went on before she could speak. "That's all right. I don't like to talk to me either. So to save us both the hassle of having to listen to me more than we need to, I will simply impart my uncle's message. He wants you to know that very soon, you will be presented with a decision, and you should make the right one."

Aklaq gave him a look. "Really?"

He shifted position. "Well, it may have been something more along the lines of, 'The decision made will either end the world or save it.' "

She raised a brow.

"All right, fine," Sabelu conceded. "Those are my words, not his."

"Something you saw?"

Now he gave her a look. "I see too much to want to make anything up. My uncle saw the same thing, but as I said, he's busy, and the White animals don't like me very much, so he sent me on this errand."

"So what is this upcoming decision?"

Sabelu sighed. "I told my uncle I would be as polite as possible and try not to direct you in such a way that it would impede free will."

Aklaq shook her head. "I don't understand."

"He believes that the choices one makes should not be of fear, vanity, or even a promise of reward like training a dog with treats. Decisions should be made with knowledge, thoughtfulness, truth, and love." Sabelu shook his head. "The problem is, any of those on their own are usually in short supply."

"But doesn't telling someone the truth sometimes provoke them to fear or vanity or hope of a reward, or a treat, as you put it?"

He did not look at her as he said, "If I told you that the next man—in Time—that you meet, you have to marry in order to save the universe, would you do it?" He continued before she could answer, "And if I told you that he was white—as white as any of the men you've fought against so far, maybe even whiter—would you still do it? Would you do it if I told you that it would be decades before your union produced these universe-saving results? What if I said that you would have to risk your life multiple times? What if I said that he would risk life and limb and ignore all of your warnings to the contrary? What if I told you that he would risk your life without your knowledge, permission, or ability to refuse? What if I told you that it would be nearly a century before you would even be able to have children again? But what if I also told you that to not do any of this would be to sentence the universe to death? Do you really want to know all that truth? Or would you prefer to listen to my uncle's 'tact and diplomacy' as he calls it?"

Aklaq blinked. "Is that what's going to happen?"

He shrugged casually and looked at her. "I don't know. Is it? Could it be true only because I have effectively frightened you into fulfilling this potentially-bogus prophecy? Considering how long I've said it's going to take to fulfill, what if you went along with it but it never came to be? Or what if you ignored it and sentenced the universe to death?"

"What if I punched you in the face and then went and did the same thing to your uncle?"

He burst into laughter. "If I thought you could, I would let you punch me just so I could go with you and watch."

"So what am I supposed to do?! Is the next Timekeeper I meet going to be a white man who I have to marry in order to save the universe? And why wouldn't you warn me about something like that sooner?"

Sabelu shrugged yet again, then took a roll of nala from his bag, put it between his lips, and lit it. He puffed out some smoke. "You wanted the truth. As I said, I know too much to want to make stuff up."

"Well, I hate you for it. And you can tell your uncle when you see him that I hate him, too, for sending you to me."

"Hate me all you want, everyone else does."

Aklaq glared at him. "You're incredibly selfish, do you know that?"

"I've been called worse."

"You claim to see all this stuff, but you never once mention any of the good things that happen. Festivals, weddings, the joy of a child. No, it's all about the bad stuff in the world."

He took another drag and looked at her. "I did tell you some good things. You're going to marry again. One day, far in the future, you will have children again. You'll even have the opportunity to save the universe. Those don't sound like good things to you?"

"Yes, well, you're cynical enough that even good things sound like bad things. You just want everyone to be as miserable as you."

He grinned around another drag. "Believe me, I do not. I would be more than content to live alone in my cabin, but, interestingly enough, I don't have much say over my life." He gave her a severe look. "You, however, do."

She searched his face. "Do the things you see change? If I were to decide not to marry this man, do you see different things? Different futures?" She blinked. "Or are you just saying this in order to get me to do whatever it is you actually see me doing?"

Sabelu sighed, took another drag, and studied the remainder of his roll, blowing smoke from his nostrils. "This is why prophets have a hard life and do not belong in the waking world, whatever my uncle thinks." He stood. "I've told you what I can."

"What you can, or what you will?"

He went on as though she hadn't spoken. "What you do now is up to you."

He turned and started walking away, still smoking. Aklaq shouted at his back, "Oh! Right! It's only the fate of the universe we're talking about! Who needs clear answers about that?!"

Sabelu did not react, just headed over the hill, conjured Galohisdi, and returned home. It wasn't much later that Yukpa showed up, as he'd known she would. They made love, then lay together a short while before she departed.

Maybe, he thought, his grouchiness came not from having to talk to Aklaq, but because he knew what was coming next. Maybe he'd hoped to put it off. He might have learned after the first couple decades that it wasn't going to happen, but still he foolishly hoped. Well, at least he got to see Yukpa beforehand.

It was early the next morning when his father and brothers visited, but this was hardly a social call.

They had all aged a little, enough that Ola Achukma looked like a father again, in his late forties early fifties perhaps. Blaknik no longer looked like a teenager, but still youthful. Galiliga had changed the least, just enough to say he looked a few years older than he used to, a man in his mid- to late thirties.

He was out in front of his cabin doing some or other when they approached, walking up the trail three across.

"So, do we need to tell you why we're here, or are you going to come quietly?" Galiliga asked once they were within conversation distance.

"Are those statements mutually exclusive?" Sabelu countered smartly.

"Then you do know," Blaknik stated.

Sabelu gave his younger brother a look. "Of course I do."

"You might have been prepared for our arrival," Galiliga said.

"That's assuming he is coming," their father piped up. His expression remained neutral, if not forcefully calm, as he looked at Sabelu. "You know what our endeavor is; the question is, are you joining us?"

Sabelu made a slow gesture. "Now that is a wonderful question. Finally, someone takes into account that I, too, am a human being, and not just some tool you can parade around with you wherever you go to show off—"

"Answer the question, Sabelu," Galiliga cut in. "Is this important enough to warrant your divine attention?"

"I like the way Itsitsa asked the question better, but the short answer is yes."

"Great, let's go. If you knew all this beforehand, why aren't you ready?"

Sometimes Sabelu wondered how life might have been different if Tsona had lived. Such hypotheticals were now a staple of his free time. Maybe Galiliga wouldn't be so up tight. He'd failed to protect one brother, so now he was determined to keep watch over the other two and didn't understand why one was so resistant to his efforts. Would he still be so hard on Sabelu if he hadn't lost Tsona? Who was to say?

"It's my job to inconvenience people," Sabelu told him. He turned and headed into his cabin.

"It's your job to help the people," Ola Achukma said calmly. "I hear you've done very well at that...when you get out and actually help people."

"I helped the people once when I destroyed the Cursed One of the Desert. There was no choice and no alternative to that." Sabelu huffed a sigh as he knelt to pack a small bag. "Trying to help people on their own..." He shook his head. "People say they want to be helped, but it's the biggest damn chore to make them see what that help actually entails. Even those who do know they have problems and know what it will take to resolve some of those problems...it's like they want to go to sleep one night and wake up the next morning with the problem magically resolved. It doesn't work like that." He waved a hand as Galiliga opened his mouth. "I did my duty. I cut off the dead, infected limb, but I'm tired of doctoring sniffles."

"Except this time, it isn't destruction," Galiliga said, butting in. "We're not trying to break anything. We're building. Quite frankly, we're only asking for help with the physical labor. You might have noticed we didn't consult you about any of the legal ramifications and circus we've been dealing with."

"I did notice, and I appreciate your consideration." Sabelu tied up his small bag and stood.

"Then what's the problem? Is there something we should know about this project? Something you want to tell us? Don't complain about never doing anything major and then keep silent on significant events."

Sabelu just shook his head. "Are we going?"

Galiliga gave him a hard stare bordering on a glare before turning and pushing his way past the others out of the cabin. Blaknik followed, more confused than cowed. Ola Achukma, however, lingered a moment, casually blocking Sabelu's path.

"What is it, Sabelu?" Ola Achukma inquired, sounding older and more tired than Sabelu was prepared for. "What is it that has you so riled up? Is something bad going to happen? Should we abandon this project now and save ourselves the time and effort?"

Sabelu gave a mild shake of his head. "No. This project is very good and will steer many wayward lives back onto the right road."

"Then what is it?" Ola Achukma went on before Sabelu could reply. "Sabelu, I have never claimed to understand you or the things you see. Nevertheless, I have tried to help any way I can. In old times, it would be your mother's brothers who would do a lot of the teaching, but we didn't really have that option after the war. And even then, how does anyone teach someone who carries all the knowledge of the past? It greatly pleased me to hear that you were communing with Anagalisgi, and yet you still seem so unhappy. This solitary living sounded good at first, that you were able to break away from the cacophony of thoughts and noise, yet you appear so bitter." He shrugged helplessly. "Your mother weeps for you sometimes, you know. Netami, too, though she's more stubborn about it, more intent on fixing you."

"Yes, she's told me that she does not intend to marry until she deems me happy enough to invite to the wedding." Sabelu barked a laugh.

"And how does that make you feel to know that you've done that to your sister?"

"Amused, honestly, because I'm not going to see her marry."

"So you enjoy making others miserable because of your own distaste for...what, exactly?"

The words exploded out of Sabelu before he could think about them. "I enjoy helping people and keeping them alive. But this project is going to be the last one you do. You will do it boldly and you will do it well and you will help more people than I ever could. But it will be the last thing you do."

It was like that moment after an arrow has been released but before it finds its target.

Sabelu sighed and added quietly, "If you knew that doing something meant you were going to die, would you do it?"

His father blinked, snapping his trance, and he nodded. "I went to war with no guarantee of living. But a certainty of death? Well, I might as well help as many as I can before I walk on."

"Yawi once lectured me on how the more time we have, the less we do with it."

"Smart wolf."

Sabelu gave his father a look.

"How long?" Ola Achukma wondered.

"Thirty years."

Sabelu flinched when his father burst into laughter.

"That long?" he asked. "Oh, you had me worried for a second." Without waiting for a response, Ola Achukma clapped his son on the shoulder. "Come on, then. We haven't even gotten started on this project yet, never mind anything that might come from it in thirty years."

Sabelu couldn't decide if he was sad or confused as he followed his father outside. Everyone knew that their parents would one day perish. Sorceries or not, death was inevitable. Sabelu had the added benefit, if it could be called that, of knowing the time and manner of his parents' deaths. Only one of them was peaceful.

Perhaps it was just as well that his father had aged some. His mother, not so much, but definitely his father. There came a time when the invincible young man realized he was no longer invincible, when he began to think more about the ancestors he wanted to join than the descendants who had grown up and were leading their own lives. At least then Ola Achukma might be more at peace when the time came.

The trip to the Old Land was about as much fun as it usually was, although the four of them shouldering the burden of Galohisdi did help to keep them upright on the other side.

The spot where they landed was unremarkable by itself. A forested slope in the state of West Virginia, it was only accessible by foot or horseback as there was no proper road. A seasonal river ran near the southern edge of the property. It was currently dry, but when it flowed, it dumped into a swampy area a little ways down the slope at the far eastern edge of the property before reforming into a river and carving its way down the steeper mountainside.

Already Sabelu could see the phantoms of the future. The footpath would be turned into a dirt road for most of the way up, turning into a paved portion that opened up into a large parking lot. One large log building would dominate the immediate vicinity with several smaller buildings around it: an office, a nurse's office, and laundry and shower facilities. A dozen cabins would line the slope, boys' cabins on one side, girls on the other.

There were also phantoms of buildings that would be built and later destroyed, either by nature, neglect, or intent. Many of them were simple roof structures or pavilions, though there was also a scattering of more traditional houses, which was what they would be building here in this first camp iteration.

"It doesn't look like much now," Ola Achukma said, "but it'll be great. First we just need to clear some trees."

If there had been anyone outside of their family in the vicinity who heard him say that, there would be instant accusations of being too white. Ola Achukma had sold the idea of this camp on the premise of taking back land from white hands. Coming here and talking about clearing the land and building this and that and such and such future plans, well, it did sound pretty white. Doing the work first and then inviting everyone else to come and see what was done, well, any violence would be reduced to fiery words and acidic accusations only.

This place would be very much a place of contention among the Krydik, but it would do a lot of good, too.

Felling the trees wasn't difficult; it was primarily a matter of invoking the sorceries to separate the wood along a certain break point. The only real difficulty came from pushing the break point horizontally across the width of the trunk, rather than vertically up the tree. Once it was down, then they stripped the tree vertically, producing a number of rough boards, many of which they later refined. As for the stumps, they did not pull them up, thereby creating hundreds of craters, but instead invoked Time to rapidly decay them and return them to the soil naturally.

Once the area was clear—not as clear as it would be later, but enough for the time being—then they could start on the actual construction. It wasn't a lot to start with: a large gathering place, like a townhouse but smaller and slightly less official, although the kids would be told it was for very official, very sacred things; a few smaller shelters for sleeping and general protection from the elements, the walls easily removed for airflow in the summer; and another large shelter so as to keep the respect for the pseudo-townhouse.

The whole project took roughly three weeks, partly due to weather, sometimes due to difficulty getting everyone together between various obligations, and partly because of the time it took to recover from such heavy use of sorceries they did not often use, such as invoking Matter to fuse structure beams back together without the need for nails or pegs.

"What do we do, now that it's complete?" Blaknik wondered as they sat in the grass and ate lunch, admiring their handiwork.

"Now we bring the kids here," Ola Achukma said, sounding a bit uncertain himself.

"Yes, but how? Not Galohisdi?"

Their father faltered a bit. "Well, it will be a bit of a hike, but it will be the first step in helping them to reclaim their identities."

"Come on, Itsitsa," Galiliga laughed, "you know how hard it was to get us to go anywhere. Even just leaving the bowl for the first time, we were exhausted, starving, and going to die before we got halfway to the pass."

Ola Achukma grinned. "Yes, I suppose you're right. Maybe we'll use horses; we can put two or three children on a horse and bring them up that way."

The horse tenders were less than enthusiastic with the idea, if only because most of the children had probably never ridden a horse, but Ola Achukma assured them that there would be experienced riders leading the horses.

A couple weeks later, twenty children and fifteen adults made their way up the slope to the new campsite. Eighteen of the children had come from the boarding schools, but the attitude toward the schools was not the same as it had been fifty or a hundred years ago. There was still opposition to them, but the economic and political pressure wrought by the government on the nations as a whole meant that some were starting to see the schools as more of an opportunity for their children to get an education and get out of poverty.

Ola Achukma intended to show the children a time when success meant more than just money. It was about family and the community, the people as a whole. Of course, this was easy to say when the Krydik had free access to nearly endless hunting lands, while the people of the Old Land had been herded onto small reserves of some of the worst land the United States had to offer, and to wander away from those lands was to invite discrimination, ridicule, and even violence.

Sabelu, following the group on his own mount, quietly watched the children on the ride up the hill. Twenty children, out of how many thousands? Studying these children now, one would go on to be successful, by the American definition, although her grandchildren would know almost nothing of their heritage except as a tool of political exploitation. Thirteen of these children would live fairly mediocre lives on or around the reserves, living in one world, knowing they were part of another, but otherwise stagnant in their ambitions. The rest would devolve into alcoholics, either suicidal or homicidal, half of them turning on their own people to become violent rapists and murderers, a tragic tale that would affect multiple generations.

But these were children now, and the Whites surrounded their group. There were no Shadows to fight yet. And when the Shadows came, much of the progress that had been made in the days of Fichik Shobota had been erased. It did not always come through violence, a force that could be readily opposed, but a quiet takeover of the mind, worry about circumstances and daily needs.

"And what have you done to stop any of it?"

Sabelu looked down to see Yawi padding alongside him. He invoked Sound so as to speak without being overheard.

"Me?" he wondered. "What about you? How many Whites were there in Fichik Shobota's time? What happened there? What happened to Ossi? Two Shadow generals destroyed and somehow the people here become too overwhelmed?"

"You do not understand the nature of the black phoenix."

"Well that seems to be a convenient excuse, doesn't it? Something goes right, look at us, we're mighty and powerful, praise to the Author. Something goes wrong, it's some existential horror beyond my comprehension. Or it's just another maneuver in the war."

"What do you want me to say? What do you want to hear?" Yawi bared his teeth. "You already know what's going to happen, so what is your problem exactly?"

Sabelu had no good answer for the wolf's question that didn't make him sound like a petulant child. He did know how it was all going to end. He knew they were going to win.

"But what about all the people who are going to be sacrificed in the process?" he asked quietly. He looked at a boy he knew was going to one day murder his parents in an alcoholic, drug-crazed rage; then at a girl who would be trapped in a lazy, loveless marriage with four kids, three of whom would become delinquent. "Why would the Author write someone only to throw them away? Why not have fewer people of higher quality? Sometimes less is more."

Yawi relaxed his lips. "I understand, human. I do."

"Some of these children...they will honestly never amount to anything in their lives. Why would the Author even make them if they're so...useless?"

"Are they, though?" The wolf made a vague gesture toward them. "They are children. None of them come from successful homes, but not all of them know that. They see the world differently, and sometimes, they are the only joy their mothers know. Do their mothers not deserve that joy?"

"They do, but...a sick vine is a sick vine, no matter how long it grows. A proper gardener will root it out."

"And yet a sick vine that eventually recovers and bears fruit is now more resistant to that sickness. Some sicknesses take longer to cure than others."

Sabelu again looked at the children, many of them excited, a few still afraid of the horses.

"The vines that are healthy should be carefully tended," Yawi said. "The vines that are sick should also be tended, cared for, until health is restored. Then they must be pushed to flourish as an even stronger vine."

"For some of them, though...that's generations away."

"Then it's a good thing the Krydik have long lives and excellent knowledge of the old ways and the sorceries."

"But I won't be there to see it."

Now the wolf gave him a look. "You've already watched it happen."

It was something to think about anyway, and Sabelu couldn't deny that the camp did give him some ray of hope that things would actually work out in the end. The sheer joy of the children as they listened to elder stories, played traditional games, and were permitted to speak their own languages, it was almost like an escape from the way things were. Or maybe this was reality, the way things were, and everything else was a fabrication. Small islands of reality amid a sea of falsehood.

That didn't mean that things were always smooth sailing. It didn't take but two weeks for the vandalism to begin. It was simple enough at first, paint and trash, maybe a drunk teenager wandering through looking to pick a fight with a dirty Indian. Ola Achukma did not oblige such challenges, instead preferring to demonstrate the art of diplomacy, but Galiliga was more than happy to demonstrate what years of hard labor, traditional hunting, and wrestling championships could produce.

Then the arsonists came. The only reason there wasn't a good old-fashioned Indian raid on the nearest town was because no one was at the camp at the time, meaning no one was hurt. More importantly, no children were hurt.

This did not mean that they were happy about it.

Sabelu walked the area with his father and brothers. All of the buildings and structures had been reduced to ash, the grass and undergrowth incinerated, and many of the surrounding trees damaged as well. Sabelu nudged a lump of charred wood with his foot, deliberately ignoring the noose that had been hung from a branch at the edge of the clearing.

"We could—" Ola Achukma began.

"Even if we found who did this, they will never be held accountable," Galiliga cut in, giving their father a look. "They're probably bragging about it to everyone in town, will probably even get a medal for it. 'Heroic White Boy Burns Down Savage Indian Training Camp' as a newspaper headline."

"It doesn't help that there are groups in the west who are training for just such occasions," Blaknik threw in. "Kah Kitowak mentioned something about a similar movement in the north among the Anishinaabek. He said he was trying to counsel against it, but..." He shrugged. "This is Kah Kitowak we're talking about." He glanced at Sabelu who just shrugged and gave a half-committed nod.

"Our focus here is the children," Ola Achukma said. "Giving them a safe place where they can be who their ancestors hoped they would be, but better. We can't fight every battle or we only exhaust ourselves."

"Us four, maybe," Galiliga said. "But once again, there are millions of Natives, all of whom have been beaten down and trodden into the dirt, some more severely than others. If they don't have an outlet, a purpose, a way of fighting back, then they're only going to dissolve into drunk, wasted shells that used to be men." He added before Ola Achukma could speak, "If the United States can send soldiers to every corner of this fucking planet to fight a war, why can't we?"

Now Ola Achukma bristled. "Did the last war teach you nothing? Or have you forgotten what that was like in the last hundred years? Have you forgotten your dead brother's face already?"

Galiliga drew a breath and straightened. "I haven't forgotten Tsona. I also know that he died because I abandoned him." He gestured to the ashy carnage. "So I will not abandon the people here."

"We—are—Krydik. I may have Choctaw and American blood, but I cannot claim loyalty to them and to the people of Hlohi. You have even more in you from your mother's side."

"Which means I have a duty to them all."

"Even the Americans that are doing this?" Ola Achukma mirrored his son's gesture. "Or do you suddenly get to pick and choose your loyalty based on convenience and who you happen to agree with at the time? Let me tell you something, that is a very selfish stance to take. Loyalty to the spirits, loyalty to the truth, loyalty to the people. And our people are the Krydik. We abide by the rules of the Krydik, and right now, those rules say that we do not engage in physical warfare!"

Galiliga made a scoffing sort of sound and stormed off. Blaknik glanced uncertainly at Ola Achukma and Sabelu, then timidly went after Galiliga.

Sabelu walked up beside his father who sighed. "He's going to be the death of me."

Sabelu nodded. "He will."

"That wasn't a question."

"But it is a statement of truth." He added quickly, "It won't be anything intentional, such as murder."

Ola Achukma rubbed his face and turned away, to the north. "He's going to go north and undermine everything Kah Kitowak is trying to do to stop the Anishinaabek aggressors." He glanced back at Sabelu. "I don't have your gifts; I just know my son." He looked around. "Will it always be this bad, the hostility and vandalism?"

"Not always, no," Sabelu replied, electing to stop there in his answer.

"Well, that's good anyway. Means we might make some progress in the next few decades."

Sabelu elected not to reply.

"Your brother is very much like Yvgidahi, I think," his father went on, "when Yvgidahi was a younger man, I mean. And Blaknik is very much like my father, very much like me."

"And me?" Sabelu wondered, hoping his tone conveyed a sort of non-threatening challenge.

"I don't know. Sixty years ago, I might have said you were like Anagalisgi, or Yvgidahi in his later years. Now...maybe still Anagalisgi, though I never got the sense that he was ever trying to run away from the people. Help in an unconventional way, but never run away."

Every word that his father spoke, Sabelu heard as a familiar, already knowing what he would say, as if from a dream, but just now hearing it for real. And yet, he was still surprised and a little hurt by the answer being spoken aloud.

"I remember you said once that you don't see children like you do adults," Ola Achukma went on. "You don't see their hopes and ambitions and dreams, and you don't know their thoughts. That's why you always preferred Blaknik to Galiliga, at least for a while. Why don't you take charge of this camp?"

"Me?" Sabelu asked.

"It would be helping the people, you don't have to deal with politics back home, and you're not inundated with the minds and lives of so many others. And you know all the traditional ways, all the languages. Why not?"

"Tsitsa, I may not know the minds of children, but yet that is how I have survived most every human interaction. It is how my social life is structured, knowing the thoughts and motivations of others."

"Sabelu, you don't have a social life. You live alone in your cabin." Ola Achukma went on before Sabelu could speak. "At least give it some thought; it's going to be a little while before this place is ready to re-open anyway."

Indeed it took a whole year, between standard delays as well as fending off the local hooligans who figured if they could get away with it once, they could do it again. It got to the point where a group of local Shawnee men were camping there in shifts so as to respond immediately to any mischief that might be going on.

Ola Achukma confided in Sabelu about it one evening over tea. They were in Sabelu's cabin, the camp supposed to reopen in just a few days.

"You said this camp would help many children," Ola Achukma said, his tone entirely lacking in confidence. "And yet we've seen, what, one hundred fifty total, and then it gets burned down."

"And rebuilt," Sabelu stated simply.

"And harassed. Circled by vultures. The Shawnee and a few others have taken up guard duty, but won't that only escalate things? With the more disgruntled people in the west and the work in the north which..." Ola Achukma shook his head. "Why...? Galiliga has seen war and he's lost a brother. Why is he so intent on...raising up an army in the north?"

"He's not raising up an army, he's just joined their movement." Sabelu took a drink. "As for why he's doing it..." He hesitated and took another quick drink. "Quite frankly, it's because of me."

His father's expression turned both confused and hurt. "You told him to do this?"

Sabelu shook his head. "No, not at all. Galiliga looks at me and sees a man who crossed the desert to single-handedly slay the evil demon and save the people, just like the heroes in the stories he admired as a child. And he looks at himself as a man who lost a war, got his brother killed, and did almost nothing to help the people or his brother when he was in danger of being murdered and later exiled."

"But he followed your directive to help the Old Land. He is a well-respected leader of Bear Clan, and he has done time on the national council as well."

"He compares himself to me. If I saved the people, he thinks he has to also."

"Surely this isn't the way to go about it. If you tell him not to—"

"Then it's my idea, my plan, my credit. He wants to emulate me, but he doesn't actually want me to be involved in any way, which is a little ironic."

Ola Achukma shifted uncomfortably. "You know what they're doing, right? It's not some minor political movement; some of the members are actively calling for violence."

"War is a tool, just as peace is a tool," Sabelu said knowingly.

His father gave him a look. "Are you going to do anything to stop him?"

"He won't listen to me."

"Have you tried?"

Sabelu knew where this was going. His father would ask him to try, Sabelu would, Galiliga would disregard him, their father would try to reason with him, nothing would change except that Galiliga would be even more convinced of his own self-righteous purpose that it would get their father killed in the end.

Would it be better, then, for Sabelu to not speak with Galiliga? Well, Ola Achukma was going to talk to him regardless. Whether or not their father would die was up for speculation, and Sabelu didn't like to speculate. It would do no good; he saw what would be and tried to limit his stress to that knowledge only.

"It's going to be a longer, more drawn-out affair," Sabelu said, cutting into his father wondering about what he might say to persuade Galiliga away from the northern radicals. "The camp is reopening in a few days, and you need to be there."

The sudden change in topic jarred Ola Achukma enough that he paused dumbly for a moment, unable to respond, before picking up on the line of thought. "I still don't understand why you want me to oversee this and not you."

"You're a better diplomat than I am." Sabelu added, "So maybe I don't see children, but I don't know that I ever truly was a child. You have the advantage of being able to meet with children in that sense of wonder and curiosity, not knowing what the day will bring. That's what they need. They need someone with whom they can discover the world, not someone like me who is going to dictate it to them."

"Children still need discipline. Even you did naughty things and threw a few temper tantrums when you were little. I'm sure you could keep them in line. Mothers and fathers exist for a reason."

Sabelu raised a brow. "Would that make me the father or you the mother?"

Ola Achukma opened his mouth, realized what was said, then closed his mouth and settled for a look. When Sabelu laughed, he said, "All right, you, are you saying we need to get your mother and sister involved in this?"

"It would be a good idea. Girls need a role model, too, in this rediscovery. You've seen some of the insane things the Americans are permitting their women to do."

A few days later, Sabelu stood before a group of nineteen children, flanked by Ola Achukma, Nendawagan, Netami, and Blaknik. Well, that was how they introduced themselves to the children. To the white men, they were known as Saul, Roland, Diane, Natalie, and Blake Aberdeen, and Wolf Clan of the Krydik people quickly became synonymous with the camp.

It wasn't what Sabelu would call fun necessarily, but it kept his family off his back about rejoining the people, rejoining the pack so-to-speak. Even so, he was happy to return to his cabin at the end of the summer, and he was even happier when he found Yukpa waiting for him.

"How long have you been waiting?" he wondered, taking her in his arms.

"Long enough to wait, then get annoyed, then marvel at the fact that you're working with children," she replied, her expression fiendishly seductive as she pushed her hands under his cotton shirt and pulled it off. Then she started fumbling with his leather belt. He did not resist; he was glad to be rid of his white clothes, like his white name. All a mirage, a disguise so he could walk around in another world. Here, he was Sabelu. With Yukpa's help, he was soon naked and even more quickly erect.

"Looks like someone missed me," Yukpa observed.

He did not say anything to that, just pushed up her skirt and took her. There was an advantage to having the intimate knowledge of all of the peoples, such as knowing what would and would not work. An advantage to knowing other people meant that he knew what she liked, even felt what she felt to a limited extent, which only propelled him further.

"All this work at some children's camp in the Old Land," she murmured afterwards, tracing his chest, "and you still don't give a thought to a family of your own?"

"No," he replied, only half awake. "I know what will be, and that's not part of it."

"Are you sure? You talk about what will be, what should be, what must be. You complain that you know things, you complain that you don't know things. Obviously you don't know everything, so how can you know what you don't know?"

"Because family is important enough that its presence or absence does not go unnoticed."

She hummed something like an acknowledgment, then said, "One day, you will father one of my children."

"Let's be honest, I'm going to father more than one of your children." He gave her a look. "I know your plans."

Yukpa just grinned. "You are too amazing of a man to waste. The people need more men like you."

"You think you know me well enough to say that, do you? There are plenty of people who think I'm a terrible person."

"Then they are, quite simply, stupid and unappreciative of your talents and everything you've done for the people. Was anyone else going to go after the demons in the desert?"

"I don't know. We didn't have time to find out."

"Exactly. We need more men like you, who know the need, see the need, and address the need." She rolled over and pressed her hips against his as she stretched. "Your sons will be great. I just know it."

Sabelu did not respond to that. Women were the givers of life, and far be it from him to suggest that she not have children. It was a little disconcerting to think that a few of them would technically be his, although blood was far less important than bonds forged in time and fire. And on top of that, children belonged to their mother first, clan second, and father third, if at all. Everyone else was merely a helper, and a hermit in the hills didn't even register.

Still, he wasn't entirely sure how he was really going to feel the first time he walked into an annual festival and met a young boy with shining gold eyes.

DᏟᏪᎪᏁ ᎠᎾᎢ ᎠᏉᏋᎢ

Atlasgone Anagwoge Adolv'i
Revenge of the Dead

Another year, another group of kids.

Car after car pulled up to the drop off area, plopped down two or three kids, and drove away. The dirt lot was too small for everyone to be able to park and have long goodbyes. It was supposed to have been expanded this spring, but it never happened.

That was all right, Sabelu thought, watching the grounds fill up with children of varying skin tones. The lot only saw this much activity twice a week, and even then it was only for a couple hours.

He stood at the door of the small office building, watching everything happen. Netami greeted the children with big smiles and bigger hugs, leading them to the main pavilion to keep them corralled and entertained until everyone arrived and received their cabin and leader assignments. She, Sabelu, and Ola Achukma were the only ones still working at the camp. Nendawagan had returned to Aktiya Waya to keep the fire warm as it were. Galiliga remained in the north with the American Indian Movement, and Blaknik had meekly followed.

Kah Kitowak, having failed in his mission to direct the movement in a less radical direction, had come to work at the camp, as if replacing one brother or the other. He, too, greeted the children and got them directed to the pavilion.

"How's it going out here?" Ola Achukma asked, appearing beside Sabelu from inside the office building. He surveyed the scene. "First camp of the season, looks good so far."

"I suppose," Sabelu said evenly.

His father did not reply. They'd had the discussion before. The world wasn't going back to the way it used to be. The gap between the people of the Old Land and the Krydik was widening exponentially.

It wasn't about the destination but the journey, they said.

If you ended life the same way you started, your life was wasted, they said.

Pithy, feel-good commentary to cover up the slow death of the people. Assimilation by necessity, fatigue, and time.

Sabelu watched a group of light-skinned, dark-haired girls sit down to play a game. They were local tribal members, though they didn't really look it. They went to a white school, and their parents, who were also mostly fair-skinned, worked white jobs. This camp was just a regular summer camp to them, like Girl Scouts, which they also participated in.

Maybe he'd been too optimistic about the role the people of the Old Land would play in restoring things. Otherwise, what was the point in keeping the Krydik separate? Surely they couldn't be expected to work together?

He'd expected great wildfires from the black phoenix, not this slow smolder.

"I think that's most of them," his father said suddenly. "There might be a few stragglers, but let's get this week started."

Ola Achukma moved off, gathering up a couple boys who had wandered off trying to catch a frog, then going to the main pavilion to address the group. Sabelu followed at a distance. There were sixty-five kids in all this week, all of them stuffed into this camp because their parents weren't ready for them to be done with school quite yet. Enrollment for the rest of the season hovered around an average of forty.

Introductions were made. Sabelu noted how, although most had translated traditional surnames, only eleven of the kids had traditional given names, and only one of them was not translated. Once they were separated into their cabin groups, the first "game" the kids played was taking a traditional, untranslated name to use for the duration of the camp.

"The good news," Ola Achukma said, joining Sabelu at the edge of the activity while the kids talked and laughed amongst themselves, "is that those who have been here before are using the same names. They probably use them at home, too."

"Some do, yes," Sabelu agreed. "But it is a bit strange when the other counselors have to do it, too." He looked at one of the male counselors, a large man of mixed tribal origin. He had never been to the boarding schools, but his parents had, and they had named him Christopher out of fear that he might be taken away from them if he did not act white enough. All of his siblings suffered similarly. In spite of heavy Native influence, especially Sabelu who was always available to answer any and all questions about his heritage, he remained Christopher Randolph Wright, though during camp he might also go by Red Crow. Didn't even bother to translate it, just Red Crow. His excuse was that his parents were two different tribes and he didn't want to favor one or the other, not realizing that in doing so, he was favoring the tribe of his captors instead.

"This is the Old Land, Sabelu," his father reminded him. "It's not our war anymore. We help where we can, but no more than we're asked."

"We're asked less and less every year."

"I don't see you running off to join your brothers."

Sabelu huffed a sigh, trying to keep his expression at least neutral in front of all the children.

Before he could say anything, his father stepped away to call their attention for something new.

Sabelu glanced at his sister, sitting in a circle with the eight girls she would be spending the week with. She wore a pleated cotton skirt with a flower pattern on it and a solid color blouse, all of the colors vibrant against her dark skin. Her hair was neatly braided, large beaded clips at the base of each braid with a few beads interwoven at the very ends. She wore a beaded necklace and several bracelets as well, though they were currently being passed around by the girls in her group. Every so often she chanced a look at Kah Kitowak. Only his age guaranteed his genetics, but he still didn't really call anywhere home. Cree by ancestry, Metis by nationality, but homeless and lost by every other measure, wandering from people to people, failing at every cause he joined.

One hundred years. A century to prepare for the rebirth of the cerberus and the wolf dog. A century to take down the serpent and the black phoenix. They were now unquestionably on the downside of that hundred year hill, and this was where they were. True, his visions hadn't changed and he still saw their victory, it just...didn't feel as great as he thought it would. He didn't want these allies. He wanted the people they had been two hundred years ago.

He'd just seen Yukpa a few days ago, but he wouldn't mind another visit. Maybe he would send her a message and see about meeting her between camps. Sabelu was only at the camp as the storyteller and authenticity advisor, which was just a fancy way of saying he answered any questions anyone had about the old ways or any history. Strictly speaking, he didn't have to stay at the camp overnight. Once the kids were dismissed from the evening fire, he could go home. He only stayed because his father asked him to in order to keep a prophetic ear out for any shenanigans. While the camp had not been burned down again, vandalism was still not uncommon.

So he stayed, tending to the sacred fire and waiting for any shenanigans. It was the closest he'd come to performing any priestly duties since he left Aktiya Waya. Well, that wasn't entirely true. He had gone to the annual festival a few times and done ceremonies there, and he had done a couple weddings and funerals by specific request.

"Am I intruding?"

Sabelu looked up as his father entered the camp townhouse. He shook his head and motioned him in.

"Nothing to be worried about tonight," Sabelu reported, placing another log carefully on the fire.

"Well, that's good to know for the camp, but what about you?" his father wondered. "The only time I see you is this camp."

"And if I were married and living in another village with my wife, the only time you would see me is the annual festival. All things considered, then, this is a luxury." At his father's look, Sabelu shrugged. "Nothing new. The life of a hermit doesn't change much."

"No, I expect not." Ola Achukma shifted in his seat. "I expect you already know the answer—maybe you even know the question—but do you know why I stopped using the sorceries and allowed myself to age, and your mother didn't?"

"Because you want to experience as much of life as possible before you die, and even old age is part of life. That, and Tsitsi isn't convinced that she's done having children. She's just trying to figure me out first."

"And having to clean up messes in your absence."

Sabelu shrugged, not taking his gaze away from the fire. "That, too."

He could feel his father's eyes on him. "How are your brothers?"

"Wait a couple weeks and you can ask them yourselves."

Ola Achukma took a measured breath. "Is this going to be a peaceful encounter?"

"The movement is less violent than you give them credit for— remember that hatred breeds exaggeration—but it's only going to be the two of them anyway, so yes."

Now his father released a relieved sigh. "Good. I didn't appreciate it when they brought more of their group here to talk to the children. They may not have told the children to get violent, but, as you've put it, they're seeking a physical solution to a spiritual problem."

He stood before Sabelu could reply. "Another season, another week. We have an early day tomorrow. Get some sleep."

And he departed.

The children visited Sabelu twice a day for traditional stories and history lessons, once before breakfast and again before bed. He always made sure to include the Whites and Shadows as much as he could, trying to get them to understand that everything in the waking world was just an echo of the spirit world.

He hadn't seen Yawi in a long time, though he would wake up to wolf tracks around either his cabin or the camp townhouse every so often. He also hadn't seen his uncle, and if Anagalisgi left similar small signs, Sabelu did not know what they were.

It was at lunch on a Thursday when Galiliga and Blaknik showed up. A few of the boys who knew them from past years jumped up from their meals and ran to greet them, begging for war stories from the north. Sabelu did not miss the expression on his father's face at such a phrase, but he managed to wipe it off by the time he got to greet his other sons.

"Camp looks busy," Galiliga observed mildly, sending the boys back to their groups.

"We're averaging about forty every week for the season," Ola Achukma replied. He gave the two a once-over. "You look good. But then, you don't spend the winters in the north, do you?"

Galiliga shook his head. "Of course not. I still have to go home for a time to see my wife and contribute to the clan. It's a bit difficult because of how the years get out of sync, and I'm never sure just what season I'm walking into, but I do what I must."

"They've missed you at the festival the last few years," Sabelu said, "but it just means your sons have less competition." He gave his brother a look. "The ones who aren't with you, anyway."

"At least I have sons to help me. At least I am including them." Galiliga made a gesture. "And Blaknik."

Blaknik flinched.

"Please, not here in front of the children," Ola Achukma interrupted, "and certainly not at meal time. Are you hungry?"

"Getting there, but I'll eat," Galiliga said, hardly breaking stride.

If there was one battle Sabelu had won concerning the camp, it was the food. All of the food was game, forage, and garden, with nothing allowed to be store-bought. Most of it was from Earth, or Earth animals anyway, but every so often he would bring in something from Hlohi, just to shake things up. He'd also convinced his father to organize a foraging activity for the campers. Every week, the kids would go out and search for a particular edible plant that would be added to one of the meals for that week. A few of the kids, those that had the option, had started to change up the week they came to camp just so they could forage for different plants and learn more.

Today's lunch was rabbit that was marinated and then shredded on fried cornbread with honeyed spring greens. Kids that were new to the camp blanched at such foods initially, but as Sabelu pointed out, if they were hungry, they would eat. Most came to love it. Those who didn't, well, they didn't tend to come back to camp.

If there was any advantage to being Krydik, it was having their own language so they could talk without worrying about the kids understanding them, even if they were arguing.

"I didn't realize the camp had been opened up to the general public," Galiliga began evenly once they were seated together with their food.

"It remains tribal members only," Ola Achukma replied, his tone equally even. "Different tribes have different rules about who can be a member. And just remember, it used to be based on character and upholding the values and traditions of the people, not their appearance. In the early days of the Krydik, it was much easier to tell who was Cherokee or Choctaw or—"

"I'm not arguing," Galiliga cut in. "Actually, I think it's great."

"Which part?"

"Separating people based on values, not appearance. It's one thing we do better than the Americans who claim they invented such a concept but don't adhere to it themselves."

The only thing Sabelu was getting from his father was pure confusion.

"When the nations rise against them, it will be far more confusing for them if they think their own people are against them," Galiliga went on.

Ola Achukma nodded. "There it is. Back to the violence."

"We're going to Washington, D.C. this weekend."

"To do what? And who is we?"

"A group of us from the movement," Blaknik answered. "We're taking a proposal before the congress."

Now their father shifted in his seat. "A proposal? Some form of legislation, then, not a violent protest?"

"Yes." Blaknik shrugged. "Well, mostly."

Ola Achukma gave his son a look.

It was Galiliga who answered, "We're not going to be tricked into thinking they're not going to try and make an example of us. In Yvgidahi's time, in his very Book, a bunch of leaders went on a mission of peace and were slaughtered. We're not going to let that happen to us. We may not throw the first punch, but we're not going to roll over if something does happen."

Ola Achukma rubbed his face. "And you're telling me this because...why? Why can't we just have a good lunch together?"

"We'd like you to come with us."

"And do what? You have capable leaders, even lawyers. What do you need me for? Obviously I can't explain that I'm the son of John Aberdeen anymore."

"We'd like a representation of elders with us, to show that this isn't just from some hot-headed young men, but from the roots and soul of the nations. Most of the elders don't like to travel, though."

Ola Achukma sighed and deliberately took a bite of food to avoid answering right away. Then, "It used to be the other way around, you know. Young men would ask for the elders' blessing before running off to do a thing. But I suppose it is easier to ask forgiveness than permission." His tone was accusatory. "Just as Nvya usurped Yvgidahi's authority because a bunch of young men thought themselves better and more knowledgeable."

"Yvgidahi and Anagalisgi were young men when they embraced the sorceries and hid the people on Hlohi," Sabelu threw in.

"You agree with them?" Ola Achukma put his hands up. "Well, maybe that was my first mistake. Sabelu, how is this going to turn out? What happens next?"

Sabelu nodded slowly. "Well, we're not going to resolve anything at this lunch. You're going to take an easy out by saying lunch is over and it's time for the next activity. Galiliga and Blaknik will stick around to help this afternoon. We are going to intentionally not sit with each other at dinner. The kids will come to hear my stories and lessons in the townhouse, as they normally do. You, Itsitsa, will be moved by some of those stories and agree to go with Galiliga and the others to Washington, D.C., provided it remains peaceful.

"It will be, at first, and you will meet with several senators and representatives and other people of various importance. There will be lots of pomp and circumstance, some media coverage, and so on. Things will appear to be going very well."

"I don't like the word 'appear,'" Ola Achukma stated sourly.

"Someone will join the group waiting outside, appearing as a friend and ally. They are going to incite the group to agitation, not quite violence—"

"Who is he?" Galiliga demanded. "We'll keep a watch and not allow him near."

Sabelu shrugged. "Well, that's the thing. They know you're coming. They have a plan for whether they are accepted into your group or not. They'll manufacture something if they need to. They might just shoot first and claim self-defense, knowing that the newspapers and general public will believe them regardless."

"We can't not go. We can't be intimidated by a little violence. If they are willing to go the extra mile, then we must be also."

"What happens then?" Ola Achukma wondered.

"Blaknik escapes. Galiliga is arrested." Sabelu paused as he looked at his father. "And you die."

"What?" Galiliga cut in. "Impossible! I'll watch over him myself!"

"Maybe he shouldn't go," Blaknik stated, and it was unclear just whom he speaking to.

Ola Achukma just cleared his throat. "Well, Sabelu, I think you're right on the first part anyway. I am going to step out of this conversation because the kids need to go to their next activity."

With that, he stood and walked to the center of the group where he whistled for attention.

Galiliga turned to face Sabelu.

"How can you say that?!" he hissed.

"Because it's the truth," Sabelu said, meeting his brother's gaze. "It doesn't care whether you like it or whether you agree, and neither do I."

"But now that we know, we can change it," Blaknik said, expression a mix of worry and guilt. "He doesn't need to come. If they're only going to ambush us, whatever we do or don't do, it makes no difference if he's there."

"Surely things can change," Galiliga stated harshly, as if daring Sabelu to refute him.

Sabelu shifted in his seat and scooped up the last of his honeyed greens. "I admit, I'm not a fan of the Old Land and what it's become, but they do occasionally come up with philosophical questions to pique my interest. Have you heard of Schrodinger's cat?"

"I have," Blaknik said simply, even as Galiliga just looked confused.

"If you put a cat in a box with poison, is the cat alive or dead? No one knows until the box is opened. Similarly, if I do or don't say something, is that what would have always happened, or could you have done something to change it? Did Asdeoha die according to plan as I told him, or not, because I do not believe my words were properly recorded?"

"Do you ever make sense?" Galiliga interrupted. "Is there a way to save Itsitsa or not? Should we just not take him?"

"He won't let you go without him," Sabelu said. "Because now he's thinking about things. His life, his work, conversations he's had with me and you and others. He's wondering about his Book, the War of the Old Land, everything. And he will come to the conclusion that he must be willing to die for something or else there will be nothing to live for."

"That's stupid; he has this camp. He's done good work with it. He likes it here."

"And yet, no matter what he does, what he tells you, you still end up running off on some other adventure, some other mission. He is convinced that he isn't doing right by you. And he will go to protect you if nothing else."

Now Galiliga blinked. Sabelu finished off his lunch.

"Maybe we shouldn't go," Blaknik said, picking at the greens. "Not the movement, but just me and you. Then Itsitsa won't have to go."

"We helped plan this. We can't back out now; we'll look like cowards."

"We're trying to save our father."

Galiliga stood, posture annoyed, mind racing, but tongue silent. He shifted his stance several times, looked around at the kids as they were being organized for their next activity, then looked back at Sabelu. "So this is just like the War of the Old Land and losing Tsona, isn't it? If I hadn't committed myself to Nvya, if we had left at any point—the war was already lost; it was just about formality at that point—would Tsona still be alive?"

"I can't speak for hypotheticals almost a hundred and fifty years old," Sabelu told him calmly, "but I do know that the war proved what it meant to be a man. And sometimes, men are called to die."

Galiliga leaned over the table, and it was all he could do not to slam his fist. "That's great, when it's for a cause, not because your brother or your son condemns you."

"Tsona went with you willingly. He made his choices, just as you made yours. And now Itsitsa is making his choice."

"But this isn't his cause. He never wanted anything to do with the movement." He straightened and shook his head. "I can't let him die for something he doesn't believe in."

"He is going to die for you," Sabelu said firmly before his brother could leave. "Because he believes in you."

Galiliga did not respond to that, just left the table. He would head to one of the short hiking trails that had been cut through the woods, then join in the afternoon activities, as Sabelu had predicted.

"Is it hard?" Blaknik asked, staring at his plate. "Knowing what you do?"

Sabelu shrugged. "I've gotten used to it."

"Yes, for everyone else. But you weren't there when Tsona died. Itsitsa is the first family member whose death you've predicted and faced."

"I've known about it since I was a child. He's known about it for thirty years."

"And I just learned about it now." Blaknik looked at him with a soulful gaze. "Is there nothing that can be done, or am I going to be facing the last few days of life with my father, marching around in some...political protest?"

Sabelu let out a breath. "Would you have done things differently if you had known?"

"Maybe. Yes. I suppose it would have been more important to find a wife and have children." Blaknik sighed. "Maybe I should have done that anyway. Galiliga is the fighter, not me. I mean, we've done some good work, but seeing that it's all been leading to this..." He shook his head. "How much responsibility do I bear in Itsitsa's death?"

"You won't even see it happen."

Blaknik grunted. "You know, reading Itsitsa's Book, I always loved the part where Yvgidahi avenges Tsona. Obviously, I never knew him, but I always loved envisioning him riding on his horse, making that final, majestic leap, and crushing our brother's killer. Sometimes, I would pretend that he had saved Tsona, and I would wonder what it would be like to have him with us. Maybe he had survived, too, and they were both with us."

Sabelu nodded. "I know."

A melancholy silence settled between them, though the sadness remained primarily on Blaknik. Finally his brother looked up from where he'd been studying his hands. "There's no way?"

Sabelu just shook his head.

His younger brother stood. "Guess I should go and help him out while I still can. Seeing how he's never stopped helping us."

Soon Sabelu was left alone at the table. The kids had all gone to a hill at one end of the camp where a wooden fort had been built just this spring. Sabelu could already see the many afternoons that would be spent trying to capture the fort for one cabin or another.

He returned to the townhouse and stoked the sacred fire, finally sitting and adding a tobacco plug. He closed his eyes and breathed in the sweet smoke. When he opened his eyes, he was startled to find Anagalisgi with him, sitting to his left at the fire.

"That was tobacco," Sabelu stated dumbly.

"Yes, it was," Anagalisgi said. "But not only."

"You had my father add more to it." At his uncle's nod, he asked,

"Why not tell me directly? Why not dream-walk to me?"

"Because I didn't want to. Because I wanted to sit in a traditional hut again, around a proper sacred fire that I didn't have to tend."

"You don't need to ask my permission, Tsidushi, and I suspect you've been doing so for a few years now. Not that I would know since I never see you anymore."

"If a man is convinced of his own superiority, and his superior reasoning tells him to do nothing, perceived inferior voices will do nothing to sway him to action."

"I'm not sure, but I think you're complaining about my ego and apparent laziness."

Anagalisgi gave him a look. "Did your superior reasoning tell you that?" He looked back at the fire. "Ego has always been your bane."

Sabelu shifted position. "You specifically referenced inaction. What are you trying to say? Should I go with my father and brothers to their protest? I've not seen myself there, at least through their eyes."

"You've sat in a long period of waiting, Sabelu, and it's not from lack of tasks to accomplish, but because you lacked interest in them. You thought them beneath you, ever since your trip into the desert."

"I'm here, aren't I? And I did some stuff, tried to help out in the wars."

"But you know your time for action is coming to a rapid close, and it will be forced on you."

Sabelu gave his uncle a look. "Is that a yes, I should go with them?"

"You are a priest and the keeper of the sacred fire. The flame must not go out while you tend it, while this camp is in use. It burns for the next generation while the previous one passes away."

"So, that's a no?" Sabelu sighed and searched through everything he could about the next few days. Netami was the easiest to use, trying to pick out any interactions or even passing glances. "Everything I see says I stay here."

Anagalisgi glanced at him. "Then why the confusion?"

Annoyed, Sabelu answered, "Because if I had been certain, you would have cited my ego."

"If a man does not know where he is going, he consults a map of some form, be it on paper or in the landscape or the stars. If he does know where he is going, does it do any good for him to brag about it?"

"Perhaps, if it's a dangerous path and he must escort others along it. They may want reassurance that he knows where he's going, where he's taking them."

"What if the path isn't dangerous?"

"The path that leads to my father's death is hardly not dangerous."

"But is he afraid?"

"My brothers are."

"Are they the ones dying?"

Sabelu scoffed. "No, but they're about to lose their father. Like Blaknik said, we've known for thirty years at least. They just found out today."

Anagalisgi nodded slowly. "A path that you and your father know. He is not afraid. The path beyond, however, you do not know. And it is one that you and your brothers and sister will have to face together."

"But I do know it. I see everything up to my death. I see things beyond my death."

"The difference between looking at a map and navigating the terrain."

Sabelu rubbed his eyes. "Tsidushi, you speak in circles."

Anagalisgi grinned. "Well, I have to bring some intellectual excitement to your dull I-know-everything-that's-going-to-happen life."

Sabelu just scowled.

"Don't be so bitter, human," a familiar voice rumbled. "Things are going to get exciting again."

Yawi appeared from behind Sabelu and sat by the fire across from Anagalisgi.

"I don't know if exciting is the word I would use," Sabelu said, "but if it means you're back by my side, I guess I'll take it."

The wolf gave him a look. "Idle stones need no guardian."

Sabelu knew full well what the wolf was saying, but he still replied with, "Obviously they do, or the Shadows wouldn't have cared so much about the ruins in the desert, or the device hidden there."

"And now they're coming to take their revenge," Anagalisgi stated.

"Then it's a good thing they don't know what's coming."

His uncle opened his mouth to speak, but before any words came out, there was a shadow at the door and Netami walked in. She did not bother to try and hide her distress as she sat down across from him, blind to both Anagalisgi and Yawi.

"Sabelu, what is this that Blaknik is telling me that Itsitsa is going to die this weekend?" she demanded.

He sighed and bought a brief moment of time by placing a log on the fire. Even then, the only thing he could come up with was, "Yes. And not necessarily this weekend, but next week."

She made a sound that was somewhere between a scoff, a cry, and a disbelieving laugh. "Obviously you've known for a long time, but this is the best you can do for the rest of us? Just a couple days of warning?"

"Some people don't even get that much."

"But we could have!"

"What would you have done differently?" Sabelu wondered honestly. "You still live with our parents, and you've cared for him very well as he has aged. You work with him here at the camp. Galiliga and Blaknik may have cause to grieve as they have been away in the north, but you, not so much."

Netami blinked. "He's our father, Sabelu. You might be able to carry all of his memories and our memories about him and recall them at any time, but we don't have that luxury. And consider this, too, that there will be no more new memories of him. It's all about to come to a very abrupt end."

"You think I don't know that?"

"You don't seem to act like it."

Sabelu shifted position as if covering for how much he was struggling to keep his voice level. "Oh? And what would that look like, exactly?"

"For one, you might be out there spending time with him." She flung an arm wide. "You might have spent more time with him in the last...seven decades that you've separated yourself from society!" She went on before he could speak. "You once said that you can't see yourself, that any visions you have of yourself have to be through someone else's eyes. You don't know how much regret you're going to carry with you if you don't do something now, and take time to appreciate Itsitsa. I don't want to see you carry any regrets."

"Is the absolute worth regretting?"

His sister sighed and shook her head, finally staring into the fire. "At least say goodbye to him. Even if it's not for you, do it for him."

Sabelu nodded. "I will."

It was the most she was going to get from him, but at the moment, it was enough. Netami stood, wiped her face and smoothed her clothes, tried to compose herself and put a smile on her face for the little girls waiting for her outside. She did not say anything more as she left. When Sabelu turned his attention elsewhere, Anagalisgi and Yawi had both vanished.

That evening, as usual, the children came to him for stories. It was a bit crowded, and in the waxing summer heat, Sabelu kept the sacred fire stoked only as much as he had to. This made the lighting rather poor, but this was nothing a little Atsvstdi couldn't fix.

Even before everyone was settled in, some of the kids were blurting out requests.

"Tell a Rabbit story!"

"I wanna hear about Crane and Frog!"

"What about the peace delegation to Charleston?"

"Do you know 'The Owl and the Pussycat'?"

"Actually," Sabelu said, putting his hands up, "I have a new story tonight." That, at least, got them to quiet down. "It's a story about a wolf pack."

"About Yawi?" a younger boy asked.

"Not this time. A different wolf pack. And in this pack there were six wolves, a daddy wolf, a mama wolf, and four pups. One day, the pack was out hunting when they were attacked by a wolverine. Now, wolverines are vicious animals, and it took the wolves by surprise. It wanted to eat the pups, because it knew that if it ate the pups, they would not grow up to be big, strong wolves.

"But wolves are pack, and they work together as much as they can. Even the pups, who were not so smart or well-trained as their parents, instinctively knew some of what they were expected to do. Father Wolf and Mother Wolf tried to direct them as much as possible, but it was difficult to coordinate the pups while at the same time defending them and trying to keep the wolverine at bay. And the wolverine bit the Father Wolf and Mother Wolf many times, especially the Father Wolf.

"The fight was long, and they were traveling near a ravine where a great river frothed and foamed at the bottom. Any animal that fell over the ravine into the water would surely drown. The wolverine knew this and became even more vicious. Finally, it got one of the pups near the edge of the ravine. One step backwards and the pup would fall in the river and drown."

Sabelu paused long enough to take a breath and gauge the reaction from the children. Wide eyes, open mouths, and blessed silence.

"But even as the pup was close to the edge of the ravine, so was the wolverine. Father Wolf leaped forward and hit the wolverine in the side with his head." He saw the hope on the children's faces. "But as the wolverine skittered to the edge, it made a snap at the pup and grabbed it in its mouth. Father Wolf lunged forward and grabbed the wolverine by the scruff before it could go over the edge with the pup.

"Now there were only two options. Father Wolf could let the wolverine go, and the wolverine would take the pup over the edge into the river with it, and they would both drown. Or the wolverine could let the pup go, but if it did that, it would assuredly grab hold of Father Wolf and, because Father Wolf was already weak from fighting, they would go into the river.

"The wolverine let go of the pup. Father Wolf did his best to release the wolverine at the same time, but the wolverine still had too good of a grip on the top of the ledge, and it started to come back, again going for the pup. So he grabbed the wolverine again and flung himself and the predator into the river."

"Where was Mama Wolf?" one girl asked.

"Protecting the rest of the pups," Netami answered behind her.

"The pack protects the young. If there are no young, pretty soon, there will be no pack," Sabelu said.

One of the boys got excited. "I would have jumped in and chomped on the wolverine! Rawr, rawr, rawr!" He made motions with his curled hands like teeth. "Rawr!"

"That's not how it works in sports, and that's not how it works in fighting, either," one of the counselors told him.

"The point is that you all here, all you kids," Sabelu said, gesturing, "are still pups. You're still learning, and that's all right. But being pups doesn't mean that monsters don't want to eat you. In fact, they want to come after you more because they don't want you to grow up big and strong. The good news is that the pack will protect you. Right now, that's your mom and dad, your family, your people. And as you get older, you'll bring more people into your pack, and there will be others that you will be willing to defend. And that's good. The lone wolf dies, but the pack survives."

There were more stories and more lessons, and at the end of the night, as the children were hustled off to bed, Ola Achukma remained. Once everyone was gone, he helped himself to a seat beside Sabelu.

"Was that you trying to convince me to stay or go?" he asked.

"You'd already made up your mind," Sabelu stated.

"Well, you're not wrong."

Sabelu poked at the fire. "Netami gave me a short lecture on how I should have been spending more time with you over the last entirety of my life."

Ola Achukma grinned. "I don't doubt that." He shook his head. "No, it's all right. In a bit of a paradox, fathers want their sons to not need them, and yet need them forever. As much as we may have our disagreements, it gives me great pride to see Galiliga where he is. Respected man of Bear Clan, respected member of this movement, husband, father, uncle, though only tangentially to his wife's nieces and nephews." His tone was lightly joking rather than truly accusatory. "Blaknik is a fine man, too, and I enjoy watching him follow in the footsteps of both his older brothers. And I'm sure Netami will make a good wife."

"She once told me that she's not going to get married until she's fixed me," Sabelu said.

"And is that true?"

"Well, yes and no. She'll get engaged, but I won't live to see her wedding."

Ola Achukma grunted. "Kah Kitowak?"

Sabelu nodded. "Mhm."

"I've seen the looks they share. What does she see in him? He's failed at basically everything he's tried."

"But he keeps trying. And you've seen the state of some of the people, the drugs and alcohol."

"That's a pretty low standard, don't you think?"

"You were perfectly fine with giving him a chance on everything else."

Ola Achukma gave him a look. "I swear, Sabelu, I will haunt you."

Sabelu waved a hand. "Well, if you're going to do that, you might as well visit Netami from time to time, too."

"That's not how that works." His father shifted position. "Besides, if I were to hang around anyone, it would be your mother." His expression changed and he shot Sabelu a glance. "How long until she remarries? I may want to rethink this."

Sabelu shook his head. "She doesn't. Blaknik will provide for her as needed, and Galiliga, too, when he's around Aktiya Waya. Netami will get married and have children of her own, after which she will also forego the sorceries so she will eventually start to age again. Blaknik will get married to a Deer Clan woman and live with her in Lehoyed. Eventually, she will want to move to Aktiya Waya to learn more about the sorceries and the Old Land."

"Do they have children? Netami and Blaknik?"

"They do. Netami has seven and Blaknik has five."

Ola Achukma took an even breath as he stared into the glowing coals. "Sometimes I wish I could see what you see. Just a glimpse."

Sabelu said nothing for a long moment. Then he took his father's hand and, like Anagalisgi dream-walking in broad daylight, he connected their minds.

He didn't understand all the fancy, anatomical terminology for it. It had to do with the nerves in the brain, manipulating the electricity in them. Anagalisgi evidently had enough experience to do it without needing physical contact, but Sabelu was not so talented. He felt his own heart, his own body. He felt the blood, the bone, the nerves deep within. He felt his brain, his mind, where knowledge flowed like a rushing river.

Netami had tried to help him once, tried to understand, and she'd nearly died. Even now, Sabelu prayed that he might just give his father a small peek into his mind, exactly what he wanted to see before he died.

Sabelu did not know if it was necessary, but he brought to mind his mother, his brothers and sister and the grandchildren they would bring.

He wasn't sure if he'd actually closed his eyes or if the images were just so vivid that he lost sight of everything in front of him, but the next thing he knew, his father was withdrawing his hand and he was blinking back to the present moment. Once he could see straight, he looked at his father and saw tears running down his weathered cheeks. But he was smiling.

"Thank you," Ola Achukma whispered.

"You're welcome."

His father stood. "Galiliga is here. He's staying overnight, so he can watch the camp. I think I'm going to pay a visit to the woman I've loved for the last one hundred and seventy years."

He left the townhouse without another word. Sabelu just watched him go, throat tight. Only now was it starting to sink in and settle in his chest like a ton of bricks. Tomorrow would be the last time he would see his father, actually see him. The last time he would actually hear his voice, look in his eyes. As Netami had put it, it would be the last time he would make new memories. After tomorrow, all he would have were the old ones.

He wanted to run after his father, clasp his wrist, and give him a hug, thank him for everything. But he was rooted to the ground, only vaguely aware that the fire needed another log. Blindly, he reached for a chunk of wood and tossed it on.

The following morning, parents arrived at the camp early to pick up their children. All of the counselors were busy making sure the kids got everything packed up, that they took home everything they brought with them and didn't accidentally grab something that belonged to someone else. Sabelu watched from a distance as he always did, gaze fixed on his father.

The difference between a map in his hands and the ground beneath his feet. The difference between someone else's memory of an experience and an experience of his own. Once all the kids were gone and it was time for Ola Achukma to leave with Galiliga and Blaknik, Sabelu couldn't have spoken any words if he tried, and he wasn't sure how or why he'd allowed himself to let go of his father's wrist. Somewhere in the background, Netami was crying. Their mother had wept, too, Sabelu knew. The two would see each other several times over the next few days, but eventually, it would happen.

Sabelu returned to his little cabin on the ridge, a line of ants marching around the perimeter even as Yawi sat patiently by the door. Sabelu paused before he entered and looked at the wolf.

"Was this planned out beforehand, or is this my fault?"

The wolf hesitated. "Time matters little to those like us, and those who use the sorceries are granted a little more flexibility. Yet it remains a force that cannot be ignored, even by us, because you are the prize, and you are bound by time. There are things that must be done. The Author asks certain people to do them. Pleasantly, at first, as honey rather than vinegar. But eventually, either—"

"My fault, then," Sabelu cut in. "My ego from seventy years ago is getting my father killed in the next few days. Even before that, because I've known about this for..." He shook his head and grouchily stalked inside his cabin. "This gift is a curse. I don't want it anymore."

"It is your calling," Yawi said, turning to face inside the cabin now, though not actually entering.

"A calling that I failed before I was even aware of that failing. Or the calling for that matter. Did the Author write me to be a failure?"

The wolf did not answer, and perhaps that was for the best. When Sabelu turned around to address him directly, Yawi was gone.

All that day, and the two that followed, Sabelu just lay in bed. He watched, over and over again, his father's final moments. The sudden surge of violence, the tear gas, the water, the gunshots. Any of those were annoying on their own, and even a gunshot might have been tolerable. But as he rounded a corner, looking for a safe place to conjure Galohisdi, he ran into a police officer. A K9 officer. While Sabelu could not physically see the Shadow within the vision, it was not difficult to imagine either a wolf dog pup or a cerberus pup suddenly possessing the dog, influencing it to ignore its training to subdue and instead go for the savage kill.

Sabelu returned to the camp the next week, but he did not leave the townhouse except to relieve himself. Netami had not come at all. He told only short stories, gave only brief lessons, sent everyone away just as soon as he could.

It was Wednesday, just after lunch, when Blaknik ducked into the townhouse. He looked bad, smelled worse. He stumbled in and collapsed by the fire, unhurt, but obviously overwhelmed and confused, looking for any solace in the flickering firelight.

"Itsitsa?" Sabelu asked.

Blaknik just shook his head. After a moment, when he looked up, Blaknik saw his eyes were red.

"Have you told Itsitsi and Netami?"

Another shake of the head.

Sabelu nodded slowly. "Let me absolve you first, then go home. Let them know, but for the sake of our mother and sister, don't say anything. Ever."

Atlasgone Achuchine Adolv'i

Semper Fidelis

The camp closed down.

Years passed.

Sabelu did not attend festivals. He did not visit Aktiya Waya after his father's funeral. He hadn't seen Yukpa in three years. Any ideas of ensuing grandeur or revenge for his father's death had faded to virtually nothing. Netami, who visited about once a month just to make sure he was still alive, failed to persuade him to return to the people, return to the pack.

He did not spend his time in the deepest bowels of sadness and depression, nor was he unproductive. He continued to hunt, fish, gather firewood, and maintain himself. The difference now, however, was the terrible arguments, with Yawi during the day and with his uncle at night. He didn't want his prophetic gifts anymore. He had fulfilled his great mission to save the people. That was it. Anything he might have done afterwards was so minor that anyone could have done it. He wasn't important anymore. Asdeoha was dead, and he wasn't going to be a priest again. Just take away his gifts and let him live out the last few years of his life as a normal human being.

He couldn't quite bring himself to suicide, at least as far as jumping off a cliff, but then he got an idea of how to best go about it.

"What do you mean you're going to join the United States military?"

Galiliga had come to visit, a yearly ritual rather than monthly. It had been four years since their father's death.

"I mean, I'm leaving," Sabelu stated. "I am going to go to the Old Land —"

"And defend the same government that murdered Itsitsa."

"I'm going for my own reasons."

"Well those reasons are stupid. I don't care what they are, they're stupid. If you want to commit suicide, you've got a cliff a hundred yards that way." Galiliga pointed.

"I know that very well, thank you. And how do you know that this isn't—"

"Oh, please, Sabelu, you haven't cared about the spirits in a long time. This isn't a mission from them, don't lie to me."

Sabelu took a breath, tried not to yell. "Fine. You want me to be honest, I'll be honest. I do want to kill myself. But I'm afraid. The disgrace, the dishonor, I can't stand it. But I can't return to the people. I can't stand to see their lives and listen to their thoughts. I can't. I can't, I can't, I can't. That's why I agreed to help with the camp, because I don't see children the same way."

"So why not reopen the camp?" Galiliga wondered.

"I can't do it. I'm out here in the wilderness, Galiliga, no one around for miles, but I feel trapped. I compare myself—all of my gifts and the things I've done—against all the knowledge of all the warriors and priests of all the people who have come before us. And I fail. I did one great thing, but was it me, or my ego? I don't know. I do know that my own ego and my own justification are what's caused me to wander."

"Then come back."

"I can't, not while I still have these prophetic gifts, not while I can still see people. But I only see our people. United States is still majority white, their military even more so. I don't see them, or not to the extent that I see any of us. Aware of them, but I don't know them before we even speak."

Even now, Sabelu could feel his brother's confusion, not just as perception through body language, but he felt it. Galiliga sighed and said quietly, "Don't go to war just to say you have, little brother. If you must go, go with a purpose, go for a reason. If you are trying to prove yourself in some way, you must know when you have proven enough, or you never will."

Sabelu nodded. "When did you realize you had proven enough?"

His brother hesitated. Then, "Four years ago, when Itsitsa told me so. I suppose I already had, but I just needed to hear it from him." He continued before Sabelu could speak. "He was already proud of you, Sabelu. He always was."

"Well, at least he doesn't have to be here to see this."

"You don't think he is?"

Sabelu shrugged. "I don't know. You're right that the spirits and I don't exactly see eye-to-eye these days."

Galiliga nodded slowly. "I don't know if I want to try and stop you. I don't think it's a good idea for you to go fight for the ones who have been persecuting the people of the Old Land. But I also don't think it's good for you to just sit here and stew in your thoughts because this isn't just going to go away." He put his hands on Sabelu's shoulders. "And the last thing I ever want to do in this life is find you at the bottom of that ravine. I also don't want you coming home in a pine box."

"You've read Itsitsa's Book, you know—"

"The side of a mountain, yes, you've said. But you say things like that, and then you talk about jumping off a cliff. What am I to believe, Sabelu? I don't see what you do, I don't know whether things can change. To me, things just happen." He continued, "Be wise, Sabelu. Seek counsel. If you do decide to leave, at least get the blessing of a priest. And make sure to tell Itsitsi you're leaving, so she doesn't go looking at the bottom of the cliff."

Sabelu had no real intention of doing any of that when he did finally make the decision to conjure Galohisdi and offer himself to the United States Government. However, unlike his father's time when a man could just walk into a tavern, sign a piece of paper, grab a uniform and a few supplies, and be in the army, the modern process was a little more complicated. He needed identification and a high school diploma or GED and a driver's license and he needed to pass a bunch of tests. Then he would be sent to basic training where there would be even more papers and more tests.

When his father and brothers had opened up the camp, they'd had to convince the government that the Krydik people existed. It saved a lot of time now, except for the fact that the Krydik did not issue any sort of formal identification for its members. Sabelu didn't want to ask for help, but he also didn't want to go it alone, and he had far less experience dealing with white politics and requirements than his brothers. Seeing how he wanted to be rid of his prophetic gifts, he was trying to use them as little as possible and did not bother looking into his brothers' memories for the things they had to do with the movement in the north.

"We've never had a problem with people trying to impersonate us," Galiliga said. "Believe me, no Indian wants to claim to be us."

"No, but there are plenty of whites and excluded mixed-bloods who might," Sabelu told him. "Honestly, I don't care. We know who we are. But the government has a little harder view of things."

They were standing in Galiliga's house in Yonhi. His children, now well grown, were moved out, though a grandchild would run through occasionally. His wife was out in the fields.

Galiliga folded his arms. "So you're still going through with this."

Sabelu nodded. "I am. It's the first direction I've had in a long time."

"Are you sure it's the right one?" At Sabelu's look, Galiliga sighed. "All right." He mulled over a few thoughts. "When Itsitsa finally got the Krydik officially recognized, the government was obligated to set aside a little bit of land, one of their infamous reserves. It did not say how big this piece had to be—it's only a few acres—in addition to converting the camp grounds to Krydik land. It might not be a bad idea to actually make use of the land as a sort of base of operations for people to use when they go to the Old Land. No one here cares about ID cards, but we might keep them there, just to use if needed."

Within a year, the tiny plot of land had a small structure on it, just a few rooms. They had electricity, running water, even a phone line in case one of the other tribes wanted to get a hold of them. All of it very modern. Then they got in a modern vehicle—owned by someone else but driven by Sabelu who had learned to drive and gotten his license—and run to the local Rite Aid where pictures were taken and cards were printed.

"Why can't the government just be grateful for any help they get?" Sabelu wondered, looking at the shiny card in his hand. "Why do they care who or what I am?"

"Times have changed," Galiliga said, shrugging. "And you're no longer fighting on home soil." He studied his younger brother. "You're still sure you want to do this?"

No. "Yes."

"Have you talked to Itsitsi?"

"Not yet, but I will."

"And a priest?"

Sabelu didn't want to, but it didn't feel right to leave without at least trying first. The blessing wasn't anything big or extravagant, but it felt rote and mechanical. Dikdi performed the blessing because he was asked to, not because he agreed with the decision.

Nendawagan didn't agree either, and Sabelu made sure to keep his visit brief. From there, it was straight back to the recruiter's office with all of his new (and sometimes forged, as in the case of the diploma) paperwork. He'd been a little anxious about the ASVAB and other testing simply because he was not that well acquainted with the Old Land. His saving grace was that the test was less about rote knowledge and more about logical application, which he could do easily. When his score came back, he had his pick of branches and jobs.

He chose the Marines for a couple of reasons. First, because his father and brother had commented multiple times on how strong and reliable they were. Second, because he didn't want to follow his father and brother quite that closely.

"Any particular job you'd like to do?" the recruiter asked.

Sabelu had been told on several occasions that it didn't matter what he answered because he was going to be placed wherever the need was highest according to his test scores.

"I didn't have anything particular in mind, no," he answered,

"Well, you'll have a few weeks to think about it."

Sabelu couldn't read the recruiter like he could those back home, but that didn't mean the man was as stoic as he might have imagined. He wanted to ask questions, but he also couldn't get too familiar with the bodies he pushed through the door. He was just here to find fresh meat for the front lines.

The following morning, Sabelu got on the bus. He didn't know anyone, and he found that he kind of liked it. Looking around the bus, he saw mostly white, some black, but no natives. None of his ancestral peoples. He picked a window seat and waited quietly. Four men went past, one woman, then someone decided he needed a riding buddy.

"Hey," the man said, holding out a friendly hand. He was eight if he was eighteen, light blond hair, and a mustache so light it might have glowed. "Name's Miles."

"Sabelu," he replied, taking the hand.

"Yeah? You're Indian, right? Trying to escape the reservation?"

"For a while, I guess."

"Cool. I'm carrying about four generations of Marines. Got to make Dad proud since I'm the oldest."

"My father and two of my brothers were in the Army."

"One-up on them, eh? Right on. Welcome to the Jarhead Club."

Those who had already been in Jarhead Club for some time, however, had a little different welcome party for the recruits as they disembarked and knelt on the yellow footprints. Thus began thirteen weeks of Hell.

This was more difficult for Sabelu than he thought it should have been. Natives by nature were more collective; survival was dependent on the cooperation of the whole village, the whole people, the whole pack. Maybe he had gotten too soft in his solitude, but he rather liked his name and he preferred to be referred to by it, not just "this recruit." He preferred to call others by their names, not "that recruit." And he really didn't like having his hair lobbed off like a great black snake falling from his neck. He didn't recognize himself even as he watched in the mirror; no way anyone at home would recognize him.

Even the initial fit test was difficult, not because he was unfit, but because he was one of the most fit men there. The other men ("those recruits") were berated for not being as good as him. He was berated for showing off.

"Fuck am I doing here, man?" someone, actually multiple someones, wondered as they were finally permitted to get some rest at some point in the middle of the night.

The rest of them had gotten to call home shortly after arrival, just long enough to let their families know that they had arrived safely. Sabelu had declined. Now he wondered if he shouldn't have at least left a message at the little office-type building they'd built on the reservation plot. His mother would be making many trips to that building, hoping for a phone call or a message. Or she would beg Galiliga or Blaknik to check on him, all the while thinking of Tsona.

He closed his eyes and forced himself to get away from that. He didn't want to use his gifts. He didn't want his gifts. Maybe, if bootcamp was as grueling as the DIs promised, he would be able to block it all out and actually learn to focus.

"You know, despite Galiliga's distaste and my own misgivings, I think I'm actually, finally finding myself."

He sat at the fire in his uncle's cave. It was the first time he'd been here since getting on the bus a few weeks prior.

Anagalisgi sat across from him. "What do you mean?"

His uncle spoke in a manner that was reserved and a bit exhausted. It wasn't that he didn't care about Sabelu, but he'd grown weary of the arguing and the anger, even as there remained a spark of hope that maybe something had changed.

"I started this for myself, for my own reasons," Sabelu said. "I thought I wanted to prove something about myself, to myself. I thought the quiet in my mind, because I can't see or hear those recr— the others, might help me. And it is, in a way, but I'm also finding that I want to be part of the group, I want to succeed, but I also want to help them succeed. Because they don't have that benefit either. We have to help each other; we have no other choice."

"And you think that this lack of vision, shall we call it, is responsible for this?" Anagalisgi wondered, sounding cautiously curious.

"Well it hasn't hurt it any. I don't need an empathetic reason to help someone or drag their sorry hide up the hill on a hike. I don't need to know everything about him, just that he is a fellow soldier and I need to help him."

"You couldn't muster up the same for your own people?"

Sabelu hesitated. "Maybe it was my ego. Maybe it...Like my father's time, or my brothers', when there is so little to do. Yes, I went in physically fit, and I know that every Krydik man is just as physically fit—and the women, too, in their own way—but the stress and the training and...it's drive and purpose, Tsidushi. I've found it."

"Once upon a time, you had that same drive, and it took you to the desert—"

"Yes. And then there came one hundred years of what? Training? Preparing? How do you keep motivation like that for a hundred years? Just like before, there is nothing to do, nothing to prove."

"What are you preparing for now? Are you defending the people, or going to? Or are you going to go halfway around the world to another man's land to fight another man's war?"

"You want to debate the righteousness of this war?"

"I question why this war is so much more important than the one you previously engaged in."

Sabelu rubbed his eyes but had no good answer.

"I'm glad that you have found something good and helpful. Maybe you can make it work for you when you remember which war you ought to be fighting."

"The physical is an echo of the spiritual, yes, but I still had to physically destroy the Cursed One of the Desert."

His uncle nodded. "And what will you destroy in this desert, I wonder?"

Well, it would be a few more weeks before he would find that out, and PTs didn't give a lot of time for introspection, but that didn't mean Sabelu didn't think about such things when he lay down to sleep at night, or on the rare day off.

He did manage to get a message through to his family to come see him at graduation. As expected, none of them recognized him at first.

"What happened to all your hair?" Netami wondered, horrified and amused at the same time as she reached up and touched his "high and tight."

"I don't get it, though," his mother said. "It used to be that you just signed up and then you went to war. You've been here for months; where is the war?"

"Across the ocean in a different land," Sabelu told her. "But first I get ten days off, then go to MOS school where they train me for the actual job I'll be doing."

"What job is that?" Galiliga asked.

"Heavy mechanic, going out to repair damaged vehicles so they can get back to a base and don't fall into enemy hands."

"In your father's time, they'd just shoot the horse if it broke a leg," Nendawagan said, grinning anxiously.

"Well, that was a long time ago."

"Are you sure this is what you want?"

"I don't have much of a choice at this point, but even if I did, yes, I'm sure."

She nodded. She'd gone through her anger and her tears and her stress, and only physically seeing her son before her was reviving her from an otherwise deadened state.

"I noticed you chose to use Wolf as your name instead of Aberdeen," Blaknik observed. "Why?"

"For the same reason I chose the Marines over the Army; I thought it was about me." He shrugged. "Fortunately, it's not anymore. But that did kind of cement my legal name here."

"It'll be easier for the rest of us to change our names to match," Galiliga said, waving a hand.

"And you chose to use your white name, your political name: Saul," Netami stated.

"That I did do, yes," Sabelu admitted. "Like I said, I did it for selfish reasons at first, but there's nothing I can do about it now. But I'm still park of the pack, whatever happens here."

If there was anything that still separated Sabelu from his Marine fellows, it was his detachment from the war itself. The vast majority of the men he met in bootcamp or, later, at MOS, had joined because of the Gulf War and everything they saw on TV, many convinced that terrorists on the other side of the world were out to get them. He had no such inclinations. As far as most civilians were concerned, the conflict was over and everything now was just damage control. Whatever he told his family, mechanics were in high demand just so they could repair everything they broke during the conflict.

Sabelu had not requested nor expected to be a mechanic; he'd expected infantry. He'd expected to be put on the front lines as an unimportant sacrifice. It wasn't impossible for him to be called to the field of battle—in fact it was very likely if there was another conflict or war—but this was far more than his father or brother had ever done.

He did not have the advantage of growing up taking apart toasters or working with his father on an old sportscar. All he had was the ability to pay attention and learn. He was not the best of his group, which he would admit was a minor annoyance, but he made it.

From there, he was given his official assignment at the logistics base in Albany, Georgia, repairing and building vehicles, machines, and the occasional coffee maker. Sabelu did not have a family, though he still saw Yukpa occasionally when he did get back to Hlohi for visits, and he had no desire to buy a house off-base, so he stayed in the barracks. The residents here tended to be the newly-transferred, especially those fresh out of Infantry or MOS, and poor bachelors who made bad financial decisions and couldn't afford a house if they wanted it.

It was easy to tell when a new class had graduated, as a dozen or more new guys walked in the door, either skittish as hell or twice as arrogant. It was also easy to tell when one of those guys was one of the people, because Sabelu knew everything about him before he even made it through the door.

"Hey," the man, Dan, greeted, dropping his pack and working

quickly to unpack everything as neatly as humanly possible. "Guess we're bunk buddies now. Name's—"

"Dan Redbird," Sabelu stated, not looking up from his book. "Of the Lakota."

"You saw the roster, I guess. And you are..." He looked at his trunk. "Saul Wolf?"

"Well, it's my legal name, anyway. Call me Sabelu if you like."

"What people?"

"Krydik."

Dan shifted his stance. Sabelu knew he was grinning awkwardly. Then he laughed. "Krydik? Really? Bullshit, man."

"What do you mean?" Sabelu still hadn't looked away from his book.

"Everyone knows the Krydik don't fight, not anymore. After you got your asses beat in the Civil War, you just hole up in your caves and watch the world go by." He snickered to himself. "Well, I mean, you're here, but only after the Gulf War, so...I guess that's not too surprising."

"I don't know, everyone seems to think that something really big is coming."

"Well, I don't think the Iraqis are too thrilled that we bulldozed their shit."

"It does seem like the United States just can't resist meddling in other people's business."

"And who knows what this Y2K shit is about?"

Sabelu turned a page, annoyed to find that it was just four sentences to finish out the chapter. "Just another hyped up nothing, trust me." He placed his bookmark and sat up.

"Holy shit, dude, you got colored contacts or what?" Dan wondered, startling. "Or is this part of the supposed sorceries your people use?"

"No, this is my natural eye color. Believe me, it scared the shit out of the recruiters and DIs, too."

The Lakota man shifted his stance. "I don't blame them. It's weird. Where'd it come from?"

"The spirits."

Dan finished his unpacking and sat down to face Sabelu. "Are the spirits on your world the same as they are here?"

"The spirits are the same for everyone everywhere. It's the message they deliver that makes the difference. The Whites will point you in one direction, and the Shadows will point you in every direction but that one."

"My grandmother was a traditionalist, but my mom is Catholic. Neither one seemed any better than the other for getting us out of poverty; that's why I'm here."

"The spirits aren't interested in material gain, although it can be used as a tool or a weapon. They're more interested in life and the spirit within you."

Sabelu hoped his surprise didn't show on his face, because he hadn't been prepared for how honestly he meant what he said. It wasn't even anything especially profound; it had more to do with his own sincerity. He noted a small White moth fluttering into the room, and while he could not see Yawi, he could feel the wolf briefly press up against his legs.

The two of them got along well enough, though Dan was a lot more outgoing than Sabelu. More than once, Sabelu thought about trying to explain that he already knew what Dan was up to—knew what he was going to do before he did it, in fact—so that he didn't have to listen to the exaggerated bragging and lies about it later. He refrained from this for the simple fact that there were going to be much bigger fish to fry in the very near future.

All anyone really knew in those first few days was that there had been an attack on American soil and someone, or a lot of someones, were going to die for it. Sabelu lost count of how many times he watched, willingly or unwillingly, the Twin Towers fall. If there was ever a time when he wished he could see everyone, including white people, it was then. What really happened? Who was involved? What was the actual timeline of events? Why did Building 7 collapse? What was going to happen next?

Afghanistan was the first target, but it was a couple months before Sabelu was called to go. The first mission was Kandahar International

Airport. Even as they were in the air, they were told that there were reports of Taliban and anti-Taliban fighting in the airport terminals and to be prepared to hit the ground running.

Fortunately, such fighting had ended by the time they landed, though there was no less urgency to their movements as they secured the airport. More U.S. troops arrived, as did small forces of Australians and Canadians. The airport filled up quickly and there weren't always enough showers to go around. The Army took over operations, and Sabelu and the Marines were transferred to a base in Kuwait, awaiting orders.

The Army may have been successful in their initial campaigns against the Taliban, but that also meant that they abused their vehicles, and Sabelu spent plenty of time trying to show Army mechanics how to fix their own shit, then pointing and laughing when they did it wrong and it didn't work. Of course, this only highlighted his inability to see non-native people as he fell victim to several retaliatory pranks. In the middle of the desert, they had to get their kicks where they could.

Sabelu knew that the children's camp had been reopened, and he knew that everyone at home was aware of the new war. He also knew that his mother was worried sick because he hadn't checked in for a while. But there was too much going on, and he was on the move too much to give her any sort of news, never mind good news. Although, just proof of life might be good for her.

What was supposed to be a quick in and out to dispatch one terrorist or another quickly turned into a very long, drawn-out game of whack-a-mole, and the moles were winning.

It was just before midnight when he was woken up, told to get ready and assemble with his squad for a quick debrief from the base commander.

"At 2100 hours, Camp Rhino lost contact with a squad of Marines. They were sent north along this road here—" The commander indicated a road on a large map of the area. "—to gather intelligence for an upcoming operation and enlist the help of some of the locals. Last contact indicated they were somewhere in this location." He circled a large area of otherwise geographical insignificance. "There are a lot of caves in this area where insurgents are believed to be hiding. There was no distress call made, or none that was received, and contacts in the destination village deny ever seeing them. Your mission is to determine what happened to the Marines. Yes?"

"Why wait this long to dispatch a search party?" someone asked.

"Communication in these parts is difficult on a good day, and nearly impossible otherwise. The insurgents are quickly learning where our deadzones are and positioning themselves accordingly."

"Is this a rescue mission?" someone else wondered.

"We do not know what happened to these men, and we do not want to send more sacrificial lambs. The first step is figuring out their location and status. Staff Sergeant Pyle will be leading this expedition, and he will make the determination if a rescue is or is not feasible at this time. It could have been a crime of opportunity, or they could be baiting us into a trap."

"This close to the base?" a third man questioned.

"Outside that fence, anything goes; you know that. Your secondary mission, if necessary, will be to ensure the return of any and all equipment to this camp so the enemy does not get their hands on our stuff."

That, at least, was met with unanimous approval.

"Do not make us come out and rescue your asses, too," the commander said, finishing his brief. "We're Marines, for God's sake, not the Chair Force."

Ten minutes later, they were on the road.

Years ago, Sabelu had vowed never to return to the desert. Perhaps this was his punishment for ignoring or abandoning the spirits for so long. It wasn't the same kind of desert as south of Anpa O Wican'hpi, but it was still a desert. Hot, dusty, and even the occasional breeze brought more warm air. Sabelu couldn't invoke any sorceries to cool himself because there was nowhere to push the heat; it was just absolute. One of the easiest ways that the soldiers had made friends with the locals was just buying local produce (at some ridiculous markups, seeing how all

Westerners were rich), all for the hope of a moment of cool fruit juice. There was always the risk that the crate of oranges had a bomb in it, but as the mercury rocketed toward one-twenty before ten a.m., sometimes the risk felt justified.

The nights were more bearable, at a chilly eighty degrees. Keeping the air conditioner working inside the vehicles was just as important as keeping them running. Sabelu, with his preconceived hatred for the desert, always made sure it was working before he finished tinkering and signed off on the job.

"If something did happen, I can't imagine why we wouldn't have heard something," one of the guys, Rhodes, commented. "Vehicle breaks down, call for help. Under fire, call for help. These bastards don't have the technology to bust our comms that bad."

"Why use technology when geography is more reliable?" another man, Jameson, said. "Look around. There's nothing out here. These people use their hands to wipe their asses after they take a shit behind a bush; I'm surprised they know how to use half the weapons they have."

"Who needs to use them correctly when paradise awaits the martyr?" Sabelu pointed out.

Rhodes muttered a curse. "Yeah, I suppose it doesn't take much skill to run a plane into the ground. Or a building."

"We're approaching the target area," Pyle cut in sharply. "Keep an eye out. Lewis, try to raise them on the radio."

Lewis, a wide-eyed PFC only four weeks into his first deployment, lifted the radio to his mouth and started calling. The humvee slowed to a tiptoe. Outside, Sabelu heard the rumble of a helicopter overhead.

"Air support?" Jameson wondered.

"Aye, taking a look around the broader area, and trying to act as a mobile relay for the radios," Pyle said. He glanced at the PFC. "Lewis?"

"Nothing, sir," the nineteen-year-old reported.

"Keep trying." Pyle picked up his own radio. "Mother Bird, do you copy?"

"Groundhog, this is Mother Bird, we read you but you're broken," a staticy voice responded.

"It's these damn mountains. See anything up there?"

"Warm bodies, two klicks to the northwest."

"The road goes northeast," Rhodes said quietly.

"Can we confirm that they are our Marines?" Pyle asked.

"Negative, Groundhog, cannot confirm," the helicopter replied.

"Mother Bird, swing around them and see if you can confirm. It's too damn hot and too damn dangerous to let them get lost out here."

"Copy that, Groundhog."

The bird rumbled away, a shadow in the darkness but for a few small lights. Sabelu looked around, sandy hills lit up bright green. He spotted a herd of goats picking at scrub on the hillside. Some of the larger males looked up, then determined that they were not a threat and went back to browsing. A few opportunistic birds that traveled with them hopped away but did not flee.

"The animals are calm," Sabelu observed aloud. "They're not fazed by our presence."

"Is that a good or bad thing?" Lewis asked.

"Bad, because it means they feel safe otherwise. Safety for them out here means their shepherd is nearby, and Mother Bird didn't tell us about any other warm bodies in the vicinity."

Jameson pointed. "What's that?"

They all looked to see a brief flash in the distance, visible only because of the dark. An explosion lit up the sky, and all they could see was the vague outline of a fiery helicopter going down, about two klicks to the northwest.

Pyle's radio barked suddenly. "Mayday, mayday—!"

"Shit!" Pyle hissed, yanking the wheel in that direction. "Lewis, get someone on the radio, tell them what's going on. We have a bird down and unknown hostiles, evacuating any injured and dead." He turned his address to the rest of them. "There were four men in that helicopter. I want those four men in this humvee in sixty seconds or less, do you understand?"

"Yes, sir," the rest replied.

"And if the missing Marines are here, if they were used as bait, I want them in here, too. Pack this thing like a motherfucking clown car and stack hostile bodies like firewood."

The second round of "yes, sir," was a little more enthusiastic.

"Wolf!"

"Sir," Sabelu said.

"If the missing humvee is there, you have sixty seconds to fix it or disable it until we can get back here later. Make the bird disappear."

"Understood."

"Lewis, anything?"

"Only static, sir."

They stopped about half a klick from the burning wreckage and got out of the humvee, crouching in the scrub and pausing for a full five seconds to simply listen. Sabelu invoked Uhnvyvgi, blocking out the natural night noises, the crackling of the flame, everything but the breathing of men. Nineteen distinct breaths in the immediate vicinity, but there was no way to tell whether they belonged to friendlies or hostiles. Considering the likelihood of most or all of the other men being dead, this was nothing less than an ambush.

They got closer until they were within rock-throwing distance of the wreckage. Sabelu saw a man crawling away from the wreckage, dragging a corpse behind him, having to pause after every progression of movement. The stench of burning metal, fluids, and flesh permeated the air as black smoke billowed into the sky like a perverted offering. Thirty yards to the east, a humvee sat quietly. Five men were positioned around or inside, as casually as you please, but none of them were moving. Using infrared, Sabelu determined that there were five warm bodies in the humvee, and not all of them were the obvious ones. Invoking Uhnvyvgi, two were struggling to breathe but the other three were strong.

Sabelu communicated his findings, although he had trouble explaining just how he had come to his conclusion. Outside the humvee, only three hostiles could be seen through the night lenses, seven with thermals.

"If there are more, they're above us," Jameson hissed, indicating the high slope and many invisible caves. "They're going to try and cut us off from an escape, crush us right here in the fire."

"Agreed," Pyle murmured. "But this is a trap, and it's only effective if we take the bait." He let out a slow breath. "Rhodes, Jameson, Lewis, move up. Take out anyone on top of us and see if you can't raise anyone on that damned radio. Wolf, you and I are going to take these guys on the ground. I want you to get to that humvee and assess. Maybe we can bust out of here in that one."

Without word or argument, they split up, slinking through the scrub. Sabelu tried to time his movements with that of any wildlife, although with all the commotion and danger, the only life in the area was human. He did not invoke Uhnvyvgi right away, not until Pyle bade them pause. He did, but not before spotting a nice, crunchy stick and intentionally stepping on it. Then he invoked Uhnvyvgi, carrying the snap to another area entirely and drawing the attention of the hostiles.

Throwing knives were not an officially issued weapon of the United States Marines, but it was something Sabelu had fair practice in. He picked the hostile at the back of the group and put a knife squarely in the back of his head, guided not a little by Nulinigv sorceries. He went down without a word. The hostiles swung in his direction. Two of them ran to the body while the remaining four raised their weapons. Confirming that their comrade was dead, the two stood and the six of them got in a semi-circle formation around the body, weapons raised. They spoke amongst themselves but did not call out to any friends on the hillside.

Sabelu looked at Pyle who made a motion. Sabelu grabbed a second knife. As the hostiles began moving outward, poorly keeping their semi-circle formation, Sabelu buried another knife in a man's forehead. He went down, the crunching scrub alerting the others who ran back to their first fallen comrade.

One man opened his mouth to shout but was swiftly cut off by a round to the face from Pyle's rifle. Sabelu followed suit, taking down a fourth man. Now there were only three on the ground. All of them were yelling to each other, firing off randomly into the darkness. Several shots rang out on the hillside.

It was nothing for Sabelu and Pyle to dispatch the three men, then scamper to the humvee for protection from any hillside snipers. Pyle went to the front door.

"Sergeant, don't—!"

As soon as Pyle wrenched open the door, his head snapped back and a hostile leaped from the seat to continue stabbing his body, screaming in Arabic. A second man jumped out of the backseat, wild eyes fixed on Sabelu. Sabelu knocked the man's gun to the side, positioning his own rifle under the man's chin and firing. He grabbed the lifeless body and used it as a shield as the man who had killed Pyle jumped up and came for him. Sabelu pushed the body into the man, then sent a bullet around the bloody neck into the hostile's head.

Sabelu stumbled as another man jumped him from behind and put a blade to his neck. A quick drop to the ground shook the man's grip, and one bullet to the shoulder stopped him long enough for a second to tear through his throat.

He turned back to the humvee. As expected, three of the men were dead, and all of them were tied in place to make it look like they were perhaps having a discussion about what to do with their busted vehicle. Sabelu freed all of the men, hauling them into the back, stacking the living on top. They'd been beaten pretty badly, but if they were going to die, they would have done so. The two still breathing could make it back, assuming they got to a running vehicle.

"Wolf!"

Sabelu looked up to see the rest of the guys running toward him. Rhodes and Jameson each had a man or corpse across his shoulders. Jameson and Lewis were dragging another corpse between them.

"Where's Pyle?" Rhodes demanded.

"If his beliefs are correct, Heaven," Sabelu reported.

Jameson opened the back door of the humvee and saw Pyle's body underneath the two men still alive. He swore righteously as he heaved his load inside.

"We made radio contact," he reported, motioning for Sabelu to follow and help with the last man from the helicopter. "We've got reinforcements from holy hell bearing down on this place, ETA eight minutes."

"What the hell, do they want five more minutes of beauty sleep?" Sabelu asked, pushing aside a bit of wreckage so Jameson could retrieve a bloody, charred corpse.

"Fuck if I know, man." Jameson hefted the corpse on his back. "This humvee operational?"

"Didn't get a chance to try before the fuckers jumped us and killed Pyle."

"Well, we need to go."

"Don't have to tell me twice."

Jameson took off toward the humvee, corpse on his back. Sabelu kept his rifle up, turning around and scanning the hillside. Night ops revealed nothing significant, and he couldn't locate any warm bodies in the vicinity.

"Pack it up!" Jameson snapped. "Staff Sergeant's orders still apply! Clown car this bitch! Wolf!"

Sabelu backed up slowly toward the humvee, certain that something wasn't right.

His attention was taken by a familiar bird scream, and he looked up at the black plume still rising from the helicopter just in time to see the black phoenix rise up and scream again. Then suddenly, everything went white.

There was no forest, no cave, nothing but white. Sabelu's vision was blurry at first, and then he was able to make out his hands. And then his uncle in front of him.

"What happened?" he asked. "Where am I?"

"The Shadows tried to kill you," his uncle answered, even as voices in the white babbled something he did not understand.

"Tried. They didn't succeed, then."

"No, human, they didn't," Yawi said, appearing off to one side. "But they did significant damage."

"What about the others? Surely there must have been some Whites there. Even if they couldn't take down the black phoenix, they could help the other men."

"The world is full of darkness, Sabelu," Anagalisgi told him, "and the Prince of Persia is a powerful titan. In this instance, it had the backing of the black phoenix."

"But once again, the Whites are stronger than the Shadows," Sabelu repeated. "And the Author—"

"Sometimes says no. Or not yet." Anagalisgi went on before Sabelu could protest. "Things are going to be confusing for a little while. Shock is normal. Let yourself rest for now. Deal with your injuries in time."

His vision blurred again and everything faded to black.

He did not dream. He was barely aware of his own consciousness, his own soul. Every part of him felt dead, and that was the first thing he perceived when he did start to crawl back to the light. He did not feel pain or relief. He could not even say that he truly felt the fabric of either clothing or blanket except as harsh resistance against his skin when he made a feeble attempt at movement. Sound was muffled and confusing, and for a long time he was too tired to open his eyes.

Consciousness came and went, and memory of such times was even more fleeting. When he did finally open his eyes and look around, it took him a minute to piece together his surroundings as a hospital. Sounds were clearer now, and he could feel the scratchy, threadbare blankets and make small movements though he still felt completely dead. He expected to feel pain of some form, but that Afghan opium was apparently some pretty strong stuff.

A man, perhaps a doctor or nurse, entered the room, and they locked eyes. The man said something in Arabic and left. A couple minutes later, the base commander stormed in the room. The first thing out of his mouth was a curse. The second was a demand, and it took Sabelu half a second to realize the demand was, "Talk to me, Wolf. Tell me you're not a brain-dead idiot."

For a long moment, Sabelu didn't know how to speak, how to use his mouth and lips and tongue to formulate the words he needed, and his first few attempts were not in English. Finally he got out, "I'm a Marine, sir, not a Chair Force."

The commander grinned. "Good man."

"What happened?"

"The humvee was rigged with an IED. Soon as the key turned in the ignition..." He sighed.

"What about the others?"

"No survivors. Except you."

The whole mission flashed through Sabelu's memory. Driving. Helicopter. Fireball in the sky. Drive up. Jump out. Pause, listen. Sneak up. Assess. Split up. Distract. Throwing knives, rifle. Pyle dead. Sabelu takes out three. Stuff everyone in the vehicle. Others join. Rescue from the helicopter. Look around. Cover. Clown car.

White.

"They tell me you're banged up pretty badly," the commander went on, "but this hospital is a third world shithole. The opium should tide you over until you get to Germany and—Wolf!"

Sabelu startled and blinked several times, coming back to the present.

"You'll be flown to Germany," the commander repeated, "see what they can do for you. Then you'll be heading back stateside. By then, you'll have your orders. Or your discharge."

"Sounds good, sir," Sabelu managed.

"It's not the outcome anyone wanted, believe me, but it's a hell of a lot better than it could have been. We could have lost all of you."

And he left.

Sabelu just lay there, staring at the ceiling.

Driving. Helicopter. Fireball in the sky. Drive up. Jump out. Pause, listen. Sneak up. Assess. Split up. Distract. Throwing knives, rifle. Pyle dead. Sabelu takes out three. Stuff everyone in the vehicle. Others join. Rescue from the helicopter. Look around. Cover. Clown car.

White.

Driving. Helicopter. Fireball in the sky. Drive up. Jump out. Pause, listen. Sneak up. Assess. Split up. Distract. Throwing knives, rifle. Pyle dead. Sabelu takes out three. Stuff everyone in the vehicle. Others join.

Rescue from the helicopter. Look around. Cover. Clown car. White.

Driving. Helicopter. Fireball. Drive up. Jump out. Listen. Sneak. Assess. Split up. Distract. Knives, rifle. Pyle. Take out three. Everyone in the vehicle. Others join. Rescue. Look around. Cover. Clown car. White.

Drive. Jump. Listen. Sneak. Assess. Split up. Distract. Rifle. Pyle. Take out three. Others. Rescue. Look around. Cover. White.

Drive. Listen. Assess. Split up. Rifle. Pyle. Others. Rescue. Cover. White.

Drive. Assess. Split up. Rifle. Others. Rescue. White.

Drive. Assess. Rifle. Others. White.

Assess. Rifle. Others. White.

Assess. Rifle. White.

Assess. White.

White.

Black.

ᎠᏓᏱᎾ ᎠᏗᏄᎳᎾ ᎠᏫᏯᎢ

Atlasgone Asonelane Adolv'i
Post Mortem

Sabelu didn't know if it was the drugs, the concussion, the shock, or some combination of the three that made it so he barely remembered what happened next. All he knew was that when he finally came back to himself, his first thought was that American painkillers had nothing on Afghan opium. He groaned in pain and instinctively contorted, trying to find a position of comfort, only to find that he was nearly immobile, and the parts he could move didn't make the immobile parts feel any better.

He couldn't move his neck, his back, his hips. His shoulders were restricted. He had bandages everywhere. And damn did he have a pounding headache.

He didn't know how long he lay there—he couldn't move his head to look for a clock—but it was easily half an hour before a nurse appeared. She wasn't the most helpful person in the world, but the doctor she finally got to come down to his room seemed to know what was going on.

"Your spine was broken in four places with shrapnel embedded throughout the backside of your body," he explained, slow enough that Sabelu could process it. "There was extensive soft tissue damage just from the concussive force. Both clavicles were broken, most of your ribs were broken, and we had to put you on a ventilator on account of damage to your lungs. There was some bruising around your heart, which we've been keeping an eye on, though nothing appears to be developing from it, which is a lucky break. At one point, you were in danger of total kidney failure, but your younger brother proved to be a match, and none too soon. You've been in a medically-induced coma for about four weeks."

Sabelu couldn't decide if it was the drugs, the concussion, or the shock that made it so that he couldn't answer right away, and even then, he had trouble finding the words. Finally he managed, "Four weeks?"

The doctor leaned back on his stool. "It was more than necessary with the condition you were in. I was surprised when they said you managed to talk to your commander after the incident. Coherently talk to him." He went on before Sabelu could speak. "So what happens next is, you're going to be immobile like this for at least two more weeks. After that, you'll undergo some more tests. We couldn't remove all of the shrapnel in the initial operations. Now that the swelling has gone down a bit and some of the organ damage has healed, we can see what we're looking at, what it will take to remove the rest. We can also get you started on walking again and strength exercises."

"Why bring me out of a coma if I'm just going to lay here for two more weeks?" Sabelu asked. His head was still fuzzy and every word was slow and deliberate.

"Because we need to assess your brain functions. We didn't know if you were going to wake up reciting Shakespeare or eating crayons."

"I might be a Marine, but I'm not an idiot."

The doctor chuckled nervously. "Okay, bad joke, I'm sorry. I'm retired Air Force, so I guess I—"

"Chair Force," Sabelu interrupted. "On full display."

The doctor stood. "Ha ha, very funny. If you're feeling up to it, your mother and siblings are here to see you. Your mother at least has been here every day since you arrived."

"That's not surprising. Fine, send them in."

"A nurse is going to be standing by as well, to gauge your mental status in your conversation."

Sabelu just flicked his wrist in acknowledgment.

A minute later, his mother appeared in his line of sight, and her soft hand touched his cheek. Sudden emotion overwhelmed Sabelu, but the best he could do was close his eyes and let the tears come. His mother evidently felt the same as she took his hand in hers.

"Welcome back," she whispered.

He squeezed her hand. "I'm not going anywhere just yet."

She kissed his forehead. "You've been gone so long, and we didn't know what was going on. All of the news on the television was always bad all the time. Then I checked the answering machine at the cabin and there is a man saying you've been terribly injured and we need to come here." She sniffed and wiped her eyes. "Sabelu, what happened?"

Sabelu swallowed. Even without his gifts, he knew what Galiliga's expression would be. Finally he answered, "I don't remember."

"The doctor said you're going to be laid up for a while," Blaknik said.

"He also said I have one of your kidneys."

"They wouldn't let us in the operating room—wouldn't let us anywhere near you for the first week—and they really didn't tell us anything about what was happening. There was too little time to stand around and think about it and see if we couldn't come up with some sorcery use. I didn't know what else to do."

"Thank you."

The most joy that Sabelu got out of the conversation, aside from seeing his family again after fourteen months overseas, was the fact that their conversation was in their own language, thus frustrating the attempts of the nurse to dissect any of it beyond social observation. Eventually, pain and fatigue started to wear on him, and he asked everyone but Galiliga to leave.

"What's up, little brother?" Galiliga asked once everyone had filed out. His tone turned gentle. "What really happened?"

"Thirteen men died. Seven of them after we got there. And I should have been one of them. But because I was outside the vehicle when it exploded, I was just picked up by the concussive force and not incinerated or turned to dog food."

"Aw no," his older brother warned. "Don't even start with that."

"The device was attached to the starter. I'm a mechanic, Galiliga. My job was to get that vehicle up and running so we could escape. And I'm the one who lived. I failed them. I should have found the device and told them to get to the other—"

"Dammit, Sabelu, if you weren't so fucking injured right now, I would punch you in your stupid fucking face. It is not your fault. All right? Okay, I don't understand modern warfare. It is very different from when I was in the Army, I understand that. But it is not your fault. And I don't want to hear another word to the contrary. Understand?"

"Thirteen men, Galiliga. Good Marines."

Galiliga leaned in closer. "Our brother. A brother you never even knew. For a long time, I blamed myself. Itsitsa blamed himself. But you know what? War is hell, and accidents happen. Right place, right time. Wrong place, wrong time. I can only imagine what the Whites and Shadows see and do, trying to save or kill anyone and everyone. In the physical world, shit happens. It is not your fault." He put up a hand as Sabelu opened his mouth. "No. Not your fault. And not another word otherwise. Got it?"

Sabelu sighed. "Yes, sir."

Galiliga straightened. "That's what I thought. I shouldn't have to lecture a priest of the Whites or Author or whomever about his own spirits."

"Just don't tell Itsitsi or Netami."

He knew his brother was nodding. "I'll never tell a word."

And he left.

The nurse asked a few questions, took a set of vitals, and left.

Lying in bed immobilized got very old very quickly. Sabelu had grown bored of it halfway through the first conversation with his family, and knowing that he had two more weeks of it did not make things better. Multiple doctors came through, assessing his mental functions and helping him improve to the point where he could hold a normal conversation without having to think about what was being said. His family came through at various times. Yukpa visited once, and even Tlistso stopped by for an afternoon, though both of them were so petrified by all of the Old Land modernity that they left early.

He also received plenty of visits from his stateside Marine buddies, including Dan Redbird.

"I heard what happened," the Lakota man said, giving him a fist bump as he sat down. "Listen, I know I've given you shit a couple times about the Krydik being passive and stuff, but...you got balls, man. You are a warrior. I hope I can be the same."

"If you can do it without breaking your back in multiple places and turning your insides into tenderized steaks, do that instead," Sabelu told him. "This way sucks."

"You know if you'll be able to come back, even as a desk jockey?"

"No, I'm done. I'm toast. They got my papers waiting for me; I just gotta be able to sign them."

"That's too bad."

"And what about you? You just got back, too, didn't you?"

Dan's tone was leery. "Yeah, for a few months. End of contract is coming up soon."

"Going to renew?"

"I don't know. What do I have to look forward to at home? More poverty, boredom, no real drive or direction in life. But then I come here and see you and...I'm the only son that isn't a worthless alcoholic. Dad's been gone for years, obviously not coming back. I need to provide for my mother and grandmother somehow. How am I going to do that if I get the shit beat out me, or if I'm dead?"

"You're a welder, aren't you?"

"Yeah."

"Start a welding business. Teach your useless brothers a skill. Guarantee at least one of them will change his ways."

Dan chuckled as if brushing him off. "Yeah, maybe. Well, I got a few months to think about it. If you're still here, I'll let you know."

"Fuck that. No way I'm still going to be here in a few months. I get out of these braces and everything starting tomorrow. I'll be up and around in no time."

As usual, his hopes were at odds with reality. He never expected sitting up to be so difficult. Or painful. Needles ripped through his arms and pricked his fingers from the inside. His legs felt almost dead until he put pressure on them, when more needles raked his skin and penetrated his muscles, and he was too weak to walk more than ten feet. Further testing revealed minuscule pieces of shrapnel cutting into his spinal cord, and he was spirited away into another surgery.

Once he was lucid, he swore off any and all painkillers, as he was determined to recover all of his faculties and invoke the sorceries for healing. There were still some pieces they hadn't taken out. He wasn't sure quite what he was going to do with them, how he was going to remove them, but he needed to know what he was dealing with. Bad enough his brother had had to give up a kidney because the doctors hadn't let them see him, given them the time and space needed to work with the sorceries.

But as the painkillers wore off and simple pain turned to writhing agony, he started to wonder just how bad his injuries were and if his family could have done anything. Healing cuts and scratches, wouldn't even blink. Set and heal a broken bone, easy. Deal with some deep tissue bruises, nothing. Torn muscles and ligaments, well, that required some skill, seeing how they were small but important pieces of the body. Damaged organs, it would take time, which could be conjured, and it might be able to be done with some thought. Restoring an organ that was in danger of imminent failure while the rest of the body struggled with horrifying injuries including nerve damage which was a major catalyst of healing? Maybe not so much, and guaranteed that his family wouldn't have been as level-headed as the normal surgeons.

Sabelu may have used the sorceries on occasion. Minor accidents while working on vehicles, avoiding accidents. At one point, he was tapped for his blood for some incoming wounded who needed emergency transfusions before being flown to Germany, and he took the time to explore the wounds and see if he couldn't do something for them to give them the best chance at survival. Of course, he couldn't regrow limbs—he wasn't sure if that was even possible—but he could help stop the blood loss and maybe do something for bruised organs.

That was all on others, though, where he didn't have to feel their pain. He couldn't run from this. According to the doctors, his heart and lungs looked fine, and everything was generally on the mend; the biggest problem was just the shrapnel still in his spine.

Maybe he could block the nerves that were sending the pain signals to his brain, or block the pain receptors. But even if he did that, what was he going to do about the pieces themselves? Well, if they got into his body, maybe he could work them back out. All right, then what he do about the damage left behind? There would be holes in the bone and frayed nerves in his spinal cord. Could he turn the shrapnel into flesh? Was that even feasible? Few of the people had ever gone so deep into the atomic matter of objects, and to change it alchemically was obscene. Did he really want to risk it in his own body?

After a few days of trying to tough it out, he gave in and accepted painkillers once again. Within minutes, he could sit comfortably again and his headache went away. Cautiously, he sat up, put one side rail down, swung his legs around, and reached for the walker. Getting to a standing position reminded him of Oko, and it was a little embarrassing. Looking around to make sure there were no nurses around, he pushed the walker away and tried to stand up straight.

"Not gonna end well, man," his roommate, a man by the name of Phillip, said. "At least use the bars on the wall."

"Doctor said that once I can walk on my own reasonably well, I can go home," Sabelu growled through gritted teeth. "Well, I'm tired of being here." He fixed his gaze on the door to the bathroom. Necessity, if not sheer willpower, would get him there. Biting his tongue, he forced one foot in front of the other. He was getting stronger and his head felt fine, just his back was in awful pain and every limb felt like pins and needles so he couldn't feel pressure correctly.

In the other bed, Phillip shifted uncomfortably. "Slow down, Jarhead, you're gonna kill yourself."

Sabelu forced a laugh. "I don't take orders from Frogmen, are you kidding?" He gave the man a look. "Especially when the frog's legs have been eaten."

He did end up using the bars on the wall once he got to the

bathroom, but not before he crossed the room on his own. The trip back was just as grueling, almost as bad as the Crucible, and the nurse who was waiting for him looked about as cranky as any DI he'd ever trained under.

"You're supposed to be using a walker or getting help," she scolded as she came beside him to help him back into bed.

"I'm bored, I'm ready to be out of here."

"You and literally every other patient in this hospital."

"I will get out of here, one way or another. Doctor says I have to be able to walk on my own. Sounds like a good place to start."

If nothing else, it provided endless entertainment as he began a series of "escape attempts." First it was just trips to the bathroom, but as he learned how to walk again in spite of the numbness and tingling, he started going up and down the hallway, visiting other rooms just to hide from and frustrate the nurses, which in turn boosted the morale of the patients in those rooms and may have spurred a few others to mischief as well.

"You are intent on starting a prisoner revolt, aren't you?" Phillip asked, amused as Sabelu was again escorted back to his assigned room.

"You could get in on this, too, you know," Sabelu told him. "Oh, wait, you can't, can you?"

The double amputee gave him a single finger salute and a grin even as he pulled his wheelchair around. The nurse was much kinder about helping him and getting him ready for his daily walk and exercise regimen.

"You better still be here when I get back," the nurse told him.

"When are you going to be back?"

She just gave Sabelu a look and headed out, Phillip at the lead. Sabelu gave them a count of ten before shuffling his way back to the door where he was met by another nurse and a doctor.

"Dammit," he hissed, reluctantly turning around and heading back to the bed.

"We've caught on to your antics," the doctor told him smartly. "We Chair Force aren't as dumb as we pretend to be."

Sabelu sat on the edge of the bed for a moment, then swung his legs up and offered his arm for whatever they needed next. To his surprise, the nurse began removing the ports and gently taping cotton over the sites.

"If you can cause this much trouble here, you can cause just as much trouble at home," the doctor went on, scribbling out a script. He leaned against the counter near the sink. "I won't lie. Your back is fucked up. It needs—"

"I've been here for almost three months," Sabelu said. "The first one I was unconscious. Ever since, it's been nothing but tests and scans and hypotheticals and an occasional surgery where I think you do more exploring and poking around than fixing. I understand that it's delicate. I don't want to end up in a wheelchair like Phillip over here. But I can't just sit here and wait for something to happen. You said that once I can walk, I can go home. Well, I'm walking."

"Yes. I know. I'm giving you a script for painkillers and a referral to a doctor who specializes in high-risk spinal surgeries. He's not part of the VA system—"

"Oh, I'm sure that'll be cheap."

The doctor sighed. "But he is very reasonable toward VA referrals."

Sabelu took the papers and scanned them. "I'm sure he is."

"Do you want to call someone to come pick you up?" the nurse asked, attempting to steer the conversation.

"No," Sabelu told her. "I'll walk out on my own."

Netami had brought him a change of clothes a week prior and he changed into them to leave the hospital.

Official discharge from the Marines was less extravagant than some men thought it might be. There was no fanfare, no parade. He got sympathy, some reassurances, a scripted thank you, and more paperwork that detailed his service and the end of that service.

He conjured Galohisdi and headed home. Unprepared for the difficulty of conjuring combined with the pain it caused him to cross through, the last thing Sabelu saw was his bed coming up fast to hit him in the face. But at least the cold felt good.

He slept but he did not dream, and warmth slowly tempted him back to life. As he crawled back to consciousness, his first sensation was one of pain, as bad if not worse than what he'd felt when he first woke up in the hospital. Worse than that, he couldn't move. He could feel, but he couldn't move. At least not at first.

Training kicked in. Push the pain aside. Small movements first, then get more aggressive. Like breaking a scab, he got his body to move and he turned over in bed.

"Good morning," Netami greeted, poking at a fire in his stove and closing the door. "When were you going to tell us you'd left the hospital? If we hadn't gone this morning and found out you were gone, you could have frozen to death! You very nearly were!"

"Sorry," was the best he could manage, throat tight and raw.

She gave him a look, then relented and moved to help him sit up. Hadn't he just been walking yesterday and causing trouble? Was it the drugs? Was it his bed? Was it the cold? The windows and doors were covered, but there was still a chill that the fire hadn't been able to drive away yet.

"You look terrible," she said apologetically. Then, more mischievously, "Are you sure they let you go willingly?"

"They couldn't wait to be rid of me," he told her, wincing when he tried to stand and finally sitting back down.

Netami sighed. "Well, you still need help. Why not come back to Aktiya Waya—"

"And be a shameful embarrassment? I can fight evil spirits but I'm nearly killed by mortal men?"

"I'd be willing to bet that there were evil spirits behind those evil men. Men don't tend to be evil on their own." She continued, "You're part of the pack, whatever happens in the Old Land. You said that yourself. And you've been part of a pack, a very tight-knit pack called the Marines. You can't just sit up here all alone, not even able to fend for yourself."

"I can fend for myself," Sabelu protested. He forced himself to stand, though he still needed support from his sister and the wall.

"No, you can't," Netami insisted.

"Just let me rest a few days and get used to my own bed again."

A few days turned into a few months as Sabelu pleaded the cold and the weather. By the time spring came, he was up and walking around, could keep a clean house and toss wood in the fire. It was just as well that he was improving during the day because his nights only got worse. At one time in his life, he thought being overwhelmed by the future was bad. Now he would give anything for that to be his worst problem.

It was a cool summer morning when he wandered out to the cliff and painstakingly sat down on the hard rock, much to the dismay of his spine. As the sun rose behind him, he heard movement in the trees. He hoped she wasn't trying to be sneaky, because she was failing miserably. Netami broke out into the open, paused, then moved to sit beside him.

"If you were hoping to watch the sunrise, I might suggest turning around," she said quietly after a long moment. Her tone suggested she was attempting a bit of humor.

"I know," was all he said.

She took an even breath. "You're alone, Sabelu. That's not good. You need someone. Someone who isn't me."

"I can't."

"Why?" When he didn't answer, she went on, "At the camp, there are a lot of kids who no longer have fathers or brothers or uncles. Some just went off to war, others went off to war and have been killed. And the things we've seen on TV..." She sighed. "What happened over there, Sabelu? Don't tell me you don't know or you don't remember, because you do know and your mind is not letting you forget. I can see it in your face, whether you're awake or asleep. I suspect you told Galiliga already."

Sabelu hesitated. Then, "Thirteen men died. I was the lone survivor."

"And?"

"And what?"

"What happened?"

He shook his head. "I can't burden you with what I see."

Netami frowned. "You often cite the end of Itsitsa's Book, your death on a mountainside in the Old Land, following a trail, presumably tracking game. The mountains of Afghanistan...hunting terrorists...we were worried that maybe that was what it was really talking about. When Itsitsi told us about the message that had been left at the office, when we heard of your terrible injuries, we feared the worst. Itsitsi invoked the sorceries to get past all the doctors, to get to you to see if she couldn't do something for you. She said that you were covered in blood and bruises, your whole body confused and panicking as it tried to fix itself, but you were so inundated with drugs and machinery, she didn't know what to do. The best we could do was Blaknik giving his kidney; thankfully it was enough, at least at the time. And, sometimes, when you're napping, I will use Asvhnisgi you, try to figure out if there is anything I can do for your pain. I have found the metal that is still in your spine, cutting into your spinal cord—"

"And?" Sabelu cut in, unsure how hopeful he wanted to be.

"I've been afraid to do much, worried that I'll make it worse. I made mention of it to Kah Kitowak, and he's said that he will consult other sorcery users, maybe even track down Nathan and Andrew, to see if there is anything that can be done." She paused. "Will there be anything? Can you see it?"

He shifted uncomfortably. "Before I left for the Marines, I told Anagalisgi that I wish I didn't have my prophetic gifts. I still have them. But these days, they're often stunted or entirely overpowered by..." He vaguely gestured to his head and face. "This."

"The nightmares."

"Yes."

"And how is sitting here dwelling on it going to help?"

Sabelu sighed and did not answer for a long time. Across the valley, the sunlight was gradually making its way down into the forest. "Fighting for the Whites...Yawi helped me to see and understand the nature of time, this whole mortal existence. Well, I got a glimpse of it anyway. The Whites can step in and out of our time, move forward and backward as needed. He once told me that he would go ahead to the difficult battles of the future so that when I got there, he would already be there to fight for me."

"Sounds like he fulfilled his promise."

"He also told me once that he would come back to the winter nights, lie at my feet by the warm stove, and just enjoy the moment. Because he had gone ahead, past my time, and he was grateful that he could come back and still be with me." He shook his head. "I wish I could do that. Just step out of this moment and go back."

"To change the past, I assume."

"Save the men who died, yes. Stop Pyle from opening the door. Move the rest of the men to the other humvee. Maybe somehow stop the first one from disappearing, then we wouldn't have to go look for them." He rubbed his face. "And...I would go back to see Itsitsa again. Make new memories instead of having only a finite collection of old ones. Maybe I would try to go back and actually meet Tsona."

Netami studied him for a moment, then put an arm around him and leaned her head on his shoulder. "I'm sorry, Sabelu. I don't know how to do any of that."

"Unfortunately, neither do I."

"But I do know that you can't keep doing what you're doing. The wolf needs a pack to survive." When he did not reply, she added, "I saw your son at the festival last year."

"Children belong to their mother first, their clan second, and their father third, if at all, or at least their mother's husband," Sabelu reminded her. "I am only Yukpa's lover; I have no rights."

"Maybe so, but you were the first child anyone ever saw who had gold eyes. I don't think it's a coincidence that your lover has a son with the same gold eyes."

"The timing of her last visit a few weeks ago was also not a coincidence. What's your point?"

"You may be special, Sabelu, but you are still human. Still mortal. Who or what do you belong to? Where is your pack?"

It took the better part of the summer, but Netami finally convinced him to return to the children's camp. It was still owned by the Krydik, but run by a white man by the name of Matt Davis. There were more cabins, a small office building, a nurse's station and camp shop, proper shower and laundry facilities. The road and parking lot had been expanded and paved. An enormous log cabin style building had been erected, the lunchroom easily converting into a small basketball court. The fort that had stood proudly just beyond the open campsite had been destroyed in a storm a few weeks prior and there was some debate over whether to clean it up and rebuild or just build a new one at a different site.

Matt had opened up the camp to any and all children, with an emphasis on Natives and anyone from an impoverished family, per Galiliga. For the state of West Virginia, poverty was the name of the game. The camping itself had been restructured so that the camps were arranged by age, and they were now two weeks long.

It was Sunday afternoon. The kids from the most recent camp had gone home, as had most of the counselors and staff. A few remained, shooting the breeze or doing a few minor chores they couldn't do with the kids around. Sabelu just stood in the parking lot, arms folded, staring at the huge log building. After a few minutes, Matt joined him.

"Your brother was reluctant to approve some of the changes, but I think it's turned out for the better," Matt commented, trying to sound non-threatening.

"Looks good," was all Sabelu could find to say about it.

"He mentioned that you did some time overseas."

"Six years in the Marines, couple years in that hellhole of a desert, yes."

"This should be a nice change of pace, then." Matt began explaining some of the different activities that the camp did now. They rented a couple buses to go to the beach for a day or two, went to a stable for a day, a zipline adventure for a day. And there were plenty of regular sports that they played right there at the camp, including some archery and firearm target practice.

"Are there still nightly stories and lessons?" Sabelu asked. "I noticed the camp townhouse is gone."

"Well, we have a fire every night—weather permitting—and we tell ghost stories and—"

"I don't know if my brother mentioned it, but I am a priest of the Krydik. It was my job to tell the kids the old stories, teach them the old ways."

Matt nodded slowly. "He did mention that, yes. He also said that you gave it up to go into the military."

Sabelu took an even breath and insisted, "I didn't give it up."

The camp director put up his hands. "That's not my call, I'm just telling you what he said. As for the camp, I have no problem letting you tell stories and teach some life lessons. Just understand that not all the kids are tribal kids anymore. Most of the counselors aren't tribal either. Lot of people here, myself included, are as white as the pilgrims. It may not mean anything to them."

"The bow is less important than the arrow," Sabelu said. "And the target."

The following morning, he was assigned nine campers to his cabin, aptly named Wolf Cabin. His own little squad as it were, although children were hardly soldiers. Their attention spans were far too short for giving more than one order at a time, and that only if it sounded fun or interesting. They weren't bad kids necessarily, but it took all of three hours for Sabelu to realize that his back wasn't able to keep up with their energy, no matter how great his willpower or how much he mentally drilled his training to himself. Eventually, he just couldn't do it.

But he did it anyway, enduring several months of having virtually no feeling beyond pins and needles in his limbs, constantly aware that a sudden, poorly-timed movement could instantly paralyze him.

By the end of the summer, Kah Kitowak had amassed enough research and more than enough self-confidence to proclaim that he could (probably) remove most of the remaining shrapnel from Sabelu's spine and heal the damage.

Two days after the last day of camp, Sabelu lay face down on his bed, Kah Kitowak, Netami, Galiliga, and Blaknik around him.

"Are you absolutely sure you don't want another roll of nala?" Kah

Kitowak wondered.

"Damn it, Kah Kitowak, get on with it," Sabelu snapped. "Galiliga, if he kills me, you have my permission to kill him."

"All right, fine. I'm just trying to be considerate."

Sabelu had already done the blessings around his house, on the implements Kah Kitowak expected to use, on the man himself, on himself as the victim, and he'd done it all while chain-smoking half a pack of cigarettes plus a roll of nala. So he may have picked up a few bad habits in the Marines, so what?

In theory, Netami was supposed to conjure Iyuwahnilvhi during the whole thing. This way, Kah Kitowak would not be fighting any natural bodily processes, such as movement from breathing, and Sabelu would not have to endure any pain or feel any lingering anxiety. As he explained it beforehand, Kah Kitowak expected to make a small incision in Sabelu's back, that way the shrapnel had somewhere to go, a way out of his body. He would use Gayalvnga to gently attract the shrapnel to a small metal rod. In fleshy places, he would only have to conjure Iyuwahnilvhi to get everything to knit back together. In the matter of bone, he intended to use ground bone powder from other animals to pack the wound, then use Agvhalvda to forcibly reconstruct the bone. He was avoiding the spinal cord for the moment, instead using this instance as a test run.

From Sabelu's perspective, then, the entire procedure lasted only half a second, if that. All he knew was that one moment he was in his normal space of pain, and the next it was like someone took a spiked club to his back. He reflexively contorted, rolling defensively, looking for the enemy. His gaze settled on a man with dark skin and dark hair, holding what might have been a knife. Images of a man stabbing Staff Sergeant Pyle's body over and over again flashed through his mind.

"There is no pain you cannot endure," one of his combat instructors had once said. "In fact, endurance is your only choice because the only alternative is death."

Sabelu was in the air before he could think, and then he was suddenly seized from behind, arms wrenched behind his back. He knew this game. Before a knife could touch his throat, he threw himself back, jarring his attacker but it was not enough to free his arms. Another came at him from the front. Sounds were distant as his only thought was freedom.

"He who has control of a situation has control of its outcome," the instructor said. "If you cannot do anything more than react, you do not have control of the situation. If you can think only one or two steps ahead, you do not have control of the situation. If you cannot envision your path to victory, you do not have control of the situation."

Victory. Get free, gain control of the situation. Visualize the path to victory and—

"Sabelu." Slender fingers touched his shoulder and a familiar woman's soft voice cut through the chaos. Why was there a woman here? How had she gotten here? There wouldn't be any women— He stopped and looked around.

He saw Netami first. Background images came into focus. His cabin. Blaknik and Kah Kitowak in front of him, Galiliga behind still holding his arms.

"I'd say it was a success," Kah Kitowak said nervously.

"Shut up," Galiliga told him. He shifted his stance though he still didn't let go of Sabelu's arms. "You all right now?"

Sabelu took a deliberate breath. As evenly as he could manage, "Get out. All of you."

The four visitors exchanged uncertain glances. Galiliga released Sabelu who stumbled back to sit on his bed, head in his hands. None of the visitors made any move to leave, instead grabbing chairs to sit down and face him.

"I told you to get out," he repeated.

"We will," Blaknik said, "once you tell us what's going on."

"It's fine, I can handle it."

"Little brother, I had to handle it," Galiliga told him. "We all did."

"It's fine."

"It's not," Kah Kitowak said firmly. "Listen, I've seen a lot of conflicts, and I've seen the guys who come home from the conflicts I haven't seen. Bad dreams are part of it sometimes. In the old days, our peoples took pride in it and believed it all just part of life with the blessing of the spirits. But things have changed."

"In the old days, warriors who lost men in war could be stripped of their social and military standing," Sabelu said. "Now, they get a promotion."

"Were those men under your command?" Galiliga wondered, his tone more than innocently curious.

Sabelu did not answer for a long moment and he just stared at his hands, limp between his knees. He looked up at Netami. "You—"

"I'm staying," she told him. "I've seen your sleep, and I've seen your wakefulness. I may not need to know, but you want someone to know, so I will listen."

The cabin was quiet as all eyes stared at Sabelu.

"A squad of Marines had gone north to a small village to gather intelligence for an upcoming operation," he began. "They never made it. Radio communication is terrible out there, impossible in some places, and it was hours, almost midnight, before anyone knew they were gone..."

In the old days, warriors would brag about splitting the skulls of their enemies and burning their scalps in the fire to consume their spirit and strength. Maybe it was different when it was your own hand, when you were close enough to get the spray of blood on your skin, rather than something as impersonal as a gun or IED. Maybe it was different when men still had to kill men, and when the enemy was dead all danger was past. Not that tricks and traps had never been utilized, but there was just something...different about all of this.

"If I had done my job as ordered and checked the vehicle first, those men might still be alive today," he finished. "And I wouldn't have all this damn shrapnel in my back. Hell, I might still be a Marine." He glanced at Blaknik. "And we'd both still have our original kidneys."

The boisterous laughter that ensued was in no way proportional to the joke that evoked it, but it was necessary for the situation.

"Matt Davis called and left a message at the office," Galiliga said once the empty mirth subsided. "Actually he called a few times. He said there were a few incidents. Nothing violent or anything, not really causing a scene, just...moments of bizarre behavior."

Sabelu nodded. "I know." He went on before anyone could speak, "With this new warfare...your enemy doesn't have to be in the same area, doesn't have to touch you at all, doesn't have to be particularly strong or clever, doesn't even have to be alive to kill you. We used to tell our sons and nephews that we were the biggest and the best, and we had killed so many enemies to prove it. How would you explain to a child that twisting some wires together and putting some metal scraps in a sack makes a great warrior?"

Galiliga's expression was sympathetic. "I don't know. Warfare has changed in the last century and a half. At least back then, if someone shot you, there was a chance for revenge."

"Well, not anymore," Sabelu said quietly, staring at the ground.

"Thank you for telling us," Netami told him.

He nodded slowly, not looking up.

"Do you still intend to just stay here in your cabin, away from the people?" Blaknik asked.

"You're not a disgrace," Kah Kitowak threw in quickly. "If you're a disgrace, then I'm on the national council."

"I ran away because I didn't like my gifts. I didn't want my gifts." Sabelu sighed. "Not having use of my gifts cost lives." He glanced around at his siblings and Kah Kitowak, hoping his expression was somewhere in the vicinity of apologetic. "I have less than ten years left, and I know how it ends."

Galiliga nodded solemnly. "What do we need to do?"

"You four must represent the Krydik. I may have saved the people and given them a fighting chance, but I ultimately failed to prepare them for what's coming. They'll be slow to react."

"And what is coming?" Blaknik inquired.

"After I die, the Shadows will come in force, very similar to what they did to the People Before. Hlohi and Earth will be cut off, the people held hostage. They will be looking for you and killing as many as they can besides."

"What do we do now, while you're alive?" Netami wondered.

"The purpose of the wolf is coordination, communication. The purpose of the bear is to fight. The purpose of the deer is to retreat. The purpose of the eagle is guidance and wisdom. Make sure everyone knows this. Teach those who want to learn the sorceries. For those who do not want to learn, ensure they are prepared to supply the people with whatever they may need. The whole of our people must become an army. Galiliga and Netami, you must be the voice of reason here. Blaknik and Kah Kitowak, on Earth."

"What about you?"

"There is only one thing left for me to do: stay at the camp and confront the Shadows."

"So they can kill you," Kah Kitowak stated flatly.

Sabelu grinned. "At their own peril, I assure you." He stood, half-expecting everything to be normal. Sudden stabbing pain in his back pushed him back down again and he lay back on his bed.

"Are you okay?" Netami asked, sliding over to sit beside him.

He gave her a look. "What do you think?" He carefully got to a sitting position and looked at Kah Kitowak. "Didn't you get anything out?"

Kah Kitowak offered him a small dish. The dozen or so metal pieces ranged in size from dust particle to a grain of sand, all of them sharp and twisted.

"I got the ones in soft tissue and in the bone, but I didn't touch the ones near your spinal cord," he said.

Netami took the dish and tilted it this way and that to see all of the pieces. "How many surgeries did you have to go through already, and there is still more?"

"Welcome to modern warfare," Sabelu told her. To Kah Kitowak, "What do you think about the rest of it?"

The mixed-blood hesitated. "Not today. I want to think about it a little first, and I don't want to risk my life a second time today."

"In the old days," Galiliga said, smirking, "you would have been called a coward." He clapped Kah Kitowak hard on the shoulder, then grabbed it with a little more force than what might be considered casually friendly. "And you think you have a right to look at our sister?"

Kah Kitowak went pale as he seemed to suddenly realize how outnumbered he was.

"Let him go," Sabelu told him, mirroring his brother's smirk. "This is one of the few things he's succeeded at; I think the phrase 'quit while you're ahead' applies here."

Galiliga gave Kah Kitowak's shoulder a hard squeeze before letting him go. The mixed-blood didn't even bother chancing a glance at Netami as he left.

"Honestly, Netami, what do you see in him?" Galiliga asked. "He hasn't even tried to properly ask for you." He didn't bother waiting for an answer as he turned his attention back to Sabelu. "What do you think?"

Sabelu looked up. "About what?"

"The two of them."

He shrugged. "They'll be fine."

"And what about you?" Netami wondered. "Ten years is plenty of time to find a wife and have a few children, or have a few children you can call your own anyway." She gave him a look.

Sabelu shook his head. "No. I've always known I would not have a family in such a way. As I said, I have only one task remaining. But that doesn't mean I can't give you guys the best chance of success, starting with the national council."

Sabelu's reception at the festival a few weeks later was far less than enthusiastic. As Galiliga had once pointed out, he had gone to fight for the same government that had killed Ola Achukma. The people may not have understood modern warfare, but they understood betrayal.

For the first time in many years, Sabelu gave his recommendation for the next year's national council. Despite the general disdain with which the people may have regarded Sabelu, the council accepted his nominations graciously. They would approve the council later, once the fervor over the messenger had died down and the message could be considered more objectively.

His piece spoken, Sabelu melted into the crowd, determined to see himself out so he didn't disrupt the festival any more than he already had. Then he turned and locked eyes with a child, a boy, around nine years of age. Like all Krydik, he had dark skin and dark hair. But there was only one other person in the entire nation who had gold eyes.

"Hi!" the boy said, grinning.

"Hello," Sabelu greeted awkwardly.

"My name is Tommi. And you're Sabelu, the White priest."

"That's right."

"They mean the same thing, just in different old languages."

Sabelu nodded. "That's right."

"Tsitsi says people with gold eyes have been touched by the sun. Is that true?"

Looking at the child before him, unable to see his future and unwilling to probe the lives of others to look ahead, Sabelu briefly found himself wondering what his own life might have been like if he hadn't been burdened with agotvhdi from such a young age. A twinge of pain in his back cut that line of thought short, though there was something almost hypnotic about the boy's innocence. He nodded again. "Yes, it's true. Maybe someday when it's not so busy, I can tell you the story."

With a grin reaching from ear to ear, his son ran off into the crowd.

DKꝺAꭴ DVꞪT

Atsosgone Adolv'i

What Must Be

Although he hadn't let on in the moment, there was something jarring about saying out loud that he had less than ten years left in his life. It was like a shift in his mind, knowing that he did, in fact, have a date of death. More than just running into a hostile situation in the desert, he knew the time and manner of his death. He'd known since he was a child, but now he was about to stare death in the face.

It didn't really hit him until the snow started melting that he'd just experienced his last winter. The last first frost, the last blizzard, all of it. Last autumn was the last time he would see the landscape awash in yellow, orange, and red. This would be the last time he would watch the buds bloom. The last time he would see and do a lot of things. And the memories just didn't cut it.

He headed to the cliff that he was frighteningly familiar with, and a moment later, Yawi joined him.

"Will you miss me?" Sabelu wondered.

Yawi made a whining sort of sound. "I can always go back in time to lie at your feet by the fire. But there is a certain sadness that, like you have said, there will be no new memories. There will be no going forward for me to you, only backward."

Sabelu nodded. "You were at my feet a lot." He looked at the wolf. "Keep me company, will you? It meant a lot, even when I was being obstinate and unproductive."

"I will," Yawi promised, pressing himself against Sabelu's leg. "I most certainly will."

Sabelu scratched the wolf between the ears as he looked out over the valley to the mountains beyond. The more time a man had, the less he did with it. Now here he was, one season left in his life, and there wasn't much he could do with it.

Eventually, he returned to his cabin, mind still a bit dazed, tipping to a point of ridiculousness, almost insanity. What if he didn't actually die this summer? What if this was some sort of cosmic trust exercise? What if there was something ulterior going on, something from the spirits that he couldn't see? There would be hell to pay when he was scrambling for firewood in the fall, plus his food stores.

But then, when he considered the visions of his brothers and sister, and especially his mother, as they mourned over him and committed his body...there was nothing ulterior about any of it. Even seeing such things, these events beyond his death, chilled his blood a little. It wasn't so much the events themselves, for he knew that life would go on without him. Perhaps it was seeing his own body through the eyes of others. His cold, dead, lifeless body. It spooked him even as it conjured visions of that night in the Afghan desert. The helicopter going down, the dead men who had been tied up, Pyle, plus every image his brain had invented about the rest of the men who had died despite not actually seeing anything.

He'd visited their graves, spoken to a few family members. He wore the bracelets or kept them close to hand when he couldn't wear them. He wondered if anyone would do the same for him. Oh, he could look ahead and see his mother and siblings visiting his grave—right there with his grandfather, father, and brother—but would the emotional impact be the same? Had he done anything to make his life worthwhile on a personal level? Would anyone truly weep for him?

The following morning, he left his cabin and headed to Aktiya Waya. There was no fanfare, no fighting. That threat had evaporated decades ago. Anymore, he was just the cranky hermit on the hill, the wolf who had abandoned the pack. He made his way to his mother's house where she was quietly working on some beadwork and drinking afternoon tea. She looked up as he walked in and broke into an enormous grin, standing and embracing him.

"I was just thinking about you," she said, releasing him and moving to get him a cup for tea as well. She handed him a steaming cup. "What brings you here?"

"I thought I should visit before camp started," he answered evasively, sitting down. He'd given explicit instruction, and his siblings agreed, not to tell their mother about his death before it happened. No timelines, no hints, nothing. "Maybe stretch my back a little before camp, too."

"How is it feeling? Any better?"

"No better, no worse." He added before she could speak, "And I'm fine with that."

She gave him a look. "Oh, Sabelu, you used to be such a strong warrior."

"Used to be?"

"Well, you still are. You are more than capable. I just don't like to see you in such pain."

"The medication helps."

His mother dramatically waved a dismissive hand. "Bah! Synthetic witchcraft. Even the sorceries could not be painted so evilly." She gave him a look. "Why not use the sorceries, if not to heal yourself, then to stop the pain senses?"

"Because the pain tells me when I've gone too far, done too much. Stopping the pain does not heal the wound. As for healing the wound...I don't know anyone with that kind of skill."

"But Kah Kitowak—"

"Paralyzed me the last time he tried so that I could barely breathe on my own. I was just lucky that Galiliga and Netami were right there and could reverse his mistake, though I think that word is too small for what he did." He continued, "I'm fine. I've lived like this for...nine, ten years now. I'll manage."

"It just seems that—"

"Tsitsi," Sabelu cut in, exasperated, "please. I didn't come here to argue or give you a burden that I alone bear."

She gave him a look. "A mother bears all of her children's burdens, whether they want her to or not."

"All the same, we know that my life has not changed much." He made a polite gesture. "Tell me what's going on here."

Now she barked a laugh. "Not very much, I should think. Little has changed here as well. The fields are inspected and cleared, the irrigation repaired. The first major trades between villages have gone out and returned. Paper from Aktiya Waya, leather and bone from Anpa O Wican'hpi, metal and stone from Yonhi, books from Lehoyed." She shifted position. "There are rumors that Lehoyed is experimenting with glass."

"Glass?" Sabelu wondered politely.

"They already make stunning jewelry." She shrugged. "So, one of their jewelers has turned his attention to glass."

"Is there demand for it?"

"Well, for Lehoyed, they might want to have windows in their homes. If they ever want to build above ground, they'll need something to protect them from the infernal wind. Anpa O Wican'hpi isn't overly interested, but Yonhi is."

"And Aktiya Waya?"

Nendawagan made a so-so motion. "Less interested. Most of the residents are Wolf and Bear Clan, so anything we absolutely need can be gotten in the Old Land."

"Tsitsi, there is something to be said for self-sufficiency so you don't have to go to the Old Land."

"Maybe so, but that's where it stands. I assume you knew all of this already; you just wanted to make me feel better about my end of the conversation."

"I've learned a few interpersonal skills in the last few years." He self-consciously took a drink of tea.

"But not enough to make you want to come back to town?"

He shook his head and gave her a look. "I know what everyone intends to do with the rest of their day, and I know what's actually going to happen. I know people's hopes, plans, dreams. I know four women who are going to try to get pregnant in the next day or so, and three of them will be successful. I know half a dozen young men who are already training for this year's festival and the young women they hope to impress. Absolutely none of them will end up marrying the girls they're trying for. And so much more." He took a drink. "The military helped me to be able to focus on the here and now, what's in front of me. The hospital helped me to realize that sometimes, walking away really is the best option."

His mother sighed. "Well, at least you're still at the camp."

He nodded. "I do that for Tsitsa. It was his camp, his dream." He let out a breath. "Even if it doesn't much resemble what it started out as."

"His spirit still lives in that place, whatever happens to it."

Where will my spirit reside? Sabelu wondered silently.

He stayed for a fair length of time, mostly just acting as fresh ears for old stories for his mother. When he finally stood to leave, she made him promise to visit more often, which he did.

Two steps out of the house, he ran into Netami.

"And how often do you plan to visit?" she wondered, her tone half-serious though her arms were folded.

He made a motion for her to walk and talk as he headed out of the bowl. "I'll visit again, between the camps in midsummer."

"And then?"

He gave her a look.

Netami slowed and let her hands drop to her sides. Finally she stopped. After a couple steps, he also stopped and turned.

"It's this year?" she asked, voice tight, face pale, every part of her mind coming to a halt before splitting between memories of Tsona and the fear of losing Sabelu.

"Ten years, Netami," he said. "Time's up." He turned and started walking away.

"But...it's not fair," she said weakly, catching up to him. "All of the things that you see, everything you know across all of time, and there is nothing you can do?"

"Can do, maybe. Maybe I just don't do the thing that gets me killed. Maybe I decide not to go to camp this year."

"Then—"

"But I can't do those things either."

"Why not?" She was trying not to cry, though her tears betrayed her.

He put an arm around her. "Because there are some things that simply must be."

She wiped her eyes and nodded hurriedly. "That doesn't mean it's fair."

Sabelu stopped and spun her around to face him. "You know what else isn't fair? That I have to die with the knowledge that you're marrying Kah Kitowak."

"You approved of him!" Netami blurted, her sudden grin confused.

"I know." He continued walking. "And you two will have a very happy life together. I just...still think he's an idiot." He glanced back at her. "He almost killed me."

She caught up to him. "And if you knew he was going to do that, why did you agree to it?"

"Maybe I wanted to see if I could change something, even something small. In the event the answer was no, that was why I wanted you and Galiliga there."

He could feel her gaze boring into him and he forced himself to not react. Instead, he said, "If, for some reason, I don't do it the way I see it, it's going to be a whole lot worse the second time around."

"How can you know that? You never entertain hypotheticals."

He shrugged. "Simple logic. The cerberus and the wolf dog are back to their full size and power, and they want revenge for the incident in the desert. As long as I let it be that simple revenge, it ends the matter, turns their attention away from the people for a time and keeps the people safe for the near future. If I don't do it this way, then my inevitable death will mean nothing."

They reached the pass out of the bowl, the sentries entirely disinterested in their presence.

"The problem is, I know you're right," Netami said quietly. She took an even breath, trying to stem her sorrow before she burst into tears a second time. "I just wish you weren't."

Sabelu pulled her into an embrace where she choked out a sob.

"Don't weep for me, sister," he told her gently. "At the very least, wait until I'm dead. Then, if you must, weep for everyone on the other side who has to deal with me again for all eternity."

She made a sound that was somewhere between a sob and a laugh and she hit him in the chest. "Why aren't you taking your own death seriously?"

He let her go. "Why should I? It's only death." He took a couple steps back. "I'll be back between camps. And remember, not a word to Itsitsi."

With that, he turned and left the bowl.

It was long past dark by the time he reached his cabin. Yawi was waiting for him, sitting by the door like a sentinel.

"I'm not dead yet," Sabelu told him.

"Maybe not, but the time is still limited," Yawi countered.

"You've already been ahead to where I am no longer living." Sabelu entered his cabin and tossed a few logs in the fire. "Why are you so emotional?"

"Because I have not yet howled for you, and I know I must."

"You're putting it off as long as you can."

"Yes."

Sabelu sat in his chair to enjoy the growing warmth. "I didn't realize Whites procrastinated."

Yawi sat beside him but did not lie down at his feet right away. "An advantage to being able to walk through time. But like you, we can't outrun it forever. Eventually, I must make the call."

"Are there others you have to howl for?"

"There have been others, but you are the only one now."

"So you don't howl for everyone who dies."

"No, or else the chorus would be continuous. It is reserved only for our charges. All Whites with a charge do something similar."

Sabelu nodded absently. "I see. But if you can jump ahead—or back— to times when I am not alive, what does the howl actually do or signify?"

"It signals the end of our charge and let's everyone, everywhere in the universe know that at that moment, a charge was lost. It is primarily for ourselves, when we carry you into death."

"Stress relief."

"A tragically oversimplified summary, yes."

He shifted in his chair, his back cramping. "Did you howl for my father, or grandfather?"

Yawi's expression was apologetic. "No. Providing assistance is not the same as having a charge." He added, "But don't worry. The ants took care of them."

"I thought the ants just formed a perimeter, laid a foundation, that sort of thing."

"They lay the foundation, and they finish it off once it's all over. They carried your kin."

"Oh."

"And I will carry you."

Sabelu nodded but did not reply. After a minute, Yawi stretched out in front of the fire. Neither of them said a word the rest of the night.

A few days later, Sabelu was back in the tribal office on Earth. He'd started a small garden plot on the south side of the building. He wasn't going to bother with the one outside his cabin, but at least the people who came through the office would have something good to eat at harvest.

"Morning!"

Sabelu did not look up from where he was planting seeds, but he recognized the voice. It belonged to Jerry Wilson, the new camp director as of a couple years ago. He had been a counselor for several years prior to taking over and a camper many years before that. Nice guy, somehow not as white as Matt Davis had been, but still very white. As far as Sabelu was concerned, the camp was Native in ownership only, and any semblance of what his father had started was going to die this summer.

"Oh, good, it is you," Jerry said, trying to be optimistic even as he timidly looked around to study Sabelu without studying him, attempting to ascertain his identity amid the dirt smudges that no doubt marred his visage.

"Would I be anyone else?" Sabelu wondered, finishing his row, returning the spare seeds to their appropriate pouches, and standing.

"Well, I hope not, but this makes it easier than trying to play the telephone game."

"I'm guessing you're here to ask if I'm coming back this year."

Jerry nodded. "Well, that, and to let you know that Joe isn't going to be there this year."

Joe was Sabelu's helper, able to handle the physical labor that he couldn't and able to anticipate his mood swings and flashbacks so there were fewer episodes of "bizarre behavior."

"I've already put out a job listing for the position," Jerry went on. "Hopefully we'll have someone before camp starts in a couple weeks."

"What if I don't want someone?" Sabelu wondered.

Jerry sighed. "Every cabin has two counselors." He went on before Sabelu could speak. "Please, Saul, you're arguing just to argue. If we find a good candidate, you'll have a helper. If we can't find someone, then you won't have one. How's that?"

"Works for me. And please, don't hire someone just to have someone. These are kids we're talking about. Can't be too careful."

"You're the one I'm more worried about." He made an awkward gesture. "But, gardening is good. Relaxing." He made a move to leave. "Anyway, I just wanted to know if you were coming back and let you know the situation. I'll see you in a couple weeks."

Sabelu made some vocalization that resembled a farewell, then knelt back in the dirt, reaching for another pouch of seeds. He heard a car door slam, an engine rev to life and slowly creep back toward the road, and then all was quiet once more. Just the wind in the trees, some birdsong, and him working in the dirt.

After a while, he sat back on his heels and stared out into the trees. He knew he was being watched. Part of him wondered if he shouldn't just go out and offer himself to the cerberus now and get it over with. But if he was going to do that, he might as well just not go to the camp, break Iyuwahnilvhi that way.

No. This was a Thing That Must Be, and it had to be done a certain way.

Two and a half weeks later, he showed up at the camp. It wasn't the camp itself, but a sort of adult camp the week before, where they would get the grounds and cabin all cleaned up and then indulge in some of the activities they were going to be doing—things like ziplining, rock climbing, and horseback riding—but without being slowed down by a bunch of kids or teenagers.

His new counselor's assistant was still a teenager himself. Dark hair, pasty white, lanky to the point of being blown over by a strong wind, Tommen was not what Sabelu would consider a good assistant, and he told Jerry as much once he got a free moment at lunch one day.

"He's young, he's energetic, he's strong," Jerry told him. "He can do whatever needs to be done, physically—"

"You know it goes beyond mere physicality," Sabelu cut in.

"I can't help you with your demons, Saul. No one can do that but you."

"He's going to be a peer of the older kids, hardly an authority figure."

Jerry shrugged. "So he gets to be a camper in your charge, and you are left with no assistant. Just like you asked." He went on before Sabelu could speak. "This is not up for debate. As of right now, he is your assistant this summer. Deal with it. Because he has to deal with you, too."

And that was that.

Jerry headed back into the main hall, leaving Sabelu standing there in the hot sun. After a moment, he dug out a roll of nala and lit it. Smoking was technically prohibited at the camp, but there weren't any kids around right now. Even when there were kids around, he'd still find time to sneak off and have a smoke, usually before the alarm went off in the morning or after bedtime.

He was halfway through his roll when Wallace, one of the kitchen staff, stepped out of the kitchen to light up his own cigarette.

"That shit's gonna kill you someday," Sabelu told him.

"You can talk," Wallace snickered, taking a drag.

Sabelu grinned and mirrored him.

"Another year," the cook said. "How do they sneak up on you so fast?"

"Lethargy the rest of the year, usually," Sabelu said, shrugging.

"I cook at the elementary school the rest of the year, and that shit sneaks up on me, too."

"Well, then, you are clearly working too much. You don't take time to enjoy the present moment."

"And you do?" Wallace raised a brow. "Man, you're always going, except for rare times like this. But when the kids are here, you are on top of it."

Sabelu took a drag. "I have to be. And I have to be even more on top of it this year with Joe gone."

"Kid you're with doesn't seem too bad."

"He's still a kid. Soft city kid with no work ethic."

"You've known him for three days. Has he been dodging work? Sneaking off to play on his phone and whatnot?"

"Well no. But—"

Wallace flicked his half-smoked cigarette into the receptacle and turned to open the door. "This isn't the military, Saul. This is a children's camp. These kids are going to be playing hide-and-seek, not running through a minefield."

"That was Vietnam; I was Iraq," Sabelu said indignantly. He tossed his butt and turned to face Wallace. "The kids didn't run through a minefield; they fucking blew themselves up while pretending to sell you a crate of fucking oranges."

"That was there," Wallace said gently, putting up a hand. "This is here. There are no enemies here, Saul. This is a camp that your family built. We're all friends here."

With that, he ducked back inside. Sabelu made a few harried paces in front of the door, glancing out toward the trees where he knew the cerberus watched him. Just waiting for the opportunity. After a few more paces, he went around to the side door. He entered the main hall and stopped, briefly stunned to find adults and not children. Why had he expected children? Well, the younger kids came to camp first, but why had he thought they would be here now? Was he that scattered?

Instead, the adults who were in the room—all the counselors, counselor assistants, and assorted other staff like the nurse and office workers—were cleaning up from lunch and starting to head out for the afternoon activity. Work in the morning, activity after lunch, to keep them all sane.

Today happened to be horseback riding. It was one of Sabelu's favorite activities, even if it was one of the most strenuous ones on his back. The stable was not associated with the camp or any tribe in any way, but after a few years, they'd learned that Sabelu preferred their less than perfect horses. He liked the ones with spark and personality, or anything but the dull plodding of a well-used kiddie hauler.

Naturally he paid for it dearly, though not right away. It wasn't until the next morning when sharp pain in his back and numbness in his limbs—worse than normal—saw him straight from his sleeping bag to the nurse's office.

"You knew this was going to happen," Michelle, the nurse, told him as she signed off on a couple pills.

He tossed the pills back without any water. "I have to get my fun where I can, while I can."

"If you stopped doing stupid stuff, you might be able to have more fun longer."

"But stupid stuff is fun."

She gave him a look, though it didn't faze him. She was too pretty to give a good scolding.

"Well," she went on, "I guess it's up to you, how long you want to last, how much you want to put on your assistant. Four weeks of camp, a week off, four weeks of the next camp, same as always."

He straightened, some feeling returning to his limbs as the anti-inflammatory started working. "Not the same as always. This camp used to be a lot different, you know that."

Her expression softened. "I wasn't even born when your father died.

I didn't know the camp before. But my parents did, and they told me stories."

He nodded slowly. "You would have liked it."

With that, he returned to the cabin to pull on some work clothes, as ready as he could be.

The good news was that the first week of camp with the kids wasn't all that bad. It was sports week, where the kids could participate in either basketball or soccer tournaments. They ran their legs off, and Sabelu just made sure they stayed on the field and didn't go running off to play with matches or something.

His assistant proved to be, well, teachable anyway, bordering on competent. He was still a hormonal sixteen year old boy who wanted to text his girlfriend and sometimes got offended by something someone said. Sabelu was almost willing to bet that he wouldn't return for the second camp, when the older kids came.

The cerberus made the first move before then, inciting vandalism in the camp while they were out on a separate camping adventure. This was frustrating, but then it escalated when Sabelu found a dead wolf outside the cabin the following morning, the last day of the younger kids' camp. His initial rage was quickly tempered by the weight of the wolf as he took it out to be buried. Once it was in the ground, he lit a small fire and sat down. While he was murmuring prayers, Yawi showed up. Sabelu stopped praying but continued to stare at the fire.

"It's almost time," he said.

"Yes," Yawi agreed softly.

"I've seen the mountainside where I am to die." Now he looked up at Yawi. "Will you be there with me?"

"I would rather be anywhere else in the universe," the wolf admitted. "But for you, I will."

Sabelu nodded and went back to staring at the fire. "You know, for a long time I couldn't understand why, if I can't see myself, I had a vision of my death. But I think I understand now. It wasn't meant to frighten me; it was to give me courage, the knowledge that every day was held and spoken for. It was all a blueprint, and I just had to follow it for everything to work out."

Yawi lay down on the other side of the fire as the rest of the pack appeared from the woods, sitting down in a circle around them. A minute later, Minotaur, Chimera, and Griffin also joined.

"Will you all be there?" Sabelu wondered.

"No," Minotaur rumbled. "We will be protecting those you defend."

Sabelu nodded. "Thank you."

He waited another minute or two before standing, putting out the fire, and returning to camp. There would be meetings and speculation about what it all meant, but none of them could appreciate what was really going on. They were too focused on the physical to give the spiritual a second thought.

He returned to his cabin in the week between camps to find his siblings all waiting for him. And Kah Kitowak.

"What are you doing here?" Sabelu wondered.

"If you don't know the answer to that question, you're an idiot," Blaknik told him with a perfectly straight face.

Sabelu shrugged. "I've been called worse." He studied each of them. "And you haven't told Itsitsi, right?"

"Not a word," Netami promised.

They had already unsealed his cabin and started a fire in the stove. On the stove was a pot of vegetable stew while a fire outside roasted some large game and fish.

"Don't you know that mourning involves fasting?" Sabelu asked cheekily as Galiliga started cutting the meat. "One would think you were trying to celebrate my death."

"Celebrate your life," his sister corrected, handing out wooden plates. "And everything you've done for the people. Even if they don't fully realize it."

For as much as Sabelu had warned his brothers and sister against telling their mother what was going to happen, he was the most in danger of blurting out everything when he visited her a couple days later. It was difficult to keep conversation light and casual, just another ordinary visit. He couldn't bring himself to tell his mother that he was going off to die, but he also couldn't bear the thought of just leaving her without a proper goodbye and ensuring that she knew beyond a shadow of a doubt that he loved her and appreciated everything she had done for him and that everything would be all right. And perhaps there was a little regret on his part, that he had no grandchildren to leave her. Well, none that could be claimed, though she had seen Tommi and a couple other golden-eyed children at the festivals and heavily suspected Sabelu's involvement.

He left Aktiya Waya feeling very much like he had unfinished business, but there was no good way to go about finishing it. He only felt worse when he left his cabin for the last time a few days later. He'd long since gotten past the idea of missing "stuff," what little he had, but it still hurt, and he returned to camp feeling absolutely wretched.

When the camp had reopened a decade ago, Matt Davis had started a camping activity, getting the kids away from the modern camp and going out into the wilderness to camp, hunt, forage, and survive. For the younger kids, it was only a few days. The older kids got a whole week. Jerry continued the tradition and included short survival classes before they went out. Sabelu was in charge of the hunting class.

Because they were camping on Shawnee land, guns were not allowed, nor was anyone thrilled about the liability involved with so many children around guns at a camp. Instead, they used bows which were kept locked away in the main office for safety. There were five that were for common use during the survival week, but most of the counselors and even a few of the older kids had their own personal ones that they brought. Sabelu removed his from the locker and paused. He stood there just holding his bow for a long moment, feeling the smooth curvature, the sinew string.

The bow is less important than the arrow or the target, he reminded himself.

He grabbed the communal bows and returned to the class. After giving a short lecture, he took his twenty kids out back for some practice.

"Basic stance for beginners," he began. "You don't hold your bow out here or here or here." He demonstrated some poor grips and stances. "Pretend you are pressed between two walls. Back straight, chin up, shoulders back, everything in line. Keep your arm straight out, twist at the hips if you must." He demonstrated as he spoke. "Do not try to roll your shoulders forward and hunch over." He grabbed the string; there was no arrow yet. "Take the string and draw. Recurve is a little different than compound, but the point is, draw all the way back. Compound, you'll feel the give in the string as you get over the draw weight. Keep pulling."

Sabelu released the string and looked at the kids. "It takes time to develop muscle memory, so you should practice even if you're not hunting. Then, when you are in the field, you will be that much faster, stronger, quieter, and more precise."

He grabbed three arrows out of the quiver and shot them in rapid succession at a target about thirty feet away. Three perfect bullseyes. Three daggers in his back though he refused to give in. He looked back at the class. "Now then, we only have five bows and twenty students. Five of you grab a bow, and you only get three arrows each until you have all gone through at least once. Begin."

Some of them were obviously hunters, some had potential, and some were probably better off just staying at the campsite.

After class was lunch and then a grueling bus ride to the trail head followed by an hour or so hike to the campsite where they pitched tents by the light of flashlights and a few small fires. There was no big group campfire, no songs or s'mores, just a trudge into the tents. Sabelu slept at the entrance, the first, and arguably weakest, line of defense for the boys, assuming a bear was kind enough to utilize the front door. There was a little arguing over ghost stories, but eventually everyone settled into sleep.

The following morning, Sabelu woke to find his left side nearly useless. He fudged it enough to get out of his sleeping bag and stumble out of the tent, but he couldn't feel his steps well enough to walk properly, and Michelle was summoned.

"I'm fine," he insisted, even as she guided him to a tree stump where he sat and removed his shirt for an examination.

"Shut up, Saul," Michelle told him. "It's bad for anyone to lie to a priest, but it's worse for a priest to lie."

"I haven't been a priest for a long time." He flinched as she felt along his spine, using her fingers to gently probe around each vertebra. Several growls and similar assorted noises escaped his throat, and he pressed his nails into his palms until he thought he might bleed. She focused on a particular area around the base of his neck, then put a hand to the area and pushed.

Something shifted. He cried out in pain and couldn't stop himself from cursing, but almost immediately his left side was flooded with pins and needles. She did the same to several more areas down his back. A few moments later, he regained some feeling, enough to function.

"Sit down," Michelle ordered, putting a hand on his shoulder and forcing him back down when he tried to stand. She moved to stand in front of him. "Now you listen to me. You are not to do any heavy lifting. Ever. Here, at camp, at home, none of it. You can't do it anymore. Until your spine is actually fixed, you're done."

"I'm still going to use my bow and hunt," he told her.

"Fine. But get someone else to carry the carcasses. You've got plenty of campers to help you."

Sabelu sighed. "Fine."

Michelle shifted her stance and folded her arms. "What is it, Sabelu? What do you need to make yourself better? What would fix your spine?"

He groaned as he stood, flexing fingers and toes. "Some very delicate surgery, some chiropractic work, and, if you happen to have one lying around, a little time travel."

She gave him a look, then knelt and dug in her bag. "Well, would you look at that? Fresh out of time machines." She pulled out a white bottle. "But I do have some painkillers."

He dry swallowed two pills, then headed to his tent to grab his bow and a roll of nala. His first stop was a shady area by the river, out of sight of the campsite though large amounts of activity could be heard. There he sat on a rock and lit up. A moment later, Yawi appeared at his side, lightly brushing him with his fur. Sabelu absently reached up and gave the wolf a scratch between the ears.

"I don't know how you do it normally, but I'd like you to howl before I'm dead completely," Sabelu said. "I wouldn't mind that eternal echo."

Yawi did not reply except to pop open his mouth so his tongue could loll out.

For as much as his pride told him to keep doing what he was doing, Sabelu followed Michelle's rule to not do any heavy lifting. One could argue that pulling a heavy draw on a bow was heavy lifting, but it was a different kind of strain, one he wasn't going to give up this close to death. If he was to die, he would die with his bow in hand.

It was the second to last day of the survival camp when Sabelu woke to find White ants dutifully marching around his sleeping bag. When he got outside, Yawi and the wolves were waiting.

Sabelu said nothing aloud, but he knew.

He let his assistant Tommen dole out duties for the day, assigning the boys in their tent to either go hunting, fishing, or foraging.

"What about you, Saul?" Tommen asked once all the boys had been assigned.

Saul gave him a look seeing how he was still chewing his food.

"Well," he said when he was done, "I figure I'll check on the pelt and see how its doing. Then I'll head out hunting one last time. The more food we get today, the less hunting we have to do tomorrow, and the less time we'll waste packing up."

"Do you need someone to go with you?"

"No, I think I'll be all right. I'm not intending on going after any deer or anything big. A couple turkeys ought to do it for us, plus whatever they bring in from fishing."

He said it so easily. But then, what was he supposed to say, that he was going off into the woods to die?

With everyone on assignment, Sabelu grabbed his bow and headed off into the trees. No one stopped him. No one questioned him. He got about halfway up the slope when he turned to look back at the campsite, what he could see of it through the leaves. He could hear the activity, the general din of loud conversation, some laughter.

A shadow hovered over him. When he looked up, he saw the cloud and the Shadow that was driving it, none other than the black phoenix.

The wolves walked on either side of him, slinking through the trees, but the black phoenix guided him from above. He knew another Shadow general stalked him from behind, perhaps the serpent, but he paid it no mind.

The trees began to thin, then ended abruptly. It was like walking out of a dream into reality as Sabelu stepped into the clearing. To his left, the slope continued for a very short distance before falling away sharply. Before him was another steep slope leading up to a rocky outcropping. Even from his lower vantage, Sabelu could see the cerberus waiting for him up there.

Domineering vantage aside, Sabelu had little doubt that the cerberus had chosen that spot because of the physical toll it took on him just to reach the area. Still he never let go of his bow.

"Well, well," the cerberus rumbled. Saul did not see which head had spoken. "He came without being told."

"I was told a long time ago," Sabelu said. "I came because it is necessary."

"Necessary?" the right head wondered, amused. The left and right head both lowered to look at him while the center head remained high. It was the left head that said, "You are but one mortal. There is nothing to destroy here. And we would only be reborn."

Sabelu just grinned. "You fail to understand time. You fail to understand destiny. You fail to understand love."

And he wasn't about to explain it to them. They were here for the kill, to avenge all that he had destroyed: the Cursed Zukatopa, the Cursed Man, their titans and puppeteers who had controlled the chiefs and the priests, their entire hold on the Krydik people.

But Sabelu was here for the sacrifice. If they believed that this all ended with his death, then they would never think to look for what vengeance was coming for them one day.

He turned his attention away from the cerberus though he never moved his body. "I know you're there. I know what you've come to do."

"Don't you want to face the one who's about to kill you?" the man asked.

Sabelu met the gaze of the cerberus' middle head. "I am." He turned his head just a little. "Don't you want to know how and why you've been led here?"

There was a moment of uncomfortable silence. Sabelu turned his gaze to the valley, lit up in bright sunlight, a breeze rustling the leaves.

"I already know," the man decided finally.

In a moment that stretched out far, far too long, Sabelu decided that, given the choice, he really preferred the IED. For the men in the vehicle, death had been instantaneous. Even he had been knocked out before he could realize what was going on. Being shot in the back was slow, torturous, excruciatingly painful, at least for the parts of his body he could still feel. Everything below his mid-back had gone completely dead. He couldn't even say that he felt his legs give way because even that seemed to require some kind of sensation. This was more of a falling sensation.

Then he hit the ground. His bow bounced out of his hand. Pain made him dizzy.

New spears lanced through him. No, not spears. Arrows. His arrows, shot with his own bow through his body, pinning him to the earth. He could feel the pressure begin to build in his chest and he had a brief memory of being trapped in the tomb after being ripped apart by the black phoenix.

There were other noises, too, otherworldly and awful, and he couldn't be sure that he didn't make a few odd sounds of his own.

Then, for a moment, all was quiet.

Finally, there was the sound he wanted to hear. It echoed in his pain-addled brain, the howl of the white wolf. A whole pack of them, in fact.

The tension in his body released and he closed his eyes as he let out a painful, bubbly, hot breath. He opened them again when he first felt a wet nose on his cheek. All he saw was white, silver, and red. The wolf whined and gave his cheek a lick.

"Good boy," Sabelu breathed, wishing to lift a hand and give the wolf a scratch but unable to find the strength.

The wolf lifted its head and howled once more.

There was some movement beside him. He could not move his body, but he still managed to shift his eyes upwards just enough to see Anagalisgi kneeling there.

"Sabelu," his uncle said, his voice the first crisp thing Sabelu has heard in the last...he didn't know how long. Time was starting to lose all meaning.

Something was pressed into his hand and he grabbed it as tight as he could, though that was difficult to gauge. His bow. Yes, he would need it.

His uncle put his fingers to Sabelu's eyes, to close them. Then he took Sabelu's other hand.

"It's time to go."

The pain receded and perfect feeling returned to his body. He hadn't felt this good and strong since he was a teenager or young man. He could feel every small pebble, sharp rock, and blade of grass beneath his body. Fresh air filled his lungs. He could smell strong pine, hardy oak, sweet maple, bitter grasses, and the dozens of animals roaming the area. Opening his eyes, he could see every grain of sand and dirt, the smooth curvature of some stones and the imperceptible imperfections in others, and the shadows of each distinct blade of grass. Every color was bold yet not overpowering, and even the faded colors of dry stones looked remarkable.

Putting his hands to the ground, he felt things he could not explain. He felt the grit of the dirt as he had never felt it, yet it felt no more gritty or smooth than it had before. He felt the wetness of grass, the dryness of stone.

When he stood, he went to the edge of the rocky outcrop and looked out over the valley. There was something going on behind him, but he paid it no mind, instead entranced by the brilliant sunlight, the shadows of the clouds, and everything coming alive as he had never seen it before. Anagalisgi walked up beside him.

"Did you walk with my grandfather and brother like this?" Sabelu asked, listening to the voice of the wind and reveling in the clarity of his thoughts. More than just not seeing or knowing things, more than just an unsettled silence, his mind was quiet, and he was okay with that. The future no longer mattered, for there was only the now.

"I did," his uncle replied calmly.

Yawi walked up on his other side.

"What happens now?" It was perhaps the first time his asking of the question was honest and genuine, lacking in sarcasm and devoid of ego.

"Begin your journey," Anagalisgi told him. "You have been called."

Sabelu did not need to be told twice, but before he made a move, he looked at his uncle. "Thank you. And tell my family, will you?"

His uncle dipped his head. "I will. Now go."

Sabelu looked out over the valley, to the west, and started walking, Yawi faithfully beside him. He left the outcrop but did not fall. He walked through the air toward the mountain peak, shining in the sunlight. Everything behind him faded, and anything in his periphery started to blur. The mountain peak grew large and the sparkling sunlight grew brighter and brighter.

Everything went white.

ᏚᏫᏗᏞ

Olosoma

The fire crackled and popped noisily in the cave, and the only other sound to be heard was Anagalisgi preparing meat for a stew. He took the pot over to the fire and hung it on the spit, then offered a haunch of rabbit to Yawi who was lying by the fire, just staring at the flames. For a long moment, the wolf did not react. Then his nose began to twitch and finally he looked up. He looked at the haunch, looked at Anagalisgi, then gently took the leg from the outstretched hand. He ripped some meat off the bone, being rather polite about the whole affair, the wolf's way of reluctantly picking at his food.

"This isn't the first charge you've lost," Anagalisgi said quietly, squatting by the fire to stir the stew a bit.

Yawi tore off a chunk of meat and swallowed. "Maybe not, but it was one of the most violent ends, from our point of view. Others have met gruesome ends, but this is the first to attract the attention of all of the generals."

"Well, as long as the generals believe Sabelu to have been the end-all vengeance for what he did, they'll leave the rest of them alone. For a time." Anagalisgi stood. "You're lucky. I just lost another nephew, and I can only carry his memory with me forward into the future. You can step in and out of time as you please."

The wolf stripped the bone clean and rose, shaking himself. He looked at Anagalisgi. "Is there anything you would like me to tell him?"

Anagalisgi hesitated. Then, "Tell him...tell him I'll be watching out for him, even at the very end."

Yawi nodded once.

Stepping out of time was not something easily explained to beings bound by linear time; it was as natural to him as breathing was to mortals.

It was winter. The air was perfectly still yet felt like thin ice. Overhead, stars struggled to twinkle against a shining full moon, no clouds to be seen. Ahead, a squat cabin with only minimal lighting peeking through the few places that were not sealed off. Yawi had no trouble pushing through the wall.

Sabelu was just relaxing in his bed, having fully stoked the fire. His eyes were closing, but they opened when he saw Yawi.

"It's a little late to be lying at my feet," he said.

Yawi couldn't help but smile as he trotted over and hopped onto the bed beside him. Sabelu grunted in surprise and shimmied over as far as he could. Yawi curled up on the other side of the bed, resting his chin on Sabelu's shoulder.

"Can I help you?" Sabelu asked, his irritation more bark than bite.

"Your kin wanted me to tell you that he will be watching out for you, even at the very end." Yawi licked Sabelu's cheek, much to his annoyance. "And so will I."

Sabelu grunted again and shifted a bit. "Lovely. Go to sleep."

Yawi closed his eyes and sighed contentedly.

ᎢᎬᏁᎢᏍᏗ ᏗᎪᎲᏪᎵᏍᎩ

Igvne'isdi Digohwelisgi

The first draft of this Book was very different from what you have in your hands now. The first draft was far more integrated with the rest of The Timekeeper Chronicles. It had Sabelu (and the rest of them) going to the Akarin fortress, going here and there, meeting a lot more people from other series or making those people more significant, and, as I said, very different.

But when I looked at it afterwards, it just didn't seem to fit. There was nothing untrue about any of it, nothing that would not fit in the grand scheme of things, except it really detracted from the essence of The Lone Wolf series. If each series is meant to be self-contained, then there was too much outside influence for that to be feasible. Not only that, but it provided too little conflict, and it made it sound like all of the Krydik's problems had been solved in Alpha Wolf, which wouldn't make any sense considering the fight just to keep Sabelu alive as an infant.

Thus began a serious rewrite, scaling everything way, way back and, really, deleting whole swaths of chapters and whole mini-adventures. Time spent in the fortress or anywhere else was traded for time spent in the cities of the People Before, bringing everything back to Hlohi and the Krydik and Sabelu's primary mission to help the people.

After that, things just smoothed right out and revealed a lot of hidden gems, both philosophically and emotionally. I really love how the relationship between Sabelu and Yawi turned out, and being able to explore Sabelu's life and how and why things happened was both fun and disheartening.

All that said, is this truly the end of The Lone Wolf series? In short, yes. There will be no "Book Four of The Lone Wolf." But, as Sabelu himself noted on several occasions, and as readers of The Chivalrous Welshman will know, the Krydik live on. They still have a role to play. The Timekeeper Chronicles is comprised of many different facets of the same story. This particular adventure is complete, this facet of the greater narrative has been explored. I don't know how much bigger it could get after the showdown in the desert. Actually, I do, and it will require the participation of more than just the Krydik, for it affects more than just the Krydik.

What about the children that Sabelu fathered? Will they show up again? The answer there is also yes. But that is another adventure for another series.

Single novels aside, this is the first series in The Timekeeper Chronicles to be completed, and while it brings a certain sadness, I can honestly say that I regret nothing. This has turned out to be a beautiful adventure, and I hope you enjoyed it as much as I did.

- Brooke Shaffer